For my 'somewhat distant' friend Andy. I hope you enjoy my stories. Thos P. MAY '20

The Chronicles of Athan

Soldier and Brigand - Book One

by
Thos. Pinney

authorHOUSE®

AuthorHouse™
1663 Liberty Drive, Suite 200
Bloomington, IN 47403
www.authorhouse.com
Phone: 1-800-839-8640

First published by AuthorHouse 8/10/2007

ISBN: 978-1-4343-2340-8 (sc)
ISBN: 978-1-4343-2339-2 (hc)

Printed in the United States of America
Bloomington, Indiana

This book is printed on acid-free paper.

Acknowledgements

Creating a book is always a collaborative effort; especially one as long in development as this one.

I particularly want to thank my Editorial Review Board:

Bil Pinney, PhD, Ruth Pinney, PhD, and Ellen Rayner, MS

They fought the grammar and punctuation wars with me and won almost every skirmish. Ruth also provided expert toxicological technical advice, ideas, suggestions, and encouragement.

I am also indebted to Sandy who is talented Illustrator, and a fine finish carpenter.

Many other friends and neighbors also helped me with suggestions and encouragement over the years including the late Julia Thorner who, long ago, gave me a book with blank pages and told me to "fill it up".

Thanks to you all.

Table of Contents

People

Prolog

The Old King- Protagonist, once known as Athan son of Medius
Thais – His beloved
Enoch – a former boon companion
Jacob, Kaj, Pelops, Tenucer (the younger) and Rasmus - his other
    hunting companions

Soldier

Athan son of Medius – Protagonist, a rising young soldier
Thaddeus son of Ajax - an old campaigner & comrade of Athan
Erinsys –The first important woman in Athan's life
Phineas – A bad man
Milo – One of Phineas' bad men
Cottus – Another of Phineas' big bad men
Ocnus – Yet another of Phineas' bad men
Persis – A very good woman, in a bad sort of way
Anteros – Persis' boy servant
Yura – Erinsys' late husband
Cyrus – An old Captain with a cottage
Baruch – A man with a bath house
Esther – A working girl with a lyre
Philo – A sergeant of the guard and a fine companion

Doreen- A would-be leader of a group of hetaira
Vania – A well endowed woman who likes men
Chara – A dancer of limited grasp
Lais – A hetaira of good education
Zita – A powerful singer with powerful ambitions
Skoripus – A criminal interested in moving up in the world
Ianthe – A singer who learned too much
Kulin – a porter and perhaps a relative

Demetrius – Also Known As Achilles, A.K.A. a disaster waiting to
    happen
Fedras – A senior captain of the guards
Karin – Erinsys' servant girl

Jason – Athan's son
Persephone and Dionme- Athan's younger daughters
Ariel – Persis' eldest daughter and Persephone's best friend
Amie – Persis' younger daughter
Beltos – A young hoplite officer of great promise
Timon – An old guard sergeant of ability
Simeon – A young peltast also with promise

Brigand
Azziz – A sorcerer priest from Tyre
Clestonese – A man who knows when to leave
Jonathan – A peltast scout with a bright future
Petra – A good fighting man
Laurel – A bold young woman worth of pursuit
Jokrastes – A former and possibly future lover of Laurel
Keros – See above
Marissa – A girl who did not have what Athan sought

Mira – A respectable matron, abducted
Rheta – Her also respectable daughter also abducted
Bea – Mira's respectable servant and former nurse to Rheta
Agalia – Rheta's not so respectable maid servant
Argo - Mira's dead husband, father of Rheta
Aorastus – Mira's cautious, but living husband
Kopria – Mira's faithful steward
Phemius – An underappreciated bard
Kirkor, Glaucus, Adrastus, and Kopria – all daring brigands
Nitsa – Glaucus' so respectable wife

Pirro – A useful red-headed man who learns things
Philip – An artisan of questionable reputation
The Satrap – A suspicious Achaemedidian potentate, with good
    reason
Drogas – The Satrap's captain of the guards
Rodas – A very capable hoplite captain with a devoted band
Endre, and Lexias – Other hoplite captains of varying abilities
Utana – The Satrap's right hand snake

Etor and Maur – Unindicted Co-conspirators

Ixon – A good man with horses, for a hoplite

Tenucer – An off again on again, long-term member of Athan's band

Talos – A man who knows the country

Theron – A hoplite and a hunter from a desirable country

Prolog– Going to Ground

The Old King's pony finally died sometime after midday, leaving him completely alone. He was prepared for her death, since the little mare had been shot in the ambush that separated him from his remaining companions. Only her willing heart and complete trust in him had kept her going this long. But now she could no longer help him; he was alone in a cold and desolate place, a long way from anyone who would not kill him on sight.

This was all his fault, of course; he had been in charge. He had been the one who had decided to go on this extended circuit of his lands on a combination hunting and exploring trip into the mountains that bounded the loosely defined the boundaries of his territory. He was the one who insisted that a ride of seven was all the escort he needed. 'If I expect my men to patrol the boundaries in rides of seven men, then I should be willing to do the same.' So he had only six men with him when they were ambushed. Of course he had not known when he left the Hold that he would be going this far and be gone for this long. Just as he had not known that he would have risen so high in the world. He had been lucky, and even with that luck it had taken him a very long time to get where he was

He pulled the leather saddle off the remains of his pony. His hunting bow had been lost in all the excitement so he left his quiver of hunting arrows behind, but before he did he broke his few remaining arrows. No point in leaving useful plunder. He pulled off the horse blanket and bundled it with his bedroll and balanced the load over one shoulder with his saddle bags over the other. Finally, taking up his water bag he headed uphill.

It was hard going with such an unbalanced load. He moved briskly until he was out of sight of the remains of his poor pony. He tried not to leave an obvious trail, but the ground was rocky and it looked like snow again, so he was not especially worried about being trailed by the bandits that had attacked him. He was more worried that wolves and birds would lead them to his pony and if they made a rapid search they might see and overtake him, so he made the best speed that he could uphill. He went uphill because bandits tended to be lazy and think a man on foot would take the easiest, most direct way back to his people; that way was downhill. The Old King stopped for a moment and sat on a fallen tree to ease his load. He reached into his mouth and pulled at a loose molar that had been nagging at him. With a twist and a pull he jerked the tooth out; the pain was not great; the relief was. He spat a bit of blood from his gums down on the ground behind the tree he was sitting on in a place where it would not be obvious. He then dropped the tooth down out of sight as well. He reached back into his gum and rubbed the new tooth coming in where his old one had once been. The King had recently lost all his teeth, which was not unusual, but having new ones come in to replace them was not usual at all, and this was not the first time it had happened to him. Getting new teeth was embarrassing. He liked to be away from his Hold while it was happening. That was another reason he chose to go on his long "hunting trip" with so few companions. He did not like to call attention to how different he was from other people. A grown man getting new teeth like some child was somewhat weird. And sure enough Enoch had teased him about it; claimed his cooking was so bad it made your teeth fall out, but so hearty it grew 'em back. The Old King had not seen Enoch die; when he looked back after that first sudden flight of javelins and arrows, all he saw was his pony standing next to his arrow-riddled body. Enoch had been with the pack animals in the middle of the line; he had not had a chance. Athan thought he had also seen Kaj and Pelops down; Rasmus and young Sergeant Tenucer had been bringing up the rear. Perhaps they had been outside the initial killing zone.

The Old King settled his burdens less uncomfortably, with the horse blanket across his shoulders, followed by the saddle and then his saddlebags, one side hanging down each of his shoulders with his little bedroll tied on top of it all. He then headed back up the hill at a steady pace. Eventually he struck a small game path that turned north parallel to the slope. Now he moved more cautiously, moving quickly across open areas, stopping to watch and listen for searchers. He did not think the bandits knew who he was or they would have made more of an effort to capture him for ransom instead of simply trying to kill them all at once. His clothing was plain, his most valuable visible possession was his kopis, a sword with a powerful down-curved blade sheathed at his side, but it was not really remarkable. His clothing, though of good quality was not ostentatious: leather boots, a stiff vest of red lacquered leather, brown trousers, a green long sleeved tunic, a wool scarf around his neck and the characteristic conical black cloth pilleus cap. His gloves were knitted wool with leather undersides, but they looked just like what they were: a gift made for a man by his woman. His gray cloak was lined and of the best quality but then they had all been wearing gray cloaks. Even his dagger was unremarkable with a wide curved bronze blade and plain polished wooden handle.

Athan wondered how they could have been so badly surprised. They were all experienced and though not alerted to any specific threat, were by nature alert and watchful. Perhaps it was because of the season; though the day had been pleasant enough, it was clear a winter storm was on the way, and the ride had been pressing to get down from the hills before full dark. The ambush had been well prepared. There had been no warning, so it had obviously been in place for some time. They were making their way single file along a narrow trail that was running halfway along a steep slope. Young Jacob and he were the only ones he was certain had not been hit by that sudden initial shower of arrows and javelins from the steep hillside above the trail. Jacob had been in the lead, and as he had been trained, he spurred ahead to get beyond the ambush. You don't fight from inside the trap," he always told his men. "Those in front get beyond, turn and fight; those behind, attack the ambusher's flank. Those caught in the middle, get out ahead or back if you can. If you can't, attack right into them. Never stay in the zone where they expect to kill you." It worked as well as anything else he had learned in his long career of conflict.

In one way it had worked this time. He was alive and unhurt. The Old King had been second in line, and after a single brief glance back at the carnage behind had followed Jacob along the trail. At a narrow place hemmed in by a tree growing on the hill on one side and a shrub next to the steep drop-off on the other, two spearmen had stepped out, one from either side. The one on the right-hand uphill side moved up and expertly spitted poor young Jacob right off his pony. But the Old King had closed by then, and using Jacob's plunging pony as a screen on his left, had simply ridden down the spearman on the right before he could extract his spear from poor young Jacob. The King knew his pony had taken at least one arrow in the initial volley; he felt it hit just behind his own leg. She must have taken another arrow on that wild dash out of the ambush angling from behind up into her ribs, but he was so concerned about keeping low and riding hard down the winding trail he did not think of it until she finally began to falter. When he reckoned he was clear, he pulled up and looked back. He saw several of his attackers hurrying after him on foot, out of bowshot range but too many to fight, and coming on at a run. The Old King turned his poor pony on down the trail, leaving his pursuers behind. He had lost at least four friends and a wonderful little pony to those miserable felons. There would a reckoning, but only if he was able to get back home. Perhaps Jenucer and Rasmus had been far enough back to escape the ambush; they could make their way back to the Hold and return with reinforcements. But that would take at least several days, if not more, considering the coming storm. And they could not be expected to pursue the bandits with vigor once they had collected the bodies of his friends, especially with winter arriving so soon. No, the King did not count on anyone rescuing him. If he was to revenge himself on these bandits, he would have to survive and lead his men back here himself.

It was well past midday now. The wind was picking up, and it was beginning to get seriously cold. The Old King knew that Old Man Winter was now a much greater threat to him than any number of bandits. He estimated that he was over half a parasang from where his poor pony lay, more than one parasang from the site of the ambush. It was time from him to start thinking of shelter and a fire. It was going to be a very cold night. He found a faint game trail that ran parallel to the slope and began to follow it; he had climbed high enough. It was time to make distance and look for a place to lay up. He started looking for a good deadfall, or perhaps even a cave in the hill that was sloping up steeply on his left-hand side. He could make a little hut or lean-to, surround it with cut evergreen branches and build a little fire inside. He had done something like that before, but not for a very, very long time. In any event, any shelter he found would have to be concealed from the searchers he was sure would come looking for him.

He paused behind some firs at the edge of a shallow draw that led to the northeast tending somewhat uphill. The draw was created by a high narrow arm of rock thrusting downhill. Looking up the draw he thought he saw what might be a cave opening near the top of the draw. He moved out from cover after taking care to look and listen for any possible watchers. Midway up the draw an old stump provided both possible concealment and a perch for a closer look at what might be the entrance to a nice snug cave. Because he was watching behind for danger the King did not glance up at the cave mouth again until he reached the stump. At once he saw this was not a cave entrance but only a shallow dimple in the cliff face. If he had been on a pony's back he would have been high enough to see that right away. The little depression in the rock was not what he wanted; it was too shallow and was exposed to what was a strengthening cold wind.

As he turned back the King noticed a set of low bushy evergreens on the far side of the draw directly below what appeared to be a crack in the steep cliff face. He carried his burdens across the draw and paused behind the evergreens to get a closer look. On this northwest side of the draw the sides were almost sheer vertical rock walls. At some point the base of the cliff had separated from the upper portion, and then apparently slid downhill a few cubits before settling back at the top, leaving a tall but narrow triangular gap in the slab of rock leaning against the west face of the cliff perhaps five or six cubits wide and ten high. A narrow triangular niche was thus created behind the entire length of the slab. The earth at the bottom appeared to be level. The King moved cautiously into the opening.

What he could see in the gloom was a space about ten to twelve cubits deep ending in a tangle of deadwood at the far end. Apparently, when the slab had fallen back against the cliff, it had been somewhat cushioned by a substantial growth of timber. But at any rate the deadwood blocked the other end of the gap almost completely; enough light remained to allow an inspection of the entire enclosed area. He stepped into the crevice and looked around. Out of the wind, it seemed immediately warmer. A quick examination revealed the floor of the space to be more or less level, with enough space against the front slab where he could build a fire. There was plenty of height for him to stand upright, and it was wide enough to make a bed against the cliff side. This was the place to spend the night. It was protected from wind, rain, and prying eyes and the deadwood drift at the back of the crevice would provide more than enough firewood. He dropped his burdens against the cliff side and knelt to make a small fire pit. Using his broad bladed dagger he scraped a small area in the shallow dirt against the downhill side of the crevice, and then made a simple hearth ring with the flat stones that littered the floor. Next he gathered some of the smaller ready bits of wood from the deadfall. He took care to lay down kindling and placed it ready to take fire. Finally he used his kopis to hack some substantial branches from the deadfall at the far end of the crevice. Although the kopis was designed as a weapon of war, the thick convex blade worked wonderfully well at chopping off branches; slicing through wrist-thick branches with a single blow.

His fire ready for lighting, the King then pulled his scarf around his neck and wrapped himself in his cloak. He was going to have to go outside to get some bedding. The brief respite from the wind inside the niche made it seem even colder outside. Pausing briefly to scan down slope for anyone determined enough to still be seeking him in the rapidly worsening weather, he moved downhill directly to a small meadow that opened up below the game trail he had been following. There were still patches of long grass there; he went to each using his kopis to cut bunches of the grass as quickly as he could. Although the inward curve of his sword was well suited to slicing as well as chopping, the blade was too thick to work as an efficient sickle. Instead, he grasped the tops of the clumps of grass put the blade at the base of the grass and moved the clumps along the blade. In a few moments he had cut a double armful. Sheathing the kopis again, he stumbled up the slope to his new lair as quickly as he could. Throwing his first load of grass down inside the mouth of the crevice, he returned downhill twice more carrying loads of grass into his den. He was struck with the idea that he was like a marmot, carrying up his fodder to his den. His harvesting left obvious traces, but he was not concerned about it being seen for it had begun to snow. He stopped at the entrance to his new lair after depositing his third load of grass inside. Although he was winded he saw one more thing he needed before settling in for the night. Just upslope were two evergreens, one slightly taller than himself, the other half his size but with full branches. He worked his way laboriously uphill to them.

Conditions seemed to be worsening by the moment and it was already getting dark, but he took the time to cut the two trees down; the smaller one went with a single stroke but the larger took half a dozen cuts from the thick blade. He put the kopis away and took the butt end of each tree, one in each hand, and dragged them down to the crevice. At the entrance to the crevice he stopped long enough to slice away all the branches from the smaller tree. These he threw into the crevice. Then, setting the larger tree upright, he backed into the triangular opening, pulling it in behind him. It fit into the opening and blocked the entrance reasonably well from both outside observers and the persistent draft caused the by the strong north wind. It also blocked the light. The King fumbled stupidly about in the gloom trying to find where he had laid the fire. He could not seem to get his tinder box out from the bag he wore around his neck under his undertunic. He took off his gloves and fumbled the little bag open. He was surprised to realize the outside of the bag was damp. Even though had he been out in a gathering snowstorm, he had been sweating.

He was feeling the strain of his efforts. The Old King had not eaten since breakfast this morning and had been working hard since the ambush: riding a dying horse, carrying his gear over steep mountain trails, cutting grass and trees, all in cold weather. Now he was cold, tired, and hungry. He could not seem to stop his hands from shaking. He peered dimly at the pile of wood he prepared and tried to remember just what he was supposed to do next. What he really wanted to do was lie down on that pile of grass just behind him, wrap himself in his cloak and blanket and rest, and maybe sleep for a while. The old man shook his head to clear it. No, if he did not start a fire and get something hot inside him he might never wake up. He rose and pushed the tree out of the opening to let in some light. There was little light to let in. Night and the storm were both gathering fast. Getting back down on all fours the King knelt beside his hope: a pile of sticks, twigs, pine cones, and a bit of tow (scorched cloth rubbed with pitch) from his tinder box. He took the steel striker and tried to hold it firmly in his right hand. In his left he held the shard of flint. He struck the flint with the striker. Sparks flew into the tow. It should have started glowing but it did not. It had been a long time since the King had needed to start his own fires. In the Hold, servants had his fires going before he awoke. There were candles and lamps lit when he needed them. Even out in the field, Enoch or someone else lit the campfire while he did more important things like sitting around and waiting for Enoch to bring him his dinner. But he was alone now. If he did not start his own fire, he would die. He had started fires before, he could do it now.

Again and again he struck the edge of the shard of flint with his striker. He could get sparks but none of them would take. Finally he stopped trying. He stood up and returned to his belongings. He took off his sword belt and let the kopis drop to the earth, then bent down and rooted around in his saddlebags until he found the bread he had left in there, wrapped in cloth, a morsel he had intended to eat at the midday stop. That and a piece of meat, venison from the stag they had killed the previous day, washed down with a swallow of water became his dinner; the first food since that morning. Steadied, he rubbed his hands together and once again knelt down to his tinder box. This time when the hot sparks hit them the tender began to glow. Carefully he blew on the embers until suddenly the tow flashed into flame. Piece by piece the King fed in bits of twigs and pine needles, growing the flame into a fire. By the time some of the pine cones had caught and the bigger branches began making crackling sounds he was stiff from bending over the fire. So glad was he of the heat that he built a bigger fire than he really needed. What was the old saying, 'a small fire is usually better than a big one.' As heat and light from the fire filled the crevice, he got up and replaced the pine tree in the entrance. Then he sat on his pack in front of the fire watching the flames and the natural draft pulling the smoke to the top of the crevice while the fire steamed moisture out of his clothing.

By now it was almost dark with a howling wind, blowing snow in wild patterns outside his sanctuary. Reinvigorated, the King ensured that there would be enough firewood from the deadfall close at hand; he would not run out of wood before daylight. He set up four stones around the fire to act as a stand for his copper cup so he could heat some tea and maybe warm up some more of the venison. When he checked his water bag he realized that he was low on water; not a good thing. Fortunately there was a tremendous amount of precipitation coming down just on the other side of his pine tree 'door'. So he once again put on his gloves wrapped his scarf around his face, and his cloak around the rest of him, picked up his broad copper plate and stepped out into the storm. He filled his plate with drifting snow six or seven times, each time dumping the collected snow into the cup that was steaming over the fire. Once he emptied the cup of snow melt back into his water bag for future use. Eventually he realized that he was getting chilled once again and he was not really getting much water for his efforts, so he abandoned further attempts to refill his water bag and replaced the pine tree in the entrance. Once the water in his cup was hot again, he added some tea, and placed another strip of meat next to the fire. He then reviewed the contents of his saddlebags: his cup and plate, a copper spoon, a bit of dried meat, some dried apples in a separate cloth bag, a spare set of socks, and small-clothes, both dirty. After some thought he took the socks out of the clothing bag and placed them on a rock by the fire to warm. There was a bit of soap, a flannel he used to dry his hands after cleaning up (most of his people thought his cleanliness to be excessive) some oil and a sharpening stone, a good-sized bag of oats intended for himself and his late pony, more herb tea, and some sewing equipment for repairs. He had his dagger, sword, tinderbox, though much of his tow was now used up, and the clothing he was wearing. He appreciated the close warmth of his silk undertunic on a night like this. Perhaps his men may have thought him a bit of a sissy for wearing silk next to his skin, but he knew that an arrow would not normally cut through silk. That meant that if you pulled carefully on the shirt, you could extract the arrow from the wound the same way it came in, so long as it did not penetrate too deeply. He would have recommended it to all his men, but the cost would have been prohibitive. Secretly, of course, he did like the way he felt on his skin, but he had never told anyone that except Thais.

And Thais was dead. And so were old Enoch and young Jacob and Kaj and Pelops and probably young Tenucer and Rasmus as well. And so were Erinsys, and Jason, who died with, for, and because of poor Kiren. And Thaddeus and Persis, and Timon, and Jonathan, and Beltos, and Rheta, and Mira, dear sweet Mira. And Simeon, Philo, Tenucer the elder, Spiros, Stamitos, Rodas, old Abacus, who had not been old when he Athan took him in service, all gone to the other side; and so many, many others as well. And yet here he remained, doing the things he had always done: taking care of those in his charge.

Since there was nothing else for him to do, the King prepared to go to sleep. He banked his fire with considerable care, he did not want to have to start a fire with his tinderbox in the morning, and then he prepared for bed. First he put down a layer of grass on the flat area next to the cliff face. Next he placed the ground cloth he had wrapped around his bedroll down and then spread the remaining grass he had gathered onto half of it, and then folded the ground cloth over the pile grass to give him a pallet to sleep on. His pillow would be the rolled up saddle pad, head facing toward the entrance and near the fire. His primary concern was not comfort, but insulation from the cold earth.

Sitting on his new bed, the King took off his stiff red leather vest. Then he pulled off his boots, pointed his stocking soles at the flames, and warmed his feet to the fire. After his socks had stopped steaming, he took the now toasty warm pair of dirty spare socks off the rock and pulled them over this other pair. Finally, wearing his undertunic, tunic, trousers, cap, two pairs of socks on his feet, gloves on his hands, his scarf around his neck and face, he wound his cloak around himself, and lay down on his newly-made bed. He covered himself from the waist down with the horse blanket and then stretched the heavy wool blanket from his feet to his chin. He sat up for a moment and placed a layer of pine boughs over his blanket as a final extra bit of covering before he lay down to sleep. He was now dry and out of the wind, although in truth his refuge was more than a little drafty. Well, he was now well insulated from mere drafts.

It had been a very bad day. That morning he had been a wealthy and powerful man, a king, surrounded by good friends and devoted companions. Now he was completely alone, his friends murdered or scattered. He was a hunted fugitive hiding in a cave with few resources and fewer prospects. But the King was not a man to agonize over losses. Within moments he was asleep. And began dreaming, dreaming of long ago before he had become a King; before he was a bandit himself, or even before he was a captain chasing other bandits.

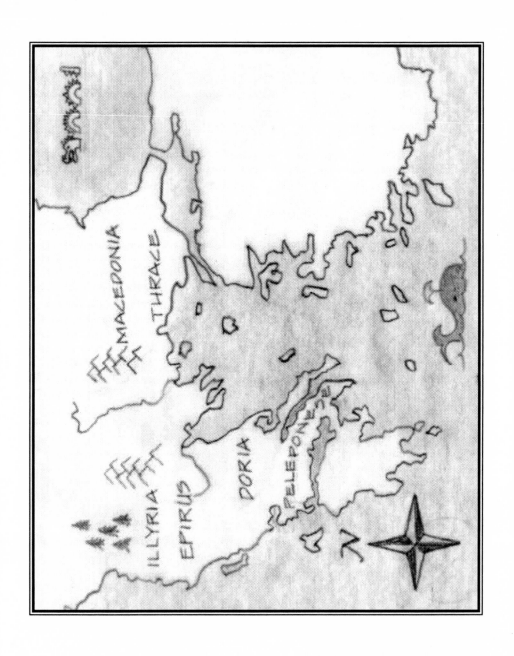

Part One – Soldier

Chapter One – A Rescue

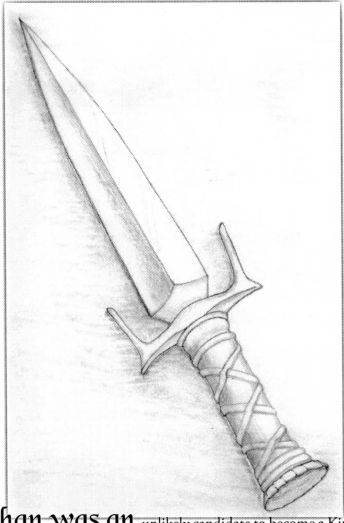

Athan was an unlikely candidate to become a King. He had grown up in the small city-state of Epiria, a part of a loosely bound confederation of cities that formed the territory of Epirus. He was the second son and sixth child of a carpenter and his unhappy wife. By the time his father had finally obliged his mother by dying of dysentery, Athan had been just old enough to persuade an uncle to get him into the city's guards. He was fortunate enough to have attracted an older mentor there. Thaddeus, a burly man with thick black hair and a face that showed some of his many fights, had taken the boy under his wing and taught him how to get along in the world of fighting men. This included so much more than learning how to hold your shield or fight with a spear and sword.

Thaddeus was an old campaigner and welcomed the chance to teach what he had learned in his life to a bright and eager young soldier. Most of their comrades thought the two companions had become lovers in the Laconian way, but in fact their relationship was more of a paternal nature. Indeed, part of young Athan's instruction included dealing with the prostitutes and other available women that seemed to congregate around the camps of fighting men. And when, several years after becoming a city guard, Athan first began to develop a reputation within the city it was because of just such a woman.

Her name was Erinsys, and she worked part time in one of the local taverns.

"What do you see in that bitch, anyway," asked Thaddeus. "She has a sharp tongue and a waspish nature. Nothing seems to satisfy her."

"One thing does," smiled Athan.

"For any man that pays her," retorted his companion. It was a measure of their friendship that he could make a comment like that without provoking a fight. Young men can be touchy about their girlfriends. But Thaddeus was merely voicing his concern for his young friend's attachment to a woman, especially one as prickly as Erinsys.

"No, it's not like that," responded his young companion, "She is a widow, three times a widow! Perhaps sometimes she does spend some time with other men but that is just because she has nothing left. It is just a way for her to take care of herself for a while."

"Is that what you are to her," replied Thaddeus, "just one of the men who help her get by?"

"No, replied Athan with complete sincerity, "what we have is different."

"Of course" replied the big guard showing nothing in his face, "that must be true."

The irony, however, was lost on Athan.

Athan was young and very self confident, and so on a fine early autumn evening some nights later he went back to the house where he usually found bread, cheese, wine, and Erinsys. It was not exactly an inn or café or even a tavern, but kind of an unofficial sort of a place where wine, food and other things could be obtained and enjoyed. But that night the man who filled the role of innkeeper could only provide three of the objects of Athan's desires. Erinsys was not available. She was not entertaining another man, she no longer worked there. An increasingly agitated Athan discovered that due to a matter of some debts, whether the innkeeper's, or Erinsys', or some of her relatives was not quite clear, Erinsys had been transferred, sold in Athan's view, to an actual full-time brothel.

"She is not a slave, she is a freewoman," argued Athan, "She is not even a prostitute. You had no right to send her there!"

The innkeeper was a man of some sensitivity; sensitivity toward danger that is. He was well aware of the dangers presented by an excited aggressive soldier, and Athan was a strapping example of just such trouble. So the innkeeper talked, and explained and eventually convinced Athan that his best course of action was to talk directly to Erinsys who would undoubtedly be glad to explain everything to him. All he had to do was go over to see her at Phineas'. Athan did not know who Phineas was or where his establishment was located. Of course the innkeeper was glad to tell him exactly how to get there.

Athan had enough presence of mind to compose himself before walking up to Phineas' place, a solid two-story walled structure. Like most buildings in town, it had a few narrow windows facing the street and heavy shutters on those. The door was made of thick timbers with a central peephole and which was firmly closed. Athan banged on the door. The peephole slid open.

"I'm looking for a good time. I hear you have some nice girls in there" Athan asked in his most matter-of-fact voice.

"Maybe" replied a thick voice, "but they're all busy just now. Come back later."

This was puzzling to Athan. Certainly a brothel had to have security to ensure that no one harmed the girls, or worse, escaped without paying, and since they did commerce after the sun went down they were as susceptible to robber gangs as any other business open after dark. But it was not as if they were doing anything illegal. Or were they?

"Well, can you tell me about the girls you do have?" he asked in his most reasonable tone. "I can go somewhere else, but I hear you have some new girls that are special."

"They're all special," the gruff voice stated. "Come back in an hour and one of them will take good care of you." And with that, the tiny window slapped shut.

Athan repaired with speed to the tavern house. The innkeeper quickly relocated himself to stand beside a large scarred man who helped provide security and cleaned up the place. That cleanup extended to disposing of recalcitrant customers.

"She is not there."

"Of course they told you that." replied the innkeeper, now thoroughly in a damage-control mode. "Believe me, she is there, she left with Phineas and one of his men two days ago. They just are shy about showing any girls that are still new until they have trained them."

"What kind of a place did you sell her to?" demanded Athan.

"I told you, I did not sell her," replied the innkeeper, "she went there for a better opportunity."

Athan looked at the innkeeper, and then at his helper who was now holding a cudgel in his right hand, and decided he needed some help. He went to see Thaddeus.

"Tough problem," admitted Thaddeus. "You don't know if she deserves to be there, wants to be there, Hades, you don't even know if she is there at all. One thing for certain, that place is nowhere that you want to go into without some help and a plan for getting out."

"Look, why don't I go over there again and try to find out if she is there. If she is, maybe I can talk to her; maybe find out what is going on. If she wants to stay, she can stay. If she wants to leave and they won't let her, then I come back here and we get some of the guard together and we go back to straighten things out."

"This may not be guard business," cautioned the older man. "But even if it is not, those people in there may not appreciate someone like you stirring things up. Look at it from their viewpoint; if they are doing nothing wrong, they are going to resent a young and not very affluent young swain coming in bothering the girls and disturbing the customers. It is obvious this is a very discrete place. And if they are

6

taking free girls and making them slaves illegally, then they want to keep the city magistrates out of their business. And if they are paying the magistrates off, then they have their approval and they will have no fear of getting rid of you. In fact to keep a low profile they will kill you just as quietly as they can and dump your body in some midden. No, you are not going to be able to just walk in there and talk to your girl. Let me round up some of the fellows and let's come up with a plan."

Thaddeus left their barracks room and headed for a common room near the mess hall where their companions often sat talking and playing dice when they were off duty. Athan watched him go. Then he went into his kit that was stored neatly beside his cot where he kept his equipment. He did not dare take any of his armor or a sword; that would be too obvious for his plan. Instead he drew out a dagger. It was his best single possession. It was of good iron, with at straight blade two fingers wide and a bit longer than his hand. It had stout quillons projected forward alongside the blade. Thaddeus and he had practiced using this quillons to catch the blade of an enemy's sword. The idea was that if you could catch a sword blade between a quillon and the dagger's blade you could twist the dagger so that the dagger in your left hand trapped your opponent's blade. Then you dealt with him using the main weapon you carried in your right hand. For this work he could only carry one weapon, one he could hide, and the dagger would be it.

He took two short strips of leather and bound the dagger's sheath to his right thigh. Then removing his everyday tunic, he examined his few alternatives for attire. His best tunic was somewhat dirty, but a few moments with a rag and brush got rid the worst of the dirt and stains off the dark blue knee-length garment. He then donned a fresh set of small clothes, then strapped on his sandals and took down his cloak. The cloak was the standard one for the watch, but that was not obvious. Using the bronze mirror at the end of the barracks, he shaved using the common razor. Athan was one of the few guards that did not wear a beard since his was still a bit thin, and being clean shaven made him feel somehow cleaner. Thaddeus had also warned him that in close battle an enemy could grab a long beard. Athan then oiled and combed his brown hair back to the back of his neck. He paced nervously back and forth in the barracks. His dagger kept slipping down his leg requiring him to retie the strips of leather, but the bunching of his thigh muscle caused it to loosen and slide down again after a few moments. Finally he poked a small hole in his tunic, and fastened a thin thong from the ropes that acted as his girdle down inside his tunic to support the dagger's sheath. That kept the sheath up satisfactorily. He was ready. He sat on his cot for a while. Then he paced some more.

Finally, after another half of an hour of waiting Athan decided that Thaddeus had either decided to go ahead without him, or, more probably, been persuaded by his friends to have a few beakers of wine and forget the whole thing. Athan felt his own ardor fading, so he decided to go over to the brothel himself before he lost his nerve entirely and see if he could find out more about Erinsys' actual situation. On the way out of the barracks he pulled out his leather script. He seldom had much money, but he did have a presentable script with a nice leather strap that carried over his shoulder. He took the time on his way out to pick up several lead markers the men sometimes used for playing dice. They looked like coins and give his script a nice fat weight. Perhaps in bad light he could be mistaken for the son of a wealthy man.

All the way to the house Athan was keyed up. He felt fully alert and alive; it was even better than before he went into a battle. There was the same sense of unreality, the same heightened senses, but this was better because he was in control, not locked in a shield wall with men ahead, behind, and on both sides. He reviewed all the possible contingencies that he might encounter and his response to each of them. Over and over he told himself that if things became dicey, he would simply walk out; just apologize and leave. If things did not get out of control he could come back another time and figure out just what was going on. Suddenly he found himself at the thick door once again. Athan resisted an impulse to just walk away. He looked at the door and took a deep, calming breath. Assuming what he thought to be a relaxed pose he knocked on the door. Nothing happened. He waited, keenly aware that he might be under observation. Finally, he reached out languidly again to knock when the observation slot was abruptly pulled open.

"What do you want?"

"A woman, I heard this was the new place." Athan replied in his best attempt at a bored rich man's accent. "Were they wrong?"

There was a long pause. "Who is 'they'?" queried the horse voice.

"Look, are you open for business or not?" replied Athan trying his best to sound as though he were a wealthy young man who was about to take his search for fun elsewhere.

There was a short pause and then the sound of two rather substantial bolts being drawn. Athan was disappointed with himself when he felt his heart began to race.

"Come on in, stripling."

Inside was nothing special. It was warm in the building. There were two couches against the far wall, a sturdy table with a bench, some nice brass lamps, fabric wall hangings partially concealing three open doorways, and two stout brawlers dressed in vests, kilts, and thin sheens of sweat. But he was inside. One of the men shot the bolts back in place and lingered by the door, which put him behind Athan. Not good. Time to be casual.

"So what kind of girls do you have?" Athan asked looking around. He noticed that the two men not only had thick cudgels in their wide belts, but each also had a substantial curved dagger as well. The door on his right was almost completely covered by a wall hanging, but the one directly opposite the entrance was open enough to show that, like many houses of this type, there was a central courtyard with an attempt at a garden in the center. A middle-aged man with thinning hair came through the left hand door. This man was smaller than the other two but obviously more dangerous. It was not just the sword he wore on his left hip, though Athan was pretty sure from the length of the scabbard and shape of the hilt that it was a leaf-shaped hoplite blade, more common on a battlefield than in a house in the city. Stuffed into his belt on the right side was a short whip with at least half a dozen short lengths of leather, each capped by a small lead weight. It looked as though the ends were wet; Athan smelled blood. But the most dangerous thing about him was hard to specify. He was so calm, so in command of himself, and so obviously ready to take decisive action. He behaved as though he was walking into his own kennel. The two big men deferred to him without a word. Athan moved as casually as he could away from the entrance and to the space between the right hand door and the entrance to the courtyard. He knew two things: he was in trouble and Erinsys was in much deeper trouble than he was.

Athan had a distinct feeling that it would be better to end up dead on a midden than to be in the control of this man. He had to get her out. If she was even in this place and still alive.

"My name is Phineas. I am the owner of this house. We do not normally take new customers without a reference," the dangerous man told Athan. "Who did you say recommended us?"

"Oh, I overhead two older men say this was the best place in the city for special girls," Athan lied.

"Girls, boys, animals, anything you can imagine, I can provide, but I must tell you that the pleasures I offer are not cheap."

"Well, I can probably afford your prices," said Athan jingling the lead slugs in his wallet with a false sense of bravado. "My family is well off, I have wealth of my own and I have wealthy friends. And if what you offer is so exceptional, I can recommend your house to those friends. If you do not take business that just walks in how can your business grow."

"Oh, my business is just fine," replied the man looking at Athan like a snake looks at a foolish bird that has just fallen from the nest. He moved around the room to Athan's right, putting Athan between him and his henchmen. Athan backed to the right as well to keep the man from forcing him to put his back to the threat of Phineas' two men. "And what family are you from? I know most of the better families in the city. Who are your friends? Are they outside?"

"No, they are back at the tavern house waiting for me," countered Athan. "I was the only one who was willing to try a new place. I haven't had a girl in a while. You said you have girls? I like them of average size, saucy, but not too hard. Someone about my own age. Do you have anyone like that I could use?" By now Athan had backed up until he was against the wall between the door that had been on his right and the center door.

"Why, yes, we had someone like that come in the day before yesterday," said the man, "Brown eyes and hair, used to work in a local place. But her training has only just begun. She won't be ready for a customer like you for a few months. By then you will find her most satisfactory, not a bit of hardness left in her. Do you want to come back?"

It was obvious to Athan that Phineas either knew or suspected that Athan was looking for his new acquisition. In fact, Phineas had faced this situation many times in the past. When a boy or girl is ripped out of their former life to start a new one in very different circumstances, it was common for a boyfriend, or brother, or father to come looking for her. Phineas felt the best way to solve the problem of friends and relations was the same one he used with his new acquisitions: a firm hand. If intimidation would not work at the first application, a beating usually would. Best of all, if an intruder could be quietly silenced permanently there was no come back and Phineas' reputation was simultaneously enhanced. The friends and family seldom made a fuss so long as nothing could be proven. This young man had presented himself here, alone, with money. The story of friends waiting for him was probably a lie, and if not, was a weak defense. The streets were dangerous, and the boy had never made it to Phineas' house. Such a pity. The main thing that prevented Phineas from killing this foolish young man on the spot was that Phineas was wearing a sword. A sword is a fine killing tool, but it kills by letting out blood, sometimes lots of blood. It would not do to have to clean up a large pool of blood in his very foyer, especially with customers due to arrive within the hour. The other small problem was that the boy was alert and held himself like a fighting man. This complicated matters; most of his victims had been angry and indignant so that it had been easy to get one of his employees behind him for a sudden blow to the head. The fatal bloodletting could be done in some alley or midden before the subject woke from the blow. All that was necessary was to get him to lose control. He did not seem to have a weapon. He was probably here for the new girl, a troublesome wench, what was her name? Ah, yes, Erinsys.

"But if you are interested in this new girl, a common tavern slut called Erinsys, you can have her. I will even give her to you for a reduced rate, but I have to warn it may be a long wait. She has many customers to service tonight so when you finally get to use her she will probably be exhausted and, how shall I say it, somewhat sloppy. Perhaps you can use her like she was a boy, but then that will probably be somewhat loose by then, too."

His words were calculated to drive a brother or boyfriend into a rage. And they had an effect on the young man in front of him too, but before Athan could reply there was a firm knock on the door. Phineas looked over to the man closest to the door. "Get rid of whoever it is."

The man obediently turned to the door and slid back the opening.

"What do you want?" he asked in the same voice Athan remembered.

Phineas never took his eyes of Athan. Athan glanced briefly to the door but his attention never left Phineas. The tension in the room was palpable. Time seemed to slow down. Athan now fully understood his folly; his dagger was concealed so carefully that it was almost inaccessible. What had he been thinking? He had not expected to be confronted so aggressively almost from the moment he entered the house. Now he was facing three armed men without easy access to a weapon of his own. Then he realized that he had a weapon hanging over his right shoulder, his script loaded with nearly a score of lead markers.

"We want some women!" came the drunken-sounding reply in a voice Athan knew well: Thaddeus!

"We only have boys here," relied the doorman.

"That's my friend," said Athan loudly enough so that Thaddeus could hear him.

"Get out," said Phineas to Athan in a flat voice. Perhaps Phineas was distracted by the resumed hammering on the door or perhaps it was this young man who was not behaving the way he should, but his eyes gave away his intentions. It was a reprieve for Athan, though probably a death sentence for Erinsys. If Phineas could not easily dispose of this male protector, he would remove the object of his desires. It would be even easier and safer to quietly get rid of the troublesome wench than it would this boyfriend. Athan took the meaning from Phineas' eyes as clearly as though the thought had been spoken aloud. The two men stood with their eyes locked; and then Phineas snapped. He turned his gaze away from Athan.

"Get rid of those idiots!" he barked turning his back to Athan.

In one sudden smooth motion Athan slid his script's stout leather strap off his shoulder down to his fist and whipped it around in a short arc over Phineas' shoulder. Phineas felt rather than saw the leather bag coming around and tried to jerk away from the blow. The script whipped over his back and lapped onto the front of his right shoulder. He gave a short scream and clutched his shoulder. There was a moment of complete stunned silence. The two thugs stood with their hands on their cudgels, Phineas held his left hand over his broken right collarbone and glared at Athan. Athan stood with the script swinging from his right hand. Then something hit the outside door with a resounding THUMP! And everything began to happen at once.

In a room upstairs at the back of the house two women lay on cushions on opposite sides of the room. They barely knew one another's names, and shared little in common beyond their current location in the same room, looking out onto the central courtyard.

One was a young woman, in a plain light cotton chemise that came past her knees. She had a young woman's figure and her face was still clear and unlined. Her hair was probably her best feature: dark, with a fine natural wave, worn pulled back and halfway down over her back. There was normally something about her that seemed to let everyone know that she was one tough cookie; small she might be but she could be very determined. Now, however, that aggressive self-assurance was gone. Her cheeks were dry at the moment but her normally pretty hazel eyes still showed the redness from her tears. Erinsys lay on her cushion in the borrowed chemise staring fixedly at nothing at all and trying not to think. When she did, all she could repeat over and over was a variation on "How did I get myself in this situation." She was ashamed, angry, and terrified but determined not to let any of that show. She did not realize that she was failing badly.

Across the room from her another woman in her mid twenties lounged on a low dining couch. Persis could make any position look languorous when she so desired. She was helped by her looks. Although she would never admit it she knew she was beautiful. Long straight dark hair, an oval face with a small chin, balanced features, a glowing complexion, perfect white teeth, and huge dark eyes. She was somewhat taller than usual with long firm legs and a wonderful hourglass figure. Perhaps she was a bit less rounded than some men preferred, but she considered herself a trained athlete and kept herself supple and fit. But what made her truly beautiful was not obvious. Sheer vitality came off of her in waves which, combined with an absolute confidence fascinated both men and women. Just as Persis knew she was desirable, she also knew that she was smarter than anyone around her. She understood ideas quicker and remembered things better even than her elder brothers who were considered great scholars. But she preferred solving human equations to geometric ones. There was nothing more satisfying than understanding what made people do what they did and then causing them to do something you wanted all the while making them think it was their own idea. Persis could have had a brilliant career as a courtesan in her eastern homeland but for one tragic flaw in her young personality. She loved adventure. When she was a girl she had seen a man with a trained bear. Persis noticed that this trainer, unlike some others had retained the bear's teeth and claws. When Persis had been introduced to him she asked him why he had not removed the bear's teeth.

"Ah, girl," grinned the man, "where's the fun in having a bear like that?"

Persis understood him perfectly. In fact, she had come to crave the excitement of manipulating people, especially strong men; in pitting her wits against the fates with her life on the line. She was a natural gambler, but one who loved to cheat. She did not always win; her presence in a brothel in this city proved that. But it was not a common brothel, and she had done well for herself, both in money and influence over the last few months. But Phineas was becoming increasingly difficult to manage. And he liked to hurt people; especially those he thought were trying to put themselves in competition with him. And he was beginning to realize how powerful his top girl had become. All in all it was time for her to leave. All she had to do was figure out how to get by six guards and the only accessible door, one that was constantly guarded. She knew she would have only one chance, but this did not worry her. Persis liked the idea of staking everything on a well conceived plan. She had an idea of what to do, but she needed a strong distraction and a clearer idea of where to go when she departed this profitable but confining existence. The girl who had been shoved into her room a while ago might be a diversion. She appeared to be local, brand new and not broken down just yet. She was pretty enough in a conventional way with a nice figure, and no visible scaring yet. Undoubtedly she had either family or a lover who might be induced to come to see her. That could give Persis the opportunity she needed.

A sudden scream came from the front door. Screams were not uncommon in Phineas' house, but not from a grown man and definitely not from what sounded like Phineas himself. Persis come to full alertness.

A dull but powerful THUMP resounded through the house.

Rising smoothly from her couch Persis went into action as though she had been waiting for an expected signal. In a sense she had. "Get up," she told Erinsys, "I need your help."

Erinsys looked up at her in misery. "They raped me," she said as though answering a question, "they didn't have to, and they didn't have to beat me, but they just laughed at me. And they raped me."

"Of course they did," replied Persis as though explaining something to a child.

"Why?"

"Because it made them feel important and powerful. Now if you don't want it to happen again get up and help me."

"I'm going to kill them," growled Erinsys getting to her feet.

"No, we are going to get some man to do that for us," responded Persis opening a secret drawer in her wardrobe. "Now, put on something suitable for the outside," Persis instructed, taking down a tasteful linen robe. "This should fit you reasonably well. Now get up and take that scarlet bag there and put these things in it," she said, indicating a rack of mostly flimsy and flowing garments lining the wall next to the wardrobe. Then, removing a small elaborate wooden box she stepped to the door. "Wait here with the bag and anything else you want to take out of here. I will be right back. Oh," she indicated another elaborate lacquer box, "take my cosmetics as well, I'll be needing them." Then, wrapping a light woolen cloak around herself, she gathered a bronze lamp from its wall hanging and turned out the door moving purposefully. Erinsys began listlessly stuffing things into the indicated luggage and wondering why Persis needed a cloak on such a pleasant evening.

Persis was back even before Erinsys had a chance to finish filling the cloth bag. Persis now had one of the houseboys, a cheeky little creature of about 10 years old in tow who was carrying another burden. She still carried the lamp.

"Leave what you haven't already packed," she commanded calmly. "We need to leave right away. I think the house is on fire." And with that she calmly held the lamp's flame to the fine curtains that framed the barred window.

Erinsys gaped at her as the flames caught, too stunned for words.

"Come on," smiled Persis, "Let's go find a rescuer to put out this terrible fire."

THUMP! The two thugs pulled out both daggers and clubs at the same time. One went to help his employer the other menaced Athan.

"I'm all right," grimaced Phineas, struggling to pull his sword from its scabbard with his left hand. Since the sword was belted on his left side and his right shoulder was obviously giving him considerable pain, this was neither quick nor easy. The delay saved Athan's life. "Kill him, Milo" commanded the struggling Phineas to the man who had gone to his aid. Athan reached under his tunic for his dagger with his left hand while sweeping his leather script around to keep off the nearer henchman. He quickly confirmed the flaw with his arrangement for the dagger. It was inconspicuous, secure, and damned difficult to get the blade out, especially with your left hand and most especially when trying to hold off two villains who were trying to kill you. He hopped around the room groping under his tunic. There was a fair amount of yelling going on, by everyone in the room. Athan found he had to retreat back to his right to prevent Milo from getting behind him. Just as Athan backed against the wall, things in the foyer got even crazier. Reinforcements in the form of two more bodyguards charged through the hangings on the right-hand door at speed and into the middle of the room. The first man, seeing the confusion, came to an abrupt stop, causing his companion to blunder into him. Athan added to their problems by hitting the second man on the back of his bald head. He went to his knees pawing at his head and bawling.

WHUMP came from the attackers outside. The pins holding the bottom latch were partially sprung by the weight of the well-directed blow. Athan leapt to his right through the center doorway into the courtyard then stopped, covering the door with his frantically swinging script. He was finally able to extract his dagger by hiking up his tunic well above his waist and jerking the blade free with his left hand. He was still holding it reversed, with the blade pointed down when Milo

16

and two companions came through the door using their clubs to block his swings and close with him.

THUMP! The top latch was now under attack and failing fast. Athan frantically blocked club blows with his dagger and dodged back and forth avoiding dagger thrusts and cudgel strokes. Phineas came into the courtyard behind his men. He had finally gotten his sword out and was holding it in his left hand while his right was tucked into the rope girdle around his tunic. "Milo, you and Ocnus go block the door before those brigands knock it down. Cottus and I will kill this one." Another WHUMP from the foyer accented the danger from that direction. "Now boy, I am going to kill you. Cottus, work around behind him."

But Athan had taken advantage of the respite. His dagger was now properly held pointed up and toward the foe. He had set his feet and gathered himself, with his heavy leather bag swinging slowly back and forth, and his mind clear and ready. Phineas was not sure how to deal with an alert, trained warrior in an open area, and his confusion showed. He started to direct Cottus again when Athan attacked. Phineas was not prepared nor was he comfortable with his sword in his left hand. And it is one thing to stab someone with a sword; it is another to fight with one. Athan blocked the weak left handed thrust with the dagger in his own left hand and, though he did not catch the blade with the quillons, he did push it wide while he slammed his shoulder into Phineas' right side, knocking him down and sending the sword flying as Phineas gave cry of pain. Athan then spun to confront Cottus, a large but slow moving adversary who seemed confused on just how to cope with the swinging weight coming at him from the right and a dagger attacking him from a left. As Athan forced him back he though he heard a woman's delighted laughter.

With a final THUMP, the latches on the main entrance gave up its resistance to a log suspended from two short lengths of rope and swung with a will by four determined guardsmen, two on each side. There was a tinkle of brass fittings shooting across the floor and a bang as the door flew open and Thaddeus and three comrades were in the house. They were experienced fighters and knew how to assault a breach. Carrying stout billets of firewood the four positively swarmed into the foyer to face not only Milo and Ocnus and the bald man who was still recovering from Athan's blow to his head but two more of Phineas' guards who had arrived on the scene as well. But, although the numbers were nearly even the struggle was not. The guardsmen blocked mostly ineffective blows and counter attacked, fighting with skill and as a team. The unfortunate bald man never had a chance to pick up a weapon before being so bludgeoned that he chose to spend the remainder of the fight curled in a ball beside the upset table. Thaddeus was in the lead, driving two of his opponents before him out the courtyard door like a cowherd driving reluctant cattle before him. In the open they threw away their weapons and fled before him. Cottus stepped away from the Athan and faced this new and more formidable threat. With a brief 'clack clack' Thaddeus blocked the big man's attacks, dodged a wild swipe, disarmed Cottus with a blow to the wrist and then dropped his opponent with a sweeping stroke that took him on the knee, leaving him writhing on the ground.

Once again Athan heard feminine laughter and clapping from above his head and to his left. Looking up he saw smoke.

"Fire!" he shouted.

Persis, Erinsys, and the boy, whose name it appeared was Anteros, made their way along the open passage along the second story of the courtyard. At each door, Persis would pause long enough to look inside. If occupied she would inform the girls inside, and (once a customer) that the house was on fire and to leave at once. At the third door there was no one inside. "I think this is Adara's room," said Persis calmly entering despite the growing tumult as more women discovered the flames. "Let me see now." And she deftly felt beneath several couches and tables before with a "Eureka" she came out with an ornate but sturdy jewelry box that she slid into the bag now being carried by a grinning Anteros. "I never liked that cow."

"What are you doing," gasped Erinsys.

"Preparing" responded Persis, "A girl has to think of her future." And with that she spilled some oil from a lamp onto an ornate cushion and set it alight. "All right, let's go on, now. No dilly dallying."

There were two sets of outside stairs that led from the second story to the courtyard, one on each side of the main entrance. As they made their way toward the one on their right side a man burst out of the foyer into the courtyard. Erinsys sucked in her breath.

"Who is that?" Persis asked interested in her companion's reaction.

"Athan" replied Erinsys. "What is he doing here?"

"Rescuing you I suppose," replied Persis

"He's going to get me into a lot of trouble," worried Erinsys.

"I don't think you are the one who is going to get in trouble," smiled Persis as she stepped back from checking another room and finding it occupied. "Oh, he is quite the young Achilles!" she laughed delightedly as Phineas went down under his attack, "and handsome, too."

Erinsys had had to use enough varied emotions in the last 12 hours to last a lifetime. Now to her astonishment she found she might even add jealousy to the list.

But before she could even sort out what she did or did not want to feel, much less say, men came boiling out of the door into the courtyard, pursued by a stocky bearded man of perhaps 30 years. The watched him from the top of the stairs as he swiftly overcame the most formidable of Phineas' men. Persis laughed aloud again and clapped her approval. "Who is that one?" she asked Erinsys, pointing out Thaddeus who was now stalking around the courtyard ensuring that no threats remained upright.

"That is Thaddeus, the captain of Athan's company" she replied.

"You may keep your Achilles, girl, I will take that Hercules!"

And she descended the stairs to claim her prize.

"Fire!"

The cry was now general, not only within the house, but also from neighbors. There was no standing organization to fight fires. The guard might pitch in to help if they were in the neighborhood, but in general, self-reliance was expected in the event of a fire. That meant you helped your neighbor not only from a sense of community but also because his fire might grow and become yours. Of course, often the only thing to do was carry out furnishings from the building and hope the fire did not spread. The house of Phineas had an evil reputation in the neighborhood, especially with the current commotion. Yet a crowd began to gather around the only open entrance.

Thaddeus was taking command of the situation down in the courtyard. He had put all his enemies either down or to flight, and now, as a captain of the guards he needed to restore order and see that people put out the fire upstairs. He noticed that there seemed to be several sources of the flames. That was strange. But before he could consider what that might mean his life was suddenly and unexpectedly changed forever.

A stunningly beautiful woman in clothing that seemed somehow to both cling and flow glided up to him. He vaguely noticed that she was closely followed by a young boy who was holding a cloth bag, and Erinsys who was burdened with what appeared to be a lady's cloak and a small wooden box.

"Captain, how wonderful of you to rescue us from this terrible place! It is on fire as you can see, but it does not seem to be too bad. We would like to put ourselves under your kind protection." During this brief speech, Persis had come to stand quite close to Thaddeus and at the end she placed a supplicating palm on his shoulder looking first deeply into his eyes, then casting them shyly down before glancing up again for his response.

Thaddeus, a worldly man of considerable self-possession stood stunned. After a moment he seemed to shake himself. "Uhmmm, yes my lady, of course, just stay close by and we will, ahhh, make sure you come to no harm."

He was distracted by cries; no those were screams for help coming from doors located on the first floor of the courtyard.

"Phineas keeps some of his people locked up," advised Persis. "I am sure he would be glad to give you the latch key to let them out. He is that disgusting man over there with the injured right arm. Your man Athan's work I believe."

Thaddeus strode over to see the indicated man. Persis took the opportunity to wander over to where Milo was helping his big friend Cottus examine his damaged knee.

"The fire seems to be spreading," she remarked to the two men who knew her well and thus were wary. "Those young ones in the locked rooms really need to be let out. That captain is asking Phineas for the latch key but I don't think he will open up the doors. He is too afraid someone will get into his treasury room."

In fact it was becoming increasing chaotic in the courtyard as more and more people lost their reluctance to come into the courtyard to help fight the fires or just look around at the excitement. "I believe the guardsmen broke in with a battering ram didn't they?"

"A log," said Milo.

"Well," mused Persis "I guess that a great big log is a kind of a latch key. You could help by getting those young ones over there out of the locked rooms before they burn alive. But be careful where you leave that key. It can open every door in the house, even specially secured ones; even the outer doors. And with so many people running about things might be looted. But then, Milo, you're a smart one." She smiled at him, "I am sure you already knew all that." And she quietly turned to rejoin her companions just in time to see Thaddeus in the corner of the courtyard administer a kick to a crouching Phineas.

'Oh,' she thought to herself, 'I do like that captain.'

"Well," she told Erinsys and young Anteros, "I think we have done all we can for this evening. Let's collect our protectors and leave this place." "Athan is not my protector," said Erinsys sulkily.

Persis rounded on her, "Would you prefer Phineas? After what happened here he would probably kill you, if you were lucky. He loves to take out his frustrations on the weak and defenseless. If your young guardsman had not come for you, at considerable risk to himself, I might add, where would you be right now? Waiting for them to continue your 'training' that's what! Do you know how lucky you are to have a brave and handsome protector like that who will risk his life to save you without even being asked? Count your blessings and thank the gods for your Athan, for he is clearly their gift to you."

Even the perpetually cheeky Anteros was cowed by her towering anger. Persis gathered herself and with a gesture for her little entourage to follow approached Phineas again. The captain was conferring with his comrades and watching the activity. The fires upstairs seemed to be being contained with buckets of water from the courtyard's fountain. Milo and Cottus were hard at work battering down the locked doors and releasing the occupants, mostly young boys, out into the courtyard. Others seemed to be helping by carrying portable valuables out of danger; in some cases they seemed to be carrying them right out of the main entrance, no doubt to places of even greater safety such as their homes. Phineas' remaining henchmen were not having much success in restraining them. On his feet again, Phineas was in a rage, but his shoulder prevented him from taking a more active role. He had lost his sword, and he wisely kept his whip in his belt. He knew that he would need to see a physician tomorrow to set his broken collarbone and that he would have to wear a sling to keep the arm still for a month or more. He had not just had his house damaged; his belongings were being looted. What was worse, his reputation was in ruins. Much of his power came from the fear and respect he engendered. Everyone would discuss and remember this night of defeat and humiliation.

"Captain," purred Persis, giving Thaddeus a sun-bright smile, "I wish to thank you and your men again for saving us. I think it is time for us to go to a place of greater safety. Could you be so kind as to offer to escort us? The streets are so dangerous after dark."

"Of course," he replied.

"Oh, thank you so much," Persis said, moving up to take his left arm. "I feel so much better having you next to me. Athan, can you escort Erinsys? Come along Anteros," she directed, deftly taking the load from Erinsys. No one seemed to notice that she had just commandeered the captain and one of his men and was now leading them effortlessly toward the entrance.

"Where are you going, bitch" rasped Phineas as they passed him in the entrance.

"I have decided to change my lodgings." She coolly replied as she walked past.

"Master," put in the bald man who still had blood dried on the back of his head from his previous encounter with Athan, "she brings in more than anyone else."

"Let her go," he responded, "she is more trouble than all the others combined."

But it must have irritated him beyond his limits or he would not have made the mistake of speaking to Athan as he left with a very subdued Erinsys at his side.

"You can have that one, boy, we all took turns screwing her. She's no good at it."

It is very foolish to be rude to a young man who has just personally defeated you not once but twice. But to insult his woman, in her presence, when he is holding a dagger in his right hand is positively suicidal. It was a testament to Athan's self-control that he did not murder Phineas. But he did smash his right fist, clutching the solid hilt of the dagger, into the man's face. The blow broke Phineas' nose with a great spray of blood. He fell back so stunned that he did not even feel the renewed pain in his collar bone. Not for a while, at any rate. Baldy just gaped as they passed through the door and followed Thaddeus and Persis into the night.

Persis took the lead, of course, all the while chatting with Thaddeus, making sure that her servant Anteros, who still had her belongings, was close by, and ensuring that Athan and Erinsys were able to catch up to them.

The two young lovers were obviously having a disagreement.

"What were you doing in that place?" was the question that had been on Athan's mind since he had first found her missing from the tavern that evening.

"It's complicated," she replied unhelpfully.

"Complicated" he echoed flatly.

They walked along in silence for a while, listening to Thaddeus and Persis chatting back and forth, getting to know each other and each obviously enjoying the experience.

"Look, my uncle owed a lot of people money," she started defensively. "I could have made a lot of money there, gotten him out of debt, and put a little aside for myself; have a little security. I am a widow you know."

"Yes, he replied dryly, "Three times."

"That is not fair!" she shot back, already becoming heated. They walked on a bit longer. "Yura was my first husband," began Erinsys in a quiet voice. She had never really talked to Athan about her life in any detail. "I was young and he wasn't. He was a widower, maybe forty years old and had grown children, but we had a nice farm. It was my bad luck that he died before we could have any children. One night he did not come home for his dinner. Finally after dark I went out with a light looking for him. The mule was still hitched up to the plow and he was sitting on the ground with his hand on the plow. At first I thought he was resting, then I though he was hurt. But he was just

dead; he must have just sat down and died out there all by himself."
They walked on for a while. "My second husband, well, he wasn't
really my husband officially, but he told me we would be married when
he came back from that expedition down to Buttrotiuria. Do you
remember that one? Did you go?"

"No," he replied quietly, "It was only a small contingent, mixed
guards and militia. I didn't get to go. It wasn't a very big deal."

"It was to him. He got killed."

"Sorry. You never told me."

"Well, I don't like to talk about it."

"How did the third one die?"

"He is dead to me." She said in an ice-cold voice. Athan was not so
stupid as to ask any further questions.

"You don't know how it is. After my father died, my mother
just seemed to give up. My sisters were all either married or dead,
so my uncle, my mother's sister's husband, arranged my marriage
with Yura, but after he died because I didn't a son with him I
had no rights to the land. I guess that's the law. In the end I got
nothing but some furnishings. My uncle told me he had too many
daughters of his own to take me in. So I wound up at the tavern
house. Until my uncle came to tell me I had to help the family
out. He told me he had arranged for me be Phineas' pallake. I
thought I had finally found a chance to get ahead. But even that
was a disaster. Phineas had no intention of treating me like a wife
of any kind."

The two walked on for a while in silence. Finally Erinsys resumed
her story.

"It's not your fault. I found out it was not such a good opportunity
before you came. I have no luck with men. But I have no idea in the
world what I am going to do now. My uncle will be furious. If I go
back to the tavern house, as soon as Phineas repairs his house he will
come get me again." She shivered a little though the evening was still
warm.

They had walked through the streets almost half-way back to the
barracks before Thaddeus thought to inquire of Persis just where they
were headed.

"Almost there, captain," she replied. "Tell me about your home, Captain Thaddeus. Do you stay in some large barracks with all those other soldiers?

"I have a section in the barracks that has a barrier, lady," Said Thaddeus. "I haven't been a captain long, but I expect to move into one of the captain's cabins soon."

"Oh," she asked, "where are those?"

"They are in our compound, not far from the barracks. They are nice, new brick buildings with three rooms. Usually two captains share one unless they are married. Then he can keep his family there. Really they are quite clean and nice." He wondered why he was suddenly so interested in impressing this gorgeous creature. What could she see in a simple guardsman, a professional soldier, like himself? But she was clinging to his arm looking up and obviously was enjoying his company. Thaddeus was a man of the world, and had known many women. But though he had drunk many beakers of wine this was an intoxicating beverage beyond his experience.

"Well, what is keeping you out of your new residence?"

'Residence', he thought, not cabin, residence; almost as if she said home.

"There is a house that has an open wing, Cyrus lives there. His wife died last year, and he has just been hanging on. He really should be retired from the guard, he says he has a daughter who has a farm, but no one has the heart to tell him to take a new lodger and all."

"Ah," interjected Persis, "here we are." They had come to a large stone building with a small but impressive portico. She stepped to the door and pulled the bell.

"Lady," began Thaddeus

"Oh, please," she replied giving the bell a more vigorous tug. "With all that we have been through together, please call me Persis. And may I address you as Thaddeus, kind sir."

"Please do, but Lady Persis, this is a bath house."

"Yes, I know Captain Thaddeus." She replied, "I come here often."

"But Lady Persis it is late and the bath house is closed."

"Baruch is in there," said Persis her temper starting to rise. She made a movement in the dark and suddenly she was pounding on the door with the pommel of a slim dagger. They all gave back a step from the flashing blade as she hammered the doors panel with the hilt and filled the air with a penetrating set of demands.

"Baruch! Baruch you indolent scut! Get up here, open this door and let us in! You are making important customers wait, you old fool! Open up!"

"The baths are closed. Who is it?" came a nervous voice from inside.

"It is Persis, as you know perfectly well you lazy hound!" Persis took a deep breath, just possibly a little shaky, and continued in a lower but still penetrating voice. "I have the watch with me. Now open up. It is important." Persis, collecting herself, turned to the others. "After our adventures this night I think we all need to clean up a bit. Our heroes still have the blood of their victories upon them and we smell of smoke and exertion." Noticing their gaze on the reflected silver blade of her dagger, still held in her right fist, she retreated slightly into the shadows turned partially away and made another movement and the blade disappeared. Athan smiled to himself. His own dagger was now thrust into his girdle and he thought he knew where that dagger had gone. Somehow she could get her weapon out from its concealed hiding place not only more smoothly than he could, but with style. She was carrying a nice little blade, about as long as her hand, slender with no guard to speak of, and a darkened bone grip that would probably match her skin up there on her thigh. That was something to wonder about. He noticed that Thaddeus seemed to be having the same bemusing thoughts.

Just then the bar to the entrance door was opened and a small wizened face peered out, balding, with a white corona of hair. "Yes, lady?"

"Baruch, this is Captain Thaddeus, son of Ajax," introduced Persis while stepping forward and pushing open the door for her companions. "And this is his comrade Athan, also of the guards, his lady, Erinsys." Erinsys bristled at that but Persis ignored her and continued speaking, "and my servant Anteros. Captain Thaddeus has just had the most astonishing adventure. Brigands broke into the House of Phineas, you know that place?"

"Yes, of course, lady," interjected Baruch as he was steadily pushed back into the baths by his unexpected and uninvited late visitors, "but…"

"Well", continued Persis unaffected by the attempt to stem her advance, "Captain Thaddeus and Athan came to our rescue, put out the fires."

"Fires!"

"Yes, without brave Captain Thaddeus and his guard the whole city might have been engulfed in fire, but he defeated the miscreants, put out the fires, and rescued us." And at that point she once again placed a palm against his shoulder and looked up at him. Not taking her eyes of the bath keeper she said, "Don't you think we should reward him at least with a chance to clean off the blood of his opponents and allow us to rid ourselves of the smell of the fires?"

And indeed, there was a bit of blood on Thaddeus' tunic, and they did have the smell of smoke still clinging to them. The rest of her speech was, of course, such an outrageous warping of the truth that the others were struck dumb with astonishment. After all, the brigands and arsonist were both right there. But Persis knew her audience well. Baruch, like many who work in gossipy places dearly loved a good story, especially one that promised heroic acts and beautiful rescued maidens (not that there were any maidens present.)

"Come in brave captain," he gestured in welcome. "We will get the baths hot for you right away. I was just damping down the fires but some water is still hot. You can tell me more while you bathe."

"The water is hot because you and Aeolus were just in them yourselves, you old scoundrel. We will need two baths, one for our heroes and one for us. We will take the green tile room. Anteros, bring our things."

The boy had enough sense to wait until Baruch had bustled away before asking, "Lady am I really your servant now?"

"Yes, you little rascal, you have moved up in the world."

"And I won't have to work at Phineas' any more."

"Never again."

"Good" he grinned.

Turning her attention to Thaddeus she said, "Anteros will attend Erinsys in our bath. We will need some private time, and do not want Baruch bothering us."

Thaddeus had picked up what she had in mind. "We will entertain him with an account of our adventures this evening. By the time his regular clientele arrive tomorrow morning he will have a story to tell them that will make Heracles blush. Perhaps you might visit your hairdresser and seamstress tomorrow morning to tell them about how we foiled the attack on the house of Phineas."

"I am glad to see that I did not underestimate you, Captain Thaddeus," said Persis with a considering look. "It is of course important that people understand what happened tonight."

"What did happen?" asked Baruch as he returned with styguls, fresh cloths, and an insatiable desire for gossip.

"Let me tell you," started Thaddeus expansively. "They were a desperate band of brigands, perhaps they had some dealings in the past with that Phineas; he's a shifty one he is…"

As Thaddeus warmed to his story the two women made their way to their separate bath, trailed by Anteros, who was clearly delighted in his new role.

The men had a leisurely bath and then had time to take a beaker or two of wine from Baruch's personal stock before the women finally returned. Both were clean, freshly dressed from the clothing that Persis had brought from the house. Despite the skillful use of cosmetics it was clear that there had been many tears shed in the green tiled bath. Erinsys walked straight up to Athan and took his right hand in both of hers.

"Athan, son of Medius, thank you for coming to take me away from the house of Phineas. I am forever in your debt." She made this speech in a low voice with downcast eyes. Then she took his hand and pressed it to her forehead, bowing as she did.

Athan was astounded. He had no idea how to proceed. Fortunately Persis, who had obviously prepared Erinsys' speech for her, once again took over.

"It is late. Thaddeus, let us find a place for the night."

He said not a word but merely offered her his arm.

Things such as inns or hotels were not common in that time and place, but they went to a large house that would take in travelers passing through. Here was one place where Thaddeus was more familiar with the hosts than his companions. Even though the hour was getting quite late, he was able to gain entrance and secure two adjoining rooms for the remainder of the evening. Thaddeus, with the cloth bag on one arm and Persis on the other and a huge smile on his face, disappeared into the larger room. Young Anteros was given Persis' cloak and settled in to sleep in the hall outside their door.

Athan and Erinsys stood outside the second room for a long uncomfortable moment. "I can sleep out here," he offered.

"Don't be stupid," she snapped and went inside.

Without looking at him she removed her borrowed gown and stood in her chemise, very aware it was really all she had left in the world. She felt stupid, helpless, wretchedly vulnerable, and totally alone. She did not even have anything to comb her hair before she went to bed, a thing she had done without fail since she was a little girl. Instead she lay down on the pallet and pulled a blanket over herself. She did have her body, she thought, men found that valuable. Well, some men did. She would be able to get by on that for a while.

Athan watched her with some dismay. It dawned on him how little she had left. "We'll get your things tomorrow." He promised.

"I can't go back there," she replied. "I just can't."

"Of course not. You will tell me where your things are and I will go there with some members of the watch and we will bring them back to you. Well, those things that did not burn up." 'Maybe I should not have mentioned that', he thought.

"Where, just where will that be? Where will I stay?" The words came out harsher than she intended.

Sometimes someone says the perfect thing. Lives can change on a single sentence. That happened when Athan said in a calm steady voice, "With me."

That did it; Erinsys began weeping uncontrollably. Athan was confused. After a bit, he decided that this puzzle was not going to be solved with words, so he lay down beside her. She stiffened and turned away still sobbing. Athan lay behind her and put his right arm over her shoulder, gently patting and giving her a gentle "There, there." He had seen it work on the little ponies the guard kept and he had seen it work on small children. "There, there." Erinsys suddenly turned toward him and buried her head in his shoulder and began that most wonderful of remedies for when things go terribly wrong: a good cry on a strong shoulder.

It would have been even better if Persis in the next room had not begun to enthusiastically reward Thaddeus for her rescue. From the sounds of it, she was very grateful indeed. By the time Erinsys' sobbing had slowed to sniffles and short gasps, Athan's tunic was actually soaked through. In the next room Persis was now apparently rewarding Thaddeus for his defeat of Cottus. The activity next door made the two young people uncomfortable; Athan was actually shocked. But he was not as shocked as he was by what Erinsys did next. She giggled.

"No wonder she is so famous," she said. "Poor Thaddeus, I fear he may survive Phineas only to succumb to Persis."

That got Athan laughing as well. "He always wanted to die in battle," he said. "And it sounds like this is the most epic confrontation since Achilles met Hector."

Erinsys was suddenly serious. "Darling," she said using the familiar address of lovers, "Can you wait until tomorrow for me to give myself to you? I will try to make it up to you." Then with another giggle, she added, "Perhaps Persis can give me some pointers."

The two lovers snuggled in together. Almost immediately exhaustion overtook Erinsys. Holding her small body Athan felt protective and strong. He would watch over her this night. And then, despite the fact that next door, Persis began rewarding brave Thaddeus this time perhaps for breaking down Phineas' front door, Athan drifted into sleep.

When he awoke it was gray dawn and Erinsys was not on the pallet with him. Then he heard her coming in from the privy.

"Sorry," she said, "I didn't mean to wake you."

"Let's go see if any of the bakeries are open," he said, going to the basin of water in the corner and splashing his face. "We can bring back bread for the others."

Before they were able to complete their toilets and slip out, from adjoining room came unmistakable sounds that Persis was rewarding Thaddeus again, perhaps this time for becoming a captain.

When Athan and Erinsys returned with bread, fruit, and a small pitcher of milk the other couple was out of bed ("Finally!" thought Erinsys) and dressed. They all assembled in their bedroom with young Anteros and shared out their breakfast. Thaddeus was wan but smiling broadly. Persis looked like a cat leaving an empty aviary.

"Now," she began briskly, "we must plan." No one had any objections. "First, we must have a safe place to stay. Phineas' standing was badly hurt last night. Not only was his house damaged, but I would be very surprised if his treasure room was not looted in addition to the many smaller things that were stolen in all the confusion. Worst of all, he lost a great deal of face. Phineas is powerful because of his money and because of fear. He has few friends but many allies. He lost most of his money last night, but many people will remember only that they fear him, and not consider how weakened he has become. Of course, to reinstill that fear and for his own pride, he will have to kill us. Well, perhaps not you and I, Erinsys. But what he would do to us might be even worse than death. I know that if either Erinsys or I go into that house again we will not come out until we are dead. The only question would be how long that would take. And I am certain that he will have both bold Athan and my handsome captain murdered as soon as he regains his power."

"Do you want me to kill him?" asked Thaddeus "I doubt if he has many of his people around him. I could do it tonight."

"No, my darling," using a familiar word that was reserved for lovers, "that would be much too obvious. You might be charged with murder, and I do not think I would like to lose you to the executioner. No, we must be careful. In the meantime we need to take measures to counter his next moves. Erinsys is particularly at risk. Phineas will undoubtedly invoke his arrangement with her uncle to try to bring her back into the house. So she will have to stay out of sight. I think we should move into the garrison's compound. He will not dare make an open move there, especially if we are careful. Thaddeus you and young Athan should never go outside the compound unarmed. And we should never go outside without you," Athan touched his dagger. "Yes," she observed, "and a sword would be better yet."

"Perhaps we should carry a shield and spear as well," joked Thaddeus.

"I will leave the decision of your armament to you brave soldiers," responded Persis. "Just be prepared to resist an attack. His favorite tactic is to present you with an obvious threat to the front and have another man strike you from behind."

"Sound tactics," agreed Thaddeus.

Athan, thinking back to his encounter with Phineas realized that was just what Phineas had hoped to do to him in the foyer that evening.

"How long will we have to hide in the compound or be escorted everywhere we go?" wondered Erinsys.

"Oh, just until Athan kills Phineas. I estimate half a month at the most."

"So Thaddeus is too precious to risk being caught in a murder but my Athan is expendable!"

'My Athan' he thought. 'Nice'

"No, your Athan is going to take care of Phineas because he is less conspicuous and I suspect will do a better job. Sorry, darling, but I think that what I have in mind is much more in Athan's line than yours."

"Well, we just can't keep women in the compound," said Thaddeus, addressing a problem that he had obviously been considering. "It's against regulations. The place would be overrun with whores and harlots, beg pardon ladies, in no time otherwise."

"Ah, but a captain can have a guest in his cottage. And you said that men could keep their wives in the compound."

"What does that have to do with us?" asked Thaddeus guardedly.

"With you and I? Nothing. Erinsys and Athan are the ones getting married."

"What!"

"How sweet. You see, dear Thaddeus, how they both responded exactly together. They already are like a couple married for years. Look, you two" she continued, overcoming inarticulate comments from Erinsys and Athan, "it is quite simple. Erinsys, if you are married, that contract supersedes anything your uncle might arrange. Can you imagine the uproar if Phineas attempted to snatch the wife of one of the guard's young heroes? And Athan needs to be married. It is obvious he is ready to settle down. And as his wife you can share our cottage."

"What cottage?"

"Ah, all three of you at once. Such unity! Anteros, you will have to keep up and join in the next reply." The boy only grinned.

"Cyrus is going to decide to move out to his daughter's farm today," explained Persis. "Do try to keep up. Now the first thing is to get some of our possessions back. Anteros you scamp, do you think you can still get into Phineas' house?"

"Of course, mistress."

"Ah, what a fine boy you are! You should all know that no burglar in the world can match a mischievous boy for getting into and out of places. The problems will be in ensuring that he retrieves only the correct items and getting them carried away. Small boys make excellent cat burglars, but poor beasts of burden."

Thereafter the two women spent some time telling Anteros what they wanted him to bring out, where they thought it was located, what messages to pass to others who might or might not be in the house, and what to do if he was apprehended. Porters were called for and additional instructions provided. Before long Anteros and two men pushing carts departed for their 'raid' on the house of Phineas. Then the two women were joined by the lady of the guesthouse who had, through some secret sense unknown to men, detected an imminent wedding. Soon several women had gathered and hasty plans were made and put into motion.

While all this was going on the two men drew off to one side. "So, are you ready to get married, boy?" asked Thaddeus.

"I guess so," replied his friend.

"You need to be more sure than that," countered Thaddeus. "After all you are promising to live with her; to support her. That is a lot different than rescuing her from a houseful of angry pimps; it's much more dangerous." He was openly grinning now.

"Why have you never married?" asked Athan.

"I'm too clever. Besides, if I were married, I would have had to miss out on Lady Persis. That was the most amazing night I have ever known; and morning, too." And right on cue he gave a jaw-cracking yawn. "But I think Persis is right. It is time for you to get married, have a couple of kids. I hope so because," Thaddeus looked at the women locked in animated conversation, "kid, you're a goner. Now, if you will excuse me I am going to conserve my strength. I am going into your room to take a little nap." Athan had no duties for the guard, so after a bit he followed Thaddeus into his room, found a corner away from an already snoring Thaddeus, and dozed off as well.

The Old King became aware of himself again. It was still pitch black and very cold. He was glad he had found shelter from the wind that was howling just beyond his little pine tree barrier. He stirred himself long enough to feed the fire; the heat it released was a pitiful counter to the blizzard raging outside in the night, but it helped, and the light greatly cheered the old man up. Watching the flames he thought about his wedding to Erinsys. They had all been so young! They were so confident and so anxious all at the same time. Everything had seemed so urgent, so important back then. Well, perhaps it had been. He made huge commitments and took desperate risks. Back in his bed under his covers the old man shivered himself warm again and, watching the fire, thought about those early days. It had been a very long time ago, but there were some things that always remained fresh in your mind; things like your wedding day.

Chapter Two – A Wedding

Things went astonishingly well. Within two hours Anteros was back with the porters pushing a cart filled with clothing, bedding, hangings, cosmetics, and virtually anything else the boy could find that could fit through the bars of a window over the alley where the two porters had waited. At least a third of the stuff had belonged to, or at least been used by, one of the two women.

"It was easy," bragged Anteros, "everyone had been up all night guarding the place and trying to put things right, so everyone was asleep. That is everyone who is not out looking for Milo and Cottus. Someone broke into Phineas' strong room and a lot of stuff is missing. Also, somebody broke open the back gate.

A lot of the boys and girls slipped out that way. Phineas is tearing mad, I'll tell you. Anyway they left Simon on watch as the doorman!" Simon was another of the boys, a teenager and Anteros was one of his favorites. "Nobody seemed to remember that I had left with you so I had the run of the place. Do you like what I got?"

"It's wonderful" Persis told him sorting through the things she wanted to keep. "Do you like these, Erinsys?" she asked holding up some drapes. "I don't know what your new home will look like, but these are nice." The two women divided the spoils with occasional items given to reward Anteros who hung around the proceedings like a dog at a feast. Persis felt that most of the goods recovered should go to her; she had been with Phineas for the better part of a year and she would need money to set herself up in the necessary style. On the other hand, Erinsys had had a much, much more difficult time in the house and she **was** about to get married. Persis was not by nature a generous woman, but on this occasion she allowed the younger woman to take a fair share of the goods. And a portion of what they did not want for themselves was put aside to be sold to support the wedding.

At this time and place, every respectable woman became a wife if she could. Women usually married young and were expected to stay at home to bear and raise children. But there were always exceptions; widows or women without a dowry could become a pallake, perhaps not a respectable as wife, but certainly more than a concubine. Her husband accepted responsibility for the maintenance of both her and any children of the union, and these children were considered legitimate heirs. This system worked well, especially for poorer families or foreign women. There was a third form of recognized relationships between men and women: that of hetaira. Hetaira did not usually live with the men with whom they were involved. These women were the intelligent, beautiful, and respected companions for men and were usually foreign. They might have sex with men and were paid for doing so, but the women were more than just socially proficient high-class prostitutes. They were usually educated in both politics and philosophy. Persis was just such a woman, and one of the most famous in this city, though if truth be told, she considered Epiria a backwater place just about as far west and north as she cared to go. It was only her adventurous spirit that had led her so far afield.

Because Erinsys had little money and her only surviving male relative was a poor and disinterested uncle, she would just become Athan's pallake. But it was a legal marriage, and she would be a wife. Therefore there would be a wedding ceremony.

Thaddeus was awakened around noon to provide an escort for Persis for a series of missions, since the man she had paid to escort her around the streets earlier that day on her errands had business elsewhere that afternoon. She had been busy all morning doing more than just getting her hair done. Apparently there had been many messengers sent to and fro while the two men were 'conserving their strength'. Persis had dealt with moving Cyrus out of his cottage by dealing directly with his daughter. With a few hints from his daughter and some gifts to ease the transition, the old widower was plucked from the cottage in the compound and on his way to his daughter's farmhouse before sunset. It was only possible because he had few possessions, and as a life-long soldier, he was used to rapid relocations. Thaddeus and Athan together moved on the Provost Marshall, the senior member of the guard who was in charge of the barracks compound, including assigning housing for the guardsmen. They struck not only before any of the competition was aware that Cyrus' cabin was open, but before the Provost Marshall even knew. Their case was helped by the fact that Thaddeus was in fact entitled to such a residence as the most senior captain not to have his own residence, and by the events of the night before.

The streets were full of gossip about the raid on Phineas' house, and almost all of it reflected well on the guards in general and Thaddeus and Athan in particular. Once he was assured that that Cyrus was finally ready to leave the compound at last, the Provost gave his approval for Thaddeus to move into the recently vacated cottage. If Thaddeus wanted to share his residence with a friend or three, that was his business. Thaddeus and Athan inspected the cottage; it was as they expected, a simple brick building with three rooms and its own privy in the back. The central room was the largest and contained a table, some couches, and a fireplace for both cooking and heat. There were two shuttered windows on the front wall, one on either side of the door, a window on the left side of the fireplace and a narrow backdoor to the right. Thaddeus chose the larger room to the left for himself. Athan walked into what would be his new room on the right. There was a window with a shutter on the far wall, low pallet, a small table with a cracked pitcher and basin. Several pegs were driven into the wall for hanging clothes. It was far more spacious and private than anywhere he had ever lived before.

Late that afternoon Erinsys, accompanied by Persis and several sympathetic women from the guesthouse, was escorted to the temple of Artemis for prayers, sacrifices, and preparations. Other friends of Erinsys, one of her sisters, and even her aunt, joined them there. Within the safety of the temple walls the women were free to engage in traditional pre-wedding feminine activities such as bathing with water from sacred streams, preparations to adorn the bride for the wedding feast, and exchanging the latest gossip. There was bread, cheese and wine to go with the conversation and preparations. Persis was the center of attention. Her lifestyle fascinated the other women; the younger women admired her courage, the older ones her freedom and personal power. It was clear that Erinsys' uncle would have no part in the marriage.

"He is furious with her," confided her aunt, "at least that is what I hear. He is in hiding from Phineas." This was greeted with gales of laughter. Persis offered to arrange for and fund the ceremony to the surprise, and general approval of the women.

"Of course," she drawled, "Phineas is really paying for it since most of the things we sold were his." This was received with uncertain, but then growing laughter, and the wine was passed around again.

The women's rituals were conducted with much less solemnity than for a first marriage. Also lacking was the sense of loss that sometimes accompanied such gatherings; Erinsys was no virgin, and she had already left her family. All in all, it was a wonderful night, with some of the women staying so long that they had no escort home and had to remain overnight with the bride in the guest rooms of the temple. But no one seemed to mind that.

As to Thaddeus and Athan, they both had guard duty that evening, after which they retired straight to bed.

The next morning dawned bright, clear, and delightfully cool. For some the morning was filled with almost frantic activity. Erinsys was so keyed up she had hardly slept the night before. As soon as it was proper she and her sister were escorted back to the guesthouse where they supervised the loading of all of Erinsys' worldly possessions (most of which were the spoils of Anteros' raid) onto a cart for transportation to the cottage that would be her new home.

Those in company of the bride to be were subjected to seemingly endless variations of protests and hypothetical questions generally on the themes of:

"What am I doing?"

"I hardly know him."

"He is too young; he's scarcely older than I am."

"This is a terrible mistake. I have no luck with men."

"Do you think he will be a good husband?"

"I must be insane!"

"She is worse than any virgin," complained her exasperated sister.

Meanwhile Persis was an absolute force out in town. Arranging a wedding ceremony in a single day, even a pallake wedding, is no small feat. She cajoled, she bullied, she used all her prestige, and ample bribes to ensure that the banquet hall, caterers, musicians, and all the other countless details would be in place for the wedding banquet that evening.

Thaddeus and Athan had guard responsibilities that morning and so worked until noon. Athan did invite a dozen of his friends, and, dipping into his thin financial reserves, purchased an amphora of wine for the guard to share in lieu of a formal feast. Cyrus had only just left his cottage bound for his son-in-laws farm when another cart arrived loaded with feminine clothing, hangings, bedclothes, and other elements of a household. In the middle of the unloading, Persis herself arrived looking spectacular and accompanied by three stout slaves who looked exhausted.

"How did you get into the compound?" asked Thaddeus. "Didn't the guard stop you?"

Persis only smiled at him and began to supervise the arrangement of the new household effects. Both men noticed that some of the items seemed to belong to Persis and were being installed in the left hand room. In an astonishingly short time the cart was emptied and the cottage had been transformed into a pleasant and well-established homestead instead of an old soldier's lair.

"This will do for now," she consented, looking around at the transformation. "I will see you both at the banquet hall in two hours. Don't be late Athan. Thaddeus darling, take him in hand. And do wear something festive." And with that she smoothly rose and departed, sweating slaves in her wake. The two men looked as though they had been caught in a stampede.

"Well," said Thaddeus to his protégé, as they listened to Persis' voice providing instructions to the slaves diminishing in the distance. "I think we better get ready."

And so it was that at the appointed time some two hours later Athan, accompanied by his friends, arrived at the banquet hall. He was dressed in a borrowed tunic that was very fine, even if it did not fit him perfectly. Thaddeus had also made a special effort with his appearance and was resplendent in his scarlet captain's cloak over a formal tunic. The bride's party had already arrived including Erinsys' aunt, her sister, her friends, and every woman at the guesthouse who could manage to get away. Though his mother and most of his relations were not living in town, Athan's older brother and all of his surviving sisters who lived close by were there, as well as a dozen of his companions from the guards. It was a good crowd, even if there were more of the women's tables than those for the men.

The feast was a triumph. Wine and honeyed sesame seed cakes were passed freely about as the meal progressed. During the meal professional singers both sang and led the party in favorite songs. After eating, the meal was cleared away the dancing began, first the men, then the women, each group aided by professional wedding dancers. At the head of the tables sat Athan and Erinsys, at different tables of course, but next to each other, each with wedding garlands in their hair. After her second glass of wine, even Erinsys began to relax and enjoy the affair. Between dances the bride and groom were presented with gifts. Erinsys received a grill for toasting barley (and teasing by the women on burning her new husband's meals) and a mortar and pestle (with many raucous jokes by guardsmen). Finally, Anteros arrived wearing a crown of thorns and acorns to act as the traditional wedding 'amphithales', the child who filled the role of escorting the bride. He moved around the tables, giving the guests bread from a basket speaking the traditional words "She fled worse and found better." And occasionally he could not help adding in a low voice "And so did I."

At the end of the festivities Athan and his new wife went outside and climbed into the rented wedding cart, and were escorted to the couple's new home. On the trip to their new home, Persis pointed out two of Phineas' men watching the procession from the shadows to Thaddeus but decided not to mention it to the happy couple.

Arriving at their new cottage, the newlyweds entered to cheers and ribald suggestions from the guardsmen. Someone had ensured that the floor had been freshly strewn with rushes and a vase of flowers was on the table. Erinsys stopped in wonder.

"Oh, Athan, this is really nice, very comfortable," she exclaimed in surprise.

Fresh cheers came from outside as Thaddeus and Persis entered the cottage. Without taking their eyes off each other, they went directly to the left room and closed the door firmly behind them.

With a gesture Athan offered his new wife the room to the right. They entered the open door and stood there looking around, and then began removing their wedding garlands. The all too familiar sounds of the night before were already coming from behind the closed door on the left hand room where Thaddeus and Persis had gone.

"Well," she told him rolling her eyes, "they're at it again. By Hera, they are just like alley cats." Then stepping close to him she looked up, gave him a brief kiss and spoke the traditional words of a wife. "Not tonight dear, I am just exhausted, all right?"

And so began Athan's life as a married man.

The Old King realized he had dozed off again. He stirred in his rough place of rest. It was brutally cold but at least there was a pale filtered light coming into his refuge. He got up, trying to keep his blanket and cloak wrapped around him, and went to the entrance. Pushing the little pine tree aside he looked out on a scene of beauty. It was still snowing, but the wind had dropped. Everything was covered in a pure, thick coating of snow, knee deep. No one was going to move in that. The Old King turned back to his make-shift hearth and bent to the fire. After a few minutes of blowing on the remains of the fire the tender he carefully placed on the ashes rewarded him first with a fresh tendril of smoke, then a tiny flame, and with care, a nice friendly fire. Fortunately he was not hungry, as there was little food, and it was clear he was going to be holed up here for a while. He did heat some water and made a cup of tea. He sat by the fire sipping his tea for a while, and then replenished his supply of wood from the pile of deadwood at the far end of the crevice. He kept the fire small; there was no telling how long he would be here and he did not want to have to seek firewood in deep snow.

Huddled in his blanket he sat by his little fire and thought about how easy it was back when he was a newlywed. He knew who his friends and his enemies were. And if enemies presented a threat to his family and friends all he had to do was figure out a way to kill them; nothing to it.

Chapter Three– A Murder

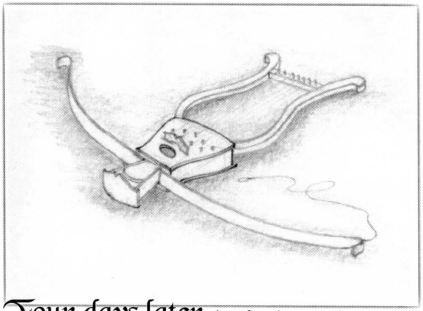

𝔍our days later three friends sat on a bench outside a tavern and plotted murder.

"Phineas has recovered faster than I hoped he would," reported Persis. "We must act soon or we will become the hunted ones."

"It is better to be on the offensive," agreed Thaddeus. "It gives you more choices."

Let us review our options," she began. "I see three: slip in and kill him in his house, wait until he is on the street and kill him in the open, or poison him somehow. I prefer poison myself. Poisoning him is more discrete, creates less public outcry, and is safer. But I do not know how get it in him. He is so careful about what he eats and drinks. I suppose I could try to get something into the bread or wine, but everyone in the house shares those things. I can't afford to kill that many people."

"Thaddeus and Athan looked at each other but did not say a word.

Persis continued without noticing the look. "Besides, he is so tough it would take a lot to make sure he died."

"Getting into the house is not going to be easy, either," responded Thaddeus. "He has replaced his broken doors, and with the cooler weather all the windows have the shutters closed in addition to the bars. I also hear he has hired more men and he has one often patrol outside the house from time to time in addition to the guards inside."

"How does he afford that," wondered Athan.

"He sold some of his boys, traded services with a few of the girls for some things, and borrowed up to his ugly eyebrows," replied Persis. "Some of his allies seem to think he will be able to pay them back. Forget killing him in his sleep. He sleeps in a different room every night, he always bars the door, and he seldom sleeps alone."

Neither man wanted to consider how she knew this.

"That means he will soon start planning to murder us," said Thaddeus.

"Oh, he's already planning. It will take him a few more days before he can start getting serious about putting the plan in motion. We need to strike before that."

"How about killing him on the street? Athan, what did you find out?" asked Thaddeus

"It is as the lady said," he replied, "he goes to the baths at about the same time almost every day and by the same route. He always has either two or three bodyguards with him, one in front, one behind, and if there are three, one next to the buildings. Even if somebody could get close enough to strike, the guards would be all over him before he could get away."

"How about shooting him with an arrow?" inquired Persis.

"Lady, I am no hand with a bow and besides, arrows are not certain to kill; it might only sting him. Now a javelin that would put him down, but it is hard to hide something that big. Maybe if I was up on one of the roofs I could get him but they would be sure to see me when I stood up to throw and dodge the javelin. I thought about dropping something on his head, but the same problem, too easy to be seen, too easy to miss."

"Did you say an arrow would sting him?" asked Persis with a considering look.

"Just an expression, Lady."

"It has to be outside and that means on the way to the baths," said Thaddeus. "We will have surprise, we can pick the time and place, and that is when he has the fewest guards."

"Agreed," said Athan, "we should hit him on the way back. That way we know he is coming so we will be ready. If we get enough men we can overwhelm him."

"No," injected Thaddeus, "that would ruin the element of surprise. The more who know your plans, the less secure they are. We can't have him tipped off and we can't have anybody blabbing afterward to the Magistrate."

"You are all correct in your thinking," said Persis, "and someone is more likely to talk after the fact. Besides we cannot afford a street brawl. That would force the Magistrate to take action. No, I think I have an idea that will combine your plan to strike him on his return from the baths, and my own preference. Do you think young Athan that you could hit him with an arrow from a rooftop across the street?"

"Yes, Lady, but I would have to stand up to draw and even if they did not see me, I am not sure if I can kill him with a single arrow."

"But could you at least stick an arrow into him to say this far in?" she said holding up a slim palm as a gauge. Athan noticed her nails were long and perfectly manicured.

"Probably that deep."

"Good. I think I have a plan. Thaddeus, can you arrange to obtain an Achaemendian bow, a horse bow I think it is called, you know the short ones they shoot from horses."

"I can try, Persis, a 'horse bow' you call it?"

"Yes, I saw men shoot bows like that from the back of a horse when I was a young girl. They are double curved and are very powerful."

"I will ask some of the easterners I know. I think they use such a bow to hunt boars in close thickets."

"Don't forget to get some of their arrows, too. Athan, I want you to find a place where you could get a good shot at Phineas from a roof, but do not let anyone see you, least of all one of his people."

"How am I going to be able to stand up and draw the bow on him with being seen?"

"I am going to see about fixing it so you can shoot a bow from your stomach."

Persis did not explain herself further. She offered the services of young Anteros to Athan to help him find a good spot for their ambush. She enjoined both of them again to be discrete and to not bring anyone else into the conspiracy, not even Erinsys.

Two days later Thaddeus presented his hetaira with a horse bow and five arrows.

"You must not call me your hetaira," she protested, "if we don't stop living together soon, I will be thought of as no more than a pallake."

"What's wrong with that?" asked Thaddeus.

"Nothing my darling, but you deserve more than that. I have plans for you, plans for both of us."

"Why do they call it a horse bow? Do they really shoot it from a horse? Or do they shoot horses with it?"

"Your attempts at humor are so pathetic, beloved. They actually do shoot it from a horse. I told you, I actually saw it when I was a girl; the horses came running by a target and the men shot the target full of arrows and then rode away. It was very thrilling."

"I am glad we have hills to hinder horses and trees to hide behind here," considered Thaddeus, "it would be hard to fight an enemy that can hit and ride away without coming to grips with you."

She took the bow and three of the arrows, wrapped them in a cloth, and finding two young guardsmen in the compound, who were willing to escort her into town, left to pay a visit to a cabinetmaker she knew. Persis persuaded the men to stay in the street until she finished her business within. It took almost an hour, and when she left, assuring the woodworker that she had great trust in his skill, she was no longer carrying her burden.

For ten evenings Athan watched from discrete places in their neighborhood as Phineas and his men took their nightly trips to and from the baths. Not once did they venture into an alley or any place where it would be easy to get next to Phineas. Athan did find a good place on a flat rooftop to observe Phineas coming to and from the baths where it might be possible to get a shot at him with a bow. He showed the place to Thaddeus one night. Together the men came up with a plan for Athan to escape from his roof after he made his shot. To explain his repeated presence in the neighborhood, Athan began to visit a near-by prostitute, which, while it provided an excellent cover to the neighbors did not go over so well at home.

"Why are you seeing that filthy whore!" screamed Erinsys. "Married less than a month and you are already tired of me! What does she have that I don't?!" Then she began to get really unpleasant. It was all he could do to keep from telling her of the plan, but instead he held his tongue and promised his wife he would stay home more. As the days went by, Persis made two more visits to her cabinetmaker, each with a different escort. The wait was proving a strain. Erinsys became touchier. Athan obsessively sharpened the remaining two of the bronze-headed arrows Thaddeus had obtained. At Persis' direction, he cut three narrow groves back from the head about a quarter of the length of the shaft. Though she did not say so, Athan was sure that these groves would hold poison. Persis and Thaddeus relieved the stress in their own way each night; the noises that came from the other side of the cottage shocked the newlyweds. They were both experienced adults, but there surely must be limits! Then one night Erinsys surprised her husband in bed with something he had only vaguely heard about.

"Persis and I have been talking" Erinsys stopped to tell him. "She says that if I am to compete with disgusting whores, I should know a few tricks, too" and she resumed.

"Oh, Persis," thought a grateful Athan, "may Artemis bless you!"

The very next day Persis received a message from the cabinetmaker that her order was ready.

"Beloved, can you get free today to take me on a picnic?" she asked Thaddeus with a significant look.

"Of, course, Persis," he replied ignoring the snickers of the guardsmen with him. "Let's take Athan and Erinsys with us as well."

Within an hour the two women were in a rented cart with their men leading the pony. It was a measure of their increasing concern that Thaddeus wore his sword and Athan, in addition to his dagger was using a spear as a walking staff. Bread, cheese, and some wine were in a small pile of hay in the cart. On the way out of town they chanced to stop at the cabinetmaker's shop where Thaddeus and Persis ducked in, Thaddeus carrying a purse. They returned before Erinsys had a chance to become restless with an object wrapped in cloth and an much lighter purse.

"It's a new type of lyre," replied Persis to Erinsys' questions, "When we get into the country I will show it to you.

Outside the city they turned up the hills away from a boggy fen and eventually stopped in a lovely secluded grove.

"I think this will do," said Thaddeus.

Erinsys, glad to be out of the compound even on such a cool and windy day took out blankets from the cart and began to lay out the food and drink.

"It is so nice to get outside in the open air. When I was a girl, Papa used to take all of us up here for picnics and to play. What are you doing? Athan, are you going to play the lyre? What do you have there?"

Then she saw Thaddeus holding the thing that the cabinetmaker had obviously made for Persis. It was definitely not a lyre. The short, heavy recurved bow now had a crosspiece of stout wood coming back from the center of the grip extending more than a cubit back past the bowstring. This crosspiece had a short metal piece running beneath the end of it until it came though a square notch near the back of the wood were it was apparently hinged. On the top of the crosspiece was a forked catch. A notched channel ran the length of the top of the crosspiece.

"I have heard of these things," explained Persis pointing out the features of the device. "It allows you to hold a taunt bowstring back until you are ready to shoot it. It is supposed to be easier to shoot, but we just needed a thing that would allow Athan to shoot while staying low on the roof. See," she gestured "the bowstring is drawn and then held in place until the bowstring is released with this lever. You have to hold the thing horizontally so that the arrow will stay on top of the cross piece in this groove."

Thaddeus drew the bowstring along the new wooden stock and hooked it into the forked catch. The bowstring remained taut held by the two sides of the metal catch. It was obvious that the arrow would be notched into the string between the two tines. He started to hold the bow in the normal fashion, vertically, but Persis reached out and took the end of the bow and turned it horizontally. Thaddeus did not like anyone, especially a woman touching his weapons when he was at work and it showed. Persis with her quick perception recognized this and covered her gaffe with an explanation and diversion, "I think that is why it is called a crossbow, not because it has a crosspiece, but because it is at cross purposes to a real bow." And she smiled as brightly as the sun into the grim clouds of his glower.

She stepped back and Thaddeus, with some trepidation, pushed up the lever on the underside of the crossbow with his right hand. 'Plong!' The bowstring released; Thaddeus, unprepared dropped it. He growled in disgust.

"Excellent," said Athan, "let me try."

After he drew and released the bow several times to get the feel of the mechanism he took one of the three arrows that Persis had left with the cabinetmaker and notched it to the drawn bowstring then settled the arrow down on top of crosspiece into the grove that ran down the length of the crosspiece.

"Look out," he warned as he lifted up the crossbow, fighting an urge to turn the bow upright. He aimed the contraption at a cork tree some ten paces away and pushed up the trigger. The crossbow jerked in his hands; the arrow flew away, never to be seen again.

"Did you see it?" he asked excitedly. "Where did it go?"

"Not exactly an effective killing machine," judged Thaddeus. "A nice idea beloved, but leave the weapons to the men."

For once Persis appeared crestfallen, but before she could reply, Athan interrupted excitedly. "No, no, I think it will work. I just wasn't ready for it, that's all. Let's find the arrow and try again."

But they could not find the missing arrow. After a futile search they were persuaded by Erinsys to stop and eat. She was determined to enjoy her outing and turn this practice for a murder into a pleasant picnic. But to everyone's annoyance, Athan continued his enthusiasm, drawing and releasing the bow several times during the meal.

"I think you just have to hold it firmly and aim down the length of the arrow," he told them, several times while they ate. "I really think it will work." And sure enough, after eating, he demonstrated that he could shoot the crossbow with growing accuracy, first firing it into a small hummock a few yards away, then with additional practice hitting tree a dozen paces off.

"Now climb a tree and see how you do," suggested Thaddeus. Athan obliged him, reaching down to take first and arrow, then the cocked crossbow. Balancing on a branch six cubits up, about the height of a rooftop, he took aim at a pine tree a score of paces away. The arrow clipped the side of the tree and disappeared into the bushes.

"Pass me up another arrow," he begged.

"This is all we have left," warned Thaddeus, reaching up holding the arrow fletch first.

Holding the arrow in his teeth Athan took the bowstring in his hands and balancing on the branch placed his feet on the bow. He then pushed out and hooked the bowstring on the catch. "Nothing to it, it's easy," he exalted. The effect was spoiled, however, when he shifted the crossbow around so he could fit the arrow in the slot and inadvertently released the trigger. 'Plong!' Down came the crossbow and very nearly Athan, who balanced wildly to stay on the branch, arrow still in his teeth.

"Sorry, pass it up to me, would you Thaddeus?" This time he confidently cocked the crossbow, shifted it around, fitted the arrow, and took careful aim at the tree without hesitation. 'Plong!' The arrow stuck deeply in the tree a little over than two cubits above the ground. Thaddeus had difficulty in pulling it out.

"Thank you Athan," said Persis with great satisfaction. "Do think you can do that to Phineas tomorrow night?"

"Easily my lady."

"Good, then our problems with Phineas will be over. And you, young lady," she said to an astonished Erinsys who was just now figuring out what this little exercise was all about, "will stay in the house tomorrow like a good wife and speak to no one, no one at all mind you, except us."

"We need to have a system for signaling'" said Thaddeus on the return trip. "That way Athan knows when they are returning and he can be ready. I have been on ambushes before where you get so keyed up that when the time comes you are worn out from waiting and so miss your chance. You want to be in position waiting quietly, and not waste your energy." Thaddeus had been a soldier most of his life; he was big on not wasting energy before an action.

"How do you do that, beloved?" asked Persis.

"Well, in battle you can signal with trumpets, flags, fires, or flashing mirrors," he responded, "but this requires something more subtle. Perhaps we can get the boy to help."

"I am not going to let you risk Anteros," protested Persis, "besides, he is known to Phineas. Seeing him waving flags or flashing mirrors would alert Phineas and his men."

"No, nothing like that," explained Thaddeus, "Athan, that place on the roof, can you see the far corner from up there?"

"Yes, easily, Captain."

"Good. You are stay down flat behind that bit of statuary on the roof, just watching Anteros, who will be on the street at that far corner. He will watch for Phineas and his men coming around the corner at end of the block. When he sees them he will just turn and walk away. Then you will know it is time for you to cock that infernal machine my devious darling has devised, and as he walks past you shoot him. Then you escape according to our plan."

"Yes, captain, but there is one thing you should know. If I stay behind that bit of stone, I will not have a good angle to shoot until he is past me."

"Yes?"

"That means I will have to shoot him from behind."

"Good. Athan, haven't I taught you anything about the art of war? All that dreck about the valor of Hector and Achilles is for poets, not soldiers. The only time you attack an enemy from the front is when it is to your advantage to do so. Or when you are sure your attack will demoralize the enemy. A surprise attack from an unexpected direction is usually better. Do you know why generals form up and attack in rigid formations? Because it is easy; most of the generals I have known are either lazy, or do not understand the art of war, or both. You must train your men so that they can maneuver effectively to your commands in battle, and that means doing a lot more than just lining up shield to shield and charging."

51

Usually when the four were together Erinsys had little to say. In fact she was a little intimidated by Captain Thaddeus and completely so by Persis, but this time she could not restrain a question, "Captain, do you mean all our generals are just incompetent?"

"No, Erinsys, war is actually very simple, but in war even simple things are very difficult. There is one more thing to remember, Athan: you will be afraid up there."

This got the warrior puzzled looks from the women.

"Everybody is afraid before a battle," he explained. "The recruits in their first battle are afraid because they don't know what a battle is like. The veterans are afraid because they do. So men do things to keep up their courage such as boasting, drinking too much wine, or going out in front of the lines to attack by themselves; anything to ease the tension. Mostly we have each other, our comrades to keep our spirits up. We don't want to look bad in front of them."

"Surely you aren't afraid, Captain. Everyone knows how brave you are," interrupted Erinsys.

"Yes, Erinsys, even I get afraid. I have known a few men that did not seem to know fear, but none of them were good soldiers. It is not being afraid that is the problem, it is allowing fear to prevent you from doing what must be done. You learn to use fear, to manage it, and, if you can manage it with your men, then you deserve to be called a captain. Of course, it is a lot easier to be brave when you have your friends all around you. Athan will be up there on that roof by himself. Even though all he has to do is shoot an arrow and run, he is going to be plenty nervous up there. He will have to manage his fear all alone."

After this little speech they walked along in silence for a long time. Athan had heard variations of his advice many times, but he never forgot what Thaddeus said that night for the rest of his long, long, life.

After their return, Persis and Thaddeus had a murmured conversation after which they collected Anteros and went into town. When they returned it became clear that it had been more than just a trip to the market for the evening meal. As Anteros served them their supper in the central room they reviewed the plan for the murder.

Persis had recruited another conspirator in town, an old woman who would be wearing a grey head cloth. She would sit two blocks down from the baths at the corner where the gang turned left. When she saw them coming out of the baths she would get up and walk away down the street, turning away at the next corner. Anteros would be stationed at the end of a three block long stretch Phineas would pass on his way home, just short of the corner where Phineas would turn right toward his house. The boy would pretend to be playing stones. When Anteros saw the old woman walking toward him, he was to pick up his stones and move to the corner. That would be the signal they were coming. Athan would draw and cock the crossbow. When Anteros saw Phineas and his men actually round the corner he would walk directly away from the house. Once Anteros was around the corner and out of sight of the oncoming party he was to skip briskly back to the garrison and wait there.

Seeing Anteros depart would let Athan know his targets were on the way; when they walked past him on the opposite side of the street, Athan would rest the crossbow on the roof coping, take aim down at Phineas, and shoot an arrow into his ribs. Then Athan would run across the roof to the rear of the building, jump down into the alley there and follow a planned escape route returning to the garrison as though he had just returned from a visit to his prostitute. He was to get home as fast as possible but not to appear be hurrying and definitely not to be out of breath when he entered the compound gates. He would discard the crossbow on the way back.

It was a good plan, but as Athan lurked behind the statuary on the roof the following night he could not help remembering the Captain Thaddeus' teaching on battle plans: 'always have a plan, it will never work, but always have a plan. It gives you something to deviate from when things go to shit. And things always do.' Athan had seen the old woman in her place when he arrived at the ambush site so he knew Phineas was definitely still in the baths. He had been even more careful than usual when he climbed up to the roof. He had hidden a ladder in the alley behind the house he would use for his ambush. The ladder was on the left side of the roof, next to the street the gang had walked up on their way to the baths. If it had been propped up against the house when Phineas was on his way to the baths, the gang might have seen it. Anyone looking into the alley immediately after the shooting would certainly see the ladder leaning up to the roof. If they realized that the arrow had been fired from the roof it would only be natural for them to wait at the foot of the ladder for the assassin to come down. That was part of Athan's plan. Athan was much more nervous than he thought he would be. Carrying the crossbow in a bag, pretending it was a lyre (Erinsys' idea) he had to restrain himself from making some idiotic comment the guard at the compound gate about singing to his girlfriend.

"Don't tell them anything; let them assume it is a lyre. What else could it be?" advised Persis.

He had his only arrow laid out beside the crossbow already pointed in the right direction, ready to be cocked and loaded. "There will only be time for one arrow," Thaddeus had told him. That arrow had been specially prepared the night before. After the evening meal, Persis has taken it from him, picked up a bag that held cosmetics and other mysterious feminine items and retired to her room for a time. Later that evening she came out holding what looked to be the arrow wrapped in a stiff bit of cloth she used to cover her hair in rain. She gave a look at Erinsys; the two women went out the back door together. They returned without the arrow half an hour later. He did not see it again until she gave it to him with the crossbow just before he left. The head of the arrow with its finely sharpened barbs had a viscous gray substance liberally smeared on it. The first third of the arrow's shaft was now covered in a dark brown substance. Persis covered it up again with the stiff waterproof cloth before putting into the 'lyre bag.' "It would be best if you avoided touching the coated places," advised Persis.

"What is it?" joked Athan, "Hydra's blood? Essence of scorpion? Are you friends with an adder?"

"Several," said Persis in a serious voice, "just handle this as little as possible."

"Phew," sniffed Athan at the brown stain on the shaft, "is that what I think it is? Nasty!"

"Yes," replied the woman with a small secret smile. "Touching the shaft will be merely disgusting; handling the tip would be more serious. I am not sure I had enough fish to do the job, so we added the extra onto the shaft just to be sure."

"Fish?" asked Athan puzzled.

But Persis merely gave him that mysterious smile. "Special fish." Then she leaned forward and gave him a swift peck on the check. "Good luck." And she withdrew to her room.

Captain Thaddeus was on duty and would be until the midnight watch. This concerned the two men, but Persis thought it provided an excellent alibi. Unfortunately this led to some additional pointed comments by Erinsys concerning Persis' willingness to risk someone else's man while hers remained safe. For once Erinsys stood up to Persis. Words became heated, then positively nasty. Had Athan not stepped in the incident might have ended in blows between the two women. The dispute did nothing to reduce the already tense atmosphere. When he gave his wife a goodbye kiss, she was tense as a post and tears were swimming in her eyes, but she said nothing. That is until he was halfway across the compound when she shrilled out after him, "Don't you go off visiting that whore again!" Athan winced as his comrades chuckled; same old Erinsys. He was halfway to his destination before he realized that his wife had given him an alibi, too. Athan was so nervous that he briefly considered actually visiting Esther, the convenient prostitute, just to relax him and really perfect his alibi, but he knew he did not have time and went directly to his assassin's perch.

Once up there he immediately saw his lookout Anteros down by his corner playing stones by himself. He could not see the old woman from there without being far too conspicuous. It did not matter; he would rely on Anteros. Athan tried to settle himself in for the wait peeking down from time to time to check on his young lookout.

Athan almost hoped that Phineas and his gang stayed at the baths until dark as they had done twice before when he had been watching them. If it was too dark to shoot accurately, the plan was for him to wait, then return quietly, leaving the crossbow hidden on the roof and wait until the next night. And right now tomorrow night seemed like a pretty good idea to Athan.

He looked down at Anteros in the street below and saw the boy had gathered up his stones, moved to the corner, and was looking right at him. That idiot! He was giving away his position to anyone who followed the boy's gaze! Making a gesture to the boy, he bend down and prepared to draw the crossbow. To his horror the boy immediately turned and skipped rapidly away and up the cross street. They were already coming down the street! Athan pulled back the crossbow but he could not get the bowstring to catch on the latch. After a frantic moment he realized the trigger was depressed. He eased the bowstring back down. Okay, they would do it tomorrow. And as the thought those words, it was as though he could hear Thaddeus' voice. 'Slow and easy is better, boy. If you want do something fast, do it slowly; slow and sure.' Letting out a breath, Athan carefully pulled back on the bowstring, and this time notched it cleanly. He then took up the arrow, first notching it, and then laying it carefully on the slot. If they were by him and he did not have a shot, they would do it tomorrow. Athan took aim down the arrow at his kill area. They had not yet appeared. He waited; then waited some more. Perhaps they had seen Anteros and were going a different way. Maybe they had seen the boy's gaze and were coming up behind him on the roof to see what he had been looking at. A quick glance back revealed nothing; he was being ridiculous. They had just gone a different way. It was beginning to get dark and a breeze was gusting. Soon it would be too dark to shoot. Then he would have to release the tension on the bow and hide the arrow.

Then he saw the bald man from Phineas' house in the lead; strange how he had never learned the man's name. He took aim down the arrow at the street below, the fingers on his right hand gently touching the trigger lever. Then his target came into view, with another guard on his left hand side, protecting Phineas from a sudden lunge out of the shadows, but leaving his right side open for a clear shot from across the street. Athan picked a point just below his target's right shoulder blade and gently pushed on the trigger so that he could hold his aim point pushing, pushing…'Plong'! The actual release of the arrow came a surprise to Athan. He watched it flash across the street and saw it hit Phineas. But it hit him all wrong; the man should have been driven straight back by the impact. Instead he twisted from left to right and screamed. The arrow had been too far back and too low. Athan was not sure exactly where he had put the arrow, somewhere between his ribs and buttocks and on the man's far side, his left, not the closer right side. In any event it was not a killing shot. He observed the scene below for only a few moments, but it was a few moments too long. One of the bodyguards was pointing right at him. Athan turned, picked up the lyre cover in his left hand while holding the discharged crossbow in his right and moved toward the ladder on the left side of the building. As soon as he was out of sight Athan turned to his right and raced to the far right hand corner of the building. As he reached that corner he glanced below him. A thin padding of sacking was still there. Holding his crossbow in one hand he jumped down four paces to the alley.

The ladder at the other end of the alley was a red herring. It also met another of Captain Thaddeus' maxims of the art of war: "Do not retreat from the scene of an ambush using the same route that you came in on."

No one was visible to Athan as he landed but someone must have seen his shape jumping down for there was an immediate outcry, 'There he goes!' The chase was on. The plan had been for him to walk out onto the street casually so as to avoid notice. Now Athan came of the alley sprinting for dear life, dodging and weaving past strolling groups of people. He made it to the next alley and turned into it before his pursuers rounded the far corner. There was no one visible in the shadowy lane, so Athan continued to run fast as he could, just concentrating on getting to the far end. His pursuers would have little trouble figuring out that he had ducked down this alleyway and they would have certainly expect him to run away from the pursuit. He slowed to a rapid walk and rapidly stuffed the crossbow into its bag before he emerged into the next major cross street. He had crossed the street and was continuing down the alley when he heard a 'view hallow' behind him. He accelerated again into a full sprint. As he dashed away, his carefully thought out plan of escape in tatters, an idea hit him, he could go to Esther's place. Then another related thought come to him so strongly he almost broke stride: she had a lyre! He had seen it before even if he had never heard her play it. Why had he not thought of this before?

All at once he was no longer fleeing blindly from his pursuers; he was executing a new plan. Instead of a wild panicky dash, he began to run smoothly and with purpose. Down the alley, a quick walk across another street where, glancing to his right he could see the bathhouse that Phineas had so recently departed. Athan made a quick left turn down a short crossway, and another right onto a street, walking again, up to a door on the other side, and into the house. A large man with a full beard and a thinning head of hair was sitting on a stool. He looked up at Athan.

"Is Esther free, Demos?"

"Hello Athan, yeah, business is slow. Go on up."

Had she been busy, Athan would have asked for her next appointment and then gone out the back door that led to the rear of a drinking house. Houses like Demos' were discrete; a man sometimes had the need to leave by a back door. But Athan had been confident that Esther would be free. It was early and she was not especially popular.

He knocked and entered without waiting for an answer.

"Sweetheart," she said getting up from the bed where she had been sitting, "it has been so long. I've missed you. What have you got there?" she asked, pointing at the bag on his back.

"Oh, wife trouble, I'm sure you understand," he said answering the first question and not the second.

"What did you expect, marrying that harpy," pouted the prostitute.

"Do you know how to play that thing?" he pointed to the lyre atop her wardrobe changing the subject and getting to his real purpose in visiting her, "or is it just for looks?"

"I used to play," she admitted, "I thought it would help me entertain customers, you know, but no one seemed to want to do anything but get straight to business. Why you are panting? Did you hurry to come and see me?"

"Can you try to teach me to play a little?" he asked, ignoring her questions. "I'll pay your usual rates, of course."

"You're the customer," Esther shrugged, taking down the instrument.

And so for the next hour and a half the tones of the lyre echoed from the room. It transpired that Esther was no hand at the lyre, but had an unexpectedly sweet voice. Athan on the other hand, had a mediocre voice but revealed a hidden talent with the instrument. So enjoyable was this unusual activity to them that they were both surprised when there was a knock on the door and they heard Demos' heavy voice outside. "Are you two going to caterwaul in there all night? We have other customers you know, and some of them are music lovers."

At a gesture from Athan, Esther got up to open the door a crack. She was aware that Athan had drawn his dagger and moved behind the door. "Sorry Demos, we just got carried away. I'll keep it down."

"Well all right. When you young man comes down, he might want to go out through the tavern exit. Seems there has been a killing of sorts and the streets may not be safe."

"My thanks, friend," said Athan from behind the door.

"Well, don't want to lose a regular customer," Grumbled the big man good naturedly as he trundled back downstairs.

"It is remarkable how clean you guardsmen keep your weapons," said Esther, looking intently at his shiny and obviously unbloodied blade.

"It's a good thing we have been up here safely practicing the lyre for the past two hours; let me pay you " said Athan quickly putting away his dagger. "Let me pay for your time and leave you. By the by, do you think I could arrange to purchase this lyre? It seems to suit me."

They agreed upon a price, and arranged for delivery of the payment the following day. Athan put down money for two full hours and a generous tip. "Thank you Esther. It was a fine lesson."

"Listen, sweetmeats," she said catching him by the front of his tunic, "It isn't quite two hours yet. I can't let my favorite customer leave without giving him a little something."

He knew that all prostitutes told their customers that each was their favorite. But he did not know he actually was Esther's. She thought him quite the bravest and most handsome man she knew. And she decided that tonight she would prove that he was her favorite. A few moments later Athan began to waver. 'After all', he thought distractedly, 'the streets are probably still dangerous and she is so good at what she does.'

One thing led to another and it was over two hours before Athan slipped finally our through the tavern with a lyre and crossbow hidden in his sack. He picked up the route originally planed and made his way back to the compound unremarked.

He quietly slipped the latch and entered his cottage almost three hours after the attack and placed his bag on the table next to hour wine goblets and a sword. Four people were waiting for him. Anteros sat with his back to the fire, grinning at him. Thaddeus, now off duty took his hand off the naked sword that lay on the table. Next to him Persis gave him a relieved smile. Erinsys was pacing in front of the door to their room. When she saw him she gave a cry and flung herself into his arms.

"Oh, thanks be to Hera, I was so worried, we heard that Phineas had been shot but you didn't come and didn't come. Oh, I was so worried!" she sobbed into his shoulder. 'Now this was more like it!' thought Athan.

Erinsys stopped sobbing to draw in a breath. She became very still and drew in another breath; no a sniff. Then she took in another sniff that had all the accusation of a formal writ by a bailiff.

"You've been with her!" she accused backing away from him, her eyes going to slits, looking like nothing less than a fierce jungle beast preparing to spring.

"No! Well, yes, I had to buy a lyre, you see, as a cover. And she was giving me a lesson on the lyre. Mostly." Even to his own ears it sounded like a weak lie. Erinsys had endured massively stressful dangers and changes in her life over the past month. On top of everything else she had been under enormous strain for the last 24 hours. Now, she just snapped.

In a shriek that could be heard throughout the compound Erinsys let him have it: "Lyre! **Lyre! LYRE**! YOU AND YOUR WHORE WERE PLAYING THE LYRE!?!? I'LL GIVE YOU LYRE!" and snatching up the bag that contained both the offending instrument as well as a murder weapon, she began failing at him ineffectually but with great rage.

"I'll take that' Erinsys," said Thaddeus calmly running his hands down her arms and removing the bag from her grasp. Undeterred, she snatched up one of the terra cotta wine goblets and flung it at him. It smashed against the wall with a spectacular crash.

"LYRE LESSONS! I CAN PLAY THE LYRE BETTER THAN ANY WHORE THAT EVER LIVED! IF YOU WANT LYRE LESSONS YOU BETTER PLAN ON GETTING THEM AT HOME!"

Athan, staggered by the ferocity of the attack, fled the cottage with Erinsys in hot pursuit, stopping only to hurl another goblet, which somehow found something to break against. Seeing he had escaped, Erinsys stopped near the center of the compound, which had suddenly gone very quiet. All the tension, rage, and frustration of the past few days boiled up and came out of her is a mighty scream. It echoed off the walls and out into the streets beyond. It went up in pitch like some giant insane teapot boiling over, up and up until it finally seemed to reach a pitch audible only to dogs. The compound was now utterly quiet. Brave men quailed; women clutched their babies, dogs slunk under shelter. Athan, by now hiding all the way over by the guardhouse at the entrance of the compound, watched in fascination and dread as his wife stalked in small circles near the center of the compound cursing him with great skill. The primal scream she had vented had not seemed to damage her throat at all; she still maintained excellent volume. Her voice echoed and reinforced itself off the compound walls, clearly reaching Athan as he cowered behind the guard at the compound's entrance.

"Athan," said Philo, the guard on duty, a big tough veteran armed with shield and spear, "if she comes this way I'm running for it."

Eventually Erinsys wound down and stalked back into the cottage, where, her emotions now vented, she went without a word into her room and fell into a deep sleep for the next twelve hours. Thaddeus found Athan hiding in the barracks and assured that it was safe to return home though Athan slept on one of the dining couches in the center room just to be safe. 'Erinsys' Rant' passed into a legend in the guards, and for many years after it would be said of some salty leather-lunged sergeant that "He could give Erinsys a lesson." Of course they never said it where she could hear.

There was immediate fallout from the attack on Phineas. "He got stuck in the lower back," Anteros reported the next day with great satisfaction. Then he went all stiff and couldn't move. "They couldn't get the arrow out, so they had to put him on a door and take him to physician, him screaming and moaning all the way and crying that he was paralyzed. They didn't know what to do at first with him all helpless like that. Finally they decided to get the arrow out even if he couldn't move. The physician couldn't get it out for nearly an hour. They say he bled like a stuck pig."

"Good," purred Persis, Erinsys nodded grim agreement.

"They have him back at his house now. He is still paralyzed, but they say he is regaining some feeling in his hands. The physician said the wound itself is not that bad and unless it festers it should not be mortal."

The two women shared a look. "I have heard that the arrow was cursed," commented Persis, "I fear the wound must soon become inflamed."

"Of course," she confided to Athan after the boy had left, "we did give the arrow some help."

"What was on that arrow lady?"

"Two things: on the arrowhead, I put some essence of a special fish that was sold to me some time ago. A girl needs to be prepared," she said blandly, as though keeping lethal concoctions with your cosmetics was a completely natural thing to do. "But I was not certain of its potency. So we soaked the first part of the shaft in what was in the honey pot out by the privy. Fitting, yes, he was a shit in life and that is what is going to help kill him."

Over the next few days rumors swirled around the city. At the insistence of Phineas, who remained abed in his house, the city fathers send bailiffs to investigate Captain Thaddeus and Athan. Both men had alibis: Thaddeus had been on duty surrounded by guardsmen; Athan had famously been with a more or less respectable prostitute; famously because tales of 'Erinsys' Rant' made the rounds of the city. This had the result that Esther's popularity spiked as brave men went to find what could arouse such fury in another woman. Indeed, the lyre was there in Thaddeus' house, and if the questioners did not bother checking the ashes of the fireplace for the remains of strange-looking bits wood, they could not be blamed. Both men found that for the next few days when they went on patrol in the town the guard's general assigned several extra guards to their bands, 'just in case of trouble'. The investigation into the assault faded as quickly as Phineas' health. The rumor mills in the town had it that the arrow had been fired by either a god or demon and was indeed cursed. Though by the third day he had regained the use of his limbs he was greatly weakened and a fierce infection swiftly took hold of him. Within four days he was burning with fever and ranting incoherently. By the time he slipped into a coma on the fifth day, his creditors were already moving in on his goods, and his men began to seek other employment. In the case of some of them this employment was out of town. Several old scores were also apparently being settled. Athan was with a patrol that found the body of the bald man whose name Athan had never learned.

The morning after Phineas died, an old woman wearing a grey head cloth came with a donkey-drawn cart and two porters to collect his body, claiming to be a distant aunt. They had not been sure what to do with the body and were glad to help load the corpse onto the wagon. The old woman followed the cart to a non-descript barn just outside the city walls. There she paid off the porters and told them she would be met by other family members.

Some little time later Erinsys, Persis, and Anteros arrived, escorted by Athan. They covered the cheap shroud over the body with hay and then the boy led the donkey out into the countryside with the three women and Athan walking behind.

In a typical funeral, the procession to the grave or pyre is called an ekphora. A typical ekphora is a solemn thing, the body followed by a line of grieving mourners, wailing and lamenting the departed. This was not exactly a typical ekphora. Instead of a fine carriage carrying the body there was only a donkey cart with the body concealed under filthy straw and a handful of the deceased's mortal enemies strolling behind in satisfied silence. The boy led the cart down the road south for a time and then turned down a track that led toward marshy fen. Just as the ground became so soft the cart was in danger of getting stuck Anteros, aided by Athan, turned it around. Then the boy and the man grabbed the corpse by its feet and pulled it out of the cart and down next to a small fetid pool. Athan ripped the shroud away from the corpse leaving the naked body on its back, staring up into the cloudy evening. It had already begun to putrefy.

Erinsys and Persis walked down to the corpse. "That's him alright. Good," said Persis. Erinsys had worn a conservative wool dress for this outing with practical shoes; she gave a vicious kick to the side of the dead man's head. Anteros giggled. Persis took Erinsys' hand and they turned away from the corpse. Erinsys walked hand in hand with Persis up to her husband.

Facing him she took a deep breath. "Husband," she began and stopped looking at the ground. They all waited. Persis gave her hand a little squeeze. Erinsys took another breath and steeled herself to deliver what was obviously a prepared speech. "Husband, on the night my uncle took me to the house of Phineas." She stopped again for a moment then continued, "…on the night I arrived, Phineas took me into his room and he raped me. He beat me and he raped me. Then he had one of his men rape me while he watched and laughed. It was one of his guards, the one with no hair." There was a long pause. "If you want to put me aside, I will understand."

She was interrupted by the sound of a thin stream of water. They looked back. The old woman had hiked up her dress and squatting down, and was urinating directly onto the corpse's face. Unembarrassed, she wiped herself with some grass, pulled down her black dress and came up to them.

"My grandson, Perseus, he was a wild one," she told them by way of explanation, "Phineas took him in. Said he would make him rich. Said all the men would want him. He corrupted him. One night a bunch of his customers got drunk and beat my grandson to death for no reason; maybe just for fun. Phineas said it was Perseus' fault. He claimed he would pay reparations. But all he ever gave us was his poor, abused body. When the Lady came to me, I was glad to help, glad to be a lookout, glad to help dispose of this rotting trash the way it deserves."

Looking down at the defiled corpse Athan wondered aloud, "Will anyone find him here?"

"Only the scavengers," said Persis, "he will not last long. He had no friends or family, only temporary allies. Let the pigs and wild dogs have him. I am sure they, at least, will appreciate him."

Athan turned to his wife and answered her question by offering her his arm. She took it they turned and walked back to their lives. Erinsys walking on her husband's arm looked up at him. "You are a good man, Athan son of Medius. I am sorry that I was angry with you. I will never scream at you again."

'But she did', thought the Old King dreaming in his cave, 'many times. She was famous for it. But she bore my children. And all in all she was a

good wife; maybe not a comfortable wife, but a good wife.' He was sorry he never got to make sure she had a proper funeral.

Outside the light had dimmed. He had dreamed away the day. He returned to his sleeping place and lay down and once again slipped into reminisce.

Chapter Four–
Crimes and Punishments

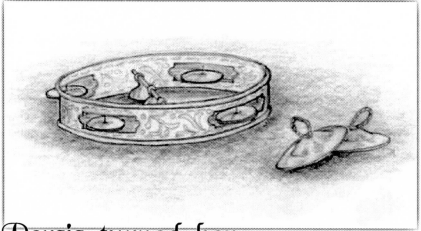

Persis turned her abrupt departure from the house of Phineas with little more than a single bag and the clothes on her back, from what might have been a traumatic disaster for most people into an opportunity to expand her influence. And expand it she did. She quickly charmed the General of the guards, the Provost Marshall, the other four Captains of the guard (Thaddeus being her first, most thorough and lasting conquest) and then the rest of the guards in general. She became a cross between an honorary captain and a mascot.

'I bring a bit of glamour and excitement to their lives,' was how she put it. When Persis entered and left the compound the guard at the gate would almost always come to attention and salute her. And she would inevitably have a few kind words for him in return.

Rather than seeing herself as a refugee living in some soldier's quarters, she viewed her move as sort of a temporary transition; her chance to spend a bit of time supporting the troops and enjoy the secure environment they provided. Soon, that was how the rest of

Epiria viewed it as well. Already well-known in some mysterious way, she now became even more famous in the city simply by being famous. She found lucrative employment attending and sometimes hosting symposia for the best families in the city. Within three months she rented new and much more suitable quarters, yet, for a while most nights she continued to return to Thaddeus and his little cottage in the compound. This arrangement continued for almost a year before Erinsys' first pregnancy began to intrude on the serenity of the household.

Thaddeus was the beneficiary of a totally unexpected development: Persis, to her own astonishment, had fallen deeply in love with him. She knew that she could do much better than a mere captain of the guards, but she knew her heart would settle for no one else. Once she realized that this tough soldier was the love of her life, Persis reacted with typical practical efficiency: if she was completely in love with a man whose social status was too low, she would raise his status. Fortunately, her instincts had not failed her; Thaddeus rose to every challenge, and his personal status concomitantly rose as well. The association with Persis did wonders for Thaddeus' prospects. Not only did he gain prestige by being the lover of the most famous and influential hetaira in the city but he also had the benefit of her excellent advice as she deftly guided him through the intricacies of developing personal influence.

Of course, he did not need advice in how to carry out his guard duties. Thaddeus's rise in the guards was primarily due to his own considerable talents. Men in the guards of small city states like Epiria had three primary duties. First, they patrolled the streets inside the walls, especially at night. They were not firemen nor were they police, but they would help with extinguishing fires, and would detain any suspicious characters (usually that meant any strangers) found in the streets where they did not belong. Second, the guards would mount periodic patrols through the farms and homesteads in the general vicinity of Epiria. This was a duty at which Thaddeus excelled. His company would sometime range far out to clear the roads of bandits. Should a farm be menaced by brigands, Thaddeus and his men, sometimes augmented by an additional company of soldiers, would sally forth and put the intruders to flight. Finally, in the event of a threat to the city, the militia would be called to augment the relatively small number of professional soldiers. And in these larger conflicts as well, Thaddeus was able to demonstrate his professional talents. His association with Persis somehow helped the free men of the city who made up the militia to follow him without the usual grumbling about status. Thaddeus rewarded their support by an unbroken series of victories, usually obtained at little cost.

In the guards there were few promotions available. Experienced men of ability could be become sergeants, which provided them with authority and prestige and slightly more pay. Typically there were two sergeants for each company, one of whom was understood to be the leading or 'top sergeant'. Men of recognized value could also be promoted to captain. The most capable of the Captains was recognized as the Senior Captain, an administrative position with greater prestige, but no additional pay. The Senior Captain was in charge of operations: the watch that guarded the streets, the troops that patrolled the areas outside the city for bandits, and the guards that made up a portion of the city's army when they went to war. The other senior officer was the Provost, who was responsible for the guard's compound and internal administration. The overall commander of the guard was the General, who might also be called upon to command the militia in the event of a battle.

The military organization was dependant on the militia and citizen soldiers for operations of any real size; war was usually limited in time to a season and at most a single battle, but it did involve much greater numbers of men. The leaders of such expeditions were purely ad hoc for that operation only. The General could command the army but a member of the oligarchy with solid military experience could also be put in charge. Much depended upon individual personalities and prestige within the ranks. This only worked in groups that knew one another well, either personally or by reputation. Despite the seemingly casual organization, each man understood the need to work together. Each was dedicated to his city and particularly his company.

Being a guardsman was not a particularly prestigious job, but it was honorable. Although his profession did not pay especially well, a man could raise a family on what he earned. And if the job was often boring, it could at times be very interesting indeed.

Things were never more interesting within the city than during the brief and terrible time of the Mad Butcher. There were no such things as newspapers or any other form of printed media in that time and place, so information was passed by word of mouth, and people being people, often as juicy gossip. And there are few things juicier than an especially brutal murder.

Although the guard did patrol the streets looking for suspicious characters, there was no such thing as a police force. Unless you were caught in the act of a crime, or blundered into a patrol literally red-handed with your victim's blood, there was no formal mechanism to investigate a crime. Like firefighting, people were expected to be self-reliant. Law and order in town existed because even though Epiria was a fairly large city for its time, most people knew one another or a least a member of someone's extended family. Strangers were not common and were watched. When a suspected criminal was captured, he could be brought before one of the city's designated magistrates. These were men of property who acted as judge and jury. They would listen to the complainants and defendants, review the evidence, and then render a judgment. Punishment could take the form of fines, corporal punishment, exile, reduction to slavery (but only if the guilty party was a foreigner) and death. Since there was no provision for long term incarceration and law enforcement was far from certain, many crimes were punished by death. Little was formalized or written down. Justice depended on the fairness and common sense of the magistrate hearing the case. To their credit, most of them were honest and decent men who took their responsibilities seriously and tried to do the right thing. Of course, not all cases made it to a magistrate; when a criminal was captured in the act, his would-be victims often took care of things then and there. But all in all it was a system that worked surprisingly well, perhaps because there were no lawyers.

But even though the level of crime was not unreasonable, the streets were unlighted, and it was dangerous for a man to be out after full dark unarmed and without a light of some kind. And it was doubly dangerous for a woman, unless she was accompanied by a prudently equipped escort. Anyone who was outside, unarmed and without a light after the third hour of darkness was drunk, desperate, or foolish; that or of the underclass of whores or criminals who preyed on the unwary.

Persis' manner of living often required her to attend banquets and gatherings late into the night and so she required a suitable escort.

Anteros, her personal attendant, who had by now become a young man, was not suitable since he would, in Persis' words 'be more likely to flirt with an attacker than defend me.' Thaddeus went with her whenever he could, and he soon became welcome in the homes of the city's oligarchs. But there were times when his duties with the guards conflicted with this, and so Athan was sometimes called to provide a trustworthy escort services for Persis.

These escorts had become more common since the birth of Erinsys' second child, Persephone, a month before. Erinsys had temporarily moved in with her favorite sister, since it was easier to care for her infant daughter and their three year old son, Jason there. Athan, though welcome at his sister-in-law's, found the accommodations a bit too crowded for his personal taste and remained behind in their cottage in the guard's compound. Sometimes he also stayed with his friends Persis and Thaddeus in Persis' spacious and well appointed house in town.

So it was early one summer's evening that Athan arrived at the house of his friend to escort her to a symposium at the home of one of the richest merchants in Epiria. The new porter already knew him and let him enter immediately, informing him that the lady was getting dressed and would be down soon. Athan, feeling at home, went to an anteroom and waited patiently until she emerged half an hour later, looking stunning. She was perfectly dressed in the classic style: an ivory-colored chiton with a pattern around the hemline that intrigued Athan. The thread was gold in color consisting of a series of connected right angles that brought Athan to mind of a series of square waves. He was never quite sure how women arranged their chitons in such variety. After all, it was only a single piece of cloth but wound and folded so artfully as to cover and highlight the feminine frame. Tonight two ornate gold broaches on her shoulders supported the dress, leaving the arms and shoulders bare. The cloth had been folded so that there was an overlap of material on the bodice. Persis had somehow managed to wrap the cloth below this bodice so that it fit her as closely as a blade fits into a sheath. Her maid had applied cosmetics skillfully; kohl darkened and highlighted her eyes, there was a faint blush of rouge, and the fine lines that had begun to appear around her eyes had somehow been disguised with creams and powders. She wore a simple gilded headband or fillet around her head with her long hair up and back in an elaborate bun; every hair somehow kept in place. Around her throat was a simple coral necklace highlighted with elements of gold. Elegant gilded sandals that matched her hem and headband peeked out from the bottom of her skirt. Athan could not help but smile at the sight of Persis' feet. She could be vain and was certainly proud, but she fretted about her feet: she was convinced they were too large and ugly. They were in fact a bit larger than proper proportions would decree, and as a dancer she had put her feet to hard work and it showed. Still, neither Athan nor Thaddeus quite understood why she sometimes went to lengths to conceal her feet; Thaddeus referred to her 'Achilles' Heels' which did not please Persis in the slightest. Persis could be prickly about being teased.

It was late in the day when they made their way to the house of the merchant where Persis had her assignment, so they did not have to put up with most of the street whores and beggars that sometimes pestered the well-to-do as they walked in the street. There was, of course, no concept of a public welfare, so those without family who fell upon hard times were quickly reduced to a truly desperate condition. They were accosted by one such waif that had such a foul mouth that even Persis, who was accomplished at ignoring such creatures, recoiled from her. Athan imagined that soon one of the criminal gangs of the city would come by and sweep the poor thing up. She would then either be forced to function as a simple prostitute working for only the food the gang cared to give her, or perhaps she would be sold as a slave, which was essentially the same thing. There was little concern for the weak or unlucky in that time or place. Persis lengthened her stride to move away. She could do this despite her long tight chiton because she had arranged the folds to that they could split all the way up to her knee where another broach, this a small golden dragon, held the folds together. The girl followed them a short way making more and more graphic suggestions for lower and lower prices. Athan suspected there must be more to the girl's condition than mere hunger. Perhaps something had happened to her that had pushed her beyond all reason and into the edge of madness. It was sad, but Athan knew from experience such creatures could seldom be succored. They delighted in biting hands whether feeding them or not.

They were welcomed into the banquet site where the host and his staff of foreign slaves and domestic servants were making final preparations for the event. Low couches were spread around the room, some big enough for two, a few large enough for four. This evening's banquet was in the form of a symposium, a form more typical farther south, but gaining in popularity in Epiria. The men would be discussing politics, philosophy, art, and women. The few women there were either entertainers or, like Persis, hetaira. Some symposia degenerated into drunken orgies. It was not uncommon when things got out of hand in such a symposia for fist fights to erupt. Persis had once confided to Athan that one of the reasons she had drifted up to a place so far from the sophistication of the wealthy city states to the south and east was that symposia there tended to be much coarser and more violent. It was not a danger of rape that frightened her as much as the fear of being caught in one of the brawls.

"One blow to the face can put an end to your business. What happens to your looks when your nose is broken and your front teeth knocked out? Who would want such woman in their symposium?" Persis had told him. "I saw it happen. A woman I knew lost everything to a single drunken backhand. Her beauty was ruined in an instant." Up in the so-called backwater of Epiria, things were much more reserved and therefore, safer. Further, in this "less civilized" region, women had much more practical freedom. The city states often expected women to remain silent and sequestered for their entire lives. That did not suit Persis at all. She much preferred banquets like the one she anticipated tonight where she would be expected to entertain the men with her wit, style, and charm. Her status as a paid she-companion allowed her to give her customers the things that men did not expect from their wives: a female that they could speak with as they did with their male friends. It was still an exotic notion to the men.

But even though Persis did not expect any problems, she was grateful she would have a protector on the premises. Athan would not leave, but wait in the house until Thaddeus arrived. Athan did his waiting in an anteroom outside the banquet hall listening to the conversation and laughter. From time to time he would hear the singers who were entertaining the guests. The merchant could afford the best, and judging from the quality of the music that was what he had gotten.

"Are they done yet?" said Thaddeus entering the room as a burst of laughter came from the room next door. His duty with the guard completed, he chose to come to the banquet hall to walk his woman home after her engagement.

"Soon, I think," yawned Athan, "It must be almost the sixth hour by now."

As though to grant his wish, the participants of the feast began coming out of the banquet hall to collect their escorts, attendants, and bearers, departing on foot, or in sedan chairs for home. Of course, the entertainers were some of the last to leave. This included not only Persis but three other hetaira, four singers, three musicians, and a dancer. From behind the door could be heard the age-old sounds of plates and goblets being bussed up from the tables and benches by the house kitchen staff. The singers and musicians departed together ahead of them, escorted by a muscular hired guard. Persis explained that the four remaining women had only an older slave as a guard and would appreciate an additional escort back to their house and would the men be so kind as to accompany them, as it was only a little out of their way.

They would be glad to escort the ladies to their residence. The two men ignited their lights, Athan had used one of Persis' stylish glass-shielded lamps hung from a shepherd's crook; Thaddeus had come straight from duty and still carried a simple pitch torch. Despite the heat the women wrapped light cloaks around themselves and stepped out into the darkness with the men on the outside. The women immediately began a somewhat technical discussion centering on the establishment of a new group of hetairas, musicians, singers, and dancers to be called the Five Sisters. The plan was to try to provide a broader range of entertainment services from a single source. The principal expounder of this idea was Doreen, a small delicate woman in her mid-twenties whom Persis had known as a friend and confidant since shortly after her arrival in the city. Athan had definitely noticed Doreen at the house, and thought her a rather tasty little bit. She had a slender but definitely feminine build, a long graceful neck, oval face, flowing russet hair and enormous dark brown eyes. The second of the group was the oldest; Athan did not catch her name at first. She was a short witty woman with an easy, confident manner that he thought would be a good addition to any gathering. Walking behind the other three women was a tall lithe young woman, very pretty, but also very quiet. On the other side of Persis, next to Athan walked the final member of this group, a lively red haired girl just out of her teens who called herself Vania. She walked alongside the others, carrying her share of the conversation all the while flirting with Athan. The little tease had brushed her ample bosom against Athan 'accidentally' so many times in a walk of a quarter hour that despite himself he found he was becoming aroused. He wondered how much she would cost, not for a symposium but for a spare hour or so of private entertainment. These ruminations were cut short when they arrived at the new house where the so-called 'Five Sisters' resided. There, with proper courtesies, the ladies were ushered inside past their porter, a suitably large doorman who called himself Porter (of course) and into the safety of their new house.

"Can you imagine?" started Persis as soon as they had moved away from the door, "They actually think they can support themselves as hetaira. Well, not just as hetaira, they have the sense to bring in singers and musicians, but there is not enough business in a city of this size to support so many entertainers."

As Persis continued her discussion Athan could not help thinking that these women did represent competition to his friend. They did not directly challenge Persis. By now she was unquestionably the premier hetaira in Epiria; a true 'she-companion' of the wealthy and influential in the city. She had quit sleeping with her clients shortly after meeting Thaddeus; her value was no longer just her sexuality, although it was appreciated. Persis was invited because she was witty and enlivened any gathering with her sophisticated conversation. Even more importantly she knew everyone of importance in the city by now. She made introductions. She provided honest character references. And she provided advice that while not always followed, was highly valued. Her careful cultivation of relationships and insight into the city's politics and commerce was also put to personal use. Through a series of agents and trusted friends she had been able to amass a nice little fortune, something that was technically illegal for a woman who was officially single. Of course, with her influence and the presence of a personal champion, Thaddeus, no one would question her holdings. But Persis had been honest enough to understand that even her considerable beauty would eventually fade, and she had done a canny job of skillfully redefining her role. In the past she had had to balance her role between that of a high-class prostitute and an entertaining companion. Now with her contacts in place she was well on her way to establishing a new balance between being a respected and wealthy matron (sort of) and a discrete, trusted advisor. Doreen would be offering something else, a single point of contact for the people who made rituals and gatherings successful, not only hostesses, but singers, dancers, and musicians, all working together.

Of course there were a number of obstacles to this goal, most of them being men. Athan and Thaddeus were aware of a number of street gangs that would need to be convinced they did not deserve a piece of the action. The gangs tried to control any element of society they could extort or intimidate into paying them off; thus the definite need for the women to have a stout defender when they went out at night. One of local gang leaders, a smirking little rat of a man who called himself Skoripus, had even tried to claim Persis owed him money since he said he was in charge of 'hired women' in this part of the city. He hastily abandoned this claim and the immediate vicinity with Thaddeus in hot pursuit; fortunately for him he was a fast runner. Though Persis herself was in little danger from such criminals, the other women would need to be especially wary.

Persis continued her analysis of why Doreen and her venture were likely to be unsuccessful. "Doreen is probably attractive enough to be moderately successful on her own," Athan thought she was damning her friend with faint praise. "but she does not have the drive to organize and run a disciplined group. Besides, she does not like men enough. Now that Vania likes men, perhaps a little too much. She is too likely to fall in love with one of her clients or let them take advantage of her." This sounded just fine with Athan. She had a pair of assets he would personally love to take advantage of. "Besides," continued Persis as they walked through the dark streets, "Vania is too young, yet and lacks education. Lais might have had some potential once." Athan decided

Lais must be the older woman in the group. Persis continued talking, "She is reasonably well educated and can hold up a conversation, but she is too old and too plain for most men. Chara is pretty enough and an adequate dancer." Here Athan pricked up his ears. Persis loved to dance and was very proud of her considerable ability. This was the first time he had ever heard her say anything complementary about another woman's dancing skills. But then she continued, "Unfortunately she is simply too shy and too stupid to hold a man's interest."

"So," Thaddeus said with a hidden smile, "One is too stupid, one is too smart, one too pretty, one too plain, one too educated, another not educated enough, one likes men too much and the other not enough. Clearly these women will not do."

"Exactly," she replied, and Athan could hear the smile in her reply. Thaddeus was the only one who could get away with teasing her on professional matters, and then only in private.

"What about the fifth member? You did say Doreen wanted to call her group the five Sisters." Thaddeus asked this question while watching the entrance of an alley they were passing. Even though there were two armed men in the party and this was their home town, both men were alert. Bad things could happen even on a quiet night in a respectable neighborhood like this. And though none of them knew it, bad things were about to happen.

"Oh, her," said Persis dismissively, "she is a singer. Her name is Zita. She came down from the north with a small troupe of musicians and singers she claims to lead. In fact that was her troupe you saw tonight. They are relatively talented. One of them, Ianthe, is pretty and seems to have enough brains to be a hetaira on her own, but she is completely cowed by that Zita character." Athan thought he knew the singer Persis was discussing. She seemed quite lovely in a shy way. "But Zita was off doing a private concert," continued Persis. "You get bigger fees when you perform by yourself. But I am afraid Zita is totally unqualified to do anything but sing. She is simply enormous."

Here Athan began to smile to himself. Persis, though slim and emphatically female in form was as tall as many men. Zita must be a veritable giantess. Now Athan realized who she was discussing. Zita was the current darling of the upper class. She had quickly developed a reputation as a great diva. Whoever had been able to engage her for a private performance was probably a very wealthy man.

Persis continued her analysis of the newly-famous singer, "She has a face like a horse and no tact at all. And she appears totally uneducated. I doubt if she can even read; of course she is a barbarian, and so I suppose that is only to be expected. She does have a rather good voice, however." Athan decided that Persis was in a very good mood; she seldom was so complimentary concerning potential rivals. "This Zita," continued Persis who was, as always, doing most of the talking, "thinks she should be the leader of the Five Sisters, even though it was Doreen's idea and she made all the preparations. I can see her point; Doreen is a bit too sweet and indecisive to be a really effective leader. And Zita is used to being in charge of a group. She did lead her musicians and whatnot down here to civilization. On the other hand, Zita is far too coarse and demanding. Where Doreen might suggest, Zita would bluntly order. Women don't like that sort of thing."

"So," said Thaddeus with the same good natured patience as before, "One is too weak, the other too strong."

They never found out what she would have replied, for at that moment Athan stopped dead and turned toward an alley they were passing, extending his lantern for a better look. Instantly, his companions reacted. Thaddeus moved up to the side of his comrade, holding his torch high, his hand on his short sword. Persis moved behind the men and turned her back to theirs, watching for any threat that might come from behind them. Athan thrust the lantern on the end of his staff forward and stepped into the alley. Shadows flickered weirdly, partially illuminating a shape on the ground next to a wall. Humans are very good at recognizing other human shapes and Athan had caught a glimpse in the gloom of just such a figure where no figure should be. Now, approaching the form that was lying lengthwise against a wall the two men could tell that there was something very wrong with this person's shape. They moved three steps into the alley with weapons out and eyes alert for any other threat. First they caught the smells of death: blood, feces, and something else not easily described; all of them horrible. Then their lights fell upon the body the two men sucked in their breath as one.

Athan and Thaddeus were veterans; they had seen many dead men, hacked open in battle and left to rot in the sun. They had come upon many corpses, some that were well decomposed or which had been gnawed upon by scavengers. Yet the sight of the dead woman in the alley, for clearly it had once been a young woman, sickened them both. Her dress, or more probably a castoff man's tunic, had been pulled up over her head leaving her body bare below the shoulders. Her thin torso had been split down the middle. Not merely cut open, but split wide; someone had cut the poor girl from groin to breastbone, and judging from the open cavity, removed some of her internal organs. Her heart was definitely gone and perhaps other bits as well. Athan turned away from the awful sight to see Persis looking over their shoulders at the remains.

"Oh, the poor girl," she said in a small voice, then, "Who could do such a thing?" Athan took the pole lantern and pretended to search the area for the murderer. Persis, with a small shudder, pulled the poor creature's tunic down off her face to cover her ruined torso. She looked at the ravaged remains in the flickering torchlight and then said with shock, "I know her, well, that is, I have seen her before. Athan, do you remember the beggar that propositioned us on the way to the banquet?"

Athan returned and forced himself to look at the body, now at least partially covered. "Yes," he confirmed looking down at her face. It was not easy to look at her face, either. Her eyes were bulging and her mouth was open in a silent scream. Her attacker had also stabbed her in the throat, though it was a single narrow wound with less blood than he would have expected. But there was plenty of blood elsewhere. Coming to himself again, Athan was able to add, "She was that nasty little whore we saw propositioning us from an alleyway when we were on the way to the banquet."

"Us?" asked Thaddeus.

"Yes," put in Persis in a shaky voice, not at all like her normal confident tone, "It was just before dark. We were in a bit of hurry to get to the symposium, and when Athan declined her offer she propositioned me in the most direct terms. Then she begged for, no, more like demanded, some money. We were late and just moved on. Poor thing was probably starving." Athan could not tell just what was in Persis' voice; was it pity for the girl, shame that she did not throw her a few coppers that would have gotten her off the street and into safety, or sorrow for a world where young girls could be so foully treated. Then her voice changed and she asked Thaddeus a question, "What happens to the dead you find in the streets?"

It was not an unreasonable question; it was not all that unusual for the men of the watch to find bodies during their rounds. Usually they were those who were indigent and had died of more or less natural causes. They were often simply removed from wherever they had breathed their last and deposited on the street like trash for pickup. But though this was not the first murder victim either man had seen, neither of them had seen or even heard of anything like the savage attack on this victim. Nevertheless, they did know what to do with a dead body found in the night, and their experience took over. They kept together and moved cautiously into the street; badly rattled by what they had found. After a brief search they were able to locate a patrol of guardsmen. Thaddeus arranged for two to report the murder back to the compound and request additional guards to reinforce the watch and look out for anyone suspicious in the streets. Two more were sent to secure one of the long hand carts used to haul long burdens such as lumber that the Guard pressed into service whenever they had to dispose of a body. Others guardsmen accompanied them back to the scene of the crime to make a more careful examination and search for suspects. Thaddeus stressed the need for all the men to work in teams of at least two; no one was to work alone. Even off-duty members of the guard were turned out to aid in the search.

While the streets, alleys, sheds, barns, and stables of the city were getting a once in a lifetime searching, Thaddeus took control of the investigation of the murder site. He asked Athan to escort Persis home, but she refused. He insisted. She, with typical tact, suggested a compromise: she would accompany the body to the local house of the dead, the equivalent to a mortuary, and once it was secure would then return home with Athan. Thaddeus agreed as long as four guards accompanied them. She objected that this was excessive. He replied that two of the men would stay to guard the body. She asked then why was he sending four men. He informed her that the other two would accompany her home before resuming the search for the killer. She demanded that he stop wasting his men's time and effort on protecting someone who already had an escort, thank you, a brave young guardsman who did not try to treat her like a delicate and fragile flower, but as a serious woman of consequence who damn well could take care of herself in her own city. He then instructed her not to tell him how to deploy his men and if his men had to work in pairs on a night when a monster was stalking, he was not about to make Athan walk home alone while burdened with the need to guard the most bull-headed, stubborn, and overconfident female in the city. Now follow that cart. Right now!

"Yes, darling," she said suddenly yielding. She stepped up and kissed him on the cheek. "I will be home waiting for you."

"Don't wait up," growled the Captain. Even though he was by now familiar with her sudden changes, he was still put off balance by her capitulation. The men who had been standing around them during their exchange were doing their best to appear to be statuary.

"Do you want me to come back and help?" asked Athan.

"No!" snapped Thaddeus. Stay at the house and protect the women. Help that new porter, what is his name?"

"Ajax," said Persis quietly, the very image of a dutiful wife.

"Of course," Thaddeus muttered. Then he took Athan aside and addressed him privately, "Keep an eye on her and the house tonight. Tomorrow we may all need to take other measures if we haven't found him."

Athan was already thinking of Erinsys and the children, but there were nearly a dozen people in his sister in law's house including three men. They would be safe for tonight, at least.

As they walked alongside the cart with its sad cargo, now covered with a cloth, Athan imposed on their long friendship by asking Persis, "Why did you give in. Did you get what you actually wanted all along?"

"No," replied Persis honestly, "but I know when my man has made up his mind. And he was right, the Guard is his responsibility. I just hope they catch the monster that did this alive. I would like to ask him a few questions."

The next morning the town was abuzz with rumors of the murder. Crime was not so common in the city that a murder would go unremarked, and the sheer gruesomeness of this one had set tongues to wagging. The aggressive response of the guard had ensured that townspeople would notice the event, and it being a slow day for gossip, everyone was repeating and enhancing their versions of the story, not the least of whom were the men who had taken part in the searches during the night. Some of Thaddeus' men thought they had seen a suspicious man lurking in the streets but he was able to escape them in the dark. The guardsmen were not even able to give a vague description of the shadowy figure. The terrible mutilation of the victim and the general air of mystery and created a sensation around what otherwise might have been a fairly minor murder.

Persis was up early, joining Athan for a cup of hot tea.

"What time did Thaddeus get in?" asked Athan, who had retired to the guestroom shortly after they had returned.

"The poor dear was up until just before dawn," replied Persis who looked tired herself. She covered her mouth as she gave an enormous yawn. "But what we must do must be done this morning. Anteros, attend us. Come along Athan, and bring your dagger. I no longer feel quite safe even in the daylight."

Athan did better than that; in addition to his dagger he borrowed one of Thaddeus' short swords. He walked beside her, well aware of the sudden and unusual tension in the city. The story of the grisly murder had spread and people were worried. Persis walked directly to the mortuary house where bodies were prepared for burial or cremation. Anteros followed behind them, a large cloth bag filled with various mysterious items bumping up against his legs.

Instead of going directly to where they had left the body the night before, they detoured to the house of a local herbalist. There, apparently alerted by a note from Persis delivered first thing that morning, a small balding man was waiting for them. Athan looked at him with suspicion. The man was getting on in years, with a stooped back that was almost a hump. He had a large nose, and wore a hat. He wore a pair of strange braids that hung down on either side of his face. Though Athan was not introduced, Persis addressed him as Zakias. As they walked with this strange man toward the house of the dead, Athan learned that he was from a place called Dan, which was far to the south, and that he considered himself to be a learned man and a great doctor. Athan was more familiar with the term 'physician' and was not quite sure what this man's specialty might be. But Athan knew that it was Persis' business to know just what was going on in the city and who had talents that might be useful to either herself or her clients. He was confident that whoever this Zakias was, he would be very good at whatever it was Persis needed.

There was a small crowd around the house of the dead. The owner made his living by preparing the dead for burial, and provided separate rooms for ritual viewings referred to as a prothesis, a cross between a viewing and a wake. He also could provide professional mourners and arrange for the ekphora, the procession to either the tomb or pyre. The proprietor had apparently not yet figured out he could make money by displaying the suddenly famous young victim's remains to the curious for a fee, but Athan figured it would not take him much longer to come to that realization. Athan, assuming an authority he did not possess, cleared every one except their little party out of the room where the young victim lay, covered now with a thin, stained cloth. Zakias went directly to the body and whipped off the cloth. Anteros, with the insouciance of a teenaged boy, peered over the little man's shoulder for a peek. Athan expected some rude joke or snide comment from the slave, who was notorious for his flippant attitude, and prepared to give the boy a clout. But this time, instead of a jest or snide observation Anteros went visibly pale and stepped back with out a word. He retreated to a corner and squatted there breathing through his mouth.

In the light of day the victim's injuries appeared both better and worse. Most of the blood had been drained away and the proprietor had washed some of the blood off the skin. But you could see the injuries better in the full light of morning. What was far worse, with her eyes now closed and her features composed by the hands of others it was possible to see not a feral little beggar/whore but a pale thin young girl. She looked to be in her early teens.

Zakias immediately began to examine the wounds. After a time he asked to examine her clothing, which was brought to him.

"See," he said in a strange accent, "here is one of the first strikes." He pointed first to a narrow blood-stained cut on the girl's lower left side. "It was a powerful stroke," he continued, "penetrating the skin, muscles of the abdomen, perforating the intestines, and look, see here," with this he half rolled the body over, "exiting the back."

Athan knew how hard it was to stab all the way through a human body, even a small thin one like this. He was the first to comment on the nature of the cut. Swords and daggers have a thick cross section; they have to be able to hack through armor and thick muscles as well as standing up to blows from other blades. This cut was wide but very narrow. He pointed this out to the other two who immediately expanded on his observation.

"Yes," Zakias said, "not a normal weapon. More like a tool. See how wide the entry wound is? Yet at the back the wound quite narrow. And see how the skin has almost completely closed over the mouth of the wound. The blade that did this had a very thin how do you say, cross section; it was relatively long, and the blade was wide at the hilt, but came to a sharp point. It is more like, how do you say, a butcher's tool than a dagger."

"You mean like a cleaver?" asked Athan.

"No," responded Persis, "a butcher's knife."

"That's it," agreed Zakias, "like the kind they use to slice up meat. As I said, long, with a thin but deep blade and an acute point. Not a normal weapon of defense at all. But it certainly did a good job for the rapid dissection that followed. Now, let's see," continued Zakias. As he examined the body more minutely, Athan noticed that he was the first man he had ever met who could dominate the conversation more than Persis. Looking over at his friend he saw that she, like her young servant, had gone pale, but there was a determined set to her chin. Athan could see a stubborn anger building in her face as well.

"Now," resumed Zakias after completing his examination, "it appears this might be the second wound, another thrust, this time to the throat." Athan, absorbed in the massive damage to the torso had forgotten the thin cut to the center front of her throat. "This thrust did not sever any of the major blood vessels that figure so prominently in a normal throat slashing. See, a straight punch right in. It looks like," here the man used his fingers to spread the wound into a wider mouth and peer inside. Persis looked over his shoulder. "Yes, it definitely cut the wind pipe. I would imagine she screamed, well, who wouldn't, if the first blow was to her belly, and then the man stabbed her in the throat to shut her up. That makes sense. He silenced her, probably more by luck than skill, but didn't kill her. Oh, she would have died from either wound, but not for a while. Now, let's look at the other major wounds."

Athan took a cloth and paced it over the dead girl's face. That made it easier somehow. He stepped back and away from the two who bent over the body to continue their examination. He was remembering very strongly the times when he had seen throats cut with blood spraying and bellies ripped open with the entrails gushing out onto the ground and men screaming. He had not been in many battles, but he had seen and participated in enough fights to have seen slaughter. He had done some of that slaughtering. It had been traumatic, and the delayed reactions from those fights sometimes caught him by surprise. He let them think he was nauseated by the sight of the corpse as Anteros had been. The boy was looking at him sympathetically from the corner, not even trying to keep up a pretense of nonchalance. Athan heard snatches of Zakias continuing on.

"I think this is the most likely the sequence of events. First a stab to the abdomen through her garment, then another hasty stab to the throat to silence her, then he pulled her tunic over her head and threw her to the ground. I suspect he straddled her and then stabbed in her, just above her groin and started ripping up. You see how the wound stopped here? Then it restarts and goes up to the sternum with this curious zigzag motion. She was probably flopping around quite a bit."

"You mean," said Persis incredulously, "he did this to her while she was still alive?"

"Oh, yes," confirmed the old man confidently, "but she probably passed out from the pain by the time he cut up to the base of her ribs and severed the diaphragm. Death would have come soon after."

After imparting that bit of horror, the doctor began showing Persis the various parts of the inside of a human body. It appeared the killer had removed several parts of the body including the heart, liver, and possibly the spleen. The primary portions of the digestive tract had been left more or less intact, but there had been some wild slashes within the torso that damaged the remaining organs.

From his position behind them Athan asked a question, "Why did he cut out her heart?"

"Impossible to know," replied Zakias without looking up. "This looks to me more like someone who was enraged, not some cool assassin sending a message. I might guess, however, that when he opened her up the heart was still beating. That would attract his attention I think. How better to totally destroy your victim. Either this poor young girl had enraged her attacker somehow or there he has a tremendous amount of rage in him; probably both." There was a pause, and then Zakias added in a low voice, "I have known some like that, constantly angry at every one and every thing."

He resumed his commentary, showing cuts on the sternum and how the ribcage had been apparently lifted to give access to the heart and lungs.

Persis slowly became interested in the descriptions of the body parts and how they were positioned. Like many other inquisitive people she had often wondered just what was inside a person's skin, and Zakias was very knowledgeable. He did not reveal how he had gained this knowledge, or why such an expert in anatomy had wound up in what was considered by some to be close to the farthest edges of civilization.

They had been at it for over two hours before the owner of the house knocked discretely and informed them that family members had come to collect the body.

Instantly Persis shifted from medical student to outraged matron. "Do not lie to me. She had no family. The Captain of the guard informed me himself. She had been in town for only a few days. You merely wish to display her to that rabble out there. Well, she suffered enough in her life; she shall at least have the dignity of a decent funeral. I will pay for the rights. We will burn her this evening. There will be no prothesis, but I will pay you for a respectable ekphora. We will depart at the seventh hour. Until then no one except your personal staff is allowed in here. You may now prepare the body."

The owner, cowed by her anger, yielded at once and withdrew to make the requested arrangements.

Why Persis decided to provide this nameless waif a proper sending off was never clear to Athan. But she was a good as her word. When the cart left for the burning ground the corpse had been pinned back together and dressed in a proper white chiton. Her hair had been washed and arranged and her features enhanced with discrete make up. Dead, she was far more beautiful than she had ever been alive. As the bier moved through the streets for the procession the mourners and singers hired by Persis were joined by others who trailed behind. Notable among the mourners were the so-called Five Sisters. They were not actually professional mourners, but they gave a wonderful presence to the ekphora. In particular, Athan noticed a large woman who was singing a somewhat generic dirge; it was hard to not notice her voice. She had a powerful soprano that could carry well without losing its sweet and pure tone. She sang with the effortlessness that takes even talented singers years of training and practice to achieve. The singer's appearance, Athan supposed it had to be Zita, contrasted oddly with her voice. Not only was she a tall, big boned, full figured woman, but she had a strong jaw and an unfortunate face. Athan decided she could be described as handsome if seen from a distance. Zita was carefully dressed, and wore her hair up in an elaborate hairdo; it seemed that she was aware of the shortcomings in her appearance, and like any clever woman did what she could to maximize her assets and conceal her weaknesses. Athan had to admit that her voice compensated for a great deal. She had two female accompanists, the young Ianthe who had a clear contralto as pretty as her own appearance and another older woman whom Athan did not know. From the occasional looks thrown her way by Doreen and Persis, they thought Zita was making rather too much of herself. Still, Athan did enjoy the music even if it was a sad, haunting melody.

By the time the nameless murdered girl was laid on the pyre there was a more than respectable crowd of mostly women, who wailed, not just for this child whom many had spurned when alive, but for all the lost children who came to undeserved ends all too soon.

Thaddeus was there with Persis, as were Athan and Erinsys. The two women stood next to each other and shared a private conversation. That evening Athan, who spent the night with his wife and child at his sister-in-law's home, found out what the women had decided.

"Husband," said Erinsys, "Persis and Thaddeus are going to find the man who did that to that poor girl. Please help them all you can."

And so the search for a madman began.

For a time the city seemed gripped by a kind of madness. Several strangers were arrested, and if they were not actually tortured, they were certainly handled roughly. But not only could nothing be proved, the men could demonstrate they were otherwise occupied when the murder occurred. The local gangs kept a very low profile. No one seemed to know who had done the murder or even why, though there was much speculation.

"I don't understand why there is so much fuss," grumbled Thaddeus on the third day after the nameless girl's body had been discovered. "If the killer had just knocked her in the head, no one would have noticed."

And in fact he was probably correct. Murders were serious things; if there was a suspect, things were often resolved by relatives, sometimes resulting in blood feuds. But this girl had no family. In fact she had been so isolated that no one was even sure what her real name was, much less where she had come from. But as Thaddeus knew, this killing had been so spectacular, so random, and so obviously unnecessary that everyone was put on edge. If the killer would make such an unnecessary mess of such a defenseless creature, who knew what he might do next?

Part of the problem was that no one had any real experience in solving murders like this. The justice system worked reasonably well for most crimes, but something like this killing was so far out of the ordinary that everyone was at a loss what to do, except for the leading Magistrate: he assigned Thaddeus to find the murderer.

Thaddeus took the assignment with a sense of inevitability. He already knew that Persis wanted the killer found, and when she set her mind to something, stopping her was like trying to stop a mountain stream in full spate. Athan too, wanted the case solved. Erinsys was deeply disturbed by the murder and refused to go out of her sister's house until Athan had disposed of the killer. This was not typical behavior for his wife, but for all his persuasion that the guard's compound was the safest place to be, she would not budge.

"How do we know it is not one of the guards who did it?" she asked him accusatorily. In fact this was not an uncommon opinion. Thaddeus announced he would only employ men in his investigation that had a firm alibi for the time of the murder. No one thought to mention that Thaddeus himself had been out on the streets alone at about the time of the murder.

Since Athan's did have such an alibi, Thaddeus chose him as his deputy, and they set to work. He also involved Persis in the investigation, but of course he had no choice in that. At least he was able to extract a promise from her that if he discussed every aspect of the case with her each night, she would not go out and try to discover anything on her own. It was a system that worked well, even if it did break down in the end.

While Persis, Athan, and the strange 'Doctor' Zakias were examining the corpse, Thaddeus and two of his men scoured the area where the murder had taken place. They also questioned everyone in the area to determine if there had been any strangers in the area or if anyone had heard anything.

Thaddeus returned to his house just before evening, a tired and discouraged man. First Persis told him of the results of the autopsy. Listening to the grisly way the girl had died caused him to suck in air through his teeth.

"Well," he declared after she finished his report to him, 'we know how, and where she died, just not who and why."

He then detailed six hours of difficult work. The girl had been in town for less than a month, perhaps only half that long. She could not find a place in any of the local houses of prostitution (or any other kind of house for that matter) because of her prickly nature and had been sleeping in odd corners and empty sheds.

"Did anyone hear anything when she was killed?" asked Persis.

Thaddeus gave a grimace, "Oh, yes, just at dark two women in separate houses reported hearing a cry or scream. One claimed she thought it was a cat, but she was lying. On the other hand, what was she to do? She would have had a hard time rousing her man out to go look in a dark alley to investigate because she might have heard a sound. But at least we have confirming evidence that the girl died shortly after dark. There were still people moving around, so that no one would particularly notice a person hurrying away, and it was dark enough that it would be hard to see the blood on his clothes."

"Yes," agreed Persis, "his clothes would have been covered in blood. But the darkness would have only helped from a distance; anyone getting close would have smelled the blood. So we now have confirmation that the killer probably did not pass outside the gates."

"Yes," agreed his Athan, wanting to be part of the conversation, "the gates were closed and the guards did not let anybody out before the alarm was given. Afterward the sergeant made sure the people leaving were examined; certainly no one with bloody clothes was let out. So odds are he is still inside the walls."

"Unless he went over the wall," observed Thaddeus dryly. "And even if he is in the city you can bet those clothes are gone or at least thoroughly washed out. So that only leaves a few thousand possible suspects."

"Well, beloved," said Persis brightly, "tell me, how do you catch criminals? I mean the ones who have washed the blood off their hands."

"Mostly we don't," Thaddeus admitted. "You talk to people. Criminals usually brag about their crimes, or somebody sees something. If that doesn't work, then what you try to do is look at the problem using the three rules: motive, means, and opportunity."

Seeing Athan's puzzled look Thaddeus deigned to explain. "See, Athan, first you look to find out why. A crime, especially a murder, usually had a reason. Of course, this one may be a result of madness so that is out the window. You also examine to see if anyone has the means. This time anyone with a big sharp butcher's knife and a strong arm had the ability to kill her. She was not a very big girl, and I doubt if she could have put up much of a fight. And the time was perfect for our murderer. There were still enough people moving around for anyone leaving the scene not to attract attention. How would you tell a murderer fleeing his crime from a man hurrying to get home? So, there is no point in investigating that angle. And as to opportunity, well, I will bet a month's pay it was a spur of the moment thing. The killer saw his chance and acted. I am almost certain if he hasn't done anything like this before, he has at least thought about doing something like this a lot."

"So it could be anybody," said Athan, discouraged.

"I think not," put in Persis. "I think the man who did this was not some big tough powerful man. I think our killer does not have any power in his life, or doesn't have as much as he thinks he deserves, and he desperately wants more. One night he gets confronted by this nasty little bit, she insults him, and he snaps. So he stabs her. She screams and he stabs her throat to shut her up. Then the madness comes on him and he takes all his frustrations out on this poor, miserable little girl, someone who he thinks should have treated him with respect and instead added to his humiliation. So he cuts her up. I wonder what he did with the parts he took?"

"Oh," said Thaddeus, "I think we found the liver and maybe some other parts. It was hard to tell. Night creatures had been at it. It was in an alley two streets down from the murder, not far from Doreen's house. He probably got tired of carrying such a messy burden." Persis gave him a look. "But we think he took something else; that is something that belonged to her. People said she wore a white apron around her waist. It had two pockets that bulged. It probably held everything she owned."

"Yes," interjected Athan excitedly, "Now that you mention it, I do remember. I remember seeing it on her. It was dirty. It seemed out of place somehow, as though it had once been a nice bit of work."

"Well, there was nothing like that near the body," confirmed Thaddeus. "We are looking for it along with a bloody butcher's knife."

"Have you talked to all the butchers in town?" asked Persis

"Of course," lied Thaddeus, "well not all of them, not yet, but we are looking into that angle. We are asking them about their whereabouts, and if they are missing any knives."

"I think you should ask about their helpers, dear," said Persis thoughtfully, "I think we are looking for someone, probably a weaselly little man who is frustrated and angry, not a successful tradesman."

"**We**," said Thaddeus emphasizing the word and getting to his feet with a significant look at has woman, "are not looking for any one. Athan and I are doing the looking. You are staying here and do some more of your thinking."

"I can't believe she couldn't get anyone to take her in. There should be a fairly steady business for a girl between travelers and the guards," commented Athan thinking about the victim.

"Apparently this girl had a hard shell on her and a tongue like a scorpion. She never once asked for help and often insulted those who might have given her a place," responded the Thaddeus.

Athan remembered his own brief encounter with the dead girl. She had indeed been and aggressive and insulting. He had been somewhat shocked when she propositioned Persis who was obviously a high class matron. It did not take much imagination to picture her insulting a tough caravan guard with fatal results.

And the mention of a scorpion turned Athan's mind to Skoripus, the street criminal who had tried to shake down Persis.

"Well, I find it interesting that our little friend Skoripus somehow failed to add her to his collection," Athan suggested.

"Me, too," wondered Thaddeus, 'but why kill her. Beat her to death, maybe, even cut her throat, but why mutilate her?"

"As a lesson to others?"

"Maybe," Thaddeus agreed, "but it doesn't fit somehow. That little bastard is certainly mean enough to kill, but this just doesn't seem his style. For one thing, I haven't heard a word about him bragging about it or using the killing as a threat to others. But I think we should ask him about it, though." From the grim smile on Thaddeus' face, Athan figured the visit to Skoripus would be a mixture of business and pleasure.

As the two men left the house, Thaddeus ordered one of his sergeants to get two men and visit all the butcher shops within 10 blocks of the murder scene. "And take a tablet with you," he continued to his subordinate. "I am going to want to hear details tonight."

It only took a few questions for Thaddeus to discover where the man who called himself 'the Scorpion' was staying. Cheerfully unaware of concepts such as warrants, due process, or rights of the accused, Thaddeus burst into the house and quickly found his man lounging with several members of what might be called his gang. Thaddeus began his investigation by smashing Skoripus over the head with a truncheon he carried next to his short sword. Athan literally backed him up, sword in one hand, dagger in the other, waiting for any of the other men to make the slightest hostile move. They slunk out of the room quietly, not walking like men, but slinking out like cats leaving a courtyard when a big dog enters. Some of them were barely more than children. None of them even looked at Thaddeus, who was continuing to 'investigate' the gangster about the poor man's head and shoulders with his club. Nobody reached for a weapon. Once satisfied there would be no resistance, Thaddeus thrust his truncheon back in his belt and sat next to the dazed and beaten man, removing a large heavy dagger from the smaller man's belt and tossing it aside with a thump.

"So," began Thaddeus, in a friendly conversational tone, "I guess the little bitch deserved it. What did she do, tell you to buzz off? She did have a harsh way of putting herself sometimes, didn't she?"

This was the first time Athan had a chance to really look at Skoripus at close range. He was not so much lean as young and underfed. He did not look tough at the moment, merely desperate, the way some young men become when they are raised hard and have little to lose. Right now he was confused and afraid.

"I never said nothing to her," he whined, "I left her alone. We ain't been anywhere near her. I swear! I ain't even seen the…" here Skoripus' self-preservation circuits clicked in and he changed epithet he was about to use to "nice lady."

Now it was Thaddeus' turn to be confused. Athan saw the problem and helpfully asked, "No, not Persis, the little tramp you cut up the other night. Why did you have to butcher her like that? Did it make you feel like a big man?" Skoripus was in fact both small and skinny.

With comprehension came indignation, "I didn't have nothing to do with that," he sputtered watching Thaddeus fearfully. "Yeah, we were looking for her, but we just wanted to put her to work. Ya don't kill the merchandise. Why would I do that?" and then followed a long rambling explanation that essentially claimed that Skoripus was busy with the 'friends' the night of the murder and was seen a long way from where he heard the killing occurred. Athan and Thaddeus quit listening before he was half way done.

"Stay where I can find you," said Thaddeus with a final slap to the back of the gangster's head.

"Think he had anything to do with it?" Athan asked when they were outside.

"No, like I said, not his style, but we had to check him out. Besides," the older man continued smiling, "it sure was fun to talk to him."

"You know that right now he is telling his friends how he is going to get even with you," said Athan.

"Yeah, so," responded Thaddeus unconcerned. "There are lots of little rats like that who would kill me if they dared. But they don't. I know there are people who would kill me if I let my guard down, so I don't. It is the people who think they are safe who find themselves on the pointy end of a knife."

For the next two days the two men continued their search without progress. Each night Thaddeus and Athan would gather at the house to talk about the case with Persis. They were able to eliminate many potential suspects, including all the butchers and their assistants.

As fear of the 'Mad Butcher' diminished, the new topic of conversation became Doreen's continuing attempt to unite the city's entertainers, or at least a portion of them. According to Persis, the major disagreement centered on whether or not Zita and her singers and musicians would join the group to make the fifth of Doreen's hope for 'five sisters'.

"Actually," confided Persis, who enjoyed gossip as much as anyone, "the problem is not if she will join, but who will be in charge. Doreen still believes that since she had the idea and has already started the group, she should be the one in charge of the group. She would decide what contracts to seek, which to take, who would be employed for each event, and of course would therefore get a commission for each event. According to Doreen, just because Zita is bigger than any of the other women and has a magnificent voice, she felt everyone should do what she said."

"Actually I am a bit surprised that Zita left Illyria, or wherever else she came from," continued Persis. "With that voice she should have found a patron. Instead, she shows up here with a half dozen miscellaneous associates and that dog of a man Kulin." She was referring to her combination bodyguard and porter, a large broad-faced simpleton who seemed to be very devoted to her.

What Persis did not discuss was Doreen's repeated efforts to have Persis join Doreen's group. Persis had no intention of attaching herself to any group. She was unconcerned about losing any of her own clients to them. In fact, Persis was so utterly confident of her own abilities that she did not even consider the 'Five Sisters' to be competition at all.

Athan and many others were becoming convinced that the murderer had been a transient who had climbed the wall and fled the city after the killing and the city began to return to normal. But all that changed on the morning of the third day. A decaying human heart was found early one morning in one of the city's small fountains by women coming to get water. The tension which had begun to dissipate once again ratcheted up. Erinsys, who the night before had spoken of returning home to the compound, immediately decided to remain with her sister for the indefinite future.

The recovered organ was brought to the guard compound for some reason. "Do you think it is hers?" asked one of the guards looking at the piece of meat.

"Know anyone else missing a heart?" responded Athan without humor.

"A few moneylenders," came an anonymous voice from the men who had gathered around to look at the grisly remains.

In the end it was taken to the house of the dead for disposal. An examination by Doctor Zakias and Persis could make nothing of the find other than it had been removed from the body by a sharp knife and apparently been wrapped in cloth for a time.

Questions of the locals revealed nothing. The item had been deposited in the fountain at night. One old drunk said he thought he had seen a big man lurking in the shadows that night, but that was all, and not enough.

Perhaps even this discovery would have quickly passed if on the very next day a woman's body had not been discovered in the largest fountain in the city, floating face up. It was another newcomer to the city, but this time she was not stranger; she had a name: Ianthe, the prettiest of Zita's singers. Poor Ianthe had not been carved up, however. Indeed, the body had no obvious marks on it at all. There was wide speculation as to how she had died and how she had come to end up such a public place. The general view was the poor girl had drowned herself in the fountain's pool. After all, it was the deepest in the city. When full, the water level in the deepest part of the fountain was chest high on a woman. In normal times, perhaps that explanation might have been accepted, but in the current climate, the worst was assumed. Thaddeus took charge of what was now an unprecedented investigation. At his direction, once again the house of the dead was visited by Doctor Zakias, Persis, and Athan.

Zakias undertook to examine the corpse with unusual care, or more precisely with his normal unusual thoroughness.

"The body has not been in the water long," he said, telling them something they already knew. "I cannot tell for certain without opening the lungs if she drowned but my initial judgment is that she did not." The strange little man did not explain himself but went on to comment on some minor abrasions on the dead woman's ears. Then he turned the hands over and examined them carefully.

"Hands tell a great deal," he said. "This woman's hands show normal work patterns, perhaps a bit less than normal. Was she unmarried?"

"She was a singer," said Persis looking over his shoulder.

"Hmmm," replied Zakias distractedly, feeling the corpse's jaw line and examining the eyes. "Help me turn her over," he requested.

Athan came over from the corner where he was looking out a window and assisted the old man to turn the damp corpse onto her stomach. The body was cold and creepy to the touch. Zakias resumed his ghoulish examination, focusing on her head. It did not take him long to find something significant.

"Eureka," he said quietly and motioned Persis over. Athan looked over her shoulder to where the doctor was pointing. There was a small round puncture wound at the base of the skull right at the hair line.

"Pithed," said Zakias.

"What?" said a puzzled Persis.

For once Athan had the advantage of her, "Pithed: when you kill a man or in this case, a woman by stabbing his spinal cord. If you need to kill a man quietly, you stab him at the base of the neck. It kills instantly," explained Athan. He had not done this himself, but he had talked to some of his comrades about this means of silencing an enemy. "But it is hard to do," Athan continued, "you have to have a firm grip on the head or they can twist away. You have to stab deep into the backbone, and that is not always easy."

"It appears that in this case, the victim may have been held in a headlock," here Zakias demonstrated with his elbow cocked out and his hand on his waist. "You can see the marks on her ears. Then the blade was driven into the neck. A round bladed stiletto, a spike, or an awl was used. Yes, an awl is most likely. After all, they are common enough. Although why a killer would carry such a weapon is beyond me."

The men speculated on how the dead woman had been transported in the night to the fountain and why she had been left in such a public place. They eventually agreed that it would be easy enough for a man to haul a woman through the streets at night either hidden in a cart or on his back, dodging the patrols. They also decided that the fountain was chosen because it was deep enough for a person to drown in and so might mislead an investigation. Zakias was of the opinion that few people not trained in his anatomical arts would have noticed the wound and its significance. But they could not decide if this was the work of "their" killer. All throughout this discussion Persis was unnaturally (for her) quiet. The men were still discussing any potential relationship between the murders when Persis came to herself and spoke.

"I think they are related and they were done by the same person. But please, we mustn't tell anyone what we found. We must merely tell everyone that the death was mysterious. That isn't a direct lie, is it?" But where normally Persis would have given one of her dazzling smiles she used whenever she was being clever, instead this time she turned away without meeting their eyes.

And with that she excused herself and returned to her house, Athan and Anteros who had carried her bags trailing behind. Both were puzzled by her silent and direct return, so different from the way she usually sauntered through the streets, chatting with friends and acquaintances. This time she was so absorbed she actually did not return several greetings, much less stop to chat.

"Something connects the two killings, I feel it but I just don't know how they fit," was all she would say to Thaddeus and Athan that evening, instead of discussing the case as they had done on the past nights. And despite their urging she would say no more.

The death of Ianthe had much less impact on the consciousness of the people of Epiria than the earlier murder. This was in part because people were not even certain she had been the victim of foul play. Her mistress, Zita, told all and sundry that Ianthe had been depressed of late and had gone out alone into the night. This was surely not the action of a woman in her right mind. In any event, the body was not visibly disfigured; people turning up dead in public were not ordinary, but it was far from unprecedented. And after all, the woman was a stranger. Zita showed up at the house of the dead shortly after Athan and Persis had left and claimed the body. Zita was not pleased that Zakias was still there continuing his examination. She chased him out loudly, claiming that Ianthe's body would not be abused any further. Her accusations about what certain sick men did with the bodies of dead women delivered with a powerful, penetrating voice followed him as he fled down the street.

Ianthe's funeral was held that evening. Disposal of a body within a day was not uncommon, since embalming was almost unknown in that time and place, and decomposition began quickly in the heat of early summer. It was not a big funeral, but all of Zita's company was there, as were the four women who made up the 'Five Sisters'. Persis, Thaddeus, Athan, and Erinsys attended the ekphora as well, staying at the back of the procession. Once again, Zita could be heard singing a dirge in her lovely voice. The effect was slightly, spoiled however, since it was the same one she had sung for the unnamed girl only a few days before.

Afterwards the two couples returned together to Persis' house for a meal.

"Were those singers with Zita her company?" asked Erinsys. "They all looked so overwhelmed and sad. It must be hard to loose someone like that when you are a stranger."

"I think they looked more cowed than overwhelmed," observed Athan. "That Zita must really make them toe the line."

"They are terrified of her," put in Persis.

"Understandable," grunted Thaddeus, reaching across the low table to take another bit of the chicken they were sharing, "she certainly frightens me."

There was a bit of laughter at this. For a while they sat together sharing a meal, and chatting about nothing of consequence, much as they had when they had first shared a little cottage together. It was a relaxed and peaceful moment which Athan ruined by asking a question he had not yet gotten Persis to answer.

"Persis, why do you think the same man who butchered the girl also killed Ianthe? After all, the way they were killed could hardly have been more different."

Athan realized his mistake when Erinsys, who had not been following the most recent investigation immediately sparked up with questions: 'What do you mean murder? Hadn't she drowned herself? Didn't everybody say the madman had run away? Do you think he is still stalking victims? It couldn't be.' Their attempts to calm her did nothing other than to reignite all of Erinsys' fears. She became so upset she decided to return at once to her sister's so she could warn them; so she could be with her children. It was with difficulty and two cups of wine that Erinsys was eventually persuaded that young Persephone and Jason were safe, she was safe, and the killer must not be tipped off that they knew he had killed again.

"We are stalking a lion; we must not let him know we are on to him. I think I can catch our murderer, but not if he knows he is being watched. Please, be patient, I do not think he will kill again, at least not for a while. Meanwhile, I must have something solid to bring before the Magistrate."

Athan never understood how Persis could always persuade Erinsys to do things for her so easily. He knew if he had tried talking to his wife, even using the same words, Erinsys would have spun up into one of her screaming rages. This might have amused the neighbors who were familiar with her temper, but there was a good chance the murderer would have been able to hear every word directly. Instead she agreed to say nothing, but she also announced she would stay with her sister until they brought the murderer to justice. Athan agreed to this although somewhat grudgingly. He had his own personal reasons for wanting to wrap this case up quickly. There was no place he could be alone with his wife when she was staying with her sister. What with her pregnancy and birth it had been months since Athan had been alone with his wife and the pressure was becoming distracting. He was either going to have to solve this case or pay a visit to that busty little red head Vania to see what her rates for a private consultation might be.

When he returned from escorting Erinsys to her sister's he found Persis and Thaddeus just short of a full row. Thaddeus was pressuring her to share her theory as to the murders.

"I can not," she maintained. "For the third and last time, I am not sure. It is just the only thing that makes sense to me, but if I am wrong I will have led us all off in the wrong direction."

"Let me decide if it is the wrong direction," said Thaddeus stubbornly.

Persis wavered, then yielded a little. "Listen, I may be all wrong on this. And you know how much I hate being wrong." This was true, but she seldom admitted it. "Let me tell you my assumptions and let you see if you draw the same conclusions I did. If so, maybe we have something to build on. If it is not obvious to you, then I don't have anything to talk to the Magistrate about. Is that fair enough for you?"

Thaddeus looked at Athan, who shrugged his acceptance. Thaddeus looked back at Persis, who understood that there was an agreement.

"I used your idea of 'motive, means, and opportunity' darling," here she flashed one of her brief smiles. "That did not help all that much on the first murder. All we decided on the first murder was that the killing was probably spur of the moment, using an unusual weapon, and the mutilation was the result of an overwhelming and probably unanticipated rage. The opportunity was pure chance: the murderer was in the right place, right time of day, right for him anyway, and there where no witnesses around. Does that seem correct?"

"Right," agreed Thaddeus, "and now we are going around looking for a frustrated and angry little man who carries a butcher knife and has a place not too far from the killing so he could clean up and change clothes."

"I never said it was a little man," interrupted Persis, "I only said the killer did not have to necessarily be a big man. Now," she continued, overriding Thaddeus' retort, "this second murder is different, yes. Different method, different location, different treatment of the victim, everything was totally different. That was what made me suspicious."

"Of course," said Thaddeus dryly.

"You must consider the disposal of the heart," she continued. This change of subject puzzled them.

"Why was the heart and liver taken in the first place? If you assume an insane rage, then you have to say that the heart was taken because, well, it is the heart. And the liver is big and obvious. I am willing to bet the killer wrapped them in the poor waif's apron to carry them away. But on the way back to safety he decided that the liver was not a suitable trophy."

"Trophy?" interjected Athan. Persis was on a roll now and ignored him.

"So it was discarded. You found it Even if the killer did not make a direct line back home you can safely assume that he was headed in the general direction of safety when he threw the liver away. So, we are looking for a house at least one block east of the murder out to a general line toward the wall."

"That is still a big area," protested Thaddeus, wondering where all this was going.

"But much smaller than the whole city. And it got me to thinking about where our killer might be. Then the heart was found near the center of the city in a place where it was bound to be found the next morning. Obviously as it began to decay it lost its appeal as a trophy. Why not throw it away in some alley? That is the most telling bit. It was left there in the fountain as a display. The killer had to know the murder was the talk of the town. I am certain he loved the fact that everyone was talking about what he had done and no one knew who he was. That is powerful, and we all think that is what motivated the crime in the first place; a sense of a lack of power. So, he left the heart where it would cause another sensation just to let everyone know he was still a presence."

"What does this all have to do with the Ianthe's murder?" asked Thaddeus becoming impatient.

"What if," here Persis paused for dramatic effect, "the motive for the second murder was to conceal the first? What if Ianthe found out who had done the first murder? There was a confrontation, leading to a quick killing not from anger, but from need. If that is the case, then the means, an awl, and the opportunity both make perfect sense and the perpetrator becomes obvious."

She looked back and forth at the two men expectantly. This was not the first time Persis had made Athan feel stupid. Thaddeus spoke first, "Ianthe left the house just after dark, alone. Zita said she had been feeling depressed and said she was just going outside near the door to take some cool air. That simpleton porter, Kulin, cannot speak, but he can answer yes or no questions and he answered yes, she had gone out alone into the night."

"He can not speak because his tongue was slit," interjected Persis. "What does that tell you?"

"That he said the wrong thing to the wrong person," responded Thaddeus. "He may be a simpleton, but he can nod and answer questions. Are you saying that she was unhappy because she knew who killed the girl and that she went out to meet him? And that he took advantage of the night to silence her and then try to make it look like a drowning?"

Persis gave him a scornful look. "If I am unable to make a case to you, if you do not already see what I am driving at, I clearly could not make a case to the Magistrate. I will need to do more work."

"What case? Do you think we are too stupid to follow your train of logic…?" Thaddeus began but in that wonderful way she had, Persis somehow maintained control of the situation.

"No, darling, not at all," retorted Persis, not wanting to argue with him. "I was merely wrong, just as I feared. And now all this thinking has made me tired. If you cannot follow my train of thought, perhaps we should focus on something you are better at doing. Please take me to bed." This was delivered with a beaming disingenuous and utterly irresistible smile.

The mood changed abruptly, Thaddeus laughed and took her hand to lead her to their sleeping quarters.

"Wife, living with you is certainly never dull."

Her response floated through the door as they exited. "Thank you darling, but remember, I am not your wife, I am a hetaira. You keep forgetting that.'

His reply was lost though a few moments later Athan could hear them laughing together.

He ground his teeth and sought out his pallet in the corner.

The next day Athan was up early and at the compound to resume his normal duties. He was surprised when, following a session of training with some new men, he was called before Thaddeus.

"I am taking you off all your other duties for a while, Athan," said Thaddeus. Athan did not know what to say, and so waited for his captain and friend to continue. "Persis and I had a long talk this morning. She still thinks she can find this murderer. Problem is I don't want him to find her, if you catch my meaning. We talked about it," Athan could imagine **that** conversation and was glad he left early. "She is certain, don't ask me why, that the killer will not strike again unless he thinks someone has discovered him. She intends to ask around to try to find some more proof of what she suspects." Athan made to speak but

Thaddeus forestalled him with a raised hand. "I know, I know asking questions might just let him know she is on to him. At any rate," he continued plowing on, "she has agreed to be discreet." The two men looked at one another; Thaddeus sighed, "and to stay inside during the hours of darkness. But she will not allow an extra escort during the day. She claims Anteros is enough of a 'guard'." Once again the two men looked at each other. In fact Anteros was as devoted to her as much his nature allowed, but both though that in a crisis he would likely run from the scene screaming shrilly. Thaddeus continued on heavily, "That is why you are off of your official duties and will now be assigned to keep a discrete watch over my wife, or whatever it is she calls herself. Try not to let her see you."

"Why me?" asked Athan. "She is likely to recognize me even at a distance. We could get some of the new boys she doesn't know yet to follow her."

"Do you honestly think any of them are up to keeping an eye on her? She would probably spot them in an instant. Anyway, if she sees you, I can always say you were worried about her and following her on your own."

"So I take the heat, eh."

"Yep," and then Thaddeus looked away and lowered his voice, "and I don't trust anyone else to look after her."

"She can be a handful," said Athan.

"You have no idea," confirmed Thaddeus.

The first thing Athan did was to borrow another tunic from a friend, then he bought a ridiculous-looking wide straw hat that at least had the advantage of keeping the sun off his head. When he arrived in the vicinity of Persis' house, he had a boy take in a letter to Anteros. The boy was always getting love letters so no one thought it strange when he slipped out of the house and around the corner to meet a man. It did not take long for Athan to get it across to Anteros that his mistress was in danger. The teenager would have been glad to help in any event, but Athan really focused the somewhat flighty youngster with a threat.

"If she is hurt in any way in this affair, I promise you, Thaddeus promises you, that you will be sold to a farmer."

The very idea of working from sun up to full dark in some dreary pastoral setting frightened Anteros more than anything else. He promised his full cooperation. He would notify Athan when he knew when his mistress was leaving where she was going, to wear an easily recognized tunic and generally make it easy for Athan to follow from a distance. He also promised to stay near his lady and do his best to keep her from harm.

And the slave was as good as his word. For the next two days Persis had the most attentive servant in all of Epiria. For her part, she resumed her normal activities, visiting people in their homes and on the street while Anteros remained conspicuously in the street and Athan stayed well back, watching the boy instead of worrying about keeping Persis herself in sight. She of course knew something was up, and Athan was pretty sure she had seen him once or twice but she took the discreet security in seeming good grace. This made Athan very nervous. He became convinced that she intended to simply give Anteros the slip and head out on her own. Anteros was also convinced she intended some trickery. The two worked out a signaling system so that Athan would know immediately when Anteros realized she had made her break. But she fooled them by not fooling them. Her attention seemed to be focused on Doreen's progress toward finally completing her 'Five Sisters' group.

In the evening Persis told the men how Doreen, through sheer perseverance, had finally managed to convince Zita to bring her little company into the Five Sisters group. Negotiations had been extended and exhausting. Major issues such as Doreen's commission and who would book the various engagements were reasonably well settled, but the details continued to be a challenge. Zita did not want to leave her house and reside with the other women. Since the two structures were typical two story buildings, nearly identical in design, and literally opposite each other, separated only by an alleyway, this should have been easily resolved; but it was important to Doreen to have all the sisters under one roof, while Zita, for her part, did not want to leave her own domicile. Zita wanted to keep her faithful Kulin as a porter, while Doreen properly felt that her own man, a large patient good natured man who answered to the name of Porter, was a much better choice than Kulin, whose appearance was apt to frighten potential customers, not to mention most of the sisters. But there was an agreement in principle; it appeared Doreen's dream of a collaboration of hetaira, singers, musicians and dancers was finally within her grasp. But it was also obvious that Persis had more on her mind when she spoke about Doreen that evening than merely finding out how business negotiations were going. She seemed increasingly focused, as though she had made progress in confirming her suspicions, but she still would not comment on what she had found. She assured Thaddeus that the immediate danger from the killer had passed. She had time to be patient and build her case carefully. But for once she was wrong, tragically wrong.

The following evening there was a celebration at the House of Five sisters to celebrate the pending agreement. Although the details still remained to be worked out, the two primary parties concerned, Doreen and Zita, had agreed to work together, and that for the time being was enough to warrant a party. Of course, the two being women, technically could not actually legally own property or run businesses on their own. And of course, the women found ways around these sorts of legal restrictions. Doreen had family in town and, as a recognized hetaira, had no lack of sponsors. Her house was "owned" by a doting uncle. Zita tended to put things in the name of Kulin whom she claimed as a brother. The agreement between the women was primarily verbal and, like most deals in that time and place depended upon trust and personal relationships.

Athan, as a close friend of Thaddeus and Persis, was invited. Erinsys begged Athan to let her attend.

"What about Persephone?" Athan objected. "We could be gone most of the night this time. She is not old enough to be left without her mother. Who will feed her?"

"Husband, leave the care of babies to me. Mia is still nursing her own and won't mind, I have fed her son; she can feed my daughter this time. And if that isn't enough, they have a goat. They will be fine. Husband, I have not been anywhere for months! And this will be the banquet of the season. Oh, please, let me go out with you."

Proper matrons did not leave infants to attend social events hosted by hetairas, but then Erinsys was not exactly a proper matron. So, dressed in the finest chiton she and her sister Mia could construct, with new sandals, and just the right amount of scent, and perhaps a bit too much kohl used as eye shadow, Erinsys left her sister's house on the arm of her husband to attend the festivities at the place to be dedicated as the House of Five Sisters.

They arrived in the company of Persis and Thaddeus just as the sun was going down. They climbed to the roof of the second story of the residence now officially named the House of the Five Sisters, where the celebration would be held. During the summer months, many people chose to spend time under awnings erected on the roof, allowing access to cooling breezes. Doreen knew how to put on a celebration. Some of the city's most influential men and their wives were circulating beneath awnings next to vases with flowers and small statuary. Oil torch lights and lamps flickered in the breeze. Young servants passed through the guests offering olives, dates, pastries, and other delicacies. Musicians played discreetly in the background on a lyre, a flute, and a drum. Athan noticed that though some of the musicians were associated with Zita, the woman herself and her singers were not in attendance. This puzzled them only for a short while. Just as the evening star appeared, Doreen and the three other members of her little organization assembled at the back of the 'House of Five Sisters' directly across the alleyway from the house Zita had rented. They were all dressed in pure white chitons and bare feet. The four women began with a sweet hymn to Athena followed by another to Artemis. Then they began a traditional song of welcome familiar to all, delivered with professional skill. Suddenly the verse was answered from the roof across the alley as first Zita in her marvelous soprano then her accompanists joined in the song. They emerged from behind a cloth screen where they had been waiting, each woman dressed like the Sisters in tasteful white chitons, each carrying an oil lamp which they lighted in turn from a shielded lantern placed on a low table. Back and forth, point and counterpoint they sang. As the song began its second verse, one of Zita's accompanists turned and walked down the ladder into the house. She emerged moments later, still holding her lamp from the back door where Kulin now stood guard. This was a higher class neighborhood and even the alleys were paved with flagstones, so the girl did not soil her bare feet as she crossed the alley and entered the back door of the House of Five Sisters, where she climbed the stairs up to the roof and joined the singers there. One by one as a new verse began one of Zita's singers would cross over until only Zita was left. Then as the final verse started she too descended and crossed over, managing to reach the roof just in time to give a final rousing ending to the song. The guests were charmed and delighted.

Once the two groups were united on the roof there was more music, followed by dancing, first formal pieces, followed by more common folk dances which the guests were invited to join. The women mingled and made conversation. Athan and Erinsys noticed that Persis made a point of speaking with each of Zita's singers and every time she did so Zita broke off her own conversation and immediately drifted over to join the group like a mother hen protecting her chicks.

"Do you really believe she thinks Persis will try to lure one of her singers away?" wondered Erinsys aloud. "I think they are all too afraid of Zita to ever leave her without her permission. Persis is just being polite but that big woman acts like a jealous lover. That can't be it; not with all of them. I believe that big woman is simply insecure despite her position and talent."

The other guests in their temporary conversation group agreed that Zita was over-protective and probably not the 'right sort' for polite conversation. But her magnificent voice meant she would always be able to find engagements.

It was a lovely evening. A cool night breeze caressed the party on the roof. Overhead the stars filled the clear night. So gracious and delightful was the company that Persis paid them the compliment of looking slightly worried. Near the end of the evening, as the wine continued to flow, Doreen approached her mentor/rival.

"I hope the event gave you pleasure," she said addressing all four of them though it was clear she meant the words for Persis.

Persis could be gracious and made an appropriate response.

"I would ask a boon of you, dear Persis. Would you, I mean please would you be willing to perform a dance with Chara and myself? It would mean so much to me. Please?"

For a moment they thought she would decline, but it would be churlish to not to accept, and Persis had secretly wanted to dance with Chara for some time. Or perhaps the wine had mellowed her. In any event she nodded her ascent and the two women went to the center of the roof where Chara waited shyly. The three women took their positions for a dance each knew well, though they had never performed it together. Chara took up a tambourine, while Persis and Doreen put on finger cymbals. The dance required the dancers to accompany the musicians with these instruments while they danced. Doreen took a deep breath, looked over at the musicians, nodded, and the dance began. Athan and Erinsys had seen Persis practice dancing many times and were aware of her skill. But despite the fact they had been to some banquets where she had danced, for some reason neither had ever seen her perform a full formal dance. The three women were magnificent. Doreen was graceful and supple as a swan; Chara more than lived up to her reputation with lovely turns, perfect timing, and elegant moves. But it was their old friend Persis who led the dance. They could not tell how she did it, but it was her moves that held the eye, that led the other two into logical responses. Together the women moved as one perfect entity, responding to and enhancing the music that guided them. The roof became still as every eye followed them until the last note when the three sank down together, arms extended toward one another, fingers just touching. The audience responded appreciatively.

Persis glided over to rejoin her companions. She was followed closely by a star-struck Chara who thanked Persis effusively for allowing her to dance with her. Then bobbing a curtsey, she backed away. Right behind the young dancer came Doreen, a thin sheen of sweat on her forehead, her huge brown eyes shining. Even the streaking of the black kohl she had put around her eyes did nothing to diminish her radiance.

"Oh, that was so wonderful! Thank you," she gushed, "I have wanted to dance that dance with you for so long! Wasn't Chara magnificent? And you led us so very well. Thank you again." And she pressed her forehead onto Persis' hand before withdrawing.

The evening drew to a close and guests began to depart. When they paid their respects to the hostesses as they departed, Athan noticed how different Doreen and Zita seemed. The big singer seemed aloof and almost condescending, as though she was a wealthy matron seeing off minor guests. Doreen, on the other hand, was gracious and effusive. She appeared flushed and excited; Athan could not tell if it was the excitement or the wine she had begun to sample; Persis had hinted on occasion that Doreen did enjoy her wine in the evenings. But all that was swept away for Athan as, when they emerged from the house, Erinsys whispered to him that they did not need to return to her sister's house that night, and could they spend the night in their own home? Immediately Athan bade Thaddeus good night and turned with his wife on his arm toward their little cottage in the compound.

The next morning, Erinsys was a little grumpy, whether from the pressure to feed her infant son or from the need to resume the demands of motherhood Athan, could not tell. But then he had never been very good at sorting out his wife's moods; or any other woman's for that matter. It was still early when he dropped off his wife at her sister's. Mia was glad but not surprised to see her sister. Clearly Erinsys had planned on staying away all night from the beginning. Leaving his wife and children with a kiss, Athan strode along the street munching a bit of bread his sister in law had given him. He had a smile on his lips and a spring in his step as he headed back to resume his surveillance duties on Persis.

He knew something was wrong as soon as he approached her house. Although he was not a policeman, he had patrolled Epiria long enough to be able sense the currents of the people in the street. There was too much hurrying and whispering, too many people sharing a secret. Obviously there was news of something that had occurred in the night. Even Ajax, Persis' porter seemed distracted. He made as if to stop Athan from entering, something he had never done before.

"You might not want to go in there, sir," he said somewhat apologetically. "She is in a taking," he said using a colloquial expression describing a person who is very upset. "Understandable I guess. Maybe you should come back later."

"I am here to talk to Anteros," said Athan both annoyed and alarmed. "What is wrong?"

"I guess you hadn't heard the news," replied the porter. Many people take an obscure satisfaction at passing on bad news; Ajax was no exception. "They found Doreen dead this morning. The Lady just got the news a quarter hour or so ago. She was in a proper taking, like I said. Never seen her like that before; she was screaming and raging at the boy who brought the news. He fled out of here like a scalded hound. She has been screaming and crying ever since."

"Where is Thaddeus?"

"Well, sir, he had been trying to comfort her. I guess she is calming down now, you can't hear her now, but I don't think it would be such a good idea to go in just now."

"Did they say how Doreen died?" asked Athan, who was shocked himself at this unexpected news.

"The boy said they found her in the alley next to her house. He said they thought she fell off the roof in the night."

Athan stood on the doorway for a long moment. He did not want to go up there and see a distraught Persis. He wanted to go back and spend the day with his wife and children. He wanted Doreen to be alive and excited about her business. He wanted to see Persis alert and calculating how to turn the establishment of the Five Sisters into her own advantage. He did not want to think about that beautiful woman who had been so alive and happy the night before lying dead in an alley. But he knew he would have to face reality sooner or later. Athan was a brave man, and so he did what he needed to do, not what he wanted.

"I better go up there," he told Ajax, "do you know where Anteros is?"

The porter shrugged and gestured the boy was somewhere in the house.

"Don't let him leave without talking to me."

Anteros had a tendency to avoid unpleasant scenes and would slip away if he could. Athan was worried he might need the boy.

Bypassing Persis' maid who tried to divert him, Athan entered a dim room where he could hear Persis sobbing. This unsettled him; he had seen the lady cry, of course. She had wept when she had a miscarriage last year, but this was different. There was an element of self-loathing in her that Athan had never remotely associated with the city's most renowned hetaira.

"Hubris," she was gasping into Thaddeus' shoulder. "I was so sure of myself, so confident. And now she is dead. That poor, poor, woman is dead because of me. I could have stopped it."

Athan could think of nothing to say. He was puzzled by her words. Did she think she could have stopped Doreen from falling off a roof? Of course she would be deeply saddened by the death of a friend and fellow hetaira but this was more than ordinary grief. What was he missing?

When Persis saw him she began to control herself. He had never seen her face like this, red, blotchy, with tears streaming down her cheeks.

"I'm so sorry," was all he could say.

"It's not your fault," she replied bitterly.

"I heard she fell off a roof," Athan said stupidly, "it is a great pity."

"She didn't fall off a roof, stupid," retorted Persis, "she was thrown off. And I could have stopped it." Then looking at Athan she caught herself, "I am sorry Athan, it is not your fault. You are not stupid, I am the stupid one, stupid and proud and arrogant. I didn't trust you and Thad and tell you all my suspicions because I thought I was in control. I wasn't anything except stupid and overconfident. And Doreen paid for my hubris."

Thaddeus continued to try to comfort his beloved. Both men noticed she had used the diminutive of Thaddeus' name, something she almost never did. Neither had seen her like this, and it upset them even more than the news of the death.

"I am sorry, Lady," Athan was reverting to his old way of addressing her under the stress, "but how do you know she didn't fall off the roof? You were not there, were you?" She sat bolt upright. "You are right. I might be mistaken. Athan, please go get Zakias and have him examine the body. Tell him to be thorough." She made as if to get up but Thaddeus restrained her.

"You are not going anywhere like this, woman," he growled. "I want you to clean yourself up; I am taking you to the baths."

Persis sparked up briskly, "I am not going to the baths!"

"Do you know how she died, truly, do you know?"

Persis shook her head, "I suspect."

"Then let Athan examine the body. I will investigate the scene. You take Ajax and go to the baths with your maid. Leave Anteros to watch the door. I want you with Ajax. And tell him to bring his club. Then when you come back we will bring you information. If we decide she drank too much wine and fell off the roof then you will be blameless. It is possible she did die accidentally isn't it?"

"Yes," bit off Persis, "but I don't think so."

"Well, let's base our actions on accurate intelligence," Thaddeus was falling back on his military training. Soon he would start talking about the folly of anticipating your enemy's actions based on what you wanted him to do, not what he might do. Athan did not want to be there if Thaddeus sprang that on Persis, especially in her present mood. He decided he better forestall that possibility.

"Lady, that is sound advice. We can find out what you need to know. Then we can take the appropriate action, whether that is to bring her killer to justice or simply to mourn a senseless death. But while we get that for you, you need to hone the best weapon we have."

She looked at him with a question.

"You mind, Lady, your mind."

She gave him a ghost of a smile. "Always polite, Athan; Thaddeus, he could give you lessons on how to manage a woman." The two men looked at each other. They could tell each was thinking of Erinsys and her temper which Athan certainly did not manage well. "There is a need for haste," continued Persis with briskness entering her voice. "Your investigations will probably be hindered from a variety of sources, Athan, yours in particular. You must get Zakias and go to the body as soon as possible."

That turned out to be more difficult than Athan would have thought. Zakias liked to sleep late, nor did he move quickly when bestirred. He recognized the urgency, but simply did not function well in the morning. Then Athan had to locate Doreen's body, which was not at the house of the dead, but instead had been laid out in the place that had been known for a single day as the House of Five Sisters. Once there he had to penetrate a variety of mourners and curiosity seekers. At the very entrance of the room where the prothesis was already been prepared, Athan and his companion stuck fast. Her family was with the body and a large unsympathetic servant flatly forbad them entrance. The body was being prepared for the viewing and only family was allowed inside. Most especially that sick, creepy foreigner would not be allowed inside to fondle Doreen's body. Things had gotten quite tense when suddenly Persis was there, pale, and drawn, but herself again. Apparently her bath had been delayed.

One thing about the Lady, when she really wanted something she got it. She overcame the objections of the servant through sheer force of will. She sympathized, flattered and persuaded the family to allow her to pay a few moments of quiet time with her dead friend and fellow hetaira. There was considerable resistance about the presence of Zakias who was beginning to develop an unsavory reputation. This was solved with an unexpected compromise offered by Persis: a great aunt, a tough old bird who was obviously the matriarch, would remain with them as a chaperone. Ahax remained with the family to tactfully prevent any interruptions.

Once the family had withdrawn, Persis addressed the crone using the most respectful tones, "Mother, I believe your grandniece was murdered by the same fiend that butchered that poor girl several days ago. We wish only to check several things. We will not remove her chiton or treat her with disrespect in any way."

The old woman looked right at Persis, "How can you tell?"

"Come and watch," she replied and moved to the body gesturing at Zakias.

The first thing Persis did without waiting for Zakias to reach her was to put her hand behind the neck and feel for a telltale wound at the base of the neck. As she did so Doreen's head flopped to one side. Immediately Zakias moved to the other side of the body. With the great aunt watching intently from the foot of the corpse the little man ran his fingers along the neck. He withdrew them with a white powdery substance on his fingers.

"There is makeup or a covering of some sort on the neck. Please pass me a damp cloth." There was a brief delay then Zakias was wiping Doreen's neck clear. Purplish marks were visible on the sides and front of her long slender neck. "The powder was placed there postmortem," he opined.

The grand aunt confirmed that they had tried to improve the body's appearance. Her eyes had been closed and were also covered with a bandage. Zakias carefully removed the cloth and murmured an apology to the corpse. Athan noticed how different his attitude was with Doreen compared to the other two bodies he had examined. Obviously the man had some sensitivity, or perhaps he was afraid of the grand aunt. He peeled back the eyelid and showed the slightly protuberant orb to Persis. "Notice," he said in respectful tones, "the bulging of the eyes and the broken blood vessels. These were not noticeable the last time you saw her, no?"

Persis shook her head mutely.

"And the bruises are also new, yes?"

Persis nodded in agreement. Apparently she did not trust herself to speak.

Then with a nod toward the old lady who stood watching him he carefully reached around and felt the back shoulders. He requested permission to roll her over for a moment. This granted, the two men gently rolled her on her stomach, her arms flopping sickeningly over. Again Zakias ran his hands over the shoulder blades and back. Then he indicated to Athan to return her to her back. Finally, as Persis and the great aunt rearranged the folds of Doreen's white chiton Zakias ran his hands along the sides of her elegant neck.

Straightening up he looked at Persis with an unspoken question.

"Tell us," was all she said.

"Madam," Zakias spoke to the great aunt, "your niece was murdered. The cause of death was a broken neck but I believe she was also strangled. Whether her fatal injury occurred while she was being choked or if she was rendered unconscious and then the neck was broken I can not tell, but she did not sustain any serious injuries that are consistent with a fall. See the marks on the side of the chin. Those are consistent with an impact. Although a fall from a second story window can certainly break a neck, in a woman of this small size it is less likely. Further she was a dancer, yes. That implies she had some balance. If she were conscious, her arms would have been the first to hit as she tried to break her fall. They are uninjured. More importantly, landing on her face like that is not consistent with this type of neck fracture. And see the marks on her neck? The man who killed her had relatively small hands." Here he indicated the dark places on her throat. "The hand is even smaller than mine." Athan remembered how Persis suspected a small and oppressed man. He looked up at her to see her staring back at him. "At any rate, she was dead before she landed in the alleyway. Her neck was almost certainly been broken first."

After that there was little to say. Zakias made to leave. Athan saw Persis speaking in low tones to the great aunt; both women looked grim and determined. The three left the old woman standing beside the body as family members filed back in, exclaiming at the removal of the makeup.

By the time they had returned to Persis' house, Thaddeus had returned.

"Well," he announced before they had a chance to speak, "if there was foul play our murderer is part ape. The door was barred and Porter is emphatic that no one who did not live there was admitted after the last guest left. The five sisters were together up there on the roof for over an hour after that talking and drinking wine. Doreen went down to her room to sleep but the rest of them spent the night up on the roof together. They think that Doreen must have decided to come up to sleep on the roof in the middle of the night and stumbled over the coping. She had been drinking."

"No," said Persis flatly, "she was murdered. Her neck was broken before she was thrown out into the alley. Where did they find her body?"

"Directly under her window, near the rear corner, away from where the women were sleeping. How do you know she was killed and then thrown out the window?" queried Thaddeus.

"Was she found face up or face down?" asked Persis challengingly.

Thaddeus thought for a moment, then realized he had not asked.

"Face down," said Persis. "She was throttled and in the process her neck was twisted like a chicken's. Then she was thrown out her window."

"How did he get in?" objected Thaddeus. All the lower windows and doors were secured. I saw no ladders or ropes anywhere around. I spoke with Porter and Kulin. Neither man indicated they heard anything during the night. Neither did any of the girls."

"Porter is a bit deaf if you haven't noticed," said Persis dryly, and the girls had an exhausting night along with some wine. Zeus' thunderbolts would not have awakened them."

"Are you saying someone slipped into the house and killed her? It would have been hard to get up into one of the upper windows without being noticed. And why would a burglar enter a house so obviously inhabited? It doesn't make any sense," protested Thaddeus.

"Her murderer was already in the house when Porter barred the door," countered Persis.

"You mean one of the guests hid in the house and then came out when the women had passed out, crept into Doreen's room, killed her, and then somehow slipped away? That seems highly unlikely. After all, the guests were some of the most important men in the city. Are you suggesting that one Doreen's guests killed her? Why?"

"Yes," said Persis with finality, "Doreen invited her killer into her home. And tomorrow I will bring a case to the Magistrate that will demonstrate who did it. Now, I really think I need that bath." And calling for Anteros and her maid she departed for the baths. Athan saw the small group walking toward the bath, escorted by Thaddeus, who Athan could see was questioning the Lady. From his posture it appeared she was not sharing anything of interest with him.

Since Thaddeus had clearly undertaken escort duties, Athan declared himself off duty. Instead of returning to the guard's compound where he might be put to useful work, he instead went to visit his wife and children. There he played with his son, chatted companionably with his Erinsys and Mia, and after a small meal, lay down for a comfortable nap in a corner.

He was awakened by a frantic voice at the door. He recognized it as Anteros. Mia's servant, a youth not much older than Anteros was trying to turn the boy away but Anteros was being uncharacteristically persistent. Athan knew trouble when he heard it. Snatching up his dagger he hurried to the door to intervene.

As soon as Anteros saw Athan he immediately began babbling his tale.

"She's gone sir, I tried to stop her but she told me to stay home. I tried to follow her but she gave me the slip. I don't know where she is." Obviously he was referring to Persis.

"Where is Thaddeus?" asked Athan as calmly as he could in an effort to settle the youth down.

"After we got back from the baths, the Lady laid down to rest; she has been in such a state since she got the news this morning. Then, while she was resting, the Master took an urgent message from one of his men. He told me he had to take care of some business; he said he would be only gone a little while but after he left another boy came with a message for the Lady and she got up and left in a flash. I don't know where she went, I tried to follow me but she cursed me and then gave me the slip in the market." This was all said seemingly in one breath.

Athan interrupted the flood. "Where is Thaddeus?"

The flow of words from the boy continued. He was so anxious that he was literally hopping from one foot to the other. "I don't know, sir, he will beat me or sell me to a farm for certain. If the Lady comes to any harm I will not know what to do. I don't know where she is."

Thaddeus was one of the few things that Anteros feared in all the city. It was clear that Anteros did not want to tell Thaddeus the bad news about Persis. No one likes to be the bearer of ill tiding, especially to a man like Thaddeus, and most especially when the bad news involved endangering a loved one through what might be perceived as your own negligence. Anteros was never one to be very brave in matters like that. Athan had no doubt he would find some excuse to avoid Thaddeus. Thinking quickly he searched for a wax tablet or a slate.

To buy time he asked Anteros, who looked ready to bolt, another question. "How long has she been gone? Where do you think she might have gone?"

This led to another long outpouring of woe. He did not know where she could be. He had not seen her for a while, he was not sure how long; perhaps half an hour or so. Clearly the boy, so resourceful and inventive in getting into mischief or playing off lovers against one another, had lost his head. Finally Athan snatched up a bit of a wooden board from the street and with a bit of chalk scrawled a message to Thaddeus.

Persis gone off alone. Come help search.

-A.

"Here," he said to the frenzied boy, "take this to the compound and ask for the sergeant of the watch. Tell them it is an urgent note for Thaddeus. Tell them to find him and give it to him right away. Then get back here as fast as you can and start looking for her. Try all her favorite haunts. If you find her stay with her! Convince her to return to the house even if just to leave a message. Now GO!"

The boy was gone in a flash, intent on emulating his own personal favorite deity, Hermes. Whereas the boy would not dare face Thaddeus, he could be relied upon to deliver a message. He had been told what to do. Soon his wits would return. Athan had no doubt that within half an hour the entire city would be keeping an eye out for Persis. As to the contents of the note he had sent, Athan knew the boy did not read, and he doubted that the sergeant of the guard could either, but Thaddeus could. He would come as quickly as he could, probably with an entire company of the guards to expedite the search.

But it would take time for that to happen. Athan had a bad feeling about the situation. He believed Persis knew who had killed her friend and she could be remorseless in obtaining revenge for wrongs. He had never seen her as upset as she was today. There was no doubt she intended to confront the killer. She could be fearless, and that was the problem. Athan and Thaddeus had discussed fearless warriors many times. They had seen a few; they were usually quickly killed in battle. In order to find Persis, all Athan had to do was figure out who had killed the women, for now he too, felt the three women had all been murdered by the same hand. Where ever the killer was, Persis would be there, and ahead of him; he had no time to waste.

Athan began walking toward the center of town. He considered what he knew that Persis thought: victim number one died in an impulse attack by someone who considered himself oppressed or otherwise held back. Victim number two died because she had somehow known or otherwise discovered who had committed the first murder. He was somehow able to lure her out of her house after dark. Victim number three had been killed in her own home behind barred doors. How could a killer get in? Persis said the killer had been invited in. What if victim two had been killed inside her house and then her body taken outside and disposed of in the night? What if that was the case? Suddenly things began to make sense and he understood what Persis had seen. He looked around to see where he was and began to run.

Persis looked behind her to make sure Anteros was not in sight. This was easy; it was a hot afternoon and there were few people out. She was glad she had been able to give him the slip. The fool boy would have gotten himself killed. At the very least he would have tipped off Athan, who had been following around behind her for the last few days trying to be inconspicuous. She had been presented an opportunity, and she intended to use it. She had a case, a fairly good case now, to present to the Magistrate, but a conviction was far from certain. She needed more; possibly things could be resolved this very afternoon. Persis felt an excitement of a kind she had once craved, one she had not felt in quite a while. She was betting her life in an effort to stop a monster. Of course, she intended to cheat, but she never knew when she would encounter someone who could cheat even better than she did.

Her heart giving a pleasant thump, thump she raised her slim hand and knocked on the door. The hulking simpleton opened the door with the usual vacuous smile on his face.

"I am expected," she said with a smile.

Without a word he swung the door open, then shut behind her.

"I know the way," Persis said climbing up to the stairs. No one seemed to be about the house. That was a little odd.

"I got your message," she said as she entered the private room in the back of the house. The little slave boy had been so anxious that she come right away and come alone. How obvious. When she asked the boy how much he would get if she came at once and alone he told her he would receive two bits, a small enough fee, but to a boy of his age and station a great deal of money. Then she asked him what he would get if she did not come. 'A beating'. How typical. She paused before she departed long enough to make certain preparations and write two brief notes on slates. The little slave boy was hopping with impatience in the front portico. Instead, Persis went to the rear of her house and hailed a passing boy in the alley behind the house. Giving him hasty instructions and some money she quickly returned to the urgent urchin waiting in the front. Ajax was surprised to see her leave with no one but a slave boy, but said nothing.

"Thank you for coming, so fast. Did you need an escort?" asked Zita with a smile that did not reach her eyes, as Persis entered Zita's sitting room in the back corner of the house.

"No," replied Persis, "I left at once. I do not feel the need for a man to come with me in the middle of the day. I noticed when I came in that the house is empty. Are the girls out on an assignment this afternoon?"

The smile now touched the eyes of Zita. "No," she answered settling back on a couch located behind a table, "they are at the prothesis of poor Doreen. I expect them back before dark. We are going to make sure she has a fine ekphora this evening. I understand she will be buried at a family tomb."

She gestured Persis to a couch near the back wall on the other side of the table. Then, seeming to make a decision, she rose and went to a set of shelves and took down two goblets made of a thick grayish metal. Persis watched her carefully as Zita took the goblets that had been placed one in front of the other and set them carefully on the table that was between them. The goblet that had been in the rear was of better make and more ornate than the other. Zita carefully set the ornate goblet closer to Persis and ostentatiously poured wine from the same container into each goblet. She then mixed in water as was common. Finally swirling the liquid to mix it she handed the better goblet to Persis.

"Let us toast to Doreen's memory. It is an old custom in my land." With that she took long pull on her watered wine. She watched as Persis brought the cup to her lips and tipped it back as well. As Zita watched the other woman's throat work she smiled with true pleasure.

'Really,' thought Persis, 'this woman would not last a week in civilized company.' She decided that Zita was not really stupid, just unsophisticated. Persis was the daughter of an Achaemendian nobleman. She had literally grown up in an atmosphere of intrigue and betrayal. She had never accepted anything to eat or drink from a potential enemy in her life. In fact her own knowledge of poisons was extensive. When Zita began her elephantine efforts to get Persis to drink from a cup that had obviously been set aside for a special purpose Persis had to hide her amusement. She was a bit surprised that Zita had chosen this method of murder. She had calculated the big barbarian woman would prefer something far less subtle and far more personal. Persis rolled the wine around in her mouth while she pretended to swallow and then quietly squirted most of it back into the cup. As she lowered the goblet she could see a trace of a dried white power on the side of the cup.

"Very nice," Persis observed. "I needed that. It has a slightly spicy taste."

"Yes," replied Zita, smiling broadly with obvious pleasure, "I prefer it that way."

Persis decided that this woman would not give her anything that would simply kill her in a few hours. No, Persis, decided, she would try to give her something that would render her unconscious or otherwise incapacitated. Now she had to try to decide what potion this enormous diva was trying to use on her and then simulate the symptoms. Persis looked about languidly, noticing an undertunic cast carelessly next to her couch. The flagons of wine and water were on a stand just behind where Zita had sat back on her own couch. Persis decided she wanted to keep the table between them. The big woman looked capable of simply leaping upon her and beating her into unconsciousness.

"I think I would like a bit more," announced Persis, rising to look out the window and shifting her goblet to her left side.

Zita turned to get more wine; in a swift motion Persis dumped most of the contents of her cup onto the undertunic, the movement hidden by her body. The cloth muted any sound of liquid splashing. At the same instant she appeared to stumble turning the garment over to cover the telltale stain on the garment with a swift movement of her foot.

"Oops," exclaimed Persis. "I had a cup before I came here. I seem to be a bit clumsy now." She wanted Zita to think her befuddled; wanted her to be confident. No she wanted her to be triumphant and overconfident. The ploy seemed to work. Zita smiled and filled the offered goblet in Persis' left hand. She did not offer to water the wine, and watched with satisfaction as Persis flopped back down on her couch. "What did you want to talk to me about?"

"First let me apologize for calling you over so suddenly on such a hot day," began Zita, sitting back on her own couch safely behind the table. "I saw your husband heading past my house in a hurry and thought you might be alone."

"He's not my husband," said Persis automatically. Then recovering she continued, "But yes, I was alone. My lazy boy had gone off to see some of his friends. I was glad to come over. It appears the murderer has left the city."

"So no one came with you," pressed Zita.

'The woman has the subtly of a bear' thought Persis. 'Any reasonable person would have been alerted by her manner. And that ridiculous message asking her to come over alone and at once; really! Either Zita was insanely overconfident or utterly unsophisticated. But she needed to be cautious. It would be a shame to be killed by such an idiot.' So all she said aloud was, "That's right."

The two women then began a strange conversation. Zita clearly had decided to find out whatever Persis had discovered and then do away with her. Persis had, in a manner of speaking, decided to do the same with Zita. Of course Persis had several advantages in this odd contest. First, she was bred to such intrigues. Second, she knew what Zita was up to and the reverse was not true. Third, Persis had her secret friend with her. Her first professional client, an older man she had loved for over two years had given it to her when his health began to fail. It was quite an expensive weapon, custom made just for her. The blade was a silver alloy that was strong, held an edge, and most importantly, was bright and shiny. The hilt had no guard, but the thin ivory handle had been expertly carved to precisely fit her hand. That double-edged silvery blade, a little longer than her hand and a bit wider than two of her fingers had proved to be very useful. She had used it half a dozen times in her career to flash in front of a threatening face, to menace genitals, and twice to slash a groping hand. Discreetly secured to her thigh in a sheath that, like the ivory handle almost exactly matched her skin tone, it was out of sight, but instantly available. Persis had practiced drawing it many times. She had never used her stiletto to kill, but that was what she was prepared to do now if threatened. She waited for the big woman to confirm what Persis already knew: that she was the 'Mad Butcher', the killer of Ianthe and Doreen's murderer. If she obtained enough additional information to make a solid case to the magistrate, then she would leave matters to him. But she afraid that any confirmation she received her would only be her word against the other woman's.

Persis waited, trying to draw the big woman out. Once she was satisfied she had her answers, well then she would take the first chance to escape. And if escape was not possible, then she had her little friend. She knew what she would have to do: thrust to the neck if possible; if not a stab into the ribs, a wiggle and withdraw the blade before it became stuck.

They sat on their couches, Zita at one side of the room, Persis in the corner of the building backed by one window that faced the dwelling known for one day as the House of Five Sisters, with another window that faced the blank wall of a stable over a quiet alleyway. Persis had heard of Cretan youths who would dance with bulls: they would face the enraged animals in an area and then at the last instant grasp the bull's horns and summersault over his back to the applause of the crowd. Persis understood how they felt and why they did it. Nothing was more exciting, nothing made you feel alive than facing death on your terms. This Zita was Persis' bull with a couple of exceptions: no one was watching, and unlike the Cretans, Persis wanted her bull dead at the hands of the executioner.

The conversation drifted from preparations for Doreen's ekphora procession, then inexorably to what would happen to the women who had worked in association with Doreen.

"It is a good idea," Zita stated, "having all the entertainers and hetaira under a single point of control. Now that Doreen is gone I will, of course, be making the arrangements."

"Whaa abou d others?" slurred Persis softly. She was a little surprised how hard it was becoming for her to enunciate clearly. There was a tingling in her lips and mouth. How potent was that poison, just how much had she sipped?

"Oh, I am sure they will come around," said Zita confidently, now with a broad smile as she watched Persis shift uncomfortably on her couch. Flies buzzed around the room. This was not unusual. It was summer and all the windows were open in the quiet heat. Persis' eyes followed them to the table in front of Zita. Apparently Zita had been putting a wide leather belt together, sort of a bodice, while she waited for Persis. The two pieces lay on the table partially laced up, the awl used to punch holes in the leather lying next to them. Flies had landed on the metal piece that jutted from the awl's wooden handle. Persis looked at them and knew exactly why flies would be attracted to a seemingly clean bit of iron. Flies could smell things that people could not. Things like blood, no matter how carefully cleaned. Zita's eyes followed Persis' gaze. Abruptly she stood up.

"Dear Persis," she exclaimed with obviously false solicitude, "you look quite unwell. Can I help you?" And the big woman came around the table toward Persis' couch. Persis saw her hands were empty. This was not the expected attack, not yet. It was time to make the final ploy.

"Can't seem ta move," she whispered. Clearly from Zita's observation of her she did not expect her victim to fall asleep, nor was she watching for signs of illness. No, Persis decided that Zita had decided to use a paralytic potion. They were expensive and hard to find, but some could be ingested with liquids. A poison that left her victim awake but unable to move, would appeal very much to this spider of a woman. It would give her power over her victim and a chance to gloat.

Persis could almost feel the woman's need to boast about her crimes. 'Oh, let her tell me,' prayed Persis as the woman approached. 'Oh, please let her stay right there and tell me all about how you murdered three innocent women.'

"It must have been something you ate," smirked Zita, looming over Persis who was now reclined on her back left hand dangling over the side of the couch. "Or drank." Her voice abruptly became angry. "You think you are so special. Acting like a respectable matron when all you are is a whore. Maybe you can fuck all those men but you can't sing, can you?" Her face was right up to Persis now, the big square chin pushed forward aggressively.

'Admit your crimes now you vicious sow', Persis thought holding perfectly still save for her tongue which licked her lips nervously. There was a long moment. So far Zita had not admitted anything except professional jealousy, and that was common enough. The tension between the women reached a breaking point.

"Hepp me," Persis whispered in a weak whisper.

A cat will watch a mouse for a long time until the mouse twitches, then suddenly pounce. So it was with Zita; the admission of weakness galvanized her. Her left hand came across with a powerful slap to Persis' face. Persis never saw it coming and so had no opportunity to flinch before the blow landed. But once struck all her dancer's agility came into play, she twisted around completely in the air and wound up on her face, left leg now thrown across the couch, right arm and right leg over the edge, out of sight where Persis now gripped her stiletto. Zita had still not admitted guilt. Persis gave some twitching motions as if attempting to rise. She was horrified to notice that her left arm continued to twitch even after she had tried to stop it.

"Why," she asked in the same hoarse whisper she had used before.

Zita stood over her looking very self-satisfied. Persis was now well below the line of sight of the street even if anyone had been outside. But there was no one out there.

"Because,' the big woman moved back around the table to lounge on her couch apparently satisfied the other woman was now totally at her mercy. She seemed delighted to be able to sit and watch her next victim lying there apparently helpless. Now at last she could openly reveal herself. "Because, you are a skinny conceited whore, that is why." Zita stopped long enough to call downstairs, "Kulin, bring around the manure wagon to the side alley again. Go now."

Then, looking back at the recumbent figure of Persis, Zita lowered her voice and continued, "You have no talent other than lying under a man with your legs spread. You think everyone is lower than you; think you are so smart. Well, you are not. Think you could find out something talking to my girls." Persis had found quite a bit from Zita's troupe. That on the night of the first murder Zita had returned from a private assignment before the others with only Kulin in her company. And that she had behaved strangely, washing herself in her room and remaining alone until all the others had left the next day and then going to the baths alone. And she no longer had what had been her favorite dress, a dark patterned chiton that she had worn that night. And that no one else had thought Ianthe appeared upset the night she died. She was a shy girl and had no men friend in Epiria as yet. And that Kulin apparently actually was Zita's brother and had little to do with anyone else in the group. And Persis was able to determine without anyone actually coming out and saying it was that everyone in Zita's company was terrified of her, men and women alike.

"Well', continued Zita, now with her arm stretched out along the low back of her couch, "you might have made trouble for me. So you have to go."

"Liiak Dorren," slurred Persis, now close to her goal.

"More like that stupid Ianthe," confirmed Zita. "The flies gave me away there just like they did on that awl. They were so interested in the back of my couch that Ianthe let her curiosity get the better of her." Zita pulled at the cloth covering on the back of her couch and reached in, producing a bloody girdle that might have once been white, wrapped around the handle of a large butcher knife. Zita replaced her trophies but did not seal up the back. "I walked in and saw her looking at this." Here Zita laughed. "She squeaked like a mouse and tried to run. I caught her right there," she indicated the corner of the table, 'fortunately the awl was handy on the table so I just kept my arm around her head and," she crooked her left arm miming a headlock and with her right gave a downward stabbing motion.

There it was. From this point on one of the women in the room was going to die, perhaps not right then and there but soon. Zita continued on, blithely unaware that her supposed victim was now merely waiting for a chance to take her case to the Magistrate. While she waited she listened for more incriminating evidence; and Zita provided it, proud of her accomplishments. "And that disgusting little street slut, like you, Persis, only she was poor, she actually insulted me. And then she laid her filthy hand on me. Well, she got what she deserved, didn't she?"

"Why," slurred Persis from her position on the couch.

"Why, what?" exclaimed Zita irritably, "You whores are all alike. Can you imagine me working for a whore like Doreen? Now that she is dead I will have them working for me. I was willing to make an accommodation with her for a while, but last night when I came down to her room, she still somehow thought she would be the one in charge. The other girls were asleep with their heads full of wine. There was no one else around so it was easy to get rid of her." Zita was so proud of herself. "People who oppose me seem to have bad things happen to them. Just ask my troupe. They know to do what I tell them."

The singer got up from her couch and came around the table. Persis prepared for action without seeming to tense. Zita paused, standing near Persis who remained sprawled on the couch, giving an occasional twitch; a lure waiting to bring in the big fish. Zita remained standing where she was looking down at Persis, just out of range. "I suppose you are wondering what I am going to do with you. I bet you think I am going to stick my awl in the back of your neck like Ianthe. No, you are not going to get off that easily." Outside the women heard a cart being led down the side alley stopping just past the window on that side.

"We all have our fates. You are about to find out yours." Zita bent down and leered at the seemingly helpless Persis. Then she stood straight up again and continued in a gloating voice. "Don't worry about dying from that little potion I gave you. It will only keep you still for a few hours. But in the meantime, I am going to tie you up very tightly, put a gag in that big mouth, and then wrap you in a cloth bag and lower you down to my brother. Kulin is a good boy, he helped me get Ianthe out of here using that cart. He used to like to talk too much. But after I had some men take care of his careless tongue, I have had much less trouble with him." Even though Persis thought of herself as a hard woman, listening to Zita talk about having her own brother's tongue slit to keep him silent made her shudder. What had this woman done before she came here?

Zita saw the tremor and giggled. "Oh, you will leave your city just the way you deserve: covered in stinking straw and horse manure. We will tie you so firmly that you will be unable to twitch even if the potion wears off. I will make sure you can breathe under there though, even if it will stink. We will all ride out of the gates, Kulin and I in our disguises, you under the horse shit. No one will even look at a pile of stable waste or the men driving the cart. Then we will go out to a nice quiet spot. I will make sure you arrive alive at our destination out in a lonely place where we won't be disturbed. Then we will get you out of your disgusting clothes. I think I will let Kulin have his fun with a famous hetaira for a while. I will be right there to make sure you do not lag in your efforts to please him. I am sure you will be quite happy to do anything he wants just to prolong your miserable life. Because when he has no further use for you then it will be my turn. I think he will leave us all alone then. Poor Kulin gets upset when I have my fun. I won't have to hurry like I did with the girl in the alley. I bet I can keep you alive and trying to scream for an hour. Of course your body will never be found. Everyone will think you just ran away with some new man." Finally in a musing voice Zita looked down and but in a final thought. "You have nice teeth. Perhaps I shall have some of them made into a necklace."

Zita had again leaned over toward Persis. She was gloating again, her words thick with anticipated passion. Then she leaned back abruptly and began moving back to her couch. "People will wonder where you went, but you certainly never came here. And with the two leading hetaira gone in the space of two days, I will certainly have a lot of commissions for my new troupe. Now I think it is time we trussed you up and put you down in your new bed."

With that Zita turned and reached behind the couch where she had apparently stashed strips of cloth to bind her victim. She was halfway across the room but her back was completely turned to Persis. This was Persis' chance, and though it was not what she had expected, she did not hesitate. Swiftly but quietly Persis moved off the couch and around the table heading for the door, knife drawn. Zita was still rooting around behind the couch with her back to the room. Persis hesitated, close behind Zita and paused. It would be so easy to stick her knife into the big woman's neck and end it all right now. But as swiftly and silently as Persis had moved it was not stealthy enough. Perhaps Zita caught some motion at the edge of her peripheral vision; the big woman did not hesitate. She wheeled about with the big butcher knife in a sweeping backhand stroke that should have all but decapitated Persis. It would have certainly slashed open almost anyone else's throat, but Persis was nothing if not agile. She leaned far back in a move that was effective and graceful. The tip of the knife barely touched her skin. Instantly Persis regained her balance and made a thrust at Zita's right breast. The blade pierced the cloth of the woman's tunic and drew blood, but before the thrust could go home Persis had to leap back to avoid a second slash, coming forehand this time. Zita staggered back from the force of her blow with a solid thump against the wall sending the wine to the floor with a crash. She recovered and attacked Persis with a series of short, vicious slashes. Zita snatched up the awl from the table with her left hand as she went around the table and spread her arms with a weapon in each hand as she moved forward toward her opponent. Zita was clearly trying to herd Persis back into a corner where Persis could be unable to dodge and the larger woman's size and weight could become decisive, but Persis countered with stop thrusts and cunning moves that kept her out near the center of the room, where she could use her speed. The two women were evenly matched: Persis was faster and more agile, but Zita was stronger and had more formidable weapons. The two women were both fit, both athletic, and both were now absolutely committed to killing the other. On the other hand, this was the first actual knife fight either had ever been in, and neither was willing to take a serious blow even in exchange for a clear chance for a killing counter stroke. So they circled, slashing and stabbing, Zita knocking over the table and pushing aside the couches, Persis leaping over obstacles and drawing blood on Zita's arm.

The fight might have gone on for a considerable time but it was interrupted as suddenly as it began; the door slammed open and Athan rushed in. Zita, on Athan's right side, drove a thrust at his chest, a blow that was intended to punch through his ribs and into his vitals. It was a good stroke. But just as Zita had seriously underestimated Persis' intelligence, once again she was guilty of overconfidence. She had never fought an alert healthy adult male. Most certainly she had never faced a trained warrior whose fighting blood was up. Athan grabbed her knife wrist with his left hand and spun inside her so that they were facing the same direction, her back against his chest. Athan stretched out Zita's left arm, turning the elbow up and reached his right arm under her elbow grasping his own forearm with his right hand pinning Zita's right arm in a figure four arm bar. As Zita went to her toes to ease the pressure on her elbow, Athan bent his knees and taking her weight on his back half turned and slammed the woman against the wall next to the door. She shrieked from the pain in her right arm.

Athan had subdued fighting drunks with this move before. The pain from an over-extended elbow usually calmed down even the meanest drunks. He fully expected this woman to open her hand and drop her big knife. Instead, Zita stabbed down with the awl onto Athan's left thigh. It was her final mistake. The blow hurt, but did no serious injury. Athan was a fighting man and could manage the pain of minor wounds; instead of releasing her he merely grunted and shifted his grip, bringing his right arm directly under her elbow. She pulled the awl out to strike again; he pushed down on her wrist with his left hand and pushed up with his right forearm. The elbow made an audible pop; Zita screamed in agony and dropped the knife. With a half turn Athan twisted and hip-threw the big woman, sending her stumbling all the way across the room, the awl flying from her hand and bouncing off the wall.

Athan had not aimed where the woman would go; he had merely used a wrestling throw to get her off him so he could draw his dagger. But there was an open window on that side and Zita went almost all the way through it back first, barely catching herself with her left hand.

Zita was still moving across the room when Persis leapt after her with stiletto flashing. Before Athan could say a word Persis struck: a slash to Zita's fingers that were clutching the window sill and a firm push to her head and the big woman was defenestrated head first. There as a meaty thud on the flagstones below

The two people in the room turned to look at each other, but before they could say a word Kulin burst into the room, club in hand, bawling like a bull. Athan was in no mood for any further nonsense. He had realized there was only one place where Persis could be. He had run directly to Zita's house and found the door unbarred. He had just entered and was about to call out when Kulin returned from the side alley. Kulin became very agitated and made urgent signs for Athan to leave. Athan did not have an opportunity to respond before he heard a crash from the back upstairs room followed by the unmistakable thumping sounds of a fight. Kulin had tackled him from behind when Athan tried to up the stairs to investigate. The two women, involved in their own life and death battle did not hear the two men struggling below. In truth it was not much of a fight. Kulin was bigger and stronger than Athan but he was no fighting man. Still he was desperate and Athan had to kick him all the way down the stairs before he could get clear of the porter.

Now, Kulin was back, this time with his club, frantic, looking left and right for his mistress. Athan, to the right of the door, hit him with a roundhouse right that landed squarely on Kulin's chin. Considering that Athan had his fist wrapped around the hilt of his dagger it was amazing the man was not knocked unconscious at once by the blow. He was stunned, however, and fell back against the wall, his hands going to his face. Athan hit him again, this time in the center of his chest. This blow must have hit the simpleton's solar plexus, for he crumpled, gasping and dropping the club. This gave Athan a chance to get in some excellent kicks to the body, and as Kulin finally lost consciousness, to his head.

"Enough," said Persis bringing him back to himself. Both of them were breathing heavily. "Let me think. All right, that will explain it. Yes, I think it will do nicely. But only if she is dead." All this was delivered in a hasty voice, so unlike her normal tones. Athan thought this was as close as he had ever come to seeing Persis flustered.

"That was a close thing," said Athan.

"What?" answered Persis distractedly, "no, not really. If things had gotten out of hand I would have just jumped out the window. I would have landed on my feet."

"No," corrected Athan, "not that. There is a cut on your throat. You are bleeding a little." He looked closely at the small wound. "That much deeper," he held up two fingers side by side as a gauge, "and she would have cut your throat."

Persis put her hand to the place where she suddenly felt a bit of pain; when she brought her had up to her face there was a trace of blood on her fingers. She remembered leaning back just enough from that first sudden backhand slash. She suddenly realized she still had her stiletto in her hand. With a glance at Athan she lifted the skirts of her chiton to slide the weapon back into its sheath.

'Yep,' though Athan admiring a very fine length of leg, 'that was how I thought she kept it.'

Persis seemed to take her time getting the knife back in place. She lifted her skirt even higher to arrange it, then with a final flip settled it back in place. Though people in that time and place were relatively unconcerned about nudity, Athan had never seen so much of Persis' leg. It was a very, very good leg. Athan stood transfixed. Some women, especially wealthy matrons, wore small clothes. Persis did not. Did he just get a glimpse of her Gates of Paradise?

"Thaddeus is a lucky man," was all he could say, still staring at her now decently clothed form.

She gave him a sudden grin and just like that was the old Persis again. "Come on," she urged leading the way, "we have to get down there. I may have to ask you to do something for me." She went over to the wall picked up the awl and headed down to the alley.

Athan had followed Thaddeus into battle several times. Each time he tried to stand either behind or next to him because he knew his friend was an accomplished warrior. Now he followed another friend because she was the smartest person he had ever known. When they rounded the side of the house they found a donkey hitched to a cart loaded with fouled straw partially blocking the way. Persis squeezed by while Athan took advantage of the tarp placed on top of the straw to climb over the cart. Zita was still lying where she had fallen. She had fallen on her head and shoulders; a singer she might have been, but she lacked a dancer's balance. She was alive, but unable to move. Persis knelt beside her for a moment alert for any tricks but it was clear Zita was in a bad way, rolling her eyes and gasping for breath. Once certain the woman posed no further threat, Persis slid the awl under a bit of straw in the cart, then hurried around the corner into the alleyway between Zita's house and the former House of Five Sisters and began screaming.

It did not take very long for people to show up. Even on a quiet hot afternoon, a woman's screams will get people's attention. Before long a small crowd had assembled. Persis told them what had happened: that crazy brute of a porter, Kulin had attacked them. She and Zita had just discovered the knife he used to butcher that poor street girl when he burst in and attacked them. Kulin had thrown poor Zita out the window and was about to kill her when this brave guardsman dashed in and saved her. This was the kind story that drew a crowd in a hurry. Before many more people had arrived, however, Thaddeus was there with one of his trusted sergeants. Soon more of the guard arrived in response to the excitement. Persis clung to her man's neck and whispered into Thaddeus' ear. Some thought he seemed irritated with his woman when he should have been consoling her for her recent ordeal. After a few moments Thaddeus set to work. He detailed some men to arrest Kulin upstairs. Others carefully lifted Zita from the street onto the only conveyance at hand, the covered stable cart. Persis insisted on accompanying her 'friend' to the residence of Zakias where her injuries would be tended. Kulin had recovered enough so that when he was brought down out of the house and saw his mistress being wheeled away on the cart he momentarily broke away from the guardsman on either side of him and tried to charge over to her. This time Athan thought he sounded more like a calf that had lost its mother, but to the crowd he was the very image of a madman trying to finish off another victim. The guards did not stop beating him until he was bloody and unconscious. Then they dragged him away to the Magistrate. Athan decided he would not mention the wound to his thigh. It was painful but it was not particularly deep, and he was able to staunch the bleeding discretely.

Zita tried to speak, but Persis who was walking next to her leaned over and spoke to her in a carrying voice. "There, there, see, we caught the murderer. Don't worry about him any more. Now we are taking you to see Dr. Zakias where we will take care of you."

Perhaps they would have, but the movement of the wagon was too much for the singer's broken neck. On the way there she simply stopped breathing.

The capture of the Mad Butcher was satisfying to almost everyone in the city. Everyone heard the story. How the brave guardsman Athan had been passing by and heard the crazed porter attacking the women; how he had arrived to save the city's most famous hetaira and defeat the monster in single combat though not, unfortunately, in time to save that foreign singer. It enhanced Persis' reputation even more as she became essential at any fashionable symposium, where she had a new and thrilling set of stories.

Even Anteros avoided a beating. When Thaddeus received Athan's hastily scrawled message he hurried home to find a note on a slate leaning face in beside the door.

> *My Darling Husband,*
> *I am convinced that the singer Zita murdered*
> *the girl we found, Ianthe, and Doreen. I am*
> *going to her house to see if I can trick her into*
> *admitting it. Please come quietly with some of*
> *your most trusted men and wait on the roof*
> *of the House of Five Sisters for my signal.*
> *With Love,*
> *Persis*

This note was most unusual: not only did she address Thaddeus as her husband, and declare her love for him; it was also as close as she could come to asking for help. And Thaddeus did help. The next day he brought the case of the Mad Butcher to the Magistrate. There was not much to it. The murder weapon and the dead girl's girdle were found in the same room where he was taken. Two respectable witnesses saw Kulin throw his mistress out the window. It seemed the whole city had seen him try to attack her when he came out of the house. The man had been seen in the vicinity of the butchered girl the night of the murder. He was a foreigner. He looked different. He could not defend himself. He was obviously guilty. There was no mention of Ianthe or Doreen whose deaths remained officially mere misadventures.

Before midmorning, poor Kulin had been condemned. He did not even make it to the place of execution. Outraged citizens first stoned and then hacked him to death on the way there as the guards stood by. His body was thrown in a garbage pit.

Zita had neither friends nor family in Epiria. Persis arranged that her body's trip to the pyre took place that afternoon while Doreen's funeral was still underway. Since Persis had hired every one of Zita's old troupe to attend that more popular funeral procession, Zita's trip to the burning grounds was a lonely one. In fact, only old Doctor Zakias was there to see her off; but at least he did get to spend several hours alone with the remains before setting the pyre alight.

In contrast Doreen had a magnificent funeral. Her ekphora passed through the city with all of singers and hetaira who were to have been part of the Five Sisters in attendance. Doreen was laid to rest with a fine stele in her family's tomb.

Lais, whom Persis thought too plain, became the de facto head of a group of entertainers who functioned much as Doreen had envisioned, and if Lais lacked Doreen's vision she turned out to be a fine administrator. The women and musicians did work together well, and prospered together for years.

After Doreen's funeral, the four friends, together with young Jason in his mother's arms, gathered in Persis' house for a somber dinner together. There, after dinner they reclined on couches drinking wine and listening as Persis told them the whole story, omitting nothing.

"I think she gave me some of poison taken from that fish that inflates," mused Persis after she finished. "It is supposed to paralyze and disorient the victim. I do not know the dosages required. I do know it is hard to find and very expensive. I wonder where she got it." Obviously Persis would like a supply of her own.

"You take too many risks," grumbled Thaddeus.

"This, from a man who has fought a dozen battles!" Persis replied instantly. "You have faced far more dangers that I."

"I am surrounded by doughty comrades. You were alone."

"I left notes!"

"When would I have received it?"

"When the boy delivered it," retorted Persis.

"What boy?" asked Thaddeus.

"The boy that I sent to deliver my notes to you and Athan. Didn't he give it to you?"

"Anteros left a note with the duty officer from Athan," Thaddeus told an increasingly disconcerted Persis.

"I gave one of the street boys two messages, one for you and one for Athan," she said defensively. "I gave him four bits to deliver them first to Athan then to you."

Ajax the porter was called in. He confirmed that the boy had returned half an hour after Persis left and returned, apparently lost and asking for additional directions to the men he was supposed to deliver the messages to. Ajax had sent him away and the boy had simply decamped without delivering his missives.

Somewhat disconcerted, Persis tried to rally, "Well, it all worked out. But Athan, if you didn't get my note to come and wait on the roof of the House of Five Sisters, how did you know where I was?"

Athan was grinning from ear to ear, "I figured it out," he said.

Persis opened her mouth to say something. She stopped and then started again.

"Well," she said weakly, "it took you long enough."

Still grinning, Athan helped up a smiling Erinsys. Together Athan and Erinsys made their courtesies and went back home together to their cottage in the compound. He was only limping a little from the puncture wound in his thigh.

Athan's fortunes rose with his friends. Thaddeus quickly rose to become the Senior Captain of the guards. As Senior Captain, Thaddeus no longer had a company of his own, but assisted the General of the

Guards in his duties. An unexpected death created an opening for a new captain, and with his recently enhanced prestige (and with Persis and Thaddeus subtly aiding his cause) Athan became the youngest Captain of the city guards in years. His promotion was just in time. The birth of his second child had begun to put a strain on the peace of the little cottage, even with Thaddeus often staying with Persis in her house. Now as a captain he was allowed to live in the cottage without staying as the 'guest' of Thaddeus. For his part, Thaddeus simply moved in full time with Persis.

Over time Persis was able to manage not only the rise of her husband, which he had in effect become, but also the transition of her own status as a respected matron. Her popularity was hardly changed as the years passed and with the births of her two daughters, one born within a year of Erinsys' second daughter, the other only a few months after Erinsys' third. Even though Thaddeus and Persis grew to a have a significantly higher social status than Athan and Erinsys, the two couples remained relatively close, with the two women often caring for one another's children. Of course, when they were with Persis, her nurse took care of them.

Another day had passed. The Old King boiled some of the oats originally intended for his pony into porridge and ate it greedily. He decided that if he was careful he had rations for ten or twelve days; well, reduced rations. After that he would be in for a hard time.

It was a strange thing, mused the old man, bad times, frightening times; times of hardship were always vivid in memories. It seemed that they lasted forever. But the good times, the times when all the problems were small and concerns were petty (in retrospect) all seemed to run together in a warm fuzzy haze. 'Those were the good old days' he decided, but individual moments of the contented times seemed hard to remember. And when he did recall them honestly, he knew that at the time things did not seem so easy.

It was cold and dark outside so he banked the fire for another night and lay back down.

Chapter Five – Battles

Athan always thought of the early days of his marriage as the 'good days'. It didn't seem like that at the time, of course. He spent most of his time in boring details around the city. And though he enjoyed the time at home with his children, he also looked forward toward excursions against other fighting men; it was a time of warfare, limited warfare, but serious enough for the participants. Even up in the 'semi-civilized' north there were battles between the armies of the various political entities in the area. Like most armies in this time and place, the Epirian forces consisted of three main fighting elements: phalangists, hypaspists, and peltasts. Only the first two were considered 'real' hoplites, but all were typically engaged in a full battle. The phalangists were considered the backbone of the army. They were made up primarily of the citizens of the city. Phalangists fought as heavy infantry, armed with bronze tipped spears, about as long as a man could reach up with his hand, roughly five cubits. This powerful weapon, referred to sometimes as a 'dorry', could be either thrown or thrust. The men wore a variety of swords, the most common being an iron short sword with a leaf shaped blade. They carried heavy round wooden shields called hoplons, each painted with an individual design, usually of monsters, fierce beasts, or other terrifying and powerful images. Some wealthy men even covered their shield with a thin layer of bronze but this was uncommon; not only was it expensive, it also made the shield very heavy. The most important part of a man's armor was his helmet. Of bronze (often highly polished) the helmets had wide cheek pieces that gave the front of the helmet a Y-shaped appearance. The top of the helmet was adorned with a crest, usually horsehair that ran fore and aft down the center of the helmet. Those were the defining elements of a phalangists' equipment. Additional armor depended upon the wealth of the individual, as all equipment was personally owned, and was not cheap. Most protected their torsos with a cuirass or corselet of layered linen and leather, or in some cases bronze. Often they wore greaves of bronze or leather to protect their shins from nasty strokes that came under the hoplons, but some fought bare legged, even to the point of fighting barefoot. Men who seldom wore shoes developed thick calluses on the bottoms of their feet and many claimed boots or sandals did not give them secure footing.

The second element of a hoplite army was called hypaspists or medium infantry, usually composed of mercenaries or professional soldiers. Normally they were not as heavily armored as the phalangists, but they were still formidable fighters. Like the phalangists, they relied on spears and swords for offense. For armor they wore helmets, but often of a different type than the men who fought in the phalanx; these helmets were almost conical and completely lacked the crests of a full helmet and sometimes had no cheek pieces at all. In fact, they bore more than a passing resemblance to the pilleus worn as headgear by most men who worked outdoors. Hypaspists' helmets were not always of bronze, but were sometimes made of reinforced leather instead. They provided less protection, but were lighter, gave better visibility, were more comfortable, and were much cheaper. On the downside, they presented a much less formidable appearance to the enemy. Hypaspists used different shields than phalangists as well. They carried light shields of layered wood or ox hide-covered wicker in a rectangular, oval, or figure 8 shape. As with the helmets, protection was reduced for the sake of reduced weight and cost. Men fighting as hypaspists would wear cuirasses similar to the heavy infantry, and might or might not wear greaves.

The major difference between phalangists and hypaspists was the way in which they were used in battle. Phalangists usually fought in tight formations four, six or even eight men deep, with hoplons overlapping, using their spears as primary weapons. Hypaspists operated in more open formations than phalangists. They would avoid the charge of a phalanx of phalangists, but could easily brush aside any peltasts who were pestering the phalangists with their missiles. The main difficulty in fielding a substantial force of hypaspists was that they required advanced training to be effective. Since they lacked the prestige of phalangists and it required a lot of time to maintain the high level of training required, they were almost always professional soldiers. A large force of such fighters was an expense few cities could afford. This was the reason those who were so employed were also used as guardsmen, acting as the civic watch to keep order within the city and in pursuit of bandits and brigands. They were also expected to help train the militia in how to fight as phalangists when the militia had their periodic training sessions.

The third element of an army in this time and place was the peltasts. These were light troops including javelin throwers, slingers, and bowmen. Powerful bows were uncommon, and even fewer men were able to use them effectively, so the weapon of choice tended to be the javelin. With little or no armor beyond a light shield, and only a long dagger as a close-in weapon, they relied on their projectile weapons to sting the enemy and their speed to stay out of the way of the real warriors. These fighters were always young active men, either from the poorer classes or younger sons who did not yet have the money necessary to become a proper hoplite.

Cavalry were seldom used in battle in this region. First, most of the horses in this time and place were actually more like ponies, too small to be really effective in battle. In fact there was little difference between ponies and horses in that time and place and the two terms were sometimes used interchangeably. Second, the rugged terrain of the area was simply not good horse country. Third, few had the time and money necessary to learn to ride and keep horses trained for war. Finally, fighting from horses just wasn't done, it was not forbidden; the culture just did not expect men to fight on horseback. Although hoplites, especially hypastas might ride the little ponies to get from place to place, they would almost always dismount when it came time to fight. This was not true in other areas. The armies of the plains had larger horses and incorporated them in their armies as cavalry. These were larger animals, trained for war and their riders knew how to use them. But true cavalry was not effective in the region where Athan lived, and besides, all the armies that used numbers of horsemen were far away to the east.

When hoplite armies of approximately equal size met, the basic plan of battle was for the two sides to form up opposite one another. Final negations were often conducted between the leaders to try to avoid the battle. If these failed, the forces would close one another on a mutually acceptable site, usually a flat area with firm footing. This was a limiting factor in regions such as Epirus, since the terrain tended to be hilly when it was not frankly mountainous. But, if a suitable site could be found, the two armies would form up and shift back and forth, trying to find some advantage before closing. During this time it would often happen that a champion or two would come out from the lines to challenge the enemy. This was a ritual that was watched and enjoyed by both sides as individual warriors met between lines and fought. These were almost always either young men looking for fame or seasoned champions eager to demonstrate their skill at arms in front of their friends and neighbors. On occasion, there would be a dozen or more of these combats in front of the lines, with the individual fights going on so long that sometimes light failed before the armies came to grips. Since all this required a good deal of time and mutual consent, full-fledged battles between the hoplite armies of city-states might only happen a few times in a generation.

When armies of hoplites did come to battle, actual combat tended to follow a fairly set procedure. Peltasts would issue from the flanks and dash forward shooting arrows, hurling javelins, and slinging stones and lead shot at the massed ranks of phalangists. Since these launched weapons were not especially powerful and their targets were well protected, the projectiles were usually ineffective against the formations of well armored men. Sometimes, however, if the formation was shifting, or the men in it were irresolute, a hail of projectiles would upset the center long enough for a charge by the other side to be effective. While the phalangists endured the peltasts, the hypaspists would move out, probing the flanks of the enemy formation at the same time trying to prevent the enemy's light infantry from doing the same. If an organized formation of hypaspists could get behind the enemy phalanx, they could do great harm. At the very least, the rear rank of the enemy phalangists would have to turn to address the threat weakening the formation and making it vulnerable to the primary arbiter of battle, the charge of a phalanx. The sight of hundreds of heavily armed and armored men, advancing with their hoplons overlapping, helmets shining in the sun, clashing their spears against their hoplons, and singing their dreadful war chants, presented a truly terrifying image. A formation might break and run before the charge, usually resulting in a slaughter as the charging phalangists overran and killed the brave men who stood to fight or the slow and wounded who could not run fast enough to stay ahead of the charge. The hypaspists would kill and harry the fleeing enemy from the flanks. Even peltasts would chase and kill an enemy in flight. If individual hoplites turned to face them, they were swept away by the oncoming enemy infantry who advanced in an irresistible formation.

Sometimes, the enemy would stand in place and absorb the charge. Then would come 'The Push'; man against man, hoplon to hoplon with each side trying to push the other back like some gigantic scrum. Hypaspists fought to keep their opposite numbers from interfering from the flanks or rear, and did what they could to attack the enemy. Peltasts stood clear and cheered for their men. Sometimes one side or the other would break, turn and run, and the slaughter would begin. Sometimes both sides would exhaust themselves until eventually both lines, still intact, would disengage. Usually such an outcome was considered a draw, and the opposing armies would withdraw the next day.

The most dramatic (and by far the least common) confrontation was when both armies charged simultaneously and met together a full speed. Over a thousand armored men crashing into each other at full speed made a dreadful sound that could be heard for half a medimnos. Sometimes both lines would hold and battle would revert to the 'The Push'. But if both lines broke at about the same time, fighting men would intermingle in a huge murderous brawl. Athan had never seen this happen, but Thaddeus and a few of the other old veterans had, and they spoke of it with awe and dread. It was a truly terrible scene, usually resulting in great casualties on both sides. Even the victorious army was usually left so mauled as to render it ineffective for battle for many months.

The force that marched out on an autumn excursion to disperse a large troublesome band of hill brigands was made up primarily of citizen militia fighting as phalangists. The militia consisted of men less than 40 years of age who could vote, and that meant all men who owned some property in or around the city. The militia was not an inconsiderable fighting force. Each man had been trained since youth to fight as part of his basic education. The men in the ranks knew one another, and many were personal friends. There was a bond between the men within the militia that translated into a comradeship that could stand the test of battle. The majority of the militia was made up of veterans of many excursions, many other battles. They were well equipped, disciplined, and organized. When the phalangists stood in their ranks, hoplon to hoplon, holding their spears ahead of them in a powerful formation, they were almost irresistible, and they knew it.

This expedition was not expected to result in a full battle and for that Athan was glad. He had participated in three battles in the dozen or so years he had been a guardsman, one of them as a captain of his own company. He had never had been in the prestigious front line, and that was fine with him. If Athan had to fight, he much preferred battling against smaller numbers of raiders or bandits with his own hypaspists and some peltasts. He had been on expeditions against bandits with phalangists before, and only once had the heavily equipped soldiers been useful.

Thaddeus was the leading captain of the expedition. Such was his prestige and reputation that when two hundred phalangists came with them, even though they comprised some of the leading citizens of the city, they followed the famous captain's lead without question. Their enemy was a group of several score Dorians and some local Dassaretae hill men, who had gone beyond raiding and had actually set up a permanent camp in a valley some 10 parasangs from the city. Thaddeus had gone ahead with a handful of trusted men, taking along local guides for a personal reconnaissance of the enemy's camp. Thaddeus and Athan had actually crept to the edge of the steep valley where the bandits had their base of operations. To their right a wooden palisade blocked the lower end of the valley. The palisade was topped with a low watchtower. To their left a stream issued from a spring near the head of the valley and ran down, past the camp, and out past the gate in the timber wall.

"Nice place," said Thaddeus. "A deathtrap if you let the enemy get past that little wall there, but a nice place. Fortunately for us they have made too many mistakes."

Athan gave him a questioning look.

"First," explained the old soldier, "if this is a band of brigands, they are too many. If they are soldiers, they are too few, especially if they expect to hold ground so close to the city. And they did a poor job in setting up this camp. That little watchtower there is too low to see far and, look you, see that dead ground?" Thaddeus pointed out, referring to a shallow gully that hid anyone inside it from the view of the watchtower. "It runs almost all the way up to the tower if you approach from that ravine over there on the far side. And they have no one watching this side of the ridgeline. Athan," he said turning to the junior captain, "do you think you can get your boys up here without being noticed from down there in the valley?"

"Yes, but what good will we do from way up here?"

"Well, for one thing, you can leave a man here to signal if they are regrouping or preparing an ambush. But once the attack starts I want you to lead your boys up the ridgeline to that spur there and come out just above the spring. There is a place where you can form up your company into a battle line. If we haven't broken them by that time, you bring your men down and attack their line from the rear. But I think we will have them on the run by then, so all you need to do is block that trail that leads up past that spring at the head of the valley and wait for them to either try to climb out the cliffs individually or surrender. You might bring a few peltasts to discourage too many of them from leaving."

"If we get there and form up we can hold that high ground forever. But what will keep them from heading up there to the same spring and forming up as soon as you attack?"

"Because they do not understand the art of war. No, I should not say that. It is never wise to underestimate your enemy. I don't think they will withdraw and form up, because I think everyone down there will focus on our phalangists at the wall. The brave ones will want to fight right there; the cowards among them will run up the valley away from the battle. Should those rascals retreat up the valley in good order, try to get up to that spring first; I will press them as hard as I can and try to slow them down. Even if they did get up there and form up, they would still have you menacing their rear. At worst it will be a draw, and we will find another way to kill them tomorrow."

Athan had heard Thaddeus say that before; he remembered he had repeated the same thing to himself the night he had killed Phineas. But he knew Thaddeus expected his officers to understand the whole plan. "How will you take the palisade?" Athan asked.

"I will use some picked hoplites and all the rest of the peltasts. They will move up to the tower late tonight using that dead ground for cover and wait until it is just light enough to see. Then they will climb the walls using ropes and ladders under cover of the peltasts. The wall is too low to be much of a barrier. Once over the wall they will open the gate from the inside and wait for the heavies to show up. While all that is going on I will bring up the phalangists and batter down the door if it is not already open. Once on the other side I can form up and move up the valley at my leisure."

It was a hard scramble up the hill for Athan's company that night. Even with two guides moving ahead leaving trail markers, some of the men lost their way. One put his foot wrong and fell end over end down a steep slope. They left him where he lay, to either recover or await burial. In either event, no one could be spared to help him until after the battle. It was past dawn and the sounds of fighting were coming up clearly from below by the time Athan reached the ridgeline. He could not make out details, but he was able to see the gates swung open wide. Tiny figures below were shouting and making their way by ones and twos toward the palisade. In the distance he saw the glint of sunlight off the spears and helmets of the approaching phalanx.

Athan, still breathless from his climb, knew he could not wait. "Come on men," he panted, exhorting others to follow him up the ridgeline to the spring. It turned out to be a long hard run for a man wearing a cuirass, helmet and greaves, a sword and carrying a spear and shield. By the time he got to his assigned place over the spring, blocking the enemy's escape, his legs were weak and his lungs were burning. He stopped long enough to take a deep draft from the cold spring water. At once he felt revived. Perhaps this was due to relief of arriving at his assigned location ahead of the enemy, or the cessation of hard work and the knowledge he could rest, but Athan decided to credit the spring. "Come, this is the magic spring of Ares!" he called to his men. "Drink from it and be revived! With this drink in you no enemy can stand before you!"

The word spread like wildfire. Before long his men were hurrying over from the ridgeline to drink from the 'magic spring'. Men who tottered to the spring, gasping for breath rose a few moments later full of life and energy. At Athan's direction, his sergeants pushed the men into formation. A few of the hill men came scrambling up the hillside, and seeing the force of Epirian hypaspists formed and waiting, darted up faint side trails that scrambled up the far ridge. Athan's men were in excellent humor; they were young and fit, standing in a position of advantage side by side with their friends, and they were winning. It was one of those glorious mornings that happen in late autumn after the heat of summer breaks but before Old Man Winter shows his ugly face. It was just cool enough to have made their exertions pleasantly warming. The sky was cloudless and the air was crystal clear, giving the men a great view of the slaughter down below.

Captain Thaddeus had formed his hoplites in a shallow V formation only two or three men deep, much thinner than usual. He had put strong but loose formations of hypaspists on each wing where the ground sloped steeply upward. Higher up on those slopes peltasts skipped nimbly back and forth, shooting down at anyone that tried to reach them. The formation was moving slowly but steadily uphill. From time to time a group of men would assault the heavily armed hoplites, but each time even with the slope in their favor they would be pushed back, leaving their dead on the ground. Athan's troops had been in fully deployed in position for almost an hour when he saw the signaler on the ridge flashing a bronze mirror at him. It was a simple code; this signal was 'advance slowly'. Athan knew what his mentor wanted. Calling his sergeants, he gave them simple directions. Form the men into an inverted wedge formation like the one they could see down in the valley. Move slowly and carefully to cut off any escape up possible goat tracks that led over the ridges. Grind them down against the hoplite formation. They moved slowly and carefully down the valley. It took the rest of the morning, but it kept his casualties low. Shortly after noon the last group of surviving Dorians surrendered. Only a handful had escaped, and few had more than the clothes on their backs. Those captives that had been held in the bandit's camp were released. The fighting men who had surrendered were bound and prepared for slavery. The bandit's camp followers were rounded up and the women were duly raped (as was the deplorable custom) and prepared for slavery as well. By nightfall it was getting cold; the miserable captives sat huddled together shivering in the shelter of the palisades, guarded by cloaked hoplites. Athan wondered what it would be like to be one of those "lucky" few who had escaped over the ridgeline on a cold night like this. Cold, alone, with no fire and with bad weather coming, many of them would probably die cold and lonely in the wilderness. As he looked at the miserable survivors of the Dorian brigands, Athan made two promises to himself: always have a means of making fire on your person, and never, never, never allow yourself to be captured.

The Old King twitched in his sleep, an old nightmare coming back to him.

Turning his back on the disintegrating Epirian army, Captain Athan bellowed in his best battleground voice, "TO ME HYPASPISTS! Form up on me! If you want to live, you miserable curs, come to me and form up! Sergeants!"

"Here Captain," came several voices in the tumult.

"Form them up; provide mutual support. We are getting off this ridge and moving to the west. We are going to wait until things settle down and then march home together. Form up and provide mutual support."

He turned his back on the army behind him, driving his men up the slope and away from the immediate danger. He knew what he was leaving behind him, an Epirian army being slaughtered and beyond them their camp, now undefended from a horde of hill brigands and Dorian raiders. The camp held the army's possessions and the camp followers. Those camp followers included his wife Erinsys, his ten-year-old son Jason, and his infant daughter.

"To me stragglers, up the hill and form up if you want to live!"

You saved what you could and gave up the rest.

The Old King awoke with at start from the nightmare that was an all too real memory. It was light out again, but it was the thin weak light of a sun trying to shine through a thick layer of clouds. He got up long enough to relieve himself and get a drink of water. He felt weak; his forehead seemed hot to him. The old man was not sure, but he suspected he was running a fever. This was more than rare,, he almost never got sick. In fact, he could not remember the last time he had been ill. No colds, no fevers, no indigestion, headaches, nothing. He knew that this was unusual, but like most of the unusual things in his life he did not dwell on it. And now, just when he was at his most vulnerable, he was getting sick.

There was nothing else to do but lie back down. Soon he was dreaming again. And he could not prevent himself from going back to a day he worked very hard to not remember, perhaps the worst day of his long life.

Chapter Six– Achilles' Debacle

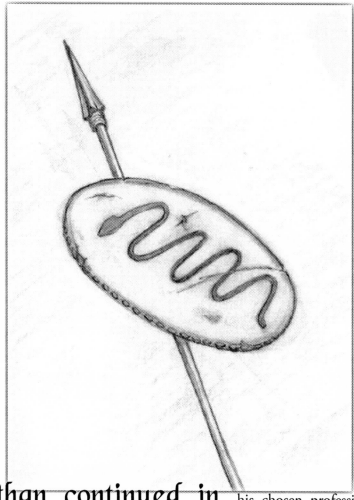

Athan continued in his chosen profession; a combination beat cop, drill sergeant, frontier marshal and foot soldier. It was interesting work, though in fact not especially dangerous. The main chance to get hurt or killed was when the guard mounted an expedition against strong bands of bandits in the hills. Sometimes these men had the support of neighboring states, and there was always a chance the enemy would turn out not to be a small band of robbers, but instead a well armed force that outnumbered the men sent out to remove them. But this was of small concern to Athan and his growing family. He enjoyed his work, was advancing in his career, his wife was as satisfied as she could be, and his children were happy. Life was good. And it might have remained that way for the rest of his life. But Athan's life, and those of everyone he loved, was to change dramatically, and all in one very bad day.

Two years after Thaddeus crushed the Dorian bandits, another expedition was sent into the hills. It started out as another routine move to counter increasing depredations of hill bandits in the hills to the north and east. The brigands had gone beyond raiding caravans and started attacking outlying villages and farmsteads. The price of food had gone up. Farmers had begun to leave their remote homesteads and move into the city for protection. Two of the four current companies of guards had been called up, along with some supporting mercenaries and the city's militia.

A man named Demetrius used his influence to be named general of the punitive expedition. He was one of the leading oligarchs of the city, a wealthy land owner and an experienced soldier with the militia. General Demetrius had served with some distinction two years before, when Thaddeus had crushed scores of similar Dorian raiders. According to scouts, this band consisted mostly of hill brigands - men of no city - who made a precarious living in the hills, mostly by preying on caravans and unprotected farms. And once again there were reports of soldiers from the Dorian cities to the east supporting the brigands.

In order to ensure his success and to justify the title of general, Demetrius was able to convince the military council to take most of the militia and two companies of guardsmen, reinforced by men from the other companies and some additional mercenaries hired for the expedition as well.

"It is foolishness," complained Thaddeus, "with that many men he won't be able to catch anyone. And while he has the main force of the city out chasing bandits, we will barely have enough to protect the city from a sudden raid. A sudden foray by a thousand warriors coming down from Illyria and the city might fall. Demetrius is a brave soldier, but I doubt he has the wit to catch these hill men. They will lure him half way to Doria and vanish in the hills, leaving him to wander home through a series of nasty little ambushes."

"Oh, you worry too much, Thaddeus,' replied his loyal friend. "I very much doubt there will be any fighting, those brigands will be long gone before we get there, but at least it will be safe. That is why I am taking young Jason. It will give him an adventure and a little taste of military life. Erinsys is coming along with the little one to keep an eye on me. And Erinsys is bringing Karin along to try to restrain Jason."

Athan had enough money now that he could afford a slave girl to help Erinsys. Karin was a girl of about 15. Taken as a captive at a child, she had avoided the usual rapes and degradations that usually accompanied such captures and for the last four years had been owned by Athan. Karin had replaced Athan as the chief source of Erinsys' displeasure; well, most of the time anyway. Although the poor girl was driven to distraction at times by her demanding mistress and the requirements of cleaning the cottage, preparing food, and watching over four young children, Karin also knew she was on the whole, lucky. Not only did Athan not sexually abuse her, but she was protected by both Athan and Erinsys from mistreatment by others. If her duties were hard, they were not altogether unpleasant. She did love the children and she was seldom beaten and then only by Erinsys. She was especially close to Jason, and was far better at keeping him out of trouble than his mother.

"Late spring is a strange time for these raids," mused Thaddeus. "We have never had raids in late spring before. I presume Persephone and Dionme," referring to Athan's two middle daughters, "will be staying at Persis' establishment."

"Yes, it is amusing to watch Erinsys when she has the girls stay with Persis. She bathes and dresses them like they were going to be presented to a king or something. Even after all this time, I think she is a little intimidated by Persis."

"Smart woman," observed Thaddeus, "she scares me, too."

"What about your own daughters?" teased Athan, "I thought they were the ones who frightened you."

"Them most of all."

"Well, while Erinsys and I have a leisurely tour of the highlands searching for brigands who will undoubtedly flee our ponderous force, you and Persis will double the number of daughters in your house."

"Well, the girls love it when Persephone and Dionme come to stay with us. Besides, it is not my problem," grunted the old soldier. "Not Persis' either; she just dresses them up during the day and tells them stories in the evening. She has her servants and the nurse to handle all the unpleasant jobs."

"Well, when you are a rich and famous hetaira with the city's leading soldier as your protector, I guess you can avoid the unpleasant jobs."

Four days later the bulk of the city's fighting force sallied forth from the city on a rainy spring day. First came the scouts, well in advance of the main body, avoiding the departure ceremony. Next a company of hypaspists marched by, wearing their best uniforms with helmets and weapons shining. This company was commanded by Captain Fedras, the most senior of the guard captains. He rode a pony with his helmet hanging from his saddle showing off his long silver hair. He was a fine soldier and a good captain, but both Thaddeus and Athan thought him unimaginative and not especially bright. Next came the heart of the army, the phalangist militia with General Demetrius at their head, riding a horse. Here were men who had undertaken their civic duty to defend their city from foreign invaders. They did not exactly march out in step, but they were walking together in well-ordered ranks. Many had flowers adorning their armament, gifts from wives, sweethearts, and family members. They were followed by the young peltasts. After them came the inevitable accompaniments of war, carts and wagons pulled by donkeys or ponies. Then came the other pack animals. Intermingled in this traffic were the drovers, quartermasters, wives, sweethearts (who thought of themselves as potential wives) whores, children, and merchants hoping to sell their goods at higher rates to soldiers out in the field. Finally, there was the rear guard commanded by Captain Athan, a junior captain but a man of very good reputation. He had had an active career, with many successful battles, skirmishes, ambushes, and lesser scraps to his credit, including a prominent place in the great victory two years before. By the time his company left the city, the crowds had thinned to nothing; his men's lines were ragged as they had to step carefully to avoid the leavings of the many animals that had preceded them. Their attitude was resigned. It was just another day of work.

Erinsys had purchased the use of a donkey to carry the family's possessions. This allowed them certain luxuries, such as their own tent, better food, and extra clothes, but it also meant additional responsibilities. Burdened by an infant just on the verge of being a toddler and a very excited 10-year-old boy, Erinsys was nearly at her wits' end. Karin was now fully engaged in leading their donkey cart and could not keep an eye on Jason. The boy took advantage to race up and down the column, easily eluding his distracted mother. By the time the rear guard came up to the little army's campsite that evening, Athan's family was more than ready to rest. Athan took his meals with his soldiers, and then attended an officer's council of war at the tent of Demetrius, who was now insisting on being called 'General Achilles'. Captain Athan was not particularly well educated, but he did know that the legendary Achilles was supposed to have sulked in his tent during the Trojan Wars. He also knew the difference between an effective, well-run council of war and the rambling discussion that went on in the tent of 'General Achilles'. He left still uncertain of the basic plan of battle in the event of a hasty engagement, the overall plan for trapping the bandits if they found them; he did not even how long the army would be in the field. There was no discussion of plans for resupply. Captain Athan could only suppose that the army would wander around the hills hoping that some of the scouts would discover the enemy before they ran out of food and had to return to the city. He was certain that any bandits in the area would know about this ponderous force long before they were themselves discovered, and would easily avoid contact. So perhaps that was the plan: an overwhelming show of force designed to cause the bandits to withdraw.

Captain Athan was wrong about two things. Four days after their departure from Epiria, a caravan of supplies reached the army. And three days after that, the bandits made contact with them.

The army was making its way back toward the city, expecting to return in only two more days, when reports came in from scouts that a strong band of bandits had attacked one of the patrols. The bandits had retreated over a hill to a valley northwest, and were apparently stopping for the night in the valley. This all seemed very odd to Captain Athan. The army had passed this spot on the way north not four days before, and there had been no sign of the enemy. He had been over the west ridge of that particular valley himself and had seen nothing suspicious. And why would they attack a well-armed patrol? There was no profit in attacking a band of soldiers unless you could easily defeat them. And why attack when there was such a strong force nearby?

"They are stupid bandits," rationalized 'General Achilles' in his tent that evening. He had immediately turned his force to the northwest and made camp near a stream less than a parasang from a low hill that sat in front of the entry to the valley. This valley ran generally north-south and was cut into a larger ridge that ran generally east-west.

Scouts reported the bandits were still camped on the other side of the hill at the foot of a valley. They could see campfires for over a hundred men. 'General Achilles' was delighted at the news. It was clear he intended to try to duplicate or even improve upon Captain Thaddeus' great victory of two years before.

"Captain Fedras, take your company and move around the hill on the right then go past them up the east side of the valley until you get to the big ridge. Then move back west along the ridgeline behind them to cut them off. Captain Athan will do the same on the west side of the valley then move east along the top of the ridge. Your two companies will meet in at the head of the valley where that road comes up from the valley below. I will advance with the main force of phalangists up the valley and push them into you."

"I beg your pardon," protested Captain Fedras, but it will be far faster for the bandits to retreat up the road than for us to make our way up to that ridge. How can we get there to block them before they escape?"

"You must leave soon enough to get a good head start. Further, I will not advance the main body until you are well up the ridgeline."

"Excuse me, general," interjected Captain Athan, "but what will prevent them from escaping behind us on the road that runs east and west in front of the valley once we have crossed over and gone up the ridge. There will be nobody to stop them leaking off left and right and they won't have to retreat north up the valley."

"Because we will be advancing in a V formation that will cut them off," replied the 'General Achilles' triumphantly. "Really Captain, I was assured you knew something of the art of war. Didn't you pay attention to Thaddeus two years ago?" His aides and militia captains chuckled. No one mentioned that this cumbersome plan required the General to simultaneously delay the advance of his main body to allow the hypaspists to encircle the enemy, while advancing the same body rapidly to prevent the bandits from escaping east and west from the mouth of the valley. Even worse, the plan required the enemy to remain where they were and wait to be attacked. This violated one of the things stressed to Athan by Thaddeus: 'do not expect your enemy to accommodate you.' But so confident were the men that not even Athan had misgivings about violating another one of the fundamental tenants taught by Thaddeus: 'do not divide your forces in the face of the enemy'. It was true that Thaddeus had sent Athan's men up the hill in his most recent victory, but Athan's company was a small part of the total force in action that day, and Thaddeus knew exactly how many enemy he faced and he had overwhelming force to oppose them. Now, even though he was still unaware of the full size of the enemy opposing him, the General intended to split his force in three parts that would be unable to support one another. It was true they had reports of campfires for only about a hundred men, but that was all the intelligence about the enemy they had.

Discussions and debates continued for some time, with the two guardsman captains protesting that they lacked enough troops to leave some men behind to guard the valley road. The various militia captains did not want to be detailed out of the battle as mere "road guards", and have to watch while their friends advanced up the valley and gained the glory of crushing this band of brigands. Eventually, the two most junior hoplite captains were each detailed a small body of troops and instructed to move down to block the east-west road against any bandits from escaping before the main body moved up to push them up the valley. The two young officers protested loudly about being relegated to this useless duty.

"We are hoplites, not road guards," one of them protested, but to no avail.

There was no discussion of contingency plans, rally points, and no mention of signaling.

Captain Athan left the council certain that tomorrow would be a long hard day's work, with nothing to show for it at the end of the day but a few unlucky bandits and a cloud of dust disappearing over the northern ridgeline. Still he was uneasy about the weak guard left for the camp. All the hypaspists were needed to surround the bandits and none of the phalangists wanted to miss an easy victory. Only a few men were left to guard the baggage train, the sick, and the camp followers. Athan knew that if a number of the bandits were able to slip past the main body, such a rich target might tempt them to attempt a quick raid.

"Beloved," he addressed Erinsys, "After I leave, I want you to pack up our things and go back to the city. I will get Philo to escort you Kiren, and the children. Perhaps some of the other women will go as well. Philo," Athan turned to an older hypaspist, a fellow guardsman he had known longer than he had known his wife, "As soon as it is daybreak take my wife and children and her servant and head them back the way we came to the city. If any of those bandits get around the lines and head this way, go straight down the hills and make for the city. I am sure with a half day head start you can stay ahead of them."

"No," said Erinsys, "we will stay in the camp. Do you think we would be safer out in these wild mountains with just one man to protect us? There are a score or more of men here. We will be safer here."

"There are things to attract bandits here," retorted her husband, and few of the men here are fighting men. Besides, the aftermath of a battlefield is no place for children. You can go home a day ahead of me and make ready for our return."

"Listen, my peach" this was a danger sign, Erinsys only called him 'my peach' when she was in danger of losing her temper with him, "you will need the talents of the mighty Philo more than I. Philo, stay with my husband and keep him safe. Husband, I will prepare our goods, and if we are threatened we will withdraw as you requested."

Athan was trapped. If he ordered Philo to force her to leave, Erinsys would make Philo's life miserable for the entire trip back; and his life miserable for months. Perhaps he was being too cautious; after all, the main body of the army was between her and harm.

She helped him decide, "Go fight our foes, my hero," she told him, "and send Philo away. We have things to discuss in private, you and I."

It was not like her to use sweetness and feminine whiles on him. He relented and sent Philo to tell the sergeants to muster the men at midnight for the night march. "And see they are fed," he directed, "I don't know how long it will be before we can get a good meal again."

When he left his wife a few hours later, she was asleep. He did not wake her or the children to say goodbye.

Things did not go well from the first. Captain Athan was not surprised; things never went well at the start of a maneuver, especially on a night march. The men were slow in forming up. The company got lost and then became scattered going up toward the side of the ridge they had been assigned to climb, so it was necessary to call a halt to regroup his tired men at the side of the hill just below the valley's rim. The first faint signs of dawn were showing before the Captain was able to get his men moving up toward the top of the valley. Athan moved over and crested the rise to a point where he could see the enemy camp off to his right. Their campfires were still burning brightly. 'Maybe General Achilles is right,' Athan thought, 'maybe they are that stupid. Why else make themselves so conspicuous?'

He had to keep reminding his scouts to pick a route below the crest of the hill that hid the men from the enemy camp as much as possible, and his sergeants to keep the men from wandering up to peer over the crest down into the valley. This western side of the ridge rose up perhaps two hundred feet above the floor of the valley; the east ridgeline, less than a third of a parasang away across the little valley was half again as high. Though neither of the slopes up to the head of the valley was especially steep, they were still a stiff climb, especially to armed and armored men. Remembering how thirsty he had been when he arrived at Spring of Ares at his last battle, Athan had insisted that each man carry a water bag, so that they would have a chance to refresh themselves at head of the valley before taking the enemy in the rear or, more likely, chasing the band over the next ridge.

By the time the last of the men were headed up the west ridge toward the head of the valley, it was full light. It was a cloudy spring day, very humid, but not yet too warm. There was rain out there somewhere, but probably not today. It would be a steaming and uncomfortable day when the sun got high. Looking behind him Athan could see no sign of the band of hoplites detailed to block the road. Captain Athan left a handful of his hypaspists behind when they had crossed the road on their way uphill as a deterrent to small groups of the bandits who might slide around the front of the oncoming hoplite army and menace the camp.

"Just stay here until you see your relief coming," he ordered them. "In the meantime, make yourself conspicuous to keep any stragglers from escaping west down the road past you."

Now that the sun was up Athan moved over the crest and stopped on a small knob half way up the valley. Looking down into the valley, he saw that things were continuing to go wrong. He could see plainly Captain Fedras's hypaspists coming over the hill on the far side of the camp. They were making no attempt at concealment, and their formation was badly disorganized. Down in the valley well ahead of them, Athan could make out over a hundred men retreating up the north/south valley road away from their camp of last night. There was nothing disorganized about their withdrawal. They had undoubtedly known about the Epirian army on the other side of the hill and scouts had certainly warned them at the first sign of movement towards them. There was one bit of good news; the main part of the enemy column was no farther up the valley than Athan's men. If he hurried he may be able to get his men to the head of the valley before all the brigands got over.

But that was probably not going to happen, because General Achilles could not restrain himself. Seeing his enemy before him and clearly escaping, he had sent his phalangists up in pursuit. This would probably spur the escaping brigands to increase their pace rather than hinder them. But there was a chance the phalangists would come in contact with the hill men's rear guard and slow them long enough to let Athan's men get to the ridge top. His scouts had found a good path that made the climb easier but sloped away west down below the crest and away from the valley on his right. This made his route longer, but on the other hand, it did help conceal them better from the bandits in the valley. He and his company headed up this route, temporarily taking them out of sight of the men in the valley below. For nearly an hour Athan's men trudged up the incline, safely out of sight of the enemy below.

He heard the shouts of dismay from his men at the front of his column before he saw the looming disaster himself. The shouts and calls were like the calls of helpless spectators on a shore watching a ship cast on the rocks by a storm, powerless to help the doomed mariners. Captain Athan pushed through his leading elements, just below their side of the ridgeline and gained the top of the ridge where he could look down again into the valley below. Behind him most of his men were still toiling toward the ridgeline that marked the head of the valley. The ridge was now only a few bowshots ahead of them and perhaps a dozen cubits up. In the valley to his right and just below him he saw the Epirian phalangists now being heavily engaged by the brigand's equivalent of peltasts. Just below the top of the valley the slope had steepened, and the enemy was hurling down javelins and stones with some effect. The extra height meant that each missile coming down had greater force while the replies of the few peltasts in front of the hoplites below were ineffectual. The Epirian formation, already thin and straggling, was slowing even more as the heavily burdened phalangists struggled uphill to come to grips with their foe. Bodies of men who had been wounded or merely collapsed from exhaustion marked the phalanx's ascent. But the punishment being given to the Epirian phalanx was not the cause of his men's dismay.

From his position on the ridge he could look down just below him to the very head of the valley. Moving over the crest of the low hill at the head of the valley, still invisible to the struggling men below, were well-ordered ranks of hoplites. These were no bandits; they were phalangists. Not a band of hill men or lightly armed raiders, but fully equipped, disciplined, well-organized, deadly Dorian phalangists. Athan estimated at nearly a thousand of them followed by several hundred hill men and Dorian hypaspists and ominously, mounted cavalrymen on tall horses. What were horsemen doing here? Where had cavalry come from? Dorians did not use cavalry; or did they?

The Epirian forces were outnumbered by the Dorians, but it was far more serious than that. The Epirian formation had become even more scattered in the grueling ascent. The Epirian phalangists were tired from the long climb up the ridge; they were downhill from the enemy, and worst of all, were utterly unprepared for what was about to fall upon them. Athan's men on the ridgeline were shouting and waving to their comrades just below them but the distance was too great. On the far side of the formation he could see the lead elements of Captain Fedras's men also trying to warn their comrades, but it was no use. 'If I had one of Thaddeus' flags or mirrors, at least the phalangists could stop, set themselves and try to form up to receive the charge,' Athan thought hopelessly.

But they had no such devices or any plans for using them. Captain Athan watched with his men from up on the side of the valley as the leading hoplites finally saw their danger. He saw a swirl of activity, saw a man sitting on a pony that had to be 'General Achilles' gesturing, and saw the Dorian formation come pouring over the top of the valley, and then smashing down on the Epirians in an irresistible avalanche. In an instant the Epirian line disintegrated, the battle was over, and the slaughter began.

Looking at the far flank he saw Captain Fedras's hypaspists were now also being attacked; that galvanized him to his own danger. Just in the nick of time he came to himself and began to give orders, bringing his shocked men back to order moments before they too were attacked from men sweeping up from the valley on their right and from the front by a mixed formation of hill men and Dorian hypaspists who came over the ridgeline in front of them.

"TO ME HYPASPISTS! Form up on me! If you want to live, you miserable curs, come to me and form up! Sergeants!"

"Here Captain," came several voices in the tumult.

"Form them up! We are going up that hill to the top of the ridgeline and to move down it to the west. We are going to wait until things settle down and then march home together. Form up in column and provide mutual support." Athan could feel sudden sweat as he realized his desperate situation. 'It wasn't exactly fair', thought Athan; 'win a score of battles all you get is your pay. Lose just one and you get killed.' He was more upset about the likely deaths of his men than his own impending demise. They had trusted in him, followed him, and now it looked like he was going to get them killed. None of this would have happened if Captain Thaddeus had been in command, but he was not even on the field. 'General Achilles' was the commander who was responsible for this debacle, but Athan and his men would be the ones to pay. Captain Athan looked down at the slaughter going on to his right; his men were not the only ones paying. The Epirian heavy infantry were fleeing down the valley and the Dorians and their hill bandit allies were harrying them relentlessly. And now worst of all, there were enemy cavalry coming over the top of the valley and spurring down in pursuit; not mounted hoplites, real cavalry. Where had the Dorians gotten cavalry? As he watched, men began to throw down their hoplons and spears and run, as if there was a chance of outrunning their doom. A man in armor had no chance to outrun cavalry. There was nothing Athan or his men could do for their comrades down there. It was time for Athan to see if he could save any of his own men.

Captain Athan refused his right flank, bending the rear of his line around to face the threat on that side, and ordered his men to make a charge uphill. That sudden attack pushed aside the hill men that stood between the hypaspists and the top of the ridge before they could be reinforced. Once at the summit, he formed a strong rear guard and moved along the ridge top which trended west; far better to stay on the high ground than to try to run. He took one last look at the battleground. On the far right side of the valley, Captain Fedras's company had disintegrated. They had been badly strung out before the attack, and they had been attacked by even greater numbers of the enemy than Athan's troop. He thought he glimpsed Fedras' pony down and thrashing. He was certain that he saw dozens if not scores of enemy horsemen down in the valley pursuing the fleeing men. That was very, very bad. The totally unexpected cavalry turned a disorganized retreat into an utter rout. In the center of the field halfway down the valley, the few groups of Epirian hoplites that were trying to make a stand were being systematically encircled and cut down. Captain Athan had hoped that the first rush down the valley would break up the Dorian formation and allow some groups of Epirians to escape, possibly to reform farther down, but the Dorian commander was keeping his troops in check and maintaining an effective formation as they moved down the hill after the broken Epirians. The hill men had no formation at all as they plunged down the ridge after the beaten men. Hill men were no match for formations of hoplites, but a fleeing hoplite was no match for a hill man. The combination of the fleet hill men and cavalry meant no one could expect to escape. Already the pursuit was moving towards the hill at the base of the valley and toward the Epirian camp. Captain Athan estimated that half of all the effective soldiers in Epiria were already either dead or captured, and the slaughter was far from over.

Captain Athan had problems of his own. His men now turned west down the ridgeline, which trended gently down on this side. This took them out of the killing zone and away from the enemy, but meant that their attackers behind them always had the advantage of height. Some of the hill men moved ahead of them to try to block their retreat down the slope. The Dorian hypaspists and the hill men together seriously outnumbered Athan's company. They pressed the retreating company hard; fierce fighting flared up and then abruptly ceased as Athan's makeshift formation held. It was fortunate that some of the Epirian peltasts who had been with the hoplites in the valley had seen the oncoming enemy phalanx and had climbed up out of the valley to join up with Athan's company. Until their javelins were gone and the slingers ran out of ammunition these light troops provided some protection to each side and ahead of the retreating force. They were fortunate that the cavalry remained in the valley and did not trouble them. The company was also fortunate that most of their enemy preferred to pursue a beaten army and loot his camp rather than engage a doughty foe still in formation and full of fight. Even so, it was a difficult and desperate afternoon. After moving west for a time, the remains of Athan's company moved down off the ridge and further away from the battle. Once down off the ridge, the opposition finally melted away and the company had the opportunity to stop, lick its wounds and count the losses. Athan had started the morning with over four score effective fighting men, his normal company augmented by mercenaries and some of the militia. He now had just over three score hoplites with less than a score of peltasts who had made it out of the valley. There were also three phalangists who had somehow managed to join up with his formation. It turned out they were part of the detachment that had arrived late for their assignment to block the road. Seeing the carnage above them they had gone west around the end of ridge and made their way up join with the only friendly force they could see that was still a fighting unit. Realizing all was lost, the detachment's officer had directed his tiny band to try to fight their way over to join the retreating hypaspists. Three of them made it. Captain Athan recognized the leader as one of the junior officers who had complained about the roadblock assignment causing him to miss the battle. The officer, Beltos by name, was staring at nothing at all. He was literally covered in blood.

"It seems you got your battle after all, young Beltos," said Captain Athan not unkindly as he gave the boy a drink from his bag.

"Why am I still alive?" Beltos asked no one in particular.

"You are alive because you are a good soldier and lucky. Almost all good soldiers are lucky. Of all the men who left camp this morning I think you three are the only phalangists who are still holding their hoplons. You fought well. Now get your wounds looked at"

"This is not my blood," Beltos replied.

In fact some of it was his. Almost every man was wounded in one degree or another ranging from the minor to the mortal. Captain Athan had been stabbed in his left shoulder and had a nasty slice on his left thigh. They were not deep but they hurt and he was stiff and sore all over from many hits on his armor and tremendous exertions of the day.

After a quick council with his remaining sergeants, the Captain gave his movement orders. They would march in fighting formation across the field in front of them and up a small knoll visible about a parasang or so to the west, where they would set up a defensive position for the night. Arrangements were made to assist the wounded. This assistance extended to opening the veins of two of the wounded, one who had a gaping stomach wound, was in great pain and begged for release. Another was a peltast with a fractured skull who had slipped into unconsciousness during the retreat and was clearly already close to death.

A parasang is the distance a horse can walk in an hour. A fresh and unencumbered man can also cover that distance in an hour if he moves briskly. It took them well over two hours to cover the parasang to the knoll, even though they were not disturbed by the enemy. The knoll turned out to be a good place for a camp. The captain first set his men in their fighting positions so each man knew where to go if they were attacked. Sentries were set and watches for the night assigned. Only then were the men allowed to stand down, settling in to camp on the west side of the hill, the far side from the enemy. The captain had the sergeants detail some men to carry the company's water bags down to a stream just to the west of the hill, some to gather firewood, some to tend the wounded, and even set up latrines. Everyone had been awake and physically active since midnight, and no one had eaten in that time. There was, of course, no food now, but the men were so exhausted in mind and spirit that few seemed interested in eating.

The sun was well down toward the horizon when the Captain found his old comrade Philo. "I have something that needs to be done tonight. Are you up to it?"" he asked the old guardsman.

"Yes sir," he replied getting slowly to his feet.

"Find three other men that you trust; good scouts, quiet and discrete. Are any such with us still unwounded?"

"I think so," was all the big man said.

"Good. As soon as it is dark I want you to scout over to our old camp. See what is going on over there. Maybe you can find some food. Bring back a prisoner if it is not too much trouble. And perhaps you can collect some stragglers." This was as close as the Captain could come to asking his friend to find his wife and children for him. Both men remembered how Erinsys had refused to leave the camp under the protection of Philo. "Try to get back before first light."

When Athan made rounds of his company, he found no fires burning. Men were trying to start fires with wood drills. "Don't any of you men know to always carry a way to make fire?" he growled to one group of such men. Reaching down under his cuirass he pulled a small bag from around his neck that contained his spare tinderbox and tossed it to one of the men. Within a minute, the man had used his Captain's tinderbox to start a fire.

He handed it back with a "Thank'ee Cap'n," and began to pass flaming brands to the other waiting campfires.

It was amazing how a campfire raised the men's spirits even on a relatively warm night like this. They were no longer hunted fugitives, but were an Epirian company camped out for the night. Athan made sure everyone drank plenty of water, and when the bags were almost all empty, he sent a strongly armed party down to the stream to fetch more. As he moved through the camp, he listened to the men and tried to gage their mood. That mood was somber at best, but he could feel the beginnings of what might eventually grow into a fighting spirit as well.

"We are really in the shits now," he heard a voice he did not recognize. The speaker was young, perhaps one of the peltasts. "We got nowhere to go; the Dorians are between us and the city. Probably they are on their way there now. They will hunt us down tomorrow or maybe the next day while we starve out here. I heard that they had a sorcerer helping them. That is why we didn't know they were there."

"Shaddup, you whiner," came a voice he recognized but could not place. It was definitely one of his hypaspists, though. "We're alive tonight, and free, and that is better than most of those poor sods that come out with us. We got water, fire, and friends all camped out safe and secure. And tomorrow we will be on the way back home. The Captain will take care of us. Didn't he get us here? Didn't he start the fires for us tonight? He's our own bloody Prometheus. Stick with and you can tell all the girls back home how you survived old General Achilles' debacle."

'That was what the men were calling today's battle,' he though, 'Achilles' Debacle; altogether appropriate. We were so confident. It was more than confidence, it was hubris'. Athan thought, 'We thought we were we too strong to be beaten. And we tried to duplicate a battle two years old. We were foolish, ignorant, overconfident, and under prepared. But mostly it was hubris.'

When the Old King came to himself, his little lair was completely dark again, the kind of thick darkness that happens in the middle of a heavy overcast winter night. From the stillness he deduced it was snowing again. Bereft of sight and sound, he concentrated on his other available senses. He could smell the wet rock around him, the fresh clean smell of pine tree he had used to block the entrance, and perhaps the fire. As to feeling, there was the heat of his feverish body, the weight of the cold on his blanket, a lightness in his head, and a weakness in his body. It was hard for him to concentrate; things seemed all jumbled up in his head. He wondered how long had it been since he had last eaten. It did not seem important at the moment. The old man managed to drink some water, from his water bag. Then he lay down again, surrendering to a delicious lassitude. He had rested in worse places. For example there was that bad night after the debacle. Yes, that had definitely been worse. That had been the very worst night of his life.

Chapter Seven –Things Fall Apart

With the men settled down, Captain Athan called his remaining sergeants together for a council of war. He had few enough sergeants remaining even before he had sent Philo on his scouting mission. Athan needed to reorganize his men to fill the holes in his ranks. The guard had always preferred to have ten to twelve men per sergeant, and they were now short of these critical mid-level leaders.

On this night the council of war consisted of five surviving sergeants, Beltos, the young hoplite officer (who had been invited out of courtesy), and Athan their Captain. They seated themselves around a fire and worked to reorganize their battered little company. The first order of business was designating new sergeants. "We need to have two or three new sergeants," began Athan, who had counted his numbers.

"There aren't that many of the men left," put in Timon. It was expected at Captain Athan's councils of war that each man speak frankly and without concern for rank. "When Philo gets back we will have six. That should be enough for this remnant. We don't want to have weak sergeants mucking things up at a time like this."

"I will have another job for Philo, so his men will need to get another sergeant. We also will have to take care of any stragglers that come in," countered the Captain, "and they will need a firm hand. If we are going to get home, I need sergeants to keep all of these men in line. Perhaps we can make the appointments conditional, subject to approval after we get back to the city."

This compromise was agreed upon. The young hoplite officer noticed that, as they spoke of returning and reestablishing the old order within the company, the sergeants began to relax and act more confidently. Soon the men were discussing the situation as though they were sitting securely in their compound, not squatting around a fire virtually in the midst of a victorious enemy. After some debate three men were decided upon, two veterans who had already been considered ready for promotion, and a surprise, a young man named Simon who had distinguished himself in the fighting that day.

"I'd say he will eventually be captain material more than a sergeant, but if this works out, we can move him into that later," was Sergeant Timon's assessment.

The selected men were called to the council campfire and told of their new status. They quietly accepted the news and joined of the council matter-of-factly. The next order of business was to reorganize the company with different men being assigned into different squadrons under the new and revised muster of sergeants. The peltasts had no surviving leaders, so they were assigned to Beltos, the hoplite officer, with Simon as his sergeant.

"I know you don't know anything about peltasts," explained Athan, "but Simon was a peltast until last year, so he knows how to employ them. You two are young enough to keep up with them. Besides, they don't have anything left to shoot with so you won't exactly be thrown in the heat of battle. You and your men can loan your hoplons to the sergeants until enough stragglers come in to start rebuilding a phalanx. In the meantime, I will need scouts; quiet, agile, active scouts."

Next, the men discussed the plan of action for the morrow. Opinion was divided between those who wanted to march immediately for the city and those who wished to wait in this spot for a few days. Those in favor of marching pointed out that they were vulnerable if discovered, and had no supplies of any kind. Those wishing to stay spoke of the many wounded and even greater vulnerability while on the march.

As was customary, the Captain held his peace until all had a chance to speak. Then he gave his orders. At first light teams of scouts would go out to investigate the area around them, particularly to the east where the battle had been fought. They would look for any enemy troops, see it they could find any supplies, collect weapons, and most especially, bring in any stragglers. Other scouts would investigate possible locations for a campsite closer to the city. The remainder would remain to complete the company's reorganization, tend the wounded, and work to improve the camps defenses. All the teams of scouts were to return and report back before dark. They would have another council at sunset tomorrow.

"So, men, you have your work cut out for you," concluded Athan. "Tonight I want you to designate your scouting teams and bring them to me for orders. And see if anyone can find anything to eat around here. Surely there are roots, nuts, berries, rabbits, birds, something. See what the men can turn up around here for breakfast."

Athan had a long night before him. Sitting down allowed him to feel his exhaustion, and he longed to stretch out and sleep, but he was not to be allowed the luxury of rest. Every time his head would begin to nod, a sergeant would bring up another team or two of scouts who needed orders and reassurance. Finally, over 24 eventful hours after he had left his family, he eased off his corselet and lay down next to the fire. He had no cloak or blanket in which to wrap himself, nor pack on which to rest his head. But once he stretched out he was instantly asleep. Sergeant Timon, bringing up a final group of four scouts for the morrow, let him sleep, and having a good idea of what was needed, gave them their orders. Then he left to see to the sentries.

At first Athan slept the deep dreamless sleep of exhaustion, but as the night wore on the dreams came. He always had nightmares or 'strong dreams' as Thaddeus called them after a fight, but these were much, much worse. They were mostly of the battle and men being killed and mutilated. But he saw Erinsys in one of his dreams. She stood before him looking at the ground.

"Husband, they raped me. Why did you not protect me?"

That woke him with a start. After an image like that he knew he would not be able to sleep again. He got up and checked the sentries. To his surprise not one was actually asleep. Nodding to the sergeant of the guard sitting by his fire, Athan returned to the dying embers of his own fire. He stoked it up again and stretched out on the ground beside it aching in every limb.

"Husband, they raped us all. Why did you not stop it?"

This time he could see her throat had been cut. Blood had poured down her linen tunic, staining it dark red.

Athan jerked awake with a cry. To his relief he could see it was beginning to get light. He could hear men moving around and there was a smell of wood smoke. It was the sound of organized activity, low voices, preparations, and gear being donned. With intense relief, the Captain rolled up, splashed water on his face from his water bag and relieved himself against a tree. He hoped that today he would be so busy he wouldn't have think about his dream. He was right about being busy, but unfortunately, he was wrong about forgetting the dream.

The good news was that there were enough active 'country boys' to bring in a half a dozen rabbits and two pigeons, along with some wild leaks and a few other unidentified tubers that the men assured him were edible. Although they had done well under the circumstances, it was not much food for over eighty hungry men. Athan decided that those going out on patrol would have the chance to get something to eat while on the prowl, so those men were chivied out of camp and onto their missions without breakfast. 'Besides', commented a sergeant, 'being hungry will keep them sharp.' The available food was prepared in three soup pots consisting of the bronze helmets of the hoplites. Though the men did not want to have their fine (and personally owned) helmets used as cook pots, Beltos set the example, cutting off his helmet's horsehair crest, removing the leather interior liner and rinsing it with fresh water. He set it upright between the stones placed beside a morning fire. Those who were wounded (and expected to recover) got a shared cupful. No one got enough and most got nothing, but the idea that some food was in the camp lifted everyone's spirits.

The morning was unusually quiet. Nothing and no one was visible from the knoll in any direction. Athan became concerned when Philo did not return at first light. In fact it was mid afternoon before the scouts began to return and report. The first few had little to add, but by late afternoon teams were coming in with useful things. Discarded weapons were easy to find; by nightfall every peltast had either two javelins or a javelin and a sling with a full pouch of stones. Food was not as easy to find, but some of the scouts were able to scrounge scraps left from the now abandoned Dorian camp behind the ridge. Two lame donkeys were brought in. One was slaughtered immediately and the smell of roasting meat soon filled the air. In fact, as the afternoon wore on, and more and more scouts came in, some bringing refugees and stragglers, any effort at making a discrete approach to the camp was abandoned. Anyone looking at the fields to the west of the ridge where the battle had been fought the day before could easily see groups of people converging on the knoll. It was almost evening when the largest group of all came in, perhaps a score of people leading four pack animals, two of which were burdened with wounded. Obviously the little exodus from the hills to the knoll had not escaped the enemy's notice, because a dozen or so men riding ponies broke from cover behind the refugees, followed by perhaps a score of other figures on foot.

Calling for two of his sergeants, Captain Athan quickly formed up two squadrons and led them out to counter this new threat. By now he knew the main body of the Dorians had moved southwest, toward Epiria, and he was no longer afraid of an attack by the enemy's main forces. This new threat was almost certainly hill men, bandits, or both, and Captain Athan knew just how to deal with those. To his pleasure, his two trotting squadrons of hypaspists were overtaken in the field by a group of peltasts, led by Simon and Beltos, both grinning hugely. They had seen the threat and acted without direct orders, but exactly as Athan would have wished. Beltos had left his helmet on kitchen duty and was wearing a conical felt pilleus. He still had his hoplite sword, but he now carried a brace of javelins instead of spear and shield. Simon deployed the peltasts in a line ahead of the two squadrons of jogging hypaspists. Without hesitation, the peltasts dashed forward past the oncoming friendly party and attacked the enemy horsemen, who where now well ahead of the bandits on foot. A long, skillful throw plucked one of the hill men right off his horse. The rest spurred back to their dismounted companions, who then stopped. The Epirians cheered and formed around the returning party.

Captain Athan moved over to greet Philo, who was leading this group back to the knoll. Athan had already seen that there were no women or children with him. Most of them seemed to be merchants, servants, or drovers. There was one pony, bearing two wounded hoplites, and three donkeys, one with another groaning man on her back. The other two animals were burdened with what appeared to be tentage, blankets, and mess kits. He recognized one of the animals. Until yesterday it has been his. It was the same donkey that he had urged Erinsys to load with their belongings and return to the city. She would not have left that donkey behind. Philo was looking at him with a peculiar expression on his face. "May I speak with you, my captain?"

He could only nod mutely in reply.

"Over there, sir, if you will," requested Philo in a low voice.

Athan moved over to the side with leaden feet. He was aware of whispered conversations between Philo's scouts and his men. He became aware that everyone had stopped now and was watching them.

"You found Erinsys, I take it," began Athan wanting to get it over with.

"No," said the big guard, "no one has seen her or the baby." But before hope could begin to blossom he delivered his blow. "We found Jason. I am sorry, Captain. He was with your servant girl."

"Karin?" asked Athan stupidly.

"They were together. It looks like the boy may have been trying to defend her. Looked like a spear into his heart." In fact it had been into his belly and the boy had obviously died in agony, but Athan would never know that. "They killed the girl with a sword, nearly took her head off. I don't think they even raped her. Her tunic was torn a little but she was still wearing it. I found a knife in her hand. I think maybe Jason was trying to protect her and they killed him. Then she went after them with the knife, or maybe it was the other way around."

It made sense thought Athan. Karin and Jason had been close; she was almost like an elder sister to him. Athan believed she would die trying to save him. And he knew what her knife probably looked like, too: not too long, narrow, with no hilt to speak of, and a bone handle. After all, he had given it to Karin and shown her where to wear it. And he had told her it was to be used only to defend her honor and the honor of his family. Yes, brave little Jason would have tried to stop the men from hurting Karin, and she would have reacted with fury to anyone threatening her beloved charge.

"One more thing, sir," Philo continued, "there was blood on her knife. Not hers."

That would be important to a warrior, thought Captain Athan. "Good. We will go back tomorrow and take care of the bodies."

"No need, sir. We buried everyone we found there. It required a pretty big hole, but we all helped and we got four hill men to dig, too. A half dozen of them showed up leading these animals. The Captain did not need to ask why only four helped do the digging. Or what happened to those four when they were done with their final chore. Four scouts and perhaps some help from a handful of stragglers against six men. None of Philo's men showed any wounds. It must have been a ferocious attack on the unsuspecting bandits.

"Well done, Philo. Thank you."

Then the Captain moved back to the men who stood silently watching him. "Let's get into camp, men, there is a lot to do." And Athan made sure he stayed very busy indeed until long past dark. A hundred hungry men (for a full score of survivors had joined them) can eat one donkey in a day, and so to save time the second lame donkey was butchered for the morrow. What equipage that had been recovered was apportioned, planned responses to attack reviewed, orders for the next day's march issued, problems with the company's reorganization resolved, and a hundred details that his sergeants could not solve were addressed. Athan even forced himself to eat some donkey stew to keep up appearances. He actively discouraged the sympathy of his men.

Late that night one of the sentries heard a man sobbing alone in the dark and, if he recognized the voice of the man, he never mentioned it to anyone. And that was the only grieving for his family anyone ever heard from their Captain.

It was a grim force that marched out the next morning. Anticipating that the Dorians would move directly against the city, then withdraw, the Captain took a more westerly route at first to avoid being on their army's return track. With about a hundred men now in his party, he had too large a force to conceal, but with so many effective fighters, he was also too powerful to attack by any but a strong force. At the council of war that night, he put forth their situation as he saw it.

"The Dorians could have arrived at the city this afternoon if they pressed straight on. We need to know what is going on there. I want three separate patrols to move out and see what is happening there. We are a still a couple of day's travel from home. Tomorrow night I want to camp at the Notch," naming a well-known if little-used pass in the ridgelines. Have the scouts meet us there as soon as they know something. We can get to the city from there in one day if we have to. If the Dorians are laying siege to the city we can move up to the Gray Hills north of the city and menace them from up there." Additional scouts were left behind as a rear guard and to collect any further stragglers and bring them into the company. They had enough food to last for two more days if they kept to short rations. Captain Athan thought that one way or another that would be enough.

The scouts did not have to tell them what had happened. By noon, a south wind started blowing black smoke up into the sky. When they crested the last ridge before The Notch, they had a distant view of the city. It was burning. Scouts confirmed the worst that evening and brought in even more bad news. The city had fallen. The city had been attacked not just by the Dorian army but by Illyrian troops from the north and Buttrotiuria forces from the south as well. The three armies had apparently been able to overwhelm the reduced defenders and breach the walls. The last scouts to come in that night had come close enough to the city to speak to refugees, see the open gates, and hear the screams from the city. It was said that the Dorians had been aided by a wizard or sorcerer who had been able to persuade the city to open its gates.

The company was numb. 'General Achilles' Debacle' had apparently been just the start of a larger disaster. The council of war could come up with no useful course of action.

Even Captain Athan was left without a plan other than to address the troops the next morning. It rained during the night and was still drizzling the next morning when everyone who was not on sentry duty assembled next to a rising piece of land to hear the Captain speak. He stood on a fallen tree trunk so the men could see him.

"Our city has fallen," he began. Every man there already knew this. "Our city was betrayed by treacherous attacks from three of our neighbors, and perhaps by some foul sorcery. Now it is being pillaged. We here are too weak to defeat the enemy. Tomorrow our food runs out. I cannot tell you what to do. But we cannot go back to our city and we cannot stay here. If any man wants to leave to see if he can find his family, he may leave. If any man wants to leave for any purpose, I release him. To those of us who served in the city guard, the guard is no more. We will have to find our living somewhere else."

There was a long silence from the assembled men; then came several questions almost at once. "Where are you going, Captain?" "What will you do, sir?" and "May we stay with you, Captain?

"You ask about me," replied Captain Athan. "I have been a fighting man all my life. I had friends and family in that city, too." There was another long pause as he thought of his fellow guardsmen he had left behind to fight a battle against overwhelming odds. Then there were his other friends in the city, tavern keepers, merchants, shop owners, slaves, prostitutes, poets, mothers, and children. And his own two remaining daughters were there, along with Persis and Thaddeus. He had let them all down. "As for me," he said, "I think I will go up to those hills and show our enemies how a band of brigands ought to be run. I think I am going to make them wish they had left this beehive alone. I am going to hunt, harry, rob, and kill those treacherous bastards all the way back to Doria. Then I am going to clean out every one of their hill folk allies from these hills. It will be hard work, and hard living, with probably nothing in the end but a cold grave. Still, if you want to come I would be proud to have any man of you at my side."

It was a grim set of choices, but at least there were choices now. Athan stepped down to the cheers of his men. He was no longer a Captain of the Guards. He had instead become what he had once fought against, the Chieftain of a band of brigands.

The Old King tossed under his covers and rested his head on a more comfortable spot on his makeshift pillow. That had been a good exhortation he had given his men. Most of them had wound up in a cold grave, or had left him, eventually worn out from the hard life, but they did give those particular Dorians a very hard time. It was pitch black dark in his little refuge; would the morning ever come? Or had it already come and gone again? He was beginning to lose track of the days. He felt hot, so hot. He kicked the blankets back. His fever had made him lightheaded and drowsy. After a time he wrapped himself back up in his covering and lay back again. The fire had gone out but he lacked the energy to try to rekindle it, especially in the stygian dark.

The old man sighed and drifted back to an uneasy doze, dreaming of the next phase of his long life.

Part Two – Brigand

Chapter Eight- The Scent of Prey

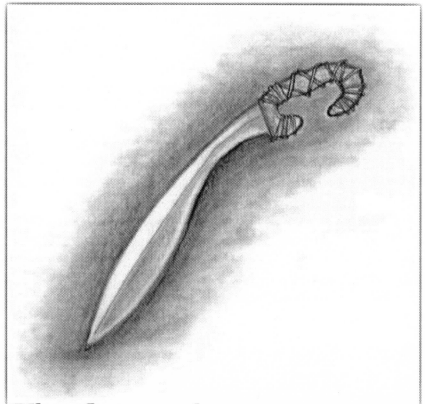

The afternoon heat reminded the men sitting on the hill that late spring had turned into summer. Perhaps three score of them squatted or lay down in the shade of scrub trees just below the summit of a ridge. Two other men waited at the top of the elevation, one watching each way. The sentinels each stood beneath and within one of the low brushy trees that lined the crest, so that their outlines were not obvious. They were not only watching for movement on the thin road that ran below them, but were also keeping an eye on three specific sites on hill tops on the other side of the valley.

Both men immediately noticed a flash from one of those sites, a clump of brush at the western edge of a summit. The western sentinel bent down and picked up a polished square of bronze a bit larger than the size of a man's hand. Bringing it to his face he peered out of a finger-sized hole in the center of the mirror and began positioning it relative to the sun. First he angled it until he could see the bright reflection on a nearby bush, then turning he aimed it at the flashing point on the far side moving it slowly up and down. The pattern of the flashes on the other side then changed to a more purposeful series of flashes.

Both sentries noted the series of flashes and spoke across the top of the ridge to each other, confirming the meaning of the sequences.

"That looks like 'Alpha' that means 'friendly', right?" called the man on the west side of the tree.

"Yes, agreed," said the watcher on the east. "Acknowledge it." The man with the metal mirror pointed his mirror at his opposite number across the valley and nodded the reflection once again. The far signaler then sent a different set of flashes.

"I didn't get that one," shouted the eastern watcher "Did you?"

"It was 'Mu' that means 'horsemen'," responded a handsome young man how had up the hill from the group of men who were now stirring and looking up in interest.

"Are you sure, Beltos," queried the first man.

"Yes," he answered shortly, "acknowledge the signal."

The next signals were unambiguous, 'One-One' which indicated 'approaching from the west'. After a quick acknowledgement came a slow side-to-side waggle flash that meant either 'nothing to report' or 'no further report' depending on the context.

"Ask them how many," directed Beltos. "No, let me, you keep watch." He took the mirror and in a matter of moments flashed over to the other side of the ridge. It took several minutes before the other side flashed back a flashing nod. "About time," grumbled the young officer. Neither of the other two men said anything. If they thought that young Beltos was being overly enthusiastic and meddling on their watch, they kept those opinions strictly to themselves. Beltos was popular enough because of his good humor, good looks, and courage so the older men could tolerate his youthful enthusiasm. After all, he came from a good family. These days the phrase 'came from a good family' was most definitely past tense. The word that seeped up to the hills from Epiria had been mostly bad. Many of the 'good' families had been either exiled or wiped out completely, with men being murdered and surviving women and children enslaved and sold to cities in the south.

Beltos flashed "Iota' the interrogative signal then 'Omicron' which meant number. After a few moments came the reply: 'few'. The signals were of necessity very simple. For numbers the signals were 'one', 'few', 'many' and 'many many' for a large number. What this signal "few friendly riders coming from west" undoubtedly meant was that messengers were coming to the designated rally point where they could be met and led to the man had once been Captain Athan and his company of guardsmen and who was now Chief Athan and his outlaw band.

When Beltos went down the slope to pass this on the Chief, he found him already up and ready to move. Although Athan had not seen the signals himself, he had heard the men talking and knew to expect visitors. With a nod at Beltos' message, Athan and his personal bodyguard moved down to where the livestock waited.

The months since the destruction of first the Epirian army, quickly followed by the sacking of much of the city of Epiria itself, had wrought changes to the men who had followed Athan. For one thing, they were leaner and harder, both physically and mentally. Rations were not easy to come by in the hills; neither were the gentle qualities of pity or mercy.

Athan looked older than he had before he lost his army, his city, and his family. His clothing was worn and usually dirty. He still shaved his face, when he could. He had taken a fine bronze razor off the body of a Dorian they had killed in one of their first ambushes after the fall of the city. It was an expensive item, the thin blade folded back into a handle, making it easy to carry. There had been a leather stop along with it that allowed Athan to keep the edge keen. He was not able to scrape his face clean of whiskers every day, but when he had time and water he would mix up a batch of soap and olive oil and shave himself by feel. It gave him a sense that he had not abandoned all pretenses of civilized life.

The men selected a mount from the small heard of animals. Athan did not especially like being burdened with the care of the donkeys, mules, ponies, and even a few horses, but they were necessary to carry the supplies his band needed, and on good days they were needed to carry some of the loot they obtained from the men they attacked here in the hills. There had been quite a few of those attacks since the fall of Epiria. Bands of hill men returning to their tribes in the north and east, and most especially Dorians returning to their city farther east, now seldom traveled in groups of less than four score, with plenty of scouts along their route and strong watches set at night to prevent the sudden attacks from Athan's band of survivors. Chief Athan had been careful in picking his ambushes and night attacks. He always ensured he had odds of at least three to one in fighting men. Every attack had incorporated an element of surprise, either by suddenly springing from ambush, attacking weakly defended camps at night, or by making a false attack to either lure a pursuing enemy into a prepared ambush, or more recently, to drive a fleeing enemy into an ambush. He had been careful with his men, avoiding larger bands of the enemy and withdrawing if he could not be certain of success. Even so, more than a score of the men who had joined him had died, especially in the early attacks, when men who felt they had nothing left to lose attacked recklessly, avenging themselves on the enemy that had killed their families and destroyed their homes. Though these were losses Athan could not easy take, they had the beneficial result in that the enemy survivors of these battles carried back tales of the utter ferocity of the new band of brigands in the hills. This reputation terrified men who had to traverse the now threatening hills to the east and north of the city of Epiria.

Not all the losses were due to death in battle. Some men simply became lost, cut off by companies of the enemy looking for Athan's band, or just became turned around in the hills and ridges that made this part of the world such a fine refuge for bandits. Athan had also lost some of his people as the fires of revenge cooled. He made it clear from the beginning that each man could leave when he so desired. All a man who was leaving had to do was present himself to Athan, request release and he would receive his share of any goods or booty and depart. The only time Athan would not let men leave was in the proximity of the enemy. But any man who wanted to leave must do so personally, during daylight hours, and when the band was resting. Even with this generous policy, some men still slunk away in the night, ashamed to leave their comrades. The remaining members of the band would sometimes pursue those men and relieve them of anything they might have taken with away them for the 'slinkers', as they were called, lost any claim on the band's booty.

There had been some recruits to the band. Stragglers from the battle known as 'Achilles' Debacle' were still being found in the hills. In the early days a few came out from the city to join the resistance to those that had captured Epiria. A very few were rescued when the band attacked parties of the enemy that carried captives with them.

Though the early recklessness was now not so evident in the band, Athan's men were still a truly ferocious band of fighters. The past months had refined their tactics and honed them into an efficient unit. They incorporated three elements that were not new, but had never before been used together by a band of brigands in an integrated manner.

First, scouts and spies were spread widely in the hills, searching for either possible targets or companies of enemy soldiers seeking the band. Using the system of mirrors and flag signals first developed by Captain Thaddeus, they provided Athan with a rapid means of controlling the band, so that they could attack where it was most advantageous while avoiding the enemy's reposts. Scouts and signals had been used before, but the band made more extensive use of them and integrated the information gained into every part of their actions.

Second, the band made extensive use of pack animals. Not only did the animals carry the necessary supplies for the band to live, but the band could move the sick and wounded along at the same pace as the main body. They did not use carts or wagons. If something could not be carried on the back of an animal, temporary travois were used to drag the item to a place of safety where it could be cached. The pack animals allowed the band to move more rapidly and over more difficult terrain than possible when using carts.

Third, battle tactics were optimized for one goal, to make their victims turn and run. The band's formation was now composed of approximately equal portions of peltasts and hypaspists. This optimized the effect of a sudden attack. Large numbers of missiles would suddenly assail a group of men not yet formed up for battle. As soon as the first wave of javelins, stones, and arrows had been launched, the hypaspists would charge from cover, forming up as they ran toward an enemy still reeling from waves of missiles. Sometime the hypaspists would hurl their own spears at the shields of any enemy that was bracing to receive the attack, and then draw swords and close before their enemies could remove the heavy spears from their hoplons. If the enemy was able to form a shield wall, the attack was to be abandoned, and the hypaspists would retreat under cover of the peltasts. But usually the combinations of missiles and a shock attack broke up any formations before they could become set. Once that happened the pursuit could begin. The men learned early not to stop to gather plunder before the enemy was completely put to flight. After the first few attacks, they also learned to let men go who immediately threw down their weapons and ran.

"We want them to know that the only way to survive is to flee," explained Athan. "Those who do not learn this lesson we will kill."

Once the enemy had fled, the band's non-combatants who had been holding back out of sight would assist in loading portable booty onto pack animals for a retreat back to a predesignated rally point. It was typical for hill bandits to rape all females (and sometimes boys) on the spot after a successful attack. Chief Athan put a stop to this. He explained that the band was not a collection of robbers, but a fighting force. He made them understand that men would be more likely to run if they did not have to protect their women from rape and murder. Finally, he reminded everyone that rape took time and made you vulnerable while it was going on. The idea was to hit hard, drive off any opposition, collect everything that was useful, and then leave the area before the enemy could regroup. That did not mean the band did not take hostages for ransom, only that once resistance at the ambush was overcome, the band continued to function in a disciplined and organized manner until they were safely back to the predesignated rally point with their booty.

So it was that the men Athan led from the hills over the burning city of Epiria had come to dominate the hills to the north and east. The hill tribes had withdrawn to the north and east, leaving these hills around Epiria unpopulated. By summer there were simply no parties coming through the hills that the band could raid. Four score men and assorted camp followers ate a lot of food, and the area had been picked clean. So the band had moved south looking for new territory, staying in the hills, and avoiding cities.

The ridges in this region tended to run on a northeast/southwest axis so it took long hours working up and down tracks and narrow trails for the oncoming riders to get to where Athan and his men were waiting. The riders were four: one of Athan's young scouts, two seedy-looking men, one quite a bit younger than the other, and Philo, who was now in charge of the advance scouts. Philo was one of the oldest men in the band, and though he had been a city guard most of his life, he had demonstrated a natural talent for not just scouting, but teaching others how to work in small groups, seeing the enemy without being seen, and reporting back to the main band.

"These men have an interesting story", said Philo grabbing the reins of the older man's pony and pulling it forward. "Get off, you, and address the Chief."

The men were visibly nervous and doing a poor job of hiding their fear. The two strangers dismounted clumsily, causing one of their ponies to snort and stamp his feet. The older man backed away from the pony and then jerked around to face the group of armed men standing in front of him. He was clearly aware that two more mounted warriors from the band were behind him. He had not noticed which of these imposing warriors Philo had addressed as the leader so now he stood facing eight dangerous-looking men desperately seeking an introduction. He looked from face to face to try to decide which of them was their leader. Beltos was the most imposing physically, and the best dressed, but he was too young. Finally he simply faced the entire group his eyes on some point a thousand spans beyond them.

"Mighty chieftain, my name is Clestonese. I bring news of a valuable caravan," he began hopefully. None of the men spoke.

His younger companion, another underfed and raggedly dressed creature, tried to elicit a response from the men facing them. "Great chieftain, this caravan carries great riches but is well guarded both by mortal men and the gods." He gulped his large Adam's apple and looked back and forth which unfortunately revealed a nasty cast to his left eye.

His older companion tried again. "We bring information to help you if you wish to take this rich prize."

"Why?" asked a lean clean-shaven man from the middle of the group. Now that he had spoken it suddenly became obvious from the postures of the men. The clean-shaven man was in the center of the men and was slightly to the front of the others.

Clestonese looked at the leader and immediately decided that this was no time for deception. "Hope of gain, sir. We hope that you will give us some portion of the huge riches you will take when capture the caravan."

Athan looked to the younger man. "Tell me about these guards. And tell me how you came to know these things."

The younger man seemed to become aware of just how precarious their situation was. His Adam's apple bounced up and down jerkily.

"Great Chieftain," interjected the older man, "forgive this fool. He spoke out of turn. He is a nephew of my sister's husband. We know of these things because we were part of the caravan. We left when we realized we had fallen in with bad companions."

At that moment every single man that heard that statement (including the speaker himself) had a variation of the same thought: 'Out of the pan and into the fire.' The ten men with Athan also shared an additional thought. 'He's lying'.

"Silence you," gestured Athan. "You," he gestured at the younger man with the bouncing Adam's apple, "tell me about the guards." He gave a hard look at the older man when he started to speak again, silencing him.

'Adam's Apple' found his tongue. "He has three dozen horsemen, sire. Brave veterans armed with lance and sword. And a troop of bowman with shield bearers, perhaps a score of each." Athan knew he was describing a typical eastern arrangement of a pair of soldiers, one with a powerful bow, the other carrying a long shield that he held to protect his partner. He had heard of such soldiers but never seen them himself. 'Adam's Apple' continued his description, "There are merchants and other travelers who are in the caravan as well. Some of the merchants have guards. I think perhaps as many as a score all together."

'That was perhaps too strong a guard,' thought Athan. 'The numbers are almost my own.'

"But they have more than mere men," continued 'Adam's Apple' warming to his subject, "they have a sorcerer,"

"Priest," quickly put in the older man. "He is a priest of some eastern religion. Some say he can do magic, but I have never seen it, Chief. He does have swordsmen with him, perhaps ten or so."

'Worse and worse,' thought Athan, but he revealed nothing as 'Adam's Apple' continued jabbering on.

"Everyone says he is a powerful sorcerer, Chief. They say he helped conquer the city of Epiria. They say he put a concealment spell on his whole army and they surprised the city's army. Then he caused the people of the city to open their gates like a whore opening her legs when she sees gold," the young man was grinning now, and animated. He liked telling others about powerful men he had seen.

There was a palpable chill from the men standing in the glade. Clestonese felt the hair rising on the back of his neck. It was obvious that these men were from that city, and had suffered personal losses there. Athan made an inconspicuous gesture to restrain his men as 'Adam's Apple' continued on, "He can make clouds and cause it to rain. And he has the gift of far seeing. I myself have seen him make coins appear and disappear out of thin air, and once a he made a dove appear out of nowhere for the General. He says his god can cause the earth to shake and raise storms at sea. And once he made fire come out from his very mouth! I saw it!" At last he looked around and he saw the faces of the men standing around him. His mouth continued to work for a moment, but no words came out. His Adam's apple bobbed a few more times. He looked to his older companion, the look of a man who realizes that once again, he has really screwed things up.

"Go on," said the Athan in a very quiet voice. "Tell me more. What is this sorcerer's name?"

'Adam's Apple' looked at the warriors that surrounded him. He did not fully grasp why but he knew that every one of them would like to kill him, and that any of them could. Now he felt with the full impact of the malice of these men. It completely unmanned him. He stood mute.

Clestonese made an effort to defuse the now explosive situation. "Sire, he is called Azziz. He is a priest of Bal from a kingdom from the south, Tyre, it think it is. His people are great seafarers."

"Then what is he doing in these hills?" came the quiet voice.

"Great chieftain, I believe he could not find a ship to take him back to his country so he is going to the sea on the other side of the hills. There he will take his booty home where he can resume his seat of power." Clestonese was sweating but he was giving these bandits what they wanted: useful information about a valuable caravan. Perhaps that would be enough to keep him alive.

"What is this booty?"

"He keeps four large chests in his tent. I have heard it is his payment for helping the Dorians. Also he and his servants have many fine garments. There is cloth, fine hangings, and many donkeys and mules to carry the effects of his household and guards. He has beautiful girls that dance in his tents. And he carries captives with him as well. All this can be yours, Oh mighty chieftain."

"How?"

"He travels to the east on a road not far from here. They travel slowly because they have many wagons and people traveling with him. Your band can attack them when they stop for the night."

"Mind me carefully. Do not lie to me again. If you do not know, tell me so. Because if I think you are lying to me than you will be of no use to me. Do you understand?"

"Yes, Chief." The man understood exactly what the brigand chief meant.

"Now, how long where you with the caravan?"

"Seven days Chief."

"When did you leave the caravan?"

"It will be four days gone this evening, Chief."

"Why did you leave the caravan?" the men around two informants tensed, waiting for the lie to be repeated.

"My sister's nephew here," a gesture to the younger man, "had an altercation with one of the merchants in the caravan. They came to blows."

"That is not usually a reason for eviction. Did the boy hurt the merchant?"

"No, he came off the worst." 'Adam's Apple' tried to protest but a preemptory gesture by the older man silenced him. "To get even he stole some of the merchant's personal things. When I found out what he had done I felt it best to leave. We were not welcome in their company."

There followed a series of quiet questions. What time of day did the caravan normally awaken in the mornings? What time did it look to stop for the night? What were the positions of the various guards around the camp? What about on the march? How did the members of the caravan get along with each other? Who was in charge of the caravan?

As the questions continued, Clestonese continued to sweat. He began conferring with his sister's husband's nephew about details. Between them they discovered that they remembered much more than they realized about the routines of the caravan. As Clestonese became more nervous, more uncertain, 'Adam's Apple' became more confident. He began to answer the questions himself without referring to Clestonese. But on the subject of the sorcerer priest Azziz he felt himself to be most valuable to the men asking him questions.

"Not only will it be hard to surprise him because of his second sight," he advised, "Azziz is a mighty sorcerer; he cannot be harmed by arrows or edged weapons! And he can take over your will. I have seen it. He just looks at the captives, points at one of the girls, even the young ones they took from the city, and snaps his fingers thus! And she rises willingly and goes into his tent and she does his bidding; whatever he wants! I have seen it many times!"

It happened so fast the move must have been thought out beforehand. Athan's sword came out of the scabbard on his left hip, whipped up and down and through the top of 'Adam's Apple's' head. The unfortunate man literally never knew what hit him. The blade clove right down through the skull and wedged in the jawbone. The corpse fell slackly, dragging down the blade. The blow was delivered so fast that no one, not even Athan's men who were trained veterans all, had a chance to react before the corpse had collapsed. A rapid heartbeat later Clestonese felt blades touching his flesh pushed through his clothing by the guards around him who had reacted to their chief's blow.

"I think your relation lied to me, Clestonese," Athan said calmly as he put the sole of his left boot on the face on the unfortunate man and tried to lever his blade free. As Athan twisted, the iron blade broke suddenly as such blades were wont to do. Athan was left was left holding half of a sword. The rest of the blade spun away out of the skull leaving a gaping wound. The right side of the head flopped over to the side, held only by a flap of skin. The brains glistened whitely in the sun.

Now that the end had come for Clestonese he was suddenly calm. "He did not lie, sir. I have heard many say that the priest has a magic to protect him from blades and arrows. I do not know if it is true, but it is widely said. They also say he does not grow old like other men. I have heard both these things from many people."

"I believed him about the protection, old man. I killed you sister's nephew for lying about the girls from Epiria. Philo, get your scouts over to find this caravan. You know where to look. Report back to me as soon as you find them. Beltos, get the men up and moving up the trail. We will go over the ridge at that notch we saw a couple of parasangs to the west. Tell the wolves we are on the hunt for a fat bullock. "Theron," Athan ordered his youngest bodyguard, "stay with Clestonese and make sure no harm comes to him." This meant 'do not let him get away'.

"What about that?" asked Theron, referring to the corpse.

"He can bury it if he wants," replied Athan, "but don't fall too far behind." With that he turned and walked away, casting aside the hilt of his ruined sword. Poor 'Adam's Apple's' grave turned out to be very shallow indeed.

Athan turned and headed back toward where his band awaited. His men scrambled away to do his bidding. Everyone was shocked; even men who had killed before were stunned by the suddenness and ferocity of the attack. More than that, they had never seen their chief do anything like that before. Violent, yes, he was after all a warrior, but to strike a blow like that without the slightest warning! The story rippled through the band and was a topic of discussion for a long time. But the comments were always out of earshot of the Chief.

"I think that it was for his daughters," said Beltos to Timon his friend and fellow captain of peltasts. "Remember, they were in the city with Thaddeus. No one knows what happened to them."

"Nothing good," agreed Timon. "We need to make sure no one talks about captives from Epiria or captive girls of any kind for a while."

It was good advice, but every man in the band already understood that by then.

The band was assembled and moving in a remarkably short time. They made good progress moving first south along the road in the valley, then turning southwest to cut through a lower point in the hills. Their rapid progress was all the more impressive, considering that scouts had to move ahead of the formation and climb the steep hills to vantage points then either signal back using flashing mirrors or flags to semaphore to the main body about what lay ahead. Thus, leapfrogged by hurrying scouts, the column moved over the rugged terrain until almost nightfall, when the band arrived at a campsite selected by Philo's scouts. They were now completely out of any territory they had ever traveled into before. At the council that evening, Clestonese was brought in and allowed to sit down. He was provided with the same tea the other men were drinking, treated with courtesy, and asked basic questions about his estimates of the ground ahead. He was encouraged to speculate on his estimate on the caravan's likely track. Other men made their comments on possible courses of action. It was almost as though they were all old business associates discussing matters of trade. Clestonese left the conference greatly relieved. He could, he thought, work with these men just as he had with other business associates. He was dangerously wrong.

They left early the next day and resumed their rapid march to the south and west, trying to position themselves to intercept the caravan. By nightfall there were still no reports. Clestonese was again invited for a time to the evening council, but this time the questions were more pointed, the route of the caravan brought into doubt, even its actual existence questioned. By the time he left the council he was stinking with the sharp sweat of tension. Fortunately for him, later than night a rider came into camp from one of Philo's advance scouts. Campfires had been observed along the major east west road to the south and east. There was at least one caravan on the route.

Athan recalled a hasty council and went over his options. As was his habit when there was time, he listened to various options and allowed his officers and sergeants to develop proposed courses of actions before issuing orders. In this case his people felt that the best thing to do would be to attack the caravan while it was on the march. They would be stretched out along a line with their force scattered, and the caravan guards could be engaged piecemeal. It was a tactic they had used almost a dozen times before with good success. Scouts were to be sent all along the track to look for a likely place of ambush. Further, the convoy would be observed on the morrow to determine route security and possible weaknesses. The attack would possibly be laid on for the day after tomorrow, depending on what was learned by their scouts.

As the band moved south, the land had begun to become flatter with lower and gentler slopes. The ridges were more rounded and there were more people. They were still mostly shepherds and small isolated farmsteads, but the numbers were increasing as the country became more hospitable for agriculture and less hospitable for bands of brigands. It was difficult to hide the almost three score men and over four score head of livestock and various camp followers that made up the main body. Summer had not yet fully come and there had been rain; still some dust was raised by their passage. In addition to the main body, there were about three dozen young fighters scouting about. Even if they were discrete, some were sure to be seen. People would notice all the activity and would talk. Athan was not going to fight a battle; he was trying to ambush a powerful foe. If the caravan heard of a strong band in the vicinity, they could change their route, hire additional guards, or even stop at a pleasant site and build defenses. Brigands could not afford to wait. So while the main band moved forward more carefully in this easier country, teams of scouts spread out to see what they could find.

One of the teams of four included two older men. Philo, who was out ahead of the band almost every day, usually with only one other companion, was one of these men; the other was the Chief. Athan had left Timon in charge of the movement of the band to a likely campsite, just over a hill from the road the caravan seemed to be following. The only concern was that it was somewhat more to the east than would be ideal. They would need to make a fast march to get ahead of the caravan the next day.

Although Athan relied on his scouts, indeed he placed his life and those of all of his followers in their hands every day, there were things that no young scout could tell him that he needed to know. So long before it was light he was riding a pony out with his old comrade and two young peltasts to a likely vantage point over the road. They pushed hard at first until they approached their destination. There they met two more waiting scouts. The two peltasts that accompanied them took the horses and retired into cover to rest both themselves and the mounts, while the next two scouts led the two leaders on foot over a hill and down to a small spur on the other side. There was not a lot of cover on the spur, but there was enough. One of the scouts stayed atop the ridge to check the western side, while they watched the track below that wound up to and around the spur and then continued on to the west. It was good that they had left early and hurried, for they had hardly settled into their surveillance before the leading elements of the caravan, a pair of horsemen, came around the bend of the track in the distance.

For the next two hours they watched the caravan go past the spur. The escort was easily the best Athan had ever seen. A dozen horsemen riding in pairs scouted the line of march. First one pair would canter ahead down the road then stop and carefully scan the area while another pair would move up pass them, and take up posts farther down the road. Further back, between six and eight horses remained together, just ahead the wagons and pack animals of the caravan proper. Never did any horseman get out of sight of the others for more that a few moments. There were always between four and six sets of eyes scanning surrounding countryside well ahead of the main elements. These men were mounted on strong horses and were armed with javelins and curved swords. A round wicker shield hung from their saddles. They wore what looked to be leather caps that must serve them as helmets. The watchers could not tell if they wore armor, but if they did, it could not be heavy. The leading element of cavalry provided excellent advance reconnaissance. They were also a formidable fighting force and could quickly come back to the aid of the main caravan in the event of an attack on the center of the column. Athan could imagine the impact of a dozen or so riders coming back to take his forces in the flank.

Leading the main body of the caravan was a score of men on foot, ten with longer versions of the curved bows Athan had once used himself, and ten with tall shields, each almost as high as a man, slung over their backs. These were the shield and archer pairs Athan had heard about, but not seen until now. They provided a portable set of walls from behind which the finest archers in the world could pour out a devastating fire. Athan knew that if his men could get in among the shields they could slaughter the men behind them with ease. The archers and shield bearers wore little armor and were only armed with daggers or light axes. But getting up to them would require enduring a hail of arrows. Bows were not often used in war here, partly because the materials and technology to make such sophisticated weapons were not readily available, and partly because arrows were not as effective against a wall of shield-protected armored men. But Athan knew how effective those bows could be, especially against peltasts. He needed phalangists in close formation coming down a hill to get to the shields to kill the archers behind them, and he had no men equipped to fight in that role. The archers would be a problem.

Next came the head of the caravan proper. An additional group of perhaps a dozen riders on horses trotted back and forth beside half a dozen wagons and an enclosed carriage. The watchers on the spur discussed this group in particular. Clearly the sorcerer /priest Azziz was in this group, but whether he was riding a horse, or on one of the wagons, or within the carriage could not be determined. The best guess was that he was one of the riders, and that his women were within the carriage. Behind this group came the rest of the accompanying merchants and fellow travelers, a long line of walkers, pack animals, and wagons. They noted that not one of the wagons was pulled by oxen. Though strong, oxen were notoriously slow moving. Indeed, the caravan was making excellent time for such a large group of people. One thing all three of the watchers noted was the presence of dozens of captives linked together and obviously bound for slave markets, and more unusually, small children. Some were so small that they had to ride in a wagon, and the cry of more than one infant could be plainly heard. Infants and small children were almost never taken as slaves; they were of no immediate use, and were costly to raise. Sometimes a mother could bring her baby with her into captivity if she were persuasive enough, but toddlers and young children, especially those without their parents were considered merely a worthless nuisance. Yet there were clearly a number of children without parents in this caravan.

'Adam's Apple' had been right about the numbers of formal guards but either he had underestimated the number of private guards for the merchants or a lot of the members of the caravan were former soldiers. Athan estimated at least two score men in the main body of the caravan were openly carrying weapons, either swords or spears. Perhaps three fourths of the way along the line came another ten pairs of archers and shield bearers. Finally, beyond the last of the stragglers, but still in sight of the main body came two dozen more riders. These remained more or less together with only an occasional foray by a pair of riders out to investigate the surroundings. If the caravan were attacked, this powerful formation not only provided protection from attacks in the rear, it could also sweep up and provide support to the archers or drive forward to slaughter attackers engaged with the caravan guards.

It was indeed a rich caravan, perhaps the richest they had ever seen. But it was also huge; there were about 200 men plus an unknown number of women and children. Not only did the caravan guards outnumber Athan's band, many were professional fighting men. Athan did not want to fight a battle, but if he wished to take this caravan it looked like that is exactly what he would have to do.

Once the last of the riders were out of sight, the three men climbed up the spur, over the ridge, and down to their waiting ponies. As they headed back toward the site where the rest of the band would camp, they discussed what they had seen.

"It will be hard to get an ambush that will engage all the parts at once, and if you let either those horsemen or the shield archers set up without opposition, they can cut you to pieces. You need to get close before you attack. We will need to watch them set up camp. The problem with attacking their camp is that night attacks are always difficult to organize. Besides you can never be sure of where they will stop for the night so it is hard to make plans."

"I know where they will stop tomorrow night," said Jonathan, the peltast scout who had held their horses.

"What did you say, Jonathan?" asked Athan, riding over closer to the young man.

"I am sure they will stop at High Meadows," replied the youngster. "Everybody does. It is a natural place to camp. It is flat with plenty of good grazing; there is a stream down the middle with a pond on the south end. It's a really nice place. But we can't attack them there."

"Why not?" By then Athan had slowed his horse, and they all circled around young Jonathan.

"Well, it's pretty flat and there isn't much cover, but it has great grass for the animals. There are some big trees near the middle that are great for climbing. We used to always put a lookout up there. You can see everything. It is all open pasture so you have no chance to sneak up on a caravan. That is another reason why everybody stops there."

"And how did you come by this information?"

"My father took me and my brother on two trips. He told us all about where to go to trade and how to get there."

"How old were you when you went with him, Jonathan?" asked Athan.

"Once when I was ten, and again when I was 12."

"That would explain the tree climbing," put in Philo dryly.

"You say that caravans stop there. Are there sometimes more than one at the same time?" Athan continued.

"Yes sir," replied Jonathan, "we stopped there four times and there were always more than one. Once there were five caravans there at once. It was like a fair!"

"How long would it take us to get there?" asked Athan, the germ of an idea stirring in his mind.

"About a day or so," answered Jonathan.

"Philo, I want you to watch them make camp," Athan told them. "Watch every detail. Once they have settled down, come back and report. Young Jonathan and I are going back to our campsite now. We have plans to make."

The old king woke in the night covered in sweat. His fever must have broken. He worried for a while about starting the fire again, but it was warm enough under his coverings and very cold outside of them; if he got up and went to the effort to restart the fire he would probably not be able to get as snug as this again. 'No', he decided, 'better just stay where you are until you are ready to get up for a while. He took a long drink of water, lay back down and in a few moments was dreaming again.

Chapter Nine– An Evening to Remember

Late afternoon the following day the sorcerer priest's caravan arrived at High Meadows. It was indeed a fine place. One other small caravan had already arrived and was camped at the north end of the large grass pasture. Azziz' big caravan turned and started making its way toward the pond on the southern side of the open area. Once the end of the caravan was safely onto the open meadow the leading group of cavalrymen began racing their horses around the meadow with wild whoops of pleasure at the open expanse of grass where they could let their horses run. As soon as the rearguard horsemen came on to the plain, they joined their fellows in dashing across the delicious open spaces and then raced completely around the smaller camp to the north simply for the sheer joy of it. Everyone, it seemed, was glad to be out of the close country where every ridge or hill might hide an ambush for it was well known that brigands had been especially active in the region lately.

"This is a good place," said Azziz to the caravan's guide. "You have led us well."

"Yes, sire, although this route is longer, it is more pleasant and much safer. We have not lost so much as a single goat to the brigands that infest these hills."

"But my bodyguard tells me we have been watched from the hills," said the sorcerer priest mildly.

"Everyone and everything is watched, sire. They come to watch the magnificent progression. This is the most imposing caravan ever seen here," responded the guide smoothly. He had been worried about an attack, not because he thought that they would be overrun, but because he would be suspected of treachery by this sorcerer priest. Now that he was out of the hills, he was beginning to relax from his fear of the bandits. The only thing he was only afraid now were his clients. In four more days, he would have them at their destination and then he could truly relax and collect his well-earned fee.

"You say this is a safe place?"

"Yes, sire. No caravan has ever been attacked here. It is too open and too far from the hills where the bandits find cover."

"Good," said the sorcerer priest. "Then let the company camp along the water here instead of forming into that circle formation, what is the word you use for it?"

"Laager, sire"

"Yes, I think we can all relax here for a time with the protection of that water on one side and all the open area on the other."

Azziz turned and began discussing the weather complaining of the growing heat and looking forward to taking ships back home. With his new riches and special captives, he would truly be a man of power and influence. Leaving home had been a real risk, but he had learned much and gained in money, prestige, and power. It was now a time to consolidate what he had gained and enjoy life. Meanwhile, behind him, the caravan guide gave the signal, and the caravan began the complicated but well-practiced nightly ritual of making camp. Azziz' magnificent blue and white tent was set up at the far eastern end of the camp this time instead of being in the center of camp. Apparently the sorcerer priest wanted a bit more separation from the rest of the caravan now that they were out of the reach of brigands.

A few minutes later a single figure rode a pony out from the woods at the far northeast end of High Meadows. He rode without haste directly to the northern caravan's laager, dismounted and began speaking with men in that camp. No one in Azziz' party either noticed or cared. Shortly after his arrival, the pickets did notice another caravan entering along the east road. Two of the horsemen trotted up closely enough to gage that it was a medium sized party with about two score pack animals and perhaps ninety or so people with at least a dozen women visible near the front of the group. The pickets cantered back to their new campsite to report. They either did not notice or did not care that there were no carts or wagons with the arriving caravan.

Two men walking on the far side of ponies in the oncoming caravan slid their bows back under the blankets of the animals. They were Athan's best archers. Had the pickets ridden close enough to discover that some of the 'women' near the front were in fact young men wearing women's chitons over their tunics, these archers had orders to shoot the pickets out of their saddles while the so-called "caravan" turned and retreated as fast as they could back into the hills. But that plan was no longer necessary. There were not many women following the band but all of them had been pressed into service to ride or walk near the front of the "caravan" so as to present a less threatening face to their target. Some of the women were *not* happy with this, but they were informed had a part to play and like it or not, they would accompany the pack animals onto the meadow. The most reluctant had been assured they would be well out of things before it came to blows.

But one of the women riding at the front of the band was thrilled with the chance to play a part in a battle. Her name was Laurel; she was 19 years old, athletic, full of life, and wild as the little stallion she rode so well. She called him Dragon; he was the spoils of one of the very first ambushes on the Dorian cavalry. Laurel had known how to ride since she was a girl, but something about having her very own stallion continued to thrill her. In fact, Dragon was nothing special, a mahogany bay perhaps 13 hands high. But for some reason, perhaps because of the nearly constant attention she gave him, the girl and horse had bonded.

Laurel had left her respectable family who lived on a large farm outside of Epiria and run away with her lover to join the band. They were some of the band's first recruits to join after the fall of the city. In short order, she left her first lover for another, then that man for another, causing a whole series of fist fights. She had acted as a lookout for one ambush, scouted fearlessly far and wide and was having more adventures than she had ever dreamed possible. Although she was no great beauty, at this moment, with her hair streaming behind her, legs gripping the barrel of her beloved stallion, she was so vital, so full of energy that every man watched her with fascination. She trotted her horse around in front of the caravan, eager for the excitement to begin.

"Not too soon, girl," Athan growled at her. He trotted past her toward the northern caravan accompanied by Philo and Petra. Petra was one of his personal guards, a man widely regarded as the best fighter in the band.

Athan had tried to prevent his old friend Philo from coming with him. "Who will lead the men if you are with me?" he asked.

"Beltos and Simeon will provide the dash, Timon will direct the battle. I am just a scout now and you already know where the enemy is. Besides, if we lose you, we are all undone. You need a nursemaid with you to make sure you stay safe."

In truth, Athan was glad for his company. He was afraid; afraid of dying, but more than that, afraid that this man Azziz whom many said was the real reason his family was killed or enslaved, his friends murdered, and his city pillaged, would escape retribution. He longed to see his enemy face to face. The three men increased their pace to a canter and headed directly toward the smaller encampment laagered to the north.

They were met at the edge of the laager by armed men.

"Easy," said Athan, "we mean you no harm. May I dismount and come among you to speak with my son?"

"Just you," replied a man who was clearly the leader. "They stay outside."

"Agreed," said Athan, "They will dismount and stay here talking with your men." Without waiting for approval, he swung down off the pony and headed into the camp.

Within a few strides he saw young Jonathan sitting in the middle of the camp, surrounded by several glowering men. Without preamble he went directly to Jonathan and said. "Did you speak to them?"

"Yes. Father, they still don't know what to do." They had decided that Jonathan's part in this would be to persuade this northern camp of the band's good intentions toward them, and serve as a hostage. A blood relative was a better hostage than a young scout, thus Athan had 'adopted' Jonathan for the duration of the upcoming attack.

"Good," said Athan. He turned to man who appeared to be the leader. "My name is Athan. I was a captain of the guard for the city of Epiria. The men with me are, were, guardsmen and soldiers from the city of Epiria. We are coming to do battle with our enemies. We intend you and your people no harm."

"My name is Pelops" replied the man. "I am the master of this caravan. We had heard the city of Epiria had fallen. You say you are soldiers from that city, how do we know you are not common brigands who will turn on us after destroying a stronger caravan?"

"I will tell you something you already know: we are not brigands," replied Athan. "Do brigands give warnings of their intentions? And do brigands leave their chieftain's only son with caravans to guarantee their safety? Do brigands attack such a strong foe? No, they would attack weak ones that are easy to take, not large strongly guarded ones with many young captives."

Pelops was unconvinced, "If you are soldiers, why do you attack with deception? Why do you not face them in open battle for a fair test of arms? And it was said that Doria and other local cities took Epiria. Those men appear to be foreigners." "We attack with deception because they took our city by means of deception, treachery and deceit. These foreigners were the ones that used those despicable tactics. They also have some of our people as captives. If we faced them openly, they would surely put those captives to death." Athan stopped answering questions and put the matter directly to the caravan leader. "Stay in your camp and give no indication that you know what will happen next. If we prevail, you will be rewarded. If we fail, then the foreigners will have no dispute with you. Remember, if you warn them or fight against us and we win, we will treat you as enemies. If the foreign barbarians win, there is no telling what those filthy men would do. They are strong; perhaps they will accuse you of secretly helping us and take your goods."

"Perhaps that is what you will do," shot back the man.

Athan laughed and relaxed, "If we can take that caravan, we will all be so rich we won't know what to do with all the booty. We will have to contract with you to help us carry it away!"

The entire concept suddenly became ridiculous. Men joined the caravan leader and Athan in laughter.

"Go then and do your work, whatever that might be. We will stay in our camp. But leave the boy."

Jonathan was thinking of what Athan had just said. He knew, of course, that Athan's son had been killed and his wife and infant daughter had disappeared, presumably taken captive by the Dorians, but he now remembered that the Chief also had two other daughters that he had left behind in the city with his close friends, Captain Thaddeus and his hetaira who was a famous beauty. Could it be that the Chief hoped to find his daughters among the children in that camp over to the south. And the hetaira was just the sort of woman that a creature like the sorcerer priest would take for his own. Was that the real reason the band was trying to swallow such a huge prize? An unexpected wave of sympathy for the Chief swept over him.

He approached his Chief with sudden emotion. "Father," he said, and to his surprise and embarrassment, his voice was choked, "Goodbye, good luck," and he embraced him.

Athan was taken aback, but the emotion was contagious, "Thank you, son," was all he could get out. Then clearing his throat, he spoke to the caravan leader, "If it goes ill with us, will you claim him as one of yours?" The man nodded.

As the three men rode south toward the far camp the leader looked carefully at Jonathan. "You do not resemble your father."

"Yes," replied the boy turning to him smiling, "I know. They tease him about that."

The leader laughed out loud, suddenly liking this bold young man very much. "He is fortunate to have such a fine son. Come sit down and eat. We may claim you as one of our own even if you are victorious."

There were strong emotions across the points of the compass in the field that evening. To the north, there was a sense of excitement and nervousness in the camp of Pontus as they variously watched the new caravan coming in from the east, rapidly completed chores that would not wait and furtively began to prepare for defense. The sorcerer priest's caravan to the south was generally relaxed as everyone enjoyed escaping the dangerous hills for such a beautiful and restful camp. This was mingled with focused concern by those who had to complete the complicated process of setting camp. The most widespread topic of conversation was whether or not they would rest here tomorrow. To the northeast, Athan's band continued to move slowly toward the center of the meadow. The people in that group were having almost every kind of strong emotion. Some of the women near the front were now frankly terrified, some of the older men who had lost friends and family were working themselves into a rage, most of the soldiers felt apprehension tinged with fear. There was a feel of being slowly carried forward like a log drifting down a river toward a cataract.

Some were excited; no one more than Laurel. She felt the same way she did when she was preparing to slip out of her house to meet a boy who might, or might not, become her lover that night. In a few minutes, she would have a chance to act out her part, leading two brave men out ahead of the band. Who could be suspicious of a couple of young men chasing a beautiful girl? Timon had arranged that her two pursuers were two of her former lovers. She just had to make sure they did not catch her too soon, and that they fought the enemy and not each other. "Soon," she said patting the neck of Dragon, who had caught her mood and was dancing nervously, "soon, my darling."

In the middle of it all, three men trotted their ponies toward the big caravan at the south end of the meadow. Their emotions were mixed. Of the three men, Athan was the only one that had any choice. He had set this part of the plan in motion; he could still call it off. He could turn his little pony and rejoin the band and attack with the rest. But then how would he explain that to Philo? Athan decided to keep going and see what happened. Philo was nervous and perhaps a bit frightened but mostly he was resigned. He had long ago come to the realization that he was going to be killed. Once you gave up hoping to live, it was easier to do your job. This was not the first time he had been certain he would die, so everything that happened to him lately had all been a bonus. The only thing he was really concerned about was that he would let his captain and Petra down. Petra was not much of a thinker and less of a worrier. If he was concerned at all, it was about looking like a coward to Philo and Athan.

Athan was pleased to note that the sorcerer priest's caravan had not posted any guards yet and did not seem to be circling into a laager. There was none of the aggressive patrolling by cavalry that Philo had reported around their camp the night before. There appeared to be only two pairs of riders on duty, and one of those was exploring the ground on the far side of the pond to the south. The two men who had already checked out his band now seemed to be racing their mounts around the far western side of the meadow. There was one man mounted over by the pond in the south but he had removed his helmet and armor and was apparently riding herd on the remainder of the horses that were being led to the pond for water and grooming. Some horses had already been released nearby and were grazing contentedly. One was rolling in the grass. It was an idyllic scene. The brusque efficiency of the previous night had clearly relaxed. Some tents, notably the one belonging to Azziz, were already up and ready, but most people were still setting up, talking with one another, and generally taking their time. The sun was still two hand's breadths above the highest hill in the west. There was plenty of time.

As they approached the camp, a man came out from the nearest group of tents that was going up. Athan noticed he was not a guard, nor was he armed.

"What do you want?" he asked them without preamble, intercepting them a few score paces from the tent.

"We need to talk to the leader of your caravan," replied Athan.

"Get off of those little animals and follow me," the man turned and walked in the general direction of the big striped tent that belonged to Azziz.

Ignoring the rude lack of hospitality, the men dismounted and led their ponies after the fellow. Well short of the Azziz' tent, however, he stopped, gestured over to a small harried-looking man with two long drooping mustaches and, turning left them. As the mustachioed man came up to them, Athan realized with a sick feeling that he recognized the man. The caravan guide was from Epiria and led caravans in and out of the city. Athan had met him at the gates several times when he was a guardsman. It had been year or so since he had seen him, but this was recognizably the same man. He did not remember the man's name, but he remembered the unusual droopy mustaches.

The caravan guide looked over at the three men standing before him holding their ponies. He saw three hard men, two of whom were obviously bodyguards for the one in the middle; the two bodyguards wore swords at their hips and looked like they knew how to use them. The man in the center was unremarkable. He had a fine dagger in his belt but no sword. A long club was shoved under his pony's saddle. Another former soldier turned guide, no doubt.

"What do you need of me? This is a busy time as you can see."

Athan tried hard not to show his inward sigh of relief. "My caravan is coming in as you can see. We always have used the southern end of the field. I can see you are here before us, but we would like to share access to the pond for our livestock."

"No," answered the guide abruptly, "we need the entire pond for ourselves. This is a major caravan and a rich one. The owner will brook no sharing. You can camp over by the stream but not within a two hundred paces of us."

"Two hundred paces! What, are you going to step it off? It seems you need a lot of space. We are going west, you are coming east and we had thought perhaps to trade some items."

"This is an important caravan," repeated the guide, "the master has no need of anything you might possibly have in that little," here he hesitated glancing over their shoulders at the slowly approaching band, "pack train of yours. Stay well away from our lines."

"Who is this mighty master of such an important caravan?" asked Athan after a quick glance at his band. They were still more than four or five bow shots away.

"Azziz bin Azziz, a mighty sorcerer and a priest of the great god Bal. Most wish to avoid him. You should do the same."

"But to meet such a man! Perhaps I can interest him in some of our poor goods?"

The guide was now more that willing to get rid of this nuisance and respond to some of the inevitable demands on him that happened whenever the caravan stopped moving, started moving, or was moving. "Hey, you," he gestured brusquely to a short, stocky dark man with a curly beard and a curving sword in his sash, "Take these men to your master."

It was not clear if the caravan guide wanted the man to act as an escort to a business meeting or as a guard bringing miscreants in for judgment. It did not matter. With a grunt and a gesture the dark man led them toward the big striped tent. Two other men, armed like the first with curving swords in their girdles suddenly appeared and fell in with them. It was clear that they had been under observation from the moment they approached the caravan. That was not promising. At once Athan began to affect a slight but noticeable limp. Smiling painfully at their guides/guards, he stopped and pulled his wooden club from under the saddle. When he looked back all three of the men had their hands on their swords. Continuing to smile somewhat ruefully, he leaned on the club which was suddenly became merely a stout walking stick. "My apologies," he grimaced. "It is painful to walk for very far." There was absolutely no change in any of the men's expressions. They gestured Athan and his two companions forward.

As they approached the tent, three more men came to surround them. They were alike in that they all were of swarthy complexion, stocky powerful builds, had black well- oiled curly beards, and wore robes with broad blue and white vertical stripes, much like the tent of their master. The six men, now all around the three visitors and their ponies, accompanied them up to a small group of men sitting comfortably on folding stools. Athan thought that a folding stool like that would probably be very a nice thing to have in the field.

"These men asked to meet you, sire," said their escort and stepped aside with a bow.

Athan had not been sure exactly what he would do when and if he got into the enemy's camp. One of the options he had discussed with his sergeants was to suddenly assassinate the sorcerer priest and then signal the others to start of the general attack. That idea was obviously not a starter. Not only was Athan's band making absolutely glacial progress across the meadow, leaving his men still too far away to start the attack, but Azziz was demonstrating proper concern about his personal safety. Athan sometimes had as many as six guards around him when he was in the field. Azziz had eight in the middle of his own caravan. These eight guards were all armed with swords; two also held spears, grounded but ready to respond. These men were in addition to the six men who surrounded the Athan and his two comrades. But things could have been worse. Although the men were alert, especially the six around him, they were not alarmed. Further, Athan felt that most of the men in attendance on Azziz, though armed, were not trained fighting men, but rather courtiers, men selected more because Azziz felt he could trust them rather than for their fighting ability. The two spearmen were probably shield bearers during the march; formidable enough, but not really a match of Athan's men. As to the six men who had escorted them to Azziz' presence, they were certainly tough enough, but he thought that from their bowed legs and curved swords they were probably horsemen, not as familiar fighting on foot as on horseback. Still, fourteen against three were insurmountable odds.

Athan looked at Azziz. He saw another swarthy man of indeterminate age with a full black curly beard. He was of average height with a stocky build, though he was not as heavily built as his associates. His ears stuck out of his long oiled hair. Azziz' features were not regular enough to allow him to be considered handsome, but there was a power in him that seemed to shine from of his dark eyes. He was dressed in a simple, but very fine, solid blue robe in the same shade as the blue stripes of his retainers. Costly rings glittered on his fingers. He wore a short sword on his hip with an elaborately jeweled ivory hilt. Around his neck a simple copper chain led beneath his robe to an unseen object, probably a jewel. He wore a red leather vest of obvious quality over his long robe. The vest was covered with a number of faint intricate designs. Although it was undoubtedly expensive, it did not seem to match the rest of his attire. Summing the man up Captain Athan realized that the odds were really fifteen to three, for no matter what occult powers Azziz might or might not possess, he certainly looked as though he could defend himself with mundane weapons as well.

Azziz bin Azziz, for his part was unimpressed with his visitors. The man in the middle with the walking stick was certainly the one in charge. He was somewhat taller and had the posture of a leader. The two men on either side of him were his bodyguards, but one looked too old for the work and the other appeared to be a fool.

The leader of the three spoke to the sorcerer priest, "Sire, I am Athan son of Medius, leader and guide to the caravan that now enters the meadow. Your caravan guide tells us you might grant us permission to camp next to your mighty caravan so that we can share our experiences about your road ahead, enjoy the entertainments such a great caravan must have, and possibly do a small bit of trading between the merchants."

"He said that, did he? Why do we give that dog money" said the great Azziz to one of his companions, "if he cannot divert rabble like this away from us?" Turning to Athan he continued "No, you may not approach my camp tonight. Perhaps tomorrow we may allow you to sell some of your trinkets to our merchants, but they will come to you. Set up your camp over there," he said gesturing to the brook on the far eastern side of the pond. "And keep your people clear of my camp. You are dismissed." This was delivered in the tone a master uses to address a slave, even the more insulting because Azziz did not even realize he was being insulting. He had long ago become used to being in charge, and the habit was now deeply ingrained.

"Thank you, sire," said Athan, bowing slightly and turning to leave. He even remembered to continue to limp. He was hugely glad that he and his friends were getting out of there alive. Athan stole a glance up to the still approaching band. He would start his little charade when they had cut that distance to the campsite in half. Just then his plan began to go wrong.

When things go wrong men tend to blame women. They have done so since Eve. But in this case, the plan really was upset by a woman. Laurel was more than merely impatient to start, she was on fire. Part of her impatience was below her waist; she desperately wanted to urinate. She had seen several of the men stopping to relieve themselves. She had waited, not out of any sense of modesty, women squatted by the trail on the march all the time, but because she just knew if she dismounted to take care of her bladder that would be the moment she was called to leave. She was supposed to watch to see how the Chief and his men came out of the camp before she set off, if they came out abreast or in a hurry she could start, but if they were one behind the other, she must wait until they returned. But as soon as she saw them mount up in the far camp she called over to Jokrastes "Let's go sweetheart!" and tossing a challenging glance at Keros who was the other man in this little escapade, she kicked Dragon into a gallop toward the far western end of Azziz' camp. Jokrastes grinned and spurred after her. Keros would have followed immediately except that Timon, thinking fast, got to him and grabbed his reins, "not yet boy, give them more of a start."

She made a fine spectacle headed out of the camp and drew every eye. Wearing a white tunic hiked up over her long legs, a bright red scarf that was failing to hold back her long black hair streaming in the wind, another red scarf around her waist to emphasize her shape, and another around her neck she was the image of the goddess of the hunt. Even from a distance her grace and bearing were arresting; in that moment dashing across the field toward the setting sun she was very beautiful. What could be more natural then for a young man to pursue her and then, a moment later another to come after as well? But she left too early and rode too fast. By the time she reined in she had ridden all the way around the western end of Azziz' caravan to the banks of pond. Jokrastes, riding as fast as he could pulled up beside her, his pony blowing hard.

"Are you crazy?" he demanded. "You are going to get us killed! Wait for Keros." Keros, who had finally been released by Timon was coming hard after them but had been left behind by the Laurel's wild ride. They were supposed to have a scene ending with her dashing toward the cavalry herd as if by accident, then scattering the horses to prevent their cavalry from mounting up to repel the attack and to draw further attention away from the oncoming band.

"Your job is crucial," Captain Athan had warned them, "if they can mount those horses and form up they will cut us to pieces."

Now, drunk with excitement, she saw the enemy's horse herd ahead of her along the banks of the pond with only one mounted man to stop her. With all the enthusiasm of a puppy chasing ducks, she gave Dragon the reins and with a joyous "Come on!" charged across along the edge of the pond toward the cavalry mounts. Keros was still coming on but was too far back to help. With a curse, Jokrastes spurred his already tired mount and followed after the girl who was now giving out a glad series of whoops. The guard riding herd must have thought her merely reckless not dangerous, for he did not draw his blade, but only moved to head her off to prevent her from scattering the herd.

She feinted close to him and easy dodged past as he grabbed for her bridle. But Jokrastes, coming up hard behind her did not see that she was clear, and fearing for her safety, reached under his saddle and blanket and pulled out one of the two short javelins secreted there. As the unfortunate guard turned to chase after the crazy girl, Jokrastes set himself, and hurled his javelin into the unsuspecting rider's lower back. The weapon entered below the man's leather corselet and penetrated almost all the way through his body. He gave a scream of agony that echoed across the meadow.

With that scream, the battle began. As soon as he released Keros in pursuit of Laurel and Jokrastes, Timon had begun to chivy the trailing elements of the band to close up. Most of them were still psychologically in the mode of behaving like a harmless caravan. It was a way some of them had to ease the tension before coming fight. Timon began to shock them out of this and prepare them for battle. He halted the leading elements and began to spread them into what would be his line of battle. But he had hardly begun his deployment when he saw the crazy little fool start her dash for the horses. Abandoning any pretense of innocence he began shout at his people, "Form up, form up in line you fools, get those packs off those animals!" Men began to move up alongside the twenty or so ponies that were near the front of the line. The women who had helped with the deception turned their donkeys and mules away and began to hastily return the way they had come. This, more than Timon's shouts alerted those in the rear that the battle was about to begin and they began to hustle up to the line, tossing off their pony's mostly empty packs and scrambling on the ponies as best they could. Timon heard the scream from the dying guard echoing across the field and knew he could not wait to get any closer to start his charge.

"Beltos! Simeon!" he called.

"Here!"

"Ready!" came the replies

"Take the men in the advanced line," which was still in truth forming up, "and go charge that camp. No shouting or cheers until you are in among them. I will follow with the rest as soon as I can form them up. Go!"

With shouts of "Come on men!" the two friends started their ponies toward the camp still four full bowshots to the south. Beside each pony trotted one or sometimes two men hanging onto the harness. As they advanced Beltos and Simeon angled apart from one another toward each end of the line, just as they planned, trying hard to keep the charge down to a trotting pace.

When they heard the scream, Athan, Philo, and Petra though mounted, were still under escort by their three original guards; the men had never taken their eyes off them from the moment they arrived in the camp. Everyone now turned to the sound of the death scream. Their guards looked back, then looked at each other and reached to draw their blades. They were too late. Philo killed his man with a single blow of his kopis before the poor fellow could finish turning around. Petra was just as fast, but his opponent was more skillful, only receiving a bad cut on the arm before he counterattacked. Athan was at a disadvantage since he had slid his weapon back under his saddle. Instead of reaching for it he drove his pony at the man nearest him. For once Athan benefited from fighting a trained soldier. The man was a cavalryman and knew what a warhorse could do to a man. He stumbled back from the little pony that in fact was not only untrained for war but was badly confused. As he stumbled back he fell under the hooves of the animal that instead of stamping down to kill skittered away trying to regain its footing. No matter, the event gave Athan time to scramble down and get his club out. The man was still getting up when Athan attacked him. Stunned he fell beneath a series of blows that ended with Athan kicking the man under the chin and rendering him unconscious. Petra had also dismounted and was engaging his opponent in a fine duel. Athan came up to the man's left only to have to suddenly retreat and parry a wicked slash. The man then turned to feint back at Petra but never saw Philo who brought the heavy blade of the kopis down chopping through his leather armor and into his lungs.

"Pretty good fighter for a horseman," remarked Philo as he levered his blade out.

The three men turned to see how they could help the attack when they were assailed by men coming from Azziz' tent. Their focus shifted exclusively to self-defense.

Laurel heard the scream of the man behind her and pulled up. She saw the guard slumping with a javelin in his back and then Jokrastes was past her shouting "The horses, the horses!" She had forgotten what her reason for being there was. Already the cavalrymen were running to catch their horses. Two who had been holding their horses, leapt on their animals drew swords, and rode bareback to intercept Jokrastes. With a yell she pointed her stallion at the rest of the now agitated warhorses and scattered them. Men ran after her from the camp with slashing swords. She dodged them easily on her agile animal and went after two other horses still standing, waiting to be caught. As they broke away from her she turned back to see Jokrastes fighting a desperate battle with the two men who had gotten astride their horses. He did not dare throw his only remaining javelin when pressed so closely, and was at a severe disadvantage against two experienced warriors on larger animals. Only the fact that his opponents just had halters to guide their mounts had kept him alive so far. His pony was quick but not nearly as fast as the cavalry horses. She had expected something like this might happen. The men of Athan's band would not hear of her carrying a weapon to the fight; her role was to keep the cavalrymen dismounted by scattering their horses, not killing the men. She turned the Dragon toward the unequal contest and reached into the small bag on the side of her saddle. She pulled out a stone a bit larger than her fist she had been able to hide there and whipping off the red scarf around her neck, tied the stone into the scarf, all done in an instant while riding a horse at breakneck speed toward the fight. As she came up on the combatants, the man on her side glanced quickly at her and then transferred his attention back to parrying a quick stroke of Jokrastes' javelin. Then she was on him and with a grunt swung the stone on the end of her scarf into the middle of his back. He grunted a deeper sound and with scarcely a glance back cut deeply into her upper left arm. The blade stuck in the bone for a moment before he could extract it and in that moment Jokrastes leaned over the distracted man and skewered him with his javelin. This left the young man leaning away from his other opponent and completely undefended to the slash that laid his back open. As Jokrastes recoiled back onto his mount, gasping in agony, the man drew back his sword for a fatal cut. Just then, Keros, catching up to them at last, rode past the cavalryman and, as delicately as any fisherman spearing a trout, punched his javelin through his opponent's throat. Both the cavalrymen fell from their horses at the same time.

"Go!" shouted Keros to the wounded pair, "Back to the band. I will hold them." Jokrastes, reeling across his pony's neck, headed slowly back the way they had come, intending to circle the camp to the west then turn north toward their comrades. As he did so Jokrastes slid forward on the neck of his pony and fainted, his animal walking out with the unconscious figure still on his back, away from the battle.

Laurel was shocked at her wound, a great gaping bloody mouth in her triceps. She reached up with her right hand and clumsily wrapped her scarf around the wound, twisting it as hard as she could before tucking the ends back into the scarf. Sensing men approaching she gripped the reins with her right hand and kicked her faithful stallion away from them. Her left arm was now numb, and she felt sick. 'At least I don't have to pee anymore,' she thought to herself. Seeing several cavalry mounts ahead of her that had stopped to graze, she steered over to them to drive them farther away. Then she saw another man trying to get close to one of the freed horses. She got there first and chased it out into the field. There were other horses to move, and she continued to move toward the center of the meadow pushing the animals slowly out and away from the camp, becoming vaguer and vaguer in her thoughts until eventually blood loss caused her to faint and collapse off her stallion. The faithful animal stood by her on the grass, reins on the ground a living monument to her fall.

Men in Azziz' caravan looked up in puzzlement. They had heard a scream near the west end of the pond, and could hear sounds of fighting to the east near the big blue and white tent. The cavalrymen's horses were now stampeding around behind them; that wasn't right. Those who looked back toward the meadow could now see almost two score men with weapons coming at them across the grass where there had just been an incoming caravan only a few moments before, but they could not seem to grasp that this line of men, approaching without shouts or war cries was a threat to them. Finally, men began to shout in alarm and search for weapons, but long before any kind of defense could be organized, the first wave of the band was on them.

Beltos and Simeon had kept their men in check almost all the way to Azziz' camp. Then as the charging band got close to the encampment, shouts and war cries suddenly filled the air followed by screams and clash of arms as the first attackers hit, then pushed through the initial defenders of the camp, killing any men that took up arms against them. One of the two groups of archer- shield pairs had the misfortune to be billeted directly opposite of this attack. They tried to form up with some archers gathering their weapons and falling in behind their shield bearers. Arrows were shot and men fell, but some of the attackers had shields, and in any event there were too many of them far too close and coming too fast for too few archers. The defenders saw that they could not stop the wave of attackers and before they could be overwhelmed they did what smart troops always did when faced with certain death; they ran. Some turned east toward their master's tent. Most were forced back toward the pond; it was not especially wide and offered a possible escape from the charging hoplites. Unfortunately for the archers though, the bottom was thick gooey mud, and the center of the pond was deeper than a man's head. Trying to wade through thick mud made them vulnerable to missile weapons, and trying to swim in heavy clothing and a leather corselet was almost impossible. Those that did make it across were able to successfully escape up the bank on the other side and then eventually to the undergrowth to the south. But the next day, men clearing the pond of the debris of war pulled out nine bodies of men who did not make it over.

Once the archer shield pairs had been put to flight, Beltos and Simeon were able to turn the thrust of their attack to what had been the rear of the caravan, camped to the west. The people at this end of the camp were mostly fellow travelers taking advantage of the protection provided by Azziz' guards. When the men in the camp found that the attackers were granting quarter to those who did not resist they began to throw down their weapons and plead for mercy. In short order the west side of the caravan had been cleared of any of the foreign soldiers. The two captains rallied their men and turned them back to the east, passing again through the camp. Behind them, the merchants and their people rose from their bellies or their hiding places and looked around. All the fighting was now at the other side of the camp and no one seemed to be attacking them. Some snatched up their belongings and fled west into the night. A few coolly hitched animals to their wagons and quietly headed north to join the relative safety of the caravan laagered just north. No one offered any resistance to the rear of the first wave of attackers.

Timon had been nearly frantic in bringing up and then organizing the rest of his people into an coliment line of battle. Some men he had to hold back from advancing, others he had to encourage to move forward. With the element of surprise gone, he needed a disciplined attack. Looking back toward the camp he could see three men that had to be Athan and his companions fighting against far too many men. Beyond them he saw one pony coming toward him with a man slumped unconscious on its back. Another rider, also slumping and apparently injured, was slowly scattering horses to the west. The last of his three riders was driving the rest of the herd east with at least ten men in pursuit. Beltos and Simeon's men had reached the outskirts of the camp and were fighting among the wagons, pushing west as was planned. He looked up and down his rapidly lengthening line, back at the men still hurrying up from the rear of the band, and decided he could not wait.

"At a walk, the line will advance."

Let those in the rear catch up as they could. He had almost two score men to lead into battle. "Form up properly. Sergeant Stefan, get the line straight!"

Athan and his two comrades would have died quickly on that field, except that they were able to keep backing away to prevent men from getting behind them, and the numbers opposing them kept diminishing as bowlegged men turned to try to catch horses, and other men turned to recover their tall shields and form a line in response to the bellowed commands of a sergeant. The archers forming up could not get a shot at them because of their own men attacking the three comrades. The sergeant was busy forming a line to stop the second wave of attackers coming down from the north, and could not be bothered with three men who were outnumbered and about to be killed by swordsmen. The farther the fight backed away from the camp, the fewer were the men opposing Athan and his comrades. The numbers opposing them were also diminished not only by men going to other parts of the fight, but because Philo and Petra were killing them. Athan with, only a club and his dagger, was limited to primarily defensive moves, but the others more than made up the difference. After Petra killed his third man and Philo simultaneously opened a bloody slash on the arm of another, their opponents suddenly backed off. "Back to the Master!" cried one, "Protect the Master." And their four remaining opponents first backed away and then turned and ran back to the vicinity of the blue and white tent.

Athan looked around; to his left was confusion of men chasing horses. To his right Timon's line was advancing across the meadow toward of the camp. A line of shield archers had formed to oppose them. He could see seven or eight of the tall shields were up and arrows in flight were visible in the evening light. Athan and his companions were well within their range, and should two or three archers decide to engage them things would become very dangerous indeed; it would be almost impossible to see the arrows coming from the glare of the setting sun. There was fighting at the far end of the camp, but unless Timon got some relief from those archers, he was going to lose a lot of his men. Athan needed to make a diversion.

"After them," he shouted, and they sprang after their now retreating foe, Athan angled to his left to try to keep the retreating men between himself and the archers. The archers could still launch arrows in their direction over the heads of their own men, but it would be hard to see who they were shooting at. In any event, no arrows came their way as the three charged the camp they had so recently left. As they continued to move ahead and left, Azziz' body guards retired straight back to the tent where the priest king could be seen gesturing wildly at his men. Athan saw that some of the cavalrymen had finally caught their horses, but instead of coming around to attack him or Timon's line, they seem to be pursuing Keros, who was now riding for his life, heading east away from the camp. Athan ran all the way past Azziz' tent and then behind it. The three men fell upon yet another small group of men standing around uncertainly on the back side of the tent. Perhaps they felt putting the canvas between them and the line of advancing enemy would grant them some sort of refuge. Athan and his men's unexpected appearance put them to flight but not before three of them went down. Captain Athan was able to close with one opponent and stun him with his club, allowing Philo to dispatch him.

There was now complete chaos in the camp. Men were fighting, some scrambling away, others standing in front of their carts and wagons uncertainly, women were screaming in fear and either trying to hide, run away, or were exhorting their companions to save them. Yet even in the madness something was penetrating the people in the caravan. The attackers were not mere brigands looking for spoil; they were primarily attacking the foreigners. And the men who were not part of Azziz' party began backing out of the fight. Realization was dawning on everyone that this was not a raid of rape and murder, but part of a battle. And that battle was still in doubt.

Azziz was a highly intelligent man of very considerable experience. Though he had spent much of his long life in study, he had also survived more than his share of adventures, and was no stranger to fighting. He saw that ahead of him on the plain the second line of attackers had stopped and were either crouching behind shields or were lying down after too many had taken arrows from his line of archers. The three spies, or more probably assassins, had been killed or driven off. His horsemen were regrouping to the east. The water behind him was an effective barrier on that flank. There was still fighting among the tents and wagons on the west side of camp, but if he could stop the initial attackers from advancing up the caravan from the west and menacing his archer's left flank, he thought he could hold the attackers still out in the pasture. Then his horsemen could sweep in and drive those men from meadow like sheep; there would still be light enough for that. Then his men would combine, and they would deal with the rest of the bandits in detail. The enemy's unexpected attack had lost momentum and was faltering. He only had to make sure the men from the western side did not get through to his archers. With a gesture he led his remaining bodyguards and associates toward the fighting in the center of his camp. They had taken the time to armor themselves and each man now had a helmet and either a shield or buckler.

Athan saw Azziz and his men as they came from the front of their tent moving toward the center of the camp - Azziz, the man who was most responsible for the death of his family. The man who might have his daughters.

"Azziz!" he screamed and charged with Philo and Petra on either side.

But the sorcerer priest was too far from him. Azziz did not even hear the challenge. The three companions were not able to get close until the Azziz was right on the front line of the battle among the wagons. Athan saw the man twist as a javelin skipped off his elaborate vest. Moving closer, Athan was aware that both Petra and Philo were engaged with opponents, but Athan remained dangerously focused on Azziz. He saw Azziz take a slash across his chest and then spit the young hypaspist who had delivered the blow. Continuing to close, Athan heard the sorcerer priest shouting encouragement to his men and saw the defender's resolve harden under the encouragement of their master. None of Azziz' men had any expectation of an attack from their rear. No one saw Athan approaching Azziz from behind. Athan stepped up and swung a terrific blow down at rear of the sorcerer priest's left shoulder. He had made no sound and was behind his enemy, yet Azziz turned to his left in time to catch most of the blow on his shield, though the impact knocked it from his arm. Snarling, he faced Athan stabbing with his short sword. Athan blocked the blow with the dagger in his left hand. The short sword's blade slid to the hilt of the dagger. Athan twisted the dagger's grip and, just like he had been taught so long ago, caught the blade in the forward pointing quillons. Azziz tried to pull his sword back for another thrust, but only jerked on Athan's arm. Athan whipped his club down onto Azziz' exposed right elbow. With a cry he dropped the short sword. But the sorcerer priest was an experienced fighter. His right arm was broken but without hesitation, he snatched off his iron helmet by its dangling chinstrap with his left hand, and swung it in a wicked horizontal arc at Athan's head. It might have worked, had Athan not ducked under the blow and in the same instant swung his club into Azziz' right knee. Azziz was a tough man; his elbow had been broken and he had not slowed an instant. There are limits; the blow to his knee caused him agony such as he had never known. He dropped screaming to his left knee, his good left arm releasing his grip on the helmet and involuntarily going to his ruined knee. He did not scream long. Athan took one step back and brought the club down in a full swing onto Azziz' unprotected skull.

There was a sound like a ripe melon, dropped from a height landing on a boulder. Azziz' skull was not merely broken it was shattered. Blood and brains flew into the air. What had once been Azziz flopped to the earth. The sound of Athan's blow to Azziz' head, so different than the screams of men and the clatter of weapons going on all around them seem to penetrate the consciousness of the fighters up and down the line.

"Azziz!" screamed one of his retainers. It was clear this was not a war cry but one of grief. "He has killed Azziz!" And with that the man rushed at Athan, all thoughts of defense abandoned. Captain Athan stopped him with a straight thrust to his face using the bloody club and Petra, coming up from the man's side delivered a mighty blow that severed the man's head from his body. For a moment the man, well dressed in a blue and white striped robe, clearly an important person staggered upright, blood fountaining from his neck. Then he collapsed and died. With him the defense collapsed as well. As one man the defenders in the camp turned, threw down their weapons, and ran away from the fight, abandoning the camp.

> Like a flock of birds in the air
> Like small fish in the sea
> They turn together away
> And flee

Archer Sergeant Modock thought he was winning his part of the fight but he was still worried. They had stopped the enemy coming across the meadow from the north, and the fight seemed to be stabilizing on his flanks, but he and his archers were running out of arrows. They had set up so quickly that no one had the chance to bring more than the single quiver of 20 they had always had at hand. He himself was without any at all. He had put them to good use. He thought he personally had put six men down killed or wounded, but with the arrows no longer coming so fast from behind the shields, the enemy was getting bolder and making short rushes toward his shields. "Boy," he called to the team's youngster who was detailed to bring fresh quivers. "Boy! Where are you?"

"Coming sergeant," he saw the youngster coming as fast as he could with an armful of quivers. He must have had trouble finding the stores, since they had not yet fully unpacked. There was a sudden burst of shouts and screams from the fighting behind them in the camp and then, the defenders in the camp were in full flight, pursued by the attackers. The boy looked around, saw what was happening, dropped the quivers where he was and joined them in flight. Modock called to his men to withdraw and raced to the fallen quivers. He had no time to do other than grab a handful of arrows and stuff them into the quiver he wore on his waist before the howling brigands were on him. He notched an arrow and fired it at point blank range into one man's chest, then had to turn and run to get some distance. He saw that his men had abandoned the shields and were now running for their lives from the surging wave of raiders coming at them from the field and western side of the camp. Modock looked over his shoulder to see if he had room to turn and shoot. He was being pursued too closely and there were too many of them for one arrow to make a difference. "To the trees," he shouted, "rally in the trees." The raiders would stop to plunder the camp. If enough men could be gathered back together, they could counterattack in the night. Modock never saw the slung stone that knocked him down. He was so stunned he was not even sure what happened to him, only that he had to get up and flee. He began to stumble to his feet to resume his flight. He never made it all the way up.

The fighters in Captain Athan's band were not like other brigands, at least not yet. Instead of stopping to plunder, rape, and murder, they continued in pursuit of the retreating enemy. Many had been trained as peltasts and chasing a fleeing enemy was one of the things such soldiers did. As hounds chase hares, so did the men from Athan's band chase the fugitives until it was almost dark and their quarry had all disappeared into the undergrowth to the east. The cavalry that might have stopped the pursuit took too long to gather their horses and reassemble. By the time they returned to the camp, all of their former comrades were either dead or vanished. The horsemen withdrew quietly back into the woods east of the camp.

Several hours after dark most of the survivors of Azziz' force had gathered approximately a parasang to the east of their former camp. None of the expedition's leaders had escaped to join them. After a bitter discussion the men decided to continue east with what little they had with them. At first light, they made their way together northeast until they struck the main track. After many hardships and adventures, most of them actually made it back to their homes far to the south and east.

Athan did not join his men in their wild pursuit of the fleeing enemy. He saw Simeon just long enough to enjoin him to keep the men from chasing their fleeing enemy too far. Then the young officer was gone after his men. Athan was very tired, too tired for the amount of fighting he had done. Petra was there beside him but Philo was gone. It was Petra who found him. Philo was face down in the dirt, sword in hand, a gaping wound in his back.

"Died instantly," observed Athan, "there is not much blood. Struck from behind."

"They were all around us there for a bit, Captain" said Petra in plain voice. Petra was one of the few men who still referred to Athan by his old title. "I doubt he ever saw who killed him. Looks like a spear."

The two men turned the sergeant over. His eyes and mouth were open. Petra closed the eyes with two fingers. "Nice sword," he said referring to the kopis Philo had always prized. Philo had paid a lot for it; he always said that a man should never stint on his tools. It had a sturdy well-tempered iron blade and a fine cross-hatched bone grip. The grip was enclosed by a brass guard that curled back all the way around to the butt of the handle, fully enclosing the hand. Not only did this type of guard protect the hand, but it could be used to smash into an enemy in really close in combat. Philo had called that type of guard his 'brass knuckles'. Though it had a useful point, the thick convex blade was primarily designed to hack through shields and helmets. In capable hands it was a fearsome battle weapon.

"Keep it," replied Athan.

"No, Captain, I think you should take it. I think he would have liked that. He always was telling us to make sure to protect you. You should wear his sword and belt. That way he can keep on protecting you in a way."

Petra unbuckled the sword belt, pulled it from Philo's body and took the sword from the grasp of the dead man. "From his hand to yours, sir," he said offering the belt and sword to his captain.

Athan dropped the club into the blood-wet earth and put on the belt, and then stooping to the dead body of the sorcerer he wiped the blood from the kopis on the corpse's robes before sheathing the blade.

"Why did you not carry a sword today, Captain?" asked Petra. He was normally the most laconic of men; tonight he was a virtually chatterbox. "We had an extra one you could have used."

"Several reasons," replied his former captain, "I thought it would make me less of threat so I could get close enough to talk to and maybe even kill this Azziz fellow. It let me limp so I seemed less threatening. And I heard that this thing," he gestured to corpse of Azziz, "could not be harmed by blade or arrow."

"He couldn't stand up to a stout bit of oak though," laughed Petra.

"Let's see what he has," said Athan.

"You look, Captain. I will examine lesser men and leave the sorcerers to the captains of this world." He turned to examine some of the other corpses for valuables.

Athan first rifled the dead man's silk purse. It made a satisfying weight in his hand and he was not surprised to see a glint of gold when he took a quick glance inside. Running his hands down the seams of the expensive robe, he was a little surprised not to feel lumps. Rich men often hid jewels in their linings, but Azziz had obviously felt so secure he did not need to resort to such measures. The rings he left for his people. 'Do not bind the muzzle of the ox that treads the grain,' he thought. He was puzzled about something. Why should such a rich man wear a simple copper chain around his neck? Why not gold? He tipped up the ruined head and lifted the chain off the neck. It supported a strange crystal. It was almost clear with a faintly milky tint. About the size of his little fingernail, it was cut symmetrically with eight facets; two four sided pyramids base to base. A sturdy-looking clasp at the top of the crystal was made of the same material as the chain. Upon examination the chain Athan decided it was apparently not made of copper after all but some strange metal he had never seen before. Athan took the chain and placed it around his neck under his tunic next to the leather thong that held his tinder. He had expected the crystal might still be warm from Azziz' body, but he did not expect it to suddenly grow warmer as it lay against his chest. He felt very odd, dizzy, disoriented, almost nauseated, but the feeling quickly passed.

There was something else odd about Azziz' garments: that vest. He undid the strange fastening on the front of the vest, sat the corpse up and pulled the vest of, twisting the body as it came off. The vest was not heavy, yet it was unexpectedly stiff. He could bend it, but it was clearly more than merely leather. He looked where he had seen the vest deflect a javelin and saw only a faint scratch. There was no sign where it had been slashed by the blade. 'Metal', he thought, 'the leather is only a seeming. It has metal beneath it. But how flexible it is! And it is so light!' Without another thought he swung the vest around and put his arms through the holes. He did not even have time to fasten it across his chest before the reaction hit him. This time he became so dizzy that he fell to his knees next to the corpse of his dead enemy. This turned out to be fortunate because the nausea was so great that he vomited into the mud.

"Captain?" It was Petra, over to him as soon as he saw him fall. "Are you injured?"

"I am all right," replied Athan from his knees, "It is just a reaction from the battle. I fear we lost many good comrades this day." He struggled up to his feet. "I have been putting off looking for the real treasures."

Then to the astonishment of Petra he walked not toward the riches of Azziz' tent, but toward the center of the camp. "But, Captain," he protested.

"Take custody of the big tent, Petra. We will hold all that is in it for common shares."

"Thank'ee Captain. Most generous. I will take care of it at once." Petra immediately trotted to the tent to secure it from all those other thieves he traveled with and to see if there were any small items inside that might just fit in his purse before they came in to divide the spoils.

At last Athan could seek what had caused him to attack this caravan. Why he had taken such a risk and caused the deaths of so many men. He could still taste the vomit in his mouth so he stopped and lifted a water bag off a seemingly abandoned wagon. He felt movement inside. He drew the kopis but his instinct or perhaps the lightness of the movement told him there was no threat.

"You can come out now," he said. "The battle is over. We are not stealing from merchants, and we do not rape." There was no reply. "Very well, but if you do not stand by your wagon and claim it as your own it may be burned."

That brought a squeak from inside, and a small face with huge brown eyes peered out over the top of the wagon bed. "Do you swear you speak truly, sir?" came a young woman's voice.

"I do," replied Athan in his heartiest voice. "Where is your husband?"

"Gone, sir, I know not where, or if he even survived, but he was not my husband, sir. He took me in service to get me away from my father."

"Ho, Mithres, come here," called Athan as he saw one of his young peltasts wandering by looking for enemies or portable plunder. "I have a mission for you. Find this wagon's animal, hitch it to this wagon and take it to the caravan to the north. Tell them that you are a friend of Jonathan's."

"Oh, Captain, there is booty everywhere tonight! Why do I have be the one to do this?"

"I think you will find that this particular wagon has ample valuables of its own."

It was almost dark now, but there were fires providing enough light for the young woman to see Mithres. Slowly she raised her curly head over the wagon seat and looked at him.

"I see, Captain," he smiled, "thank you."

"No, Mithres," enjoined Athan, "I charge you to do no harm to this woman and to protect her. Will you do so on your honor?"

"I will, sir," replied the peltast looking at the girl who was looking at him.

"There young lady, you are under Mithres' protection now. Find your donkey and go with him."

"It's a mule," she said, "with a leather harness and bells. Tell me sir, are these men really all yours to command?" she said watching Mithres heading off toward some of the livestock. "Yes, that is him over there," she called out to Mithres gesturing toward one of the animals.

"Yes girl, they are."

"And are they all as handsome as he is?" Her eyes were still on Mithres.

"No, miss," lied Athan, "he is the most handsome of them all."

"Thank you Captain," she smiled up at him. "I heard your promise Mithres," she called to the young man, as he led the designated mule to her wagon. "You must protect me now."

Poor Mithres never had a chance. By the time they were admitted into the north caravan's laager, she had reminded him that his promise to protect her did not have an end date on it. And the next day, when they found her former master's body, she was able to persuade Mithres that he should take his share of the booty and escort her back west, since now she now had a fine mule, wagon, and trade goods by way of a dowry. Mithres was a man of his word; he did continue to protect and provide first her and then their children until his death, forty-one years later.

Elsewhere on the field things were much grimmer. There were many wounded; some hurts were minor and required little more than bandaging and rest, but others needed help that was not readily available. One of those was Timon. He had taken an arrow through the meaty part of his thigh while out in the meadow. Although the wound was not immediately life-threatening, he was very concerned that it would become infected, and more directly, it hurt like Hades itself. The arrow was out of the leg now, and he was sitting in what had been Azziz' tent being tended to by seven of Azziz' eight former dancing slave girls.

In fact, the girls did much more than dance. They listened, they comforted, they consoled, and they made everyone else envious of Azziz, which was the point. Life as a slave was almost always hard, but these young women, through their looks, talent, athletic ability, and good luck, had landed in a prime spot: one with a not too demanding owner, adequate creature comforts, and a degree of security. Most of them actually loved the dancing part; it made them feel free. All that had disappeared in an hour. They had waited in the tent with dread until Petra arrived with two of his men he had snagged on his way to Azziz' tent. Posting the two men at the entrance as sentries, he ordered them to admit only the wounded who were to be tended within the tent. Then after a brief consultation took one of the slave girls, he retired to an enclosed area of the tent for a 'personal consultation' with her.

When Timon's men came in bearing their leader, it did not take the seven remaining girls more than a moment to decide that, based on Timon's appearance and the way his men were treating him, this was the man in charge and thus was the person best able to protect them from general rape. They immediately put aside their day-to-day jealousies and petty rivalries and began to work as a team to make sure that this man needed them. At least until they could find someone better.

Athan continued searching the heart of the caravan. There was some isolated noises of destruction now, crashing, breaking of crockery, splintering of locked chests, screams and shouts. Plundering had not yet become general, and the fighting seemed to have stopped altogether. Although it was now dark, he was able to find his way to a high-sided wagon where the young captives were being held, led by unmistakable sounds of crying children and vain attempts of someone inside to quiet them. His heart began hammering in his chest as he opened the door into the back of the enclosed wagon. It was hot and stank of unwashed diapers and sour milk, smells a father knows well. There was a dim lamp showing three young women holding two infants each and perhaps six other children ranging in age from two to four, all looking back at him in fear. There was no six-year-old girl with curly brown hair who was already beginning to resemble her mother. There was no bright-eyed girl of eight who would run to hug his neck.

"Who are you?" he asked more harshly than he intended.

"Marissa," came a very meek reply from the oldest girl, who was perhaps 20 years old.

"What are you doing with these children in this wagon?"

"We are supposed to take care of them and keep them quiet. We were to feed and care for the little ones."

Wet nurses then. Probably one of the infants they were holding would belong to them. There was a bag next to the door that smelled of milk, most likely from the little herd of goats he had seen with the caravan.

"Are you from Epiria? Why did they take all these little ones?" his questions were to Marissa, who seemed to be the least cowed of anyone in this strange wagon.

"Yes, sir," she replied. Then her voice became hard and bitter. "They gathered all these orphans or babies that had no mother to care for them. They are going to kill them."

"What!"

"They take them from us and throw the babies into a fire inside some idol that Azziz has up in his wagon. They think we didn't know, but they have taken three babies and they burned them. It's for their god."

Athan was shocked. He was familiar with infanticide; unwanted newborns were sometimes left exposed on a hillside where they quickly perished. He had heard of human sacrifice. But never had he heard of throwing a baby on a fire to propitiate some god. This was more than just some filthy foreign worship; this was fundamentally wrong.

"Is one of those your baby?" he asked for no particular reason other than to try to recover from what she had just told him. It was the wrong question.

"No," she said in a flat voice, her face showing bleak despair, "she is dead. I do not even know what their names are." Next to her one of the other young woman still holding two infants began to sob uncontrollably, while the other clutched her two children to her breast even more tightly. All the other children picked up on the mood and began to cry as well.

"It is over now," he told them pulling back from the entrance. "You can go home now." Then a final forlorn question, 'Are there any more children?"

Marissa mutely shook her head. Athan left the door to the wagon open, but no one in the wagon seemed to want to go outside.

There was a strange feeling in the camp; it was as though everyone, victors, vanquished, and victims alike, were all waiting for someone to tell them what to do next. In a matter of moments this relative hiatus would pass and men would start taking things from the wagons, and then taking the women, and killing anyone that tried to stop them. It was a testament to their discipline that it had not already started.

"Hypaspists! Sergeants! To me!" It was his rallying cry, taken up by his men. Within minutes he had over a score of men with him. He ordered them to gather up their comrades and assemble at big blue and white tent at the east side of the camp. He did not answer any of the questions his men shouted at him, but left them imagining a new threat. On his way to the tent he saw a figure under a fine wagon; the caravan guide had apparently survived the fighting.

"You," Athan directed the man, "get out here." As Athan was now surrounded by half a dozen stout fighters, the man was dragged from under his wagon and set on his feet.

"You are from Epiria. You have my leave to take any wagons or carts that were not with Azziz' company and move them next to Pelops' caravan, that group of wagons at the north side of the pasture. Laager them there and await my visit in the morning. Take nothing that belonged to any foreigner or it will go hard with you. Do you understand my orders?"

"Yes, Chief."

"You have one hour. And make certain that the little children in that wagon are well cared for. I am holding you personally responsible for their safety."

"Yes, Chief."

Then he directed his men to form a line to sweep through the camp rounding up stragglers and wounded men; searching especially for any enemy who was hiding in the camp. They found several of each, pressing their own men into the line, caring for their own wounded and killing any of Azziz' men they found. The rally cry worked well. By the time Athan arrived at the tent most of his survivors including all the wounded that had been found were assembled by the large tent. Timon caused himself to be carried outside for orders.

The first order of business was to reinforce the order to every man that all the loot would be shared out and individual looting was forbidden. Second, he announced that the fellow travelers who were from Epiria would be allowed to relocate away from the scene of the fighting and laager with Pelops' group. They would be thoroughly investigated in the light of the next morning. Scouts were sent out to look for any remaining enemies and to take care of any wounded found outside the camp. That meant bringing them to the big tent where Timon's girls (for so effective were they in attaching themselves to him that this was already how they were known) would provide them succor. In the case of the followers of the late Azziz, the wounded would be taken care of in a different, grimmer way. Watches were posted, teams organized, and order restored in short order.

Timon, who was still in pain, but thanks to the ministrations of the girls was feeling much better about life in general, asked if he could show his captain what was inside the tent. Timon presented the eight dancing girls to Athan, naming each without hesitation. Petra stood proudly next to a series of chests. To Athan's surprise, one of the girls was standing next to Petra and actually seemed to be flirting with him. He was smiling back down at her. On the far side of the tent was a low portable dais with a round black iron stove-like idol. One look at the large opening in the upper front of the device and Athan knew that Marissa had not lied. Next to idol was a foreigner on his knees with his arms bound behind him. He was of middle years with the thick curly black beard that all of Azziz' company seem to favor. He wore a fine robe, expensive rings, and had large jeweled golden earrings. He looked at Athan with as much pride as a man could muster under the circumstances.

The interrogation did not take long. He discovered that the man was a famous priest of the god Bal. The man told Athan that if they would let him go, he would assure them of the protection of the god. Were he to be injured, Bal would certainly bring catastrophe to them all.

There followed a series of questions concerning their destination, goods, size of the party, and purpose of coming. From the long, disjointed and contradictory replies, Athan became convinced that the man was simply lying in an effort to save his life. Finally he asked the question that had been puzzling him for the past hour.

"Why do you burn babies?"

There was a long and convoluted reply which when condensed came down to this:

"It gives us power."

Athan leaned forward and took one of the man's earrings in each hand. Then he yanked them down and out accompanied by a muffled scream from the man. Turning to Petra he said "Sergeant, take two men and carry this one to the pond. Tie a rope around his foot."

"Around his foot?" questioned Petra.

"So you can haul the corpse out after he drowns."

And so it was done, though they discovered the priest could swim surprisingly well with his hands bound. It wasn't until one of the men hit him in the head a few times with the butt of a spear before he finally went down for good.

Athan stopped and spoke to the girl who standing next to and smiling up at Sergeant Petra. "Do you know Petra?" he asked.

"Oh," she smiled, "Is that his name? No, I only met him a short while ago. But he is a sweet man. You see, he was the first to come into the tent. We knew what would be expected of us, so I approached him first. I am older and more experienced than some of others," she explained. "But he did not ravage me in front of everyone as I feared. He took me into a private area. Then he asked me, he **asked** me,' she repeated in astonishment, "if I would do it with him. Me, a slave girl! He asked if I would mind." She shook her head in mild disbelief. "Of course I couldn't say no, but I think if I had, he would have found another instead. Fortunately I did not refuse him," she gave a radiant smile. "He is a powerful lover."

Athan could not think of a single thing to say to that. He handed her the two earrings he had just removed for the unfortunate priest. Then he walked over to where one of his quartermasters was opening the latches on a heavy wooden chest. As they stood together, the man opened the chest and for the second time in a minute Athan was struck dumb. The chest held bars of what could only be precious metals, gold on one side, and silver on the other. Quickly Athan and quartermaster counted the bars.

"There is over three year's salary for every man!" marveled the quartermaster.

"That is how we will share it out, then," said Athan. "Let's see what else is here."

There was plenty. There were precious and semi precious gems, fine cloth, ivory carvings, and enough clothing to deck out the entire band. In addition to Timon's eight girls, there were a score of other slaves and bonded servants that slowly returned to the tent as it became clear that they would not be harmed. In short, it was a prince's ransom, a haul of amazing proportions. Before Athan left the tent, he added two additional guards to the tent 'to provide security for those inside.' They would count the goods and divide them in the morning.

There were no wolves in the area to trouble the survivors that evening, but there were wild dogs and feral pigs that were worse than the dogs. They devoured portions of the dead that had fallen at a distance from the camp, such as poor Keros.

Keros had been the true hero of the battle. Without him the cavalrymen would have probably caught enough horses to mount a charge against Timon's group that was caught in the open and the cavalry would have slaughtered them all. Though his agile little pony was able to dodge and escape for a while, eventually the enemy cavalry were able to cut him off then cut him down. But that took so long, and they had come far from the field, that by they time they could get back to the scene of the battle, it was all over. Instead of being able to turn the tide of battle the cavalry were only able to help their surviving comrades retreat from the scene.

Periodically during the night screams came from out of the darkness as a wounded man was shocked into consciousness when he began to be devoured by the night prowlers. Perhaps that is what would have happened to Laurel, out there on the grass, but her faithful Dragon remained beside her, acting as both protection and a marker so that when one of the peltasts accompanied by Jokrastes, who had regained consciousness with his back already stitched up, found her lying there in the field. The two men had some difficulty placating Dragon, who at first did not want them near her. After soothing him down they placed her on the back of stallion with Jokrastes walking alongside holding her up all the way to Azziz' tent. There they found that the bandage that had prevented her from bleeding to death had also ruined her arm. Two days later when the arm began to show signs of gangrene, they were forced to amputate it halfway between the elbow and shoulder. Jokrastes held her hand until she mercifully fainted from the pain. He fainted himself a moment later.

The Pelops' caravan stayed in High Meadows for two more days. In fact, a brisk trade between the two camps sprang up as the suddenly wealthy members of Athan's band found they could now purchase all kinds of things they had not realized they needed until they were able to afford them.

When Pelops' caravan did resume its westward journey, it had almost doubled in size. Athan had called the band together after awarding them their shares of the goods, which totaled almost four year's salary for a guardsman, and offered each of them their release from the band. With the destruction of the sorcerer priest and his men, Athan declared that their revenge was complete. Athan would go back north into the hills with anyone who wished to accompany him. Those who wished to go elsewhere could go east with the remains of the captured caravan and the new caravan that had come in the night before. Those who wished to return to Epiria could go west with Pelops' caravan. Even Clestonese, the man who, with his late companion-cousin had first told the band of Azziz' caravan, was rewarded and sent on his way. Looking at his share of the loot, Clestonese decided he had more than a fair exchange for the loss of the nephew of his wife's sister's husband.

Two of those who returned to the west with the caravan were Jokrastes and Laurel. With their joint share of the booty, for Athan decreed that she should have the same share as any of the men, they set up a successful trading concern. They had nine children together, all of whom survived to adulthood, though many of them felt they narrowly avoided being bored to death listening to stories of their mother's wild youth. But in time her many grandchildren loved to hear her now considerably enhanced stories that eventually led to the legend of Laurel, Queen of the Hill Brigands.

He awoke in the morning light. He was not sure if he had slept one night or two nights and a day. But he did feel better, even if he was weak. The first thing he had to do was to restart the fire. Fortunately he had adequate dry tinder and some of his pitch-smeared tow left. This time he was able to get a flame to take on the very first spark. He concentrated on building up his fire until it gave him a fine, healthy blaze. He heated up the water and added some of the oats to it. After the cup had reached a roiling boil he supplemented the oats with some pieces of the dried apples. When his breakfast was ready he poured the oats onto his plate, wiped out his cup, refilled it with water and put it on the fire again for some tea. The oatmeal was devoured long before the tea water could boil. The oats helped fill him up but he could see his stock was running out. The Old King wiped his plate clean and then served himself tea which, if not boiling, was at least hot.

The hot food had a wonderful restorative effect. After his first real meal in days, his morale was greatly raised. The snow outside was still high and the nights were killingly cold, but he could wait here in safety for a while longer.

As he drank his tea he thought about his days as a brigand. Things changed after he killed Azziz. The old man touched the crystal he still wore around his neck. His life was never the same after that fight in High Meadows. In time, Chief Athan had led a greatly reduced band up to a small village in the hills, where they had lived for over a year. Athan and his men had all they needed, nowhere special to go and nothing better to do.

'Much like now,' thought the Old King and he sat back on his little bed, wrapped himself against the cold and remembered.

Chapter Ten- Gains

As time passed men came and went from Chief Athan's band. The shares of booty had included the eight dancing girls. Since there were seven surviving officers and sergeants, the girls were divided among them. The general consensus was that Chief Athan should have two, but he deferred to Timon who had decided to retire. Timon found his wounded leg bothered him too much for an active life, so he took his share, including both offered girls, and retired to a small city by the sea. They lived together comfortably for several years, until he suffered a fatal heart attack, some said due to exhaustion brought on by his two devoted companions.

Petra stayed with the band for a while, but his girl quickly became bored with village life in the hills, and so he too took his leave. In fact, none of the girls enjoyed the quiet life. At about the same time Athan, Beltos, Simeon, and the other sergeants found they either did not care for or could not afford the lifestyle required by a high-quality dancing girl and eventually sold them to wealthy patrons to everyone's general relief. For the women, it put them back in a sophisticated society with a good chance to achieve the status of hetaira. As for the men, although having a beautiful and high-spirited girl provided exciting pyrotechnics, after a while, even pyrotechnics became tedious.

One odd fallout from the captured booty was entirely personal to Athan. Two months after he took Azziz' vest and began wearing the sorcerer priest's strange crystal around his neck, Athan's teeth began falling out. At first he was upset; a man without teeth was in a bad way, limited to soft foods, soups and the like. It was the first sign of decrepitude. To his complete amazement, he found a new set of teeth coming in. Even the two teeth he had previously lost were replaced. Not only were they replaced, they came in straight, white, and strong. His dancing girl teased him at first about his new teeth, but Athan thought she was also a little unsettled by his new dentition. He also noticed vaguely that after the battle he no longer ever seemed to get sick. He had always been healthy, but as the years passed he could not help but notice that now he never became ill. He did not mention his new teeth to anyone and soon it was forgotten by his men; neither did he bring attention to his unnaturally good health, and no one else seemed to notice. He continued to wear the crystal, and came to value it as perhaps the most precious item he had taken in that caravan's rich plunder. He openly wore the chain around his neck, but kept the crystal inside a little bag of tinder he wore in case he needed to start a fire in some crisis. Inside the leather pouch his talisman was safely out of sight even when his tunic was off.

Even the biggest hauls of booty are eventually exhausted. So in order to live, the band still needed to conduct occasional raids on travelers. And even the best known and wealthiest bands sometimes go through dry times where there is little income. You can become

236

a victim of your own success. An area known for bandit activity is avoided or the caravans that pass through are too heavily guarded for attack. Chief Athan had to always balance an equation for the number of men he should keep in his band. Too many, and they required frequent robberies to feed them; too few and they were limited in the actions they could take. Eventually he found that a group of between a dozen and a score or men was a good balance.

He had two faithful officers in these years - two friends who met on a battlefield, Beltos and Simeon. They came from different backgrounds. Simeon had, like Chief Athan, become a guardsman because he had few other options. The middle son of a farmer, he disliked agriculture and had thought to move to a city, where he might become educated. He had become a member of the guard more by accident than design. Like his chief, fighting was the only trade he knew. Beltos' family, on the other hand, had been part of the oligarchy that ruled the city. Though he was a second son, there was enough wealth and influence in his family to assure him a bright future in almost any career he cared to try. He had still been in the process of completing his education when he chose to perform his civic duty as a hoplite and marched off to 'Achilles' Disaster'. Like Athan he had lost his entire family. Unlike Athan though, he knew their fates. His father and three brothers had all died while under arms, either in the Disaster or in the fighting when the city fell. His mother had been murdered. The new city oligarchs had proscribed the rest of Beltos' extended family. His uncles, aunts, and cousins had either been killed or were exiled to foreign cities. So beyond their shared friendship and bonds of battle, the three comrades stayed together, in part, because they had nowhere else to go. Following the departure of the exotic but unsuitable dancing girls, each of the men had a variety of generally unsatisfying liaisons with local girls. And, though it did not seem to trouble either Chief Athan or Simeon, as years went by in the hills, Beltos began to feel a vague pull back toward the civilization of a city.

Bandits can employ a number of strategies to take goods from passing travelers. Some wild and desperate groups would attack and kill everyone in a party, take everything and leave the bodies behind. There were problems with this style. First, travelers who cannot surrender may fight to the death, and such struggles often resulted in casualties to the attackers. Successful bandits do not suffer losses readily. The band tends to melt away. Further, such a brutal method is a significant threat to the entire region, and causes a much swifter and determined response. Armed companies hunt down such bands, both for vengeance as well as to provide safe passage for traders.

A more sustainable system was to use overwhelming force to compel the travelers to surrender their goods, and leave them alive with at least some of their goods intact. There were levels of this system ranging from taking almost everything to merely collecting those valuables that were easily portable. Chief Athan preferred a milder variation of this method. His band would suddenly appear out of ambush in a position of overwhelming superiority but withhold their attack. They would then either negotiate a fee for safe passage or offer to protect the caravan through this dangerous area, also for a negotiated fee. When done properly, such arrangements could be undertaken by a single negotiator approaching a laagered caravan about to enter a dangerous passage. These arrangements then started to be set up over a beaker of wine in a tavern house, talking with caravan guides who had paid such fees in the past. In fact, Chief Athan's band had successfully defended a caravan under their protection from an attack by other outlaws. No matter how discrete and civilized the arrangement, it was still outside what passed for law in that place and time. From time to time groups of armed men would come into the hills to hunt Chief Athan's band. All he could do then was leave whatever village he was paying to stay in, or whatever permanent camp he had established, and retreat farther into the hills. There was no profit to be made attacking armed men, and after a few years, Chief Athan had given up fighting for any reason other than the purest necessity.

One winter a series of these brigand-clearing expeditions forced Athan's band to repeatedly relocate and run for shelter. Several other groups of bandits in the hills had not been as alert and had been annihilated. All the retreating with limited opportunity to obtain any plunder brought the band to a new low. Both funds and supplies were in short supply. Even worse, they were farther south and west than they had ever been before; unfamiliar territory was dangerous territory.

The band was vulnerable. They needed to bring in some money, and soon.

Athan, Simeon, and Beltos sat in a tent one rainy night in early spring and considered their possibilities. It was early in the year for caravans to be moving, but Simeon had heard an interesting rumor from one of the informants in a city to the east. A wealthy widow had remarried, and had a daughter from her previous marriage. This young woman was now being shown about with an eye to making a good match. Allegedly they had been all the way to Delphi, whether to visit the oracle or to meet with families in that city was not known. In any event the visit had not resulted in an offer of marriage. The mother and daughter (and presumably the dowry) were returning to their home city of Buttrotiuria in a carriage over roads not too far to the south from where they were. The rumor was that the voyage over by sea had been most difficult, and the women had insisted upon returning home by land. They would be escorted, of course, and with the recent destruction of so many bandits the risk was now considered low. Perhaps there was a chance to take this target.

"There is no way to know just how much dowry there will be," mused Simeon, "but there is another possible way to get some cash. We could take the widow as hostage and ransom her. Her new husband, Aorastus, is said to be rich as well. Surely he would be willing to spend some of his new bride's money to recover her."

"No, women are too much trouble," objected Beltos.

"There is a risk that the husband would not want a wife back after she has been carried off and presumably defiled by brigands," put in Athan.

"You do not appreciate our good reputation," countered Simeon. It was true that Chief Athan's band was known to be 'civilized' with murders and rapes very rare. This was in part due to the belief that if men knew that they could surrender without paying too great a price, they would not fight as desperately. It was also because Beltos still retained some of his aristocratic feelings that might even be characterized as chivalrous. He preferred to flirt with rather than rape female captives. Thus if Athan's band were to offer assurances of a safe and unsullied return, there was a chance that a ransom could be arranged.

"Well, if the dowry's big enough, I say we let the women go," grumbled Beltos, giving in to the idea of an ambush of the returning women.

They almost missed them. By the time Simeon's contact got the word to them of the target's departure, the women's party, consisting of an enclosed carriage, a wagon, and six outriders, had left the city and was well on its way. Obviously intending to spend as little time as possible in wild country, they set a cracking pace and had camped in a secure location nearly out of the hills before the first of Chief Athan's scouts located them. It took a long night riding over back trails before Athan's band of just over a dozen men were able to reach a good position on the road ahead of the party. The level of anxiety was raised when a scout checking to the west signaled them that there was another caravan approaching from that direction. The signals were not able to give exact estimates, but the sense of them was that the oncoming party was large and would arrive before noon. It was a real relief then when only two hours after sunrise another set of signals from the east let the band know their intended quarry was approaching.

The site of the ambush was a curved place where the road, relatively wide at this point, curved around a hill. A cut had been made to level the road, with a short embankment next to the rising hill on the right, and a shallow descent to a heavily wooded ravine to the left. Stopping a rapidly moving group of wagons and riders without killing anyone requires some art. In this case, once it was confirmed no other groups would arrive before the target, a small bushy tree was uprooted and pushed down the slope onto the road. A horse could get by the blockage but not a wagon. There was little cover on the bare upslope on this part of the trail. This would provide a false sense of confidence to the escort since attacks almost always came from above and, in this case, it was more than two bowshots to the crest of the hill.

This ambuscade was an exception. There were a few small places of concealment upslope hiding three members of the band, but the rest were well concealed on the down-slope side of the road and well before from the obstructing tree.

As hoped, the four horsemen leading the two vehicles were too close to the lead carriage and did not see the barrier around the bend of the road until it was quite near. They pulled up with some confusion, looking uphill in concern. As if to validate their worry, three armed men, two with bows and one with a brace of javelins, revealed themselves some distance up hill. What the leader of the escort would have done had that been the only threat will never be known because, with all attention directed upslope, they did not notice the men who had been concealed down slope until the brigands were among the horsemen, taking reins, menacing those who tried to draw weapons with spears and javelins. In a moment entire group was captured without a single blow being struck.

"Down, all you down from your mounts and wagons," cried Simeon in a commanding voice, "you will not be harmed. Down and draw no weapons." The guards, with men all around them and nowhere to go, began to dismount and climb down from the wagon and enclosed carriage.

"This will only take a short time and you will be on you way again, no worse for the wear," Simeon assured them.

Simeon climbed up onto the open wagon, which was ahead of the carriage. It was packed with covered chests and crates. "Tell me good man," he addressed an older man who appeared to have some official function, "where is your mistress' dowry? It would save us all time and effort if you would just show us where it is located, so we can all be on our separate ways."

The old man looked flustered. "There is no dowry,' he spluttered, obviously flustered. "We brought no dowry with us, so there is none to return. She had no offer pending so did not have any reason to bring a dowry with us. Don't you understand that bringing a dowry before there was an understanding between the families would be uncivilized?" The clear implication was that barbarians like them could not possibly understand such sophisticated concepts of culture. It was also clear that he was telling the truth.

"Arthos, Persus," directed Simeon to two of his men, "get up here and check these trunks for anything valuable." Simeon was certain that the only things in there would be necessary household goods and womanly fripperies, neither one of which would help the band. "Chief, it looks like we will have to go to our alternate plan. This looks like a complete washout."

Athan walked back to where Beltos stood on the uphill side of the carriage. It was completely still behind the closed windows. "Madam," Athan addressed the enclosed carriage, "I must ask you to all to step outside." There was quiet whispered conversation inside. Athan raised his voice slightly. "Mira, wife of Aorastus, I would have speech with you. We know you and your daughter are within. Please do not make us come inside and drag you out."

There was a sound as the latch to the door worked and a lovely, well-dressed woman stepped out and onto the carriage step.

She looked around herself apprehensively. She saw a rough group of armed men who had disarmed that worthless escort she had hired. The bandits were dressed strangely to her eye; tunics with baggy trousers covering their legs like the barbarians but they also wore the familiar cloth pilleus hats on their heads. The man who had spoken to her was obviously their leader. He wore a dark red vest, a sash around his waist and a wide sword with a strange down curved blade that he had either put back in its sheath or possibly never even drawn at all. He was, she decided, rather handsome in a raffish way. There was a strange air of conventionality about him considering he was a bandit. In a sudden moment she felt she could trust this man; why, she did not know.

'A bit old to be a bride,' thought Athan, 'no wonder they had to shop her about. I wonder what is wrong with her; she is too far too pretty to be unmarried.'

Speaking kindly he said, "Young lady, I wish to speak with your mother. Pray have her come outside."

The woman smiled. Her confidence was suddenly restored, and she stepped gracefully down to the road. "I am she, but I must ask your intentions," she spoke with great poise staring Athan right in the eyes, "If we are to be raped, I would prefer my daughter and maids be dragged out kicking and screaming rather than to willingly submit."

"Lady," said Athan meeting her gaze and using the formal address of respect, "we will neither rape nor harm you or your party."

"Do you swear this by the gods?"

"I do," a vow easily given, as Athan had little belief in, or respect for the gods he knew.

"Then we must trust you. Rheta, please come down."

The door to the carriage that had been partially closed swung back open and a young woman gripping the edge of the door stepped out onto the step. She was in her late teens; her head was uncovered, revealing her long brown hair pulled back informally by a black velvet ribbon. The morning sun brought out the highlights in her hair, showed her clear complexion and made her large brown eyes sparkle.

'She just can't resist making an entrance,' thought her mother not realizing how similar in style it was to her own exit.

'Now there is a beauty. Why couldn't they find such a one a husband?' thought Athan.

Rheta's glance swept the little group watching her and then focused suddenly on Beltos, who was openly staring at her. She looked directly at him for a moment, then cast her head down, and almost immediately glanced upward again looking at him through her long lashes.

'I had no idea bandits could be so good looking,' thought Rheta.
'Now THAT is what I have been looking for,' thought Beltos.

There was a feeling in the air like some giant invisible static spark.

'Uh Oh' thought Athan.
'Uh Oh' thought Mira.

There was a long moment without any sound at all. Then Simeon jumped down from the wagon and strode up to them.

"Looks like there's nothing worthwhile in the wagon, Chief. Has anyone checked the carriage yet?"

With a slight start Athan stepped forward to hand down Rheta and said, "Ladies, I am Athan, son of Medius, late of the city guard of Epiria. This worthy gentleman is Beltos, son of Ajaxus, late oligarch of the city of Epiria. His companion there is his fellow officer Simeon, son of Simeon, also late of the city guard."

With equal formality Mira introduced herself, her daughter, and then more informally her daughter's maid, Agalia, and her own maid, Bea. Agalia was a lively young thing a few years younger than Rheta, slender with mop of curling hair. It took a confident woman to have a maid so pretty, but with her height and bearing Rheta easily dominated her servant. Bea was past middle age and obviously devoted to her mistress. Of the four women, she was the only one that was obviously frightened. Young Agalia was looking around with excited interest; Mira maintained a cool demeanor, and Rheta was seemingly unable to take her eyes off of Beltos. Her mother artfully managed to interpose herself between the two while addressing the bandit chief. "It is as you have already discovered, we have no real money or jewelry with us, certainly nothing like a dowry. That would have been sent by separately should we have been able to find a suitable match."

"So she is not betrothed yet," interposed Beltos eagerly.

'Oh gods,' thought Athan, 'he is worse than a dog chasing a bitch in heat.'

"No," said Mira, peering around her mother to look at Beltos. "I found no one interesting there."

'Hera protect us all!' thought Mira, 'she is ready to run off and lay with the first handsome bandit she sees.'

"Lady," interrupted Simeon, "we intend to ransom you and your daughter from your husband. "You there," he continued, looking back at the older man who had remained back in the lead wagon. "What is your name and rank?"

"He is Kopria, my personal steward," cut in Mira.

"Can he be trusted?" Simeon asked.

"Yes."

"Can he read and write?"

"Of course."

"Good, Chief, this man can bear our note to her husband."

"Very well, Simeon. Lady, do you or any member of your party have paper or parchment and a pen that I might employ?"

"You write?" asked Mira in surprise.

"Not as well as Beltos, who was a scholar, but yes, Lady, I write. I have not always been a brigand."

'Now why do I want to impress this woman,' he wondered.

Mira directed young Agalia to fetch her writing box from the wagon. While all this was going on, the escort, servants, and drivers were herded away from the women down the road to the west. They were allowed to keep any personal effects they could grab. All were allowed to maintain their knives or daggers as well as their cloaks and headgear. They were even given two water bottles and some of the provisions from the wagon. They were told to move down the hill toward the west and that a caravan would be along soon to help them. The horses that had been ridden by the escort were brought back up the road to the wagons. The draft mules were also unhitched and led back past the wagons. Some of the more portable and pilferable things in the wagon, were hastily loaded on the animal's backs. The women were allowed to bring some of their luggage containing their clothing. By the time Athan had carefully if somewhat laboriously finished his draft of a letter to Mira's husband, all was in readiness for departure.

Handing the missive to Kopria, Athan told him of the contents of the letter. He assured the recipient that the women would be held safe and unsullied and provided a rendezvous to discuss the required ransom. He did this in a loud carrying voice so that the other men beyond could hear him. Athan wanted to eliminate the possibility that a treacherous servant might betray his mistress in some way. With so many knowing of the ransom, it would be the talk of Buttrotiuria within a day. It would be impossible for her husband to refuse to pay without a major loss of prestige.

Then, with some of his men on the horses and the women mounted double on the slowest-looking of the animals, the band headed back down the trail to the east. The remainder of the brigands loped along holding to the harness of the horses and mules. They left behind a greatly relieved group of escorts, servants and drivers who immediately began making tracks to the west toward the promised oncoming caravan.

After a journey of half an hour the group turned off the road onto trail up between two hills. Just over the top of the little pass, two men waited, holding ponies for the rest of the band. Then there followed a long journey over hills, down dales and beside streams. It was not a pleasant ride for any of the women. They were all well aware that it was entirely possible that, despite the assurances of the man the bandits all called 'Chief', they might be merely be taken to some remote location where they could be raped more thoroughly. None of them were dressed appropriately for riding, and there was concern about how much bare leg they showed to these dangerous men. Things were not helped by a sudden late spring shower that soaked them.

The parings, mother and daughter, older faithful retainer and new servant also led to much contentious argument as they rode. Worst of all, none of the women were riders. They were all tense, chaffed and terribly sore by the time the band paused shortly after noon for a rest and bit of bread and dried goat meat. Mira approached the Chief Bandit and requested that the women be allowed to have a place where they could respond to urgent calls of nature. Though normally people were not particularly shy about relieving themselves, the women were still very nervous and felt a strong need to separate their gender for a bit from this threatening band. Once off behind a big rock they briefly considered attempting an escape, but they had no idea where they were and were afoot. It did not take long for them to decide to return their captors.

When the journey resumed, the women still rode double, but thanks to a discrete gift of ointment from Athan and an adjustment to riding partners, things were easier. Mira came to the realization that having her daughter with her on the horse would not provide any greater protection for her child and would prevent the harsh words that had passed between them on the first part of the ride. She was much more comfortable riding with Bea. The two women could share and ease their personal fears by worrying about the young women. Likewise, the two young women could manage their fears by speculating about the men. Both liked the looks of young Beltos - Rheta almost obsessively so.

Soon a kind of game began as the two young women attempted to maneuver their mount close enough to engage Beltos in conversation while the older women did all they could to thwart any such discussions, and curtail them when they did occur. The elaborate contest engaged not only the women but Beltos as well; he was very interested in finding out more about this intriguing young woman he had just met, but her mother somehow seemed to always be positioned between the two of them, asking about his family, a sensitive subject, his life as a bandit, another sensitive subject, and his chief, at last something he was comfortable in discussing.

By the time they arrived in the band's camp, it was late afternoon, and the women were well and truly tired. There was a brook near the camp so there was water for washing as well as drinking. A tent was prepared, and as soon as they were able to eat some of the surprisingly good stew, they all retired. They were too exhausted to worry very much about the morrow and were asleep before it was fully dark.

Mira jerked awake in the early gray light before dawn. All of her fears came back to assail her at once. 'Don't be foolish' she thought, 'nothing happened yesterday, there is every reason to believe that nothing bad would happen today.' Trembling, she took out a set of clean dry undergarments and a robe from one of the small chests that had been brought from the caravan. She did not remember it being placed in the tent. She had been so tired last night she doubted she would have noticed anything. She stood up outside the tent and winced from the effects of the ride the day before.

"Sore?" came a quiet question from her right.

She nearly leapt out of her skin. "You frightened me!" she told the bandit chief, her heart pounding. "What are you doing lurking around our tent?!"

"I relieved the guard so he could eat."

"You are afraid we would try to escape? We have no idea where we are. Four women alone and on foot trying to flee an entire troop of mounted brigands? Don't be ridiculous," she did not try to keep the scorn out of her voice.

"I was not worried about you trying to escape," he said as he began to move away from the tent, "but I wanted to provide for your security in the night."

Mira stood there feeling foolish for a moment, thinking of her daughter sleeping in a tent surrounded by thieves and murderers. A guard was very welcome. Then she said, very belatedly, "Thank you," but he was gone. Curse that man!

After the others were awake, the women went in a group to perform their morning ablutions in an area protected by bushes and set aside for their use 'while you are our guests.' They were then escorted to a fire where a breakfast of whey and bread was provided.

"I notice that you ladies are somewhat stiff from yesterday's exertions. I suggest we all go for a walk. That usually has a beneficial effect."

"That would be lovely," said her daughter immediately. Too late, Mira noticed that the handsome Beltos was standing to one side. He obviously was going to be one of the escorts. Bea protested that her old bones would rather lie down again in the tent, so Mira felt compelled to accompany her daughter and maid on the offered walk since it obviously would require strong ropes to prevent the young women from going.

They were accompanied on their walk not only by Beltos and two additional men, but by Athan as well. Mira was glad she went. Not only did her presence provide some restraint for the younger women, who immediately began flirting, Rheta with Beltos and Agalia with the other two men, but she found that a stroll up the hill did help ease the soreness in her muscles. It felt good to climb to the low hill that stood on the north side of the camp. And, despite her reservations about an escape attempt, Mira thought it might be a good idea to try to get some idea of where they were. She noticed that this had apparently been a winter camp for the band because the men were housed in rough huts, not tents, and there were indications that measures for long-term hygiene were in place with privies and midden heaps located downstream. The rain of the previous day had cleared out. It was a gorgeous spring day, cool, fresh, and invigorating. A respectable matron like Mira did not normally get much exercise, and she found she rather enjoyed it. The view was quite nice, with the typical ridges of that region humping away at right angles to their view south. She was reminded of the view of the sea from the cliffs of her home. When she commented on pleasant view to her daughter, it was Athan who answered.

"Lady, I could take you to places here so beautiful that you would remember them for the rest of your life."

For some reason, his comment stuck in her mind.

That walk up the hill was all they cared to do for exercise that day. Returning to the tent she was invited to inspect the band's camp. Leaving Rheta (chaperoned by Bea) seated on stools in front of the tent still talking to Beltos (what else), Mira accompanied Athan on their tour. Mira had not been out in the world a great deal, and she certainly knew nothing about setting up a campsite in the wild, but she was a wealthy matron, used to managing a significant domestic establishment. At first she was taken aback to find half a dozen other women in the camp. Her assumption that they were fellow captives was quickly proven wrong as first she heard their good-natured laughter then spoke with them. She realized that they all considered themselves to be the wives of husbands who were simply trying to provide for their families. One of the women had a small child and another was visibly pregnant.

'Well,' Mira thought to herself, 'if we are going to be here we might as well make ourselves useful. This place needs some serious cleaning up.'

Athan watched with first amusement then respect and finally awe as through some mysterious feminine magic, Mira assembled the women, and politely, graciously, but firmly gained ascendancy over them. She asked questions, made suggestions, overcame objections, assumed compliance and in less than an hour had the place abuzz with activity. Never once did she actually order anyone to do anything. She was deferential to the men, but somehow everyone was willing to follow her suggestions. She asked one of the men to escort her maids and daughter to her; when they arrived she immediately put them to work as well. It was spring, and the camp needed a spring cleaning. Mira was filled with a seemingly boundless energy; it was most strange.

"Lady," broke in Athan, as she finished asking one of his men if he thought it would be a good idea to get more firewood for heating water for cleaning, "I only had you stay in a tent because it was late and there was no time to prepare one of the huts for you. Please choose one of these huts for you and your party."

Mira smiled. She had planned on asking him for one of the huts, and now it was freely offered. "We'll take that one," she pointed at one of the larger huts. "It is clean, neat inside and well maintained. The men who live there should be commended. Where will you have them stay? In the tent we slept in last night?"

"Madam," he said using another formal term, "that place was mine. I slept there alone."

"Oh," she said suddenly confused, "I did not mean to displace you from your home, sir."

But she had; she had chosen his hut. Why did that bother her? She had thought nothing of moving out any number of other men from their hut. She felt the heat come to her cheeks. Why was she blushing? She had not blushed in years! 'I wonder what he meant when he said he slept alone?' she thought 'Was he telling me he had no woman? That he is lonely? Is he trying to make advances? Does he think I would be willing to sleep with him? Beltos said the Chief had been married once. What did he mean when he told me that he now sleeps alone?'

What Athan meant, of course, was that no one else slept there but him.

"I will find a place, Lady," he smiled at her confusion. "Do not worry about me."

This set off another unsettling round of thoughts in her head as she wondered just what he was trying to tell her. Finally, she came to the conclusion that there was considerably more to this bandit chief than met the eye. Not that what met the eye was unpleasant, not at all.

Mira resumed her personal mission to overhaul and improve the temporary camp of her abductors. She not only organized and supervised activities but did not deign to lead by example, cleaning, carrying, and hauling with the rest of her troops. The men were glad to go stand sentinel just to escape the activity. It was strange; the women in the camp, rather than resenting this newcomer who was stirring things up so, found the way she subtly bossed the men around to be amusing. Mira had a way of pleasantly making something she wanted done seem so reasonable that it was impossible to resist her.

There was a lengthy break for a midday meal of bread, cheese, oil, and olives. The women all ate together, and by the end of the meal had formed a little union of sorts, with Mira as shop foreman. Perhaps it was the perfect spring day, or the expectation of funds coming in for the hostages, or just the influence of the newcomers in the camp, but for some reason everyone seemed to be in a good mood at the end of the day. A goat was sacrificed and an impromptu feast was held with wine, and singing. The women were invited to eat with the men, an unusual honor. The women used blanket-covered logs for banquet couches. Chief Athan brought out his lyre to play a few melodies, something he seldom did in public. Rheta and Beltos stretched out head to head talking and jesting, just like a young couple at any formal affair in any civilized city. Mira sat watching her daughter while having a perfectly respectable private conversation with a lyre-playing bandit chieftain. After a time Athan handed his lyre over to one of his men who could play with greater skill. Somehow their conversation drifted around to spouses.

"Beltos says you are a widower. I lost my first husband. I know how difficult that is."

"I don't know if my wife is alive or dead," he replied somewhat stiffly. She was in our camp after we lost a battle. I never found her. I never found my daughters. I did find my son," his tone made it clear how he had found him.

"I'm so sorry. I do not think I could bear it to lose my children."

"How many children do you have?" he said redirecting the subject.

"Mira is the only one from my first husband," she replied. "I have a young son by Aorastus. He will be three soon. He is at home his father and nurse in Buttrotiuria."

"It must have been hard to leave them."

"Less than you think," she smiled. "A young boy can be exhausting. Besides, I have the house to run. The nurse cares for my son. I needed to get my Rheta settled. I worry that I have not been a good mother to her. She was six when Argo died, and for a time we only had each other. We were very close. Then five years ago I married Aorastus, and we seemed to drift apart." She could see him mentally adding up the dates. "Yes, I am respectable old matron; much too old for you." 'Why did I say that?' she thought.

Now it was his turn to smile, "No, Lady, I think not. My son would have been almost of an age with your daughter. And I was not a child bride."

Pleased with his gallantry, she chose to change the subject. Of course, he was correct; she had been married at 16. "At any rate," she continued, "My family was given some hope of arranging a suitable liaison for her with some of the young men that live on the eastern coast. It did not work out." What she did not tell him was that Aorastus had so stinted on his stepdaughter's dowry that even with subtle additions from her own private resources, she could not interest any of the better families. It was a bitter blow and she was beginning to despair of ever finding her daughter a suitable match.

She changed the subject again and tried to engage him in talk of politics. This was perhaps an error.

"Buttrotiuria helped Doria, Illyrian, and the hill tribes conquer my city. We had no quarrel with them." There was accusation in his voice.

"Oh, no that was not what I have been told," she objected, "our men went there when they were informed of the invasion. They arrived after the city had opened its gates. I think they negotiated surrender. Some said a powerful sorcerer helped the Dorians. In any event, our men did not attack the city. In fact, they prevented the sack from becoming general. Many in the city fled to the citadel and that did not fall. The Illyrians did take part in the overthrow of the leading citizens and some were killed, but many people from Epiria passed though Buttrotiuria afterward. I saw them." She was speaking earnestly now, trying to persuade him that her city had not been part of the alliance that had cost him his family. "We still have some people from Epiria living in Buttrotiuria. I think Beltos may have relatives who settled there. He did not want to talk about it with me, but there may be some of his family living in Buttrotiuria." She knew she was babbling now, but she didn't know how to stop. "Not everyone was killed. Yes, some were exiled, but others of quality were able to leave under terms. There was Karpos and his family, Demetrios with his whole household, Ligeia and his wife's family, General Thaddeus and his famous hetaira, and all of Akakios' people."

"What did you say?" he asked with an intensity that took her aback.

"There were many who were able to leave Epiria with their possessions."

"No, about General Thaddeus and the hetaira, Persis."

"Oh, did you know them? I did not see the general, but I did get a chance to see Persis and her daughters before they left. She is very beautiful. She had all her daughters with her as well. To think, twins. I have my hands full with just one at a time."

Again he cut her off. "Twins, she had twin daughters? How many daughters did she have?" He had gotten up and was speaking in a low voice. He had taken her right arm and was squeezing it so tightly it hurt her.

"She had four," she answered twisting her arm free with a grimace.

"Describe them." He was looking directly into her face in a way that was most disconcerting; hungry, like a starving wolf watching a lamed doe.

'Is he going to attack me?' she wondered.

"I don't remember very much. It was years ago. They were only in Buttrotiuria for a few days before they left for the south. I think they were going to somewhere in Attica, but I don't remember." Before he could speak again she collected herself, drew a deep breath and tried to remember. "Persis was wearing a pale white linen chiton, sort of an ivory color with a particularly nice pair of white sandals." She held up her hand to stop him from interrupting. "This is how I remember things." She took a breath and continued, "I saw her with the wife of one of the oligarchs. They were staying there and I paid a call. She was there, and I remember being very impressed at her poise in spite of all that had happened to her."

"She's had worse happen to her," growled Athan which got him a startled look from Mira.

"I did not actually meet her", she continued after another deep breath, "but I did see she had kept her children with her, which I put down to unease in her surroundings, though she didn't seem uneasy." She stopped again and drew another deep breath. She tried not to look at the Chief whose gaze was burning a hole completely through her. 'Stop babbling' she told herself. "Her eldest daughter seemed the saddest. She had on a robe that looked to be a bit too small. She had long brown hair and was about eight. Her middle daughter was the best dressed, she looked to be a year younger than her older sister. The twins were about six years old. They were wearing identical tunics; they were not identical, but looked like sisters."

"Yes," he said, "they always did." He had not taken her arm again but remained crouched close by her still staring at her intently.

"Do you know Persis?" Many things had surprised Mira over the last two days but this above them all. How could a brigand who claimed to have once been a guardsman have known a woman like Persis?

He said nothing for a moment, then, "Did she have any other women with her? Any friends, servants, maids?"

"She had only one, a nurse. She was a young stout girl with breasts just made for babies. I remember thinking she was very good-natured. Did you meet Persis when you served under General Thaddeus?"

"I met Persis when I rescued her from a brothel." That shocked Mira right down to her toes. Then he went on to completely astonish her. "Thaddeus and Persis were my closest comrades. They arranged my marriage with Erinsys. When Erinsys came with me to that final battle she brought our son and youngest daughter who was too young to be left behind." There was a long pause before he continued in a quiet voice. "We did leave our two other daughters with Thaddeus and Persis. Persephone had just turned eight; she was Ariel's best friend; Ariel was a year younger. That had to be the well-dressed one. My Dionme and Amie, Persis' oldest daughter, were almost the same age. They were very close." There was another long pause. "I had hoped perhaps Erinsys and the baby had made it back to Epiria."

There was another long pause. 'Say something,' she thought.

But Mira, a woman of intelligence, poise, and finely developed social skills could thing of absolutely nothing to say. It was all just too much. But sometimes saying nothing is the right thing to say after all.

Athan leaned close to her and softly kissed her forehead. "Thank you for giving me back my daughters," he whispered so quietly she wasn't sure she had heard him at all.

She could see line of tears streaking down his cheeks. Answering tears came to her eyes, and at last as he rose to leave into the darkness, she was able to whisper back, "You're welcome."

In their new hut Mira and Rheta were able to resume a small ritual they performed before bed. In the bleak times after Argo had died and she felt alone in the world, she had taken to combing out her daughter's hair before putting her down for the night. One night her six year old had asked if she could comb out mommy's hair. From that time forward whenever possible mother and daughter had combed one another's hair at the end of the day and talked. It was a special private time just for the two of them, and they both treasured the moments spent together. This night Rheta could not stop talking about Beltos. So excited was she that she did not notice how silent and distracted her mother was. Her mother made only one comment, "I think young Beltos has family in Buttrotiuria." This comment set off another long series of discourses on the man in question and speculation about his past, present, and future. Neither woman noticed that Agalia did not come into the hut with them. Nor did she return until late, slipping in just before dawn, tired but very happy.

If, by the end of her second day as a captive, Mira had led the spring cleaning of the camp, by the end of the fourth day she was the de facto camp provost in charge of all things domestic. No one was quite sure how she had done it, but everyone seemed to think that with Mira in charge things were in fact better. Checking the status of supplies, she found there were more things available than anyone had thought, though less than she considered acceptable. She politely requested that Chief Athan provide some men to escort her to the nearest market. When informed that this was imprudent, she graciously offered to provide them with a list. When Athan told her with some reluctance that there were not enough funds in the camp to pay for all she required, she reached within her chiton, removed a purse and provided the lack asking only when the men would be able to return. That took them aback.

'It was so nice' she thought 'to be the one doing the surprising.'

The days fell into a routine; each morning the women would all go together to an area now screened off with material formerly used for tents. The men established a place where the abductees could get water from the stream, use a privy now designated as just for women and prepare themselves for the day. On the third day one of the young camp follower/wives had shyly peeked her head around the edge of the screen and asked if she might use the facilities as well. By the fourth day all the women were using the area. By the fifth day it was a sacrosanct tradition that women had this special place for their special needs, and no men were allowed.

Following the morning ablutions, Mira and Rheta would take a walk with Athan and Beltos. Bea always pleaded her age, and Agalia asked to stay behind and 'clean up a bit.' In fact, every morning she immediately retired exhausted to snatch a nap. First Bea, then Mira and finally Rheta came to realize that she was so tired in the morning due to her exertions after dark. It was difficult trying to decide among her suitors, and she could not make up her mind and so continued her extended sampling.

"I don't know why she even bothers coming into the hut in the mornings," grumbled Mira to Athan as the walked along the ridge. The walks had grown longer as the women became accustomed to the life. In fact, Mira felt wonderful. Perhaps it was the glorious weather they had been having or the regular exercise, or the sense of purpose she had as honorary camp provost. Today she was going to have to start looking into the men's health. And Kirkor and Kopria should be back from the market so there would be food to be distributed. She turned to ask her daughter if she was ready to return when she saw Rheta and Beltos were not behind them.

"Come on, Athan," she called to him. She didn't know just when she had begun calling him by his name. No one else in camp did. But somehow it seemed right. At the moment all she was concerned about was the fear of her daughter being lost again. She rounded a broad low fir with Athan coming up fast behind her and there, just down the slope, Rheta and Beltos were guiltily breaking an embrace.

"I can't leave you for a moment," she fumed at her daughter. "Must I have a chaperone for you every instant?"

"Mother!" came the exasperated reply traditionally given by daughters. There were high spots of red in her cheeks.

"And you young man, taking advantage of a captive like that! Chief Athan, you promised we would not be injured or raped. Can't you control your men?"

And without waiting for a reply she grabbed her daughter by the arm and hustled her down the path back toward the camp, a full mother-daughter debate starting to heat up as they departed.

Athan was wise enough to wait until she was safely out of earshot before he said "Can't you control your daughter?" Then he looked at an embarrassed Beltos. "Beltos," was all he said.

"I am sorry, sir, but I love her. And she loves me. I can no more stop this than I can stop breathing."

"To what end my friend? Will you take her as your pallake? A girl like that up here? How long would she be willing to live in a hut or a tent on the march? She deserves better than that from life. You must know there is no future for the two of you. It's hopeless."

The women's return from the walk, a return heard by everybody in the camp, ended with screams of "Get into the hut!" and "I hate you!" provided by mother and daughter respectively. Everyone in the camp had enough sense to make themselves scarce. To Mira's credit, she did not let her anger affect her dealings with others. All day long she was unfailing polite, even if it was with gritted teeth. Everyone knew exactly what the problem was and appreciated her forbearance, just as they tried to ignore the shouting and sound of thrown objects followed by the sudden ejection from the hut of a surprised Bea and a sleepy Agalia. Fortunately, Kirkor and Kopria returned before noon with the requested supplies. Shortly thereafter three other members of the band, out on a scouting mission, returned with not only provisions but coins as well, taken by way of a 'road tax' on two merchants moving between cities. It would have been a very good day indeed but for the absence of Rheta and the periodic sounds of sobbing from her hut.

Before the evening meal Beltos found Mira and apologized for his behavior. She returned the apology a bit shamefaced. "I don't know what Athan must think of me, screaming at him like that."

Beltos smiled at her. "You call that screaming? His first wife used to scream and curse at him all the time. She was famous for it. No, I doubt he even noticed."

"There is no future for the two of them," Mira told him that evening, "it's hopeless."

Another part of their routine had become the invitation to eat the evening meal with the men. This was a most unusual, but welcome change from normal society, where men and women usually ate apart. The two women would join Athan, Simeon, and Beltos to share not just food, but conversation. They would talk of civilized things: philosophy, art, politics, and music. The women's presence eating with the leaders of the band clearly enhanced their status. Mira began to feel like a very sophisticated hetaira; heady stuff for a respectable matron.

So it was that she felt able to approach him before the evening meal and talk to him about the problem of the two young lovers.

"It is not that I dislike Beltos," she continued, "he is a fine man. He comes from a good family. He is brave, handsome, courteous, educated; he is exactly the type of man I would want for Rheta. It is just that, well…" she could not finish.

"He is a penniless brigand with no living family and no prospects."

"Well, yes, something like that."

"Do you think he doesn't know that? Do you think he wanted to become a hill bandit? He was respectable once and now he has a woman right in front of him that he can't have. If there was a way..." his voice trailed off. "I just can't see how to do it."

'I wonder just who he is talking about?' thought Mira.

"I will think about it," said Athan suddenly standing. "Perhaps there may be a way. When it comes to children, all we can do is just love them and hope for the best." With an abrupt change of subject ending the previous discussion, he continued, "We have something different tonight; dried fish, but only a few days old. And there will be a poetry competition tonight. Will you and Rheta be joining us?"

"Yes, she said, "I'll go get ready."

The poetry singings, for that is how poetry was normally delivered, were well received. Some were simply bawdy rhymes; a few tried some verses praising the beauty of women or the valor and cunning of Chief Athan's band. Beltos drew hoots with his efforts at love poetry. Phemius, the most accomplished of the band's poets, gave some wonderful verses on the epic (in his terms) battle between Bold Captain Athan and the Evil Sorcerer Priest Azziz.

As the wolf scatters the flock
Seeking only the ram it desires
Seizing it with his strong teeth
Robbing it of tender life
So the Captain fell upon the enemy
Neither shield nor spear did he carry
But stole the life from the barbarians
With his mighty club

And on he went in that vein for what seemed to be another hundred or so verses.

This too drew hoots and calls of 'that's not how it went', 'you weren't even there' and the like. Perhaps Phemius would have been well advised to wait until all the participants of the battle were either dead or distant before trying to perform his epic. Actually Mira thought the poetry was not bad under the circumstances. Finally Athan impressed her by quoting several dozen verses from the Iliad, all full of blood and bravery. The men loved it. Finally, at the end of the night, it was decreed that Athan won the prize for the best recitation and Beltos for the best original composition.

"Where are our prizes?" asked Athan expecting a crudely constructed wreath.

"Here," said Rheta bending over and giving him a soft kiss on the forehead.

"And mine?" asked Beltos joining in the general cheers and laughter.

"Here," said Rheta and bending over, giving him a long, slow, lingering kiss on his open mouth. Cheers and more laughter.

Rheta looked up at her mother and said with a cool direct look, "Shall we retire, mother?"

Without a word the two women glided from the group, which began to break up into smaller groups all heading for bed. Mother and daughter prepared for bed combing each other's hair. For the first time since she had met him, Rheta did not talk about Beltos other than to compliment his poetry. They made comfortable small talk, about the meal, the route of their walk for the morrow, Chief Athan's new hut located up the hill some distance away from the camp and other small things. They each then rolled over and slept as they had every night since their abduction, next to but not touching one another.

Mira did not awake when Rheta left the hut or when she returned. Yet when she awoke she was aware somehow that Rheta had been gone sometime during the night. Perhaps to relieve herself she thought. Then she bent over her sleeping daughter and smelled a certain musky odor and faintly, the coppery smell of blood. Suddenly she knew with certainty why her daughter had left that night and what she had done. Mira was overwhelmed. She was not aware of her tears until one splashed on Rheta's face, awakening her. Mira rocked back on her heels and peaked her hands together covering her nose and mouth. Rheta propped herself up on one elbow and looked at her mother.

"Oh, Rheta, oh Rheta, what have you done? What have you done? What will we do now?" this very softly and bringing up her hands to fully cover her face, she began to quietly cry.

In an instant Rheta was there putting her arms around her mother, the two women rocking back and forth.

"What it is?" asked Bea from her corner.

"Nothing, go back to sleep," said Rheta. Then, "No, better yet, go wash up. Leave us please. Mother and I need to be alone." Although Rheta had never before spoken to her like that, the older woman obediently got up and left without another word.

"Oh, daughter, what are we going to do?" Mira continued rocking back and forth.

Rheta was nonplussed. She knew eventually she would have to face her mother, but she didn't think it would be so soon, and she certainly didn't expect this reaction of grief. "It will be all right Mother," she said patting her on the back while she embraced her still rocking form.

"Don't you understand, girl? Who will marry you now? No man will keep a wife who is not a virgin. One who has lain with a hill bandit? He would put you out after the wedding night and keep the dowry."

"Then I will marry Beltos. He loves me and wants to marry me."

"And then what, Rheta? Live in the hills with bandits? How will you raise your children in the hills?"

"Grace is raising her boy here."

It was such a ridiculous thought that Mira only looked at her daughter. They each mentally reviewed Grace's child. He was happy and healthy playing naked in the stream. And they both knew that when he grew up he would have little more than he did right now.

"Mother," began Rheta, "I was too young when you were with Father, but I see you and Aorastus. You do not love him. And I know about all the other good dutiful matrons. Few of them really care about their husbands. Husbands provide for us and give us our babies, but few women really love their husbands. Well, Mother, I have been given a gift from Aphrodite herself. I love Beltos, and he loves me. When you have a gift like that, a gift of such worth from the goddess herself, isn't it wrong not to take it? Life is so hard Mother, can't we accept a little joy, even if it is just for a short time."

There was a long pause. Then Rheta tried again. "Mother he is a wonderful man. Can't you just be happy for us, even if it does only last a little while?"

There was another time of silence. Finally with a ragged breath Mira answered her daughter, "All I can do my darling child is love you. Be happy."

The two women held one another for a time and had a good cry before they went down together to wash.

If Rheta was surprised that her mother knew so quickly about her change in status to full womanhood, she was amazed at how fast everyone else seemed to know. Was it posted on her forehead? Was she so different? Beltos told her the truth when he assured her that he had confided in no one. One look at the two lovers was enough to let most people know that they had consummated their obvious love. The whole camp seemed bursting with high spirits, and when the Athan, Mira, Beltos, and Rheta departed uphill for their daily walk, they returned greetings and salutations on every hand.

"I should have given you a wreath instead of that kiss," muttered a slightly exasperated Rheta.

"They are going to give him a wreath this morning if we don't get out of here," responded Athan.

Today they had planned a long stroll, and so brought bread, cheese, wine and water with them along with cloaks and hats against the possibility of rain. They went south this time, over the brook and up the far ridge. Spring was at her wonderful best with flowers, green vistas at every turn and an unexpected deer with her fawn. It was midmorning before the anticipated shower finally caught them. They saw the squall coming from the top of a hill and sought shelter. The men knew of a place where they sometimes placed lookouts. It was a shallow overhang facing south and just wide enough for four good friends to stand beneath. Laughing and hurrying they made it there just as the first drops started falling.

With the wind from the north they stayed dry enough and with a strong male arm around their shoulders, the women were certainly warm enough. Mira thought it was very comfortable indeed as she looked down over the green valley through a warm spring rain. She had her left hip against her daughter, and was leaning into Athan on her right, her arms under his cloak and around his chest while his left arm went across her shoulders. She wondered just how long it had been since a man had held her like this? Never. Not even Argo had held her so. She had been even younger than Rheta when she married him. Argo was a good man, but he had not been one to spend much time with his young wife. And as she remembered, he often smelled of sour sweat. Now this man she was holding here had a nice scent. She brought her nose to his shoulder and breathed slowly through her nose. This man Athan smelled very pleasant; there was wool of course, leather, and an earthy green-wood man smell. Then she caught a whiff of the sweet fragrance of flowers from somewhere outside. Flowers? Where could that smell have come from? And she remembered what her daughter had told her that morning? 'A gift from Aphrodite herself.' Was that smell of flowers a sign of the goddess' presence? Was it for her or her daughter?

Leaning back from Athan she asked, "Rheta?"

"Mmmhh?" came a somewhat sleepy and very contented reply.

"Did you just smell flowers?"

"When?"

"Just now."

"No," a pause, "but did you smell them last night? The air was thick with their fragrance."

That did it. The goddess had given a gift first Rheta, then to her. The gift was this man she was leaning against with her arms around in a most familiar way. Now did she dare accept her gift, even for a little while?

After the shower passed, the four rather reluctantly come out from their snug lair. They walked a bit farther off the top of the hill, admiring the scenery all the way. Half way down the slope they stopped in a copse that was not too wet, spread their blankets and shared out the bread, cheese and wine. It was good wine, and perhaps a bit strong for the ladies. There was a lot of giggling by the time they finally packed the comestibles away. Beltos took the two blankets and blandly asked Rheta if she would like to see some flowers around the next hill. Rheta looked at her mother, then at Beltos. "I'd love to," and off they strolled, Beltos with one arm full of blankets and the other of Rheta.

Mira watched them go with a sigh and then bent to repack the rest of their lunch into the basket. Athan had already put most of the things away.

He saw her surprise and shrugged. "I became used to doing things for myself. I don't have a servant."

"Or a woman," said Mira.

And just like that he stood straight up, took a step, swept her into his arms and kissed her. It was a very good kiss. After a very long moment she broke the kiss and leaned into his chest.

'Oh I could feel that right down to the core of me,' she thought.

"Athan," she said into his chest, "when did you learn to kiss like that?"

"Just then," he replied and gently taking her chin he brought her face up for another kiss. This one was even better than the first. Their embrace became more ardent their hands moving on one another.

Suddenly she broke the kiss and stepped back from him breathing a little unsteadily. But her voice was very steady when she spoke, "Darling, I am afraid I am too old to go rolling about in wet grass; the youngsters took the blankets."

He laughed softly and took her in his arms again. As they stood in one another's arms he began to tease her with suggestions such as leaning against trees, standing up, and other possible ways of making love that both scandalized and fascinated her at the same time.

"Where did you learn all these things?" she asked in mock outrage.

"I have been thinking of little else since I first saw you step from that carriage," he lied sweetly.

"Well, unless you know a way to do it without taking off our clothes," she countered, "I must disappoint you."

He made several more suggestions that Mira had never even considered.

They spent the next hour most pleasantly, flirting, teasing, talking, laughing, holding hands, and ambling around in a leisurely fashion. Athan made certain that in their strolling they did not go the same way as Beltos and Rheta. Mira was aware of his discretion.

"I doubt if they would even notice us," she commented a bit waspishly.

"Lady", replied Athan, "a woman will always notice her mother."

A short time after that exchange the two young lovers reappeared. Mira was relieved to see that they had tried to maintain some semblance of propriety. Their clothing was dry and neat, and aside from Rheta's glow and Beltos' ear to ear grin, the couple looked almost respectable. Well, aside from a few bits of grass that Mira plucked from her daughter's hair with a sigh.

When they returned to the camp news was waiting. A messenger had brought news. Aorastus had agreed to pay a ransom for his wife and step-daughter.

The Old King moved to the entrance and looked out. It was the early part of another morning and still cold; the sky was gray and a thin chill rain was slowly falling. He stamped into his boots, put his piloi on his head and stepped out to get some water for himself and provide a little water to the closest tree. Getting water should have been easy, but the old man did not want to have to go to the trouble of melting snow again. He found a likely puddle that seemed relatively clean. He filled and drank from his water bag twice before deciding he had sufficiently slaked his thirst. Then he filled it again and went back to his lair. As he walked back downhill he was aware of just how weak he was.

By now he had lost track of the days. He was now supplementing his dwindling rations with 'saddle soup': thin bits of leather cut from his saddle boiled to relative softness. At least he had plenty of herbs for his tea. As was his custom, he boiled a bit of tea now, savoring the warmth of the hot liquid as well as the little fire that heated it. Then he fluffed up the grasses, as much as it was possible to fluff up a few armloads of grass. It was now more like straw now. Then he lay back, conserving his energy and heat. And he had done every day since he had first taken refuge in his lair, he sank back into his reminisces.

Chapter Eleven- Losses

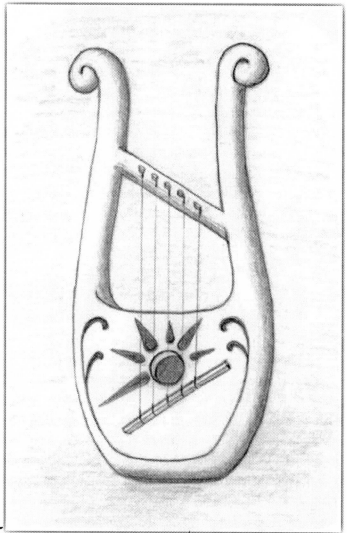

The arrangements were fairly standard. There were places in the hills where the parties could meet and negotiate the specific terms and conditions of the exchange. They were to meet at one such place at noon on the following day. They were to bring Aorastus' wife to prove she was still safe and unharmed. The band quickly picked up the moods of the two leaders upon hearing the news and a pall descended on the camp. Even the prospect of significant money coming into the camp did nothing to lighten the mood.

Only Bea seemed upbeat. "I knew Aorastus would redeem us, my lady."

"When will we have to leave?" Mira asked Athan.

"Well, it will take the messenger a day and a half to get back to Buttrotiuria after the meeting tomorrow, a day or two, probably two to gather the ransom," Athan flinched a little at his use of that word but continued, "then a couple of days to return. It will be slower coming back. We have perhaps six days."

"No," she said, "I mean tomorrow. What time will we have to leave in order to be at the place where I can show them I am alive and unhurt?" 'So he is counting the days he has left with me,' she thought with a secret smile. 'He doesn't want me to leave.'

Rheta was obviously upset. She did not come to the evening meal. It was a strained meal. On this night there no exhilarating discussions of philosophy mixed with wit and not a small amount of flirting; instead they discussed the details of the meeting set for noon on the morrow. They would be riding, something that Mira dreaded. She was assured that she would find this to be much more pleasant than her first experience on horseback. She excused herself before the meal was over to return to her hut to try to console her daughter, then Mira stopped and turned back to Athan.

"Everyone says you are the cleverest brigand to ever ply his trade in these hills."

Uncomfortable with her choice of words, Athan could on mumble some vague disclaimers.

"No, do not try to dissemble; you are clever, Athan, clever as Ulysses. Tell me this, do you care about my daughter, I mean do you think well of her?"

"You know that I do," said Athan defensively.

"And Beltos?"

"He is like a brother to me."

"And me?" 'Why did I ask that?' she wondered.

"Yes. I mean, not like a brother." There was a pause, then "yes, Mira I care about you very much."

Before he could say more she interrupted him. "Then, oh clever bandit, find a way to make your friend and my daughter happy. That is what I want from you. Can you do that?" Without waiting for a reply she picked up the hem of her chiton and walked away.

Athan watched her go, then turned back to stare into the fire. There was a long dull pause.

After a long while Athan looked up at Beltos, who had not moved. "Beltos, how do you hide something, I mean something people know you have?"

"I don't know," his friend responded diffidently, "bury it where no one will look for it, I suppose."

"Then people will keep looking until someone eventually does look where it is buried. The best hiding places for some things are right out in the open. Put a goat in a sheepskin and let it graze with other sheep. No one will ever think to look right there in the open because they know that those are sheep."

"What are you talking about? What goat?"

There was another long pause, but this time it was an expectant pause as Athan began to work something out.

"That's it!" exclaimed Athan animatedly, "Beltos, how do you hide a bold hill brigand?"

"Stay in the mountains. Keep out scouts, know the countryside, and move around; like we have been doing all these years." Beltos clearly thought his boss had lost his senses.

"No, not hide a band, hide one man," retorted Athan, now clearly excited. "How do you hide a brigand? By wrapping him in the mantle of a hero. Ho! Phemius! Where are you?"

The bard was trying to get in a nap before taking one of the night watches. He was roused and brought before the two men. By that time Beltos had been apprised of the outline of Athan's plan. He was frankly dubious.

"Captain," he protested, unconsciously going back to his old form of address to his leader, "I am known. We will fool no one. I will taken and executed."

"They might remember Beltos of Epiria, fallen hero, but no one really knows what you have been doing since then. We have to tell them. Phemius, I need a couple of poems. Tell me, do you love Beltos there?"

"You know that I do, sir."

"Then I need for you to make him famous. It will have to be your best work. Can you do that?" And Athan outlined what he had in mind to the bard.

"Well, Chief," wheedled the slender man, "it will be hard with all my duties and such. A man has trouble being really creative when he is up all night and has to cut wood and go on scouting parties and such."

"You are exempted from all watches and duties of any kind until you finish a poem for me, but I must approve the quality. And it must be completed in three days."

"That is asking a lot of me, sir. If you could see your way clear to perhaps provide a trifle of extra incentive to me..."

"Here are incentives: finish a good poem in three days and you will have no duties for a total of 20 days. And I will pay you an extra month's wages."

"Do you want me to perform these poems somewhere?" asked Phemius cagily. He was beginning to grasp what his chieftain had in mind.

"You will have leave to perform them in three towns," said Athan

"Five towns over a month's time; and I want full payment for expenses such as food and proper clothing. I can't go into a town looking like some brigand."

"Six towns, a new set of cloths, and an escort to make sure you are not robbed. As to expenses, you can pay what you need from whatever profits make as a bard."

"Can I teach others and have their performances count toward the total?"

"If they are of good quality you may. And you can keep any profits you make for these performances."

"Done."

"Good," dismissed Athan. "Now go make Beltos a hero."

It had been a difficult night for Mira. Rheta had wanted to go out to Beltos, and Mira had tried to persuade her to not go. She just did not want her daughter's inevitable heartache to be even worse. At first, Mira had prevailed, but some time after lying down for sleep she heard Rheta get up. There had been words between them, becoming tense then heated, and at the end Rheta had left the hut. Agalia, of course, had spent the night elsewhere, leaving only Bea lying tensely in the corner. Mira sighed and went back to her pallet. Sleep was difficult, even after Rheta returned before first light.

Mira was tired, grumpy, and not at all glad to see that Athan was in high spirits the next morning. 'Probably looking forward to getting his money,' she thought grimly. 'A bandit, that is all the man is, a bandit. What was I thinking? I will be glad to have my daughter back safe in civilization again. And I do miss my little boy. And Aorastus, too', she thought. But she knew she was lying to herself. It had been a bad morning. Rheta was weepy, Bea disapproving and Agalia had disappeared altogether. Good riddance. And now Athan wanted her to wear some ridiculous trouser thingies.

"You can wear them under your chiton," he explained. "They will protect your legs from the sun and brush. You do not want your legs scratched, do you?"

She snatched the offending article of clothing from his hand and stalked into the hut. She held the garment up and examined them. She was surprised: they were a beige color and made of what appeared to be silk. The thighs were cut loosely; they were tighter below the knees, ending just past mid calf. The waist was held by a drawstring. Hiking up her skirt she pulled the new undergarments on with some difficulty. The waist and length were perfect. Dropping her skirts she bent to examine herself to see if the ridiculous item could be seen. To her relief it was safely concealed beneath her hemline; the only things visible were her practical sandals. She moved around the little hut finding the sensation of the new silken undergarment clinging to her legs not altogether uncomfortable.

"Where did you get these things?" she asked Athan when she emerged from the hut.

"I had them made for you," he replied. "We used some of the cloth we picked up on the road."

For some reason she could not explain this infuriated her. "You mean stolen from honest travelers. And then you had one of your women tailor this ridiculous thing just up for me."

This whole conversation confused Athan. Of course he had stolen the cloth; he was a bandit. Where else would he get fabric like that? And one of the women had made it just for her. Mira liked the woman. It was done to please her. What was wrong? Athan mumbled something to himself and withdrew.

Her memory of her first experience of riding was still fresh; all her apprehension reappeared when they brought a little pony for her to ride to the meeting. This time however, she had a saddle, and with a bit of help was able to mount the animal without difficulty. They were six in the party; she noticed that Beltos was not with their group. They set an easy pace to start the journey with her pony's halter held by Arthos, one of the men who had originally captured her. Mira immediately noticed that this pony was not nearly as uncomfortable as the animal she had first ridden immediately after her capture. In fact, she soon began to almost enjoy the trip.

After a time she persuaded Arthos to let her hold her own reins and let her try riding herself a bit. Holding the reins of her pony, riding through rough but beautiful country on another absolutely gorgeous spring day, she felt like a girl again. Sometimes she had played games with her sister and closest friends called Pirate Queen where they pretended to be brave pirates. Never had she thought she would be a bandit queen, but that was almost what she was. The entire experience was both novel and much easier than she had expected. Mira did not consider that she had a proper saddle, had on more comfortable clothing was relatively fresh and rested, and was astride the band's most docile pony. Perhaps most importantly of all, she had been exercising every day for the past six days and was much tougher than she had been on her first ride. Still and all her legs and bottom were starting to ache when they stopped for a midmorning break. That was when she found that relieving herself was a lot more complicated with the extra undergarments.

She was still flustered from her experience behind the bush she had used as a screen when she encountered Athan. Perhaps that explained the short response she gave to Athan's greeting. This had the effect of chilling any conversation for the remainder of the morning's travel. Mira wanted to apologize, to share the sights and sounds of this really very pleasant outing, to reassume their easy personal conversation she had come to so value, but she couldn't seem to find the opportunity.

The men seemed to be moving erratically, stopping just below the crests while one man dismounted and moved ahead for a while and then suddenly moving ahead at much faster pace than she could maintain. Two of the men left their group and went off left and right. Their progress slowed even further. Mira realized that they must be moving with caution to forestall the possibility of an ambush. She finally was able to move her pony up to where Athan was watching the leading man who had once again dismounted and was peering cautiously over the top of a ridge.

Instead of trying to smooth things over, she made matters worse. "I am sure that Aorastus will not try an ambush. I am the only one he asked to come here and the bargain is for all of us. Besides trying some rescue is simply not his way. He is a practical and prudent man." 'That was not what I had meant to say,' she thought, 'it came out all wrong. Why does this man make everything so hard for me?'

Before she could try to rectify things, Athan responded without looking back. "You are the only one that matters. If he loses a step-daughter, all he loses is the cost of her dowry. Besides, this place is always dangerous. Go back and wait with Kirkor."

Gritting her teeth, she managed to actually turn her little pony and ride back to the brigand, where she waited for a hundred heartbeats before the little group was signaled forward again. Just below the top of the next hill the men dismounted, as did Mira, with some relief. She was directed to wait with the horses while Athan and one of the men peered with more than the usual caution at the terrain on the other side.

After a time Athan come down and addressed the men. "Water the horses and get a bite yourselves."

Then, taking a bit of jerky and a water bag from his pony he climbed back up to his perch on the ridgeline where he shared out a drink and meal with his fellow.

'So, that is the way of it,' she thought, 'just when you think you mean something to a man, it turns out all he wants is whatever he can get from you. I don't know why I expected more from a simple bandit.'

They had waited for perhaps half an hour, the sun beginning to get quite warm, when she noticed activity at the top of the ridge. The two men were clearly watching somebody or something. After a bit longer, Athan rose and went over the hill. There was a considerable delay, during which time Mira had to endure the unpleasantness of arranging her new garments to relieve herself again. She was just coming back from that chore when she noticed that the three men where all gesturing to her. At first she leapt to the conclusion that they were making fun of her and her clothing, but then she realized she was being called up to the crest. Obviously she was to be shown safe and sound to her husband. Taking a moment to arrange herself appropriately, she walked up the short grade to the top with as much dignity as she could muster. Kirkor and Glaucus walked with her, one on either side. They had apparently intended that she stop on the top of the hill, but when she crested the top she could see Athan less than bowshot away, so she simply continued down the trail, easily ignoring the efforts of the two men trying to convince her to stop. Athan was talking across the width of a small ravine perhaps twenty cubits wide by ten deep with two men, her personal steward, Kopria, and Cletus, her husband's personal bodyguard. A small swift stream at the bottom of the ravine had cut steep banks so that though the men were within easy speaking distance they were separated by a safe barrier. There were some small boulders nearby but few bushes to hide an ambush. No wonder this was a safe place to meet. By the time any attackers could come out of hiding, get down the steep banks, cross the stream and climb the far side, the parties on the other side could easily retire to their mounts and escape. Crossing the ravine with any animals would be completely impossible, and anyone approaching the site could be seen before they could come within effective arrow range.

Mira walked straight up and stood beside Athan. If he had any feelings of uneasiness having her so close to her husband's men, he hid it well.

"Hello, Kopria," she greeted her steward. "I am glad you were able to get home safely. Thank you for coming to this meeting. Is all arranged?"

"We were just discussing that, Lady", replied the wiry old steward who was plainly not at all comfortable being here in such a place and talking with such a man. "It is good to see you. Are you well?"

She was glad to see her old steward; a man had served her faithfully for over 15 years. Seeing his honest old face there across that unreachable divide caused her to experience a sudden rush of home sickness. Kopria had been of enormous help to her during the difficult time after the death of Argo and had never once taken advantage of her vulnerable position. She knew his wife and family well and also knew he thought about Rheta as though she were one of his nieces. With a broad smile she sought to reassure him, "Rheta and I have been well treated, thank you. How is my little man?"

"I assume you mean your son, Lady," he said with a dry humor. "He is well; as is your husband."

"When will I be able to return to them?"

"That depends on in part on these brigands," he replied. "We have been negotiating that very point. It remains contingent of course," here the remarks were for Athan, "on his continued good treatment of you and your daughter."

"Have no fear," countered Athan with a smile, "if we don't complete the transaction soon, she will have civilized my band completely." This brought smiles from Kirkor and Glaucus standing beside her. "She has already brought the camp to new standards of hygiene and order."

Kopria was relieved to see from the reactions of the bandits that held his mistress that far from being threatening or mocking, they seemed to have genuine respect for her. He could not quite contain a small smile, partly of relief, "I can well believe that. Lady, please give my felicitations to Rheta, Bea, and what is that young servant girl's name, Agalia?"

He was clearly anxious to be gone, now that he was satisfied she was unharmed, but as she turned to walk back up the slope, she had a parting word. "I shall do so, but I fear young Agalia is finding the mountain air to be a bit too much to her liking."

"Young girls can be foolish," he replied. Then he resumed discussion of delivery of the ransom with Athan. Just before she was out of earshot she clearly heard Athan tell Cletus, "And no more of your people attempting a rescue." The reply was unintelligible but Athan's response was clear, "We have seen them sneaking around the camp. I know what you are up to. Stop it at once, or we will have to renegotiate to include the extra expense."

273

'Extra expense indeed!' She thought as she continued on down to where Persus was holding the ponies. But what was Athan talking about when he referred to people sneaking around the camp? She would have certainly been aware if anything like that had been happening. And Athan would never have risked going off with her and Rheta if he had been concerned about a possible rescue. Putting it down to a negotiating ploy, she went to her pony and began stroking its nose. She would never be able to go out on a ride like this again, and the knowledge of that lost freedom pained her. But at this moment losing this freedom seemed a small price to pay to be home again and see her son.

Soon enough Athan returned over the top of the hill. He immediately had them all mount and move away at a brisk pace. Before they had gone far, the two lookouts rejoined them from their posts on the flanks, each reporting no signs of interference. Even so they moved at such a rate that it took all of Mira's fledgling riding skills, along with some discrete help now and again from Persus, for her to stay within the group. After about an hour of this pace, Athan drew up for a stop. They all dismounted just over the top of one of the seemingly endless series of ridges, leaving one man peering over the crest to watch their back trail. It was the first chance for his men to ask about the negotiations.

"I was able to delay it eight days. He was beginning to wonder why I was not in a greater hurry for my money. He was also suspicious that we agreed to his terms so easily. I told him it was because we were anxious to complete the deal but then that did not square with our delays in accepting the ransom. That fellow Kopria is no fool. Tell me Lady, does he have some attachment to you or is he your husband's man?"

'So,' she thought, 'he is asking my advice again. Well, I might as well be civil for the time I must stay here.'

Walking up to him she said, "I have known Kopria for a many years. He was my late husband's man, and after his death he managed my property for me. I believe him to be devoted to me and most especially to Rheta, who he holds in great affection. But why were you saying there were people sneaking around camp? Aorastus knows no one that could arrange a rescue and besides, that is not how he does business. He is prudent, cautious, one to negotiate and settle, not chance some wild rescue."

He stepped closer to her; she did not retreat though she was suddenly very aware of how much larger he was than she. His voice was low and confidential. "I am sorry I did not have the opportunity to speak with you sooner. You asked me to find a way for Rheta and Beltos to be happy. That means together, married, in civilization. Yes?"

"Yes," she agreed wonderingly.

"So, we are going to arrange for civilization to find out about Beltos. Not Beltos the brigand, but Beltos the hero. Beltos returning like Ulysses from a long absence, covered in glory from far distant parts. Then he can rescue all of you; well maybe not Agalia, but Rheta, Bea, and you."

"What? Rescue us? Why?" she asked, clearly not yet grasping the idea.

"So you can all make a triumphant entrance into Buttrotiuria on the arm of a handsome hero. Aorastus saves the price of a ransom and can therefore afford a dowry. You said Beltos has some of his extended family living in Buttrotiuria. They can vouch for his lineage. Beltos and Rheta marry and live happily for the rest of their lives," he concluded triumphantly.

"That is your plan?" Mira said with her hands on her hips. "That is the stupidest thing I have ever heard in my life. Beltos will be recognized, taken, and executed. My daughter will be ruined, and you will be out of your ransom."

"Well," he relied a little defensively, "it was the best I could do on short notice."

"Hummph." she snorted. "Just why do you think that anyone will believe Beltos spent the last, how many years, out being heroic in far distant lands?" all this was delivered without heat and just the faintest encouragement.

"Because," he said taking her arm and starting to walk, each holding the reins of their ponies in their off hand, "we are going to tell them,"

"And how, brave brigand, are you going to do that?"
"Poems," he replied triumphantly, then seeing her puzzled look expanded further, "epics, you know, sung by bards." She continued

to look at him. "Phemius is writing an epic that will describe Beltos' fabulous adventures in foreign lands." This was delivered a bit weakly.

"Phemius," she said flatly.

"No, really! You heard him on an off night. Really, he's very good. We are going to spread the stories ahead of you. That way people will be more interested in seeing a hero, not looking into where he has been all this time. They will expect heroic acts from him, such as rescuing a beautiful woman and her daughter from a desperate band of brigands."

"It's a beautiful woman and her mother," corrected Mira with a small smile.

"Both are beautiful," quickly countered Athan.

"Don't try to sweet talk your way out of this one," Mira returned tartly. "Just how are you going to make our Beltos a hero in, what did you say, eight days?"

"I haven't completely figured that one out yet," admitted Beltos.

"Some Ulysses!" crowed Mira. "Have you considered hiring some of the bards in neighboring cities to learn and recite this as yet uncompleted epic?"

Now it was Athan's turn to question a plan. "Hire them? How would you pay them? No, Phemius says he can persuade them to perform his epic on their own. He says bards are always looking for new material to supplement the old stuff." Without waiting for a reply, he put his hands on her waist and with a deft toss swung her up and onto her pony. The animal started and moved sideways, leaving Mira to snatch at the reins. "We can continue this discussion while we ride."

And so they did, riding alongside one other, discussing and debating every possible angle of the proposed plan. It came as a small shock when Persus rode back to interrupt them.

"I do not mean to intrude on your bickering, but we are almost back to the camp, and there is a messenger coming for the Chief."

"We were not bickering," shot back Mira, "we were planning."

The brigand merely looked at them and turned his pony. Without a word, Athan spurred his pony after him. Mira could tell from the set of his back he was nettled.

'We were bickering,' Mira admitted to herself. 'Just like an old married couple.' That was a strange and not unpleasant thought. 'The fact is, that I am more comfortable with Athan than any man I have every known. I think, no, I am certain I know him better than my own husband.' And unexpectedly a wave of longing swept over her. She wanted to ride up to be beside him. She wanted to listen to his crazy plans for the rest of the day. She wanted him beside her at meals. And she wanted him in her bed. 'So this is what Rheta must be feeling. No wonder she is so crazy. If me, a twice-married woman can be so scattered by a man, how can my poor baby cope?' And at that moment she decided that she would do all she could to make this insane plan of Athan's work. No matter the risk, no matter how unlikely the chances of success she would have to give her darling daughter a chance at happiness.

The camp was in a fine state of activity when Mira and her escort arrived a short time later. Women were moving around in a rapid purposeful way, men were assembling and moving about in apparent agitation, a group of some were at the far end of the camp apparently singing.

'Singing?' Wondered Mira to herself.

Others were clearing an area near the center of camp. Mira dismounted to try to make some sense of it all.

Rheta came racing up to her with Agalia close behind. "Mother, Mother!" she blurted out, "I'm getting married!"

"What?" Mira was totally taken aback. "When?"

"Tonight. In a few hours. As soon as we can get ready."

"I'm getting married, too," chipped in Agalia. Mira ignored her.

"You are not getting married in some brigand camp! I forbid it.'

That ignited the fire fight. Mother and daughter went at it nose to nose, with poor little curly-haired Agalia circling around trying to support her mistress and getting roundly set down by Mira when she did. There were mock retreats, vain threats, pleading requests on both sides, and raised voices. Everyone else in the camp, with the exception of poor, desperate Agalia, stayed well clear. After a while the argument became a negotiation, which was exactly what Mira had hoped for. It was agreed that Rheta might wed in the camp but not that night. Proper vigils and rites would be observed first. They would also promise to keep this ceremony a secret when they returned to civilization and have a proper, public, second marriage. "I will gladly marry Beltos as many times as you like, Mother'" enthused Rheta.

To counter the argument that preparations for the wedding feast were already well advanced, Mira gave permission for Agalia to wed Adrastus, who had apparently won the competition for her hand (and the rest of her as well). The maid disappeared with the news like a gale-blown leaf.

Agalia was a radiant if somewhat hasty bride. Mira acted as her eldest female relation with Athan as her male relation. The two surrogate parents sat comfortably together side by side at the head of the wedding feast. Though the ceremony was brief, the feasting was enthusiastic. The chief entertainment was the singing of latest (partial) version of the 'Tale of Beltos'. Mira was pleasantly surprised to find it was not bad at all. The broad sweep of his supposed adventures was set as a man's struggle against his fate, leaving his ruined city and seeking the evil demon that had destroyed it, sent by the empire of the east. There was a reference to the defeat of the sorcerer priest, Azziz; though in Phemius' version Beltos, not Athan, was hero. In the end, the hero finds and defeats the empire's demon and escapes, returning alone to civilization. The epic was met with wild approval, though Athan agreed with Phemius that it could do with some more work.

"How did you create so much in one day?" Mira asked the bard.

Phemius looked a bit abashed as he confessed, "I have been working on it for a while. I just had to change the hero's name to Beltos and add the bits about the fall of his home city."

Mira and the two men discussed ways that they might get the poem distributed as widely as possible. They eventually agreed that Phemius would have a final version ready to perform again at Beltos' and Rheta's wedding the day after tomorrow. He would leave with an escort the morning after that, six days before the ransom was due, and go to a local town for the epic's first public performance. Unless there was a serious problem with the performance, he would leave to seek out some fellow bards he knew at a city to the southwest. There he would try to persuade them to learn and perform his work. Money might be necessary to help them decide to undertake the work. In that time and place it was expected as a matter of course that a bard should learn a relatively long epic poem by heart in just a day or two. In the absence of wide literacy, memorization was a well-honed skill. Mira agreed that she would finance this with the last of her funds. The goal was to have one or more bards enter and perform the epic in the next town along the road at least two days before Beltos and Rheta made their entrance. That would give word time to spread. The idea was to plant the idea of a rescuing hero in the minds of the people of the city and then, when Mira and Rheta arrived escorted by Beltos it would be almost expected.

"Do we really need to do all this?" questioned Mira at one point, "It seems awfully complicated. Why not just let us go with Beltos. We can explain that he rescued us."

Phemius looked offended. "Madam", he said somewhat stiffly, "you underestimate the power of poetry."

"He's right, you know," added Athan, "when people want to believe in something they don't look beyond it. Maybe all this won't work, maybe no one will have heard of the mighty hero Beltos before you get there. If that is the case you can still explain it all yourself and you loose nothing. But think about it; sooner or later doubts will arise, whispers will start, people will begin asking about this man who shows up with your daughter, and eventually you will have to start telling lies. First you start with exaggerations, then you try half-truths, then little lies, and eventually you will be accused of arranging the entire ransom with your lover to cheat your husband."

Mira felt her cheeks begin to burn. "Well, this will be a complete lie."

"Exactly," said Athan triumphantly, "when you lie, you must grasp the nettle firmly. Tell a huge lie and tell it to everyone, but don't tell them too much. Let them draw it out of you. We will help Beltos learn how to tell a story that is so entertaining that the audience will long for it to be true. You, Mira, and Bea will have to practice your story, from the time he rescues you until your safe arrival back home, before you get there. Can you trust Bea; I mean trust her with your life? If she tells tales after you get home this whole thing could collapse."

"Yes, I think so. She has been with me since before I was married. She was Rheta's nurse." Then Mira noticed something. "What about Agalia?"

"She will be staying with us. She is far too flighty to be trusted with secrets as juicy as this. Besides, her husband is here. She will stay with us."

"But can't you come with..." her voice trailed off. What was she thinking? He was a wanted bandit. He couldn't come back with her. She had just wanted him along with her for a while. Yes, that was it, she just wanted him to stay with them for a few more days, that was all.

Athan was looking at her with a strange expression on his face.

They were saved from the moment by Phemius. "I will need to have two companions go with me," the Bard interjected, "how about Glaucus and Aeolus the younger? We can get down to Ionnina. They know some people down there who know some bards. I may be able to find some old friends there myself. We can try the poem there. Maybe polish it up a little more. Perhaps we can even get some other bards known in Buttrotiuria to go to and present it there. If we leave before noon, we should be there in a by dark on the following day."

"Leave the day after the wedding. You can take Kirkor with you, no one else. He will stay back and watch how thing go. Send him back as a messenger the next day when you can tell him how things went." Athan gave the orders without shifting his gaze from Mira.

Adrastus and Agalia departed the festivities, she making the ritual protestations before being thrown over his shoulder and carried off. The wedding was rapidly winding down. Various members of the band were heading off to bed. Mira collected her daughter from where she and Beltos were talking with surprisingly little fuss, and went off to their hut, trailed by Bea. Mother and daughter combed out one another's hair, discussing the wedding just held and the rituals for the women that would start tomorrow evening ending in Rheta's own wedding the day after that.

"Beltos thinks that we should depart three or four days after the wedding. That should give us time to find a caravan and make our way home before they return from the place where the ransom is to be delivered. After Aorastus finds out he won't have to pay a ransom, he will be so happy that he won't care how we return."

"He'll care," responded her mother bleakly, "especially if he thinks he is being made a fool of. He will deny you your dowry, disown you and put me away."

"Don't say that! Mother, everything will work out. Aphrodite and Artemis have taken us under their special protection. Think of it Mother, we were abducted by brigands! But of all the bandits and brigands in these hills, we were taken by Beltos! And Athan, of course," she added quickly.

"This thing we are doing in two days is not going to be your real wedding. If this wild plan works, we will have a proper wedding, with all the proper ceremonies, and you will behave like a proper bride, not some hoyden eager for the embraces of her lover. Is that clearly understood?"

Nothing could penetrate Rheta's happiness. "Yes, Mother, once we are back in civilization I will be a proper young maiden again until we can be married," a pause, "again." Then with a rush, "So since we will only have a few days before we will be apart again I am not going to waste a night, an hour, a moment. Oh, Mother, haven't you ever been in love? No, no one has ever been in love like we are! Can't you smell the flowers? They are a sign from Aphrodite! I will be back before dawn," and without waiting for a comment, she rose gracefully, kissed her mother on the forehead, saluted the scandalized Bea sitting in the corner, and left.

"You have always indulged that girl," sniffed Bea, "smelling flowers! I don't smell any flowers."

"I do," answered Mira. With calm dignity she rose and picked out the best gown remaining in her chest to put on. She bound back her hair with a bone clip; it was honey colored and set off her hair to excellent advantage. She put her feet back in her best sandals that she had worn to the feast. She lacked a looking glass and so could not check her appearance. She had no real cosmetics to speak of, though she did the best with what she had, leaving some for Rheta's wedding. She had no perfume. Yet she was clean and as well dressed as she could manage under the circumstances. It would have to do. All the time she made her preparations, Bea, normally a relatively quiet woman, had expostulated on Rheta's outrageous conduct, running off with the first good-looking rascal she found, on her certain ruination, and how she had not helped to raise a common trollop.

"Are you going after her, mistress," asked Bea, obviously unsure of Mira's state of mind.

"No," said Mira, "I'm going to collect my gift." And completely ignoring Bea's questions she left the hut and went out into the night and uphill toward Athan's solitary hut.

No one looking at the tall woman walking with such calm composure that evening would have had any idea of the turmoil of her thoughts:

'This is absolute lunacy. I am a married woman who will be reunited with her family soon. I am not a silly young girl anymore. This is a terrible risk; what if he rejects me, sends me away? What if I offer him my heart only to have him throw it on the dirt? What if he uses me cruelly and then brags about it to his band? Why am I going to him like a common strumpet?'

But in her heart she knew her fears were groundless. She knew that he would treat her with love. This was a gift from the goddess, the flowers told her so. In fact, no one saw her on her ascent to Athan's new hut, and no one would ever know of the struggle she had with her own doubts and fears.

There are many kinds of courage. Not all are admirable. But Mira faced her personal crisis of confidence alone in the dark with no one even aware of her test. And as she stood outside the door of a man she had only known for a few days, she had the courage of her convictions, convictions that she for the first and only time in her life genuinely loved a man and that he loved her. There was only one way to really find out if she was right. She reached out and scratched on the lintel beside his door.

"Who is it," came his familiar voice from inside, pitched low.

"It's Mira, may I come in?" without waiting she pushed aside the door covering and entered. Even in the gloom she could see he was lying propped up on one elbow, awake and alert.

"What is it?" he asked again in a quiet voice.

She did not speak, but stepped up to him and kneeling beside him, placing her face close to his. She gently took his face in both hands and kissed him deeply.

A considerable time later Mira lay on her back in Athan's hut while he snored gently beside her. 'Well,' she thought languidly, 'that explains a lot.' Even though she had been married twice, she really was not very sexually experienced. Now some of the comments she had heard from other women made sense. The whole experience could last much longer than she ever expected, and when your partner cared about you, 'loved you' she thought with a gentle touch to Athan's sleeping shoulder, everything became wondrous.

'Thank you Aphrodite' she prayed in thanksgiving as she snuggled next to her sleeping lover and dozed off.

When she awoke, the first faint gray glimmers of dawn were showing. Today would be a busy day, with preparations for the ceremony on the morrow. She gathered her scattered clothes, quietly dressed and prepared to slip out. She bent over Athan to give him a brief kiss. This resulted into a considerable delay as Mira discovered three things: Athan could make love to her three times in a single day, they could do it with her on top of him, and it was not necessary to disrobe to complete the act.

It was almost full light before she was able to tear herself away and head directly down to the women's washing area. Mira was certain that just as the other women had known what Rheta had done the night before, they would instantly sense the change in her relationship with Athan. She felt as though the word "adulteress" would be blazoned across her forehead for all the women to see. To her surprise, none of the four women present seemed to notice the change in her. They were busy talking with each other, washing and preparing for the day. Mira went down to the stream, disrobed, placed her robe and undergarments on the boulder they normally used for that purpose and eased into the cold waters of the stream. Some of the soap root was still on the rock, and she scrubbed herself clean.

"Getting ready for the ceremony tonight?" came a friendly inquiry from Nitsa, a Peloponnesian girl who considered herself Glaucus' pallake. "I see you have a new robe. Do you have another for the wedding tomorrow? I don't have another robe to wear, but Vania is going to help me embroider my other dress today." The young woman prattled on pleasantly as Mira completed her bath. Mira was glad for the diversion, especially when Rheta arrived to giggles and teasing comments from the other girls present. Mira was able to keep her dignity as she climbed out of the stream to dry and dress herself. She merely gave her daughter a sympathetic smile, a 'good morning, darling', and glided back to the cabin.

Back inside the hut Bea was there in a most agitated state. "I was so worried! Where have you been all night! I thought you had been taken away! I started to ask for help, but I did not know who to ask or where to go or how to look for you. Where have you been?" Mira made soothing, reassuring noises, but Bea was too wound up to be easily placated. "Where you out looking for Rheta? I know she was with Beltos; you would think she could wait two days until this little so-called wedding takes place, but you know young girls. But where were you?"

Mira made no reply and began to change into a simpler linen chiton.

"You were with him, the chieftain, weren't you? It is bad enough your daughter running off with some brigand, but you're married! What are you going to tell Aorastus? Are you going to stay here? What will become of me?"

"Be still!" ordered Mira is a tone that would brook no argument. "Sit down and listen." Bea sat right down. "Now listen, nothing happened. I was here all night, do you understand?" Bea nodded mutely. "So was my daughter. We spent every single night together. We stayed together until Beltos came to rescue us. When he came, or rather comes, Agalia will not be with us. We will say she had gone to the privies or something. But no one, I mean no one, is going to talk about what happened here. We will not even talk about it among ourselves. Not now, not ever. Do you understand me?"

Bea looked up at her mutely. She had never seen her mistress like this, so fierce.

"Say it," said Mira putting her face close to her maid. "Say where we stayed the entire time."

"We all slept together all night long," parroted Bea.

"Good," said Mira, don't forget. "Now, we have to get ready for this 'so-called' wedding tomorrow."

"What wedding?" asked Bea sulkily, "I will be spending the night in this hut."

"Good," said Mira with a grim smile. "Remember that later."

She barely had time to wash the next morning before she was swept away with the preparations for the ceremonies that night and the feast to follow. She did not have time for a walk with Athan, but she did make time to stop for a short nap in the early afternoon. For a change the other three women in her party were there. Agalia and Rheta were talking animatedly; Bea sitting in silent disapproval in the corner. There was some discussion about the evening's upcoming vigil, as well as tomorrow's ceremony and married life in general. Mira sensed Bea's growing unease, and so put a stop to the conversation.

"I am sure we have been through far more changes in the last days than any of us ever thought possible. One thing is certain. Today will probably be the last day we will be able to spend together. Do you remember how we set out for the east? It seems so long ago."

And the four women, each with their paths now so clearly divergent, sat on the floor of their little hut and talked of their adventures and difficulties; the challenges, failures and minor triumphs that they had endured together over the last eight months. After a time three of them dozed off; Bea alone remained awake, frowning.

Three of the men had left to obtain more supplies from the market of a local friendly village. The recent entertainments occasioned by the band's four abducted guests had severely strained Athan's meager finances. The kidnapping had resulted in a significant net loss, rather than the expected windfall. First had been the impromptu evening feasts, now it had come to weddings; two so far. Should there be three? Athan had come to look forward to seeing Mira every day; to conversing with her. He admired the way she had taken over the internal management of the camp. She had skills in dealing with people that far exceeded his own. What would it be like to have her as a wife? With her looks, education, and wit, she would have been a magnificent hetaira, a she-companion. But she was a respectable married woman, and a wealthy one at that. He had not thought she would ever consider leaving that life, at least not until he heard her approach his hut last night. She had hesitated a long time by his door before she requested entry. Was she willing to give up the only life she had ever known to live this wild outdoor life with him? He remembered the conversation they had about Rheta and Beltos. When all was stripped away he, too, was a penniless brigand. Except that he had no family and no reputation. What he had was a small group of men who scratched out a precarious living by taking from others. No, it was hopeless.

This wedding was better planned than Agalia's two days before. But though there was better food, a well prepared bride, an actual set of bride's relations, including her mother and a surrogate father who was now experienced in the role, and it must be admitted, a better-looking bride and groom, still the ceremony seemed stale. Perhaps it was because they had just had a wedding. Perhaps it was because the mother of the bride and her nurse kept referring to this as a token wedding or maybe because the weather had turned hot and humid after a long succession of perfect days. Whatever the cause the gaiety seemed a bit forced and the festivities ended sooner than expected.

As members of the band left following the departure of the bride and her new husband to their 'home', his hut that he shared with Simeon. Simeon for his part approached the chieftain. "Ah, Chief, I wonder if I could stay with you in your hut until Beltos and Rheta leave. They will be staying in the cabin Beltos and I used, and I thought they would like to spend this time alone."

"No," said Athan a bit roughly, "the chieftain sleeps by himself. You know that."

"Well I just thought for a few days," stammered Simeon, taken aback.

"No," said his chieftain turning away.

Surprised, Simeon left grumbling.

Athan turned back to Mira. She looked at him; the faintest trace of a smile traced her lips for a moment. Only lovers could transmit so much information with such a minimal expression. Athan smiled and visibly relaxed.

Later that night Mira lay in Athan's arms and tried to decide what she enjoyed most. The sex was amazing; how had she had been married so long without knowing how enjoyable it could be? And lying here, pressed skin to skin was wonderful; a feeling of closeness she had never known with any man. But she thought the quiet conversations they had together in the darkness were the best of all. They talked about everything, without reservation, without fear, on topics both serious and frivolous.

"I wanted you so badly," he told her "but I was afraid to speak to you."

"Afraid? You, a mighty warrior and great slayer of men, afraid of a mere woman?"

"I did not want you to think I was taking advantage of the situation."

"You did not. I did."

"And I am glad you came. Did you like the flowers?" he asked

"What flowers?" she replied genuinely puzzled. Getting flowers was not something a woman fails to notice.

"Oh, I had Glaucus and his pallake pick flowers the other evening and put them around the back of your hut. You said you liked the smell."

There was a long considering pause. 'Glaucus and Nitsa. Ah, Aphrodite,' thought Mira, 'you chose some strange assistants.'

"Why do you shave your beard?" she asked changing the subject. "I am sure you could grow a fine beard."

"I don't know," confessed Athan, "Thaddeus used to say a beard could be grasped by your opponent in battle, but he wore one, although he kept it cut short. I guess I just like it because it is easier to keep clean."

"Is that why you wear your hair cropped short? So no one can grab it in battle and to keep it clean?"

"Well in battle you better have a helmet over your hair or you are in trouble. Besides, I am not really a great warrior. I have only killed a few men in battle. I did kill two men in cold blood, though," he confessed.

And he told her of the murder of Phineas and then how he had once broken off his sword in the head of a stupid youngster just because the young man had offended him. "And to make a point," he concluded lamely.

"Did you?" she asked very quietly.

"Yes, the man with him, a distant relative, was very cooperative after that. But I killed that boy in rage and in haste. I can't afford that luxury ever again."

There was a long pause.

"So if you are not afraid of having your enemy grabbing your hair in battle, why do you not grow it over your shoulders like my son-in-law?" she said steering the conversation back to safer ground.

287

"I really hate lice, and long hair has to be groomed every day or it gets dirty."

"I know," she smiled in the dark. She would really miss combing out her daughter's hair in the evening. Then a question occurred to her, "How do you get rid of your beard? Do you pluck it out?"

"I have a razor," he explained, "I will show it to you tomorrow. It is a straight bronze blade with a blunt tip. I have to sharpen it on a leather strap every time I shave. I put soap and water on my face and scrape the whiskers away. Did you know Persis shaves the hair under her arms?"

"What, really?" Mira was fascinated. "Why? How do you know?" The last slightly accusatory.

"I think she said it made some of her gowns look better. She said it was less like some hairy man and more like a girl. You could see her arms on some of her gowns that were cut down to here."

"I'll show you 'here'," growled Mira playfully, starting another bout of lovemaking.

"You know you really are incredible," she sighed a half hour later.

This time Mira was prepared to go straight to the washing area for her early morning ablutions and was experienced enough to not wake Athan when she departed. She was the first one there and had finished washing her body, then cleaned her teeth using a splintered twig and salt. She was leaving the area just as the first of the other women were arriving. When she entered the hut she found Bea sitting in there all alone.

"You are a fool," the older woman hissed. "You upbraid your daughter and yet consort with one of these brigands yourself. You will come home to your husband after all these months bearing him a child. Rheta would be shamed, but you will be put to death by your husband; yes, and me, too for allowing it to happen!"

"Calm yourself, Bea; I am not going to allow myself to become pregnant. Do you think I am some girl who does not know the phases of her moon? Rheta's courses and mine come at the same time. We are past our time when we can get pregnant, or at least I am. That fool girl could not wait the few days to be sure, but now she is committed to her new husband. If she delivers us a grandchild a few days too soon after the wedding, there will be no damage. So calm yourself; all will be well."

"Why, Mira, why do you take this risk? Are you going to leave Aorastus and stay here? What will become of me?" It was a measure of her agitation that she addressed her mistress by her name, something she almost never did.

Mira came and knelt by the older woman, taking her two hands in hers. "No, Bea, I am not going to leave my husband, and yes you will go home as our honored nurse. I will expect you to help Rheta with her babies and grow old with us in Buttrotiuria."

"Why, mistress," repeated the faithful old servant starting to break down in tears. "Why must you put us all at risk? Rheta is young and foolish, but you..." she could go no farther.

"Because," Mira said to the sobbing woman, "I was given a gift by the gods. I have been allowed to know love, true love for a man for the only time in my life. I know I must put it aside soon, but for these days, let me be happy. That is all I will ever have, just these few days. Will you let me do that?"

The sobbing slowed and then died away. "Yes, mistress, but be careful."

"I will. Now I will do all the things I have done since we first came here. That includes taking a walk with the chieftain. Will you come as a chaperone?"

"Yes," Bea gulped, "but just for a little while. Then I will have to stop and rest. You two can go ahead."

"That will be fine," said Mira with a smile.

Phemius and Kirkor rode off on their hill ponies well before noon that morning, though not as early as Athan had hoped. Phemius was as well-dressed as any bandit Mira had ever seen. She said a fervent prayer that his poem would be well received, received at all, and that Athan's wild scheme would work.

The days went by in a golden flash, and the nights drifted on as a strange dozing dream. Though they were as discrete as practical, the connection between Athan and Mira became obvious and, to all the people around them, natural. Beltos and Rheta, who were seldom seen following their wedding, were wrapped up in learning about one another; they had the luxury of having leisure time to do so. Athan and Mira, on the other hand had to be visible and active in maintaining the structure of the band. Both had been married before, and so fell into married habits; this sometimes made things easier, sometimes more difficult. But any newcomer to the group would have immediately assumed that they had been a married couple for many years; this seemed to suit both of them.

Of the many things that Mira loved about this time was the chance to lie together with Athan late at night and talk. They told one another secrets. Athan confided to her about his extra set of teeth. "It isn't natural," he said. "Some of the ones I lost were still fine, maybe a bit worn, but not missing or chipped or decayed or anything."

"Did any of your family get an extra set?" she asked.

"Not to my knowledge," he replied.

"Well, to my way of thinking it is not all that strange. And if you are going to have a something unnatural, getting an extra set of teeth is certainly a nice unnatural thing to have. I could use three new ones myself."

She was interested in his little amulet he wore around his neck. The simple coppery chain had a leather bag tied to it with a leather drawstring. Her womanly curiosity was aroused as to the contents.

"The bag holds tinder and flint for a fire. But the chain and this" he untied the drawstring and lowered the bag off the eight-sided crystal attached to the chain, "I got it from Azziz the sorcerer priest after I killed him."

"You mean that poem was true!"

"No, most of that is pure exaggeration, but I did kill Azziz. This was around his neck on the chain. I always carried a tinder bag around my neck anyway and thought I should keep something valuable in the bag as well."

She lifted the crystal off his neck and held it close to the small lamp burning low. She stared at the way it reflected and refracted the tiny light. "It's beautiful," she said.

"Do you want it?" he asked casually.

"I can't take it," she said retying the bag it to and then placing the chain back around his neck. "All I can take from you is memories. Remembrances of times like this."

Shortly before noon, on the fourth day after Rheta's wedding, a message was flashed to the lookout from Kirkor.

"Alpha Delta Four One," reported Simeon to his chieftain.

"That is good," said Athan, "that means Phemius was successful in making contact with his poet friends.

"There is more," reported Simeon, Rho Delta four dash two dash four dash Mu dash four. Why is he telling us about a caravan, especially a big one? Does he think we should try to hit a big caravan? This makes no sense?"

"It makes sense if he has heard about a west bound caravan that might be a good candidate for our hero to join with his rescued captives," said Athan bleakly. "They must be on the south track. Please tell Beltos and the women to make ready to leave early tomorrow."

His orders caused an immediate stir within the camp. Men ran to notify Beltos. Glaucus was dispatched to relieve Kirkor on signal post so that he could make a full report in person. Athan went to find Mira to give her the news but found she already knew.

"Are we leaving tomorrow? She asked.

"There is a signal that there is potentially suitable caravan on the south road. I am sending a scout to find out more. I also need to know how the poem is being received."

"Does that mean we are leaving tomorrow?"

"Unless you stay here with me. Will you?"

There it was. Sometimes it was better to be blunt than to dance around the problem. Mira just wished with all her heart that this wasn't such a time, but she knew it was. She closed her eyes and took a deep breath. "I cannot leave my children. I have a family there, friends, a life."

"A husband," said Athan.

"That, too," admitted Mira, "but that is not why I must leave. You must know that," there was pleading in her eyes for him to understand.

"I understand," he said, "it is no use for us to fight against our fate."

She leaned forward and placed the side of her face against his chest, a palm on either side. She could hear his heart beating powerfully. She knew she had to say something to provide closure. She was a skilled conversationalist. The right words always came to her, but not this time. Instead she leaned into his strong chest and wept. First his arms went around her, then she embraced him, shaking with grief.

The storm passed, as they always do. Mira broke the embrace, excused herself, and went to the women's outdoor lavatorium they had made by the stream to clean herself up. Athan spoke to Beltos to ensure certain preparations for the departure were in hand, arranged for a three man team to scout the caravan and set requirements for the type and frequency of their reports back. Kopria was detached to get a complete report from Phemius, including how his poem had been received. Arrangements were made for a possible meeting with the bandit/poet just outside the town, if deemed prudent. The women were told to prepare for a departure, possibly as soon as early afternoon the following day.

Shortly before sunset Kirkor arrived on a tired pony. He immediately went into a council of war with Athan, Beltos, and Simeon. When they emerged, the evening meal, a rather somber affair, was already underway. Athan had sent word to Mira that the women were to eat apart. Although she was disappointed, in one way, in another she was glad for a chance to make her initial farewells to the other women who accompanied the band and also to suggest some final ideas. The women's meal was far less tense than it might otherwise have been, and by the end of the gathering there was as much laughter as tears. Beltos had already informed his wife that she would be staying with her mother until they were married "again". This did not go well with her, but pleased Mira and most especially Bea. Agalia would remain here with Adrastus, presumably until death did them part. Mira had to wait very late that night before she was sure the other two women were asleep and she could slip out of the hut. When she completed the familiar journey she found the hut empty. A noise behind her made her start.

"I'm here," was all he said.

She made to rush to him, but the poor light made her rush turn into a stumble and she would have fallen to the ground had she not fallen into Athan's arms instead.

"What are you doing out there?" she asked, trying to catch her breath.

"You must go back to your hut," he told her before she could ask anything else, "Beltos is coming to your hut to take you away any time now."

"Why, what," she stammered, "we were going to leave tomorrow after noon."

"The caravan is perfect but it is further along than we thought. You will need to move quickly to join it as soon a possible. Simeon had the idea that you should leave just as you would if Beltos, is in fact, rescuing you. That way the timing will work out and your stories will match your arrival."

She could think of nothing to say. Athan continued on relentlessly, "We will not have a tearful goodbye, you will walk down that hill and go to the hut and wait with your daughter and your maidservant until Beltos comes to take you away."

"I will never see you again."

"You will never see me again, nor I you," confirmed Athan. He could have said something else, how he would hold her in his heart or remember her forever, but he did not. The silence stretched.

She gave a great sigh, "Goodbye, then," she said. "May the gods protect you."

"Goodbye," he replied, "thank you."

"The pleasure," she replied giving him a brief kiss on the lips before pulling back, "was mine." Then she turned and walked back down the hill. She turned back to look once but it was dark and she could see nothing. She stumbled and returned her attention toward watching where she was going instead of where she had been.

As she approached the hut she saw a man bending by the door: Beltos. "You are here already?" she asked quietly and saw him jump.

"Shhh," he quieted her, "we have to leave right now."

Entering the hut she lit the lamp from the small candle that was burning in the corner and awakened the others. "This man has come to rescue us from these bandits," she told them to their evident confusion.

Mira tried to pretend that this was an actual rescue, a fiction somewhat marred by her daughter's cry of "Darling" as she leapt into her lover's arms, but with whispered explanations, they quickly grasped the idea. There was no time to pack or even bring much with them.

"How will we get away?" asked Mira.

"We have two horses," replied Beltos. In fact there were only two horses in the entire camp, the rest were small hill ponies. One horse was used almost exclusively by Beltos and the other by Simeon, Athan preferring the low and sturdy hill ponies.

"One horse can bear two women," responded Mira, but the other cannot be expected to carry both you and one of us as well, not to mention anything else we might need. I will ride a pony."

Their astonishment was obvious even in the faint light.

"I can ride," she assured them. "That way, Beltos can lead the other horse, and we can make better time."

"Kopria is coming with us," Beltos told her. "He can lead your pony."

"We will decide on the way," she compromised, "now, what can we take?"

They had brought little enough with them and left much of that. Mira shooed Beltos out of the hut while they changed into traveling clothes. She put on the silk bloomers Athan had made for her. "They make riding easier," she explained to the others. Some of their extra clothes were left for Agalia. Mira left her writing box. Within was a note: 'Thank you for your many kindnesses.'

The women slipped out of the hut with Beltos leading them, exactly as though they were escaping from a hostile camp. Beltos took them straight to were the animals were waiting. The horses were saddled with Kopria standing by his pony. There was some delay while the stolid little pony Mira had previously ridden was found, awakened (much to its displeasure) and saddled. The party then led their horses down beyond the camp before they mounted and slowly rode out the camp and the lives of those who remained.

It was early evening, just as a caravan was coming into a village where they expected to camp in safety for the night, when they were overtaken by five people on two ponies and two horses. The two men claimed that they had rescued the women from hill bandits, a story supported by the women. There was some initial skepticism, which was heightened when the men were asked to identify themselves.

"Beltos, eh," said the caravan leader, "like the hero?"

"What?" said Beltos genuinely puzzled

"Like that character in the poem," explained the leader. "We heard it in Vissana two nights ago. Did you take his name?"

"I have been in the east for a long time," replied Beltos cautiously, just as he had practiced now that he understood what was going on, "and this is the only name I have ever had." He went on to say he had traveled with some fellow who had 'claimed to be a poet' for a time 'a few months ago'. Mira and Rheta were loud in their praises of the young hero and Kopria was fulsome in his praise of his companion 'of some months' carefully repeating his agreed-upon stories. The caravan master agreed to allow them to accompany his caravan for the next day for 'mutual protection.'

By the time the caravan had traveled another day they had come to accept the stories of their fellow-travelers. When they arrived at Dodona, a small city, and found the Beltos' Epic already being quoted there, the entire caravan was quick to claim him as their own. Mira found out the poet responsible for this performance had been none other than Phemius, who joined them that evening. He was discreetly glad to see them.

"It has gone better than I expected," he enthused, "we found three old friends of mine, really established and respected bards. They were looking for a new bit of material, and were glad to have my little effort. They made a few improvements and off we went. I had to persuade them to travel west with it or otherwise they would have scattered in every direction. One of them headed for Buttrotiuria. He is probably there by now."

The caravan master had a variety of merchants with him and, as they approached Buttrotiuria, for that was their next city of call, he sent ahead messengers letting the city oligarchs know that the famous hero Beltos had rescued captives belonging to the city and was returning them to their families. The news electrified the city. The news of the capture of Aorastus' wife and step-daughter had been something of a sensation. The possibility that they had been rescued by the hero of a new and popular poem was almost too good to be true. But despite some skepticism, a large crowd met the incoming caravan.

And so it was that Beltos and his companions made a triumphant entry into Buttrotiuria. When it was confirmed that this hero, who had rescued the wife and daughter (the fact she was a step-daughter was now being ignored) of one of the city's wealthiest men was in fact Beltos of Epiria, the remaining elements of his family embraced him with open arms. Many refugees from Epiria had established themselves in Buttrotiuria, and to them Beltos was a gift from the gods. It did not take long for opportunities to be presented to him. When it was revealed that he wished to wed the girl he had rescued, the city's enthusiasm knew no bounds. It was the wedding of the year.

Mira met Aorastus with some trepidation. He was outwardly gracious and polite in public, but as soon as they were alone he turned on her.

"Did you do it with him?" he almost hissed.

Mira felt a cold shock and could reply with at faint. "What?"

"Did that young man, that hero, Beltos, did you and he, you know, do it?"

So her husband did suspect her of infidelity, but with the wrong man. Relief flooded through her. She stepped close to her husband and looked directly at him. She concealed how aware her body was that her husband was shorter and softer than the man she had been sleeping with only a few days before.

With a little laugh she said, "Husband, Beltos is so besotted with Rheta that he scarcely noticed me."

Visibly relieved he said "Cletus told me that you said the bandits had not molested you."

"No, husband, they treated me with respect. No one forced themselves on any of us. That fool Agalia ran off, but other than that we were well treated."

"Truly"

"Yes, truly. Now may I see my son?"

That evening Mira returned from the baths to her chambers to find her husband waiting there. She dismissed her maids and went into to him. She saw he had been examining the few things she had brought back with her. In his hand was the only incriminating thing he could have found. Her silk, riding underwear, cut to fit her.

"What are these?" he asked with cold suspicion.

What she did not say, or even think until much later, was that 'they were undergarments made from stolen material, so that I could ride over the hills with my wild bandit lover.'

Instead, without the slightest hesitation she said, "Remember when you left us Delphi, there were only a limited number of acceptable suitors. After your uncle died there was little for me to do so I came to know and spend time with a group of other women left without male escorts. Some of them were hetaira. We discussed fashion and clothing as women do. This," she said taking the garment from his fingers, "is the latest fashion, but is meant to be seen only by a woman's husband. Would you like to see it?" Without waiting for his answer she walked very carefully behind a screen and disrobed. She pulled on the long silk pantaloons and using a small bronze mirror tried to check her look. Fortunately Bea had rinsed the silk garment out after they joined the caravan or they would have still carried the odor of horse. Coming from the baths she was clean and her maids had done her hair, but there was no time for cosmetics. Well, she had a healthy glow from her outdoor life and her exertions, traveling and being a bandit queen and all, had left her firmer and more fit than she had been in years. On impulse she took a long scarf, nearly transparent and quite expensive and wound it artfully around her breasts and over and behind her neck. Aorastus was making impatient noises on the other side of the screen, so taking a calming breath she stepped from behind her screen. She was amply rewarded by her husband's reaction. He sucked in his breath and stared.

"Oh, Mira!" he choked, his voice full of passion.

She swayed up to him and cast her eyes demurely down. "Yes, husband?"

Neither Mira nor Aorastus had any idea he had such passion hidden within him. They scarcely left the house for a fortnight. Perhaps it was the suddenly awakened passion or the prestige of suddenly having a famous son-in-law, or perhaps it was the daughter Mira presented him just less than nine months later, or perhaps it was just that time in his life, but Aorastus found himself deeply in love for the first time in his life and with his own wife!

They named their daughter Athena, in thankfulness, said Mira, to the goddess for her rescue.

The Old King smiled as he recalled his days with Beltos, Rheta, and Mira. He looked out of his crevice and realized it was dawn. A cold gray dawn with the promise of later snow, but there was light. He put down some kindling on the remains of the fire and blew it to life. Once it was crackling, he gathered some ice and put it the fire to start some morning tea.

He wrapped his body in his cloak and his mind in memories. He later heard what had happened to them. With Rheta's dowry, Beltos had purchased some land outside the city where they raised wheat and a house in the city where they raised children. Aided by loans from other Epirian expatriates and surviving members of his extended family, he and his family had prospered. Based upon his reputation, Beltos was made a captain of the city's militia. He was fortunate to win a minor fight against another city. He then cemented his status with a successful campaign against brigands in the hills around the city. Of course, by then Athan's band had moved far from Buttrotiuria. The morning after Beltos and the women had departed the band had packed up and moved out north and west, heading up into safer terrain, and leaving behind places with too many memories attached to it.

The Old King laughed at another memory. Beltos' Epic had been popular for several years; Athan had heard it quoted in a city over a hundred parasangs from Buttrotiuria. There was also another poem with a hero named Beltos with quite a different slant. It told the story of a hero, like Beltos, who was returning from adventures in the east when he saw a woman being held captive by bandits. In this version he takes her

> **As a hawk flying over a flock of pigeons**
> **Sees the fairest one**
> **And choosing it from all others**
> **Stoops down**
> **Seizing it with his strong talons**
> **And holds her close to his breast**

In this epic it turns out that this pigeon is a lure for a falconer and the hawk is captured and bound with jesses. He becomes a provider for that which he once thought to capture for his own.

The old man thought that was about right. The last word he had of them, Beltos was a wealthy oligarch in Buttrotiuria and his wife and widowed mother-in-law were running his household. 'Not a bad fate for a former bandit,' thought Athan, with no irony at all.

Chapter Twelve– Opportunities

"**It will be** a rich caravan, Chief; there is money to be made!"

The spy, Pirro by name, had every reason to be enthusiastic. Pirro was a small, spare, red-headed man of about 25 who had been with the band off and on for over a year. He had been very helpful in locating potential targets, using his contacts on the east coast. He apparently thought this opportunity would provide the band some much needed income. Since Beltos had left the band there had been flush times and lean times. Over time, though the flush times had been less and less fulsome, and the lean times seemed to last longer.

Membership in the band had changed over time. Some men left to take up another life. Some became injured and were forced to find a less strenuous occupation, not easy to do in a strenuous time. Some men died from disease, or from accidents, a few were killed. Only Simeon, Tenucer, and Adrastus still remained of the group that Captain Athan had led from the wreckage of 'Achilles' Debacle' The latter two had both left and then rejoined the band several times over the years. Adrastus would leave the band, sometimes for over a year, to live with his wife Agalia, only to return when the marital seas became rough. Eventually, he decided it was less stressful to live as a hill brigand than as the husband of such a wild and flighty woman and he remained permanently with his comrades.

Very few men in his band ever addressed Athan as Captain any more and only Simeon would occasionally refer to him as Athan. Almost everyone addressed him as 'Chief', the normal titled of a band of brigands. The size of his band had waxed and waned along with his fortunes. In the early years he had commanded as many as hundred men, and later as few as dozen. Right now he was approaching that lower number.

In all that time Athan's band had never been trapped and never been defeated. There were a few times when he called off an attack, and several times when the band had been forced to flee its camps ahead of enemy troops, but there were never heavy casualties in the band. Whenever he felt the time had come to move his area of operations from regions that had become familiar he would find a new area of operations, because as areas became more familiar, to him so did his band to their would-be victims and enemies. Caravans became too cautious and well guarded. Groups of armed men would begin to hunt for any band of brigands that were too well-known and successful. Over the years he had been generally moving farther and farther east and north until they eventually found more or less steady work on the Thracian coast, along the eastern 'wine dark sea' where Ulysses was said to have once sailed. Athan had transitioned his band almost entirely from banditry to other occupations, usually providing security for caravans instead of preying upon them.

Now Pirro had arrived with an opportunity for employment for the band.

"When will this caravan leave?" asked the Chieftain.

"It should leave in not more than a fortnight, Chief," replied the scout. "I hear that they plan to depart from Stavros and travel along the coast of Thrace all the way to Golibolu at the Hellespont."

"How many guards?"

"There will be many. It depends on many things. The leader of the caravan is the Satrap of the province, a very cautious man; he trusts no one. He brings at least two or three score horsemen with him as scouts and outriders. He always hires three or four different bands of mercenary hoplites. He likes to have different bands in order to reduce the danger of conspiracy. So, besides the cavalry, he will have at least two and perhaps as many as four score infantry. This will be in addition to his personal bodyguard of another two score or so. Then, of course, there will be the sailors; sometimes I hear there are as many as a hundred of them, though they are not heavily armored. They are expected to fight off pirates more than bandits. Still, they are experienced fighters in their way."

That was far too many to overcome. He could not let his men know that he was turning down a chance at a good payday or so many men might leave that he could not sustain the numbers needed to maintain the band. If his band dissolved, there would be few options for him. He could consider trying to join the guard of some city-state, but who would speak for him? Should he be recognized as a long-term brigand chief, he would be executed. Even the so called "wild, free life" of a brigand was not really free.

Just then Simeon poked his head in the tent and requested to come in. The two old comrades were much alike. Lean hardened campaigners, with hair cut short, both wore similar wool tunics over baggy trousers and a conical felt pilleus hat; both men wore vests, Athan the red vest he had taken from Azziz, Simeon a plain brown one in conscious imitation of his chief. The most obvious difference was that Athan was clean shaven and Simeon wore a beard. There were other differences: though the men looked to be of an age, adult men in their prime, in fact Athan was more than ten years older than Simeon. Simeon was somewhat shorter and stockier and had a dark hair and black eyes compared to Athan's lighter brown hair and hazel eyes.

"Heard about the caravan," said Simeon.

"Come in and let's talk about it," invited the Athan. The two old comrades sat and listened to Pirro. The three men sat on folding stools around a small table that held a pitcher of wine, a pitcher of water, three goblets and the lamp that provided the only light in the space. Athan's tent was adequate to his needs and actually comfortable for one man. There was a fine bronze brazier on the rug that made up the tent's floor, unlighted in the warm summer weather. There was a low folding cot with a thin pallet (stuffed with cotton not straw) and associated bedding. The winter blankets, along with the rest of Athan's winter clothes, were in the bottoms of two wicker panniers on the other side of the tent. The panniers held the rest of Athan's rather small stock of spare clothing. He liked to wear high quality clothing in dark unobtrusive hues. He had a spare pair of sandals neatly laid out where they could be quickly donned or replaced back in the panniers. His toiletries, such as a fine bronze mirror, razor, brush, and twigs for cleaning his teeth were on top of a chest next to a basin and pitcher. Two other small chests completed the furniture. Everything including the tent itself could be loaded onto a single pack mule. Though his things were of good quality, the tent held everything Athan owned in the world.

"Pirro says that this caravan will be carrying the semiannual tribute from the conquered Ionian cities back to the Empire. He says it will have 200 talents of gold."

Simeon indicated his appreciation with a low whistle. "I assume," he said, "that it will have lots of guards."

"He expects well over two hundred fighting men," said Athan dryly nodding to Pirro, "but that is not all."

"Indeed," said Pirro, "it is how he moves this treasure that makes it so secure. He sends the treasure by ship stopping at night. But he has some of his troops move along the shore so that whenever he comes in to camp, he already has a strong force ashore, ensuring there are no surprises. Then the guards take the treasure chests up and put them ashore inside a strong camp, sometimes with a ditch around it. There is a strong guards around the camp with many sentries, watchers on the beach for anyone who thinks they can attack from the sea at night, and horse patrols to prevent and if necessary counter attack any night raids. So you see he is safe; should he sight pirates during the day, he need only put into shore where his fighting men are waiting. At night, he is secure from all but the strongest attacks, and a body of men large enough to overwhelm him is very difficult to conceal. That makes surprise out of the question. So even if you did put together a big enough force to overcome the guards, there would be time for him to move the treasure to the boats, and if necessary put back out to sea."

"What if there were ships waiting to attack him at the same time he was attacked by land?" asked Simeon.

"The problem would be coordination," replied Athan. "Can you imagine how hard it would be to get pirates to work with a bunch of bandits? And to have them all attack at the right place and same time? Just putting together a band big enough to challenge over a hundred men supported by quality cavalry, and they are quality men aren't they, Pirro?"

"The best," he confirmed.

"Would be nearly impossible," continued Athan. Even trying to put together a force powerful enough to attack them would certainly alert Achaemendian spies. But a question, Pirro, how do the foot soldiers keep up with the ships? Horses can move as fast as ships at sea, but foot soldiers cannot."

"It is all planned out very well, Chief," responded Pirro. "Half the mercenaries ride the ships, the other half leave all but their weapons on the ships. Troops marching light with the way clear ahead of them can move pretty fast. The horsemen provide route security and the roads are good. If they are fresh it is not hard for them to cover eight or even ten Parasangs and still be in place before the ships come to shore in the evening."

"It sounds like you know these caravans well," Simeon put in.

"Certainly," replied Pirro, "I helped guard one two years ago. I was thinking we could do the same this time. Even if we don't figure out a way to pilfer some of the other merchandise, the pay is good."

"Two hundred talents," mused Athan, "that would weigh over 200 medimnos. That is a lot of weight. How is it carried and stored?"

"You don't think I meant that we could steal the tribute do you? Great Zeus! That is not what I meant. The Empire would hunt you to the ends of the earth. They take that sort of thing as a direct attack on the Empire itself. This is not to mention the satrap's reaction. He is personally responsible for that tribute. He would go **beyond** ends of the earth to recover it and put an end to anyone who tried to filch a single drachma." Pirro was agitated just at the thought.

"I was just wondering," protested Athan with injured innocence. "How do they get over 200 medimnos off and on the boats every time they camp? Why not just leave it on the boats?"

"Because the Satrap is a suspicious bastard, that's why. He doesn't trust anybody; in fact he acts like he is certain that everyone intends to betray him. He splits the troops up so that no one group is able to have the upper hand. He is afraid that if he leaves the gold on the ships the sailors would sail away one night, taking it with them. That is why he puts it in a treasure tent each night with guards within and without. He always hires three or four different bands of mercenaries, so that no one band is ever in charge of the gold. His personal guards oversee the movement of the gold. It is kept in special stout wooden boxes, each with an imperial lead seal. There must be about two talents in each box because they weighed over two medimnos each, and there were a hundred boxes; they counted them every morning and every evening when they were moved. They have iron straps on the sides with places to fit in wooden poles so you can carry them like a litter. Believe me, between the boxes and what is inside them, they are a load for two men, even with that setup. We formed teams and carried them in from the boats to the big tent, we called it the treasure tent, each night. Then in the morning, we loaded them back up. With a couple score men it only took five or six trips or so to unload them. In the evening after the gold was inside the tent, the guards were set. Four men from two different bands were inside, four more from the Satrap's own guard stood on the outside, one at each corner. Other men watched the perimeter along the edge of the camp, and there were also other men from his personal guard assigned to move around the camp. They were sort of the guards of the guards, and a right set of bastards they were. They threatened to cut your throat if they found you asleep on watch. Seven men were flogged for not keeping a sharp enough watch."

"You got tired," Pirro continued, "so it was always nice when you rode the ships, because you could rest and even get some sleep if you didn't have to help row. Of course, the real reason we got to go on the ships was the Satrap wanted us as a counterbalance if the sailors tried anything, and I suppose we could fight pirates if we were attacked, but I know we would have headed for shore if we saw anything like enemy ships."

"So there were men inside the treasure tent each night?" asked Athan.

"Yes," confirmed Pirro, "but always from two different bands."

"Well, no wonder no one has ever tried to steal such a well protected treasure," said Athan blandly. "Where does the caravan end and how do we get paid?"

"We were paid off in silver at Golibolu near the straits," said Pirro. "It was hard work but safe work, and they paid the standard rates. After the tribute was loaded onto the treasury at Golibolu we were paid off in full and told to go home. Then it was up to the Empire to see the tribute over the Hellespont and the rest of the way back to where ever they take the tribute."

"Did they ever open the boxes so you could see the tribute?" asked Simeon who was showing a great deal of interest in the details of the tribute.

"No, why would they do that? Everybody was afraid to get to close to them. That is why they were covered with a tarpaulin in the ships and in the tent to keep anyone from trying to get too good a look."

"But you got a good look when you carried them back and forth, didn't you?"

"Sure, but the personal guards were right there, keeping a stink-eye out on everyone."

"So, tell me, I am curious about such riches. What kind of seal does the empire use?" Simeon continued.

Pirro went on to describe the thick oak boards of the boxes, the iron hasps and hinges, held closed with a heavy copper wire held secured with a lead seal with an impression on it. "No one can get close to those gold ingots," he concluded.

"How do you know they are gold ingots?" Simeon pressed.

"I know some people that helped to load the boxes. There are two layers with four ingots in a layer. Each quarter talent ingot is in an individual space cut from a wooden tray so they won't shift around. They weigh each ingot, put it in the cutout then place each tray in the box. The boxes are specially made. They don't just put the trays in the bottom of the box, no, that would make it too hard to get the trays out. The trays rest on sideboards inside the box, one set just above the bottom and one set about halfway up."

"You mean," Simeon interrupted him, "when you open the lid you only see the top half of the box with four of the eight ingots?"

"Yes," replied a somewhat puzzled Pirro. The other tray is underneath. When the second tray is put in, they close the lid and seal it."

"How do they know the second tray of gold is underneath the top one?" asked Simeon.

"The weight of it, a talent gold weighs about a medimnos." Athan answered for Pirro. Then he continued musing aloud, "Four quarter talent ingots in each tray, each ingot must weigh about a quarter of a medimnos. With the weight of the wood, the boxes have to weigh nearly three medimnos each." He said calculating in his head. "Gold is heavy."

"Just you wait until you have to carry it through the surf out to a boat," replied Pirro.

"Do you think you could get us signed up as guards," asked Athan. "The band could do with a bit of pay and some steady rations."

Pirro assured them he knew the man to talk to, and for a suitable bit of money could make the arrangements. "How many men should I say we have, Chief?"

"Put us down for an even score," replied Athan, rising from his seat to indicate that Pirro should withdraw. The red headed scout made his courtesies and departed.

Once he was gone from view Simeon sat back down and looked at his Chief. "You are thinking about stealing that gold," Athan said.

"Not all of it," replied Simeon carelessly.

With a small sense of disappointment the old man realized he had completely lost track of the days. It hardly mattered. He had decided he would wait until the snow was mostly gone, so he could move about without having to exhaust himself pushing through drifts. Also, he knew that if he were caught in a storm he would not survive a night outside. He was weak, but no longer hungry. He would wait here and think about things he had done long ago.

Chapter Thirteen–Preparations

"Do you remember Jonathan?" Simeon asked Athan later that evening, after they had discussed various options for stealing the Empire's gold.

"My former 'son'?" responded Athan, "of course. I haven't heard from him in years though."

"I understand he has a wife and family now and is captain of a small group of guards in Stavros. I think I could get in contact with him."

"What do you have in mind?" asked Athan.

"I'm not sure yet," replied the younger man, "Jonathan might be able to help us make a connection for employment guarding the tribute. He is a smart man; perhaps he will have some ideas."

In the event, it turned out to be easy to contact Jonathan. He walked into their camp the very evening they arrived outside the low walls of Stavros. Even better, he immediately asked if they would be interested in a job guarding the tribute for the Empire. The three men sat on stools together in Athan's tent, sharing an amphora of wine.

"The Satrap likes to hire three or four bands with between one and two score men each. How many hoplites do you have with you, Captain?"

"Almost a score," exaggerated Athan.

"Good," said Jonathan briskly, "I think we can both get work as tribute guards. My group worked with them two of the past four caravans."

"Why not more regularly?" asked Simeon, passing his old friend a small amphora of wine.

Jonathan poured some into his cup and added water before answering. "Because the Satrap is notoriously suspicious. I do not think he has ever trusted anyone in his life. He doesn't want anyone to be able to anticipate his next move. So he tends not to hire the same guards too often."

"So we've heard," grunted Simeon.

"I understand you are supporting a family now," said Athan, changing the subject.

"Yes," grinned Jonathan, "I have a wife, two sons, and she delivered me a set of twin daughters this spring."

The men made the expected compliments on his virility, followed by good-natured chaffing and jokes. As they caught up on old times, it became obvious that Jonathan was more or less respectable now. He clearly loved his wife, adored his children and worried about providing for them. Unfortunately, he had no land, no regular trade and no steady source of income. He did have a band of men at his command, but they only worked together when he could find work as soldiers or guards. The income was only sporadic, and the work often took him away from his family, sometimes for months. His wife was a refugee from Attica and had no family here so she was dependant upon friends when he was gone. It was a tenuous situation, and Jonathan was worried about it. There was no hint that he wanted to resume the wild life of a bandit up in the hills, nor did he seem interested in resuming his once intimate relationship with Simeon. He was now just a man looking to take care of his family. But Athan thought he detected a spark in his old friend, indicating that he would not flinch from a risk if the reward was high enough.

It was Simeon who broached the subject. "So, is there any chance someone might try to steal the tribute?"

Jonathan shook his head and proceeded to give them a long list of reasons why a raid would never succeed. Too many guards, too well protected, no chance of surprise, no chance of getting enough men to betray the guards, secrecy about the departure, unexpected stops and delays to prevent any planned attacks, different groups watching each other, the Satrap's personal guard watching everyone. In every major particular he confirmed what Athan and Simeon had already heard right down to the lead wafers that sealed each of the specially made oak boxes. While this was going on, Athan noticed that Simeon went from deep thought to rapt interest to enthusiasm.

"But if there was a plan," Simeon said, stopping Jonathan's monolog of the difficulties in taking the gold from its obsessive keeper, "would you be willing join us?"

"I do not think you understand," returned Jonathan, "this tribute belongs to the Empire. They would not, could not, let anyone intercept the tribute. Of course, the Ionian cities would have to pay the tribute again, so they would do everything they could to catch the perpetrators, as well. The main problem would be the Satrap. He would never rest until he found the stolen tribute and punished those who took it. He could never return home without it. Not only would he be severely punished, perhaps even executed, his family would also suffer as well. Actually, I think the blow to his pride would be the greatest affront to him. He would chase you until he died. If he died before he caught you, he would come back as a spirit and haunt you."

"If we did it right, brother," Simeon said using a term of masculine endearment, "no one would know we did it. They would not even know **how** we did it."

"This has to do with the seals on the boxes doesn't it?" Athan asked, remembering a caper Simeon had pulled off some years before that involved seducing a merchant's mistress so he could get access to the mold for the lead wafers the man used seal his treasure chests. Simeon had broken the seals, stolen the silver within the chests and resealed it with the purloined mold so that the theft was not discovered until he was safely away.

Simeon only smiled.

"The Satrap doesn't have a mistress to seduce, does he?" a grinning Athan asked a thoroughly puzzled Jonathan.

Before he could put together a coherent negative to that question Simeon asked him two more questions. "Can anyone see inside the treasure tent? I mean is it open at the front or sides? And where does he keep the mold for his seal?"

By now Jonathan was thoroughly flummoxed. The questions had been so diverse and unexpected he was not quite sure how or what to reply. He chose to answer the one question that to him was actually apropos of the subject. "No, you can't see into the tent. They lace it up tight. It gets pretty hot and stuffy in there, too. Those personal guards of the Satrap come in there once in a while and sort of look around. Sometimes they actually counted the boxes. As if someone could move one out past the four men guarding the outside of the tent!"

"And the guards inside are always made up of men from different bands."

"Yes, the assign men from two different bands to the watches inside the tent. That way the men can't conspire with their friends. Everybody watches everybody else."

"But you are our friend, Jonathan," put in Simeon placing a familiar hand on his knee. "Only, no one knows that. That is why after tonight we can not meet openly. That is, if you are willing to try to lift some of this Satrap's gold."

"First I have to know your plan. How are you going to get the gold out of the boxes? How are you going to get away after you do? Why do you need the Satrap's seal, to reseal the boxes? You will need a big head start once you do get away. I would not like to try to outrun those Achaemendian cavalry, especially carrying 200 medimnos of weight."

"As I told you," countered Simeon, "they are not going to know who took the gold, because they are not going to know it is gone." And then Simeon told Jonathan about the caper of the merchant's mistress, and how he used a purloined seal to reseal the lead wafers on the merchant's treasure chest. When he was done, Jonathan was nodding his understanding.

"So you think if you can get the Satrap's seal, we wait until you and I are on guard duty together with a trusted companion each, then we open the boxes, take out the gold, and reseal the boxes. What do we do with the gold then?"

"You said the tent is pitched on the beach."

"Usually; oh, you mean to bury the loot in the sand."

"And refill the boxes with sand to replace the weight," said Athan making his first comment in a long while. "Sand is not nearly as heavy as gold, but there is room for quite a bit of it under the upper tray. I think it will be close enough to not attract notice. After we finish our commission, we take our pay, go back and dig up our buried treasure. We think they will not open the boxes until they get into the Empire. I wouldn't want to be there when those boxes are opened."

"How would we know when we would be on guard together?"

"We wouldn't" answered Simeon. "We just wait for a time when we are together on the beach and do it then."

"If we do this I will have to leave Stavros," said Jonathan. "Once they find the gold missing, they will stop at nothing to find out who is responsible. I am sure they will torture anyone associated with the transport until they get answers. They will eventually find out. I intend to take my family a long way away. My wife has family in Attica. I think we will have to make an extended visit there, very extended; extended for the rest of my life. I think Attica is out of the reach of the Empire, at least for now, and we should be safe. I was getting pretty tired of Stavros anyway. Two hundred talents should buy a lot of security."

"It will be a lot less than that," responded Athan. "We are not going to be able to take it all; maybe we will get half. Your share will be a third of what we get and you will have to pay any accomplices and other expenses from that."

"A third?" interjected Simeon.

"An even share for each of the three of us," responded Athan, "I estimate we will be able to lift maybe half the shipment. That is about 100 talents of gold. That would be about 200,000 drachma for each of us. I think a man could jog along on that for the rest of his life; that is if he can keep it."

"Do you mean the gold or his life?" asked Simeon with a smile.

"Both," replied Athan seriously.

As if the idea of stealing that much money was too much to contemplate, the three men abruptly changed the subject and began discussing the various details required for the band to apply as guards for the shipment.

"There must be no further open contact between us until we leave; you and Simeon must only meet secretly and seldom. No comments about your old friends to your band," cautioned Athan again as the men parted. "The next time I see you I hope it will be as fellow guards. One more thing, Jonathan, I think it would be better if you could arrange for your family to depart for a visit to her relations sooner, rather than later. If you are caught it would go hard with them. And you may be moving fast when you return."

The next day Athan and Simeon found the headquarters of the Satrap's guard after having spent the morning securing the services of a few new men to bring up the numbers of the band to a full score. They reported to one of the Satrap's captains, a big, bearded formidable-looking man. They were invited in and took tea with him. After the proper amount of small talk, they got down to business. This captain, Drogas by name, wanted to know their background, how many men they could bring, their experience, how their men were armed, any references (thin in this part of the world, and positively scurrilous in others) and why there were two of them when only one could be in command.

"This is my sister's cousin," explained Athan. "I took him in to teach him the trade."

Captain Drogas looked at the two men with skepticism. Although Simeon clearly deferred to Athan, the two men looked to be of an age. No matter, they looked capable, and were not on the list he had describing the known bandits in the area. He outlined their expected duties: march with the cavalry one day, sail with the boats the next two days unless otherwise ordered, stand watch at night according to the schedule posted each evening, obey the orders of the Satrap or his authorized representative, and above all, protect the 100 wooden boxes with their lives.

"That is what you will do," Drogas assured them, "for it we should lose them, we will most certainly pay for the loss with our lives." His mouth made a smile that was not reflected in his eyes.

"That is not likely," said Athan easily. "With this guard we could go anywhere. And Thrace is safe and well traveled. My only fear is pirates."

"Mine as well," agreed the big captain, "but my master leaves nothing to chance. You will see him; he is everywhere, checking everything."

"What sort of a man is he?" asked Simeon.

"He is young yet for such responsibility, but his spirit is old. He is careful, careful, careful, and watches us all. I do not know if he sleeps." He sat back, an old soldier doing a bit of gossiping about his commander. "This may be one of the smaller the provinces in the empire, but it has its own challenges, being on this unstable border. The Satrap is not a General; however, he is a good judge of men." This good judgment obviously included the wise decision to make Drogas the leader of this caravan's guard force. "I think he will be called back home soon to govern a larger province. He is not one of those to obtain a position by influence alone. No, he must rely on being faithful to the Emperor and getting results." Here the big captain leaned forward, looking at these two mercenaries. "Just like you and me."

Athan moved his men to the designated campground, setting them up in a defensive position, just as if they were in the hills, vulnerable to attack, not on the outskirts of a prosperous and well-defended city. As soon as they were settled, Athan called them together to explain their new job and their duties. After reviewing their expected responsibilities both to the band and to the caravan as a whole, he brought them in closer so he could speak to them discretely. He dropped to one knee, the men nearest him doing the same, the rest crowding in; a group of 18 men dressed in sweaty tunics and sandals and leather belts with weapons hanging down. Simeon prowled around the outside of the circle watching for any spies. Athan looked at the men around him. Most wore beards, but a few were clean shaven like himself. All of them had thick dark hair, often curly, and they had the characteristic olive complexion of men in that time and place. They smelled of sweat and garlic, wool and leather. He had known some of them for years. Three were new to him, but came well-recommended. They all believed his leadership would keep them alive. Now he was going to involve them in the biggest gamble of his career as a thief. He knew that, if he tried to steal the tribute and was unsuccessful all these men would be either killed outright, or if captured, first tortured then executed. None of them knew of the plan Athan and Simeon had hatched and the danger they faced. And Athan was not about to tell them; not just yet.

"Men," he began, "this is a big job. These barbarians (using the word for strangers or foreigners) are taking the annual tribute of the Ionian cities back to where they live. We are to make sure nobody comes in and steals it until we deliver it to Golibolu, almost all the way to the Hellespont. The Satrap himself will be traveling with us just to keep an eye on things. His personal guard, a group of truly nasty bastards, will be coming along, too." Here there was general acknowledgement by the surrounding men of the unpleasant reputation of the arrogant barbarian guards. "There will also be spies among the caravan as well. This Satrap fellow trusts no one. If he thinks you are a suspicious character, he will get rid of you, and maybe not by just sending you off, if you get my meaning. He has hired five different bands because he is afraid we might start thinking about working together to steal the tribute. Now I know that you have friends and comrades all around this part of the world. You will probably see some old companions among the caravan guards. I think it would be best if you didn't let on you knew them, especially at first." Here Athan took time to look at the hard faces around him. "Because if this Satrap fellow thinks we are too close to the other bands, the best we can hope for is to be driven out of camp with no pay. So we will have to keep to ourselves at first. Even better, don't get too friendly with anyone from another band until we get to the end of the journey and get paid."

This was a long speech under the circumstances. It provoked comments and questions. No, they did not have to pretend they did not know someone, they just needed to avoid fraternizing with them.

Athan talked about the expected march routine. Yes, they would be expected to keep up with the cavalry on route marches, but not every day. When they had to march their personal effects would be kept on the boats under guard by two picked members of the band, while the rest were hot-footing it trying to keep up with the horsemen. Yes, they were expected to stand guard at night even after a long grueling march that day. Yes, they had to ride the boats even if they did get seasick. No, they would not need to carry rations; food would be provided. Yes, they would all be paid, in silver, when the band reached the Golibolu. Yes, Athan was returning back to Stavros, and they could return here in the band if they so desired. In fact he told them that he intended to purchase livestock and return here on horseback just as soon as he could. He did not tell them that he hoped to pay for the animals with some of the stolen tribute, and he would be traveling fast to avoid possible pursuit. Yes, they could leave some of their personal gear here. Athan intended to do so himself, and no, he would not cover the cost of their storage while they were gone.

After more review of the details Athan broke up the meeting with a final admonition to avoid others outside the band, reminding the men that there would be spies and secret watchers all around them.

Simeon then took the men in hand and made normal arrangements for the ordering of the camp. That evening he came into Athan's tent and passed him a note.

"A boy slipped it to me when I was in the market," he explained. "I think it is from Jonathan."

Simeon did not read often or well, so he waited for Athan to open the scrap of bark and read the message aloud:

"*No one has ever seen her. She does not come here.*"

"Well, do you think Jonathan is looking for another woman?" asked Athan, half in jest looking up from the paper.

"I guess he is referring to the Satrap's seal. He has apparently not found anyone who knows anything about the Satrap's seal. He must think the Satrap leaves it back at his stronghold. That would make sense. Why carry it around with you?" responded Simeon smiling back.

"There goes your plan," smiled Athan, secretly relieved.

"I already estimated that we would not be able to purloin the seal of a man like this Satrap," responded Simeon. "We are going to go into town to visit a man tomorrow who will give us the final piece of the puzzle that will open those chests of gold."

"Must be a talented man," said Athan.

"As we all will be, soon," came back Simeon, laughing at his own pun.

The next morning Athan and Simeon arrived early at a small shop in the suburbs just outside the city. Like many other places in this quarter, the business was on the ground level and the proprietors lived in apartment above it. In the summer, residents would often sleep under awnings on the cooler roofs of their apartments.

"What is this place?" asked Athan.

"An artisan's shop," replied Simeon, 'he does artistic metal work, castings, coins, medallions, things like that."

"Things like lead seals?" Athan guessed.

"More like the dies that imprint the lead seals."

"How do you know what the seals will look like," Athan wondered.

"I don't," said Simeon cheerfully, "not until we spend some time in the tent. Then he can make a copy."

"What!" expostulated Athan, just as a small, balding man in late middle years entered the front room. The little fellow peered at them myopically for a moment then stepped closer and smiled up at Simeon.

"So you are willing to pay my price after all," he cackled.

"Yes, but you will have to earn it old man," shot back Simeon. "For that kind of money, there will be both risk and hard work. Are you prepared to travel with us as a member of a band of mercenaries, stand watch, bear arms, obey the orders of the Satrap's officers, and defend his property to the death?"

"I don't know about all that," said the old man, "but for 500 drachmae I will go with you and for 500 more I will make the seals. And if the endeavor is successful I get another 1000. You say I have to be a mercenary? Well, I suppose I can carry a shield and spear as well as any man, I just don't know if I will be able to keep up on this march you described."

"You are going to be the permanent guard for our gear that stays on the boat. Have you ever sailed on a warship before?"

"Been out fishing on small boat a time or two, and down to Attica once; that was on a ship. It has been a while though."

"Excuse me, old man," said Athan taking Jonathan by the elbow and steering him out of the shop.

"My name is Philip," chirped the artisan helpfully to their departing backs.

Athan stopped with Simeon in a quiet corner and squatted down, his friend joining him, and began a low conversation.

"Where did you find this old fool," Athan began.

"He is far from a fool," countered Simeon. "He is the one who made copies of those coins that had everyone so angry over in Thessalonica. That is why he is willing to join us; he thinks it would be best to move on. He is good, he is discrete, and thinks like a thief more than an artisan."

"He is old, he is near-sighted, he is skinny, and he is not someone you would mistake for a fighting man. How can we possibly convince Captain Drogas that little mongrel over there belongs in a mercenary band?"

"We tell him he is an honorable relation. Tell him he was once a fine hoplite though now fallen on hard times and will stand watch at night. We tell him he will work for half wages. I bet the good captain will put him on the ledger at full rates and pocket the rest."

"How does he intend to make copies of a seal he has never seen?" asked Athan.

"I don't know, but he says he can."

"Do you believe him?"

"I believe he is the only man we can get who has a chance to pull this off."

"Listen, Simeon," responded Athan looking directly into his comrade's eyes, "this is a different type of job. This is big, the biggest thing we have ever tried. And it violates one of the main rules we always follow. Do you know what that is?"

"Always have a way out," said Simeon dutifully.

"Line of retreat," corrected Athan.

"Same thing," said Simeon, "retreat, escape, way out, what you always taught us is that you need to have a plan to get out if things go sour. And we do; if the seals don't match, we don't do the job. There are only going to be five of us who know what we are planning, so there is little chance of someone talking. If it doesn't look right, we simply walk away; just like you always say."

"Once we break one of those seals, we will be totally committed, with no way out, and no way to run, well, no way to outrun cavalry, which is the same thing. And once those chests are opened, and they will be opened eventually somewhere, they are going to come looking for us like no one has ever looked for us before. We are not robbing some merchant or even taking on a sorcerer priest. This time we are stealing from the richest, most powerful empire under the sun. This job will be the last one we can ever pull in this part of the world for a long time, maybe ever."

"This job is so big we won't **have** to do another one," replied the younger man. "Listen, Captain, we have been living the hills for a long time, ever since Epiria fell. It has been long enough. We need to start thinking about the rest of our lives. With the money from this caper, we can set ourselves up down south in Peloponnesus, where the empire can never reach us and live the good life. No more rough camps and short rations. We can be wealthy merchants living in a fine house with a devoted wife and a beautiful mistress; mistresses" he added with a grin. "It is time to quit living day to day and look ahead. You know, grow old and fat in peace."

"This thing we are doing is not a good way to get any older," grumbled Athan.

"Captain," said Simeon, changing the subject dramatically, "I have never mentioned it before, I have known you over ten years, and you still look the same to me. I mean, you and I look the same age now. You even have more hair than me, now" Simeon ran a hand through his black locks that had begun to thin lately, "and that new set of teeth you got...."

"I don't know, and I don't care," Athan cut him off, "what I do know is that what we are planning will be like a leap off a cliff at night into the sea. Even if we land safely, there is no going back. Once we cut the first seal, the die will be cast." He smiled at his inadvertent pun. "If we are caught it is not just us, the whole band will be killed. You know this. Now, for a final time, do you trust that little stick of a man over there?"

"Philip," put in Simeon.

"That minuscule reprobate," continued Athan undeterred, "to create a die that can make replacement seals good enough to fool everybody else until we get to the end of the trip, and beyond; until we have time to get well away."

There was a long pause. "Chief," said Simeon formally, "if we are going to make the attempt, he is the only man for us. I am willing to make the gamble."

"Well, then" answered the man who would one day be the Old King, "I guess this will end our careers as bandits, one way or another."

The two men clasped arms, hand to forearm, got up, and walked back to Philip's shop.

Athan got right to the point. "Philip, can you create a die that can replicate lead seals, like the kind that seal a box?" he asked, looking back and forth between Simeon and the little man.

"Yes," Philip answered directly.

"Can you do it in a camp without attracting notice?"

"I think so. I am willing to make the effort."

Athan looked back and forth between the two other men. He drew a deep breath.

"Very well, you are hired."

There was a good deal of talk after that, of course. Athan wanted to know everything he could about this so-called artisan, this 'coiner', and how he would do his work under the very noses of the guards. Philip talked to him about some of the methods he used to create dies; first making a wax image of a desired symbol for the seal, then pressing the wax form into a sand mold, finally pouring in molten metal, iron if he could get a blacksmith to melt some for him, into the sand indentation. The die was then cooled and attached either onto a heavy pestle stamp or put on the end of a hinged set of handles.

"That is used if you have a double sided seal," confided Philip. "Do you know if it is a double sided seal that I will be replicating?"

Simeon admitted he did not know. Philip wanted to know as much as possible about the seals in advance, including the size, thickness, type of metal "They are usually a standard lead disc wafer pressed onto wire, although I have seen copper used, or strips of lead. It is usually copper wire and lead wafers."

Philip wanted to talk directly with their source of information but Athan forbad a meeting with Jonathan. He would not even let the old man know Jonathan's name. The men agreed to try to find out as much as they could about the treasure seals without arousing suspicions and meet the next day to decide if the project was feasible.

"You know, Simeon," said Athan as they walked back to the camp. "As you said if it this does not feel right we can decide to not go forward with it. Until we open the chests, we will have nothing to fear."

"Either way, sir, I will be leaving the band. You have been good to me, and I am grateful for all you have done for me, but it is time for me to do something else."

"Like Beltos, eh?" smiled Athan. "Have you fallen in love, too?"

"Not yet," grinned back Simeon, then he was serious again, "I think it is just time for a change. Now I need to meet with Jonathan."

"Be careful, I don't want you two seen together."

"Do not worry; I have set up a signal that tells him to meet me in a private place."

"You are not going to fall in love with Jonathan again are you?" teased Athan, "After all he is a married man now."

"No, nothing like that," responded Simeon with a quick smile, "Jonathan can not give me what I need now. His wife would be surprised if he suddenly started producing babies."

By the next morning, when the Athan and Simeon returned to Philip's place, they had learned a lot about the specific security of the chests, and Philip had a plan. The seals on at least two of the previous trips had been thick cooper wire with lead wafers, just as Philip had expected. There was less agreement about what the design pressed into the seal looked like. Most of those who had seen the boxes had been more concerned with carrying the weighty boxes back and forth from the ships and treasure tents or trying to stay awake in the stuffy tents during their watches (the Achaemenid guards taking a very dim view of guards sleeping on watch) than in examining the designs on the lead seals. They did get descriptions that it appeared to be a bird or a crown, and perhaps some symbols that might have been writing. It was also possible the seal was changed for each trip.

Philip was unconcerned. "I will make an impression of one of the seals," he declared, "and then I will create my own set of identical dies."

In answer to their looks, the older man explained his idea. "I will bring a candle with me when I go into the treasure tent. I will melt some wax into the seal. That will make an exact impression of the image that is pressed into the lead. Then instead of making a sand mold and pouring in hot metal, I will use a thin sheet of copper, like this," and here he held up a copper sheet thinner than a piece of vellum and somewhat larger than his palm. "I will mold this around the wax until I have a perfect image of the impression. Now, how, you ask, will that thin sheet of copper, molded onto the delicate wax impression ever stand up to crushing into a lead wafer?" That was exactly what they were wondering. "With this," he said holding up a pinch of gray powder taken from a small mortar on the table next to him. "This, some water and a bit of time will form a stone likeness that will provide a firm backing for the copper form."

Neither Athan nor Simeon had ever heard of cement before. The idea that you could mix up a powder with water and have it solidify into a rocklike hardness was alien to them. The two men doubted that Philip's magic powder would hold up, thinking it would be like mud caked in the sun, hard, and brittle. They made Philip show them, though he complained about the cost. He took a sample seal he had in his little room and pressed a bit of the thin copper sheet onto it, using a thin wooden stick to carefully outline every line in the sample seal.

"This might mar a lead seal, obvious to a casual inspection, so I will use wax to create a mirror image of the seal and press the copper around it."

Athan wanted him to do just that. Philip protested his way was safer, because it took less time with the actual seal. It took Philip some persuading, all the time working with the little wooden stick to press out an indentation in the copper sheet. He ended the discussion by taking the lime-based cement, mixing it with water in the marble mortar and pouring it into the mold he had created. Athan and Simeon peered down at the little pocket of wet cement expectantly.

"It will take a few hours," explained an exasperated Philip, "so we have time for a cup of wine or two." His new comrades passed on his implied invitation for them to buy him a drink and went off to make preparations for the upcoming mission. When they reported to the Satrap's camp, they were shocked to find that their band was expected to muster and be fully ready to depart in the second hour after dawn the next day. Apparently, although no one would confirm this, the shipment of tribute was coming in sometime that afternoon, and the expedition would depart the next day after that. This sent the two men scrambling to make the innumerable last second preparations necessary for the band to be ready. Simeon took one of the men and departed with all their livestock, intending to sell it. They could not use their own animals for the trip and could purchase replacements after they completed their journey. In the meantime Athan drew an advance from Drogas to purchase extra rations for his men and give them an advance on their pay to complete the final items anyone needed to ensure his personal equipment was up to the coming march. This included buying gear for Philip. Much to Athan's disgust, Simeon had to obtain almost a full kit for the little forger.

It was just before dark when the two men finally were able to return to the shop to pick up Philip. The little man had heard that the band would be mustering the next morning and had the belongings he was taking with him already packed; these belongs were, in fact, all of his earthly possessions. The rest he had sold or given away. He was sitting on an empty crate just inside the door, ready to depart. First he brought out and showed them his new copper clad cement-backed die. He took a small block of wood as a backing and demonstrated to them how lead seals took the new die's impression.

"I have enough materials in here to make three full sets," he told them, tapping his leather script, "just in case."

Shouldering the rest of Philip's gear, Simeon led the little artisan out toward their encampment. At the door Philip stopped for a moment and looked around at the little shop. Athan suddenly realized that this little place had been Philip's home for years. Perhaps he had been happy here. Certainly he was leaving in the full expectation that he would never return. Athan and Simeon were not the only ones who were jumping off a cliff into the sea at night.

"Go on then," said Athan a bit more gruffly than he intended, "and keep up with Simeon. The streets are not safe at night for such as you."

There was no one else in the space. Nothing of value remained. Undoubtedly the landlord would come in the morning to prepare it for a new tenant. Athan stepped out the door and turned away from a camp to complete his final preparations for the muster tomorrow.

It turned out that the simplest of these chores was the most frustrating. Athan needed a new pair of sandals for the march. His old ones were showing wear and he did not want to be mending them on the journey. He might wind up trying to march in his winter boots or barefooted. Such details had led to the loss of men before, and he was a careful man. But when he arrived at the sandal maker, he found the pair he had ordered had been sold to another guard with the same need but more coin than Athan. There was an ugly scene as the cobbler protested and Athan insisted. Neighbors and passersby gathered to watch the excitement. Eventually a slightly worn set of sandals were found and provided at a significant discount. Though not new, they were better than his old pair and were comfortable. Athan paid the man from his still bulging purse. He would give his men their partial pay at the muster the next morning. They could afford to wait until the night before departure to pick up necessities. Athan knew from long experience he would be engaged with business all day tomorrow.

It was late, well after sunset, when Athan finally shouldered his various purchases including his 'new' sandals and headed back through the now quiet streets toward the encampment. It was a dark, hot summer night, with clouds obscuring the stars and thick humidity that caused a man to begin sweating with even light exercise. Athan was hot, tired and hungry. He used the walk back to review the many things he still had to check before the morning. Planning a theft of a hundred talents of gold from underneath the noses of a large and alert set of guards was only one of the preparations he had to oversee.

Perhaps the combination of worry, fatigue, and hunger is why even a cautious and prudent man like Athan let down his guard. He did not consider that, not only was he walking alone at night through deserted streets, but he was burdened with the cloth script over his shoulder holding his purchases and, worst of all, had been seen to be carrying a fat purse.

Now he was being tracked by a man who made his living by solitary theft. An outcast from a robber band, he lived with a woman in the city who tolerated him well enough, but expected him to bring in money from time to time for her support. This money was usually obtained from the bodies of men he either killed or rendered unconscious. The robber was not a large man, and could not easily intimidate victims, so he either knocked them in the head with a short heavy club he kept hanging on the wide belt of his tunic, or he quietly killed them with the long knife he kept across the small of his back hidden in a cunning sheath inside his belt. As he moved parallel to his intended victim, he decided to use the knife. The target was carrying his package high on his shoulder, was a bit too tall for the killer to make a certain strike and had a felt pilleus hat on his head. There was no telling how much that hat would soften the blow. It would have to be the knife. The killer slipped up behind Athan as he passed an alleyway. The thief could move with great stealth; his life depended on it. Athan never heard a thing.

The killer knew several ways to kill a man (or woman) from behind. A stab through the throat could sever both the carotid artery as well as windpipe, making it impossible for a man to cry out. This did not kill quickly, and the only time he had cut a man's throat his victim had flopped around alarmingly, spraying blood everywhere and making a great mess. A better way was to place the left arm on the victim's shoulder, reach around with the knife hand under the victim's arm and drive the blade up between the ribs and into the heart. That killed quickly and left little blood. It was a difficult stroke; the victim could block the stroke if he felt it coming. Further, the heart is on the left side, making for a long reach. That attack was best used for small, weak targets such as women or men deeply drunk. By far his favorite killing stroke was to place his left hand on the victim's left shoulder and simultaneously drive the blade into the lower back. A perfect thrust severed the spinal column, killing instantly. Even a miss would usually hit one of the kidneys causing such agony that the victim could not even cry out. A wiggle of the embedded dagger would quickly put him down. He had used all these methods before. For a target like this one the low thrust was undoubtedly the best choice. He moved up behind Athan and struck.

Athan felt the hand grip his left shoulder just as he received a powerful push in his lower back. He whirled around swinging the cloth script off his shoulder, wildly to gain some distance from his attacker. His right hand found the hilt of his knife he kept in his sash. It was a simple weapon with a wide curving bronze blade he obtained to replace his fighting dagger that he had given to Simeon as a gift. It was no weapon of war, but it was useful for a wide variety of tasks and could even provide some slashing self defense, as it did now. There was a flurry of blades flashing in the dark as they disengaged. The two men faced each other, dim shapes a few paces apart, each with a blade held low, Athan swinging the script from his left hand ready to be used for offense or defense. The murderer knew many ways to kill a man; none of them involved facing an armed and alert opponent. He stepped back two quick paces, turned and ran, disappearing into the gloom.

Athan backed away one step at a time, suddenly whirling around to look behind and all around. He took ten quick steps down the street to clear what might be a kill zone, then slowed and moved down the center of the street as quietly as he could, knife in his right hand, script swinging from his left. He was breathing hard, and his heart was pounding. Athan had been fishing before when a fish struck powerfully at his bait and then was gone before he could set the hook. The blow to his back made him feel like a grasshopper on a fishing hook; just like that, a powerful strike, then nothing. He was very frightened and more than a little angry with himself for being so careless. He thought about pursuing the man, but knew he could not catch a man in his own ground, not on such a night as this. Even if he caught him, then what? How would he recognize him? Athan turned back toward the camp, moving quickly and now fully alert. He kept the cloth script hanging from his left hand and did not resheath his dagger. A group of three young men armed with short staves had had the same idea of robbing the rich stranger and lay in wait not far from the entrance of the camp. But when they saw him, armed, alert and ready, they faded silently back into the night before he could see them.

Athan entered his tent in a strange mood. His heart was still pumping hard, and he had sweated completely through his tunic. He tossed his pilleus on the cot and sat heavily down on his stool. After a moment he stood up again and took off first his vest then his tunic. The sleeveless tunic, though damp with sweat, showed no ill effects. The back of his dark leather vest had a very thin slice where apparently the point of a knife had been turned, sliding the blade up and away. Looking carefully at the cut, Athan could see a thin layer of white metal beneath the leather, apparently a layer between the inner and outer layers of leather. Athan had worn the vest almost every day since taking it off of Azziz' body; what had it been, ten years or more? He liked it despite its stiffness. It had become sort of an emblem. It had undoubtedly just saved his life on that back street. Athan thought back on the encounter. As they disengaged, Athan had exchanged wild slashes with his assailant. Now he remembered the touch of a blade on his left forearm as he spun away from the attack. He stepped over to the lamp that was burning in his tent awaiting his arrival. He looked carefully at the place where he had been touched by the knife. There was a very faint white line on the outside of his arm. Apparently the edge has just barely touched him, not even enough to break his skin.

Athan stood there for a long time thinking about a lot of things. Finally he shrugged to himself, and picked up his bathing sponge to clean off the day's grime before retiring to his bed. Just before he blew out the lamp and lay down to sleep Athan spoke a single sentence into the air as though he had been having a conversation with a friend for the last half hour. "I guess it was I good thing I used a club on Azziz after all."

The Old King's life in his hideout assumed a slow rhythm. He would sleep late until the sun (when there was a sun) had warmed things up a bit. He would build up the fire and heat some water for the tea he made from his herbs, supplemented by bits of leaves he plucked from bushes and pine needles. Then he would check outside and, weather permitting, go outside for a bit, collecting bits of wood, leaves for his tea, and ice to warm for his water. He drank a fair amount of water, since it temporarily filled his belly. Even though he had gradually reduced his morning oatmeal ration to only a few bites, eventually it ran out completely. Now he had nothing left to eat worthy of the name food. Even the leather of his saddle was almost gone. He slept a great deal, as much as he could, sometimes all night and most of the day. It saved energy, and besides there was nothing else to do; nothing else to do but sit in his stone shelter and think about the past.

Chapter Fourteen· Guards again

The escort job turned out to be much harder than expected, harder than anything most of the men in Athan's band had ever done before. The muster the next morning had begun as a chaotic disgrace, with bands of hoplites milling about in disarray amidst detachments of sailors. Forty five surly Achaemendian soldiers that had to be the Satrap's personal guards stood around and glared at everyone, and no fewer than seventy five horsemen stirred through the milling groups of men. Drogas was driven to near distraction trying to bring some order to the gaggle of armed men. The hoplites seemed to delight in the disorder with old comrades breaking what passed for ranks to greet one another.

There were five separate bands of hoplites that would be guarding the treasure. In addition to Athan and Jonathan's bands, there was another band led by an acquaintance of Jonathan's called Endre. The other two bands were smaller; each reflecting their leader. One was led by a man with the unlikely name of Rodas. Perhaps Rodas (which means Rose) was so named for his reddish brown hair. This Chief Rodas and his men had been together for years and were a tight-knit group with a good reputation for dependability. Not so, the other band which was led by a local man of bad reputation known as Loxias. His band gave every appearance of being just a group of local toughs assembled for this specific job.

Some of the bands had apparently thought that they could bring along camp followers despite strict and repeated orders from Drogas that no one would be allowed in the camps during the journey except authorized guards. Others tried to include their own pack animals, also specifically forbidden. Athan did his part in adding to Drogas' problems.

"You said an even score of men. You have 21," challenged the big man.

"Surely you did not expect me to count myself?" countered Athan, who then launched into a long self-justifying ramble explaining why he needed to be paid a greater salary than his men. Drogas was so irritated at this distraction that he agreed to pay for the full 21 at the agreed-upon rate (no special salary for Athan) without checking to see that the twenty-first hoplite was a slightly-build man in his 40s. By the time things in the encampment had settled down, it was almost midday, and the men retired to their respective camps for a brief rest and a small meal. Athan had to admit it was a powerful force that had been assembled to guard the tribute. In addition to the substantial Achaemendian bodyguard, a formidable force by themselves, there were over three score hearty sailors, almost as many hoplite mercenaries, and nearly four score of the finest cavalry in the world. Nothing less than the full might of a city-state could expect to safely take on a force like this. In fact, Athan thought the escort was almost ridiculously large. A strong force of Achaemendians would be expected to accompany the treasure but why include so many hoplites? What Athan soon learned was that the Satrap, a treacherous man himself, suspected his own guards of plotting to steal the tribute. The hoplites were a counterbalance to prevent the guards from conspiring to murder the Satrap in the night and steal the treasure. He had taken five separate bands of hoplites in addition to his own men partly just to deter the possibility of collusion.

There were changes to the previously promulgated plan. Three of the bands, including Athan's, were detached after the noon siesta with a small group of screening horsemen and sent marching east along the coast road. This was considered most unfair by the men, who would now miss a final night in town. Athan saw the advantage in the plan. The first day of any march was always the most disorganized and made the worst time. The gold was held securely in the city's treasury and did not need any extra protection that night. By sending out the slower foot soldiers early they could get a good head start on the next day's march. Of course, the Satrap also calculated it might upset any conceivable plots against stealing the treasure on the first day out.

Athan's men left their gear in the care of Philip and two other members of the band to be loaded on the ships and stepped out following Jonathan's band down the long hot road. They set a standard pace, settling in for a long walk. For this first leg they were accompanied by some of the Satrap's pack animals carrying food and a few of the other items needed for a two-day hike. A few camp followers tagged along vainly hoping that they could stay with their men one more night. Horsemen turned the women back before they could get too far from the city.

After the departure of the hangers-on, they made a respectable distance before stopping and setting up an austere camp in an open area near the beach. One thing they had not carried with them this first night were tents. Of course, it rained.

The next morning was miserable with wet men trying to repack soaked and sandy gear and get moving while the rain and wind beat at them. The weather continued rough until well into the afternoon. Most of the men assumed that the fleet would delay their departure until the weather cleared, but just, as the horsemen led them to the previously agreed-upon campsite for the first night, three ships were seen in the offing, headed for shore.

The ships were in the formation they would assume for the entire journey. The largest and slowest ship with the Satrap and his treasure was closest to shore with one of the escorts ahead and one to seaward far enough away to avoid any chance of collision though still close enough to provide mutual support. Using a combination of oars and sail, the long boats could make respectable time even when carrying a substantial burden of men, equipment, and treasure. Despite the moderate surf, the boats pulled up to the strand and grounded, one at the time.

Even under good conditions, bringing a boat to shore could be a disaster and was undertaken with care by expert sailors. There was a standard system for the landings: first the lead escort boat would approach, using the oars to hold just outside the surf zone while lines were thrown in to men waiting chest deep in surf. The two lines, one from each side of the bow were thrown in from the boat and were led up to the beach to other waiting groups of men on the beach.

Meanwhile, the boat let down a heavy iron grapple from the stern and firmly set this anchor aft. Then the boat moved towards the shore under heavy tension from ahead and astern. The men ashore pulled at a 60 degree angle on either side of the bow, not only bringing the boat in, but striving to keep the boat from yawing left or right and broaching in the surf. Men at the oars pulled for the beach, expertly adjusting their stroke to keep her bow and stern perpendicular to the shore. Opposing them, another group of men had the anchor line (which they called the 'anchor rode') leading back out to sea. This 'rode' was wrapped around a wooden bit and played it out gradually, preventing the boat from surfing in to the beach on a large swell and getting out of control. Other men manned the steering oars aft, also working hard to keep the bow pointed to land and the stern to the swells.

Should a boat have the great misfortune to be picked up by a wave and rushed into shore, she would almost invariably broach, turning sideways to the waves. Then the next wave would roll the narrow boat over in the surf, dumping crew and cargo into the water, often rolling on top of struggling men, holding them down until they drowned. Fortunately, this stretch of coast had many protected bays and inlets that sheltered the landing sites from the prevailing winds, and plenty of sloped sandy beaches ideal for landings.

The problem with landing the treasure fleet was compounded by the Satrap's obsession with security. Before the first ship could make an approach, cavalry screens were spread widely to provide warning of the approach of any possible enemy. Hoplites formed a second closer ring, ready to give warning and engage any threats to the boats during this vulnerable stage in the journey. After the treasure boat had safely landed, the third escort boat, which remained off shore watching for pirates or any other possible water-borne threats, would come in to land on the other side of the Satrap's treasure vessel.

Once the ships were safely beached, the intense activity continued. Guards stood watch, others set up tents, dug latrines, and prepared fires for the evening meal, sailors looked to their boats, and Drogas and the Satrap would review and inspect the arrangements for security. At some of the camps, men might be directed to dig a trench around the landing site. After the Satrap was satisfied, a working party of the hoplites stacked their arms and moved the chests of gold from the treasure boat to the newly erected treasure tent, now surrounded by the members of the Satrap's personal guard.

This night was Athan's first chance to observe the Satrap at short distance. He had seen him briefly at the muster the day before, now he could take the measure of the man. The Satrap (Athan never heard him referred to by any other name) was a small, neat, well-formed man in his early middle years. He was carefully dressed with a long flowing robe of the best material and wore silly little slippers with turned up toes. He wore a turban-like wrapping around his head secured in front with a jeweled pin. His complexion was darker than most, and he wore his well-oiled black beard trimmed in a careful mustache and goatee. He could have passed for a typical palace courtier or minor functionary, except for his alert and restless attitude. His black eyes were never still. From watching him, Athan got a clear impression of energy, ruthlessness, and a decidedly hostile view of the world in general and his fellow humans in particular. Athan had the impression that this man could order a friend tortured and then retire to his tent for a hearty meal and a good night's sleep.

The Satrap spoke most frequently to three of his staff; his personal secretary, a harassed looking young man, to a soldier that appeared to be in charge of his personal bodyguard, and to Drogas, who was in charge of all the other guards. They all were wary in the presence of the Satrap. Even big, tough Drogas was careful around this elegant little Satrap fellow.

Though each of the hoplite bands had its own leader, and the cavalry were clearly of the opinion that they were their own masters, Drogas was the overall commander and established the schedule of watches and provided the route for the next day. The Satrap had been carried dry shod to the beach leaving his finery dry and unblemished, but he quickly demonstrated he was no simple dandy. Accompanied by bodyguards, he made a tour of the camp, asking questions of his two commanders and giving a long series of observations to be recorded by his sweating secretary who followed, wax tablet in hand.

When the duty assignments were posted, Athan found that he was assigned to the middle watch on the outer perimeter with six of his men. Of course, he immediately complained to Drogas' lieutenant, a slender young man who was apparently related to the guard captain in some obscure way.

"We marched yesterday and all day today to get here and now you are making half of us take the second watch! And why do I have the midnight watch? I can delegate any man in my band to stand where I think is best. That was the agreement!"

"You only marched three parasangs yesterday," countered the lieutenant using the measure of distance that equated to the distance a horse would walk in an hour. "I bet you didn't even set a watch last night," he continued with a sneer.

This was not true, but only two men were posted at a time and the watches were only one hour long each.

"It rained," Athan countered, not willing to give up the point. While you were snug under a dry roof, we were stuck on that miserable beach in the rain with only mosquitoes for company. Now we have to get up in the middle of the night and make ourselves targets for these little flying monsters again. And why do I have to be out on the perimeter?"

"Because it is your turn, that's why," responded the lieutenant, "and each watch must have one of the captains in charge. You will act as sergeant of the guard for your watch, responsible to the captain of the guard from the Household Troops."

"Is that what you call them," growled Athan, who was suddenly seeing his plan in jeopardy. How could he steal the gold from the treasure tent if he were required to stand watch outside on the perimeter? Where is this 'captain' going to be, snug in some tent I'll bet."

"No, we –and by that I mean all of the Satrap's officers including myself - will stand watch just like you," interjected the young man with irritating self-satisfaction. "You will muster with your men at the designated time and take your assigned duty. Do you understand?" this a clear challenge.

"Who will decide when the watch starts and finishes?" Athan asked with feigned suspicion, avoiding the provocation. He needed to know as much as possible about the camp's security, not just so that he could rob it but also so he could carry out his responsibilities with a minimum of fuss. That avoided problems during the trip and most especially after the trip. He did not want to stick out in anyone's mind if they started thinking about how 100 talents of gold just disappeared.

"The captain of each watch will make that decision. You must let the watch know where your men are sleeping so they can be awakened with a minimum of disruption to those not who are sleeping."

"What if it is cloudy? I know these tricks guards play at night. I have stood the last watch of the night that began four hours early because no one could see the stars to tell what time it was."

Here the young lieutenant smiled, "We have an innovation. We have a bit of precision equipment: a glass device the measures the flow of sand through a narrow opening. When the sand in the top half of the device has sifted down to the bottom, precisely one half of an hour has passed. When the glass has been turned four times, the watch will be changed."

Athan was impressed; he had always liked gadgets. Why hadn't he thought of something like that? It would certainly help end the inevitable grumbling of night guards. He decided to try being agreeable. "That will help," he said feigning a show of reluctant acceptance. "But will I always have to be out checking the outposts every night watch? Who gets the easy duty inside the tent?"

"We will alternate your assignments," the lieutenant informed him. "None of us know just where we will be assigned until Drogas tells us at the evening muster."

For a moment Athan was concerned; to steal the gold from the treasure chests either he or Simeon had to be on watch in that tent, and whomever was inside would have to be there with the ridiculous Philip. Further, they would have to be on the same two hour watch with Jonathan and his picked man who would be in on the caper. Also these conditions had to be met several times. The first time they had the chance, Philip would take the impression so he could make the substitute seals. Then every time they had four co-conspirators in the treasure tent together, they would steal and bury as much of the gold as they could. Athan knew that he could not empty all 100 chests in a single two hour watch.

He and Simeon had worked out how to minimize their exposure from a surprise visit to the treasure tent of the captain of the guard or one of the Satrap's roving household guards. First, they would dig a hole in the sand in preparation. One man would keep a discrete watch at the front of the tent to warn of any activity headed their way. When they were all in place Philip would lift the tarp over the chests and remove the sealed lead wafer from a treasure chest's hasp. Two of the men would lift the top tray of gold bars out and then remove the bars from the lower level. One man would shovel sand back into the bottom of the chest while the other put the pilfered bars in the waiting hole and covered them with sand. As soon as this was done they would replace the top tray of gold, close the lid, and Philip would press one of his forged lead wafers onto the hasp. If all went well they would then go on to repeat the process on the next chest. Philip, Simeon, and Athan had tried to estimate how long it would take to open, empty the chest of the bottom tray of gold, refill the bottom with sand, bury the loot, replace the top tray and reseal the lid using an elaborate walk through simulating each action in Athan's tent before they left. It took a surprisingly long time, and that was without the pressure of knowing that, at any moment a guard might walk in and discover the act of theft, with fatal results for everyone. It would be more efficient to open several chests at once, but far, far more risky. They all understood that they would have repeat the operation over several nights, leaving little treasure troves buried under the sand of beaches along the way.

This was not a serious concern to them. Even if they did not get a chance to pair up under the tent every night, they would still have plenty of opportunities to remove the gold. The journey was about 65 parasangs long. If they covered five parasangs a day, a fairly rapid but unexceptional distance, they would have 13 nights to stand watch. Even if they were able to cover seven parasangs between camps, that was still nine nights. They would have plenty of chances to pilfer the gold from the chests.

With a start, Athan realized he had not been listening to the lieutenant, "Sorry sir, I was wondering if my second in command and I can alternate who gets to stand watch under the tent."

"You Yauna," said the lieutenant using the term the Achaemendian soldiers used for anyone who might be from either Skudra or the Peloponnesus, "always looking for an easy way out. I can tell you that tent gets pretty hot and stuffy. And even if you don't have to walk about, you can't sit down on watch; there are very strict rules about that."

"I know, but it is out of the rain and bugs and such. My second's uncle needs to be in the tent for all his watches. He is reliable, but he is no spring chicken, and he is a bit short sighted. Good man, but we promised to keep him out of trouble on his last trip. You understand don't you?"

"Look, just keep him out of the way," snapped the lieutenant, truly peeved with Athan, "we don't have any room for supernumeraries. Can he do his job or not?"

"Oh, yes, we just don't want him getting a chill. And after all, our elders do get a little respect, don't they?"

The lieutenant walked away muttering. Athan felt he had accomplished his goal: Philip would be in the treasure tent with himself or Simeon whenever either of them was assigned to the inside. Whenever they were paired up, with Jonathan and whomever he had picked from his band to be his co-conspirator, they could execute their plan.

Athan found Simeon to confer. Simeon had had the chance to talk with Jonathan ostensibly about details of the watch, but primarily to confirm the plans to stand watch together in the treasure tent. "He has a man he says he can trust," confided Simeon, "a fellow called Maur. Simeon has arranged that his lieutenant always has watch on the perimeter, so anytime he gets watch he will be in the tent with Maur."

"What do we know of his friend?"

"Jonathan says he is steady and discrete. He won't go blabbing to his comrades about gold hidden in the sand, if that is what you mean."

"That's what I mean. There is no surer way to get us caught. Or for us to come back and find empty holes in the beach where we left our booty."

"That is the thing I am most worried about," confessed Simeon, "what if someone discovers our little stashes? Or someone is told where to go to look for them. We can not just slip away and keep a guard over them, now can we? And 200 talents of gold is a powerful temptation."

"I told you we are not going to steal 200 talents," said Athan looking around. The two men had been talking in a low voice, but Athan did not want anyone to overhear them, "we are only going to steal half of it, just the bottom tiers. That may save us if they give one of the boxes a quick inspection."

"A hundred talents! A man could set up in luxury for his whole life, for two life times, with only a dozen talents."

"Well, you should get a lot more than that," smiled Athan. "That should set you up for several lifetimes."

Then it was time for the two men to start the work of guarding the treasure they intended to steal; well, partially steal. There were about four score hoplites to stand guard. These were divided into watches of 10 men each; usually from two different bands. There were a total of six two-hour watches set during each night, in place before sunset and not relieved until after sunrise on the short summer nights. The hoplite bands were responsible for three watch stations; four men were assigned to stay inside the treasure tent, five men were to guard the perimeter, and one man who acted as sergeant of the guard. The sergeant of the guard walked between the outer guard posts ensuring they were in place and alert. That meant that sixty men had one two-hour watch each night with a night off every fourth day, usually after they had been called upon to march with the cavalry the day before.

These guards were in addition to the cavalry who had half a dozen horsemen periodically riding out beyond the perimeter, as well as a man who guarded their picketed horses. The sailors had lookouts to watch for the approach of vessels from the sea or along the beaches. Inside the camp were the Satrap's personal guards, who not only defended his private tent and the outside of the treasure tent, and also periodically roamed about the camp, ensuring all was secure. Within moments of an alarm hundreds of armed men could be up and ready to defend the perimeter of the camp, as well as the treasure inside it.

In reality there was no one to threaten the camp. A few locals were able to come in to provide some limited provisions to the camp before dusk, but once it was dark, the glowering Achaemendians cleared them out. This night Jonathan had drawn the so-called midwatch, lasting for the first two hours after midnight. After his watch was over he could then retire until just before dawn, when the camp awakened and prepared for the next day's travel. Simeon would be inside the treasure tent, and had been assigned the first watch, set once the treasure tent was pitched. This gave him a chance to watch those men not assigned to watches that night assist the sailors in bringing in 100 chests of gold. The chests were actually rather small, made of brass (not iron) bound oak, with two hooks on each side where horizontal poles were inserted so they could be carried like a litter, one man in front and one behind. From the way the men staggered under the burden, it was clear that the small chests were heavy; a man could lift one and put it on his shoulder, though it was a load he was glad to walk with slowly and not for very far. Sailors rigged a block and tackle to swing groups of the chests from the bow of the largest ship to the shingle. Two men, giving each of the small chests a sort of sedan car ride, were able to carry them from there to be counted and stacked in the center of the treasure tent under the watchful eye of one of the Satrap's personal retinue. Once the last of the chests was secured the four assigned guards (including a ridiculous-looking Philip in a helmet and stiff linen cuirass that were both too big for him) took their stations inside the tent at each corner of the pile of chests, and the tent flap was closed. Four of the Satrap's personal guards stood around the outside of the tent as an additional layer of security.

On any journey the first night out is always the least settled. Even though Athan's band had already spent one night out, this was the first night with the full complement of guards required to guard the treasure. Though for a mercy it did not rain, it was not a good night. It was late before things, both within Athan's band and the camp as a whole, were finally arranged and Athan was able to lie down for some rest. He tossed and turned on his cot worrying about the watches and how his men would perform on duty.

It seemed he had hardly slept at all when he was awakened by a gruff call to take his watch. He pulled his tunic over his head, put on his vest, stepped into sandals, placed a light bronze helmet on his head, strapped his kopis around his waist and taking his spear and shield up, headed to the main camp fire where the watch was to muster. It was a hot humid night. His eyes felt gummy and his mouth had a horrid taste in it, as though he had drunk too much wine the night before; or perhaps a small animal had chosen to crawl into his mouth and die. Since neither of these things had happened, Athan was at a loss as to just why he felt so rocky; this was not the first time he had been awakened in the middle of the night to supervise a watch. He was grateful for the water skin handed to him by a member of the off-going watch. He splashed some water on his face and drank deeply. He was even more grateful when Pirro put a hot cup of spiced tea in his hand. Athan took a long pull of the bitter mixture and looked around for the man he would be relieving. One of the men assigned to the watch from another band had to be found, reawakened, and castigated for his indolence. Then Athan and his little watch of Pirro, three other men from his band and five others from Rodas' band took their stations. Pirro and three of the men headed over to the treasure tent. Athan and the other five men walked out to the perimeter guard stations. They were accompanied by the off-going sergeant of the guard who led them to their places, the little group of men replacing each watcher with a fresh lookout until each of the five sentries were replaced. The off-going watch then trudged back to the camp's fire, where they were released to return to their beds.

Athan poured himself another cup of tea from the pot hanging over the fire and looked about. He saw on the east side of the camp the tents of the Satrap's personal guard around what must be his tent. On the northern or land side of the camp were the camps of the five hoplite bands, each subtly different than the other. Opposite the Satrap's troops on the west side were the cavalry with their tents and strings of horses. South, next to the three beached boats, some of the sailors were sleeping. From the numbers he could see many of them were asleep in the boats as well. In the dim light from a gibbous moon, Athan could see movement that must be the sentries near the boats watching the beach and looking out to sea for any waterborne threats. In the center of the camp was a simple rectangular tent notable because it was surrounded by four guards armed with spears and shields; this was the treasure tent. It certainly looked secure. He heard a challenge from one of his men, and putting down his cup, walked out to check the situation.

It marked the start of a long two hours of almost constant minor alarums and diversions. The first challenge was to the cavalry's outer patrol coming in to be relieved. Later a whole set of challenges came when the captain of the guard, a supercilious officer of the Satrap's personal guard, came out to inspect the pickets. Another challenge came when one of the men thought he saw movement in the dunes. Athan went out to investigate but only found shadows in the pale moonlight. Then the cavalry patrol that had gone out again to make a long sweep around the camp came in too close, and was spotted by the guards as they crossed the front of the camp. There were also several false alarms from the sailors who thought they might have seen something first at sea, then along the beach. It was a busy, tense, and irritating two hours, not helped when Athan returned from one of the false alarms to find the sand glass which marked the time had run out without being turned; ensuring that he would have more than two hours on watch. Finally, however, he was able to awaken the relief watch. He went out with them replacing each of his own men with a man from the oncoming watch, and finally returning to the camp's fire. Before releasing them, he provided the men with a few choice words of guidance on standing watch. Then, his watch over, Athan allowed the attraction of his pallet to pull him into his tent, were he scarcely took time to shed his clothing before falling asleep.

He awakened with the rest of the camp in the gray dawn to the smell of bread, baked in the early morning for the camp's breakfast. When he went to the cook fires to draw a mug of tea, some cheese and a big hunk of fresh bread, he heard the news. On the watch following his, the captain of the guard had found one of the hoplite pickets asleep. There was considerable gossip and speculation about the specifics of the event. Some said the guard was only sitting down on his post;

others that he was upright and resting his eyes while leaning on his spear. Others implied the man, who was from Lexias' small band, was discovered curled up and snoring. Whatever the case, before the company left that morning the man was dragged out in front of the company and savagely beaten. The negligent sentry was fined, as was the sergeant of the guard for not keeping a tight watch. Every man was warned that in future, dereliction of duty might be punished by death. It was a somber group that prepared to depart as the sun rose over the horizon that morning.

Athan watched the ships getting off the beach with interest; all three of the long narrow boats were manhandled off the shingle until they were almost floating free in about waist deep water. The treasure tent was the first struck down. Even as it was bundled into the treasure ship, a line of men began to queue up and carry the hundred precious boxes onto the ship. Athan and Simeon took their turn as well, each making three trips, commented to each other about the weight of such small-looking boxes.

They brought the rest of the baggage, supplies, and tents into the three boats. First off was one the two smaller guard boats. While the boat was loaded, sailors maintained tension on the anchor rode attached to the grapple left off-shore. They gradually moved the boat deeper as it was loaded, so that as the boat's draft increased, the boat continued to remain barely afloat. Once the boat completed her loading, the crew and the hoplites assigned to ride in the boat that day clambered aboard over the gunnels. The men on the beach pushed the boat out to deeper water, aided by sailors in the stern who heaved in on the anchor rode and the oarsmen backwatering as hard as they could until the ship was beyond the line of small breakers. Then one side of the oars began pulling forward while the other side continued to backwater. The ship twisted around first horizontal to the beach, then pulled offshore and headed out to sea to serve as lookout for possible pirates. Athan saw men recovering the grapnel from the sea as the boat moved away from the shore.

As the last of the gear was loaded onto the treasure ship, the men boarded and she too, was pushed out into deeper waters by strong hands, and followed the first boats headed off shore.

Athan and Simeon moved to the final boat which was now ready for her own launch. They hauled themselves over the low gunnels and were directed to sit facing the sea each next to a sailor who was already manning an oar.

"Ever rowed before?" asked the wiry young sailor sitting on the outboard end of bench where Athan had been pushed and given the inner end of the oar.

"No," confessed Athan, "I have never been in anything like this before." He knew he would be expected to help row, and he was somewhat familiar with the process, but the practical experience was not exactly what he had been expecting.

"Look here," directed the sailor in as gruff a manner as he could manage when talking to a larger man, especially a larger man who made his living by fighting. The sailor showed Athan how to wrap his hands over the top of the oar. "Now you just follow my lead and pull when I do. Try not to get in the way."

Athan shifted his wet bottom on the seat, the salt water was causing his skin to tingle, which he was sure would turn into an itch as the salt dried. His men had stored all their trousers and wore only short summer tunics, but the sailors made them all look positively overdressed. Some wore charamys, a briefer version of the himation, over their shoulders, the little squares of cloth providing a bit of protection from the cool morning breeze; some did not. Most wore peculiar loincloths with a flap of cloth covering their backsides; some did not. Not a few were naked, and all were barefoot. Athan decided that the loincloths would provide some padding and protection for the men's backsides when they were rowing.

The boat heaved slightly on the swell, grounding with a slight crunch as each wave receded. Athan was not worried about the danger of going to sea for the first time in his life, but he was concerned that he would embarrass himself by getting sick. As the boat pitched up and down he was acutely aware of things around him, the feel of the seat beneath him and the water that was sloshing on his sandals (should that water be there?) the salt sea-smell, the cries of the seabirds, the heave of the men over the side against the hull as they pushed the boat off the shore. These new sensations made him feel intensely alive. An unintelligible order came from the boat's master in the stern. Following the sailor's lead Athan helped push the oar away from him. He was clumsy on the first raised upstroke but by the third stroke he had the rhythm. He could feel the boat was free of the strand and backing out into deeper water. On the sixth stroke the other side of the boat was commanded to begin pulling ahead while Athan's side continued to push the oars forward, driving the boat back. As they turned parallel to the beach the narrow hull rolled alarmingly, but they kept the stroke. In four more strokes the boat had twisted around, and his side was ordered 'together give way'. Now they were pulling on the oar, lifting the oar clear and pushing it back on the backstroke. The boat hesitated briefly as the anchor was brought aboard and then they were away. The boat began moving first parallel to the shore, then curving out to follow the treasure ship responding to the steering oar in the stern.

As they rowed out to sea Athan could look back and see the cavalry and remaining hoplites forming up to begin their long march to the next landing place. The hoplites were stowing their helmets on spare pack ponies and before the boat was too far out to sea, Athan could see the column heading out. Some of the horsemen had a hoplite, hanging on to the saddle on either side and running alongside. That would make the trip much easier so long as they did not try to go too fast.

They pulled together until they were well out offshore. Athan could see the land, but he knew he was probably not a good enough swimmer to reach it if something happened to the boat. The swells made rowing a little tricky, and he spent his time concentrating on just rowing. After a time the sailor left the oar to Athan with an admonition to 'just keep pulling regular like' as he helped his mates step the mast and raise the big striped square sail. Just before they raised the sail the order 'up oars' was given and Athan had enough sense to stop rowing and pull in his oar though judging from comments directed at him by one of crewmen he apparently did not do this in the appropriate way. The wind was from the south and their direction was to the east, so Athan was not sure just how the sail would help. He soon saw how. Once the sail was up and filled, the sailors twisted the crosspiece at the top of the sail so that the 'boom' as he heard them call it ran at a 45 degree angle fore and aft instead of perpendicular to it. For a moment the boat heeled over in a most alarming way. Hoplites scrambled to the high side as gear not properly stowed (that was almost everything) slid down to the leeward side. Athan was very nervous but he watched the reactions of the sailors and saw that there was no particular concern in their demeanor. Then the helmsman eased the boat off the wind with his steering oar, the gust diminished to the gentle but steady breeze it had been a moment before, and the ship moved out ahead to take station to seaward of the treasure ship. Men were put to work bailing water out of the boat and storing equipment while the sailors trimmed the sails, stowed lines and attended to their nautical business. The wind was mild and steady and the sparkling waters had only a mild swell.

It did not take Athan long to realize that he was not going to be afflicted with the same sickness that had so troubled some of the others on the journey the day before. Even Philip seemed in better spirits. As soon as things had settled down Philip, Simeon and Athan settled, facing each other on a pair of benches near the bow, as far away from the other men packed into the ship as they could without being too conspicuous about it. They began by gossiping in low tones about the conditions in the camp, the poor fool who was caught sleeping on watch, how much better the weather was today than yesterday, and the pleasures of traveling by sea vice hanging onto a trotting horse.

After a time Athan asked the question he wanted answered from the first. "Did you get it?"

"The impression of the wafers?" responded Philip in a quiet voice, "No, there were two men from another band in there. It would have been far too dangerous. I will need to be there with your friend Jonathan and his partner to take an impression. I did get a good look at the seal on the wafers though. It is one sided and looks to be a simple design; a bird with open wings over a man's head. The workmanship is shoddy. You would think a man that rich could afford at decent seal."

Simeon immediately changed the subject to the related but much safer topic of the small and amazingly heavy treasure chests. Unspoken in his comments was a fear that even refilling the bottom half of a chest with sand would not provide enough weight. Since there was nothing to do about it, and it was far, far too dangerous to talk about the subject in the boat, they kept their conversation on safe topics until the midday meal of bread and olives. Aside from a certain drowsiness and a dry mouth, Athan could not detect any sign of seasickness. In fact he rather enjoyed the day. He manned his oar with more confidence in the afternoon when a dropping wind caused the ship's master to order the sail lowered. He enjoyed watching the crew skillfully land on another fine beach. His boat was the last to land, and by the time he reached the shore, the treasure tent was already going up, and the working party to offload the treasure had already been formed. Instead of having to help with the offloading of the treasure, he went directly to the sergeant of the guard's watch meeting. There he and his fellow leaders of the hoplite bands were subjected to a stern lecture about discipline and the need to keep the men alert. The captains of the bands would be required to personally supervise their watch until further notice. That meant that Simeon would be getting the tent duty for the time being, while Athan stalked from sentry to sentry for his two-hour watch. But there was good news: he had the second watch, which meant he would not be awakened in the middle of the night. Further, the moon would not be up by then, so there would be fewer shadows to spook the guards. Best of all, Jonathan's band was assigned the same treasure tent watch as Simeon. Philip would be able to get his impression of the seals tonight. Unfortunately, the same directive requiring Athan to stay out with his watch also applied to Jonathan. He would not be able to be in the tent with Philip and Simeon.

"I have another man we can trust," Jonathan assured Athan quietly after the sergeant of the guard muster that evening. "His name is Etor. He has been with me for years. We can trust him."

"Can we trust him not to talk, I mean not talk to anyone. All we need is for one person to blab and this whole thing goes up in smoke."

"He is discrete," Jonathan said.

"How much will this cost us?"

"I will pay him out of my share," Jonathan said.

"Remind him," Athan warned, "that if he keeps his mouth shut he will get rich. If he talks, he will get us all killed. All he has to do is nothing."

Athan was nervous all during his watch and so was relentless in duties. Drogas, who was the captain of the guard for that watch, commended him for his diligence.

"That second of yours is no good, though," he told Athan.

"You mean Simeon? Why do you say that?" said Athan at once alert.

"I was just in the treasure tent," said Drogas, Athan was glad the darkness made it difficult for the big head of the Satrap's guard to see his tension. "Do you know what he was doing?"

'Taking impression of one of the seals?' thought Athan but all he said aloud was "No".

"He was taking a dump right there in the tent!" said Drogas in disgust.

"Well," said Athan in a practical voice, "once you are in the tent you cannot leave until you are properly relieved; in a manner of speaking." Drogas did not respond so Athan probed a bit further. "Did he get any on the chests?"

"No," admitted Drogas, "he had dug a hole in the corner of the tent."

"So he will cover it up when he was done," said Athan with satisfaction, "and no smell, no problem. He did dig a deep enough hole didn't he?"

"He had dug a hole deep enough for a week's worth of shit."

"Well, there you go," said Athan with satisfaction at his second pun, "hygienic; and he was still able to keep his eye on the chests. That is much better than holding your belly and waiting with your mind on your insides and not your duty."

"You Yauna are disgusting," said Drogas moving off.

"No," countered Athan, "Only if you go digging in the sand after someone has filled it. Now that would be disgusting," laughed Athan.

'Simeon, you are brilliant!' he thought. 'What a great way to distract Drogas from Philip and explain any marks in the sand. No one would go digging into the sand if they thought they would just uncover a cat hole. Of course,' he mused still to himself, 'it might have been that Simeon just had to do his business, and the whole thing was a coincidence.' But he finished his watch in high spirits.

Of course it had been no coincidence. "I must have squatted over that hole with my tunic pulled up and my small clothes around my ankles for nearly an hour waiting for someone to check on us. You should have seen his face when he saw me," chuckled Simeon to him in Athan's tent, which the two men were sharing on this trip. "It only took Philip a few moments to do his magic with the hot wax. He took three impressions. Since we had the tent watch tonight, I figure we will have a day or two before we are assigned to the tent again. By then we will be ready to start changing gold into sand."

"What about Jonathan's men?"

"They seem all right. Maur is the one Jonathan told us about before. He is an old partner of Jonathan; they have been together for years. He is the short, dark one; I think he will live up to Jonathan's recommendation. The new one, Etor, is very quiet. I don't think he said ten words all watch. Maur says he has a new wife and is looking to move south with Jonathan's family."

"No wonder Jonathan picked him. He has his wife as a potential hostage. So he is quiet. Quiet is good. How is his nerve?"

Simeon shrugged. "How are all our nerves? So far, so good; in two nights or so we will find out just how good all our nerves are."

The next day they rode the boats again. A tired-looking Philip confided to Simeon that it was difficult to find a place to do the required fine work without curious men prying into what he was doing. The men decided that they would have Philip stay in their tent, telling the band that the old fellow was having trouble sleeping, and Simeon wanted to ensure his relative did not fall asleep on watch. That would give him the time and privacy to create his replacement dies.

Their plans were upset when they received their assignments that evening. Although the head of each band was supposed to act as sergeant of the guard, a change was made and this night Jonathan would act in that role. Philip and Athan were assigned to the treasure tent with Jonathan and Maur on the first watch that very evening. Athan could not resist reminding the little coiner that they could have begun their robbery on the second night out if Philip had been able to make the dies. Of course, it was still light for most of the first watch, so it was not the one they wanted for their first effort at turning gold into sand. Athan made sure that the men moved around periodically to accustom the outer guards to movement from inside the tent. He even dug a hole in the corner and squatted over it just for practice, though he had no need to relieve himself. Eventually he settled for having the men urinate in the hole and then covered it up. When Drogas made his rounds, entering the tent just before the watch was over he looked at the marks in the sand suspiciously and then at Athan but said nothing. Athan gave him a bland, innocent smile. Drogas withdrew from the tent muttering.

When they completed their watch they took their evening meal and retired immediately to their tent. Simeon, who had the last watch, the so-called dawn watch, was still awake in their tent waiting for the two men. Without a word, Philip took his equipment from their personal baggage kept in the tent and went to work. Before the middle watch had been called, he had created no fewer than four dies and set them aside to dry.

"We will see which one is the closest match," he explained to Athan and then, carefully packing his equipment up, returned it to his baggage and immediately lay down and went to sleep. To Athan's eyes the dies did not look very much like the seal on the wafers he had seen sealing the chests, but he had never seen anything like them before, so he put the matter out of his head and went to sleep as well.

The next day Athan's band would be moving by land. The band stood guard on the perimeter until the treasure ship had been launched, and then moved down to help get the last boat off the beach. It was a calm hot day, and it looked as though the boats would be rowing all day. They had had to row for a fair part of the day yesterday and even the tough hands of the soldiers in the band were raw from the rowing. Most of the men were glad to be ashore today. The men stowed water and their few provisions for the march on the packhorses. Most managed to also tie their helmets on to the packs, and a few even offloaded their cuirasses onto the horses. In addition to Athan's 18 men (Philip and Idas, who had twisted his knee, were accompanying their baggage on the boats) there were six of the Satrap's personal guards coming with them, led by a grizzled sergeant called Cishpi.

"All we are is insurance that there has been no treachery," grumbled Cishpi. "If he sees us on the beach waiting, that suspicious little prick knows it is safe." Clearly Cishpi preferred to ride in the boats and had a low opinion of his boss; a typical sergeant.

The men moved over to the horses, most of the hoplites held onto the pack animals, since many of the cavalrymen did not particularly like being burdened with a smelly Yauna. Athan found one of the horsemen who liked to talk and arranged to hang on to his animal as they traveled and so was able to jog along in companionable conversation. No one knew exactly where they were going until they were joined by another member of the Satrap's personal entourage, who spoke to the captain of the cavalry detachment. It did not take long for word to filter back that they would be moving seven parasangs to their next camp. This news was greeted with groans and complaints. It was said that an unencumbered man can walk a parasang in an hour, but after the first hour that same distance will take an hour and a quarter or more for the rest of the day. Seven parasangs would probably take between nine and ten hours. It was going to be a hot day, so the group pressed the pace early on while it was still relatively cool. By the time they stopped for a midday meal the men on foot were genuinely fatigued. Even after the rest, they were unable to maintain the pace. Some of the horsemen who were unencumbered by hoplites rode ahead to check the route. Others scouted to the land flank and watched their rear. It was a tired group that turned off the coast road to a crescent shaped beach well before the sun was down. They were relieved to find no ships waiting for them in the offing. The Satrap's man bustled about, talking to the cavalry captain, and trying to reassure himself that he had the right place. They set men to watch on the dunes while others rested and washed. The sun was just above the horizon before the lookouts saw the ships approaching the shore. The Satrap's envoy was visibly relieved.

'I bet he was worried he had come to the wrong beach,' thought Athan. 'And I bet that would be a fatal mistake for him.'

On that night Athan's band stood no watches. The next night, after an uneventful passage, they were not scheduled to share a watch in the tent with Jonathan's band. The night after that they arrived in Xanthi. Instead of camping beneath the city's walls with his guards, the Satrap took the treasure off the ships and, escorted by his personal bodyguards and Rodas' band, had it carried it into the city. Watches that night were lighter with no one posted in the treasure tent. This was a welcome relief, but other types of relief were denied them; the men were forbidden to enter the city. Even the hawkers of goods and prostitutes were kept out of the camp. In a way, having the comforts and pleasures of a city close by but unattainable was worse than being on a solitary beach. The slight lessening in security allowed Jonathan to meet with Athan and Simeon in their tent. The men were becoming worried.

"I did not expect us to move so fast," admitted Jonathan. "At this rate we may only have four or five nights before we get to Kadikoy. From there he might even be able to leave us behind and go to Golibolu in a single trip. That means we may only have one or at most two nights when we are on watch together."

"We will have to try to get as much buried as we can when we have the chance," agreed Simeon.

"Let's not force it. If it is not to be, we can walk still away; all we will lose is Philip's fee."

As day after uneventful day passed, the Old King actually had come to value this opportunity to think back on his life. What did that philosopher once tell him? 'An unexamined life is of no value.' It was something like that. He looked out at the sky. It was going to be another cold rainy night. His firewood was becoming depleted again. He would have to collect enough to last for at least another half a month. He was now living on nothing but tea and bits of boiled bark. He would have to find some source of food if he wanted to be strong enough to walk out of these mountains when the snow melted.

He tended his fire, a skill in which he had grown quite proficient, and lay back down for anther extended nap and another long reminisce.

Chapter Fifteen– The Heist

The next day was physically easy but hard on the nerves. The south wind, which had been blowing steadily if weakly for the past five days, increased in force during the night and shifted to the west southwest. There were white caps on the sea, and it took additional men from the garrison at Xanthi, along with several rowing boats pulling on the sterns of the beached ships to haul them off the beach. Long before even the first boat had gotten off, the hoplites assigned to the march had gone, leaving elements of the cavalry and the garrison to protect the fleet as it was laboriously hauled off the shore. It took over an hour longer than usual before the ships were out to sea and moving east in formation. With the favorable wind there was no thought of using the oars. This was just as well as many of the landsmen began to feel the effects of the short choppy sea.

Things were reasonable on board Athan's boat, the first one launched this time, until one of the men vomited over the side. He had been clinging to the high side of the heeling boat and being inexperienced he let fly over the windward side. The wind caught his 'offering to Poseidon' and cast it back to over the boat in a fine disgusting spray. The smell tipped the balance for many of the men who had been holding their own nausea in check. At first in ones and twos, and then in almost a communal rush, the hoplites staggered down to the leeward side to empty their stomachs into the sea. The sudden shift in weight briefly put the lee rail under, shipping water into the boat. The steersman, cursing fluently, eased the steering oar to fall off the wind and ease the heel. After a time, sailors restored order, putting the nauseated men in the bottom of the boat giving them containers in which to puke. Athan was embarrassed to be one of the victims. He had used his helmet, and it was some time before he was able to wash it out. A rumor that the marching men would have to cover no less than eight parasangs in one day did little to quench the fervent envy most of the seasick hoplites felt for the lucky men with their feet firmly on the ground. The wind remained fresh, and seawater, mixed with vomit, sloshed around the bottom of the boat. Sailors put the hoplites to work bailing and the work, along with the fresh air, helped most of the men to gradually overcome their affliction. With such a strong breeze behind them the boats made excellent time.

By the time they arrived off what was apparently the designated landing site, Athan had recovered; in fact, he was experiencing that special feeling of wellness you get after having been seasick. The air was fresh and bracing, and Athan was actually very hungry. He knew they had made very good time, so he was not surprised that even with a head start of well over an hour, the hoplites and cavalry that were supposed to be on the beach waiting for them were not on the designated landing site.

The lack of supporting troops ashore was the least of their problems; Athan could see breakers pounding the beach. There was a low sandy headland less than a parasang farther down the coast, and Athan heard some of the discussion with the ship's master and one of the Satrap's entourage concerning the advisability of landing in the calmer water in the lee of that point. The ships lowered their sails and closed together, bobbing in the substantial swells, as the masters shouted their advice, opining that attempting to land on such an exposed beach with breakers of this size would be more than merely imprudent. For almost an hour the ships maneuvered back and forth, conferring about the best course of action. Those men who were still seasick were reduced to groaning wretches in the bottom of the boat. It was hot, even in the fresh wind, and tempers were frayed. The master confided to the senior officers aboard his boat (which seemed to include Athan) that there were two reasonable alternatives: spend the night at sea rowing gently into the wind and remain off the designated beach or make for the shelter of the headlands just to the east, land there and await the men coming along the coast road. Finally with the sun well down toward the horizon, a decision was apparently made for the treasure ship abruptly hoisted her sail and sped off toward the headland. The other two boats followed attempting to regain their normal formation.

When the three boats rounded the narrow little headland, they found something that caused immediate concern: four other boats were already hauled up on the beach. Though this was disconcerting, there was still room on the shore further down the beach for the three vessels of the treasure fleet to land in protected water. While the treasure ship lowered her sail, apparently to begin a new round of discussion, the master of Athan's boat plowed straight to shore, barking orders for his men to prepare to beach. Even without men ashore to help him and with a nasty cross-swell running, the old seaman brought his boat in to the beach as rapidly and smoothly as any landing Athan had yet seen. Men poured off the boat, glad to be on land. Some carried spring lines to either side of the bow to hold the boat perpendicular to the strand; some dragged it forward, while Athan led his band up the shingle looking for any potential foes.

The most obvious threat was the four small boats already safely beached just to the west. Athan approached the four boats at a jog with his men behind him. The men on there were arming and assembling to respond to the possible threat represented by Athan's band. It did not take Athan long to determine that the boats and their crews were not a threat. He then had to assure them that he and his men represented no threat to them. The impromptu assemblage of boats consisted of two merchant ships headed west and one headed east; all had spent the day here in shelter from the winds. The fourth boat was a large fishing boat that had sought shelter just before noon. Athan sent back a runner with his report and, keeping his band together, started a reconnaissance up the low dunes inshore from the landing site. The coast road veered inland a bit at this point, perhaps to meet a thin road that headed up into the hills. A small campsite was visible beyond the coast road on that track heading north. It appeared to be a shepherd with a small flock of animals being herded to market, not a potential group of bandits. Anyone coming down that trail from the hills would stir up the herd and its protecting shepherds first; good.

By the time his band had climbed the dunes and verified that there were no enemy in sight, the sun was approaching the horizon. Athan gave the ship's master an 'all secure' wave. The beached ship in turn waved an 'all clear, safe to land' signal. Yet the two ships still hesitated. Finally the treasure ship began a slow approach under oars. Athan finished posting his men in five separate groups spread along the dunes and headed down to the beach. The master of the boat he had ridden in had already manned the small boat they towed behind them and sent it out through the surf to lend what aid it could. He could hear the master commenting aloud to no one in particular as the treasure ship slowly headed in.

"Come on," the master encouraged the treasure ship in a low tone as it put out its anchor well beyond the surf line, "With the surf up like this you have to bring it in handsomely. This is no time to be cautious. If you tarry among breakers this size, one of them will decide to take you. Come on, bravely now. No! No! Speed! Put your backs into in! Oh don't wait, this is no time for hesitation. Get out of those breakers! Drive her in. Oh No!"

The master's fears proved well founded. Beaching the ships in big surf was not done the same way as when the waves were smaller and more manageable. It still required using a grapple off shore and precise timing, but since nothing could restrain a big wave, instead of passing the surf in a slow and careful approach, it was necessary to come in as fast as reasonable in order to minimize the time in the danger zone. It required fine judgment and not a little luck.

The big treasure boat, coming in much slower than the first boat, was swept up by a large swell. The boat pitched wildly then suddenly the anchor rode parted, and the boat accelerated toward shore.

'Well,' thought Athan, 'that is faster.'

Then he saw what the master had feared; the boat was not under the control of the crew but of the surf. For a long moment, the boat continued in straight to shore, then, slowly at first and then with increasing speed, the boat slewed to the left until it was broached broadside to the waves. With the whole length of the narrow craft to play upon, the wave rolled the big vessel right on its beam ends and threatened to roll it right over. The oars protruding from the low side prevented that disaster. Before another large roller could come in to finish the destruction of big boat, men dashed into the water to rescue the craft. Many hands pushed her bow and pulled her stern. The master of the ship Athan had ridden had left his ship and waded up to his waist in the water, and directed the efforts of the men in the water in a stentorian bellow. Under his guidance the men grabbed the closest end of the vessel, the stern, and began to pull the boat up onto more solid ground. More men piled out of the wallowing craft, and finally, together, they were able to drag the big ship up onto the beach, stern first.

'Well,' thought Athan who had plunged in to assist along with every other able-bodied man 'that went well.'

There was much shouting and confusion. The Satrap came up, soaked and furious as a wet hen. His attendants were making a great deal of fuss around him, but his primary focus was clearly on safeguarding the treasure. His personal guards arrayed themselves in a wide circle around the stern of the treasure ship where the Satrap stood fuming. After being reassured that the ship was now safe, he turned to look at the other boats pulled up down the beach and at the low dunes inland.

"What of those vessels," he gestured.

There was consternation from his entourage and shouting for the captain of the Satrap's personal guard, a self-important snake of a man called Utana, and for Drogas. Drogas had the great good fortune to be on the third ship, which just then was coming in through the surf with much commotion, but safely enough. As it was dragged securely up onto the beach on the far side of the visibly damaged treasure ship, which was obviously, wrongly, pointed in a different direction than all the other vessels. The Satrap looked at little fleet then down at the four strange boats down the beach. Athan could read his expression clearly. The Satrap was angry, frightened, and frustrated with the collapse of his elaborate plans. Someone was going to pay for this; someone was about to die.

Athan did not want to be that man; he knew he had to say something before the Satrap began to order executions. Once that started, who knew where it would end. He addressed the Satrap directly, answering an open question that had not actually been addressed to him.

"We have inspected the four other boats, sire," said Athan with a confident self-assured tone. "They are mere merchants and fishermen, sheltering from Poseidon's wrath as we have done. My men are watching them, of course, as they are watching from those dunes." He waved at the closest group of his sentries. For a wonder one of them was watching and waved back. "This is a good place you picked, sire. Not only are we sheltered from the sea, but it is a good place to defend. We could hold off an army from here." This came in the tone of a trusted retainer reassuring his master. "I see the wisdom in your plans," continued Athan, now the sergeant complimenting the general on a battle well fought, "even this fierce tempest hardly disturbed your arrangements." Athan thought that the Satrap might be armored against direct personal flattery, so he tried complimenting the man's precious plans instead.

The man looked at Athan, his self-confidence returning, "Of course," he said in an oily supercilious tone, "that is why we take such precautions."

"Yes sire, I see. May we set up the camp now and establish the watches? And I request permission to send a runner back to the original site to inform the horsemen where we are. I imagine they are worried sick, thinking we have been swallowed by the waves. They will be amazed to find us all secure in such a snug hole."

"Yes, of course," dismissed the Satrap, turning to Drogas, who was hustling up from the recently arrived boat.

"Well, Drogas, we have arrived safely. Set the camp. When the cavalry finally arrive, have their captain report to me in my tent." The men around the Satrap released a breath, and the tension eased slightly.

"Utana," the Satrap said, calling the captain of his personal bodyguard, "Attend me."

The two men went off up the beach, heads together while Drogas went into action. Before dark the tents were erected, treasure offloaded, and repairs on the treasure ship begun. The injured, and there were many, were being treated by firelight. Most of the injuries were caused by the action of the oars as the ship rolled on her beam ends. They ranged from bruises and separated shoulders to broken arms and legs, and one poor man who had been thrown from and had his legs crushed under the ship. But there were dead men, also, two of them. One was the master of the treasure boat. The other one had been one of the Satrap's entourage who had recommended leaving that morning and then had suggested trying to land on the beach. Both men had drowned, which Athan found odd since he distinctly remembered seeing them after the ship had been pulled ashore. He had not seen them, though, after the Satrap had pulled Utana aside for a word.

At the evening meeting of the sergeants of the watch, a few changes were implemented. Due to the number of injured men and the continuing absence of the land portion of the guard, most especially the cavalry, they would reinforce the outer perimeter with foot patrols and reduce the number of men around the treasure tent. Instead of four inside and out, there would only be two inside and two outside. The first watches were assigned to Athan's troop in recognition of the work they had done that day. As the meeting broke up, Drogas even pulled him aside.

"I understand you helped calm him down this evening after the, well, you know..."

"Just doing my duty, sir," said Athan with a smile.

"Well, you haven't seen him when he gets in a temper. He could have had us flogging one another all night long. It was a good thing you said whatever you did." Without waiting for a reply, he turned back to the business of guarding the camp.

Athan hustled over to Simeon. Philip was standing next to him. "You two have the first watch inside the tent. Keep a good watch, no one else will be there with you." In a lower voice he looked at Philip and asked, "Do you have your things?"

"I will go get them now," replied the coiner, scurrying off toward their tent.

"It will be harder with only two of you," said Athan to Simeon in a quiet voice. "You make sure he is watching when you are doing the boxes. One at a time, now. If it doesn't feel right, we can do this the next time."

"There may not be a next time," said Simeon with determination. "I will get all I can tonight."

Athan's duties as sergeant of the guard swept him away; it was to be a busy watch. One hour into it the remainder of the guards came marching in. The very worried-looking leader of the cavalry arrived and was immediately escorted to the Satrap's tent. Less than a quarter hour later the remainder of the hoplites and cavalry came in with their pack horses.

Athan watched the Satrap, accompanied by Utana, Drogas, and some of his personal guards, come out to observe the latecomers. The head of the cavalry was nowhere to be seen.

Athan, emboldened by his earlier success, looked at the shadowed figure of the Satrap and called out, "Look sire, you chose the finest warriors in the world as your guards! See, nine parasangs in one day and still ready to fight!"

The Satrap gave a sour grunt and returned to his tent.

Athan was waiting in their tent when Simeon returned from his watch. Philip was not with him. Athan had heard no uproar so he knew that at least they had not been caught in the act. But Simeon's expression warned him all was not well.

"We have seven talents of gold buried in the sand under the tent," he began without preamble, "we could have done more, but after the others came in we were worried that someone would come in to check on us."

"Seven is good," said Athan. "What went wrong?"

"The new seals don't match the old!"

"What?" said Athan, shocked.

"The little shit said he could make a die that would make an exact replica of the seal of the wafers. Well, they are not replicas; not even close. Look." Simeon took two lead wafers from his purse. One had been split open with knife. It had an image of a man's profile near the bottom. Over his head was a bird of some kind, a hawk or eagle perhaps, with its wings spread. It made the man look as though he had a wreath or perhaps some sort of wild hair style. Athan did not know who the man was supposed to be. He himself would not like to be portrayed as about to become a perch (or worse) for some big bird.

"Now look at this one," said Simeon handing him another wafer. Although there was the bust of a man and a bird with outstretched wings at the top of the disc, it was different. The new seal was obviously cruder and lacked even the basic finish of the original. Side by side it was obviously a fake.

"I was in a hurry," lamented Simeon, "after all this time and planning and when time came to pull it off I got in a hurry. I started digging a hole and by the time I had finished he had pulled off two of the seals. We worked furiously moving the gold, covering it up, piling in the sand and then replacing the top layer. I didn't notice what he had done until we decided to stop at seven boxes. I was checking them to make sure there was not sand or anything on them, you know, so they looked all neat and official. When I looked at the seals I thought they didn't look quite right. So then I checked one of the other seals. Side by side, well, you can see."

A thousand worries took flight in Athan's brain like a flock of birds lifting from a field. He had thought that it might be possible to sneak the band away when they were all on watch one night, but tonight they had already stood their watches. Besides, the countryside was relatively open for more than ten parasangs. He did not fancy his chances against the cavalry when they caught up to the band as they certainly would. A score of men could neither fight nor run from several score of cavalry. And he would have to bring out his entire band. He would not leave the men who had followed him so long to be tortured and killed. They had not even known what was happening. Thoughts ran through his head like a bird trapped in a cage fluttering against the bars. After a few moments one of these thoughts came to him and he snatched at it in hope.

"You said you only noticed the bad seals after you were done."

"Yes," replied a distraught Simeon who sat on a stool with his head in his hands, "when we were doing our final check."

"And you said that you had to compare them before you could be sure."

"They are different," pointed out the younger man, "look, see for yourself."

"I am not talking about a comparing the seals. Think, when they move the chests all they do is count the boxes and look to see they are sealed. Nobody even looks at the seal on the wafers; they just make sure the lid is sealed."

"Sooner or later one of the Satrap's men will notice the difference. Then he will compare the seals. Then the torturers will start in. How long do you think Philip will last?"

"So we change all the seals," said Athan. "Next time we get a chance we replace all the seals. That way they will not be able to compare the fakes to the originals."

"But you saw this," here Simeon flung the counterfeit seal to him, "it is nothing like the original. It looks like a pile of goat droppings. It is not going to fool the man who put the seal of the wafers."

"The man who put the seals on has other things to do than check for fake seals. He will be attending to the Satrap and supervising. Philip will just have to bring in enough seals to replace all the originals the next time we are in the tent with Jonathan and his man."

"Men," corrected Simeon, "he brought in Etor, remember?"

"Look," said Athan, "we are not going to panic. If the seals are discovered every man in the camp is a suspect, and a lot of us will want to leave in a hurry. We will have a better chance to fight our way out with if there are lots of suspects, not just one band. If no one notices the substitutes before they load them on the boats, even the sailors will be suspect." And with that he went out to find a despondent Philip to tell him he had some extra work to do that night.

But they did not load the treasure chests onto the ships the next day. The new ship's master of the treasure ship, formerly the master of the boat that Athan had ridden in upon the day before, declared it would take at least four days to repair the damage to the treasure ship and replace the broken oars. This was not to mention the various deaths and injuries to the members of the sailors and guards. Replacements needed to be assigned and bruises healed. The morning remained fresh and gusty, so the Satrap allowed himself to be persuaded to remain in this place for another day. As their luck would have it, full watches of four men were reinstituted inside the treasure tent. Worse, even with the additional watches during the day, the men from Athan's and Jonathan's band did not pair up inside the treasure tent. As each watch changed, Philip, Athan, and Simeon waited for someone to discover the bogus seals and raise the alarm. Simeon added to their anxiety when he reminded the other two that if someone started digging in the sand in that corner of the tent they might find the buried gold. It was a long day, spent buying spare oars from the other ships, bringing in long timbers to cut new oars, diving for and recovering the lost grapple, and reorganizing the guards and sailors. It was full dark before Athan was finally able to share a cup of wine in his tent with Jonathan.

"How was your watch?" he asked his fellow captain.

"Hot, boring; but a relief after that long march yesterday. When we got to the rendezvous and the boats were not in sight, the Satrap's envoy nearly fainted. He and the head horse boy got into a shouting match. Then they tried to blame it on me. I was certainly glad when Pirro came running up with news of where you were."

"I don't know about the envoy who was with you, but I understand the cavalry leader got off with a severe dressing down. So, did you notice anything unusual in the tent?"

Simeon hinted that he was able to make some transfers before we came in last night," answered Jonathan with a smile.

"He made a deposit of seven," answered Athan. "Could you tell?"

"I stayed out of the corners just to make sure," smiled Jonathan. "You know, I really need to make sure I can find this place again. I may want to come back someday."

"Yes," smiled Athan, "but I am glad you did not notice anything out of the ordinary with the treasure chests." He went on to explain the problem with the counterfeit seals. The blood visibly drained from Jonathan's face. Then Athan explained his plan. "So you see when we have our next chance, we must carry four score and three blanks into the tent so we can replace all the seals. That way they will all look the same."

It took some time for Jonathan to recover from the problem. "I knew we should have made him show us an example with the tools he would actually use," he growled, "I am going to kill that little bald crab."

"If this doesn't work, the Satrap will do that for us. If it does, then we will all be too rich to kill. For now we need to work out a plan to get out if they find out before we see those chests loaded into the treasury at Golibolu."

The two men worked out a plan for all the hoplite bands to unite and stand together in the event of the discovery of the missing gold. Even innocent men will fight to avoid being tortured. Almost five score hoplites had a possibility of cutting their way out, especially if the sailors and personal guards were also under suspicion.

But the plan was not needed. The next morning the wind and seas had moderated, the Satrap declared the treasure ship adequately repaired after only one day, and the vessels departed as though the intervening day had not existed. The gold chests were carried to their storage lockers in bottom of the somewhat battered treasure ship, and the vessels were launched without incident. It was the turn for Athan's band to accompany the horses along the coast road. They were happy to find they had 'only' five parasangs to go. The day was hot, but the road was good, and they made excellent time, arriving at the designated place just as the ships did. In marked contrast to the last landing, this one went smoothly. Better yet, the offloading of the gold went without a hitch. To top their good fortune, Athan's and Jonathan's bands were paired in the tent for the last watch; things could not be working more perfectly. And this troubled Athan more than anything else had. With the solution to their problems in hand he was becoming obsessed with a premonition of disaster. He could not sleep but remained awake on his cot awaiting his summons to the Satrap, who would start by asking him if he knew what his men were up to. Athan did not think he had slept at all when the watch captain came in to get Simeon and Philip up for their watch. The two men left with a soft clinking of lead disks concealed in leather pouches.

Athan lay in the tent, sidewalls up to catch any vagrant cooling breezes, listening for shouted questions as to why his men were carrying so many blank lead seals? 'And what was this thing that little Philip had in his pouch? What were they up to? Fetch the torturers!'

But there was no outcry. Athan thought about what must be going on in the treasure tent. They were almost at the end of the journey, and this was the first night that they had been given the chance to lift the gold the way they had actually planned. The ground here was harder than some of the sandy beaches they had camped on previous nights. Would they be able to hide the gold without anyone noticing the disturbed earth? What if they were caught in the act? It was not unusual for the captain of the watch to poke his head in the treasure tent. He was jerked to wakefulness when Simeon came in with the light behind him; his watch finished.

"All the wafers have been changed and thirty talents hidden," said Simeon cryptically; then he smiled. "Now get up. We have a boat to catch."

Athan dressed rapidly trying to get his mind around the idea that they had actually stolen 37 talents of gold from right under the noses of the strongest, best organized guards he had ever heard of. And there was a chance to get even more.

Three days later they arrived in Kadikoy. The conspirators had not been matched up inside the treasure tent again so no more gold had been removed from the chests. As before, the treasure was carried into the town's citadel, and the guards remained outside around the little fleet. Here the land turned back to the southeast. They were only seven parasangs from Golibolu, where the ships would offload the gold, which would then be escorted into the city and across the straits by Imperial troops for the remainder of the long journey to the Imperial treasury. They would be paid off there and released from service. The rest of their (illicit) payment could then be collected from the sands of the beaches where Athan and Jonathan's bands had cached the purloined portions of the treasure. Much to everyone's surprise they waited three days on the beach beneath Kadikoy. Once again the hoplites were confined to camp, though the Satrap's personal guard came and went freely. On the second day the men were allowed to go to one of the closer bath houses, where they could get a proper bath and have their clothes cleaned. Otherwise, there was little for them to do.

The enforced indolence seemed odd after the previous days of activity and haste. It did give Athan and his co-conspirators time to worry about some sharp-eyed functionary spotting the counterfeit seals.

Three days is a long time when you know you have more gold than you can ever expect to spend lying buried alone and unguarded behind you on a desolate beach. The strain was beginning to tell; each morning Jonathan and Athan would meet to confirm that the other four co-conspirators were still in camp and had not left in the night to sneak back and steal the buried treasure. Perhaps the very size of the haul dissuaded a would-be thief. That much money would need protection in a violent world. They needed each other to reach a place where their wealth could be permanently safeguarded. The other four indicated they intended to go south, perhaps as far as the Peloponnesus. Athan began to firm up an idea he had been considering for a long time. He would take as many of the band as wished to follow him and go west, past Macedonia and over the mountains. With his share of the loot he could set himself up, perhaps north of Illyria. He had heard it was nice country up there, a little wild and tribal, but with a number of small kingdoms and enough civilization to have some of the finer things in life. He knew he would have to leave this part of the world forever. The mountains on the far side of Macedonia should be far enough.

Everyone was ready for the job to be over. One more good day and they could finish. But the Satrap had another surprise for them. Late on the morning of the third day, the camp was roused by orders to prepare to leave. Men from the garrison were seen coming down from the city surrounding the Satrap's personal guard who in turn were surrounding a long line of familiar chests, being carried by two hundred sweating porters. There was instant activity, and by the time the gold arrived, the ships had been hastily packed and pulled out to the edge of the beach ready to load the treasure which was already arriving.

There was concern that the Satrap's sudden and unexpected departure was the result of dire news, or perhaps because of some insult given or received, causing his presence to no longer be welcome at the citadel. One look at his smirking self-satisfied face and everyone knew this was just another example of the Satrap's arbitrary decisions. He did the unexpected, he claimed, because it upset conspiracies against him. Of course it also demonstrated his power. The Satrap was an easy man to hate; not only did he blatantly state that he knew he was better than all those around him, he often demonstrated to his own satisfaction that he was better. And since he was the only judge of events, he was always right. After being in his service for a while, a man began to doubt his own judgment and to defer to the Satrap. Athan thought he knew the Satrap's problem - when no one tells you "no", a man must have his head screwed on pretty straight, or he began to assume everything would be just as he wanted simply because he willed it so. So the Satrap made arbitrary and sometimes foolish demands on his underlings, in part just because he was shielded from any negative consequences. Well, thought Athan, this self-assured popinjay was soon to get his comeuppance.

It now appeared that the Satrap wanted to go a few parasangs down the peninsula that afternoon so that they could have all the next day to get the treasure into the treasury at Golibolu. With luck they might even be paid off tomorrow night. In addition to the late departure, there was another change. Apparently the Satrap was feeling confident enough heading southeast on this peninsula so close to his destination that he would allow the troops marching along the road to arrive after the ships made camp. He only required a cavalry screen to act as sentinels during the landing; the marching hoplites and the replacement mounts would arrive as soon as they could.

In the event it did not matter; it was a hot and breathless day, and they had to row the whole way. Athan and his band took their turns pulling an oar under a hot sun. In the late afternoon a breeze did come up. Unfortunately it was from the southeast, dead onto the eyes of the ship. Although the wind was cooling, it slowed their progress even more. In the end the three and a half parasangs took longer to cover by sea than even the hoplites walking along the coast road. They were waiting in the shade of a few scruffy trees when the ships finally started into the beach.

There was anticipation as the camp was made; this would almost certainly be the last camp, and tomorrow the men could expect to end the job. They would have a chance to enjoy the comforts of a city and anticipation of the journey home, unencumbered by watches, responsibilities, and Satraps. Unexpectedly, Athan was offered his choice of watches and locations. He asked to stand the second watch in the tent. That was after dark and late enough for things to have settled down, though not so late as to make Drogas wonder why he was taking an undesirable watch. Most men considered either the first two or final watches to be the least undesirable.

"Who do you want to partner with?" asked Drogas.

"My lieutenant's uncle, Philip; he has done a good job in there," responded Athan offhandedly.

"Any preference with for your other watch mates?"

Athan was astounded. Never before had anyone had the opportunity to choose anyone from another band. Some of the men got along better with some than others, which was natural. For example, no one seemed to like or trust the men from Loxias' little band of hoplites. They were shifty and argumentative. "Someone from Jonathan's band, I guess," Athan requested. It was known that members of the two bands got along pretty well. "Why the special treatment?"

Drogas shrugged, "You did a good job, especially there when we had that problem during the storm. You earned a little consideration."

'I probably saved you at least a flogging by calming down that little weasel you work for' thought Athan, but all he said was "Thanks."

As he spoke he continued to watch the big guard captain for any signs of suspicion; the man turned only nodded and went on assigning watches and reminding the watch captains to keep a sharp guard and to be prepared for an early departure.

So it was that that Athan relieved the watch in the darkness that night with Philo, Maur, and Etor. As soon as they were alone in the tent, Athan gestured the other men in to him. Looking at Etor he asked," do you know what we are doing?"

"Enough," said Etor cryptically.

"Can you do this tonight? How are your nerves?"

"My nerves are very talented," the quiet man said with a thin smile. "What do you want me to do?"

"Just what you were paid to do, stand guard; but tonight you are to keep watch in case anyone comes toward the tent. You see or hear anything unusual give a hiss."

The man nodded and moved to where he could peer through a slit in the entrance flaps.

Athan reviewed each man's job before they started. They reminded him that they had done the same thing before. Athan was very nervous; to cover this, he nodded and went to the back of the tent and, drawing his wide bladed dagger, began digging in the beach sand. After a few moments Philip wandered back to where he was digging. "How many are you planning on putting in there?" he asked quietly. All the men were acutely aware that there were four members of the Satrap's personal guard only a few paces out from the corner of the treasure tent.

"We have two score discs with us," he replied, "I want to use them all."

"Well," commented Philip with a dryness unusual for him, "That hole ought to hold them."

Athan looked down at the gaping hole he had made. He must have been digging like a badger; he was nervous indeed. And little old Philip was calming him down! Athan smiled. "Are you ready?" he asked. He got a nod and moved up to the chests. He lifted the tarp and examined the wafers. The seals on them really were crude. How had the change been overlooked? Drawing a breath he looked at Maur standing on the other side of Philip, and then looked up to Etor still standing guard at the entrance. Etor nodded.

"Begin," Athan said.

Philip split open the lead seal with a practiced flick of his knife, pulled the wire loose, flipped open the latch, opened the lid and stepped back as Athan and Maur reached in to lift the top tray of gold from the chest. There in a polished wooden tray were the four golden ingots, each in its own hand-carved depression, each worth a quarter of a talent, each ingot more than enough to provide for a large family for years. They lifted the tray out using the hand holds cut into the wood at the end of the tray and set the tray on the ground. The tray was astonishingly heavy for its size. The two men then lifted out the bottom tray and carried it over to Athan's hole. Athan started to set the tray down so they could lift out the ingots but Maur shook his head no. Placing one end of the tray on the ground he flipped it over dumping the ingots on the ground with a noticeable thud. Athan flinched at the sound. They filled the tray with now empty tray with sand and carried it over to the chest and dumped the sand in the bottom. They made two trips with sand before Maur nodded that it was full enough. The men then put the middle tray back in the box, and placed the tray that still held its gold on top, hiding the sand. Philip gently closed the lid and while Athan and Maur covered the ingots down in the hole with sand, threaded the wire through the hasp and pressed his die, fitted with a hinged set of wooden dowels for greater leverage, against a new blank lead wafer, affixing the counterfeit image onto the soft metal. The two men brushed sand from their knees and looked at Philip. Then they looked at Etor standing just inside the closed flaps. He looked back, nodded and resumed his watch. The three men stepped to the next chest on the top of the next row. One talent of the gold was gone, thirty nine to go.

The first problem came on the third box. When they opened it they saw grains of sand on the tray. Maur blew them away and lifted the corner of the top tray. Sure enough, the bottom half of the box was filled with sand. Athan had a bad moment thinking that someone else had also been into the treasure. Then he remembered that 37 (now 39) of the treasure chests had been already pilfered. They sealed it up and went on to the next one. Over the next hour and a half they found three more chests that had been already opened and looted. Still, they took out the bottom trays of gold from 22 more boxes, stacking the gold in the hole Athan had dug in the beach and covering it with a layer of sand, slowly filling in the sandy trench. When they opened the second previously robbed chest, Athan found something else to tighten his already strained nerves. He noticed that the seals on the chests they had opened that night were different than the other seals; not dramatically different, but subtly and noticeably different. When confronted with this in a furious whisper, Philip confessed that he had changed seals to one of his other versions.

"The one I was using was getting all worn out. You can't expect one made with copper and concrete to hold up like a proper brass die can you? I had to make hundred impressions with it! It was getting so worn that it wouldn't make a good seal! Besides, nobody has noticed so far. We will be done tomorrow."

Athan was coldly furious, "Tomorrow they will be putting the chests into imperial custody. There will be imperial guards, imperial treasurers and a formal hand-over of the chests; don't you think they just might examine the seals?"

There was no help for it. They had already used too many of the new and inferior seals.

It was difficult, nerve-wracking work, with the added irritant of not knowing if the next box would have gold or sand in the lower level. In the end, it was one of the previously opened boxes that saved them. They had just lifted the tray of a fifth 'empty' as they called those chests that had already had the gold removed on one of the previous night and were settling the tray not down onto the beach but back into the chest when there was an urgent 'pssst' from Etor. They hastily covered the chests with the tarpaulin again. Snatching up their shields Maur sprang to the left front of the tent, brushing his knees as he did while Athan leapt to the right rear. Philip was still in the far corner, partially concealed behind the low stack of chests. He was bent to the hasp, fitting the seal over the wire when the tent flap was opened and the Satrap accompanied by Utana and three more of his personal body guards came abruptly into the tent. Athan held the Satrap's, eyes moving toward him, hand on the hilt of his kopis. The guards immediately moved to interpose themselves between the two men. Now, for a tense moment, everyone's hands were on the hilts of their weapons. All at once Athan dropped his hand from the hilt of his sword and placed it over his heart.

"My apologies, sire, I was not expecting anyone, and when I saw armed men suddenly come into the tent I just reacted. I did not recognize any of you at first. My deepest apologies," and he bowed deeply.

The Satrap had not really been concerned, and it showed in his off-handed acceptance of the apology. He even complimented the guards on their alertness. "But what about that one," he gestured to the far corner where Philip stood behind his shield. "Why is he hiding? Come here you coward." Athan could tell the Satrap had been drinking from his flushed face and slurred voice.

Philip came around the left side of the stack of chests, drawing attention away from the half filled hole behind him. "I am no coward, sire, that corner is my assigned station. I am to stay alive and sound the alarm. Should anyone enter the tent without your leave the four guards outside will probably have already been silenced. I am to call for help and act as the reserve until we are relieved."

"Four men would only get in each other's way," confirmed Athan. This way he can protect our backs should someone slit the tent and try to get the treasure that way."

The Satrap's eyes took on a crafty look, "Very wise." Then he looked at Athan's knees. "Why do you have sand on your knees?"

"I had to relieve myself, sire."

"You Yauna are so disgusting, like animals. Didn't Drogas tell you not to do that in the tent?"

"I was only pissing, sire."

"So why are your knees sandy?"

"I knelt to do it, sire," and seeing the puzzlement on the other man's face explained further, "that way you get less splashing. We don't want anything to get on those crates."

"Hmmm," said the Satrap with no answer to such a strange situation. "Well, you have done well for me on this journey."

"We each do our part, sire."

"You did your part well; you are a clever Yauna," repeated the Satrap unaware, or more likely unconcerned, about the insulting term. He glanced at the neatly stacked crates and smiled a smile of self-satisfaction. He reached into his purse and tossed a golden piece into the air. It hit the top of the tent and bounced into the sand. No one dared to comment on that.

"Thank you, sire," said Athan and put his hand over his heart again and bowed. The entourage exited the tent, the guards glowering at them as they ducked out. For a long moment the tent was quiet, then Athan stepped forward and dug his hands into the sand sifting it through his fingers again and again until he brought up a the gold piece. "Look men", he joked, "there is gold in sand." The guards outside the tent wondered at the laughter inside the tent.

Athan's good humor was quelled when he looked at the impression on the coin. It had a man in profile with a spread winged eagle over him. It looked like the design of the seals only much, much better. Athan stepped over to the smiling Philip. "Look familiar?" he asked in quiet savagery. The little man quailed away from him.

"That is gold," he protested, "and freshly minted, from a hard bronze die."

"Ahhh," growled Athan disgustedly. "Let's clean this up." There was no thought of trying to open any more of the boxes.

Etor resumed his post while the men filled in the rest of the hole where 24 talents of gold now lay and smoothed over the sand generally cleaning up. Athan took an odd-shaped little rock he found in the sand and placed it in the right rear corner of the tent. He was thinking how long it took him to find a gold coin in the sand that had fallen right at his feet. He was worrying how hard it would be to find gold in the sand buried for many days. He was certain that when the Satrap realized he had been robbed, suspicion would fall on him in part because the Satrap and his men would remember the 'clever Yauna'. At the very least the torturers would want to have a long probing conversation with him. Athan would certainly like to see the Satrap's expression when he realized he was not as smart as he thought he was, but he was unwilling to give his life for that sight.

The next morning was full of excitement. Despite the fact the men had broken camp almost a dozen times before, for some reason on this morning everything went badly from burned breakfast bread, to a fist fight that broke out between one of horsemen and one of Loxias' hoplites. The worst moment came with one of the crates was dropped into the edge of the surf when it was being lifted up onto the treasure ship. A member of the Satrap's entourage dashed over and inspected the crate while members of the personal guard stood around with hands on their hilts glowering at everyone. Athan watched with fascinated horror as the man checked the bogus seal, gave it a tug, and then waved the men to lift the box up onto the boat.

'No one really wants to find anything wrong with those crates, thought Athan, 'so everyone will pretend they didn't notice anything. They know what will happen if anything happens to those treasure boxes. So they will refuse to admit, even to themselves, that they see anything different or odd; just so long as nothing can be blamed on them.'

Athan's band helped launch the boats and then set off for the four-hour hike to finish the delivery of the Ionian tribute. By the time they arrived at Golibolu, the ships had beached under the watchful guard of a portion of the city's garrison. Between the cavalry, the garrison, and the hoplites there were enough different types of guards to create complete chaos. It was early dusk before the men arrived outside the city. This time they would be allowed into the city to sleep under a roof and in a bed if they so desired. The gold would remain in the city treasury until the three ships could round the end of the peninsula ten parasangs down and come up the Hellespont to the east side of the city to transport the tribute across the water and into the custody of the waiting Imperial caravan. The five bands of hoplites were disappointed that they would not receive their wages that night. Athan went to a money changer and converted the gold piece he had been given by the Satrap into local currency. He was shocked at the value of the coin. With all the money he obtained he was able to give his band an advance on their wages and still have enough money left to consider buying a good pony. His men spent most of their money becoming popular with the local women and wine merchants.

The next day dragged on. The Imperial treasurer did not want to pay the agreed-upon rates. Eventually the matter was brought to the Satrap with Jonathan acting as spokesman for the guards. It was late afternoon before a compromise was reached that had primarily to do with arranging the appropriate compensation for the treasurer. Simeon used the delay to arrange purchases of horses and ponies for the band. They had come by ship and on foot, they would return riding. Just before the hoplite captains finally received the wages for their respective bands Simeon heard a rumor that had him waiting for Jonathan and Athan when they came out of the citadel with their full purses.

"I heard a rumor in the market," Simeon told them as soon as he could pull them off into a quiet corner. "They say some of the gold fell into the sand and was lost."

"Somebody blabbed," said Jonathan bleakly.

"Maybe they are referring to the chest that was dropped yesterday," said Athan hopefully.

'Somebody blabbed," said Simeon. "It doesn't matter. If the rumor gets around, the chests will be examined. Then the hunt will be on."

"How many animals do you have?" Athan asked Simeon.

"Not quite a score, even counting donkeys. Not enough. It is going to take some time, or we will just get skinned in a seller's market."

"Listen," said Athan, "here is what we have to do. We have to get out of this town as quickly and unobtrusively as possible. Leaving at night or riding out hell for leather is bound to attract attention. We have to get back to Kadakoy as soon as we can. We will not be under their direct observation there, and it will buy us some more time. How can we get our comrades out of here?"

"Yes, how do we get four score horny hoplites with their pockets full of money out of town before they have had their fun?" asked Jonathan.

There was a long pause as the men pondered how to ruin their men's long anticipated spree. They discussed a number of plausible lies, such as making Kadakoy more attractive by claiming a big caravan had just arrived. They considered claiming that the citizens would be trying to rob them. This was actually true, but a tough hoplite just considered attempted robbery as part of the fun. Someone suggested claiming that they all needed to get home to repel some raids by enemies. That seemed thin. What enemies would they be? Besides, the news would be old and the men were many day's travel from home. They could not possibly return in time to repel any raiders. Then someone suggested to tell the men there was a plague back home and they needed to return to their loved ones.

"No," objected Athan, "nobody runs to a plague." There was a moment as everyone digested what had just been said. The idea came to them all at the same time.

"I can spread a rumor about a plague here with some girls I know," mused Simeon.

"We could say the plague came with the gold. That would make everyone glad to see our backs," suggested Jonathan.

"I will tell some of the boys that the girls have been spreading this new disease," contributed Athan. "It's probably true anyway."

"Which version should we spread?" wondered Simeon.

"All of them, and let Philip, Etor and Maur spread a few as well." answered Athan. "You know how rumors are. If we do this right we will have a dozen versions out there by morning. Jonathan, have you given your men an advance on their pay?"

"Only enough for a drink," replied Jonathan a little defensively. "I couldn't afford more until I got our wages."

"Good," said Athan with satisfaction. "Tell your men the one about the girls here spreading plague and tell them you will pay them tomorrow after we have left."

"They won't like it," warned Jonathan.

"Yes, but if you hold their pay, they will leave with you in the morning," countered Athan. "Now we should try to get as many of the others who came with us out of here as we can."

"I will talk to Endre, I know him a little. Maybe you could approach Rodas and tell him about the plague," Jonathan suggested.

"What about Loxias and his people?" asked Simeon.

"I am sure when he finds out that we have left, he and his men will take the hint," said Athan dryly. "Anyway, I never cared much for that lot."

"Well," said Jonathan getting to his feet, "I guess I had better go break the bad news to my men."

The winter weather remained difficult, turning cold and rainy followed by snow. On the occasions the old man could see the sun it was bitterly cold. He ventured out far enough to confirm that the drifts down in the trees at the foot of his little gully were still a significant impediment to travel. And there was always the problem of the bandits that had originally attacked him. They had probably moved on, but there was a chance they were still in the area. Finally, he knew that in his present weakened state he would not be able to maintain a pace that would get him back to his people before he collapsed. He had subsisted on hot tea for longer than he cared to admit. Before he left, he would have to find food somewhere, somehow.

Chapter Sixteen– The Getaway

Jonathan had his men, grumbling and unhappy, formed up and moving out shortly after full daylight the next morning, accompanied by a handful of pack animals that carried their gear. Athan, still rounding up his band, came by to promise he would be along as soon as he could. Everyone was surprised to see that Rodas' little band of 15 was with assembled and in good order; ready to march out. This morning they were tight lipped and eager to leave. It did not take Jonathan very long to discover that their eagerness to leave was not based on the rumors of plague, but had more to do with an even more disturbing story Rodas had heard - that some of the gold had been diverted somehow from the tribute caravan.

Rodas spoke quietly with Jonathan as soon as they were out of sight of Golibolu. He motioned with his head to Jonathan that he desired a private conversation so the two men moved off the route march of the hoplites and spoke with their heads together where Rodas passed his news to Jonathan.

"If there is even a suspicion that there is something wrong with the tribute, there will be hell to pay," said the other captain to Jonathan. "You know who the first ones will be to get the blame. At the very least we could be held up there for days and days. If there is anything missing there will be many piercing questions from very unsympathetic men. I talked to the boys, about it and we were all of the opinion we would rather spend our money in a more secure environment."

Jonathan looked at his fellow captain. Rodas was a year of two older than himself, a stocky man with long straight reddish hair, often held back with a headband, a closely cropped beard, and intelligent brown eyes. Though a long scar on the left side of his face could give him a grim expression, he was unusually good-natured for a fighting man. The other captains considered him to be tough-minded but fair, and his humor made him a good companion. Jonathan was not at all unhappy to have him and his men with him.

Looking the man in the face, Jonathan put on his most bland expression and spoke offhandedly, "Really, the Satrap is far too clever for that. Do you think anyone could have stolen any of that gold without us knowing about it?"

"I wasn't sure until just then," said Rodas with a shrewd look. "Perhaps we should pick up the pace."

"No, we are to camp just beyond the place where we made the last camp on the way in. Athan and his men will meet us there."

"So," asked Rodas, "you think a lot of this Chief Athan. Tell me about him. Have you known him long?"

And so the two men began talking as the hoplites continued along the coast road at a mild pace, Jonathan speaking first to Rodas, and later to a wider group of the marching men. He shared stories of Athan, things he had seen and other things he had heard. Lives can change on chance encounters, casual meetings, or listening to someone on a walk. That morning would dramatically change the lives of many of the men who marched along, listening to Jonathan talk about his old friend and mentor, Captain Athan formerly of Epiria.

But 'Captain Athan' was having his own troubles back in Golibolu. He had trouble collecting his men, who had just settled down that night to what they thought would be at least a three-day debauch. Philip, of all people, was one of the last to be found and was absolutely the most reluctant to leave. He and the two women he had ensnared (or vice versa) actually tried to fight off his comrades who eventually found him. It appeared he had contrived to spend his entire advance in one fabulous night. Adding to Athan's headaches was the problem of managing the livestock. Athan had experience with animals, but he was not especially skilled with them. Fortunately, a member of the band, one Ixon, was a natural at handling horses. Without his help they would not have been able to leave as soon as they did, though it was almost noon before they were able to depart. Only one man from Athan's band, Idas, was missing. Idas had claimed he needed treatment for his bad knee and was last seen entering a house of prostitution with one of Loxias' men.

"He has probably gotten himself robbed and murdered," grumbled Simeon. "Serves him right. Well, we can't wait for him any longer. We need to get back to our goods."

Athan gave him a sharp look. It was best not to even hint about what they had left behind. Simeon had become increasingly concerned about the treasure they had left buried in the sands. He was clearly becoming concerned that Jonathan might take the gold for himself.

Jonathan's warning had been delivered to Endre, but Endre's band was not ready to leave by noon, when Athan departed with his band. Some of Athan's men were now mounted, and the rest placed their equipment on a variety of donkeys and mules. Endre was there to see them off, much as Athan had been for Jonathan. He promised to follow as soon as he could assemble his men. They made arrangements to try to rejoin the other hoplites at their old campsite outside of Kadakoy.

Though most of his men were still lost in the fleshpots of the city, Endre had located six of his band and brought them with him to the gate. Endre asked permission for these men to leave now with Athan's band. Endre was worried, and that worried Athan.

When Athan pressed him, all the other chieftain would say was that he would feel better away from Golibolu. "Too close to the Empire," he muttered.

Once clear of the town, Simeon pressed the men forward at a brisk pace. There was some grumbling, but his sense of urgency infected them, and every man stepped out smartly, putting distance between themselves and Golibolu. Athan caught men looking over their shoulders, even though they did not know what they were looking for. Athan was looking over his shoulder, too, and he knew just what he feared to see: a dust cloud over a formation of Achaemenid cavalry.

Such was the pace they set that well before dark the men with Athan rejoined the other two bands, just past the place where they had camped three days before and where (hopefully) 96 quarter talent bars were buried in the sand. There was considerable camp management to be figured out with the new arrivals and their livestock. It was dark, by the time the men and animals had been fed, watches established, and a war council scheduled.

Inside Athan's tent a plan to recover the buried gold was confirmed. Simeon was insistent that he lead the recovery effort. They would use an excuse of a scouting party and would be mounted. Since there had been horsemen scouting around the camp every evening on the way out, it would seem less strange, even though the hoplites were not real cavalry. Only one of the captains could accompany the scouts without drawing considerable interest of the men. Etor and Maur, who were already aware of the scheme would go, of course, but they still needed at least one more man to make up the scouting party. Philip was out of the question; using the skinny old artisan as a scout would immediately attract attention. The men liked him but knew he was only along by way of a sinecure. They would have to let another man in on the secret. After a brief debate, they decided upon Pirro; he would be told what they were doing after they left camp and would be sworn to silence.

The four men rode out just as the sun was approaching the horizon. Officially, they were checking their back trail to see if any of the other two hoplite bands were coming, and then they would take a swing around outside the perimeter looking for possible enemies foolish enough to attack three score hoplites. Simeon was eager and headed the men down the beach toward their old campsite at a high canter.

Jonathan, Rodas, and Athan retired to Athan's campfire where they traded stories around a small amphora of wine. The other chieftain clearly knew something was up, but was too polite, or too discrete, to ask. It was long after dark when the horses returned obviously unburdened. Simeon, tight-lipped, merely shook his head once and jerked his head toward Athan's tent. Athan and Jonathan looked at one another, then at Rodas. An unspoken decision was made.

"Pirro, Etor, Maur," directed Athan, 'could you ensure no one disturbs us?" Unspoken was the order to prevent any prying ears from hearing the conversation that would be held inside. Jonathan's men looked to him for confirmation, and nodded, moving to either side of the tent. Pirro took the horses back to the picket line where Ixon waited.

The three men entered Athan's tent. Simeon was in a taking. "What is he doing here," he all but snarled.

"Our circle is expanding," said Athan calmly.

"I am not paying him out of my share," Simeon stated. He was frustrated and looking for an argument.

"Very well," said Athan, 'So be it. I take it there was a problem."

Simeon looked at Rodas then at Athan.

"Perhaps I should explain," he said to his fellow captain. "Please be seated. We have contrived to remove some gold from the chests and bury it on the beach at our last campsite."

Rodas gave a whistle. "No wonder you wanted to get out of the city. Do you mind if I ask how much you got?"

The other men looked at each other and said nothing.

Rodas tried again, "When the theft is discovered my men will be in danger. All of us will be. What is our share for this risk?'

"One talent of gold," said Athan, and then looking at Simeon continued, "from my share. And your men must stay with us at least to Xanthi, defending us if we are attacked, and respect our goods."

"You must have taken a lot. You know they will hunt us to the ends of the earth. All of us; they won't care who actually took the gold, they will kill us all if they can."

"And each member of your band will get a horse when we get to Kadakoy," Athan continued. There was a pause, "and you will get three donkeys to carry your goods."

"Done," said Rodas reaching out a hand.

"Now," he said turning to Simeon, "why couldn't you find the gold?"

Simeon poured out a tale of frustration and woe. They found were the camp had been, but there were so many tracks they could not identify where the treasure tent had been. They had repeatedly plunged their swords into the sand finding nothing. Finally, they returned to camp hoping for some suggestions.

"We can go back tomorrow and set up a line of men, using probes," suggested Jonathan. "Of course, that will mean taking every man in camp into our confidence and surely such strange activity will be noticed and commented upon by travelers. That will let the Satrap know something is up right away and when he finds his gold is missing he will immediately know what happened."

"We could abandon it," suggested Athan, stopping when Simeon visibly flinched.

"How many of these caches do you have?" grinned Rodas, "Did you leave nests all the way here like the turtles laying their eggs of the beach?"

Simeon started to speak; Jonathan provided a soft answer first, "Some, some, you will know in time."

Before anything else could be said, Athan decided to take charge of matters himself, "I put it in the beach, I should have gone to get it. Simeon, let's tell the men that you saw something back on the track that you thought needed my attention. We could get our animals and go back for a second look. Maybe I can find where I put it."

So it was done. Less than half an hour later the men were headed back down the beach, Simeon on his tired horse, Athan on his pony. Fortunately it was a clear night, and the moon had waxed almost full so that there was enough light to find their old camp site. Athan took out two lamps from his saddle bags and, with a few tries, struck a spark into the oily wick. Each man took one of the metal lamps and walked down the beach in the eerie bluish moonlight. Instead of looking at the many tracks on the sand, Athan took bearings on a patch of brush and a tall cedar located back from the beach. Then looking at a rocky outcrop he mentally aligned their angles. "I think the entrance of the tent was about here." He stepped in the direction the tent had been pitched looking for marks where the chests had been stacked or perhaps where he had dug. Simeon began thrusting his sword into the sand. Athan continued to look with his lamp held low, casting about back and forth. Once or twice he stooped to examine something in the sand. Suddenly he bent down to pick up the odd little stone he had placed on the sand inside the treasure tent. "Here" he said. And orienting himself to the corner of the tent took two steps and began to thrust his kopis into the sand. Simeon joined him pushing in sword in twice for every one of Athan's slower thrusts. It was the older man who felt his weapon strike something hard.

"It was deeper than I thought," was all he said, concealing the thrill he felt.

The two men fell to their knees and began digging furiously with their hands. Simeon gave a cry as he first touched, and then drew out, a heavy ingot from the sand. He held it to the moonlit sky with an inarticulate cry.

"We did it" Athan said quietly. "I never really thought we could pull it off." The two old friends looked at each other across the hole they had dug and embraced. Then they resumed digging.

After they had uncovered several of the bars, Athan got up and retrieved their animals, bringing them to the expanding hole and began putting the ingots into the saddle bags they had brought. Before long, the bags were straining at the seams, and the animals were stamping at the load. Somehow even these careful men had not realized the weight of the load they would be carrying. Two dozen talents of gold meant 96 quarter talent bricks; each talent weighed about a medimnos. Since even a big man with full gear seldom weighed four medimnos, it was unreasonable to expect any horse to carry more than that, and Athan's pony was protesting at three and a half talents. They decided to partially offload Simeon's horse; he would ride back to camp with four ingots to give to the other captains. Then the captains would take Ixon into their confidence. It would be impossible to conceal such a burden from the man who was responsible for all the livestock. Jonathan, Pirro, Etor, and Maur would return to the cache leading a pack animal. All five men and nine burdened animals would bring the gold back to camp where it would be stored in the leather bags brought for that purpose. They now realized that they had far too few bags, but they would suffice until they could purchase more in Kadakoy.

Athan watched Simeon ride his horse back toward their camp, less than a quarter of a parasang away. There was little surf; it was quiet on the beach. His pony stamped his foot. Athan led him to the patch of brush just past the edge of the beach and there stacked 14 ingots of gold in the shadows. He walked back to his hole and got back to the business of excavating almost four score gold ingots out of the sand and moving them to the growing golden pile beside the brush. It was hard work and more than a little spooky. Athan was glad for the company of the little pony; once the pony stamped and snorted sending Athan's heart into his mouth as he snatched out his kopis. He relaxed when he saw it was only a pair of feral dogs trotting up the beach to see what things the sea might have cast up for them. They barely gave Athan a glance as they continued along the shore toward the camp. A dozen ingots made a load for the pony, then Athan would lead him to the stacks by the bush, offload them, then lead him back, tying the reins to his left foot so he wouldn't wander. Finally, when Athan calculated that he had five dozen bricks stacked up under the brush he tied the pony to a branch and went back to expose the remainder of the gold ingots. He knew he needed to find and additional three dozen. He found to his distress that after bringing up an even score he began to have trouble finding more. Even after significantly expanding his hole, he was unable to find more than 88. He went back up to his exposed stash and recounted. He now counted 90; four were gone with Simeon, two more to find.

Athan sat atop his horde on the edge of that lonely beach. It would be midnight in an hour of so. He was keenly aware that he was sitting on an immense fortune all alone in no place in particular. It was a lonely feeling and not a little frightening. Simeon had been gone a long time. Athan knew that some men are driven mad by gold, and he had seen some signs of that in his friend, but surely he would return for more gold. Suppose he had been ambushed on the way to camp? Or had some of the men found out about the gold and there had been a riot? Athan decided he would wait for another hour and then leave the gold where it was, go back to camp, and find out what was happening.

He was just getting up to resume his search for the last two ingots when he heard horses approaching from the direction of his camp. He waited beside the brush, strangely reluctant to come out of the shadows even though he could see there were four men each leading another animal. It was not until he heard Simeon's concerned call "Chief?" that he stepped out into the moonlight.

There was a problem when Simeon was told about the two missing ingots. He insisted upon going back and looking for them. The men had brought a shovel so they were able to work more efficiently, still it was some time before Pirro struck an ingot with his shovel. Bringing the golden brick out of the sand had a profound impact on him; he stared at it transfixed.

"Only one more to find," said Simeon taking the shovel from Pirro, who continued to stare at the heavy ingot in his hand, and began moving sand again.

Athan took the ingot from Pirro, and spoke to him as though he were talking to a man found sleep walking. "Look at this, Pirro." he said, taking the ingot out of his hand. "Do you know what it is?"

"It's gold chief," the red-headed spy replied a bit defensively.

"Yes, the most precious thing in the world. But it can also be your destruction. Listen, what happens when you don't get enough to drink? You die, yes?" Pirro nodded, somewhat befuddled. "But when you are thirsty and you come to a river do you drink the whole river?" Pirro shook his head. "And what happens if you swim out into the middle of a big river and try to drink it all?"

"You drown," Pirro said. Athan was aware that Etor, and Maur were also listening.

"You drown," confirmed Athan. "We have an ocean of gold here, enough so we can live comfortably for a very long time. But we have to be careful that we do not drown. We need to keep this gold secret until we can each get our share into a safe place. If we are not careful every man will be after us to steal our share. So we need to be prudent, cautious, and careful. There is plenty for all, but not if we do not keep our discipline."

"Hey," called Simeon from the hole where he was still enthusiastically throwing up dirt, "come on, help me find that ingot!"

The three men turned their heads looking at Simeon, and then, as one turned back to Athan.

"Drink," he repeated, "don't drown."

Athan had the men load the ingots onto the horses and then turned back to his friend.

"Brother," he said, using the term of endearment, "perhaps we miscounted, we have enough."

"It is a quarter talent of gold!" insisted Simeon.

"Give it as a gift to Poseidon," said Athan in a gentle voice. "Now let us cover our tracks and take our selves and our belongings home."

Simeon stopped and stared up at Athan. Then, like a man coming out of a delirium, he passed up the shovel and climbed out of the hole. Together the two friends filled in the hole and obscured the marks of their digging as well as they could. All five men walked their horses (and Athan's pony) over their digging, obscuring it even further. Finally, they arrived back at camp, passing the guard with a word and awakening Ixon who was sleeping by his animals. He took charge of the bundles and arranged them so they would be the first items loaded on the pack animals in the morning, before prying eyes could wonder at the new and heavy load. Athan left word to have Philip awakened before dawn so he could assist Ixon; helping the horseman would be his new duty.

The next day they passed Kadakoy well before noon and made camp not far west of where they had camped on the way out. Simeon had taken one of the ingots and cut it into over a score of unequal pieces. Simeon, Ixon and Jonathan went into the stables around Kadakoy to look into purchasing horses and additional pack animals. The plan was to wait here for anther day so that Endre and any of the other hoplites could have a chance to catch up to them for the return journey. As promised, two thirds of the men were allowed to go into town for a bit of relaxation, with a strict rejoinder to return by noon the next day for a muster. The mood of the camp was upbeat, all except Athan, who was uncharacteristically tense and nervous. He was able to persuade one of his men to ride his new horse back along their trail and look for anyone following them. He specifically warned him to beware of any cavalry coming from Golibolu, advising him to avoid them and return back to camp at once if he saw anything unusual. Unfortunately for Athan's piece of mind the scout, who did not appreciate the importance of his mission, was overtaken by a great thirst shortly after passing their old camp and returned via a wine shop in Kadakoy, where some of his comrades had taken refuge. He did not make his report that there was nothing at all behind them until well past the time that Athan's patience ran out.

The next morning Jonathan, Rodas, and Ixon went in to complete their purchases of horses and secure additional provisions, while Athan rode out on his pony with two men, one from Rodas' band, one from Jonathan's, to look for Endre's men. Just before they returned in the late afternoon they saw in the distance what might be a band of hoplites, but it was getting late and obviously whoever the men were they would not arrive in town until the next day. Satisfied they would not awaken to a vengeful cavalry raid, Athan rode back to camp to make preparations to move out on the morrow.

The departure was not smooth. The men were experienced campaigners, but they normally traveled on foot, not on horses. Adding to the confusion was the fact that there were three separate bands, and they had not yet fully settled the new relationships for the return trip. Three men did not care to accompany their comrades or, at least, did not appear at the morning muster. Despite the measures the leaders had taken to maintain secrecy, some of the men also seemed to know about the "special cargo" being carried by the four mules and two donkeys recently purchased.

Jonathan and Phillip had gone out away from everyone else melted some of the cut up pieces of the ingot. Philip melted the gold in a pot over a hot fire and created some rough coins using a disc-shaped mold, impressing an image in the gold with his tattered dies. The idea was to make it not screamingly obvious they were paying with pieces of a golden ingot. It was gold, however, and it did attract notice. Still and all, despite the difficulties in breaking camp, the men were away and gone and out of sight of Kadakoy before noon.

Athan watched them go with enormous relief. He was remaining behind with Pirro, Stamitos, one of the men from Endre's band, and Yure, one of Jonathan's men who claimed to know horses. The plan was for the four men remaining behind to buy some more horses and additional provisions while the rest of the hoplites, under the command of Jonathan, were to cover the two days journey to the place where Simeon had left the largest cache. There they would recover the gold, openly this time, and make some payments to the men. Then the bands could choose to either travel together or split up for the return journey home. The first and smallest cache was still kept as a secret; only the original five men in on the caper knew about the seven talents buried there.

While Jonathan was leading the main body toward the buried treasure, Athan intended to stay behind and see if that was indeed Endre's band he had seen the day before. He would offer to buy more horses for them to ride, and, if it felt right, possibly even invite them to join the larger band. The four men wandered around the markets examining some of the available animals. They bought another pony and an excellent jenny along with extra grain and additional sets of sturdy panniers. Athan periodically checked for anyone arriving from the east. Sure enough, some time after the four had a noon meal and a nice siesta, Endre's dusty little band came straggling in. Athan went down to welcome him. Athan escorted him to a house Athan knew would provide food and wine and a quiet place where the two captains could sit and talk. Endre had the remainder of his band plus two men from Lexias' group and one additional Thracian all of whom wanted to return home. It appeared that Lexias had not paid all of his men their full salaries and was now nowhere to be seen. His little band had disintegrated with some men searching for him, some seeking passage home by sea, and the two who said they would walk back in company with their countrymen.

Endre thanked Athan for the offer to join up and ride home with the larger band but declined.

"I would like some pack animals," he admitted, "but a hoplite on horseback is like a duck on land. We are better in our own element. Thank you, but I think we will stay here tomorrow and then go home on our own." Athan promised to check with him before he left in the morning and wandered off to find his own men.

Life turns on little things; Athan could not find his companions, so he went to the city and climbed the inside of the wall to a guard post, where he thought he might be able to catch a glimpse of them below in the streets. If that did not work, he would return to the house where they had paid for lodgings and rejoin them there. It was still hot, and off to the west there were thunderstorms. The wind had shifted to the southwest again; perhaps it would blow some rain their way. The sun was low on the horizon, filling the air with long slanting rays. Athan thought he would stay there and watch the sunset which promised to be very nice. Shielding his eyes from the sun, he turned with the guard and faced east to escape the glare.

It was hot, and Athan changed his mind; he would go down into the cool streets below and see the sunset tomorrow. Just as he was turning to leave the guard said in a casual tone, "That's unusual."

Since the man had not spoken before, just speaking was unusual enough to catch Athan's interest. "What?" he asked.

"See the boats? It is awfully late for them to still be sailing. And look, they are tacking."

Athan expressed his ignorance of what that meant. The guard explained that with the wind in an unfavorable quarter, the boats would row into the wind to get to weather, then raise their sails and slant down toward their destination, sometimes taking many such hitches and slants to arrive at their destination. If the wind was favorable enough and strong enough, it could be faster than just rowing. "But even so, it will be dark before they can get here. I wonder why they are in such a hurry?"

Athan felt a chill run through him. With a sense of unreality, he took a good long look at the three boats. The air was clear and the sun was behind him so even at this distance he was confident he recognized those sails. He had ridden with those particular boats all the way from Stavros. They were supposed to be rounding the headland to carry the tribute over the Hellespont to the Imperial coffers. Athan felt as though he were in a nightmare. Turning, he looked very carefully east down the beach road. With a sense of inevitability he saw, very faintly, a cloud of dust. He was absolutely certain that there would be a troop of cavalry under that cloud of dust, a troop headed for Kadakoy and vengeance. The hunt was on.

He did not say another word, walking down the stairs built into the inside of the walls. It was now urgent for Athan to find his companions and find them at once. A quick check of the stables and market, where people where now closing their shops, was unproductive. Athan felt as though he were in a giant trap with the door slowly closing. He returned to the house where he had left Endre drinking wine under an awning, and there, with their feet up were Endre, Pirro, Stamitos, and Yure, all drinking and laughing together. They welcomed Athan and smiled at his dusty and anxious expression. He sat down heavily and stopped their good natured banter with three terse sentences.

"There is a troop of Achaemendian cavalry from Golibolu riding here hell for leather. The treasure boats are also headed back this way as hard as they can come. They will be here just after nightfall."

There was a silence. It was a puzzled silence on the part of Endre, shocked by the rest. Athan had their full attention. He had been thinking of what to do since he had climbed down from the walls.

"Stamitos, Pirro, get all our things together as soon as you can. If anyone asks why you are leaving, say you have been invited to see some girls or something. Don't try to get a refund, just leave. Yure, can we buy any horses this late?"

"No, captain, I think everyone has put up their livestock for the night."

"All right, go to the stables and get all our horses out, saddled and ready to go. Say we are going to camp out on the shore because of the heat and want an early start in the morning. Wait for us there. We will come as soon as we can." Athan looked at the staring faces around him. He noticed for the first time that Pirro had freckles on his face. Then Athan realized that Pirro had gone deathly pale beneath his dark complexion. "Don't just sit there," he snapped at the men, "go!"

They were gone like startled birds.

Endre had his feet firmly on the floor. "What is amiss?"

"You heard the rumors about part of the gold being stolen," asked Athan carefully.

"Yes,"

"It is true. I believe that the cavalry on the way here is to look for the Yauna they hired to guard the shipment. I saw the same boats we came over in headed this way, too. I think there are some men on those boats who are looking for us as well. I think they all want to ask

392

us some questions. I think it would be very good not to be here when they arrive. Can you leave with us?"

Endre shook his head, "We did not make a camp; the boys are scattered all over Kadakoy. Even if I could collect them we walked six parasangs today. We are in no shape to try to outrun horses."

"If you could collect them in the next few hours," suggested Athan, "perhaps you could slip out the north gate and get into the hills. I think the main pursuit will be down coast after us."

"I will try," accepted Endre heavily. "But I do not like our chances. Still, that is probably the best chance we have."

Athan looked around to confirm they were not being watched, and then reached down the front of his tunic. He pulled a leather pouch from where it rested against his chest on the inside of his tunic. Opening the pouch he pulled out a three big chunks of a golden ingot and put them in Endre's lap.

Endre looked around, covering the gold with his hands, then he opened his hands and looked down at the pieces. They were beautiful: shiny, massy, with a part of imperial seal pressed onto one of the bits. Endre took in a breath.

"So you did it," he said as he wrapped them in a piece of cloth. There were several layers of meaning in his statement. "How?"

"Best if you not know," said Athan grimly. "If you are asked just say you heard we had help. I would chop that up even more. It is hard to spend big chunks like that in one place."

"How many ingots do you have," asked Endre hefting the covered bundle.

Athan shrugged, "A couple hundred."

Endre whistled a long low tone. "They will never stop looking for you; for us." Athan nodded.

"Just when you going to let me know about this?" Athan could see he was getting angry. "Is this little bit our whole share," he sneered, "we will be running all the way to Peloponnesus on three little chunks?"

"This is all I have with me. I did not want to tell you before," confessed Athan, "I was afraid word would get out; which it did. But you know I tried to get you out. And I waited here so you could rejoin us in safety."

Endre nodded mutely.

"If you get out and can find me, I promise I will give you a full share. I am sorry. That is all I can do."

Endre said nothing else for a moment then asked, "What about Lexias' boys?"

"They are on their own," said Athan, "there is nothing I can do for them."

Athan's fellow captain nodded his head and then stood and took Athan's hand, elbow to elbow in the warrior's grip.

"I will try to get my people out," Endre said. "This will help," he said indicating the gold. "And thank you for the warning."

The two men embraced. As Athan headed for the stables, Endre called after him, "I intend to get out. I'll see you again. Don't forget my share."

By the time Yure and Athan had the six animals saddled and ready, Pirro and Stamitos were back with their gear. It took only a few moments to load the bundles on their animals and head for the east gate. It was after sunset but not yet dark when they arrived. Although technically the gates were supposed to be closed at dark, in practice they seldom were. There was a guard who was mildly curious about why they were leaving at this late hour. Athan's offhand comment about going down to meet some ships that were arriving late, along with a small bribe, ended the discussion. By this time it was so dark that they dismounted and led the horses along the road. Athan did not start to feel even slightly secure until they were a quarter of a parasang from the city and beyond any reasonable chance of being seen in the night. It was a hot night with scattered thundershowers grumbling off in the distance. After another hour of walking, the moon, which was now full, came up and reflected off the sea, providing enough light for the men to remount and ride safely, if slowly. Shortly before midnight one of the thunderstorms in the area swept down on them, soaking but also cooling them down. The rain also erased all the tracks on the road.

When the moon went down Athan called a halt and had the men feed and water their mounts and then eat themselves. He decided to stop for a few hours of rest. He had hoped to overtake Jonathan by now; the others must have made better time than Athan had thought they would.

The sun was just lightening the eastern horizon when they remounted and headed down the coast road at a brisk pace. The sun had not been up for an hour before they come to what had probably been the hoplites' campsite. Athan was encouraged at the distance they had covered and hoped to catch up to Simeon and Jonathan before much longer. Their comrades were also apparently also moving fast. The four men were not able to easily follow the other bands' tracks after they passed a small herd of cattle being driven east to market in Kadakoy.

Athan spent the morning running over the time and distance calculations in his mind. He estimated they had at least a five-parasang head start on his pursuers. The cavalry had apparently ridden hard the day before, and Athan knew that there were few acceptable remounts to be had in the city. This meant the cavalry would be riding horses that were not fresh. Making up a five-parasang lead on another mounted group that was also moving fast as possible would not be easy. The animals would have a hard time maintaining a hot pace for very long. Athan was cautiously optimistic that they could stay ahead of the pursuit if they were not delayed somehow.

It was well late before they finally caught up to Jonathan's three bands just as they had finished setting up camp at the 'golden campsite' where they had hidden the 30 talents of gold.

Athan lost no time in sending back two of his men on horses to set up a watch on their back trail with a set of signals to warn of approaching riders. He found Jonathan, Simeon, Maur, and Philip searching the site of their old campsite in preparation for recovering the buried gold. The marks of the old camp were far from clear after all that time. Still, the men were confident they could puzzle out the location of the treasure. Simeon and Philip seemed unconcerned to learn that the troop of Imperial cavalry was less than a day behind them.

"We will find it tonight and be gone by the time they get here," said Simeon confidently.

Jonathan and Maur were less confident and more worried. They discussed various options. It was agreed that the cavalry was unlikely to come on them after dark, and if they left early enough they could stay ahead of the Achaemendians. Simeon and Philip convinced the others to continue the search. This cache had been buried on hard shingle, farther than usual from the beach. Even though Athan was not sure they could find the cache soon enough, they persuaded him to send Etor out with some spears to help them poke into the earth.

He found the camp in turmoil. Everyone seemed to know about 1) the pilfered gold, and 2) that the Achaemendians were in pursuit. Some wanted a share of the gold, others wanted to decamp and flee at once. Athan took immediate and positive measures to stop the developing chaos. He assured the men that the cavalry was at least a day behind them and that there were watches posted well back, so they would not be surprised in the night. He glossed over the demands for a share of the gold with vague promises of additional bonuses, not because they earned it by helping steal the gold, but to compensate them for the additional danger and inconvenience. Had they not all been provided a horse which was now theirs to keep? Not one man objected to the actual theft. Indeed, there was widespread admiration for such a cleaver caper. Athan promised them that they would be leaving before first light. Had he himself not stayed well ahead of their pursuers all day today? In two more days they would be at Xanthi, where they could scatter to the four winds. And if that did not suit them, tomorrow afternoon he personally would be on a little road heading north into the Rhodpe mountains from where he intended to move on into Macedonia and points west. Any of them would be welcome to join him. He elicited endorsements from the members of his band. He cajoled them about the freedoms of life in the hills, this time with a nice little nest egg to sustain them. It even sounded convincing to him.

The men were used to being told what to do on the march when so they obeyed when Athan ended his pitch and gave them orders: feed and care for their mounts, stay alert on watch, wake the company up before first light, be ready to move and move out fast as soon as they could see to pack up.

"What about Simeon and those others?" called out a man, "what are they doing?"

"Looking to make us all even richer," responded Athan. "Don't worry about them."

Thus began a nervous night; it was cloudy and time passed slowly. Athan wished he had one of those sand glasses that marked the half hours. He made many rounds of the sentries to ensure they were alert. When he did take a few moments to rest he dozed fitfully, never even taking off his sandals. He made three trips down to where Simeon and his crew were working. Despite a well-organized and efficient system with the line of men walking side by side thrusting spears into the ground every few feet, they had yet to discover any of the buried treasure.

"I am certain no one has been here before us," said a confident Simeon shortly after they started work, "the ground has not been disturbed. In fact it appears as though no one camped up here at all since we left. The ground is hard; perhaps we are just not looking deeply enough." Athan just looked at him. "I am certain this is the right place," continued Simeon to the unspoken question. "Don't you think so?"

"Yes," agreed Athan, who then turned and walked back to camp.

All that long night Athan kept expecting Philip to return and call for pack animals to load up the gold they had found. The last time Athan returned to where Simeon and his gang had been working all night, he was a very worried man. He joined a group of five tired men, standing beside what looked like a plowed field. They had not discovered a trace of the thirty talents located somewhere just beneath them.

"We have to go," said Athan, stating the obvious. "It will be light soon. Even if you found it right now we could not get it out of the ground and onto the animals before the cavalry would be on us. No," he raised a hand to stop Simeon's protest, "we cannot stop and fight them. First, they are too many, but more importantly, they don't have to defeat us, they just keep us from getting away until they send to the garrisons in Xanthi. We have almost 24 talents. It is enough, let's go."

"Brother, there are 30 talents of gold here, right under our feet," Simeon's eyes were red in the light of the lamp Athan had carried with him. In his voice there was pleading and, beyond that frustration. "We just need a little more time. Do not miners spend years digging gold from rock? This is mere dirt." The little speech sounded like something that had been said many times before on this long night.

"They will be here soon," explained Athan gesturing with the lamp back to the east. "Let it go."

"We can find a place of concealment and come out after they have passed," responded Simeon. The other men had gathered around, their shapes looming in the dim light of the lantern.

"We are too many," said Athan. He was speaking to him as though he were consoling a parent on the loss of a child. "We cannot hope to just hide three score men and almost a hundred donkeys, horses, and mules. They are following our tracks, you know that."

"Yes," immediately responded Simeon. It was clear he had been thinking hard about the problem and had come up with a solution; one that would not be welcome. "We will stay here. Six can hide up in the hills until it is quiet and then we can come down and recover our gold."

"No," it was Jonathan who replied. "I will not wait with you. I have to get out of Stavros before the word gets out. Otherwise I may never make it home. The Ionian cities will almost certainly have to make up the difference in tribute from what we took. They will be searching for us too, just as soon as they find out about the theft. How can we get 30 talents of gold past so many who are looking for it? What good is gold if you cannot get it to your family?" Maur nodded his agreement.

To Athan's surprise, Etor and Philip seemed to favor Simeon's plan. They knew that it was risky; even so they were willing to make the gamble. Athan was not happy with the plan, for he knew that once separated, there was no real expectation of ever seeing his friends again, no matter what happened. On the other hand, he could clearly see the three men were truly gripped by gold fever, and they would not leave their cache by anything less than main force.

Athan tried to use a golden lure. "If you stay, we may not be able to get together and divide our shares later. Will you let us take what we have with us until we can reunite?"

The plan did not work; Simeon had become so obsessed with his buried gold he was willing to let the gold in hand escape in exchange for the larger cache in the earth. Jonathan, Athan and Simeon stepped away from the other three men to confer on how to handle the division of both men and gold. In a few moments an agreement was struck.

Jonathan provided the catalyst by reaffirming that he had always said he would be satisfied with 10 talents; he grinned as he said it. Athan then said he was willing to give up his share of the 30 undiscovered talents. Simeon might be addled but he had shared life and death with the two men facing him, and they were his friends. He agreed to let them have his share of the gold they had already recovered in exchange for all of the gold still here. Athan then offered him half a talent of gold, two ingots, 'to cover expenses.'

"Make it four ingots," bargained Simeon with a cocky smile.

"Done," said Athan at once.

"Oh, brother of mine, you will never make a merchant," chuckled Simeon.

"There is one more problem," said Athan raising his voice to speak to the other three men who had been listening silently, "I think Maur is coming with the rest of us." The man nodded concurrence. "How about you Philip, and you Etor?" Both men indicated they would be staying for a share of the larger horde. "But three men can not manage 30 talents of gold. That much weight would require either six or seven horses or a couple of wagons. You will need some extra men to keep you from being robbed by those dangerous hill brigands." He smiled at the reference to his recent occupation.

"I will see if anyone up there in the camp will stay," said Simeon. "May I choose three or four volunteers?"

"Of course," said Athan, blowing out the lantern that was now no longer needed in the predawn light. "Let's go ask them."

The camp was almost completely struck, and the men were rapidly preparing for departure by the time they returned. The three captains first called Rodas over and assembled the men while Philip, Maur, and Etor scrambled to collect their gear and prepared to depart. As the sun began to break over the horizon, Athan explained the situation to the men: they had stolen gold from the tribute they had been protecting (which everyone already knew) and there was another cache near here (which everyone also knew) but they had not yet relocated it. The problem became quickly clear to everyone: stay and take the risk of getting trapped or leave the extra gold behind. Some men started asking about the size of their shares and general hubbub ensured.

Athan used his command voice to silence the men. "It is very simple," he continued in a penetrating voice, "stay with Simeon or come with Jonathan," here he glanced at Rodas who nodded, "and Rodas and me. Any payments will be worked out later. We have no more time. Mount up and follow one group or the other."

With that he walked over to Simeon and gave him a quick hard embrace. Then he moved over to his pony which had been saddled for him, mounted, signaled to the sentry watching their back trail, and turned his horse to the west. Simeon and Jonathan watched him for a moment. Tears flowed from both men as they shared a deep embrace, then Jonathan also mounted his horse which was held for him by Maur and followed the rest of the men and horses down the road.

At least a dozen men stayed behind to talk with Simeon. When the rear guard came past, he was quickly brought up to date on the division of the party. The guard never dismounted, continuing down the road to catch up to Athan's band, which was moving briskly down the road. After a brief hesitation, about half of the men around Simeon joined the sentry and rode to rejoin the main party. Those remaining behind mounted up and led their few pack animals down the coast road for a short distance before turning north and heading into the concealing hills.

Athan pushed his somewhat reduced band west as hard as he dared. He knew that he would need a good head start over their pursuers before the band reached the little trail he remembered diverted from the coast road up to the mountains. That was where the bands would have to split again. He had seen the trail when they spent two days laying up in the lee of the little headland where the treasure ship had almost come to grief. He knew that shepherds used the trail to get their flocks down from the hills. The intersection was about five parasangs farther on from the camp, and Athan intended to get there before noon.

Athan was sure he had forever lost his best friend that morning. Now he urged the pace with the unhappy expectation of losing another old friend by noon. Athan and Jonathan rode together talking of old times, current plans and future hopes. Riding together, moving up and down the line, they were able to speak to every man and determine the general mood of the bands. Athan could offer immediate safety (or something like it) to those who chose to accompany him north into the hills. Jonathan offered a quicker, more direct return home by outrunning the news of their theft along the coast road. Fortunately the wind had been light and from the west, so it was reasonable to assume no boats from the east had gotten ahead of them. As was expected, most of men decided to follow their own band, though some family men decided to risk the rapid return with Jonathan, and others without any prospects in the southwest, decided to head north with Athan. Rodas informed Athan that he and his men had decided to cast their lot with Athan and his band that would be turning north.

Despite Athan's urging for speed, it was just after noon before they arrived at the split in the trail. As they were approaching the trailhead to the northern road, a heavy thunderstorm grumbled over them from the west. The men dismounted and led their tiring beasts through the downpour. Though it cooled the air, it only added to the increasing melancholia that seemed to infect the men. As soon as the rain stopped, they called a halt to feed and water the livestock and themselves. After confirming that the scouts had seen nothing behind them, Athan ordered the division of the personal goods and stores. This was the first time most of the men had actually seen the gold. It created quite a stir. The men had known they were carrying gold, but to actually see it being divided, to know some of it was their share, prompted a variety of responses from wild hilarity to suspicious stares and avaricious glances. Some thought to protest when Jonathan took only 10 talents of the gold instead of eleven and a half, the amount offered by Athan.

"I said I would be happy with ten talents," he repeated again laughing at his own words. "I will not tempt the fates and take more."

Jonathan was determined to move on as soon as he could divide the spoils. With so much money available, details such as the ownership of specific horses or bits of harness seemed positively petty. Jonathan was generous; he expected he might have to have to get rid of the animals as soon as he reached Stavros and hire a boat to take him, his men and their goods south and west. In any event, he was more interested in taking the animals that were in the best condition at the moment rather than the overall quality of the beasts. He took only a few pack animals, enough for the gold, some possessions, and food for a day. He hoped to be in Stavros before sunset the following day and he would either be riding or sailing southwest the day after that with all the supplies and equipment he needed. The men ate their dried fruit and flat bread while they worked, some glancing with concern at the sentry who was watching from atop a nearby dune for any signs of pursuers.

All too soon, Jonathan had the remains of his band formed up. He was weeping again as he embraced his old friend, "Goodbye, 'Father',," he told Athan. Rodas, who did not know of the deception Jonathan and Athan had used when they attacked Azziz' camp so long ago, looked startled. Jonathan broke the embrace and took another long look at Athan. As Jonathan mounted his horse, Athan reached down to pick up one of the heavy quarter talent gold ingots and tossed it up to him.

"Here," he told Jonathan as his friend juggled the unexpected weight, "a little something extra for expenses."

Jonathan grinned and stuffed the gold ingot into has saddle bags, turned his horse, rode to the front of his band and then led them down the coast road at a canter.

Athan's remaining band began restowing gear that had been disarranged in the transfer and making preparations for their own departure up the little road into the mountains. The thought of the gold departing with Jonathan's men prompted Athan to take a stroll down to the beach to see if he could find the spot where Philip and Simeon buried the first seven talents of gold they had purloined. Athan had not actually been in the tent for this portion of the theft, and he was uncertain of just where the treasure tent had been erected. Time, wind and rain had erased virtually all traces of the encampment; however, the lay of the land seemed familiar to Athan as he stood on a low dune looking down on the deserted strand. He could not help himself from walking down to where he thought the treasure tent might have once stood.

As he walked down, a gust of wind tugged at his side from the departing thunderstorm which was still doing its best further down the coast. A glint in the sand caught his eye. Athan stopped dead. He felt a sense of unreality creeping over him. He was not a religious man; he disliked priests and all those stories of the gods and their escapades seemed vaguely ridiculous to him. Now looking down at the sand three paces ahead of him he saw the corner of a gold ingot sticking up and shining in the suddenly returned sunshine. For a long moment he stood there transfixed, then he abruptly stepped forward and began digging in the sand. As he removed the visible ingot his knife made contact with another just below the sand next to it. Clutching the quarter-talent ingot to his chest, Athan looked around somewhat wildly. To the west, Jonathan's men were out of signal range; to the east no pursuing cavalry was yet in sight. He drove his dagger into sand to mark the spot and turning, broking into a clumsy run back to where his men who were preparing to depart in their turn.

"Rodas, I need two more pack horses to the beach! We just got a little richer!"

Athan's men were well up the track leading into the hills when they saw the dust over the Imperial cavalry headed west down the coast road. The advance warning allowed Athan to get his men and the pack train out of sight, leaving only a single rearguard, Theron, posted on a fresh horse where he could observe what happened when the patrol reached the spot where the bands had split.

While he retreated with the band, Athan pushed scouts out well ahead to make sure the trail did not just peter out into some pastures, leaving them nowhere to run. Athan knew that the farther they could get into these hills, the safer they would be. He intended to make haste, but with care. There was no need to flee at top speed; this was a controlled withdrawal. Athan waited near the back of the column for reports from his rear guard on how the cavalry would react when they saw the tracks of some horsemen continuing west down the road and others headed up into the hills. He was almost certain their pursuers would split up with at least some following his band's clear tracks up the track into the hills.

Part of Athan wished that the Imperial cavalry would follow the path of least resistance, continuing straight to Xanthi, and leave Athan and his band alone. Putting himself in the place of the pursuers he knew that they would come to the obvious conclusion that honest merchants and other travelers do not turn aside from the main road and head for the hills. Logically, at least some of the enemy would turn and follow his band, so Athan prepared to lead them on a merry chase. He was fairly certain that the pursuers had few supplies with them and their horses would be tired. He was certain that he could avoid being beaten by cavalry in this rough ground so long as he maintained discipline and had a line of withdrawal.

Athan did not have long to wait to find out that the cavalry commander had decided. Theron was seen coming up fast making his signal of 'enemy behind' superfluous. The leading Achaemendian scouts soon made contact with Athan's retreating forces and before sunset no fewer than three score Imperial horsemen were visible coming over the far hill. Theron reported that although he was not sure, he thought that a few of the enemy had continued heading west and at least one was sent back east; undoubtedly a messenger reporting developments.

Athan made a great show of calmly setting camp on top of a gently rounded hill in full sight of the enemy horsemen. The track they were following came up the incline almost to the top before it wound around the hill and then continued on though a low pass to the north. Athan put alert sentries around the camp with another set on the track leading around the hill, and then allowed the men to unload their horses. Athan had made sure that the men had watered the animals and filled their water skins when the track crossed a stream earlier in their retreat. Now that they were in camp, he took special care that the beasts were well tended, sharing out the grain that still remained from the stock he had purchased in Kadakoy and letting the animals graze on the thin grass on the hill. At his evening council he set the schedule for the sentries, stressed the need for maintaining a sharp watch, reviewed plans for repelling a night attack and discussed plans for the following day. He then retired with the expectation of a busy night.

The Achaemendians did not disappoint him. There were several probing advances of the perimeter by dismounted men. These were not serious enough to cause him to rouse the entire troop. Then, about an hour before dawn, a group of horsemen tried to lead their mounts past the sentries on the track to get behind the camp. This led to some actual fighting, but the horsemen were at a severe disadvantage. It was a dark night and they could not use their projectile weapons effectively, nor could they exploit the mobility of their horses in the rough terrain, especially in the dark. The actual fighting was limited to a few brief encounters that all went to the hoplites.

The little bit of fighting did rouse the camp, and the men rose and began preparations for departure. Athan had stressed that they should take time to make sure all the animals were fed and watered and the loads were packed carefully to avoid chafing or slippage. Even taking the extra time, the men were ready to go before the sun had broken the horizon. It was well that they were well prepared for a difficult day, for the men chasing them did all they could to hinder, delay, harass, and block their movement deeper into the hills. Men uphill from their enemies have a significant advantage. Missile thrown or shot down have increased effect, while those below are usually ineffective. Charges rushing downhill can have an unstoppable inertia. Thus both sides worked to get their enemies below them. The two parties would accordion up and down the hills, the mounted hoplites dawdling upslope where they were safe while the Achaemendian cavalry remained as close as they dared. When the main body reached the top of the hill, the hoplites would set a rear guard that would hold back the horsemen until the rest of the band had started up the far slope. Then those men holding back the enemy would scurry over the hill and retreat in a hasty but disciplined formation. The cavalry could not overrun the band as long as they remained in a compact body, so they tried to get around ahead of the retreating band and cut them off before they could get down the hill and start up the next slope.

All that day the horsemen menaced the band, probing, trying to pick off stragglers and making feints to see if they could break up the formations. It was nervous, dangerous work and required considerable patience, courage and above all, experienced warriors who knew their craft.

As Athan's band withdrew north, the countryside became rougher and wilder. They passed no water that day and began to ration their supply. But they were carrying both food and water, so that when they camped on the second night at the crest of a steep set of hills, the men and their animals had a real opportunity to eat, drink, rest, and recover.

The next day the Achaemendians were fewer and much less aggressive. Their horses were obviously played out; on two occasions, the band saw hard-used horses collapse under their riders. By the third day only a few riders were keeping watch on them as the hoplites intersected a real road and turned west. The band camped peacefully that night in a meadow with a small pool which was obviously used by passing caravans. The next morning, still watched by only a handful of riders, they continued west, passing one small caravan heading east and overtaking another headed west. In both cases, the body of armed men with so little dunnage made the members of the other caravans very nervous. By the time they camped that night, Athan and Rodas were wondering how long it would be before they left northern Thrace and entered Macedonia. It hardly mattered, for there were no border guards or passes required, the demarcation line being rather casual.

The following day they entered a town where there was a small market. There Athan used some of their freshly minted gold coins to reprovision, exchange some of the animals for better stock, and purchase some donkey carts.

When they left the following day they almost appeared like a normal caravan having picked up two other groups of fellow travelers. They had far more scouts than a normal caravan, however. In particular, these scouts watched two Achaemendian horsemen who were watching them. The two continued to trail the band from a careful distance all the way across Thrace, over the river Strymon into Macedonia. The distant horsemen were still watching when Athan's men left the Macedon city of Therma, now up-equipped to include not just carts, but wagons as well. The watchers were more discrete but there were still occasional sightings of what might have been Imperial scouts, even after the caravan took the ferry over the Axius River. The distant observers did not leave until the caravan entered the Macedonian metropolis of Pella.

Old King woke up abruptly. His little lair was completely dark again, the kind of thick darkness that happens in the middle of a heavy overcast winter night. From the stillness he deduced it was snowing again. When would this winter end? He was not sleepy in the least. Even though it was probably still the middle of the night he decided to rekindle the fire. He built the fire up until it actually heated up the little crevice and provided a warm cheery light. Then the old man melted some ice; there was plenty just outside the entrance of the cave, and drank his fill. He stared into the fire, wrapped in his bedding. 'It did not do to get comfortable', he thought.

Comfort could trap a man, take away his drive. Like a child's hoop, a man needed to keep moving or he fell over.

Despite all his grim thoughts he found himself smiling at some of the memories of that 'comfortable time' in Pella. It had been a wild time. In truth, having that much fun had been exhausting.

Chapter Seventeen- Retirement

Athan was perturbed to find out that easy riches did not result in an easy life. Some of his old problems were gone, but they were replaced by a greater number of different ones. He discovered that he had to spend more time and energy keeping money than he ever had trying to get it in the first place. Further, he still had people who were dependent on him, and they all had problems, which by extension became his.

His band of about two score men had finally stopped their westward trek in Pella, a promising city in Macedonia, about ten parasangs northeast of the royal capital. There was already talk that the King of Macedonia might move his court up to Pella. For now, however, it remained a non-royal but prosperous city. Athan had contracted with a wealthy merchant family to lease their villa, a compound actually, for the remainder of the summer.

So forty hearty hoplites moved into their new home, not without considerable conflict concerning who would share what space in which room. Located outside the walls to the west of the city in a suburb of other large family estates, the buildings were in the characteristic hollow square, with residences on three sides and space for animals on the far end. Athan took the suites on the second level next to the strong room where he deposited his golden talents. One of the first things he did was hire a coiner to convert three of the quarter-talent bars into coins. With this he was able to pay his men and cover other pressing expenses. He quickly found that now that he was rich, everything seemed to become so expensive!

His men, paid what would be triple wages for a year, set a poor example. The courtyard was filled with hairdressers, musicians, wine merchants, haberdashers, prostitutes, hawkers, and anyone else who could think of a way to cash in on the unexpected sudden wealth from the hoplites. The house quickly became well known for a wide variety of entertainments, mostly of the lower variety. It became necessary for a guard to be set, not just on the storeroom, where the treasure was kept, but even on the entrance to the compound itself, just to control the chaos. There was grumbling about 'shares' and a general experience of all the unhappiness sudden wealth can bring. After a little over a month of loose discipline and riotous living, three events shocked the men back into sense.

It was not surprising that with money in their pockets and little to do, that after a month or two of this life some of the men decided to leave the band. Two men from Athan's band and another from Rodas' old band, who had grown up in neighboring villages decided that they wished to cash in their shares, leave the band and retire back to the homes of their youth. Athan and Rodas tried to dissuade them; they persisted in their request to leave. Others were watching to see if they, too, could leave. Athan felt his grip on his men beginning to weaken. In the end he lived up to his share of the agreement he had maintained with the men: they could request to leave and return home whenever the band was in camp and not under immediate threat. The villa certainly qualified as a camp, and the men were certain that their days of living under constant threat were over. So one fine autumn morning the three headed out of town, each with an additional bonus of a full year's salary. They rode ponies and were accompanied by two other acquaintances from town who led the pack animals.

This departure sobered the men began to think about how they would spend the rest of their lives now that their wild days as brigands were over. This decision was made for two of the men - they spent the rest of their lives right where they were. Two days after the departure of first three men, two other members of the band did not return from an excursion into town. This was not especially worrisome as the musters had become fairly slack; but one of the men, Adrastus, a good man who had been with Athan off and on since the Debacle, was scheduled to stand watch that afternoon. His friends went looking for him and were met halfway to into town by friends from town bearing bad news. The bodies of the two men had been found in an alley. This was troubling for a variety of reasons. The two men had been armed. They were not carrying a great deal of money. And they had apparently been killed before they had arrived at their intended destination, the house where their girlfriends lived. That meant they had been killed before it was fully dark and probably had still been sober when they were attacked. The streets of any city were dangerous at night, but Pella had a good reputation and murders were uncommon. What set everyone talking was the lack of motive for the murders. Why would anyone attack two stout armed hoplites that had little to steal and would be expected to make a vigorous defense? There was something else very odd about the murders; the men had been killed by arrows, and then the bodies dragged out of sight. This was unheard of in the streets. The town was still buzzing two days later went the next load of bad news arrived.

A caravan arrived with a two extra ponies and a story. They had come on the scene of an ambush. Five men had been camped along the road in a spot often used for that purpose. The road was well traveled, but that night the men had apparently not camped with other travelers. Three of the men had died near their beds. One, perhaps a sentry, had died next to a tree where he had evidently been standing too lax a guard. Four of the men had died from arrows, not the normal weapon of bandits in this area. What was worse was that one of the hoplites had apparently only been wounded. He had been tied to a tree and cut up with a knife before someone had finally cut his throat. Two of the ponies had apparently broken from the picket line and were wandering in the area when the eastbound caravan made the gristly discovery. Once again it was more than a merely unusual attack. The assailants had used arrows to kill when they could have simply overwhelmed the sleeping men and taken what they needed without murdering them. They apparently deliberately kept one man alive long enough to torture him apparently for information. But what could they want to know? All the goods were taken, but the killers did not make even the relatively minor effort to recapture the two stray ponies. What kind of bandits were these? It almost seemed as though they were more interested in killing than in stealing.

That was what the men in the band thought, too. Every man was well aware of the way the Achaemendians had tracked them almost all the way to Pella. They also knew that Empire's cavalry favored the bow. The men stopped going into town after dark, and Athan set a second guard on the compound walls. There was unease throughout the once carefree compound, and not a little concern. There was no way to tell how the situation might have ultimately played out had not the third major event, far greater in import than the first two, not overwhelmed all other considerations. On a sparking fall day, urgent news arrived in Pella from a dozen sources. The Achaemendian Empire had invaded Macedonia.

They held a council of war for all the men, almost two score of serious faces arranged around Athan and Rodas. Athan put their choices to them. They could stay where they were and hope that this was a fall raid intended to capture plunder or aimed at the capital. But the murder of five of their comrades had convinced most of the men that though they might be gone, they were not forgotten. They no longer felt comfortable in Pella and did not want to stay. They could join up with the Macedonian army as mercenaries and fight the invaders. There was not much enthusiasm for that idea either. This was not their country and the Empire was apparently coming in great strength. That left the third option, one that had served them well during their entire careers: when faced by a powerful opponent, head for the hills.

After a short debate the men all agreed it would be best if they took their leave of Pella. Athan and his officers immediately went into a council of war and began planning their departure. If it was not a full retreat, it was at best a prudent retirement.

Later that morning, Athan took three men and walked into several of the major merchant houses. All were scenes of intense activity. It did not take long to find employment for his band to as caravan guards escorting a caravan heading away from the invaders. Although the reputation of his men was far from spotless, he was a relatively known quantity. His men would escort two of the merchants who would be leaving in two days for the city of Aegae and possibly beyond. Each of the merchants would have their own retainers with them and would bring an additional dozen guards. Athan gave them favorable terms for his protection, since everyone suspected that his band would he leaving regardless. Athan chose not to buy any additional animals for the journey as the prices of live and rolling stock had skyrocketed. Fortunately, the band still had their ponies, carts, and wagons, and was action ready to depart the next morning.

Since they were already prepared for departure, Athan declared their last day in Pella to be a feast day. The men were able to convince some of the cooks and other entertainers to come out to the compound. Girlfriends and women of professional affection thronged to the feast, looking for excitement, a final goodbye, or just a chance to earn a bit of extra traveling money. There was a wild gaiety about this final feast, with an entire ox roasted on a spit, good wine flowing freely, and women dancing shamelessly with men to the beat of a professional group of musicians. Most of Athan's men did not go to bed at all but merely shifted to final preparations for departure as the sun began to come up the next day.

The caravans departing the city took on the aspect of a small exodus. Athan's people were the first to the agreed-upon departure site in a meadow just west of the suburbs. People had been leaving the city since early dawn; Athan's men rested beside the carts and wagons of their company watching them pass. The other members of the caravan did not appear until the sun was well on its way to noon. Athan immediately saw part of the reason for their tardy arrival; there were no less than a dozen wagons drawn by oxen. Oxen are strong, steady beasts, capable of pulling great loads, docile and easy to manage, but they are very slow. With most beasts of burden, horses, ponies, mules, even donkeys, it is possible to adjust the length of each day's journey from four to five or even occasionally six parasangs if the road was good, making it much easier to camp in better locations. Oxen can not be hurried. They would pull their loads for three parasangs and not much more. It was possible to get a little more distance from them, but not for two days in a row. Even a child walking could keep up alongside a wagon pulled by oxen. Perhaps this was fortunate, because the caravan was looking like more of an evacuation than a trading venture.

The man who was most unhappy at the sight of the oxen was the guide Athan hired to lead them out of Pella and into the west. It hardly required a guide to find Aegae, but Athan had plans to go significantly farther, and so this man was necessary. His name was Talos of Pella. His appearance was a bit unusual; he had short bow legs, large ears that protruded from the side of his head, and was almost completely bald, with only a fringe of curly hair around his bald pate. This was compensated somewhat by a fine, full, curly black beard, still, the overall impression was distinctly odd. He was well recommended as a guide, claiming to have a better knowledge of the ground west of Pella than any man living. No one Athan found could dispute this. But those who knew him also smiled when they discussed his personal habits. He kept to himself, was abrupt, jerky, and distinctly strange in his relations with others. Yet he was also considered honest and competent, even if no one could name a man who considered him a close friend. Athan decided that this Talos fellow would do; of course, he was not only the most experienced guide he could find, he was the only one available who claimed to know the way all the way across Macedonia to Lake Lychnites and even beyond.

Considering that many of the people on the road headed west that day were leaving behind their homes and businesses in the face of an invading army, the mood was surprisingly upbeat. Most people were confident that, either the Macedonian army would defeat the Imperial incursion, or the enemy would only make a small advance and retreat with the onset of winter. Even if the Empire did take Pella, there were worse things than being in the Achaemendian Empire. Once the conquest of the city (with its initial high potential for pillaging and rape) was completed, the people could come back and do business in

414

security. They would simply be paying taxes to a different set of rulers. At the moment they had their goods, their families were together (for many of the merchants had brought their families to avoid the possible troubles), the weather was fine, and it was for many a most excellent adventure.

Athan, on the other hand, could not help feeling concerned. He knew that the presence of his band, instead of deterring attack, might actually invite it. In the back of his mind, he could not help wondering if the invasion was somehow connected to the loss of part of the tribute from the Ionian cities. The Empire could not be that concerned about a mere burglary, and if so, certainly that Satrap fellow would be the one blamed for the loss. He was probably either dead or in a dungeon somewhere along with Drogas. Athan felt a bit bad about Drogas, who was also probably in considerable difficulties; he had not been a bad sort. But Athan had no sympathy at all for that little snit of a Satrap. Athan certainly hoped he had been removed from his province. This invasion of the kingdom where the robbers had fled could have nothing to do with the lost tribute could it? No, of course not, invasions took a long time to prepare. His men had probably been murdered by a few Achaemendian cavalrymen who had deserted, become brigands and were looking for some of the loot from the highjacked tribute.

Nevertheless, when the caravan came to camp that evening just less than halfway to Aegae, Athan set a strong set of sentries, one at each corner of the camp. Additionally one man was assigned to walk between the stations, and there was an acting sergeant of the guard stationed near the center of the camp. Since these guards were in addition to the guard each merchant might also have around their own encampment, there were protests that this would require too many watches depriving the guards of sleep. Athan let Rodas deal with the objections. The stocky redhead faced down those who dared to complain and ensured them that any sentry who did not maintain an alert watch would be beaten and then expelled from the camp without pay. He went on to detail specific duties of each band of guards in the event of an alarm.

"There is an army back there," he told the now cowed merchants and their guards. "That means there will be lots of bandits and masterless men of all kinds in these hills. Do you think they don't know there are rich pickings ahead of an army? Do you think they don't know that fat merchants with their goods leave the safety of their cities and move ahead of an invasion? Do you think they don't know your families will be with you? Think of how much the ransom will be to recover your wives and children?"

The merchants directed their guards to stand the watches as ordered by the caravan master.

In fact, though there were no fewer than eight men standing watch at any given time in the night and with over three score fighting men to share the duties, the requirements were far from onerous. Athan was delighted to discover one of the merchants had an hour glass, so he was able to regulate the length of watches with greater certainty.

When they moved on the next day, Athan put out patrols ahead and to either side to watch for ambushes. This was probably unnecessary as there were so many people on the road headed west that there was no real danger of being surprised. Athan's caravan alone had total of over a hundred men who could wield a sword or spear, and furthermore, along the road caravans came to each other's defense. So they plodded west in some security, being overtaken by more lightly burdened parties, each with fresh news of momentous events to the east. They stayed beneath the low walls of Aegae the next night. One of the merchants decided that this was far enough for safety and set up his goods for an extended stay. The other was bound for Armissa and then Cellae, two smaller towns to the west, planning on doing business in each. To Athan's frustration, they not only took a full day to travel the three parasangs between the cities, but they were persuaded to wait there an extra day while the merchants did business. He gritted his teeth and also engaged in trade with what goods he had. Though he was making a tidy profit, he regretted the real cost, the lost time.

After a day of business in Cellae, their caravan headed for Heraclea, a town three days journey to the northwest, where the merchant intended to make an lengthy stay, remaining with members of his extended family, trading and keeping an eye on events back home in Macedonia. He expected to return after things settled down before the winter snows closed the roads. The scenery since their departure from Pella had gone from lovely to spectacular. They were traveling up a wide valley with wild and seriously high mountains on either side; Mt. Bernius dominated the scenery to the south and Mt. Borus to the north. There was a narrow line of thin clouds running across Mt. Borus just below the summit, giving the mountain the improbable appearance of some giant maiden peering over a diaphanous veil. The road tended steadily upward, making a trip of three parasangs a hard all-day trudge for the oxen. As they climbed the air grew cooler. The trees were making a fine show of their fall colors, making the onset of winter not just a distant inevitability, but a real and present event that would come all too soon.

On the first day after leaving Cellae, the seventh day of travel, they learned from a passing rider that a column of Achaemendian troops had arrived at Pella. Later that day, another group not only confirmed this but brought news that the Macedonian army had been beaten in a battle and other Imperial forces were en route to the royal capital. The next day a group with only pack animals and no wagons arrived in their camp with more news: Pella had fallen.

Actually, the city had been occupied following a negotiated surrender. The travelers did not know how the occupation was going, since they had left as soon as the terms had been announced. The answer to that question came the next evening, when they were passed by four men on tired ponies. Things were not too bad in Pella, and the invaders seemed to be behaving themselves. These four had left in a hurry when they discovered that they were on a list of proscribed individuals that agents of the empire were seeking. They had declined to wait to find out just exactly why the grim men wanted a word with them, and chose to leave that very night. The really bad news was that they had left only three days before. That meant that a hard-riding troop of cavalry could come up to the caravan by tomorrow evening.

"Fourteen parasangs," fumed Athan to Rodas that evening. "Seven days out and we are only fourteen parasangs from the city. We are just waddling along. We are ripe for the taking."

Rodas was taking a calmer view of the matter, "We don't even know if they are coming this way. After all, there really isn't much out here to interest them. And don't say 'us' because they probably don't even know we exist."

"They know," rejoined Athan grimly. "If Achaemendian agents killed five of us when they didn't even hold the city, think what they will do with an army. I didn't think they would care this much about a score of talents."

"Rather more than a score," put in Rodas blandly, "perhaps it is the principle of the thing. They can't let a pack of bandits rob from their Emperor, now can they?"

"Who is this Emperor, anyway?"

"To be honest, I don't even know there is an Emperor," said Rodas, remaining calm, "and I am certain he knows nothing about his loss. No, I suspect there is someone less important but still powerful and very determined behind this pursuit, if pursuit it is."

"Oh, it's a pursuit all right;" replied Athan, and we both know someone who would go to the ends of the earth to avoid being humiliated."

"The Satrap," confirmed Rodas.

"But I must tell you brother," confessed Athan, "I am not sure what to do next. I knew they would try to come after us, but even I did not expect them to invade Macedonia. Do you think they will go after Attica if Jonathan made it down there?"

"We do not know that they invaded Macedonia just because we pinched some of one of their colony's tribute. Seriously, that seems all out of proportion doesn't it?"

"Well, yes," admitted Athan, "but it might have tipped the balance, made them move their timetable forward or something. That is not what matters to me." Athan leaned forward and looked Rodas directly in the eye. "Brother, what are we going to do next? I always have had a way out in the past. All my life, if I ran into a problem, I always either wait things out or run away."

"So why don't you? Why don't we ride out tomorrow morning and leave these ox-bound slugs behind us?"

Athan shifted and looked uncomfortable. "I am their caravan master. I took their money and have responsibility for these people."

"Why did you take their money?" interrupted Rodas. "And you chose to sell some of the goods back there in Pella before we left. Aren't we rich enough now?"

"You can never be rich enough," chuckled Athan. Then, serious again, he answered, "I arranged to be paid for guiding the caravan and sold those goods we were leaving behind because that is what people expected me to do. If I had done anything else people would have noticed, wondered, remarked on it. I have enough people knowing I am rich without being rich and with a reputation as an easy mark. Besides, we went through a lot of money in Pella. I don't even know where it went. We spent almost three talents in a month an a half. What do we have to show for it?"

"Well, I myself had a pretty good time," drawled Rodas.

"Right," grunted Athan with a quick flicker of a smile. "What do we do if the Empire really is looking for us? I mean looking for us in a fairly serious way."

"You **have** been doing a lot of thinking," commented Rodas. "Responsibilities of command and whatnot, I suppose. Well, I have been thinking on it, too. I talked to the boys about it, too. Do you remember Theron? He has always been the best hunter in my band. Theron is from north of Illyria. Are you familiar with that area?"

"Yes," replied Athan grimly. He did not tell his friend that troops from Illyria had been part of the alliance that had come south to help overwhelm Epiria.

"Well," continued Rodas without noticing his captain's expression, "anyway he is from that part of the world and says that there are a lot of little kingdoms over there. He says that any time a man sets himself up in a hold or fort somewhere and has a bit of land under his control, he can declare himself to be a king. Theron says there are lots of little places like that in northern and western Illyria. Says it is good country, too; rich land, winters are not too hard, and, best of all, no empires."

"No civilization, either," remarked Athan sourly.

"You know, Chief, we aren't all that civilized ourselves. Besides, with enough money we can buy a fair amount of civilization and have it delivered. Remember, we are rich." Neither man noticed that Rodas had unconsciously begun addressing Athan as a subordinate to a senior.

"So what are we supposed to do, find one of these little kingdoms and offer our services to the king?"

"Chief, you are thinking too small. We should set up our own kingdom. You can be king, and I will be your trusted chancellor and general." Rodas was grinning at Athan seated on the stool across from him in the tent. The lamp flickered as an early tendril of winter sent a draft across the space. Rodas was unprepared for his captain's silence. He watched his captain who was obviously deep in thought.

Athan suddenly broke the silence. "Just how will we conquer some kingdom? We have about two score men, not exactly an army."

Rodas put aside his easy bantering tone and became serious. "I don't know sir; I hadn't thought about conquering any existing kingdom. I was thinking maybe we could make one of our own or something. But no matter what, I think it can be done. I think you are the best chieftain of any band I have ever seen. I know that everyone who serves under you seems to come out all right. I still can't believe you pulled off stealing that gold without anyone knowing it." There was another long pause before he continued, "Chief, I have been thinking about this for a long time, even before I met you. I am not cut out to be a king. I know I am a good chieftain, but I like things that I can keep under control. That is part of the reason why I kept my band small. I didn't want the hassle of a big band. It is more trouble than it is worth. But I would like to have a place of my own, a real home, maybe with a family. My family is either dead or scattered to the winds. I want to be somewhere where I can make a difference; for my city and my own family. And the only way I can do that is to find a kingdom where I can influence the king; and the best chance I have to do that is to help get a kingdom started. I have been looking for a man who would make a good king." Here he leaned forward and stared directly into Athan's eyes, trying to persuade him by sheer intensity. "Chief, I think you are that man. They say when you were a captain of a city guard you won battles." Athan nodded. "Is it true you really killed a sorcerer priest and captured his entire caravan?"

Athan thought to explain more fully, but instead limited his answer to a nod.

Rodas' curiosity got the better of him, leading him momentarily off track, "And did you really capture eight beautiful dancing slave girls and then gave them away to your sergeants?"

"Well, yes, but they were more trouble than they were worth," said Athan dryly.

"Chief, I have watched you for months. You are a good leader. You could lead a kingdom, maybe a little kingdom but our kingdom. You might even settle down and start a dynasty."

"I had a family," put in Athan trying to change the subject.

Rodas would not let him off the hook. "Chief, how many men have you commanded at one time?"

Athan shrugged, "Perhaps a couple hundred," he replied indifferently.

Rodas was impressed, "You had a couple hundred? And you fought a battle in command of that many?"

Athan simply nodded.

"Chief, you are a good leader. You have experience with city government and real soldiers." Athan made to protest but Rodas rode over him. "You really take care of people; I mean you take responsibilities seriously. It is like you to worry about staying with this caravan when you may have a troop of Imperial cavalry after you. In addition to that you are a proven battle leader; you even know how to handle money." Athan looked at him in astonishment. "Yes, sir, think about it. You have had a real treasure in your control for over two months, and you still have most of it! You did not throw it away like most men would have. You paid everyone a reasonable share; enough money so there were not too many complaints, but not so much that the band splintered. You are holding back for a greater purpose, for the future."

Athan had shifted his gaze to the lamp. After a pause he drew in his breath and asked a question that answered Rodas'. "So just how to we set ourselves up as kings?"

Rodas grinned from ear to ear. "Just one king: you. I am going to be the chancellor and general."

"No, my friend, there is more work as a chancellor and general than you would care to do. You will be my magistrate. You seem to have a knack for solving disputes."

"Just a magistrate?" joked Rodas, his earlier bantering tone back. "I asked for two jobs?"

"All right," grinned Athan, "you said you wanted to bring in civilization; well, once we have this kingdom set up, you can be magistrate and inspector of all prospective dancing girls."

"Done," said Rodas and the two men leaned forward clasping arms to seal the bargain.

Somehow, once they had a plan and a destination, even a murky one, Athan's morale lifted and problems that had seemed insoluble just an hour before were quickly resolved. Athan called Pirro, the little redheaded spy, and three other men into his tent. Pirro and Ioannis were detailed to pick the best horses available and ride back to Cellae to find out what they could. They would let the band know if there were any problems coming up the road behind them.

"Like a whole troop of Achaemendian cavalry?" grinned Pirro.

"Something like that," admitted Athan with an answering grin. "So keep a good watch and don't get snapped up. I am more worried about a few scouts taking you unawares. Don't let that happen. Just spend one night there, finding out what you can and then catch up to us. Of course, if you do see a whole troop of cavalry charging up the road, come on back and let us know."

Athan assigned another pair of men to follow well behind Pirro and Ioannis to keep an eye on the two rear guards. They were Stamitos, one of the men from Endre's old band who had made the long ride out of Kadakoy with Athan, and Sergeant Nikolas. Nikolas had only recently been designated as a sergeant. He was a genuinely brave man, so he was cautioned about staying far back so they could not be captured with the leading pair. Nikolas and Stamitos were both excellent scouts. If anything bad was coming up the trail, Ioannis could signal back to the others who would have a big head start. That way, Ioannis and Pirro would have a chance to take evasive measures from the enemy troops while Nikolas and Stamitos raced back to warn the band. No one mentioned the real possibility that Ioannis and Pirro might also fall into an ambush and be taken. In either event the band would have warning of enemies behind.

"We can safely watch your demise at the hands of those barbarians, and be able to provide the details to the bards," teased Nikolas. All four men were in high spirits. Athan realized that standing guard around a bunch of plodding merchants was boring to them. These men had lived a life of adventure. That very summer they had taken part in a wild escape from the very clutches of the Empire; then they had had time to enjoy the fruits of their escapade. Now, riding in wild and beautiful country they were, like wolves, feeling the call of the wild. Adventure beckoned, the odds were in their favor, and they were more than ready for a little excitement.

The next day the scouts rode out, two by two, maintaining a good long distance even in sight of camp, heading down their back trail.

The other members of the band, even the new men who had joined the band in Pella, had caught the mood and were all in great good spirits. The other members of the caravan became distinctly nervous at this sudden change of attitude in their would-be guards. Athan and Rodas took pains to ride up and down reassuring their more peaceful fellow travelers. He also kept an additional rear guard remaining on the crest of each rise behind them watching for any of his riders returning to the band at speed. For the first time since they had first entered Macedonia, all their gold was moved from carts and loaded onto pack animals. In the event they had to flee, the band could abandon their remaining carts and wagons and move at speed ahead of any pursuit.

Athan remained conflicted about his duties to the caravan. In his mind he decided that if they were menaced by a weak force of pursuing enemy, he would try to stand them off to try to let the caravan escape. If they were attacked by several squadrons of Imperial cavalry the best thing Athan and his men could do would be to abandon their slower companions' vehicles and flee hoping the enemy would continue to chase him, and not stop to molest the caravan.

None of his precautions proved necessary. On the third day of travel, they arrived at Heraclea, the end of the line for many of the people traveling with them. Late the next morning, as Athan was negotiating with a group of travelers to travel on to Drucida, a town on the border between Macedonia and Illyria, he saw Nikolas and Stamitos, the first of his two sets of scouts arriving in town. Athan was immediately put at ease from their demeanor, and, in fact, Nikolas reassured him that Pirro was safe and sound and would be there to give him a full report within the hour. They could not resist spoiling the effect by telling him the gist of the stories they had picked up. There were reports of elements of the Imperial army headed down toward Cellae. But they were not moving rapidly and were apparently only an occupying force. There was no sign of a fast-moving troop of cavalry behind them. The pursuit, if there ever had been one, had apparently lost the trail. The four men on their fresh horses had covered the distance up to Heraclea in two days. They had at least three days head start on any possible pursuit, and from now on there would be no oxen in the caravan. They would be traveling light to get over the passes before winter set in.

And winter was coming. The men awoke the next morning to see a dusting of snow on the higher elevations of the Barnus Mountains to the south. Now they were more concerned about getting over the mountains and less with any potential enemies behind them. They spent that day selling the last of the wagons and buying instead provisions and winter clothing. They would need coats and cloaks, bedding and blankets for the upcoming winter no matter where they spent the season. Athan took obscure pleasure in discovering that, even with the expenses of the men and seasonal purchases, he had turned a small profit on the retreat from Pella. In the event this 'king' idea of Rodas' didn't work out, he could always become a caravan leader and trader to make a good living.

It was here that their guide Talos really became useful. Up until now his only use had been to let them know what the road ahead would be like and to advise them on good camping sites when they were not in towns where they could find lodging in houses or barns. Now, as the road became much less traveled, and towns even further apart his knowledge of the road ahead became really valuable.

Unencumbered by oxen and with only a few carts, the small caravan that departed the following day was able to make good time. Although it was almost as far from Heraclea to their next destination, Drucida, as it had been from Cellae to Heraclea, and the road was steeper and much worse, they made the trip in two easy days. After the distant hint of winter the days turned fine again, and the party of travelers, almost four score people including the fellow travelers, began to take the air of a holiday. It was almost like a bunch of men out for a camping trip. Their hunter, Theron, even brought down a stag one evening which he shared with the entire company.

Once they arrived in Drucida, the tenor of their journey changed. To reach the next planned destination, the town of Lychmidas, located well over the border into Illyria, they would have to jog north around a set of high mountains, more than doubling the distance a crow would need to reach their intended destination. There were no other parties going so far west, and the weather began to look threatening. They were already high enough to make men short of breath. These passes were normally closed once the winter storms set in. Athan and Rodas wanted to be well over them and established somewhere to the west before that happened.

When they departed the next day it was a very different type of travelers than those that had left Pella. They no longer looked like a well-guarded caravan; now they looked more like a war band on the march. Only two small groups had decided to travel with them. There was a heavy preponderance of armed men leading pack animals with only a few two-wheeled carts. There were no children and not many women.

Of the men in Athan's original band that departed Golibolu at the far end of Thrace that summer those with families had tended to remain with Jonathan on his dash to the west. There had been romantic attachments since then, and some of these women had left Pella with the band. Of those women only four still remained with them. Two were young women, who were probably pregnant and did not want to leave the fathers of their first child. Two were older women who had formed more or less comfortable attachments with veterans and had decided to hang on to what that had.

Only three women traveled with the fellow travelers who would be traveling to Lychmidas. All of those who started the climb up to the pass, both men and women, were less concerned at this point with transporting goods from one market to another than in getting over the mountains and into Lychmidas.

Talos confirmed that they were only about four or five parasangs from the pass. He assured them that it would take them a full day of hard traveling to reach the top. He recommended they plan on stopping a place he knew some distance short of the pass where travelers often camped before attempting the pass. Talos warned them that there was no place suitable for camp for a parasang on the far side of the pass. It was possible to rest at the saddle of the pass itself but the place was exposed. Cool breezes that were fine in the heat of summer became freezing gusts in late autumn. Further, he that recommended that they collect firewood on the way up and carry it with them as there would be little as they climbed higher. The combination of the steep rocky slopes and usage by other parties before them would make firewood difficult higher up.

"We will be glad to have a fire tonight," he said in his strange staccato voice. "It is always cold up there and colder than usual now."

Athan had begun to chafe at the repeated delays to their progress. They had not made one good day of traveling since leaving Pella, and even though he had no indications they were still being pursued, he was still nervous. The idea of stopping on the way over the pass in a lonely place selected by this strange guide unsettled him.

Rodas, too was uneasy, "How do we know we can trust him?" he whispered to Athan. "He has hardly spent any time with the main group at all; he is always going off ahead on his own."

"That is his job," replied Athan, "he is supposed to be looking for the way ahead. Besides we kept him under observation. Nobody ever saw him doing anything overtly suspicious."

"He talked to every eastbound caravan."

"Of course, he did. He asked them about the road ahead. We had men with him some of the time he talked with those caravan masters," Athan was trying to explain the man's behavior, though he had had the same thoughts that Rodas was now expressing.

"We didn't have men with him every time he talked to someone. And there were plenty of times when he was out front that our scouts couldn't see him."

"Rodas, we hired this man to be our guide. He came recommended. Let's let him do the job we are paying him to do. We will take his advice and be vigilant. If he can lead us into an effective ambush without our being alerted, we are not the men I think we are."

So all that day the men collected all the fallen wood they could reasonably carry as they made their tedious way up the steep winding trail northward toward the pass. Talos had spoken truly when he said that firewood would be scarce as they gained in altitude, and the men stopped grumbling about the extra weight and made more of an effort to find billets of wood even as it became harder to locate them. The sun was just above the top of the high peaks when they came to a level wide place in the road that was an obvious campsite.

Both Athan and Rodas were reassured at the location. The place was secure from a surprise attack. The site was backed up against a cliff on one side with a steep drop on the other; any approach would have to come up or down the road with only the trail giving access to the little plateau. Not only was it a flat open area big enough for them to encamp, there were even some shelters standing against the rising slope where previous travelers had erected simple huts with rude wooden roofs that provided a measure of protection from wind and the worst of the rain.

And rain they would soon have; they had been watching a storm building ahead of them to the north all that afternoon. They immediately set to making camp. The men had tenting, which they either spread over the roofs of the shelters or, in the case of the smaller tents, pitched them entirely inside the structures. Some of the stone huts were turned into stables for the donkeys and ponies while the remainder of the animals huddled together inside some of the other unoccupied shelters. There were provisions and water for man and beast and firewood to warm the party from the gusty north wind that was providing the first real cold of the season. There was much sympathy for the men who would have to stand the night watches and much praise for Athan's foresight in having them collect wood on the way up (for there was little wood left in the site beyond the structures themselves). He, in turn, passed the credit to Talos. There is a good feeling about being relatively snug when the first gusts of approaching winter are felt; that feeling is intensified when your are snug, thanks to your own preparations. Everyone was fed, the watch was set, fires banked with ample spare wood to last for the night, and everyone was settled in before it started to rain.

It was still raining the next morning; a cold, sullen autumn rain that promised to last all day and might get even worse. Breaking camp in a cold rain is always uncomfortable, especially when there is every expectation of a long cold ride with a wet camp at the end of the day. Talos approached Athan shortly before they departed. He rode a pony no larger than Athan's so that the two men were scarcely higher off the ground than if they had been standing. Talos' pilleus seemed to be perched on top of his ridiculous ears.

"Sir," he began, "We will be through the pass in less than an hour." Here he hesitated, "I know a place. It is off the normal track, but not far out of the way. About two or three hours from Lychmidas. It is real pretty most of the time. I don't know how it is on a day like today. Might not be so good. I think it is a good place. We can stay there if it pleases you. We won't be bothered, and we might get out of the rain."

All of Athan's earlier suspicions returned with a rush. "Where is this place," he asked blandly.

"Two hours downhill over the pass," responded Talos in his jerky style. His eyes did not quite meet Athan's but they never did. "Off to the west of the trail a little. There is a nice spring. Won't need the water in this," he looked up at the rain. "There are some nice trees, good wood, some caves, too."

"Is it secure?" Athan asked diffidently, looking around, seemingly interested in the departure. "It would be good to not have to set a watch on a foul night like last night." Athan cut his eyes over to gage the guide's reaction to this.

For once Talos stopped looking around when he spoke. Holding Athan's eyes he spoke, "A man would have to be a fool not to set a watch in these mountains." There was a pause. "And you are no fool." Another pause. "Do you want me to show you where it is?"

Athan nodded watching the man.

"Good. Once we are over the pass." And Talos heeled his little pony away up the slope.

The weather continued cold and gray all morning, with rain showers suddenly blasting down, soaking the wet travelers. The pass was wide enough, but the steep walls rising on both sides seemed to funnel the cold winds down from the northwest. Everyone was relieved when they passed around the corner of the mountain and turned down and southwest, putting the wind behind their shoulders instead of into their faces. Once through, Athan detailed no fewer than four scouts to follow Talos down to his recommended spot.

Less than an hour later they came upon one of the men waiting by a small trail that turned from the main trail and led steeply down to the west. It was a difficult trail for the carts but they were able to negotiate it with care. Soon after they took the track another of the scouts come back up the new trail with an enthusiastic approval of the proposed campsite. He led them down past a steep cliff on their left through a series of low canyons until they came to a place where another large gully emerged from their right. The canyon, which had a noisy stream running down its middle, opened out into a broad area perhaps two bow shots wide and five times that long. There were trees along the banks of the stream and up the slopes on the southern and western sides. There was a small relatively level meadow in the center the canyon. On their left side the cliff had a series of overhangs, some with dark holes of caves in the back. His scouts had already hobbled their horses and turned them out to pasture in the meadow. Athan saw them coming out from the overhangs where they had apparently been exploring the caves. A fire was already going back in the protected area under one of the overhangs. Even in the cold rain, it was a lovely place. The promise of a good fire and shelter from the rain made it even more desirable.

Athan and Rodas rode out into the middle of the pasture to inspect the site. Back to the northeast the small valley ended in a cliff, which in this rain was now sporting a little waterfall. The resulting stream ran down beside a low cliff to the south before joining the stream coming in from the right, and then the combined stream exited out the end of the canyon to the southwest. Once again, the night's campsite was a strong position, approachable from only two directions with the added advantage of ample water, shelter under the overhangs, plenty of firewood and even some grazing.

Talos walked out to where the two men sat on their ponies. The caravan was already settling in, men unhitching the few carts and unloading the pack animals under the cover of the overhangs. Others were collecting firewood from under the trees and bringing it back to where it could be dried next to the fire the scouts had burning. The women were collecting water from the stream. Soon bread would be baking and hot tea would be provided. Tents were going up beneath the shelter of the overhangs providing a windbreak and providing a chance to dry things out. There was a general air of relief for the chance to be out of the rain and cold. Clearly the company found this to be a very satisfactory site for a camp.

Talos looked up at the two men. He seemed almost shy as he waved an arm around at the little area. "It is better in the spring. With the trees putting out shoots. And the flowers, sometimes here in the meadow. It is really pretty. Nice place to camp, too." He looked around at the activity. Even though there was still plenty of light left and no one had given the order to stop for the night, there was no thought of continuing.

"How long will it take us to get into Lychmidas tomorrow?" asked Rodas.

"Perhaps three or four hours. Maybe less. Depends on the weather," shrugged Talos. "Where are you going next?"

"I think we should talk about that," said Athan, "would you care to take some tea with us?" The three men, two mounted one standing turned and walked back through the rain to where their camp was being set up.

Long before dusk, dinner had been prepared and consumed, watches set, and the camp had settled down for the night. The camp had almost a festive air. Some of the younger men had begun to explore the caves that led back from under the cliffs.

The women found a more practical use for one of the smaller caves, a short head-high nook that reached back perhaps a couple dozen feet. First, they had some of the men drag two logs into the space. They then set up a hot fire to heat some stones and blocked off the entrance with ground cloths. Soon they were able to create their own little heated mini bath. They had a husband and boyfriend guard the entrance, and the women entered their enclosure with fresh clothing and buckets of water. The two men periodically passed in fresh supplies of hot rocks. Soon the sound of animated conversation and laughter could be heard from behind their screen. This fascinated the men. What they did not fully appreciate was the strain the women were under, surrounded by rough armed men, living in difficult and uncomfortable circumstances and required to maintain a strenuous existence. Their little heated enclosure not only provided a chance to get clean but to be warm when they did so. And the barrier gave them a sense of security and relief from the stress of a long and arduous journey that was almost over. The chance to clean themselves up in a semblance of a civilized bath was as liberating as a glass of wine; maybe even two glasses of wine.

While the women found their source of relaxation, three men sat in Athan's tent sipping the promised hot tea.

Talos looked over the top of his teacup from Athan to Rodas, clearly uneasy.

"So," began Athan, "when will we get to Lychmidas tomorrow?"

"Like I told you, two or three hours. Steep trail but no worse than getting down here."

"And what are you going to do after we get there?"

"I don't know for certain. I need to find a place to stay the winter. No one needs a guide in winter. Myron, my cousin, may take me in. Lets me do some work."

"How well do you know this side of these mountains?" probed Rodas.

"Very well. I live in Pella but I was born over here. I have guided people from one side of the mountains to the sea and back again."

"I have heard that there are a lot of little kingdoms on this side of the mountains," remarked Athan conversationally. "I mean in northwestern Illyria and west of Lake Lychnites. I hear there are lots of little kingdoms out here; lots of places where men can set themselves up like, well, kings."

"This looks like a pretty nice spot," Rodas commented casually. "Do you know if anyone has a claim on it?"

"No," said Talos dismissively in his short abrupt style of speaking. "This place is too small. You might support a shepherd or two up here. No place to grow anything. I think you like it just because it is dry." This apparently was Talos attempting some humor.

"Maybe we can find something out when we get to Lychmidas. Do you know anyone to talk to about places where we can set up?" Rodas persisted.

"Yes. Me. I will ask some friends. After we get in, come with me. We will ask some people. Maybe I have an idea that will interest you."

They tried to draw their strange guide out, but he would give them nothing else of interest, and after a few more moments of uncomfortable probing, he abruptly got up and bid them good night.

After he left Athan made the rounds of his sentries. It was now fully and truly dark with gusty winds and rain spraying down, not cold enough to freeze yet, though it was certainly cold enough to make a man uncomfortable. Athan checked to make certain the three sentries he had posted were comfortable enough to remain alert, but not so comfortable as to be tempted to sleep. Then retiring to his tent, he wrapped himself into his blankets and immediately fell into a deep sleep. For the first night since they had left Pellas, Athan was able to sleep throughout the night without being awakened even once.

The next morning dawned cool and clear, the storm having blown past them during the night. They got an early start, and were able to reach Lychmidas, a pretty little walled city situated on a hill on the northeast shore of Lake Lychnites, around noon. True to his word, Talos immediately went to look up his friends. Rodas, Theron, and Pirro accompanied him to get word of what might be to the west, while Athan took a letter of introduction to a merchant's counting house with a view to safely lodging his bags. Of course, he had no intention of letting the men there know just what he intended to leave with them was. He did expect that the counting house would provide reliable security for all his possessions in a locked and guarded space.

He had completed his bargain with the men at their facility and made arrangements to off-load his baggage discretely. There were several options for securing security ranging from sealed chests to entire rooms. Athan contracted for a small room that would be both locked and sealed. He insisted his own men would offload his goods into the house. Athan made sure to add some additional goods beyond the two dozen leather bags that held the gold, disguising as best he could the nature of his stash.

Deciding he could do with a bite to eat, Athan was heading back to the house where he and Rodas had arranged to stay when he passed a large shop that offered cloth goods. On a whim he stepped inside to see if they had any good winter clothing. Two men were completing a transaction beside a counter at the back of the shop. Athan approached the two men and saw a set of dark gray cloaks spread across several chests. He picked one up to admire the work; it was of quality wool, simple but well made and of the best material. A thought came to him that this might be a good way to reward his men.

"I see you have several of these cloaks," he commented gesturing to the three he saw spread over the chests. How many cloaks do you have?"

The merchant smirked at the travel-worn figure Athan presented. He took up another cloak and then dramatically swung open one of the large wooden chests. "I have five score, all identical!" And seeing Athan's expression of doubt he began opening the chests and bringing out cloak after cloak all with the same cut, the same material, the same shade of dark gray. Athan had never seen so many things that were exactly the same. Perhaps with his gold finally secure he was feeling generous, or maybe it was the supercilious attitude of the merchant and his supplier, but the seed of an idea that had been in the back of his mind suddenly took root and sprouted.

"How much do you want for this cloak?"

Clearly pleased to already have interest in his innovative merchandise the merchant began to extol the virtues of the garment. Athan watched with interest and inquired how it was possible to make so many cloaks so nearly identical.

The supplier smiled and informed Athan that they were made in Lydia by special factories where workers were trained to make a single item and to make it well. He expounded the advantages of large scale purchases of cloth and dyes, and the efficiency of only training workers to make a single pattern.

Athan again asked the price for the cloak.

"Ten drachmae," said the merchant with an oily smile. He went on to assure Athan that this low price for such a fine garment was offered only because he was the first customer and he wanted others to see his fine work and… Athan quit listening to the man while he did some quick calculations in his head. A talent of gold was worth about 6000 drachmae so one of the quarter talent bars was worth 1500. The cloak probably cost the merchant no more than three, or at most four, drachmae each so he would probably sell them for as low as six or seven. Athan, looking around the shop, noticed some of the ubiquitous pilleus felt caps stacked upon another chest. Though not all identical they were such a common piece of headgear, dark wool with a slightly conical point, that they were almost the same. A pilleus like those would normally cost three or four drachmae. There were perhaps a dozen of them there.

"I will make you one offer," said Athan in the tone he used when he would brook no argument. The merchant looked uncomfortable. This gave him no room to maneuver. His supplier looked amused. Athan looked the merchant "I will give you 750 drachmae in gold for the cloaks, the chests they are in, all those pilleus, and that blanket over there, all delivered to my dwelling here in town.

At the mention of 750 drachmae the supplier sucked in his breath and the merchant visibly jerked. Clearly they had made the biggest single mistake of their professional careers in underestimating this plainly dressed man. The man tried to rally, to protest that selling his entire stock to one buyer would not be right, he could not do such a thing; Athan shrugged and turned to walk out the door.

In the end Athan only got two of the chests, but he did get the hats, cloaks, and blanket. He returned to the counting house and privately withdrew one of his bars. Using a chisel he cut it in half and brought both pieces to the now obsequiously polite merchant, who was allowed to choose which half of the golden bar he wanted. With a spring in his step Athan walked back to the house where he and his officers were lodging.

He had just prevailed upon the lady of the house to give him some bread and cheese when Rodas, accompanied by the guide, Theron, and Pirro all burst in, anxious to talk with him. Even the laconic Talos seemed agitated. Athan's first thought was that they were about to be attacked by the Imperial army. But it was good news that had them excited.

Grasping his arm Rodas spoke quietly and earnestly into his ear, "We have news, Chief. Talos' friends say they know were there is a little place west of here that is falling apart; it is ripe for the taking if we act fast. We may have found you your kingdom!"

'That was the start', the Old King thought as he lay back down for his regular midafternoon nap. 'Well the second start, and a lot easier than what it was like after Achilles' Debacle. He had almost forgotten his wild life before he became respectable again. What had that philosopher from the south said? 'An unexamined life is not worth living.' Well he certainly had time up in his hiding place to examine his. It was odd that so many times things that led to major changes in his life were initiated by others. It was Jonathan's idea that made me rich, and Rodas' that made me a king. It was strange how things had all worked out. When he was a soldier all he wanted to be was a captain. He had certainly not wanted to be a bandit, but when he was living the life of a brigand, all he wanted to do was make enough to retire. And when he finally did steal enough to retire he had to become a king just to hang onto what he had. And being a king was a lot more work than anything he ever done. And now here he was, wintering over, in a crack in the rocks some wild

animal. Well, at least his life had finally slowed down enough for him to look back on his life and his loves.

The old man settled back into his lair. Nothing to do but wait for now; his time would come again.

Chapter Eighteen: Going Home for the First Time

The news was not exactly what Athan had expected. He and Rodas had some vague idea that they would find some under-populated area where they could build the band up into a more or less permanent regional force. Instead, Talos was presenting them with an unexpected opportunity; an existing kingdom that was weak and ready to fall right into their laps.

Talos had gone to visit a friend who lived in Lychmidas. There Talos found a cousin of his who had just arrived from the west. This cousin, Myron by name, had just come from Epidamnus on the west coast. On the way Myron had to pass through part of the Candavian Mountains which was rough country; rough not just in terrain, but because the local people were unusually rapacious. Protected by the local king, bands charged tolls to use the roads. This was not unreasonable, but the collection of the tolls was sporadic, and the amount of tolls was more related to the ability of the caravans to defend themselves from the bands rather than anything else. Worse, an unhealthily large number of travelers passing this region never arrived at their destinations. The root cause of this problem was the kingdom of Dassaria. The five men, Talos, Myron, Tenucer, Rodas, and Athan sat under an awning outside the house where Talos had encountered his cousin and listened as Myron told them the unhappy history of the little kingdom known as Dassaria.

Dassaria was not technically speaking a kingdom at all. It was actually an area inhabited mostly by the Dassaretae tribe who were primarily small farmers and herders. A bandit chieftain named Ratimir and his band had descended into this area of small towns and villages almost two decades before. He and his men had come down from the north, initially as raiders, but eventually set up a permanent camp on a hill west of Lake Lychnites. At first he was little more than a typical brigand chieftain, but he soon distinguished himself in a number of important ways. He was a very large man and a mighty warrior, killing many men in open combat. But he had other traits that set him apart from others of his kind. He was ambitious and cunning; cunning meaning intelligent in finding ways to get what he wanted. These traits were emphasized by his utter ruthlessness. A dangerous sociopath, he completely lacked empathy for anything outside himself. He had the same lack of understanding of and contempt for those who had any scruples in killing other humans as an old shepherd might have for a young maiden who refused to eat meat because she did not want to hurt the sheep. He could be merciful or incredibly cruel, but not because he was either kind or vicious; his actions were based solely on what he thought would be best for his personal interests at the time. Not surprisingly, in that place and time a man like Ratimir quickly gained a following, and because he was a successful bandit chieftain, his following grew.

He had several hundred men when he got his big break: his men were hired as mercenaries to assist the Dorians in conquest of some cities in Epirus. The sack of the city of Epiria alone was enough to make him a rich man. When he returned north with his booty he decided to build a stronghold. Using hired architects from both Egypt and the Peloponnesus who with skilled masons and slaves brought back from the sack of Epiria he had constructed a stone fortress which came to be called the Hold. It was constructed on a hill not far from the west side of Lake Lychnites. It was not an especially imposing structure but it was strong enough to allow Ratimir and his men to reside in safety free from the threat of punitive expeditions. At first the brigands supported themselves by raiding caravans. As time passed they began to charge tolls for passage along the roads in their declared territories. From there Ratimir and his men graduated to exploiting the local peoples. His men became very effective at gathering "taxes" and had excellent compliance from the area's villages and homesteads. Few men were willing to risk skimping on their taxes when the penalty might be watching your home burned and women raped from the vantage point of an impaling stake. There had been resistance of course, and the more powerful tribes and the city states had put definite limits to Ratimir's little kingdom, but within its borders, everyone eventually got used to the situation. His men would ride down at harvest time and take a portion of a farmer's crops or a shepherd's flocks. Merchants expected to pay a handsome fee to allow them to continue to conduct business in the region. Travelers were taxed for their right of passage through Ratimir's little kingdom.

There was a problem with a leader like Ratimir, of course; since the concept of loyalty was alien to him he delegated nothing of importance. Anyone who showed any initiative was viewed as a threat, and anyone who was viewed as a threat was likely to be killed out of hand. Not only did the people in his kingdom fear him, his own men lived in a state of considerable anxiety as well. Ratimir did not care. Over time fewer men came to serve with him and fewer still were accepted. The numbers of his men began to decline and those who still served grew older and softer. They were still able to terrorize the locals, but after more than a dozen years it was almost by habit on both sides. The threats were made less frequently and carried out even less often because the people came to understand what they could and could not get away with; so did Ratimir's men. Besides, Ratimir's men came to know the people. It is far more difficult to torture someone you have known for 10 years, even if you do hold them in contempt. Ratimir's men were not all sociopaths, but of course their leader was and that was enough.

The social situation in Ratimir's little kingdom had been stabilized for a number of years. After a time his domain had roughly defined boundaries recognized by his neighbors and more importantly, by the people who lived within those boundaries. His subjects recognized his rule even if they generally did hate his minions. He was formally referred to as King Ratimir, but more and more often he began to be called simply the Bear. With his huge size, hairy body and penchant for wearing heavy furs in cold weather, the name suited him. And if the people in his kingdom were not exactly prospering he was utterly unconcerned. He had every one of his limited needs met to his satisfaction. He grew fat and complacent. Perhaps it was fortunate for those around him that he was also a man of little imagination and was content to leave things as they were; he could have easily made them much worse. He had little interest in women other than raping them as an act of dominance. He had no interest in a family. The few children attributed to him all died young. The Bear also had no interest in what would happen to his kingdom after he died just as he had no interest in the fate of his followers. His life was just perfect as far as he was concerned right up until the night he had a stroke.

His men had no idea what to do at first when he was struck down by this sudden infirmity. They were greatly relieved to see him on his feet again after a few days but the fierce man who they referred to as the Bear now had a distinct limp, his left arm hung useless, and the left side of his face became immobile. They also found he was now all but blind in one eye. This was partially hidden by his long beard and greasy hair that covered most of his face, but there was no mistaking his infirmity. He became increasingly suspicious, and his once self-satisfied air became sullen, angry, and dangerous. Once he suddenly attacked a member of his bodyguard who had quietly approached him on his left side; the man only escaping the king's slashing sword through a combination of his own quickness and the king's now unwieldy bulk. Physicians were sought, healers requested, and the word leaked out from the Hold that The Bear was ill and infirm. It was clear to everyone that King Ratimir would soon be either dead or totally incapacitated, no one was brave enough to admit interest as a successor while the Bear still lived. What made a difficult situation completely impossible was that Ratimir refused to admit to any weakness. Things continued as they had in the past with one critical difference: the strong hand that had once held the reins of power had gone slack. On the Bear's good days he would limp around his stronghold, a terrible figure, wearing a bearskin draped over his shoulders, his left arm hanging limp but a sword at his side, drool escaping from the left corner of his mouth and his one good eye glaring about looking for possible traitors. He had held absolute authority for so long, and his men were is such fear of him that none would challenge him. As he grew weaker he became even more fierce and arbitrary. Twice he ordered impalements of men who had served him for years simply because he decided they might be becoming a threat. An aura of doom hung over the Hold.

With King Ratimir incapacitated, and no one to take his place, things began to spin out of control outside the Hold as well. His men began demanding additional taxes from the locals, knowing that the extra take would not be accounted for and could be safely retained for their own use. Other men began to raid even the caravans that had paid for safe passage. There was increasing unrest in the little kingdom. Some of the Bear's men who were careless outside the safety of the Hold were attacked by locals and slaughtered in revenge for many years of repression. Other men who had severed the Bear began to slip away from the Hold, fearing the imminent collapse of Ratimir's rein considering the unrest that was bound to erupt after his fall to be a danger more than an opportunity.

Athan listened carefully to the sad story of Ratimir's little kingdom of Dassaria. He was not quite sure he understood what Myron was implying.

"Why are you telling us this?" Athan asked him outright.

"Because," interjected Rodas, "we can take over from Ratimir. We can seize the stronghold and make ourselves master of the whole kingdom!"

"How do you figure that?" asked Athan mildly.

"Because," answered Myron for Rodas, "Ratimir's chief lieutenant, a man called Borna, has sent a message to Bardhyllus and some of the other kingdoms of Illyria, asking for some men to help 'stabilize the situation'."

"That is stupid," said Athan, "a request like that is an open invitation for Bardhyllus to take over. Dassaria isn't even really part of the Illyrian alliance. Those Illyrian troops will be taking orders from this Illyrian king, not some local. Why did he ask them for help?"

"Because Borna **is** stupid," replied Myron, "stupid and scared. He is afraid of what will happen to him if the local people find out just how weak Ratimir is. He has made many, many, blood enemies. So he thinks that if he can get some outsiders in to stabilize the situation, things will keep on the way they have."

"And how do you know this Borna sent a message?" asked Rodas shrewdly.

"Because I talked to the messenger himself," smiled Myron. "He shared a camp with us and was glad for the company. He only had two companions, and they were none too happy to be in those hills without more men with them. He even invited us to read the request he was carrying. You see, none of them could read. I rather expect Borna selected them for that reason. They, being prudent men, wanted to know what the message they were carrying said. I was tempted to make up some story about the message telling the King of Bardhyllus to put the bearers of the message to death, but the poor fellows were already nervous enough. I must tell you their fears were not eased by finding out the request they carried. I suspect they will carry their message at a measured pace; they may even decide to simply throw it away and seek their fortune in more hospitable climes. So the help Borna is requesting may never come."

"Unless he sent more than one messenger," put in Pirro.

"But no matter whether he did or not, the main thing is that Borna will be expecting a troop of armed men to arrive soon. He will open the gates and welcome them in."

There was a long pause as the men digested this then looked at one another.

Suddenly four of the five men who had listened to Myron's story spoke at once in an unintelligible babble.

Athan, the only one who had remained silent, stopped the excited chatter with a sudden "Silence!" The men looked at him with anticipation. Athan sat looking at them and he felt one of those moments where significant events were about to be set in motion; or not. He took a deep breath, aware that what he said with that breath would either change or end his life.

"What you are suggesting is that we can take this stronghold," started Athan. Pirro and Tenucer nodded enthusiastically. "But what I mean to do is not to pillage it but to take it and hold it. I think we should try and replace this King Ratimir and his men; to take over the entire kingdom."

There was another long pause followed by another excited burst of gabble.

After a moment, Athan looked at Talos and Myron, "That is what you were thinking isn't it?"

Myron nodded, "After I saw that message I had the thought of how easy it would be to capture that Hold. They say he has much treasure there. But I had no men to undertake such a venture. When Talos told me about your band, I first spoke to him about attempting a raid. It was Talos who whispered to me of a possibly greater plan."

"You would make that place a good king," put in Talos in his blunt and choppy style.

"How do you know?" responded Athan a bit nettled. Until that instant he had not really grasped of what becoming a king might entail; it had all been sort of a vague day-dream, a distant concept. Now he was being literally given the chance of a lifetime and he was a bit daunted. It was too big a thing, coming at him too fast.

"Because you would be," said Rodas in a level voice looking right at him.

Athan looked at the four men from his new band; they all were looking at him and nodding their heads. Athan glanced at Myron who shrugged, grinned, and said, "Talos speaks well of you."

"Tenucer," said Athan looking at the man who had been with him for off and on since the fall of Epiria, "you know the men. Do you think they would like to settle down if we had our own kingdom?"

"Yes, sir," Tenucer answered directly, "I think they would like that. More security, better future, yes, I think it is time to settle down if we can."

"Pirro, what do you think?"

"Well, Captain, it's bound to be warmer."

The men laughed. The decision was made. Athan suddenly became a man of action.

Pirro and Thereon were dispatched to muster the troop at the stables with all possible speed. They were to tell them only that it was urgent and to be ready to leave at once, this very day.

As they left Myron, looking up at the sun which was past noon asked with surprise if the captain actually intended to depart that very day.

In reply Athan began peppering him with questions – How far was this place, Dassaria? What was the best route to get there? How were the roads? Could he describe the stronghold? Did he know how long it would take for a messenger to get from Dassaria to Illyria? How about a force returning back from that country? When had he seen the couriers? Did soldiers from Illyria ever come to Dassaria? What kind of scouts did the Bear's men send out? How many sentries were posted and where? Did he know if there were any granaries of food stores in the hold? What about the people in the village, would they support or oppose him?

Poor Myron was a bit overwhelmed and was seldom able to give specific answers to the questions. Fortunately Talos was able to provide more answers to Athan's questions than his cousin. In answer to the unspoken questions in Rodas and Athan's eyes he admitted that he had worked in Dassaria for a 'season or two', helping out some of the men sent out by King Ratimir to collect taxes and look for travelers attempting to pass through the kingdom without paying off the king's men. This earned him some curious looks, but he explained it with a "Sometimes a man must do what he can to get by." Well, after all, thought Athan, he had not been so very different. Did he not have a fortune in stolen treasure himself?

By the time Pirro came hurrying back to say that almost all the men were assembled at the stables and were making preparations for an immediate departure, he had sketched out a plan and had his orders ready. These he confirmed with Rodas on the way over to the stables. They stopped on their way to the assembly point just long enough to pick up their gear in the house where they had been planning on spending the night. Making their apologies to the landlady they were coming out again when the encountered a mini-caravan coming from the merchant's bearing the hundred gray cloaks other purchases. Athan directed them to follow him to the stables.

It was a fine afternoon, the storms of the previous days had blown away to the south and the air had a clean crisp fresh scent. It was just cool enough to encourage activity and the bright sun provided warmth rather than heat. Athan had expected the men to be anxious, but perhaps they had picked up the feeling of excitement rather than fear from Tenucer and Pirro, or perhaps it was just too beautiful a day to be frightened. In any event, there was a bustle of purposeful activity. It appeared the men indeed would be ready to ride out in short order. A quick muster indicated all but two men had assembled; one man, Xenos, was out still looking for them. Since the two missing men had women with them it was assumed they would be found together.

First, Athan the called over the porters carrying the cloaks and other freshly purchased clothing. He had them dump it all on an open patch of ground where his men could gather around with fewer prying ears. He called them in to him and indicated the cloaks lying on the ground. "First, I want to give each of you a gift as partial repayment for our trip over the mountains; one of these fine cloaks. Each of you take one. From now on when you see a rider with one of these cloaks you will know him for a comrade. Or at least a man who is brave enough to take it from one of us." There was general laughter and the men move forward to begin picking up the cloaks.

"What if we already have a cloak, captain?"

"Keep it or sell it, but from now on, when you ride with me wear this cloak, weather permitting."

Again there was laughter as the men milled about finding that there was little difference between the garments and then sharing them out. "Only one per man, mind you," cautioned Rodas, "there will be others joining us soon enough and we want them to have a cloak, too."

There was general but good natured grumbling at this:

"Let them get their own cloaks,"

"They didn't help us diddle the Achaemendians or cross the mountains,"

Athan ignored the comments but stepped in to try to make sure that each man only had one cloak. "Put on your cloaks and headgear," he ordered. Some of the men had to go back to get their hats, but within a short time they had reassembled, all wearing the cloaks over their shoulders and almost all wearing the ubiquitous pilleus. Those who did not have such a hat were tossed one from those he had purchased. Soon they were standing there, all aware that they were dressed more or less identically, wearing baggy trousers, tunics, and identical hats and cloaks.

"Now, listen," Athan began, "I did not call you here just to add to your wardrobe. There is a prize afoot. Captain Rodas is going to tell you about it."

The two men had agreed to this on the way over, Athan would get their attention, Rodas would issue the orders. Rodas knew the orders he had to give, but he could not resist giving them a rousing speech; which he did. He extolled their daring robbery of the gold from the Achaemendians (though in truth few of them had even known it was going to be stolen until they were compelled to run for their lives), he praised their fighting prowess recalling how they had turned back the cavalry in the hills, and reminded them of Athan's generosity in rewarding them in Pellas. Then, warming to his subject, he spoke of what a great Chieftain Athan was, getting some of his men to speak up as to his many daring feats of war, his fairness, and his general competence as a leader. The men ate it up. Athan was secretly embarrassed by this though he did not show it, standing impassively off to one side. He was beginning to get worried about the time, the sun was well down in the sky and he intended to get where he was going as fast as possible. But he also knew that sometimes it is better to make haste by going slowly, and this speech was necessary; there would be no time later. Rodas then shifted the direction of his exhortation; now, he told them, they had a chance to do something great. There was a country just over those hills who were oppressed; who cried out from relief from foreign occupation. These people, much like their own families had been conquered by barbarians from the north, who had most cruelly abused them. They would welcome liberation from people like themselves and doubtless make them all feel their gratitude. Rodas made it sound as though fair virgins would come creeping out from behind every bush to personally do her best to reward the members of the band that had freed them from the barbarians. Athan knew this was a load of claptrap; maybe the men knew it too, but they loved hearing it.   Finally, Rodas appealed to their self interest: who among them would not like a safe place to find rest.   Every wolf has its lair, every bear its den, but they had to shift constantly for a home.   Now, thanks to the Great Captain (as he referred to Athan) the had a chance to right a wrong, find a permanent home, and accept the thanks of all those maidens, all while turning a tidy profit.   Who would come with them to make the attempt?   Who was with them?

The men were ready to run on foot the whole way.   Three of those present were dismayed to find they were to be left behind.   Aorastus and Stamitos both had women with them.   They would stay behind along with Yure the Elder, Xenos, Pontus, and Tracy.   They and the three men, who still had not made the muster, would provide a presence here.   The band would be traveling fast so they would need to leave most of their goods and all the gold in the counting house. Athan was not confident enough in the merchants to leave everything in their care without maintaining a presence in Lychmidas.   Yure was a responsible sergeant, and was put in charge.   There would be three men from Athan's old band, two from Rodas, and Stamitos who had originally been with Endre but had attached himself to Athan during the retreat with the gold.   They were all trustworthy men but would also be unlikely to form an alliance and try to steal the gold.   Further two of them had girlfriends and two had wives.   Athan did not want them leaving their women behind just as he did not want to bring them with him on such a desperate venture.   The number remaining seemed about right to him.   Six would be a strong enough group to bring up the gold if it were called for after (and if) they took the stronghold at Dassaria but not so many as to weaken the band.   Yure was to put out the story they had gone on a hunting expedition.

"Tell them we are looking for bear," smiled Rodas.

The band took all the best animals, Ixon choosing as many remounts as were fit.   They carried weapons, three days provisions for themselves and the animals, and minimal personal gear.   Now that they had committed to the venture, everyone understood the need for speed.   The men were experienced campaigners, and in a short time were mounted and ready.   Talos, Myron, and Cadmus, one of Myron's companions were to ride with them.   Rodas came up from the back of the column and notified Athan they were ready to move out.

"How many are we?" he asked.

"Counting the Talos and his two friends we are exactly two score and you," answered Rodas.

"I am trying to conquer a kingdom with 40 thieves," mused Athan almost to himself, then raising his voice addressed Rodas, "Well, let's find out about this Dassaria place."

He moved them out at a measured pace; no sense in their sudden departure arousing even more comment than it would anyway. It was fortunate that like most of the cities they had visited, they were in the suburbs and not inside the walls or their departure would have been slower yet.

The road out of Lychmidas ran along the shore of Lake Lychnites, a large body of water bounded on all sides by mountains. The terrain next to the lake consisted of low hills covered with heather and gorse; there were a few trees some distance back from the lake. The road was good and as soon as they were out of sight of the city Athan increased the pace to a hard canter which they held with only a few breaks until it was almost dark. He allowed a stop to feed and water the horses, and eat some bread and cheese, but they soon were leading their horses onto the road again. After about an hour they remounted and headed west along the shore of the lake. Shortly after dark a three quarter moon came up over the lake. Athan was reminded of his desperate night flight from Kadakoy the previous summer. But this was different and better. For one thing he was surrounded by his band and they were all in high spirits, laughing and talking among themselves. And on this night march he could set the pace without fear of being overtaken. That was the main reason it was better: he was going on the offensive, not fleeing enemies. He let his spirits soar along with his men. The rode at an easy but steady pace until just before midnight when he finally called a halt more to keep the horses fresh as any need for rest for his men.

As soon as they settled down Athan met with Rodas, Myron and Talos to talk over plans and tactics.

"I was only about four or five parasangs west of the Hold when I spoke with the courier. He had left the Hold that morning, so he was not exactly tearing up the earth to get over to Bardhyllus. We stayed on a little trail that circled around on the far side of the hill the next day so we did not have to pass through Dessaria proper because the main road is just below the Hold, and if things were to go rotten that would be a bad place to be. Come to speak of it, it's a bad place to be most of the time. The main road is a lot better but the back track is a safer way if you don't have carts or wagons or such. Anyway, it is about four days from Lychmidas to the Hold; maybe you can do it in three long days. If you want to fool them into thinking you are coming over from Illyria you will have to swing around the hills to the west, avoid the scouts, and approach the Hold from the west. That will add about a day or so."

"Tell me everything you know about the Hold," said Athan looking at Myron and Talos in the light of the setting moon.

The four men talked for an hour. Myron did most of the actual talking with Talos confirming bits and adding considerable details about both the building and the men who lived there. By the time they had finished, Athan had a fair picture of the structure called referred to as the Hold.

The Hold sat on the top of a low narrow hill, about three score cubits high. The hill itself was really two hills connected by a narrow ridge about two or three bowshots long and a few score of feet wide running east west giving it the shape of a narrow double teardrop. The sides of hills and ridgeline were steep except on the western end of the hill where the Bear chose to build his fort. The location was good. The Hold overlooked one road that wound through the hills going north south, and had a clear line of sight to an intersection where anther trail came in from the west to join the main north south road. The little village of Dassaria was situated around this intersection, with a few buildings running up closer to the Hold itself. The only path up to the Hold made a gentle S turn directly up the front of the hill, and was dominated by the walls of the Hold. It was possible to clamber up the sides of either of the hills or the ridge behind where the Hold sat, but the narrow approach to the back of the Hold precluded any massing of attackers. The Hold could be approached on the facing west side, but the milder slope meant that defenders at the top could safely counterattack without fear of stumbling down too steep a slope.

The Hold itself was made of large blocks of local stone, hauled laboriously up the slope by teams of oxen and set in place using an ingenious set of counterbalanced timber cranes, rollers, and levers. The architects and their builders had done a good job. The thick dark stone blocks were cut too smoothly and fitted too well together to allow a man in armor to climb them unaided. These walls were not especially high; however they were high enough that topping them would require ladders or grapples. The building inside had two stories, the first had higher ceilings, especially on the western side; they estimated that not even a tall man could jump high enough to touch the ceilings on the ground floor. The ceiling on the second floor was a more typical height; a tall man could reach up and brush it with his fingertips. There was a crenellated curtain wall topping the walls a bit less than chest high protecting the wide fighting step so that men might defend the walls while others passed behind them running along the reinforced roof of the second story. The wall on the west side was as high as five men, perhaps 20 cubits high. The height of the walls was multiplied by their dominating location on the hill. A man approaching had to crane his neck to look at the top. The walls were a couple of cubits lower on the sides and back of the Hold, but the steeper approaches up the hill more than compensated for the lower height.

Adding to the impressive defensive capability of the Hold were no fewer than four bastions, one at each corner. Perhaps the architects had studied the works of the Egyptians to the south for they fully understood the value of crossing fires. At each corner of the Hold a three story high bastion extended past the wall. In the third story of the tower arrow slits looked down the length of the wall so that any attacker would be struck by arrows fired from the side as well as facing the fire from the men on the wall. Other men could be posted on the top of the tower of the bastion, adding stones and javelins to the missiles coming down on anyone attacking the walls. Since the bastions themselves were higher and stronger than the walls, an enemy was faced with a daunting choice if assaulting the Hold. They must either attack the higher, stronger bastions directly, or suffer their unimpeded fire while attempting to clear the wall. Even getting over the walls would not ensure an attack would be successful. Counterattacks could be launched from the strong points at the corners. Over the main gate, the fighting step and curtain wall were raised perhaps another two cubits or so higher than the rest of the wall, giving the defenders along the wall atop the gate area even stronger protection.

The structure of the Hold was fitted to the shape of the hill. The western face was wider to fit the broader face of the hill. Each of the north/south walls were brought in closer to one other as the hill pinched in giving the Hold a trapezoidal effect. The menacing western face was about a bowshot wide. The wall at the eastern end that faced ridge running away to the sister hill was only a stone's throw wide with a lower wall. To cover this back wall and perhaps to provide aesthetic balance (the architects were Hellenes and so considered themselves artists as well as builders) there were two bastions in the rear in close and looming proximity.

There were two gates into the Hold, front and rear. The front gate was a high iron-bound bivalve with an arched top. When both doors were flung open, the opening was wide enough for two men to ride through side by side. Once inside the Hold it was necessary to pass though a kind of arched tunnel as the stables on either side were walled off from the entrance way. It was very imposing to pass through two wide doors under an arched entranceway and clip clop down the enclosed flagstone entrance until you emerged into the central courtyard. Of course for day-to-day use, there was a sally port, a door of regular size, cut into the right hand door of the gate. Most people walked through this smaller and more convenient portal on their regular business. The rear gate was high and broad enough for a single rider to pass through while mounted. It was constructed like the main gate of thick oaken timbers banded with iron well set and flush with the wall. Unlike the front gates, the back gate gave directly into the courtyard.

The Hold's interior structure had an unusual feature. Because of the almost triangular shape imposed by the terrain, and the requirement to be able send out riders quickly, the stables were placed not discretely in the rear, but right up front against the west wall. Two large and comfortable stables were set one on either side of the main entrance way. The smell and sounds of stables did significantly reduce the grandeur of the entrance but Ratimir paid for the structure and he had no more concept of grandeur than a duck. He did have some very clear concept of how hay and other silage could burn.

The first smell to greet visitors was that of the wide stables that took up the entire west side of the Hold. The contrast between the imposing walls and entryway into the very mundane central courtyard was striking. Between (literally) the stables and the flat muddy courtyard the impression was that of entering a rather large barnyard, rather than the center courtyard of an important keep. Some of the courtyard had been half-heartedly flag stoned, but in the main part the courtyard consisted of dusty earth, except of course when it rained when the dust turned into mud for a while. Instead of the fountains and garden area planned by the architects for the courtyard, Ratimir decreed there should be four silos placed in the middle of the courtyard surrounding a simple well. (One of the architects burst into tears upon hearing this). In the event only two of the silos were completed. The third was only finished half way and was converted to a cistern when the builders realized that digging a well from on top of a hill would be a more difficult proposition than initially envisioned. This allowed most of the fodder to be kept in separate structures inside the walls, but not in the barns attached to the walls of the Hold. Thus, the first thing a visitor saw when coming out of the main entrance tunnel was a pair of rather ugly light brown stone and masonry silos about 15 cubits high standing one behind another. Behind them a lower and obviously unfinished silo was surrounded by wooden watering troughs completing the odd collection of structures in the courtyard.

The other jarring element of the inside of the Hold was the closed-in feeling. Most large buildings in that time and place featured a central courtyard such as this one, but almost all had open galleries running along the top providing a covered outside corridor for the upstairs rooms as well as a covering for porticos along the ground floor. Here, however, the interior walls ran right up to the roofline. There were windows to be sure, and doors on the ground floor, but it lacked the cool airiness of the typical porches. The ground floor was dedicated to business. The north side of the fort held tack rooms, storage spaces, and a small smithy. On either side of the smithy were the laundry, bath house; farther back were more store rooms, with the armory at the far end, next to the northeast bastion. The bakery and kitchens were located on the center of the south side of the quadrangle, with the dining area next to them. There were store rooms on either side of the kitchens with the treasury and a guard room at the far end, opposite the armory. There were multiple indoor washing areas and latrines on the ground floors, with outfalls directed via tile pipes down the hill and into pits dug well away from the walls.

If the ground floor of the keep was intended for work and storage, the second floor was for people. Entrance to the second level was intended to be made through the stairwells in each of the four bastions. That way comings and goings could be more easily monitored. Over time, however, two additional ways up to the second level were developed. On the south wall a wooden ramp had been left so that heavy objects could be more easily pushed up to the fighting platforms on top of the second level. The ramp went by a high window on that second level and it was commonly used as an entrance to and from the ramp. People would often congregate in the shade beneath the wooden pillars that supported the ramp. On the north side, ladders were usually left propped up into some of the second story windows so men coming down to ground level did not have to walk to the stairs located in the corner bastions.

"I did not go farther back that the start of that ramp" confessed Talos who it developed had been in the Hold much more often than his cousin Myron. "The Bear's quarters were at the back of the Hold. Nobody likes to go back that far if they could help it. It was bad enough walking back to where the ramp started up to the top. That was close enough for me!"

Almost the entire top level was given over to quarters for men with a few storage rooms. Some of the barrack rooms were open from inner to outer wall, requiring you to pass through the open bay where men were sleeping, talking, and taking their ease. In other stretches, an internal corridor alongside the inside wall made a hall past smaller berthing areas and individual offices. Ventilation came from arrow slits on the outside wall and larger windows on the inner walls. Though an effort had been make to try to allow air to flow through the upper spaces, in summer the Hold could be stuffy and hot. On the other hand, in winter, there were enough fireplaces and, with shutters over the windows, the place was reasonably snug.

Because it tended to be warm inside, during the summer nights most of the men slept on the roofs or fighting steps of the walls. The roof of the second level was pitched in toward the courtyard where cunningly placed gutters caught the runoff from rains and directed it to collection tanks that stood on the ground along the walls. To protect the roof tiles and give the men a level surface to defend the walls from, a flat wooden deck extended out from the fighting step over the pitch of the roof. A wooden railing provided some security at the inside edge. Most of the men brought bedding up to this wooden deck and artfully spread awnings above them, positioned to keep off sun and rain while also capturing the breezes usually available this high up on the hill. Others slept on the third level bastions where more or less permanent awnings remained in place to provide shelter for sentinels that kept watch up there during the day. All in all, the Hold was tolerably comfortable for such a strong place. Ratimir had hired talented architects and paid a great deal of money to construct the place. It had declined with its master but even in its current state it was still a solid fortress.

Talos and Myron finally ran out of things to say about the Hold. A stillness came to the four men sprawling on the grass just above the lake.

"Well, I think we have a pretty good idea of the structure," said Athan at last getting to his feet. "Best if we caught some sleep. Tomorrow will be a hard ride." After a moment he turned to Rodas "I'll check the guards before I lay down." And he pulled himself up to make his rounds.

For men in a hurry, they did not leave especially early the next morning. Athan wanted to make sure they were ready for a difficult day. Every man fed and watered his horse and ate a solid breakfast. Although Athan allowed the armor and spears to be carried on packhorses, as they had for almost the entire journey, he did direct every man take his shield out and carry it with him. Further he distributed the company's javelins so that every man had at least one in addition to his sword. Now they were better prepared to respond should they encounter enemies; not that he expected to this day, but they were coming into potentially hostile territory.

Distances in that time and place were usually best measured in time. Although the distance traveled the next day would not be considered much by a crow, for the band it was a long and tedious march. Athan continued his normal practice of keeping scouts out ahead to keep watch along the route. This required either Myron or Talos to be in the van with either Rodas or Athan to direct the scouts along the intended line of travel. The country was wild and strangely beautiful. There were many hills, and though none were big enough to be called mountains, many were steep enough to be called a variety of other choice names by the men who had to traverse them. Even though the tracks and trails usually led them along the easiest way, even the easiest way could be difficult. The hills were covered with gorse and other low brush, with few trees except along the banks of the streams that made their way among the hills. These streams and not the slopes were the real barriers to the paths through the hills as they were often in deep cuts or were plunging along at such as pace as to make fording them too hazardous for men and horses. This required the men to make long and often difficult detours to places where the streams could be crossed.

They saw only a few lonely farms that day interspersed with the occasional shepherd watching his flocks protectively, and the riders with suspicion. Once they came close enough to a flock of sheep to attract the violent attention of three large wolf-like dogs. The dogs menaced the horses, barking and growling fiercely. Some of the men unlimbered javelins and prepared to defend their mounts. The shepherd came up hastily but hesitantly. Athan did not know if he had ever seen a man so obviously conflicted. He obviously wanted to keep the men away from his sheep, and prevent his dogs from being killed, but he also desperately wanted to avoid offending these dangerous men. He alternated between savagely cursing his dogs and apologizing profusely to the riders; dragging a dog back with on hand and making cringing motions to them with the other, all the while keeping a wary eye on the javelins in the men's hands. Athan could not decide if he was a craven hero or courageous coward. Eventually he was able to drive his dogs back to his flock while turning and keeping an eye on the riders over his shoulder.

"Nice country," remarked Athan dryly to Rodas who had ridden up from the end of the column to see what the problem was. "Like you said, what was it 'good country, rich land'?" Athan gestured to the bare and empty hills. "That shepherd is about the only man we have seen close up all day."

To partially deflect this criticism Rodas began to ask Myron and Talos about the people and land around the so-called kingdom of Dassaria. The told him that the land was roughly bounded on the north by rugged hills, thinly populated by bands of the Paeonia tribe. Lake Lychnites made up the eastern border, and the peoples of Illyria lived to the west and south. These included the kingdom of Bardhyllus to the west and the Dassaretae tribes inhabiting the southern regions, though the Dassaretae tribesmen, like the Paeonia tribe had no real city. The land was rougher to the north and east near the lake, but was both more level and more fertile to the south and east, although it was never anything like a plain. There was adequate water with springs and streams that flowed all year. Although winters could be cold and summers hot, they were certainly no worse and often better than other places the men had traveled.

There was one town in the little kingdom, Dassaria, about a dozen villages, several score farmsteads and 'many' small farms in the area. No one had a good idea just how many people lived there because no one had ever thought to try to hold a census. The closest anyone came to trying to find out was when bands went out in the spring and fall to collect 'taxes'. Myron thought there might be thousands of people in Dassaria; Talos thought there were fewer than that. Both agreed that the number of people and their standard of living had declined over the past years. It was difficult and dangerous to get goods to market, money was tight, and the harvests had been bad. The people of Dassaria looked poor, but of course it was in everyone's interest to appear to be poor when the taxman came.

The people tended to be a proud and independent lot. They would fight one another for the slightest perceived insult. The men could react violently to threats to their women and so rape was relatively rare unless conducted by an overwhelming force. But they were by and large honest and hard working folks. It was not unusual for neighbors to help one anther out in times of crisis, putting aside previous disagreements to bring in a crop when the man of the farm was incapacitated or loaning a draft animal for plowing in the spring if your neighbor's animal had died over the winter. They would undertake a blood feud under the right circumstances, but were less likely to do so than most people in that part of the world, in part because tribal links were looser in Dassaria. People often moved into these remote hills to escape pressures from outside, or just to have a chance to start over in a new place.

The discussion continued for most of the afternoon as the rode along until Athan was called away to deal with a missing scout. It was not unexpected that scouts covering new ground would loose their way when trying to return to the band. Fortunately, all of them were eventually able to cut the band's trail and rejoin their comrades before dark. The weather continued cool and mild which was a blessing, but by late afternoon they could see storm clouds building in the north for the next autumnal storm. They spent the night in a valley near, but not too near, a mountain stream. Though it was not raining, the men had a healthy respect for the speed with which a small rivulet in the hills could grow to a dangerous river. They took time to erect small shelters put down ground covers. Being wet and cold was not only a miserable way to spend a night but could lead to exhaustion and illness.

With camp set, Athan called a council of war with, Rodas, Tenucer, Ixon, and the two cousins, Myron and Talos. Myron estimated that they were only about five or at most six parasangs from the Hold, and with easier going on the morrow they would be able to reach their destination if they went directly there in seven or eight hours. But there was a problem with merely riding up to the Hold. Ratimir's men were expecting support from the Illyrian kingdom west of them.

"We," pointed out Myron with exquisite simplicity, "will be coming down from the north. We need to swing around to the west to pick up the eastbound road into Dassaria. That way it will look like an advance troop of Illyrian cavalry."

There was a problem with this easy solution: it added three or four more parasangs, much of it over rough terrain with poor trails. The detour might add as much as five hours of travel to the journey, more if the storm behind them broke. That meant that unless they made a very early start the next day and pushed hard they would not reach the Hold before dark. It would be much harder to get inside the place once the night watch was set, so they might have to wait until the morning. There were not many places to camp near the Hold, and there was a strong chance they would encounter people, including scouts from the Hold. They could not pass as Illyrian troops beyond more than a casual inspection. Myron recommended that they move up to the road tomorrow and camp out of sight, coming in along the west road in the early afternoon the day after tomorrow. If they timed it right they could arrive around the midday meal when the watch changed and take advantage of the typical disruptions that occurred during the shifting of watch personnel. The off-going watch would be tired and eager for a break, not looking to sound an unnecessary alarm.

"Is the watch so lax, then?" asked Athan.

"Yes," answered Talos, "they play dice, drink, and talk. Sometimes they look outside; but sometimes not for a long time. Standing watch there is easy. But they think it is punishment."

Athan always came to decisions in his councils, even if it was to delay a decision until a specified later time. He always provided orders for the next day's march. But this time he did not. He only told the men to prepare to leave after it was fully light and then dismissed them. Then he walked out past the camp guards and up a hill. There he stood staring north up into the darkness for a long time.

The next morning the normal routine of the camp was strangely unsettled. The advance scouts would normally be heading off as soon as they had been fed, but they had been given no route and so stood by their shaggy little mounts, waiting to be told the plan of advance. Athan had long been up; he let his lieutenants know not to depart until he provided them with the plan for the day. Tension grew as the last of the men finished their breakfasts and loaded the pack animals with no instructions provided. Their chief had always been decisive in the past; now he was visibly hesitating. Finally he motioned to his little council of five men to join him next to his horse. This too, was unusual. Athan always held his meetings in private, allowing his representatives to speak frankly. Once the decision was announced he depended on them to execute his orders whether they had been in favor of them or not. His officers had a vote, but the band was not one of those democracies like some of the cities in the south; once he announced a decision his men were expected to obey regardless of their preference. Now he was speaking right out in the open, so that everyone could hear that the orders were coming from the captain directly.

Athan started with a question to Myron. "The direct road to the Hold is there off to the left; it winds down to the southwest."

Myron nodded.

"That is the road that you say comes out to the north of the Hold and curves down below the hill the Hold is on, and goes into that little town there below the hill."

Myron again nodded mutely. He wanted to speak but could tell now was not yet the time.

"That road continues past the town to the intersection of the west road. That is probably the way the Illyrian troops will be coming."

"Yes, sir."

The road that comes down from the north; that road goes into the town and then turns back west up the hill and goes to the front gate of the Hold. Is that the only way up to the gate?"

"No, sir, but it is the main one. There is a track that goes from the north road right up to the gate, but hardly anyone uses it."

"The road coming down from the north is a pretty well traveled track isn't it? There are a fair number of travelers who use it to go north and south past the town aren't there?"

Myron looked at Talos who shrugged. Talos answered, "I suppose. Not too many people come that way. Some do. It is not strange."

"How long would it take us to go from where the tower on the Hold can see us until we enter the town?"

Myron and Talos were confused; Athan had asked variations of these questions on the past two nights. This time it was Myron who shrugged, "For all of us? Perhaps half an hour. But they will certainly see us and that is not the direction that the Illyrian troops will be coming from. They will be coming up the west road, or maybe possibly even the south road."

He was to explain the ground again when Athan silenced him with a loud call to the entire band. "Ho, to me! Everyone. Even the sentries! Come on in and listen."

It only took a few moments as most of them had been listening anyway. There was some bustle as the men moved in, and a few conversations sprang up.

"Silence!" Athan ordered loudly. The men became still. "Listen carefully. See that storm up there?" Athan gestured to the north. There was a general craning around and shifting as the men looked at the dark clouds to the north. "I intend to be in our winter quarters by the time that gets here. Safe, warm, and settled in. And I intend for us to take our new home without having to assault any walls, either!" There were murmurs of agreement; no one was eager to storm a fortress on a hill. "Here is what we are going to do today. Stamitos, Ioannis, and Nikolas, you go with Myron as fast as you can until you get to a place where you can set a discreet watch the Hold. Stay out of sight, mind you! Ioannis will signal back to us how things are when we catch up to you. If the Illyrians have gotten there first or the people in the Hold are too watchful we will camp out of sight and figure out what to do next. But I think they are going to be lazy and be more worried about keeping warm than keeping watch. I intend to ride directly down into the town, then turn and ride up to the gates like we belonged there."

Myron interrupted him, not a popular move with the other men at that point, "But they will certainly see us! They are not that incompetent!"

Athan was prepared for objections and was glad it came from an outsider.

"We are not going to ride in like a band of mighty warriors on a raid. We will straggle in, at no particularly fast pace with our pack animals near the front. We will have our amour on but under our cloaks. We will have shields, but on our backs. We will have our sword at our sides, but keep our spears on the pack animals. Once we all get into the town, we will form up and get our spears out and put our shields on our arms. Then we will head up that road to the Hold in a disciplined column of twos. Once we get up there we are just going to talk our way in. All we need is to open that door just a crack and we are home!"

There was a cheer and excited chatter from the men.

"Myron, you Tenucer, Ioannis, and Nikolas leave now get to your watching spot as soon as you can. We will have another council just out of sight of the Hold. Meet me there when we come up." Myron delayed wanting to say something else but Athan reiterated: "GO!" and Myron was left to scramble up onto his horse and ride hard after his three scouts who were already moving south.

Soon it became clear that they were not only in a race to beat an unseen and merely potential foe coming up from the west but an obvious and highly visible enemy piling up in the dark clouds and sweeping down from the north. This was clearly going to be the first really strong tempest of the oncoming winter.

"Is that why you decided to go straight for them?" asked Rodas looking over his shoulder at the oncoming weather. The two men were riding abreast with Talos now that the road had widened. This was a more commonly used track than the one they had covered the day before. They even saw more hamlets and other isolated dwellings as the continued south. The three men were discussing the various courses of action they might take when the got to the Hold. Athan had held the men back after sending Myron and his scouts ahead long enough for everyone to don their armor. Some of the had been allowed to men don their helmets, not the bronze helmets of a phalangist but lighter ones of leather shaped with a forward curving point at their tops in the shape of a typical pilleus. These he let the men wear, the rest had to sling their bronze helmets to their saddles. They all had their shields on their backs over their gray cloaks that were now flapping forward in the increasing north wind. Spears been divided up and some were carried on every pack animal so that the men could get to them more easily. And of course, they all wore their swords as usual. They looked a proper warlike band and the few people who saw them on this raw and threatening day gave them a wide berth.

"I'm not sure," confessed Athan, "I just had a feeling we needed to get there as soon as we could." This might have been considered a sign of weakness but Athan said it in such a way that neither of his two companions took it as such. "I think the sentry will not know what to make of us. I am counting on them not viewing us as a threat but more of a curiosity. I get the impression things are not being run very well. Men who don't know what to do usually do nothing. The only tricky part will be you talking your way into the Hold."

"What!" exclaimed an alarmed Talos.

"Not you," smiled Athan, "Rodas."

"What?" said Rodas almost as surprised as Talos had been.

"Talos will be with you, of course," said Athan reassuringly. Talos did not look especially delighted to get this bit of news. Athan continued before anyone had a chance to make a comment. "He knows the layout best and he may even know some of the men on guard. That might put them more at ease. I think you should head up there with a ride of seven men ahead of the rest of us. When we come up will have to have our spears out and look like we are a real legitimate troop, but you seven can go up first and smooth the way, go inside, and be ready to overcome the watch and open the gates so we can just ride in."

"Just how are we going to do that?" asked Rodas, intrigued despite himself.

"I'm not sure," admitted Athan. "But put yourself in the boots of the watch. There has never been an attack on the place, right?" this with a look over to Talos.

"Right," admitted the squat man. With his hat pulled down to his fringe of hair and his cloak pulled tightly around his throat he looked a little less strange than usual.

"You said they never even used a password."

"I never heard one," said Talos.

"So an attack is the last thing on their mind. The watch will see us go into the town. They will wonder about that but I would be very surprised if they do anything, especially if we are discrete. Then they will see a small group head up the hill without spears followed a distance later by the rest of us with shields and spears displayed, riding slowly in a column up the hill. What is the sergeant of the guard going to do?"

"Close and bar the gates and turn out the guard," answered Rodas grimly.

"No. He is going to want to find out who these men are. And he will think that is obviously what you are coming up to tell him. The sergeant of the guard or whatever he is called will want to talk to you so when he makes his report he doesn't seem like a fool."

"We are coming in from the wrong way," interjected Talos, "we can't be Illyrians."

"He won't know who we are," responded Athan, but he will want to find out. So he will meet with the advance group. And where will he meet with them on a foul night like this?'

"In the tunnel," admitted Talos.

"Right; he won't want to keep the visitors out in the cold. He will have you dismount and come inside. And that is where you will do your magic, Rodas."

"You mean I figure out how to get in the gate and hold the entrance until you get up there?"

"Exactly; you are a good talker and you think fast on your feet. And you are a better fighter than I am. I would be very surprised if you and five picked fighters could not hold that tunnel with shields and swords until we arrive and put our spears to work."

Before Rodas could agree Talos surprised them. "Six picked fighters." He was clearly including himself into the mix. "And we can bring javelins with us. They are useful in close fighting."

After that what else could Rodas do but agree; if a man like Talos was willing to try, Rodas had to as well. After a time he and Athan began discussing who they would pick to accompany Rodas in the first ride of seven to begin the assault on a fortress that had never fallen.

The storm had almost caught up to them by the time they came up to their rendezvous with Myron. They already knew from Ioannis' signals that the Hold was quiet. Athan and Rodas had already ridden up and down the line of men, apprising them of the plan and selecting men to accompany Rodas and Talos. There was controversy as most of the men asked to join the select seven. It was a chance for glory; they all knew that this was the most important and difficult part of the operation. Finally, the chosen men were notified. They immediately coalesced and began riding together, talking and chaffing to conceal their nervousness now that they had been committed to such a dangerous venture.

At the brief council of war just out of sight of the Hold, Athan explained his plan again:

Part one: get into town without unduly alarming anyone, most especially the guards up on the Hold.

Part two: the first group of seven men under Rodas head up to the Hold at an easy pace while the rest of the men retrieved their spears, put their shields on their left arms, and formed up. Pack animals would bring up the rear, just like a transiting group of guards.

Part three: while the band rode up two by two, Rodas would get inside and open the gates, delaying any alarm as long as possible.

Part four: once inside the gate the band would dismount, giving horses to designated horse holders, form a shield wall, and clear the tunnel.

Part five: the band was divided into four parts; the advance ride who would keep the gate open and then remain in place to secure the critical entry way. Athan would take a dozen men seconded by Linus, one of Rodas' sergeants, and go to the right to clear the guardhouse on the south bastion and then climb the interior stairs to take the bastion, baring the doors that led into that stronghold from the barracks on the south side. Prokopios, a tough old sergeant who had been with Athan for several years would take another dozen men and go up the north bastion, likewise isolating it from the rest of the fort. While the leading men were taking the bastions the final group would secure the horses, (both theirs and any they found in the stables) and act as a reserve under Rodas. In the worst case they would also be securing the band's escape route. Once the band held the west side of the Hold with its two bastions and the gate they would be in a commanding position and would decide which way to move depending on the situation. They could deal with any attack from the courtyard, and secure the west gate from any possible relief force that might come up from the town.

"Of course," said Athan using an old joke, "how long does a plan last?"

"Until the first clash of spears," came the punch line from several of his men.

"So, remember, be flexible and respond to changing circumstances."

The wind had picked up, a cold north wind from their backs and heavy rain drops, drops so heavy they felt like frozen rain, began to scatter down. It was going to be an evil autumn storm; if it lacked the full power of a winter blizzard it compensated by sheer nastiness. It was not quite cold enough to snow, but there was plenty of moisture in the air that was going to come down soon, spreading misery to anyone unfortunate enough to be in the open. Rodas led his initial group of seven out in a rough and scattered group. Athan gave them a short head start and followed with the rest of the band. He had thought he would have to work to keep the band from looking like a coordinated force but he need not have worried; the storm was doing that for him. The men straggled out looking exactly like a weary group of travelers who were just interested in getting into shelter. Although it was still afternoon the heavy clouds and rain made it seem much later. As the band rode down toward the town of Dassaria it began to rain harder. Athan stole a glance up the hill to his objective. It looked bigger than he had thought it would and had a menacing air. It seemed to squat on the hill, dominating the ground below.

He was near the rear of the band when he entered the collection of buildings that made up the town. He was pleased to see that his men were screened by buildings and out of sight of the Hold's watching bastions. He was not pleased to see that the arrival of two score horsemen was creating a lot of interest among the few people looking out on the street where they assembled. Speed was now the issue. Moving over to Rodas through his milling horsemen he asked a question.

"Are you ready?"

Rodas looked around to verify his six companions were still with him.

"Yes," was all he said.

"Then go. The gods be with you."

Rodas turned his horse and headed toward the road that led around some buildings and up to the Hold. Just before he rounded the corner he twisted around and made a final jest. "Come on men, we need to open the door to our new home for these lazy follow-behinds." And the seven men kicked their horses out of the press and away up the hill.

Athan ordered his men to get their spears from the pack animals and unsling their shields. By this time it had become clear to anyone watching in the town that this was an invading force. Those doors and shutters already closed to keep out the wind were being bolted and barred to keep out intruders. Athan had thought he would have to hold back his formation until Rodas was over halfway up the hill, but it took far longer than he had anticipated to get organized with all their helmets on, spears distributed, and the men in some semblance of a column of twos. By the time he led the rest of the band out and cantering up the hill, now with the stinging cold wind and rain in their faces, blowing their fine gray cloaks back they could see Rodas was already up to the gates.

"Come on men!" Athan shouted back to the men behind who made a brave showing with matching cloaks, shields on the left sides, spears held upright on the right. "Let's go bear hunting!" and he kicked his pony into a trot.

The old man peered outside into another gloomy morning. The weather remained miserable. It was rain now instead of snow, but it was still cold and dank. How often had he had to go out into weather as foul as this? Well today he was going to stay in bed. He went back to his fire and stoked it up good and hot. Then he rearranged his gear and brought over some more firewood for later. He ritually fluffed up what remained of his grass bedding and then he wrapped himself up and lay back down.

The weather outside was almost as bad as was the day he become a king. He lay his head down on the saddle and thought back on the circumstances that led him to become royalty of a sort.

Chapter Nineteen - Housewarming

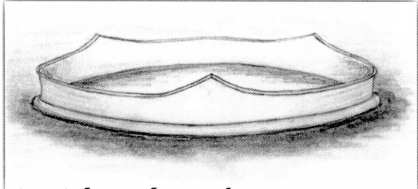

As Athan cleared the last buildings of the town and headed up the road that led to the Hold. Even though he could see Rodas and his men were at the gates he did not want to hurry up the hill; his men must look like cold tired reinforcements heading up to shelter, not an attacking assault force. And right now getting into shelter seemed like a very good idea. The north wind had picked up, alternating spits of frozen rain with bands of the heavy showers that soaked through warmest cloak. Although still it was still light, all that did was let you see the dense threatening clouds coming down from the north. Looking back at his column they did look like professional soldiers, although every man was universally ducking down using his shield as protection from the wind and rain that was coming from their left side. Athan was already chilled to the bone and welcomed the chance to pick up the pace as they headed up the hill.

As Rodas trotted up the hill trailed by his men he wondered how he had gotten himself into this position. Why was he the one riding up to this impregnable fortress while the Chief the rest of the men waited to see if it was safe? Athan had said that Rodas was a better talker and that might be true, but that business about being a better fighter, though also probably true indicated that he and his men were somehow expected to prise open the gates by themselves and hold it against the garrison while the rest of the band trotted up. The idea of trying to hold back a garrison with just six other men did not seem viable. Rodas made up his mind he was going to wait to come to blows just as long as he could.

Rodas and his men slowed down as they approached the gates. Just as they had been told the gates were two large reinforced doors as high as two men at the top where they met in an arch. They had iron rings set into the edges, so they apparently opened outward. The normal-sized sally port had a small covered peep hole where the watch could look out and examine who was at the door. There was a simple metal latchkey sticking out from a slot just like any ordinary door; obviously this small door opened inward. But for the fact this entrance was set into such an imposing set of double doors the sally port door looked like nothing so much as a rather more substantial version of a door to any well-to-do house. Well, Talos had said it was the way most people came and went into the Hold.

He expected to be challenged, but the place seemed deserted. He did see some movement near the top of the southern bastion's tower, but no one seemed to be about otherwise. He pulled his horse up to the gate and dismounted. He raised his fist to pound on the door when a happy chance caused him to push down on the tarnished latchkey of the small door. The level depressed, the latch lifted and the door opened. He stepped inside. The tunnel was just as it had been described, an enclosed white-washed passage with a arched roof that matched the two arched main doors. The floor was of flagstones, well set with masonry. The only surprise was a closed door set on the right side of the passage about half way down. There were no doors at the end of the tunnel leading in to the Hold which was the only source of light in the dim tunnel. He was inside! Scarcely believing his luck, he turned to his right and saw heavy iron holders for the bar set into the inside of the main gate doors. The bar that went into these iron crutches was a long thick timber that would withstand a considerable battering; it stood leaning against the far right wall. The gates were not even barred! Rodas pushed on the gates to open them. This was too easy! But the gates did not open. He heard men at the far end of the tunnel, and was aware at the same time of some of his men coming in the sally port. He pushed harder on the big doors; they would not open. What was holding them? Rodas was a steady man in a crisis but he began to panic. Why wouldn't the doors open?

"Here, what's all this?" came a call echoing from behind him as he pushed harder at the stubborn gates that were not barred and should open easily.

Then Talos was there, bending down and pulling up a metal bolt that fitted into a hole in the flagstones; then the strange little man was opening one side of the gates and moving to lift the right hand floor bolt and open that side. 'Of course', thought Rodas, 'a floor bolt!' Relief flooded through him and his confidence was instantly restored.

"What are you doing?" came from behind him.

Rodas turned and addressed the man who had apparently come into the tunnel from the door in middle of the passage and was walking toward them him. "We are getting in out of this appalling weather," Rodas said with an assertive and irritated tone approaching him. "Have you not seen what it is like out there?"

The man was wearing a dirty tunic, leggings, boots, no cloak but a blanket wrapped over his shoulders and no headgear. If he had a sword it was under the blanket. Rodas' confidence soared. He continued past the man toward the courtyard as his men began to lead their horses in the now fully opened gates.

"Here, now," protested the man following Rodas as he walked toward the entrance to the courtyard, "who are you?"

"We are the scouts for the reinforcements. Didn't anyone tell you we were coming?" Rodas made sure the man could see anger visibly being held just below the surface. The watchman did see it and was cowed. Athan had reached the end of the tunnel and stood looking around at the courtyard. It was just about as had been described, down to the mud and ugly red stone granaries in the center of the courtyard. Two men came over from the stables on the right, curious. They were dressed as casually as the watchmen and though neither had a sword one held a big hammer.

There was an overhang over this western end of the Hold and the rain was dripping down from it, some of it already trying to form short icicles. The stable walls extended back about a quarter of the way back, left and right from the gate entrance, before they open into a broad entrance. As promised, he could smell the horses. Behind him he could hear his men in the tunnel, dismounted and coming up with their horses. If he could not hold a narrow place like this for an hour with half a dozen picked men he deserved to die.

"Close the doors," said one of the newcomers that had come from the stable. "It lets in a draft."

"More like a gale," put in his companion who held the hammer.

"My captain is coming up behind me," said Rodas moving toward them. "They will be here soon. We need to get our horses into the best stalls before they get here. Where do you want us to put them?"

This was just the kind of problem the men looking at him expected. One of them began to complain that they were not expected until tomorrow but before he could get well started Rodas interrupted him turning back to what must have been the watchman. "When is dinner? We have come a long way. We are cold and hungry. Where do we eat?" Then turning back to his men he gestured to them to move up. One man, Spiros, remained standing by the side door in the center of the passage holding the horses. The other five came forward; they had their shields up, the lighter oval shields of hypastas not normal shield of Illyrian cavalry, and they were holding either javelins or swords in their right hands. Two other men from the garrison had appeared from somewhere to join the three confronting him. None had a sword showing and aside from the one man holding a hammer their hands were empty, but Rodas could see they were becoming uneasy. One man crossed in front of them moving toward the north bastion.

"I'll get the sergeant of the guard," he called.

"I don't think so," said Rodas and turned to one of his men. "Stop him," he ordered and drew his sword menacing the others. 'Now it begins,' he thought. The man heading for the bastion sprinted for safety, but was dropped by a well-thrown javelin. Rodas circled around to get behind the other four men to cut off their escape. The man with the hammer tried to defend himself with wild swings of his hammer, but a clean thrust by a javelin put him down. The watchman was grabbed by Talos and relieved of the short sword he had under the blanket. The other men surrendered meekly. Rodas looked into the stables on the south side. Two men in the far corner were making themselves scarce. No one else was visible. Two enemies down, three captured, the doors wide open, and still no alarm had sounded. He stood there uncertainly for a moment, glancing back to see if Athan and his men were in sight. It was eerily quiet; he could actually hear the rain dripping from the eves.

Then Rodas looking to his left saw that the door into the north bastion where the fugitive had apparently been heading was slightly ajar. They had thought that they would need to batter those doors down once they were inside; Athan's men had two stout logs on the pack animals that where coming up the trail. 'They'll get here someday,' thought Rodas impatiently. If they could get into the north bastion they would have half the battle won. It was time for action.

"Arsene take two men and go over to that door. Make sure nobody closes it." The three men raced over to the designated entrance, pulled it open, and disappeared cautiously inside. Their dash had apparently attracted attention. Several men on the south side of the Hold about half way down the courtyard over by where the mess hall was located stood under the eves and began talking and gesturing toward the gate. "Spiros," ordered Rodas to the man holding the horses, "get those animals over to the stable here on the right." They would need to have the tunnel clear when Athan and his troop finally showed up. Rodas was thinning out his guard on the entrance; there were so many opportunities that were opening up. Perhaps their plan was working a little too well. A head peeked around the end of the wall from the stables on the left side.

"Hey," called Rodas to the man, "come here, I want to talk to you."

The head disappeared. There was a corpse with a javelin sticking our of its back right in front of the stable, armed men were racing around the courtyard up into the bastions, the invaders were stabling their horses and still no alarm! What was this place?

It was almost a relief when he finally heard an alarm being rung; by the sound of it someone was hammering,' clang, clang, clang' with metal bar on what must be a piece of iron up from the top of the south bastion.

'Okay, let's get started,' he thought. And still nothing happened. And then Rodas heard the sound of laboring horses coming up the path and into the Hold. As though the arrival of the main body was the cue for the actors, everything suddenly started happening at once.

A horn blew from somewhere back in the Hold. Along the south side of the Hold armed men came running from the general location of the mess hall, and down the ramp from the upper level. A small party of men waving swords rushed out of the south bastion toward the gate. From the north bastion came faint sounds of weapons clashing where Arsene and his men must be introducing themselves to some brand new friends. And then Athan led his men, their horses blowing from the dash up the hill out of the tunnel and into the courtyard like a gust of armored wind.

As Sergeant Prokopios dismounted and led his assigned men to the left and up into the open door of the north bastion, Athan led a group of men, all still mounted, first to head off small party of men coming around from the south bastion, then to cut them off from retreating back into their exit as they realized the extent to which they were outnumbered. One man made it back to the door closely pursued by Athan who thrust his spear at the man as he dodged inside the door. The thrust drew no blood, but it did prevent the door from closing. Athan remained astride his pony holding his spear in the door while dimly seen hands tried to push it out. The other defenders in the yard had either surrendered to the men menacing them on horseback or scattered into the stalls of the stables. Horses were screaming and kicking the stalls.

"Hey," gasped Athan, "Over here! Don't let them close this door!" Most of the men assigned to go with Athan to the south bastion had dismounted and were chasing after the men who had dodged into the stables. "Let them go!" ordered Athan. Linus, a big blonde northern warrior led men over to where Athan was struggling with the defenders who were still trying to push his spear out of the doorway so they could slam it shut and secure it. His men put their shoulders to the door and heaved. After a moment the door gave back and vicious fighting broke out as the men pushed in attacked and were attacked by those inside. Athan dropped his spear which was now hindering his own men. Before he could dismount Talos came pelting up to him on foot. His pilleus had been pushed down over his bald head to his ears which were sticking out to either side. With his strange little beard and flushed pace he looked like some large maddened dwarf. In fact, even with a naked sword in one hand and shield held in the other he looked faintly ridiculous. But what he made Athan understand was not ridiculous at all; it was brilliant.

"Sir, sir," he shouted, "the armory! It is still closed! They are going to try to open the armory!" Seeing Athan's blank stare he prompted him some more with gestures and additional explanations. "Most of the weapons are there! We can stop them from issuing weapons to the men in here!"

Athan now understood. They had not really expected to be able to stop the defenders from arming themselves. If they could stop the men inside from getting to the spears, bows, armor, helmets, and other weapons the garrison would have to fight with just the personal weapons they had with them. Talos had said the Bear did not like his men being armed inside the hold when they were off duty. That made sense. Why allow such valuable items out where they could be damaged, lost, or stolen? And the inevitable fights between his men would be limited in intensity. But in order to be used to defend the Hold, they had to be retrieved from the armory, and for some reason, the defenders had not done that yet.

"Linus," he called, "take over. Hold the bastion until I get back." Then kicking his little pony he galloped a few strides up to the entrance where Rodas was holding as planned with perhaps a dozen men, some still mounted. Pulling up savagely on his mount, Athan called out to his lieutenant, "We can take the armory. They will have to fight us naked!" Laughing insanely at his own joke Athan turned back to his men milling near the entrance, "All you men still mounted, follow me!" And he yanked the poor little pony around and headed it around the north side of the silos away on the opposite side of the courtyard from where biggest concentration of defenders that had clustered near the mess hall. Athan feared they might be an impediment to his dash to the armory at the northwest end of the Hold. Eleven men followed him, some swinging up onto their mounts to follow. Talos and another man started to follow on foot but before they had gone more that a few score feet the two men heard Rodas bellowing at them to reform at the gate. At about the same time the decided that two men running across the courtyard, unsupported were extremely vulnerable to even the scattered resistance being put up by the defenders. There were a growing number of men in the courtyard, and most had a weapon of some kind in their hands. The two dashed back to the entrance just as they saw one of their comrades emerging from the top of the north bastion tower. The northeast bastion was already secured!

It did not take Athan very long to gallop even his tired pony the length of the courtyard, but he seemed to have plenty of time to consider all sorts of things. He remembered how Thaddeus always held back some of his forces, 'a reserve' he called it. Thaddeus always advised holding the reserve to the critical moment. 'The one who commits all his forces first is the one that usually loses,' was how he put it. And Athan had committed his reserves to an unplanned and unsupported charge on a mission they had not envisioned. On the other hand Thaddeus also counseled initiative, and keeping an unbalanced enemy unbalanced. 'Get them running, keep them running. Get them scared and keep them scared.' So he was going to try to unbalance the defenders to death. He had to do something, because Athan was already aware that this Hold was too big and had too many defenders for his little band to conquer. All his life he had been a cautious commander. That was why he was still alive. It was part of the reason men followed him willingly. He won or he ran. And now for the first time in his life Athan was committing himself and his men totally to the outcome of a battle; because if they did not win and win quickly, there would be nowhere **to** run.

The armory was on the north wall near the northeast corner where the northwest bastion jutted out. The armory door was opening even as Athan and his little group of men came charging up. Athan pulled the javelin he had put under his saddle getting his grip just in time to throw it after a man who was pushing inside the armory. Dismounting in a rush, he let his pony go as landed hard and staggered all the way to the wall before catching himself and pulling out his kopis. Despite the fact he had been leading the group he was not the first to the door of the armory. A wild and sudden fight scattered the few defenders by the door and then his men were plunging inside. Athan gestured to the rest of his men to watch the courtyard and entered the door stepping over a stream of blood that was already flowing out the door. Most of the blood was coming from a man lying on his belly, the blood coming from beneath him giving evidence of mortal wounds to his front. Another man somewhat further in was lying on his back writhing feebly with a javelin in his back; that was apparently Athan's work. He saw three of his men menacing two of the defenders who were cowering against the right-hand side of the wall, both now unarmed and one holding his left shoulder trying to staunch the blood coming from a wound there.

"Secure those men," he snapped and looked around in the gloom. There was only one lamp burning, and little light was coming in from the open door, but Athan could see that the sizable room was filled with arms and armor, racked, piled and stacked in poor order. But there had to be enough equipment in there to equip two hundred men. "Tenucer you and Eustathios help guard this place. Don't let anyone get this stuff. Now get those men out of here." Athan gestured to the two pathetic men who were obviously expecting their lives to end soon.

Going outside with the two prisoners shuffling along behind him he was just in time to see Nikolaos and four other men disappearing into the door of the northeast bastion.

"They saw some men going in there and Nikolaos went after them," explained Vissilios, one the men from his old band.

The situation was moving too fast, his men were completely out of control; they were diving after the defenders like terriers after rats into unknown rat holes. That was a problem, this was home for the men who lived here; they knew every door, hiding place and ambush site in the Hold and his men had only sketchy descriptions. "Come with me," he ordered Giles, a young man who had joined the band in Pella, grabbing him by the arm and heading after his increasingly fragmented little band. "Stay here with Tenucer and hold that armory!" this to Vissilios who turned to help take charge of the two prisoners while trying to keep and eye on several men who were watching them from the south side of the hold. That left four men preventing the defenders from accessing their weapons until he could catch up to his men and recover them to their duty. The four could take refuge inside the armory if pressed and hold out until he got back with the rest of his impromptu collection of fighters.

The door into the bastion led into an open stone-floored room with a stair running around two sides of the walls. At the far end on the second floor the last of his men was disappearing through a solid-looking door at the head of a landing. He ignored Athan's angry shout to wait. Cursing, Athan pounded up the stairs to his right and around the second flight that led to the door, kicking it open to find another, smaller bare room. This one had a ladder leading up to a trap door in the ceiling and doors opening left and right. He knew that the ladder led up to the lookout post on the top of the bastion. Athan pulled the ladder down to delay anyone who might be up there and with Giles close behind him pushed open the door on the right that was ajar; this entry led to the rooms on the north side of the Hold and apparently was the one his men had used. He was heading back toward the main gate but now he was one level up.

It was dim in the room beyond, the shutters were closed on the arrow slits that opened to the outside, and there were only two lamps lit. Athan could felt the room was relatively large and open. Dim shapes that might have been cushions or couches were scattered around the floor, but there were no people in evidence. Hearing noises coming from an opening ahead of him Athan did not pause but still closely attended by Giles continued through the opening on the left side down a short passage. There were shuttered windows that must open into the courtyard. The shutters did not fit well and let in a mighty draft of cold air, but they also let in enough light to reveal a door into what must be a room on the right. At the end of the passageway there was another large room that appeared to be better lit. And from that opening came the sound of men fighting; fighting in desperate close combat. Nikolaos and his companions had disturbed The Badger.

The Badger, he had another name but he preferred his self-anointed nickname so much that he no longer answered to any other. He was in his own way as much a character of the Hold as the Bear himself. The Badger was a short man. Some short men can be very pugnacious; like everything else he did The Badger took that tendency to the extreme. He had a personality that went well beyond determined into the absolutely obsessive. Any contest, any challenge became a contest of will for The Badger, and he hated being bested at anything. Even in a culture that valued athletics, The Badger was extreme in his fitness regime. Even now with gray streaks in his closely curled beard, he was as solid as a tree stump and just as reasonable. His personality would not allow him to have close friends, for he was in constant competition, always proving himself. Only the Bear himself, easily twice The Badger's size was exempt from constant challenges and prickly concerns about honor. The Badger was utterly convinced that if a man was completely committed to a goal and refused to give up he could accomplish anything. In his youth he though he had been in frequent fights, and because of his size sometime beaten, but he would never surrender. The Badger was still a wild young man when he first met Ratimir, before either man had their nicknames. Ratimir was at that time merely the new chieftain of a small but growing band. A disagreement between two such strong personalities was inevitable. The Badger, fighting the much bigger and stronger man, was beaten into unconsciousness. Upon being revived he had merely washed his battered face, sought out Ratimir again, and resumed the fight. After being knocked out a second time, he waited until the next day to resume the battle. Eventually Ratimir grew tired of beating the youngster up and amused at his persistence. Instead of killing him Ratimir made peace with the short man, bringing him into his band long before the Hold was built. The Badger had been there when the Bear had helped sack Epirus. He had watched Ratimir become rich, and famous. He was content with his role as a sergeant just so long as he was given the respect he demanded. That he was still alive was a testament to his toughness and fighting prowess. It was a deep indelible part of his personality and self image that he, The Badger, would never, never, ever give up. And in his mind, he had never done so.

Time had not mellowed The Badger, but even he was relaxed that evening. It was the start of a quiet autumn night; he had known thousands of evenings like this before. Men were lounging about on cushions and low couches. Half a dozen lamps supplemented the fire that made the room cozy on the foul autumn night. He was watching some of his fellows dicing by the fireplace set into the outside wall, waiting for the evening meal when he heard a disturbance outside. At first the men ignored it but then a man ran into the room from the direction of the main gate shouting they were being attacked. The dicers and onlookers stopped their idle conversation, the dice game paused, and they could hear, faintly, the alarm calling them to arms. There was general stirring, and everyone got to their feet, some producing their personal daggers, but no one was quite sure just what to do. Some began making toward the main entrance, either to head to the bastion or to reach the outside ladder that led down from the next room onto the courtyard, others began looking for their cloaks and heavy over-tunics. The decision about what to do was made for them when two men from the garrison dashed in from the opposite side of the room hotly pursued by five strange men bearing spears and shields. They were being attacked from the rear!

The room exploded into pandemonium. Some men fled out the far door from the attackers, others hurled furniture and anything else that came to hand at the strangers, causing them to pause in the door way and shelter behind their shields. Others, The Badger leading them, brought out daggers and charged. The Badger had a snatched up stool in one hand and his long dagger in the other as he drove into the men at the entrance. He was an old and experienced soldier and immediately achieved his first goal of splitting the enemy's force. While his compatriots pinned two men near the door against the wall on the courtyard side The Badger drove the other three away from the door toward the outside wall. The attackers had shields and spears, and were able to kill several of the defenders before their more numerous foes closed with them. Then spears became a liability in the close quarters. Only Yure the younger, caught with Niomiki near the door was able to draw his deadly leaf-shaped sword which he had began to use with good effect. He was able to keep the men of the garrison back and undoubtedly saved both their lives, but he was now separated from and could not help the others.

Things were not going so well for Nikolas and his two comrades who were pushed along the wall by the press of the men who had turned on Athan's wayward group. Poorly armed and surprised the defenders might be but they were fighting men, desperate, and they had numbers. The Badger ran under a spear thrust, knocking it up with the stool and slamming his shoulder into Nikolas' shield. There was no room for him to either use his spear or draw his sword. The Badger and his fellows began slowly pushing the men down the wall toward the corner. They resisted of course, but the three were outnumbered. All they could do was flail ineffectually with their spears on the backs of the men pushing against them. What had been a wild chase had suddenly become a microcosm of a battle of hoplites, with men pushing against one another, too close to use weapons effectively. That closeness did not bother The Badger. He dropped the stool and griped the edge of Nikolas' shield with his left hand as he worked to get his long straight dagger behind the edge of Nikolas' shield. He kept his short powerful legs driving the shield against Nikolas' body, keeping him from either using his spear or drawing his sword all the while pushing him inexorably back away from the door. Nikolas for his part was using all his strength to try to hold his shield's edge right up against the wall to keep his stocky opponent from getting past his only defense.

"Its like opening an oyster," said The Badger in an almost conversational voice. Aside from screams and curses, it was the first words spoken. The effect was so strange no man in that room ever forgot that moment. Then, with a cunning twist of his blade The Badger slid his dagger past Nikolas' shield and into his thigh just above his bent knee. Nikolas screamed in pain and his shield shifted as he tried to pull away from his opponent. He beat down frantically with the staff of his spear on the back of the man who was hurting him but to no avail. The Badger bore in ripping up the muscle on the front of the leg, feeling to position the dagger for a cut to either hamstring the man or slice the femoral artery. Either way, he had won again.

The Badger did not see the spear that took one of the men battling Yure and Niomiki near the entrance, but he felt the change in the battle. Two more attackers had entered the fray from that same damn door. In fact, Giles had made a wonderful cast of his spear from the close confines of the corridor over Athan's shoulder in into the chest of a man who was engaging Yure with a long knife and a chair. He then pulled his short sword and followed Athan into the room. Athan felt the spear go past him, watched the face of the man it killed change from rage to agony, then kicked the dying man out of the way and thrust his kopis at a man on his right. Giles moved up to his left and engaged another man. Instantly the battle had changed. The pressure against Yure and Niomiki lessened as the men drew back from this new attack. Niomiki was able to pull out his sword. Now instead of two men trapped against a wall, four men were formed up with shields and swords, ready to sweep the room and rescue their trapped comrades in the corner.

The Badger did not think. He did not need to think. He understood at a visceral level that a flanking attack can sometimes be flanked itself. Pulling out his dagger from Nikolas with a final agonizing twist he leapt across the room to kill the clean-shaven man who was trying to thrust his long down-curved sword past a chair. So sudden was his counterattack that Athan did not have time to bring his shield around. Dropping the handle of his shield and leaving it to dangle by its arm strap his left hand grabbed the top of The Badger's right wrist as the dagger came in for a curving thrust intended to go through his cuirass and ultimately his ribcage. At the same instant, Athan's own down stroke with his kopis was caught and held by The Badger's left hand. The two men posed of a moment each straining with all their might to both hold and break their respective holds. Then The Badger went to work. Once again, his thick legs began to push, twisting Athan inexorably to his right, away from support from Giles, and opening their little line's right flank. The dagger had been checked but it slowly descended toward Athan's body. It had already penetrated the layers of lacquered linen and leather armor Athan was wearing. It was a good piece of gear; light and comfortable, it did not constrain the wearer and offered excellent protection against arrows, stones, and slashing blows. It was not as effective against thrusts, only heavy metal armor was proof against thrusts. Both men knew this perfectly well. Using his great upper body strength, aided by his powerful legs, The Badger pushed the dagger through the final layer but then found he his thrust baulked by a new layer of armor. The two men were grunting and straining and stamping while this was happening; though time seemed to have stopped, it was in reality only a few score beats of their pounding hearts before the situation dramatically changed.

Athan began rolling his right wrist against The Badger's thumb. You must be very much stronger than someone to hold their wrist when they twist it. Although The Bader was extremely strong, he was not strong enough to hold Athan for long. Recognizing this he tried to break Athan's grip so that he could get another stoke of his dagger into Athan's body; this thrust would certainly punch through the armor and into his opponent's heart. But his dagger was stuck in the layers of Athan's cuirass hindering him from generating a strong enough twisting motion. Athan broke The Badger's grip. Athan raised the kopis over his head, avoiding The Badger's left hand that was trying to regain its grip. For an instant they posed, the smaller man's arm waving up like a questing snake's head. Keeping his arm high bending only with his wrist Athan cut down on the reaching hand. Blood flowed as the sharp blade sliced down; the second slash severed a little finger. All the while Athan was hanging on to The Badger's right wrist for dear life. He knew he could not let him withdraw it for another blow; neither did he want to allow the weapon to push any harder into his body. He worked his hand on top of the other man's and pushed down on the handle of the dagger wedging it firmly in his armor. It hurt, but had not penetrated his red vest yet.

Athan could not believe this man was still trying to kill him. He had taken bloody wounds, fighting a larger armed and armored enemy, and instead of behaving properly and surrendering he apparently thought that killing Athan was worth any wound. He would just not stop. For the first time since they had entered the Hold Athan became very frightened.

The Badger abruptly shifted tactics. Realizing he could not free his dagger he let go of the hilt, twisted out of Athan's grip, sweat and blood making that easy, and tried to give the hilt of his knife a blow with the heel of his hand, hoping a solid blow would accomplish what his pushing had not. The two men wrestled for a moment, Athan twisting his body and using his left hand struggling to block The Badger's right. Now Athan's shield, dangling down, was more of a hindrance than protection. Then The Badger's foot slipped. He had been lounging around before all the excitement wearing only woolen stocking in the room and had no opportunity to don proper footgear. His foot only slipped a little, but it changed the entire dynamics of their match. Athan still waving the kopis high over The Badger's head was able to slip past his blocking left arm just long enough to hammer the butt of the sword down on top of the short man's head, once, twice; then both of The Badger's hands were gripping Athan's right arm above the elbow, trying to stop any more blows down to his skull. But The Badger was stunned and could not prevent Athan from twisting the blade down and slicing it down across the side of his thick neck.

A kopis is a heavy blade. It is designed to hack more than slice and so does not need to be particularly sharp. But on the two nights riding to the Hold, Athan had eased his nerves, like many other soldiers, by obsessively sharpening his sword. The kopis was still as keen as the razor Athan used to shave his face. The inward curving belly of the blade sliced though thick cords of The Badger's neck muscles and partially severed the carotid artery.

It is amazing how much blood a healthy man's heart can pump. Every man in the room became aware of that as The Badgers heart, as strong as the rest of him, shot blood into the air well over the heads of the men fighting there, drenching them in red. The Badger pulled back for the first time. What happened next caused the hair on Athan's neck to rise. With an obviously mortal wound, The Badger calmly dragged the collar of his tunic up and held it in place with his left hand to partially staunch the blood. The dirty white garment immediately was stained red. Then he resumed his attack, ducking his head and trying to get a solid blow onto the hilt of the dagger that still stood out from Athan's armor. Athan backed, his kopis held high. Perhaps this unexpected attack would have worked, but as he charged The Badger staggered, perhaps from blood loss, or perhaps he slipped in the blood that pouring out of him. Athan stepped aside and brought the heavy blade down on the back of his opponent's thick short neck. The Badger dropped to the floor. The last thing The Badger learned before he died was that no matter how determined you are, no matter how strong your will, your body will not respond when your spinal column has been severed.

By now, thoroughly spooked, Athan hacked down at the body again. This time he nearly severed the head, only a thin strip of skin held it on. As the head rolled up, Athan saw the eyes still glaring at him in unexpended fury. Then the eyes blinked. With a yell Athan kicked the head. The bit of skin that was holding it parted and the head rolled over to the other side of the room toward the defenders who had been pressing Nikolas and his two companions. Fighting in the room had come to a stop while the two champions had battled. Now, as the head of The Badger rolled to a lopsided stop the defenders looked as one man first to the severed head, then to Athan who stood, sword in hand, completely covered in blood. There was the sound of weapons being dropped to the floor and calls for quarter. Two of the men ran out of the room down the far corridor. The fight in this room was over.

In fact the fight was over all down the length of the upper level on that side. Athan collected his men. Nikolas needed support to stand, and one of the men who had been with him in the corner, Toxeus, was beyond any further help. Six of the defenders were dead; the rest huddled sullenly in the far corner.

"You men are my prisoners," panted a deeply tired Athan to the dispirited group. "Put down your weapons." Since they had few weapons to begin with and these had already been dropped they merely stood there uncertainly. Realizing he had to make them do something or the situation would get out of control, Athan gave them another order in a more commanding voice.

"You are going to go out into the courtyard. Pick up a blanket. It is cold out there."

This they could understand and made sense. The survivors responded with alacrity, a few surreptitiously picked up their knives as they wrapped themselves in the bedding that lay around the room. They led the way out of the room down a passageway heading toward the main gate. Some moved rapidly ahead and clambered down the wide ladder that led to the courtyard below. Of necessity the line of men backed up a bit as more men waited to go down; everyone was nervous. Some of the garrison tried to slip over to the northwest bastion, but the door there was secured on the other side. They hurried back toward the ladder. Men began dropping out of windows to the flagstones below. Athan and his four hale men kept pushing through the rooms. Aeetes who alone had survived in the corner unharmed was helping Nikolas whose left leg was badly wounded. They stopped long enough to wrap a cloth around it to reduce the blood loss, but he could not put any weight on it at all, and though he did not complain, his involuntary groans indicated he was in great pain. They could not wait, nor could the leave him. So hanging on to Aeetes' left should he limped along, trying to stay up.

What Athan and his men did not see happening behind them were men (and a few women) rising from hiding places and from the rooms Athan's little group had not opened quietly making their way toward the back gate.

Tenucer was still holding the armory. His three companions had each taken advantage of the equipment available to them and while the others stood guard one at the time emerged from the armory with excellent heavy armor including bronze greaves, breastplates and helmets. The also were now holding heavy round hoplons. They made a splendid sight, especially Eustathios who was both the tallest and biggest man in the band. He had thick arms, broad shoulders, and legs like tree trucks. Perhaps he was not exactly the smartest member of the band, his beetling brows and vacant expression gave that away, but he was good-natured, brave, and well-liked. Now, splendidly arrayed in shining armor, holding a big war spear, Eustathios was a veritable Ajax. It would have taken a brave man to face such a hero. He was flanked on either side by a similarly armed comrade; additional spears were leaned against the wall behind them. Tenucer had only added a bronze breast plate to his armor, but he had found an excellent bow in the armory along with several quivers of arrows. Tenucer had once been a peltast and had always favored that form of fighting perhaps because he was not as tall as most and had a lean build. On the far side of the courtyard, a large group of men had gathered, talking among themselves, and trying to get up the nerve to do something about getting into the armory. The three hoplites stood in a menacing line; Tenucer stood behind them with his bow, keeping an eye on things, and putting arrows in the direction of anyone who seemed to be working himself up into doing anything rash. Arrows might not be a serious threat to a shield wall of armored men, but they could be dangerous to men in a situation like this, and these men knew it. Whenever anyone seemed to encourage the men to move against the heroes guarding the armory, Tenucer shot an arrow at him. Sometimes he hit his mark, too. Because he was keeping an eye all around them, he was the first to notice that the back gate was open and people were slipping outside from both the two western bastions. Tenucer was not sure what to do about stopping this flow. After consideration, he decided they had enough enemies inside, and the more that left the better.

At the other end of the Hold another member of the band was looking at another group of men, but there were very significant differences in their intentions. Whereas Tenucer was watching a dispirited group of unarmed men slinking out of the fight, Spriros was watching a group of men heading uphill toward the Hold from the town. Spriros had taken the first group of horses into the stable and then had been detailed to watch the front gate by Rodas. He stood there now by the open gate with his friend Jason watching the men coming closer. He could not be certain in the poor light but he pretty certain they had spears. They certainly had shields. Jason stood next to Spriros and watched the approaching men.

"Maybe we should tell Rodas," he suggested.

"Yeah," agreed Spriros "Go get him."

But Rodas had gone up into the bastion and Jason was having trouble finding him. Spriros decided that it was time to close the gate, even without orders. It was letting in the cold wind anyway. He stepped out and went around to the south gate, which had been blown completely open by the north wind and was now flat against the outside wall. When he tried to close it again he found that between the poor footing, the strong wind, and the sheer weight of the door itself he could not seem to get it closed again. Huffing and puffing he stopped with the door half closed, a gust trying hard to push it wide open again. Spriros stole a glance downhill. The men coming up the hill were now running. It was now clear that they were armed, and had no good intentions toward him. For an instant he considered letting go of the door and running away. But where would he run? A flood of energy poured through him and he heaved the door around and closed with a slam. Hoping it would stay that way, as he dashed over to grab the right door which was being held back by a stone placed there by one of the entering raiders to keep it open. It was upwind so once he kicked the rock aside, and got it started it slammed shut for him. Of course, this left Spriros on the wrong side of the gates. He had his second moment of panic in less than a hundred heartbeats. But then the smaller door set inside the right hand side door popped open from the impact of the larger door slamming shut. Spriros ducked inside. The bar was still leaning against the right hand side. Spriros leapt to pick it up and fit it into the iron cradles that would bar the gates. He quickly found that he had problems. The bar was heavy, but the real problem with maneuvering it was that it was an awkward load, long and unbalanced. Worse, he had forgotten to close the small door and as the door open inward, it kept him from dropping the bar down into the cradles. Swearing he kicked the small door shut and with a terrific effort heaved the bar up and then down onto the upturned iron crutches, barring the outer doors from opening outward, and the smaller door from opening inward. Then he fitted the pins into the top of the crutches that prevented someone on the other side from slipping a blade in the crack of the door and lifting up the bar. Then he leaned back against the door and sank down to his hams. He was sitting like that, feeling someone beating ineffectually on the far side of the thick doors when Jason came running up the tunnel to him.

"Rodas says to close the gate right away," he said.

Spriros just sat there looking up at him and didn't say a word.

Athan's band moved through the rest of the length of the upper story without further drama. By now everyone in the Hold understood they had been invaded, and no one, at least in this part of the structure, was willing to stand and fight. Athan arrived at what had to be the door to the north east bastion. It was the only substantial door he had encountered that barred his path down the length of the second level, and it was set into a solid wall. It was also barred on the other side. Athan beat on the door with the butt of his bloody sword. No answer. Now what? Yure, a strong man, hammered on the door with his spear butt. When he gave over, the door showing the marks of his pounding, a voice came from the other side.

"Who goes there?" They recognized the voice of Theron, the hunter from Illyria; he had been assigned to clear this bastion with Prokopios.

"It's me, Athan," he replied with considerable relief.

"Who?" The door was thick but the suspicion in the reply came through.

"Athan, son of son of Medius of Epiria; your Captain you sorry son a harpy! We have cleared this end. Now open up and let us in! Now!"

A chorus of other voices now chimed in hurling additional abuse at their fellow on the far side of the door. Theron hastened to release the pins and lift the bar on the other side. He was taken aback when he saw the men on the other side that pushed into the square room on of the bastion, and his hand involuntarily went to the hilt of his sword. There had been fighting on this level, but the men who came through the door had visibly been in a real struggle. Athan in particular was covered in blood and gore literally from head to foot; his sword dripped blood onto the wood floor.

"Sorry, Chief," said Theron, abashed, "I didn't know your real name."

"Me, either, or if I did I forgot it," said Prokopios, entering the bastion from the other side, "and I have known you for years." He had been in the center rooms over the gate on the west side of the Hold and was on his way down. The old sergeant looked at Theron and addressed both men, "We just always called you Chief or Captain."

"You are going to have to call him King after today," put in Rodas who followed Prokopios in followed by the rest of the men. "By Ares!" he exclaimed looking at his fellow captain, "you look like you have been swimming in blood. What happened to you? "

"A fight," answered Athan tersely. Speaking of being a king suddenly made him irritable. "And I am long way from any titles. There are a lot more of the Bear's men in here than we counted on. Let's get to it before they figure out they have us outnumbered."

Aeetes was detailed to close and bar the door back to the second level where they had come from and stay with Nikolas and two other wounded men.

"There are some bows and quivers full of arrows up there," Prokopios informed him. "Bring some down and discourage that lot down there." He gestured out the arrow slit to where almost a score of men were milling around outside trying to get inside or at least determine just what was going on.

The rest of the men trooped down the stairs, slick with blood in some places, past several corpses, and out into the corridor where the rest of the band was assembling.

It was getting dark outside; it had stopped raining but the wind was even colder now. Athan felt sticky and befouled and he was deeply weary; weary, sore, and sick to his stomach. He just wanted to bathe and put on a nice clean tunic and forget about this entire enterprise. He stopped long enough to go to a bucket of water, probably used to water the horses and splash water on this face and rinse his hands. Turning back to the courtyard he quickly took in the situation. His men were armed, confident for the most part, and quickly assembling. Over on the other side of the Hold near the ramp that ran up to the top of the wall was a large group of men. Some were watching his four men guarding the armory but most were turning to face the larger threat that had now assembled by the front gate.

Prokopios and Rodas come close to speak with him. Both looked uneasily at the gang of men down at the far end.

"Let Prokopios take some men and move down the south wall flush the ones on the second floor back to that end. Then we can bottle them up."

"No," said Athan, "form them up. We are going to attack those men in the courtyard right now. We are going right down the yard."

"They will just climb up the ramp. Then we will have to dig them out of the passageways. They can get right up on the wall. This is no time to be hasty."

"This is exactly the time to be hasty," snapped Athan. "They are beaten. Don't give them any time to forget that; Prokopios, a wedge if you please, to the right side of the courtyard. Take the lead; I will form up some of the boys to be your hypastas. There is your enemy. Drive him off."

These were orders that Prokopios, and old guardsman could appreciate. "Form wedge," he bellowed waving his spear over his head, "On me!" The men immediately began to fill in on either side of him, each a half step behind the man ahead of him forming a broad wedge.

Other men hurried to provide spears to those men in formation who had lost theirs in the fight. Rodas and Athan stood behind and back from Prokopios helping direct men into position, and selecting a few to act as the hypastas who would guard the flanks. Ixon, who had initially been with Athan and had charged into the south east bastion came trotting up carrying the spear Athan had used to keep the defenders from closing the door to the bastion.

"Here's your spear, sir," he said with a wide grin, "a bit battered but still good. Glad you were able to keep them from closing that door."

Ixon was referring to several cut marks on the shaft where frantic defenders had tried to hack off his spear head. The spear had been lying in a puddle of blood on the floor of the bastion and was stained blood's brownish red from the head most of the way down the shaft.

Athan took the weapon distractedly as he assigned Ixon to the right wing of the formation. He was still holding his filthy kopis; he looked for something on which to wipe off the blade, found nothing handy that was not already soiled, shrugged, and slid the unclean blade into his scabbard, taking up the spear in his right hand as he shouldered his shield. Rodas stared at him. He knew Athan emphasized caring for your armor and weapons. He had never seen Athan fail to clean a blade before sheathing it. But then he had never seen blood-soaked Athan in a battle before, either.

Prokopios turned to examine his formation. There were about a dozen men on each side of him with two loose groups at the end of the wedge. He looked at Athan. Athan nodded and pointed to the far end of the compound.

"Formation, advance," ordered the battle-scarred old veteran, and the men began moving forward, shields up, spears out. The fell instinctively into step; someone began a low chanting battle song, which was picked up by the other men. It was a very male sound: rumbling, rhythmic, powerful and primal. A third of the way to their enemies the chant gave way to three grunts. The men emphasized these by clashing their spears against their shields: whump, whump, whump! Their right feet began to come down in a stamp as one. The men at the other end were now giving the formation their undivided attention. They know what that formation of men meant, and what it could do. Prokopios was now half-way to his target, approaching the top of the ramp. Again the chant came to the point when the men clashed their spears, Whump! Whump! Whump! Some of the clustered men began to break from the blatant threat and run, a few sought shelter by ducking into doors, some up the ramp, but most retreated toward the rear gates. Two men sought to hide behind the silos in the center of the courtyard. The hypastas on that end of the formation saw them and speared them both to death before they could either attack or flee. The four men guarding the armory had begun to move up and were clashing their spears in time with the main body. Tenucer had traded his bow for a spear and shield as well. The formation came even with the end of the ramp that let to the top. The hypastas on that side impulsively charged up the ramp, scattering the few men on it. The formation was like a huge dog, straining at the leash. The chant, a low powerful thing, came around again to the three beats, WHUMP! WHUMP! WHUMP! At the third stoke, Prokopios, and the entire formation behind him broke into a charge. Those men still in the courtyard fled like startled birds. Most made it out back gate, but it became congested by the fleeing men and Prokopios and his men now augmented by Tenucer's little group butchered the unfortunate laggards. A few of the band pursued the fugitives out of the gate slaughtering all in their path until they were recalled by a furious Athan and Prokopios. Athan collected the last of the men coming back inside and had them bar the back gate.

Athan directed the sergeant to clean out the south wing of the fortress of any enemy stragglers. "Take half a dozen men or so with you; be sure to bring Nomiki along. He knows what it is like in there." Nomiki swallowed but resolutely nodded his head. "And be sure to include Tenucer and his little band along as well. They are armored for it. Eustathios alone should be enough to put them to flight."

Tenucer, who was standing by smiled, and tried to hand a bloody javelin to Athan, "This is yours, chief. Nice cast; if you hadn't gotten him he might have gotten into the armory and we would have had a hard time digging him out of there."

Rodas and Prokopios stared at Athan, then the big sergeant shook himself and smiling asked, "Mind if we visit that armory before we start? I would like to get some of that heavy stuff on if it is going to be hand to hand."

"Just don't take too long," cautioned Athan. "We have a lot to do. When you have cleared it out, leave a man in each those two bastions there and rally back at the main gate."

While these orders were being given Rodas had a chance to examine this man he wanted to make a king. Only half an hour before he had secretly wondered about why this Athan had been sending him into danger while staying back in safety; he had even wondered if this was a leader who was perhaps a little shy of battle. Was his reputation as a great fighter overblown? After all, little of the talk was from men who had actually seen him fight, and most of his exploits seemed to have been conveniently far away and a long time ago. Now Rodas saw him in a different light altogether. While he himself had not struck even a single blow, this Athan had been in the thick of the battle; there was a large rent in his cuirass right over his heart. All his weapons and every part of his body were covered in blood. Not only that, but he had apparently been the hero at every crucial part of the battle. Looking around at the strength of this place and all the defenders here, Rodas realized it had been insane to try to take it with two score men. No wonder they had completely surprised the garrison. It was impossible to capture this place. No one but a true hero could have pulled it off. What kind of man was this Athan? With a start he realized his chief was giving his orders; he attended closely to his next assignment.

Rodas was directed to take another group of men and examine the lower levels of the north side, then assemble at the main gate. He set two men on guard to keep it closed. Assembling the remainder of his force, he started to mirror Rodas' sweep of the ground level of the south side of the Hold. He did not get far.

The very first door he came to, located next to the entrance to the southeast bastion was barred from the inside. Beating on the door had no effect, so Athan was forced to find some stout pieces of lumber to use as a battering ram. The delay irritated his already touchy state to a point of near fury. After three resounding swings of a log by powerful hands that started the hinges a voice from inside cried out to 'leave off, I'll open up.' There was the sound of muffled disputation behind the door. After a moment, Athan, his patience now completely gone, curtly gestured toward the door. The log slammed into the door again. This time the sounds on the other side were of a bar being lifted. Athan pushed inside, his shield up, spear forward. The room was dim and fetid, with only a single lamp augmenting a low fire in the corner. Indistinct shapes moved in the smoky gloom. Too late Athan remembered that a spear was a poor weapon for indoor combat. Moving to one side so as to clear the entrance he dropped his spear and slid along the wall, hand on his kopis.

"Who are you to disturb the rest of King Ratimir?" came a voice that tried to sound imperious but came out frightened and thus pathetic. Athan tried to pull his blade out of his sheath but found to his intense discomfiture that it was stuck. 'Another reason to clean your blade' he thought. Then to his great relief Giles moved past him and took up a place on his right, unprotected side. Giles had his short sword out and ready

"We have taken this place by right of conquest. Who are you?"

There was stirring in the far corner. Athan could make out at least three figures standing in the room, though one was smaller and bent over. Could that be the ailing Bear?

"King Ratimir has many men, and many strong allies are already coming to his support. I cannot promise you mercy, but if you leave now you may be able to make your escape if you do not take too many things."

It was an obviously hollow threat. Athan ignored it. "This is our place now. If you leave quietly you will not be harmed."

Apparently this speech was more than the Bear could stand. There was a slurred growling from the corner that might have been words, perhaps they were 'get out of my' something or other. Then the Bear stood up. He was wearing, appropriately, a bearskin. There was enough light still shining in from the door to see him rise. It took a long time, not just become he did so with slow careful majesty but because there was a lot of him to bring up. Athan was taller than most, but this huge wide monstrosity was more than a head taller than he and the bearskin added to his already considerable bulk. A long time before, as a young man Athan had gone bear hunting with his old mentor Thaddeus. A group of guardsmen, using dogs had brought a bear to bay where, with much effort and the loss of several dogs they had killed it. This man seemed considerably bigger than that bear had been. He dominated the space with his size and something else harder to define;

even in his reduced state Ratimir still possessed considerable force of personality.

Once again that slurred voice gave a command. It definitely sounded like he wanted them to get out. Such was the power in that hulking figure that had he been alone Athan would have obeyed. But he was under the eyes of his men and he was in a very bad mood. Holding his shield loosely he stepped up to the wreck of the big man and craning up to look at him said.

"This is my place now. It is you must leave."

Ratimir's left hand hung limply by his side. This close he could see the droop on the same side of his face and saw him swaying. He did not see the big right hand coming around until it was too late. The open handed blow caught the edge of the shield and ripped it off the strap and out of his hands, Athan's helmet flew off and hit poor Giles in the side of his face. Athan knew he could not draw his sword, so without giving the matter the slightest thought he charged in taking the big man with his shoulder. Another old memory flashed through his mind. He remembered Persis once had a tall piece of furniture she called a wardroom in her apartments. One time he and Thaddeus and he had come in a little drunk, Thaddeus had stumbled into this wardrobe and either through his clumsiness or a defect in the workmanship, a leg on the tall piece of furniture gave way and the whole wardrobe came crashing down with a magnificent crash. That was how Ratimir went down when Athan put his shoulder into him. First he staggered back, then the left leg buckled, and the whole animal crashed down, upsetting a table in his fall. Athan's men filled the room and instantly had blades against the others in the room. The two men, one a youth, held perfectly still while the old woman who must have been the smaller stooped figure he had seen tried to go to help her fallen hero.

"Who are you?" Athan repeated to the middle-aged man who had first spoken. It was clear he would brook no further nonsense.

"Borna, sire."

"Get them out of here," Athan ordered turning to his men. This led to wails of protest from the old woman. As she came near to the door Athan could tell she was scarcely past middle age, though she acted much older. She pleaded for mercy for her lord who was sick.

493

Borna took up a cloak and hat and prepared to leave along with the youth. The smirking young man, out of his teens but pretending to still be a boy with an elaborate tunic and smeared makeup was as nasty a weasel as Athan had seen in some time. He offered himself in service first to Athan than to several members of the band. The men only growled and hustled him outside without giving him the opportunity to grab a cloak. The woman was trying to lift the Bear to his feet, a task well beyond her strength even if he had been helping. In the end it took two men to get him up to all fours. He looked up at Athan from there with rage and fury. Had he been the man he was a year before Athan would have been in immediate mortal danger and even now he felt a chill from the sheer malevolence of that gaze. Something glinted reflected in the dim light of the lamp in the ruined man's hair.

"Wait," ordered Athan and he reached in to touch a circlet of gold in the man's tangled and filthy hair. Drawing his dagger he hacked the diadem out of the hair ignoring the Bear's thrashing and slurred protests.

"Get him up," was all he said holding the narrow circlet in his left hand. As the big man came up swaying and muttering what must be curses more jewelry was revealed: a torque around his neck, an arm bracelet, and several rings, all of gold. The men on either side of him stripped him of these valuables. The Bear struggled against this indignity so strongly that he fell heavily once again.

"Those belong to me," said Athan, reaching out his hand. The men obediently handed them over although Athan was well known for being fair and open handed in sharing out booty such as this. Deep inside him there was a feeling that these things belonged to a king. For the first time, deep inside a secret place Athan began to think of himself as just that: a king.

They got the Bear outside but once the men who were supporting him let go he fell to his hands and knees. It was obvious he could not walk unaided. The woman came to his side to provide support but a man of his size would need more support than she could provide. Some of the men began to mock him, calling him a real bear now.

Athan stopped them. Then he called the two captured men over to where the Bear crouched on all fours. "Help him up. Once he was your lord. He deserves to walk out of here." Ixon had been clever enough to search Borna before they let him approach the Bear. He found a cunning little dagger and a purse holding many gold coins. He offered it to Athan.

"No, keep it. Better yet share it around."

Each man got two pieces of gold. There was one piece left over. Athan told Ixon to give it to the woman. "You will need that to get started again."

Athan gestured to the rear gate. The Bear seeing the gesture stood up as straight as he could, looked directly at Athan and shook his head. He nodded toward the front gate. It was hard to ready any expression in that sagging face but sometime people can communicate at a deeper level.

"You don't want to be thrown out the back gate of your own castle, do you?"

The big man kept looking at him and shook his head slowly.

"You don't want to go, but if you must you want to walk out the front gate, is that it?"

The big man nodded slowly.

Athan thought about the stories he had heard of this man's cruelty. Of the many murders committed, the rapes casually enjoyed, the tortures ordered, and lives ruined. Then he looked at what was left of the man. "All right." For the first time Athan noticed the Bear was barefoot. Turning to the woman he asked, "Does he have any footgear in there?"

"Yes, lord," she said. And then recognizing his meaning she darted into the sick room. The two men stared at each other in silence. The woman was quick; she returned holding two impossibly large leather sandals, a pair of woolen stockings, and a blanket. She had also brought a large shawl which she had wrapped around her head as it was threatening to rain again. She tried putting the stockings on his feet but he shook her off with a growl. Finally she gave up and put his feet in the sandals lacing them up quickly. He clearly wanted to leave as soon as possible.

Athan walked in front of the Bear, Giles at his side. Looking up the big man he addressed him, 'This is Giles, my personal shield bearer." He felt Giles stir at his side; this was new and the young man was proud of the honor. "Will you let him help you to the gate?" Again the big man nodded. The two prisoners who had been helping him stand were herded back with the others. Athan had no intention of letting any of the fighting men they captured leave, especially not with their former king.

Giles came to his left side and taking the Bear's weight helped him the long length of the courtyard, Ratimir's three remaining courtiers trailing behind. People, Athan's men, former defenders who were now prisoners, and servants who had hidden during the battle stood and watched, or leaned out of doorways or peered out of windows as the slow little procession made its way to the tunnel. Rodas, catching Athan's mood arranged for a sort of honor guard of six men who stood on each side of the entrance tunnel. Athan walked ahead and verified with Spiros who was still guarding the door that there were no enemies outside, then opened the larger right hand door. As he turned around to see Ratimir emerge leaning on Giles Athan saw tears streaming down the right side of the man's face. Athan wondered just why this man was crying now. Certainly a normal man had reason to weep under the circumstances, but this was not normal man. Certainly it was not from pain, or guilt for what he had inflicted on others. Was it frustration because his body's great size and strength would no long respond? Perhaps in part that was it but Athan felt it was something more complicated. The Bear did not want his reign to end, and he especially did not want it to end like this, with a pathetic retinue, given token honors by smaller men who had stolen away all he had built. It would have been far better to end your life in the heat of battle and be struck down like a bear at bay. But not an ending like this, limping off with a sad little sort of ceremony. This ending must be particularly bitter. 'Good or bad, we all come to the end, one way or another" thought Athan.

Once outside Athan gestured to the two men who still followed their master to take over support of the Bear. Borna took the crippled left side while the youth ineffectually took his right arm. The woman continued on behind, softly weeping.

They passed under the arches of the outer gate and turned down toward the long road that led to the town at the bottom of the hill. Athan reentered the hold. The big gate closed behind them with a soft inexorable thud. They had not taken two steps down the hill before the youth released his hold on his former master and skipped off down the hill. The woman, still wailing, moved up attempting to help steady the Bear as they slowly made their way down. It began to rain again.

The big gate closed on the four miserable people with a soft inexorable thud. In the Hold men barred and secured the gates, cutting off the sharp wind.

Athan turned and took a deep breath. He realized he still had the golden diadem in his hand. He had put the other bits of golden jewelry he had taken from the former King Ratimir and stuffed it into his purse without thinking but he had kept the crown in his left hand. Athan looked down at it. Unlike much of the stuff the Bear had kept this piece was simple, a flat gold band almost as wide as his little finger. Except for three small prongs that jutted up from the circle it almost looked like an oversized ring. Athan picked off a few strands of coarse black hair left from where he had taken it off of the Bear's head. It did not look as though it would be big enough to fit around the Bear's head. Seemingly by their own volition his hands took the narrow crown and lifted it to his head. The metal seemed to contract somehow as he put it on. The crown fitted Athan perfectly. For a moment he felt a little silly wearing the thing. It would be poor protection from the rain. On the other hand, his head was already wet. A second, stronger feeling come over him; putting on the crown was the right thing to do. If he was going to be a king he needed to start acting like a king. Athan was not sure how a king was supposed to act, but wearing a crown seemed to be a good start.

He did not, nor did any of the men with him realize that he had just begun his reign as King of Dassaria. But unknowing he began it in the exact way he would continue for his long reign; he began giving instructions on how to make things better.

And that was how he had become a king. Old King who had not always been a king smiled at the memory. In his long reign he had come to understand that most kings took their thrones in a great, glittering ceremony. He had just had a handful of comrades with him when he crowned himself in a stone passageway between two stables.

The Old King wondered for the hundredth time since he had been forced to winter over is some cave like some old bear. Athan smiled again at the similarities. Old King Ratimir and he had both won their kingdom by bloody force of arms. It looked as though there was a fair chance they would end their reigns the same way as well; cold and alone. There any resemblance between their reigns had ended. Well, there was one other similarity; neither man had left a designated heir.

Athan sighed. He had certainly come down a long, strange road. Looking back, it had all started when he went looking for his girlfriend. That had led him and his comrade Thaddeus to Persis, which in turn led to his marriage to Erinsys and rise in the guard. Would he have been at Achilles' Debacle if he had not chosen that path? It was impossible to tell. He certainly would never have attacked Azziz' camp if he had not been looking for his family. Athan touched the talisman he wore under his red vest. He was certain those two things he had taken from the sorcerer priest had caused his to take yet another turning in his life. What had possessed him to let Simeon convince him to steal the Satrap's gold? Why had he let Rodas persuade him to attack the Hold? It had been beyond rash to try to take the Hold with two score men, much less found a kingdom. Yet they had done it, and it had all worked out.

Even so in the end he had wound up in a small stone lair, looking out over a winter landscape. He was not disappointed. He had lived an adventurous life, had close comrades, loved and been loved by good women, and certainly risen farther in the world than he any right to expect.

And he had been a good king, too. But that was another story.

Glossary

Definitions

Andron – The dining hall in a formal house, constructed in the southern style

Andronitis – The men's hall, normally located in the front of a large formal house

Charamys- An article of clothing, worn in cool weather by women over a chiton and sometimes by poor men as their only garment

Chiton – A female tunic-like garment with an over fold at the neck to create a flap.

Gynaeconitis – The women's hall in a formal house; a place where men must be invited

Hetaira – A "she-comrade" another kind of wife, another kind of woman

Himation – a wool blanket or cloak worn over the left shoulder

Hoplites – A generic term for any organized infantry carrying spears and shields

Hoplon – A heavy round shield typically carried by phalangists

Hypaspists – Medium infantry, normally in looser supporting formations

Katadesmoi – A lead 'cursing tablet' used by witches

Kopis – A heavy chopping sword with a convex blade

Pallake – A kind of wife

Peltasts – Light infantry, mostly armed with missile weapons

Phalangists – Heavy infantry, normally in a tight formation

Pilleus –A felt or soft wool cap which rises to a forward curving point at its top

Prothesis & Ekphora – Parts of a funeral similar to a viewing and the burial procession

Stele – A gravestone or memorial tablet

Strigil – a curved metal scraper used in the baths for cleaning skin

Symposium (plural symposia) – A social gathering of men (and select women) for dinner, drink (sometimes lots of drink), and conversation

Yauna- A term for anyone from the general vicinity of Skudra

Weights and Measures – <u>All are rough approximations and are relative, often varying according to subjective conditions or local variations</u>

Numbers – Counting was more casual with terms such a dozen (12) or a score (20) used instead of exact values. The larger the value, the less exact the number: a hundred may represent 95-105, a thousand anything from 900 to 1200

Medimnos – A measure of weight about 55 pounds

Talent – A measure of wealth, about 6,000 drachmae – a lot of loot

Parasang – A measure of distance. About 5.5 kilometers or 3 ½ miles

Cubit – A measure of distance. A bit less than half a meter or ~19 inches

Foot – The length of a man's foot. Roughly 10-12 inches

Pace – The length of a man's stride. About 2 feet or a bit more

Bowshot – A very rough estimate of length, about 50-75 meters

Time - <u>All are approximations and are relative, often varying according to subjective conditions</u>

Month – A period of twenty eight days based on the moon

Hour – One twelfth of a day or a night, the length changing with the seasons

Moment – An indefinite but short period of time; less than a few hundred heartbeats

Heartbeat – A very relative measurement indicating an even shorter period of time (depending on how excited you are)

Organizations

Band – Armed men of varying size with often with no allegiance to a fixed place

Guards – The soldiers who protect a city or kingdom from threats within and without

Oligarch – A collection of wealthy men who are the leaders of an independent city

Ride - A group of about seven mounted warriors

Section – 10-20 Guards including an assigned sergeant

Squadron –Three Troops and a few more men led by a captain - about 100 men

Troop – Four rides plus a leader and sometimes a few more men - about 25-30 total men

Watch – A group of men of widely varying number assigned to work together for a specific task and limited time, usually involving sentinel or patrolling duties

Places

Epiria – Athan's specific hometown; a part of

Epirus – A region of loosely bound allied cities and kingdoms all to the west of...

Doria – A region around a city-state east of the region of Epirus

Illyria – A region of kingdoms, tribes, and cities north of Epiria and south of Dassaria

Buttrotiuria – A city-state south of Epiria

Skudra – A general region (not a political entity) south and east of Buttrotiuria

Achaemenid Empire – The world's biggest empire, to the east

Thrace – A peninsula south and east of Skudra

Macedonia – A mountainous kingdom north of Skudra and east of Epirus

Stavros – A city of departure

Xanthi – A city between Stavros and...

Kadakoy – A city at the turning point toward...

Golibolu – A destination city

Pella – A wonderful place; if you are a lotus eater

Printed in the United States
87143LV00005B/100-141/A